The
BRIDES
of WEBSTER
County

The
BRIDES
of WEBSTER
County

4 Bestselling Amish Romance Novels

WANDA *&*
BRUNSTETTER

BARBOUR BOOKS
An Imprint of Barbour Publishing, Inc.

Going Home © 2007 by Wanda E. Brunstetter
On Her Own © 2007 by Wanda E. Brunstetter
Dear to Me © 2008 by Wanda E. Brunstetter
Allison's Journey © 2008 by Wanda E. Brunstetter

ISBN 978-1-64352-680-5

eBook Editions:
Adobe Digital Edition (.epub) 978-1-64352-682-9
Kindle and MobiPocket Edition (.prc) 978-1-64352-681-2

Scripture quotations are taken from the King James Version of the Bible.

All German-Dutch words are taken from the *Revised Pennsylvania German Dictionary* found in Lancaster County, Pennsylvania.

This book is a work of fiction. Names, characters, places, and incidents are either products of the author's imagination or used fictitiously. Any similarity to actual people, organizations, and/or events is purely coincidental.

This book contains some Amish home remedies that have not been evaluated by the FDA. They are not intended to diagnose, treat, cure, or prevent any disease or condition. If you have a health concern or condition, consult a physician.

For more information about Wanda E. Brunstetter, please access the author's web site at the following internet address: www.wandabrunstetter.com

Cover Photography: © Rekha Garton / Trevillion Images

Published by Barbour Books, an imprint of Barbour Publishing, Inc., 1810 Barbour Drive, Uhrichsville, OH 44683, www.barbourbooks.com

Our mission is to inspire the world with the life-changing message of the Bible.

 Member of the
Evangelical Christian
Publishers Association

Printed in the United States of America

Going Home

To my in-laws in Pennsylvania
who make "going home" a joyful experience.
And to all my Amish friends
who make me feel at home whenever I come to visit.

Without faith it is impossible to please him:
for he that cometh to God must believe that he is,
and that he is a rewarder of them that diligently seek him.
HEBREWS 11:6

Chapter 1

Faith Andrews stared out the bus window, hoping to focus on something other than her immediate need. She feasted her eyes on rocky hills, scattered trees, and a June sky so blue she felt she could swim in it. Faith had always loved this stretch of road in her home state of Missouri. She'd traveled it plenty of times over the last ten years, going from Branson to Springfield and back again, making numerous stage appearances in both towns. She had also been in Tennessee, Arkansas, and several other southern states, but her favorite place to entertain was Branson, where the shows were family-oriented, lively, and fun.

Not like some nightclubs where her husband, who had also doubled as her agent, had booked her during the early days of her career. Faith hated those gigs, with leering men who sometimes shouted obscene remarks and people who asked dumb questions about the getup Greg insisted she wear for a time.

"You need to wear your Amish garb," he had told her. "It can be your trademark."

Faith shook her head at the memory. *I'm glad I finally convinced him to let me go with the hillbilly look instead. Wearing Amish clothes only reminded me of the past and made me feel homesick.*

Whenever Faith was onstage, the past, present, and future disappeared like trees hidden in the forest on a foggy day. When she entertained, her focus was on only one thing: telling jokes and yodeling her heart out for an appreciative audience—something she had wanted since she was a child.

Faith closed her eyes, relishing the vision of a performance she had given six months ago at a small theater in the older part of Branson. Her jokes had brought down the house. She liked it when she could make people laugh. Too bad it was a talent that had never been valued until she'd become a professional entertainer. Her family had made it clear that they didn't care for humor—at least not hers. Maybe she wouldn't have felt the need to run away if they'd been more accepting of her silliness.

Faith's thoughts took her back to the stage as she remembered receiving a standing ovation and basking in the warmth of it long after the theater was empty. How could she have known her world would be turned upside down in a single moment following the performance that night? When Faith took her final bow, she had no idea she would be burying her husband of seven years a few days later or that she would be sitting on a bus right now, heading for home.

Going back to her birthplace outside the town of Seymour, Missouri, was something Faith had been afraid to do. So near yet so far away, she'd been these last ten years, and never once had she returned for a visit. She feared that she wouldn't have been welcomed, for she'd been a rebellious teenager, refusing baptism and membership into the Amish church and running off to do her own thing.

During the first few years of Faith's absence, she had sent a couple of notes to her childhood companion Barbara Raber, but that was the only contact she'd had with anyone from home. If not for the necessity of finding a stable environment for Melinda, Faith wouldn't be going home now.

She turned away from the window, and her gaze came to rest on the sleeping child beside her. Her six-year-old daughter's cheeks had turned rosy as her eyelids had closed in slumber soon after they'd boarded the bus in Branson.

Faith smiled at the memory of Melinda bouncing around while they waited in the bus station. "Mama," the little girl had said, "I can't wait to get on the bus and go see where you used to live."

"I hope you like what you see, my precious little girl," Faith murmured as she studied her daughter. The little girl's head lolled against Faith's arm, and her breathing was sweet and even. Melinda had been sullen since her father's death. Maybe the change of scenery and a slower-paced, simpler lifestyle would be what she needed.

Faith pushed a wayward strand of golden hair away from Melinda's face. She looked a lot like Faith had as a little girl—same blond hair and clear blue eyes, only Melinda wore her hair hanging down her back or in a ponytail. In the Amish community, she would be expected to wear it pulled into a tight bun at the back of her head, then covered with a stiff white *kapp*, the way Faith had done for so many years.

Will Mama and Papa accept my baby girl, even though they might not take kindly to me? Will Melinda adjust to her new surroundings, so plain and devoid of all the worldly things she's been used to? When I'm gone, will she feel as though I've abandoned her, even though I'll promise to come and visit as often as I can?

As Faith took hold of her daughter's small hand, she felt a familiar burning in the back of her throat. She relished the warmth and familiarity of Melinda's soft skin and could hardly fathom what it would be like for the two of them once they were separated. Yet she would do anything for her child, and she was convinced it would be better for Melinda to live with her grandparents than to be hauled all over the countryside with only one parent. She'd been doing that ever since Greg had died six months ago, and things hadn't gone so well.

Besides the fact that Faith still hadn't secured another agent to book her shows, she'd had a terrible time coming up with a babysitter for Melinda. At times, she'd had to take the child with her to rehearsals and even some shows. Melinda sat offstage and one of the other performers looked after her as Faith did her routine, but that arrangement was anything but ideal. Faith had finished up her contract at a theater in Branson last night, and this morning, she and Melinda had boarded the bus. Faith wouldn't go back to entertaining until she felt free to do so, which meant she had to know Melinda was in good hands and had adjusted to her new surroundings.

Faith had left her name with a couple of talent agencies in Memphis and Nashville and had said she would call them soon to check on the possibility of getting an agent. She hoped Melinda would have time to adapt before Faith had to leave her.

Faith gripped the armrest as she thought about her other options. When Greg's parents had come to Branson for his funeral, they'd offered their assistance. "Remember now, Faith," Elsie had said, "if you need anything, just give us a call."

Faith figured the offer was made purely out of obligation, for Jared and Elsie Andrews were too self-centered to care about anyone but themselves. She wasn't about to ask if Melinda could live with Greg's parents. That would be the worst thing possible, even if his folks were willing to take on the responsibility of raising their granddaughter.

Elsie and Jared lived in Los Angeles, and Jared was an alcoholic. Faith had met her husband's parents only once before his death. That was shortly after she'd married Greg. She and Greg had stayed with the Andrewses for one week while they visited Disneyland, Knott's Berry Farm, and some other sights in the area. It hadn't taken Faith long to realize that Greg's parents weren't fit to raise any child. Elsie Andrews was a woman who seemed to care only about her own needs. During their visit, the woman had talked endlessly about her elite circle of friends and when she was scheduled for her next facial or hair appointment. Greg's father always seemed to have a drink in his hand, and he'd used language so foul Faith had cringed every time he opened his mouth. Melinda would be better off in Webster County with her Plain relatives than she would with grandparents who thought more about alcohol and mudpacks than about having a relationship with their only son and his wife.

Faith let her eyelids close once more, allowing herself to travel back to when she was a teenager. She saw herself in her father's barn, sitting on a bale of hay, yodeling and telling jokes to her private audience of two buggy horses and a cat named Boots. . . .

"Faith Stutzman, what do you think you're doing?"

Faith whirled around at the sound of her father's deep voice. His face was a mask of anger, his dark eyebrows drawn together so they almost met in the middle.

"I was entertaining the animals," she said, feeling her defenses rising. "I don't see any harm in doing that, Papa."

He scowled at her. "Is that a fact? What about the chores you were sent out here to do? Have you finished those yet?"

She shook her head. "No, but I'm aimin' to get them done real soon."

Papa nudged her arm with his knuckles. "Then you'd better get up and do 'em! And no more of that silly squawkin' and howlin'. You sound like a frog with a sore throat, trying to do that silly yodeling stuff." He started for the barn door but turned back around. "You've always been a bit of a rebel, and it isn't getting any better now that you've reached your teen years." He shook his finger at Faith. "You'd better start spending more time reading the scriptures and praying and less time in town soaking up all kinds of worldly stuff on the sly. You'll surely die in your sins if you don't get yourself under control and prepare for baptism soon."

When the barn door slammed shut, Faith stuck out her tongue, feeling more defiant than ever. "I should be allowed to tell jokes and yodel whenever I choose," she grumbled to Barney, one of their driving horses. "And I shouldn't have to put up with my daed's outbursts or his mean, controlling ways, either." She plucked a piece of hay from the bale on which she sat and snapped off the end. "I'll show you, Papa. I'll show everyone in this family that I don't need a single one of you. I'll find someone who appreciates my talents and doesn't criticize me for everything I do."

As Faith's thoughts returned to the present, she tried to focus her attention on the scenery whizzing past. She couldn't. Her mind was a jumble of confusion. Was returning to Webster County the right thing?

I'm doing what I have to do. Melinda needs a secure home, and this is the best way to make that happen. Faith thought about Greg and how, even though he wasn't the ideal husband, he had secured plenty of engagements for her. Never mind that he'd kept a good deal of the money she'd made to support his drinking and gambling habits. Never mind that Greg had been harsh with her at times.

It's sad, she mused. *Greg's been gone six months, yet I grieved for him only a short time. Even then, it wasn't really my husband I missed. It was my agent and the fact that he took care of our daughter while I was working. If he hadn't lined up several shows for me, I probably would have returned to Webster County sooner.*

Faith popped a couple of her knuckles. It was a bad habit—her parents had said so often enough—but it helped relieve some of her tension. *I'll never marry again—that's for certain sure. It would be hard to trust another man.* She drew in a deep breath and tried to relax. She'd be home in a few hours and would know whether she had made the right decision. If her folks accepted Melinda, the grandchild they knew nothing about, Faith could be fairly certain things would work out. If they rejected her, then Faith would need to come up with another plan.

Noah Hertzler wiped his floury hands on a dish towel and smiled. He was alone in the kitchen and had created another cake he was sure would tempt even the most finicky person. Being the youngest of ten boys, with no sisters in the family, Noah had been the only son who had eagerly helped Mom in the kitchen from the time he was a small boy. In Noah's mind, his ability to cook was a God-given talent—one he enjoyed sharing with others through the breads, cookies, cakes, and pies he often made to give away. If he heard of someone who was emotionally down or physically under the weather, he set right to work baking a scrumptious dessert for that person. He always attached a note that included one of his favorite scripture verses. "Food for the stomach and nourishment for the soul"—that's what Mom called Noah's gifts to others.

Noah stared out the kitchen window into the backyard where he had played as a child. Growing up, he'd been shy, unable to express his thoughts or feelings the way most children usually did. When his friends or brothers gathered to play, Noah had spent time either alone in the barn or with his mother in the kitchen. Even now, at age twenty-four, he was somewhat reserved and spoke only when he felt something needed to be said. Noah thought that was why he hadn't married yet. The truth was, he'd been too shy to pursue a woman, although he had never found anyone he wanted to court.

Noah figured another reason for his single status was because he wasn't so good-looking. Not that he was ugly, for Mom had often said his thick, mahogany-colored hair was real nice and that his dark brown eyes reminded her of a box of sweet chocolates. Of course, all mothers thought their offspring were cute and sweet; it was the way of a good mother's heart to see the best in her flesh-and-blood children.

Instinctively, Noah touched his nose. It was too big and had a small hump in the middle of it. He'd taken a lot of ribbing from his friends during childhood over that beak. He could still hear his schoolmates chanting, "Noah! Noah! Nobody knows of anything bigger than Noah's huge nose!"

Forcing his thoughts to return to the present, Noah's gaze came to rest on the old glider, which sat under the red-leafed maple tree in their backyard. He had seen many of his brothers share that swing with their sweethearts, but Noah had never known the pleasure. Since his teen years, he'd shown an interest in only a few girls, and those relationships didn't involve more than a ride home in Noah's open buggy after a young people's singing on a Sunday night. He had never taken it any further because the girls hadn't shown much interest in him.

Most everyone in the community thought Noah was a confirmed bachelor; some had said so right to his face. But he didn't care what others thought. Noah was content to work five days a week for Hank Osborn, a local English man who raised Christmas trees. In the evenings and on weekends, Noah helped his mother at home. Mom was sixty-two years old and had been diagnosed with type 2 diabetes several years ago. As careful as she was about her diet, her health was beginning to fail so she needed Noah's help more than ever—especially since he was the only son still living at home. All nine of Noah's brothers were married with families of their own. Pop, at age sixty-four, still kept busy with farm chores and raising his fat hogs. He surely didn't have time to help his wife with household chores or cooking. Not that he would have anyway. Noah's father disliked indoor chores, even hauling firewood into the kitchen, which had been Noah's job since he was old enough to hold a chunk of wood in his chubby little hands.

Bringing his reflections to a halt, Noah began to mix up the batter for two tasty lemon sponge cakes in separate bowls. He would make one of the cakes using a sugar substitute, for him and his folks. The other cake would be given away as soon as he found someone who had a need. Noah had already decided to use Hebrews 11:6 with the cake: "But without faith it is impossible to please him: for he that cometh to God must believe that he is, and that he is a rewarder of them that diligently seek him."

"Is someone in the community struggling with a lack of faith?" Noah murmured. "Do they need a reminder that will encourage their heart and help strengthen their trust in God?" He felt confident that the Lord would direct him to the right person. He could hardly wait to see who it might be.

When Faith and Melinda got off the bus at Lazy Lee's Gas Station in Seymour, Faith picked up their two suitcases and herded Melinda toward the building. The unmistakable aroma of cow manure from a nearby farm assaulted her. She was almost home, and there was no turning back. She had come this far and would go the rest of the way as soon as she found them a ride.

Faith didn't recognize the balding, middle-aged man working inside the gas station, but she introduced herself and asked him about hiring someone to drive them to her folks' place. He said his name was Ed Moore and mentioned that he'd only been living in Seymour a couple of years.

"My wife, Doris, is coming in for some gas soon, and since we live just off Highway C, she plans to stop by an Amish farm out that way and buy some fresh eggs," Ed said. "I'm sure she'd be more than happy to give you a lift."

Faith wondered which Amish family from her community was selling eggs. Could it be Mama or one of her sisters? "If your wife is willing to give us a ride, it would be most appreciated," she said.

"Don't think it'll be a problem. Nope, not a problem at all." Ed grinned at her, revealing a set of badly stained, crooked teeth. "You can wait here inside the store if you want to."

"It might be best if we waited outside," Faith replied. "I wouldn't want to miss your wife."

"Suit yourself."

Faith led Melinda outside, and they took a seat on the bench near the front door. "You'll be meeting your grandpa and grandma Stutzman soon," she said, smiling at Melinda, whose eyes darted back and forth as she sat stiffly on the bench.

Melinda's nose twitched. "Somethin' smells funny. I don't know if I'm gonna like it here."

"That's the way farms smell, Melinda. We're in the country now."

Melinda folded her arms but said nothing more.

A short time later, a red station wagon pulled up to the pumps, and Ed came out of the building and proceeded to fill the tank with gas. When he was done, he said something to the dark-haired, middle-aged woman sitting in the vehicle. After a few minutes, he motioned for Faith and Melinda to come over. "This here's my wife, Doris, and she's agreed to give you a ride." Before Faith could respond, Ed opened the back of the station wagon and deposited their suitcases inside.

"I appreciate this, and I'll be happy to pay you," Faith said to Doris as she and Melinda climbed into the backseat of the vehicle.

"No need for that," Doris said with a wave of her hand. "Ed and I live out that way anyhow."

"Thank you." Faith tucked her daughter's white cotton blouse under the band of her blue jeans; then she buckled the child's seatbelt just as Doris pulled her vehicle out of the parking lot.

Melinda pressed her nose to the window as the station wagon headed down Highway C. "Look at all the farms. There's so many animals!"

"Yep, lots of critters around here," Doris chimed in.

Faith reached over and patted Melinda's knee. "Your grandma and grandpa have all kinds of animals you'll soon get to know."

Melinda made no comment, and Faith wondered what her little girl was thinking. Would her daughter find joy in the things on the farm, or would she become restless and bored, the way Faith had? She hoped Melinda would adjust to the new surroundings and respond well to her grandparents and other family members.

Closing her eyes, Faith leaned into the seat and tried to relax. She would deal first with seeing her folks and then worry about how well Melinda would adjust. She only had the strength to work through one problem at a time.

Twenty minutes later, they pulled into the gravel driveway of her parents' farm. Faith opened the car door and stepped out. Letting her gaze travel around the yard, she was amazed at how little it had changed. Everything looked nearly the same as the day she'd left home. The house was still painted white. The front porch sagged on one end, the way it had for as long as Faith could remember. Dark shades hung at each of the windows.

A wagonload of steel milk cans was parked out by the garden, and two open buggies sat near the barn. Her folks' mode of transportation was obviously the same as it always had been. Even as a child, Faith had never understood why their district drove only open buggies. Traveling in such a way could be downright miserable when the weather turned cold and snowy. She'd heard it said that the Webster County Amish were one of the strictest in their beliefs of the Plain communities in America. Seeing her parents' simple home again made her believe this statement must be true.

Faith noticed something else. A dark gray, closed-in buggy was parked on one side of the house. How strange it looked. Her mind whirled with unanswered questions. *I wonder whose it could be. Unless the rules around here have changed, it surely doesn't belong to Papa.*

"Is this the place?" Melinda asked, tugging on Faith's hand.

She looked down at her daughter, so innocent and wide-eyed. "Yes, Melinda. This is where I grew up. Shall we go see if anyone's home?"

Melinda nodded, although her dubious expression left little doubt of the child's concerns.

Once more, Faith offered to pay Doris, but the smiling woman waved her away. "No need for that. I was heading this way anyhow. So I'll be off to get my eggs over at the Troyers' place."

Faith thanked Doris, grabbed their suitcases, and gulped in another breath of air. It was time to face the music.

Chapter 2

Faith had only made it to the first saggy step of the front porch when the door swung open. Her mother, Wilma Stutzman, stepped out, and a little girl not much older than Melinda followed. In some ways, Mama looked the same as when Faith had left home, yet she was different. Hair that used to be blond like spun gold was now dingy and graying. Skin that had once been smooth and soft showed signs of wrinkles and dryness. Mama's face looked tired and drawn, and her blue eyes, offset by metal-framed glasses, held no sparkle as they once had.

"Can I help you with something?" her mother asked, looking at Faith as though she were a stranger.

Faith stepped all the way onto the porch, bringing Melinda with her. "Mama, it's me."

The older woman eyed Faith up and down, and her mouth

dropped open. Then her gaze came to rest on Melinda, who was clinging to Faith's hand as though her young life hung in the balance.

"Faith?" Mama squeaked. "After all these years, is—is it really you?"

Faith nodded as tears stung the backs of her eyes. It was good to see her mother again. She hoped Mama felt the same.

When Mama stepped forward and gave Faith a hug, Faith nearly broke down in tears. Despite the resentment she'd carried in her heart for the last ten years, she had missed seeing her family.

"This is my daughter, Mama. Melinda's six years old." Faith gave the child's hand a gentle squeeze. "Say hello to your grandma Stutzman."

"Hello, Grandma." Melinda's voice was barely above a whisper.

Mama's pale eyebrows lifted in obvious surprise, but she offered Melinda a brief smile. Her brows drew together as she looked back at Faith. "I didn't even know you were married, much less had a child. Where have you been these last ten years, daughter?"

Faith swallowed hard as she formulated her response. "I followed my dream, Mama."

"What dream? You ran off the day you turned eighteen, leaving only a note on the kitchen table saying you were going to become part of the English world."

"My dream was to use my yodeling skills and joke telling to entertain folks. My husband, Greg, made that happen, and I've been on the road entertaining for quite a spell now."

Mama's eyes glistened with unshed tears. "It broke your daed's and my heart when you left home, Faith. Don't you know that?"

"I—I did what I felt was right for me at the time." Faith dropped her gaze to the slanting porch. "Greg was killed six months ago when a car hit him." No point telling Mama that her husband had been drinking when he'd stepped in front of the oncoming vehicle. Mama would probably think Faith also drank liquor and then give a stern lecture on the evils of strong drink. Faith had endured enough reprimands during her teen years, even being blamed for some things she hadn't done.

"I'm sorry about your husband." Mama's voice sounded sincere. Maybe she did care a little bit.

Feeling the need to change the subject, Faith nodded at the gray, closed-in buggy sitting out in the yard. "Mind if I ask who that belongs to?"

"Vernon Miller, the buggy maker. He's out in the barn with your daed."

"Does that mean the Webster County Amish are allowed to drive closed-in buggies now?"

Mama shook her head. "Vernon built the Lancaster-style carriage for an English man who lives out in Oregon. The fellow owns a gift shop where he sells Amish-made items. Guess he decided having a real buggy in front of his place would be good for business." She lifted her shoulders in a brief shrug. "Vernon wanted to test-drive it before he completed the order and had it sent off."

"I see."

Faith was going to say more, but the young girl with light

brown hair and dark eyes who stood beside Mama spoke up. "Do I know these people, *Mamm?*"

Mamm? Faith felt a jolt of electricity zip through her body. Was the child hanging on to Mama's long blue dress Faith's sister? Had Mama given birth to a baby sometime after Faith left home? Did that mean Faith had three sisters now instead of two? She could even have more than four brothers and not know it.

"Susie, this is your big sister," Mama said to the girl. "And her daughter's your niece."

Susie stood gaping at Faith as though she had done something horribly wrong. Was it her worldly attire of blue jeans and a pink T-shirt that bothered the girl? Could it have been the long French braid Faith wore down her back? Or was the child as surprised as Faith was over the news that each of them had a sister they knew nothing about?

"So what are you doing here?" Mama asked, nodding at Faith.

"I—I was wondering if Melinda and I could stay with you." Faith held her breath and awaited her mother's answer. Would she and Melinda be welcomed or turned away?

"Here? With us?" Mama's voice had raised at least an octave, and her eyes, peering through her glasses, were as huge as saucers.

Faith nodded.

"As English or Amish?"

Her mother's direct question went straight to Faith's heart. If she told the truth—that she wanted her daughter to be Amish and she would pretend to be until she was ready to leave—the door would probably be slammed in her face.

Faith nibbled on her lower lip as she considered her response. She had to be careful. It wouldn't be good to reveal her true plans until the time was right. "I. . .uh. . .am willing to return to the Amish way of life."

"And you'll speak to Bishop Jacob Martin before you attend church with us in the morning?"

Faith gulped. She hadn't expected to speak with the bishop on her first day home. She'd probably be subjected to a long lecture about worldliness or maybe told that she must be baptized into the church before she would be fully accepted.

Melinda tugged her hand. "Are we gonna stay here, Mama?"

"I–I hope so." They couldn't be turned away. They had no place to go but back on the road, and Faith was through dragging Melinda all over creation. It wasn't good for a child to live out of a suitcase, never knowing from week to week where she would lay her head at night. Melinda should attend school in the fall, and she needed a stable environment.

"Will you speak with Jacob Martin or not?" Mama asked again.

Faith gritted her teeth and gave one quick nod. She would keep up the pretense that she planned to stay for as long as it was necessary.

Mama stepped aside and held the screen door open. "Come inside then."

Wilma's legs felt like two sticks of rubber as she motioned Faith and her daughter to follow her into the kitchen. As each year had passed without a word from her oldest daughter, she'd become more convinced that she would never see Faith again.

But now Faith was home and had brought her daughter with her—a grandchild Wilma had known nothing about. Did Faith plan to stay, or would she be off and running again as soon as she felt the least bit discontent?

"Who was at the door, Mama?" Grace Ann, Wilma's seventeen-year-old daughter, asked as they stepped into the kitchen.

Wilma motioned first to Faith and then to the child who clung to her mother's hand with a wide-eyed expression. "Your big sister's come home, and this is her daughter, Melinda."

Grace Ann's mouth opened wide, and she nearly dropped the plates she held in her hands. "Faith?"

Faith nodded, but before she could say anything, fourteen-year-old Esther, who had been placing silverware on the table, spoke. "Mama, is this the disobedient sister you told us about who ran off to the English world so she could yodel and tell silly jokes whenever she wanted?"

Wilma could only nod in response. When Faith had left home at the tender age of eighteen, Grace Ann had been seven, and Esther had just turned four. If not for Wilma telling the girls about Faith and her desire to be an entertainer, she was sure they wouldn't even have remembered that they'd had an older sister.

Esther eyed Faith up and down. "Did you come here for a visit, or are you home to stay?"

Faith shifted from one foot to another, looking like a bird that had been trapped between the paws of a hungry cat. "I brought Melinda home and"—she paused and moistened her lips with the tip of her tongue—"we're. . .uh. . .here for more than just a visit."

Grace Ann set the plates on the table and scurried across the room. "It's good to have you home, sister," she said, giving Faith a hug. "Papa and the others will sure be surprised." She patted Melinda on her head. "How old are you?"

"I'm six," the child replied.

"Just a year younger than Susie." Grace Ann glanced around the room. "Where is our little sister, anyway?"

Wilma's brows knitted together as she turned to look behind her. She thought Susie had been with them when they'd headed for the kitchen. "Esther, would you run upstairs and see if Susie went to her room?"

Esther hesitated as she looked over at Faith.

"She'll still be here when you get back," Wilma said with a wave of her hand.

"Okay." Esther scampered out of the room.

Faith smiled, although it appeared to be forced. Wasn't she happy to be home and seeing her family again?

Wilma motioned to the table. "If you'd like to have a seat, we can visit while I finish getting supper on."

"Isn't there something I can do to help?" Faith asked.

"Grace Ann and Esther have the table almost set, and the stew I'm making is nearly done." Wilma released a soft grunt. "You can start helping tomorrow with breakfast."

Faith pulled out a chair. Once she was seated, she hoisted her daughter into her lap, and the child snuggled against Faith's chest. "How are my brothers doing?" Faith asked. "I imagine they're pretty big by now."

Before Wilma could reply, Grace Ann spoke up. "John's courting a woman named Phoebe." She chuckled and waved her hand like she was swatting at a fly. "Course, he's been kind of sneaky about it, and I'm sure he thinks we don't know what's up."

"I remember when John was a boy he always kept things to himself." Faith glanced over at Wilma. "And how is Brian now?"

"He says he's still looking for the right woman." Wilma moved over to the stove and lifted the lid on the pot of stew. A curl of steam rushed up, and she drew in a deep breath, savoring the delicious, sagelike aroma. "Your older brothers, James and Philip, are both married. They each have four *kinner* of their own, and they've recently moved their families up north near Jamesport."

"How come?" Faith asked.

"Neither one likes to farm, and there's more work available for them."

Faith released a sigh. "I can't believe how much has changed since I left home."

Wilma resisted the temptation to tell Faith that if she had stayed home the way she should have and not run after a worldly dream, she would have been part of that change and things wouldn't seem so strange to her.

Several minutes later, Esther returned to the kitchen without her little sister. "Susie wasn't in her room, Mama. I don't know where she could be."

"Maybe she went outside," Grace Ann suggested.

Wilma was about to tell Esther to go out and check, when the back door swung open and Susie rushed into the room, followed by Wilma's husband, Menno, and their two youngest sons.

"Susie said Faith has come home." Menno's face was red, and he huffed as if he'd been running and was out of breath. "Is it true?"

Faith set her daughter on the floor and stood. "Yes, Papa, I'm here." She motioned to the child. "This is my daughter, Melinda—your granddaughter."

Menno looked down at Melinda, and his forehead creased, but he didn't comment. He just stood there, staring at the child.

"Susie told us that your husband died and that's why you and your daughter have come here to live." John stepped forward. "It's good to see you, sister. Welcome home."

"*Jah,*" Brian said with a nod. "We've missed you all these years."

"I–I've missed you, too."

Menno cleared his throat loudly. "Where have you been all this time, Faith, and what have you been doing?"

"She's been yodeling and telling jokes for English folks in places like Branson," John said before Faith could respond. "Not long ago, I saw her picture in one of them flyers advertising shows at Branson." He glanced over at his father. "Remember when I told you and Mama about it?"

Menno mumbled something Wilma couldn't quite understand as he ambled across the room toward the sink. She waited until he had washed and dried his hands, then she motioned to the table and said, "Supper's ready now, so why don't we all find our places? While we're eating, Faith can answer everyone's questions."

Chapter 3

Faith cringed as her family joined her and Melinda at the table. She didn't want to answer anyone's questions. Truth be told, she didn't really want to be here, but bringing Melinda to live with her folks was the only way she knew to give her daughter a stable home.

You had a stable home once, and you left it, a little voice niggled at the back of Faith's mind. She shook her head, trying to clear away the disturbing thoughts. She had to stay focused on her goal for Melinda.

Faith glanced over at her father, a tall, muscular man with a good crop of cinnamon brown hair and a beard that was peppered with gray. He cleared his throat loudly, the way he'd always done whenever it was time to bow their heads for silent prayer. Faith leaned close to Melinda, who sat in the seat beside her. "Close your eyes now; we're going to pray."

Melinda's forehead wrinkled, and Faith realized that the child didn't understand. How could she? Faith had quit praying a long time ago, and she hadn't taught her daughter how to pray, either. "Shut your eyes," she whispered in Melinda's ear.

Melinda did as she was told, and everyone else did the same. Several seconds later, Papa cleared his throat again, and all eyes opened. Everyone's but Melinda's. Faith squeezed her hand, and when Melinda still didn't open her eyes, she quietly said, "You can open your eyes now."

Melinda blinked and looked around the table. "But nobody said nothing. When I watched *Little House on the Prairie* on TV, Laura's pa always said the prayer out loud."

Mama opened her mouth as if to say something, but Brian spoke first. "We offer silent prayers here."

"But if it's silent, how does God know what you want?"

"We pray in our minds," Grace Ann said. "God hears what we think same as when we speak."

Melinda seemed to accept that explanation, for she gave one quick nod, grabbed the glass of milk sitting before her, and took a drink. She smacked her lips as she set the glass down. "Umm. . . that's sure tasty."

"It's fresh milk taken from one of our best milking cows early this morning," John said, smiling over at Melinda.

"Can I milk a cow?" she asked with a look of expectation. "Laura helps her pa milk their cow on *Little House*, and it looks like a lot of fun."

"Milking cows is hard work, but I'd be happy to show you how," Faith's father said. It was the first time since he'd come into the room that Faith had seen him smile. Maybe he was glad to have her home. At least he seemed pleasant enough with Melinda. To Faith, he hadn't said more than a few words, and those were spoken with disdain. Well, it didn't matter. Faith would be leaving in a few weeks or months—however long it took for Melinda to become used to her new surroundings. The only thing that really mattered was Melinda developing a good relationship with her grandparents, aunts, and uncles. Everyone in the family could give Faith the cold shoulder for the rest of her life, and it wouldn't matter.

She looked around the table at the somber faces of her family. She couldn't allow herself the luxury of caring about these people or worrying about whether they accepted her. Her life was on the stage, yodeling and cracking funny jokes for English folks who paid money to enjoy the entertainment she offered. It wasn't here in Webster County, where everything she did was under scrutiny.

"I wanna learn about all the animals on this farm." Melinda nearly knocked over her glass of milk as she wiggled around in her seat.

"Be careful now, or you'll spill something," Faith admonished.

"She's just excited about seeing the animals," Mama said, smiling at Melinda.

Susie, who sat on the other side of Melinda, reached over and touched Melinda's hand. "If you'd like, we can go to the barn after we're done eating, and I can show you the kittens that were born last week."

Melinda's head bobbed up and down. "I'd like that."

Faith remained silent throughout most of the meal, only

responding when she was asked a question or Melinda requested more to eat. Susie made up for Faith's lack of conversation, as she chattered nonstop, offering to show Melinda all sorts of interesting things in her father's barn and telling her how much fun it was going to be to have someone close to her age living with her.

Melinda, too, seemed eager, and it was almost as if the girls had known each other all their lives. It made Faith feel guilty for not having brought Melinda to meet her family sooner. *Well, better late than never,* she thought as she poured another glass of milk for Melinda. *Besides, we might not have been welcomed before.*

They had just finished supper and the women were clearing away the dishes, when a knock sounded on the back door. "John, would you get that?" Papa asked before he drank some coffee from the cup Mama had placed in front of him moments ago.

John slid his chair away from the table and left the room. A few seconds later, he was back with Bishop Martin at his side. Except for his hair and beard turning mostly gray, the portly man looked almost the same as he had when Faith had left home ten years ago.

"Come in. Have a cup of coffee," Papa said, motioning for the bishop to take a seat at the table.

The bishop smiled and shook his head. "I can't stay. Just dropped by to let you know that tomorrow's church service, which was going to be held at Henry Yoder's home, will be held at Isaac Troyer's place."

Papa's eyebrows rose. "Oh? Why's that?"

"Henry's mother, who lives in Kentucky, is real sick, and Henry and his family had to hire a driver to take them there."

"That's too bad. Sorry to hear of it."

Mama moved from her place in front of the sink and gave Faith a little nudge with her elbow. "Since the bishop is here now, don't you think this would be a good time for you to tell him what's on your mind?" Before Faith could respond, Mama looked over at the bishop and said, "Our daughter Faith's come home, and she wants to join the church."

Faith swallowed hard and nearly choked. She hadn't expected to see the bishop quite so soon. She needed more time to prepare for this—to think through what she wanted to say.

"Is that so?" Bishop Martin eyed Faith curiously as he tipped his head. "Where have you been all these years?"

"She's been on the road, yodeling and telling jokes in the English world," Papa spoke up before Faith could formulate a response. He motioned toward Melinda. "Right out of the blue, she and her daughter showed up on our doorstep a little while ago."

The bishop opened his mouth as if to say something, but Faith spoke first. "My husband died a few months ago, and I decided it would be best for Melinda if we came here."

"I see." He gave Faith a quick nod. "Since you weren't a member of the church when you left, you won't be expected to offer any kind of confession to the church, but I think, given the circumstances of your leaving home in the first place, it would be good for you to give yourself some time to readjust to things before you take instruction to join the church."

A huge sense of relief settled over Faith as she nodded. "Yes, I think that would be best." This would give her a chance to get her daughter settled in, and no one would suspect that her real plans were to leave Melinda here and be on the road again.

"I still can't believe our daughter's come home," Wilma said to Menno as the two of them got ready for bed that night.

He pulled the covers to the foot of bed. "Jah, well, it sure seems odd to me that she would return home after this much time. It makes no sense at all."

"You heard what she said, Menno. Faith's come home because her husband is dead and she wants a stable home to raise her daughter in."

"You think she's telling the truth?"

Wilma took a seat on the edge of the bed and pulled the pins from the bun at the back of her head. "What reason would she have to lie about her husband dying?"

"That's not what I meant. If she says her husband's dead, then I'm sure it's true." Menno flopped onto his side of the bed and punched the pillow a couple of times. He had a hunch there was more to the story than Faith was telling. Unless their daughter had changed a lot from when she was a girl, it was quite likely that she had something more up her sleeve than just looking for a stable home for Melinda.

"I sure hope she stays for good this time," Wilma said as she began to brush her waist-length hair. "I don't think I could stand losing her again."

"I'd like to believe she will stay, but she's been living in the world these last ten years." He reclined on the bed and raised his arms up over his head as he rested against the pillow. "Do you really think she can give up all the modern things she's become accustomed to having?"

"Well, I don't know, but I'm hoping—"

"I don't trust her, Wilma. I think Faith is probably down on her luck and can't find a job now that her husband's gone, so she needs a place to stay for a while." He frowned. "Mark my words. In a couple of weeks, Faith and her daughter will be on the road, and we'll probably never hear from them again."

Wilma's eyes widened, and her chin quivered slightly. "Oh, I hope that's not the case." She reached over to touch the Bible on the nightstand beside their bed. "Proverbs 22:6 says, 'Train up a child in the way he should go: and when he is old, he will not depart from it.' We did our best to teach Faith and the rest of our kinner about God's laws and His ways, so now we must trust that she has come back to those teachings."

"Jah, that's all we can do. Trust and pray," he mumbled as his eyes drifted shut.

As Faith helped Melinda get ready for bed that night, her head pounded like a blacksmith's anvil at work. It had been all she could do to keep from telling her folks and the bishop what her true intentions were, but she knew Melinda would never adapt to the Amish way of life unless Faith stayed for a while and helped her fit in. It would be too traumatic for both of them if Faith left the child with strangers. No, the best thing was for her to pretend she was home to stay until she felt the time was right for her to leave. She just hoped she wouldn't be pressured to join the church, because that would be impossible if she planned to leave.

"How come everyone in your family kept starin' at me during supper?" Melinda asked from where she sat on the bed. "And how come they dress different than us?"

"They were probably staring because you're so cute and they were happy to meet you." Faith tweaked her daughter's turned-up nose. "And they dress different than we do because they're Amish and they believe God wants them to wear simple, plain clothes, not fancy things like so many other people like to wear."

Melinda's forehead wrinkled. "Maybe some were happy to see me, but not Grandma Stutzman. She frowned when you told her who I was."

"That's because she was so surprised." Faith sat on the edge of the bed and took hold of the child's hand. "As I told you before we left Branson, I hadn't seen any of my family for ten years, and they didn't know I had a daughter."

Melinda sat with a sober expression, as though she were mulling over what Faith had said. Then her face broke into a smile. "Susie's real nice, and I think she likes me."

Faith nodded. "I'm sure she does. I believe you and my little sister will become good friends in no time at all."

"When we went out to the barn after supper, she let me pet the baby kitties and even a couple of the horses." Melinda crawled under the covers and snuggled against her pillow. "I'd better go to sleep now so I can get up early and help Grandpa Stutzman milk his cows."

Faith smiled and bent to give her daughter a kiss. It was seriously doubtful that Melinda would be awake early enough to milk any cows, but it made Faith feel hopeful about things, knowing her father had shown an interest in Melinda. Too bad he hadn't taken much interest in Faith when she was a child.

As Melinda drifted off to sleep, Faith lay on her side of the bed, wondering how she would handle being separated from her daughter when the time came for her to leave. Would she be welcome to return for visits? How long would she need to stay here in order for Melinda to fully adjust?

Chapter 4

Noah looked forward to going to church at his friend Isaac Troyer's place. Isaac and his wife, Ellen, had been married four years and already had two small children. Noah enjoyed spending time with other people's children. He figured that was a good thing, since it wasn't likely he'd ever have any of his own.

"Got to be married to have kinner," Noah muttered as he scrambled a batch of eggs for breakfast.

"Couldn't quite make out what you were saying, but I'm guessing you were talking to yourself again, jah?"

Noah turned at the sound of his mother's voice. He hadn't realized she had come into the kitchen. "I guess I was," he admitted, feeling a sense of warmth cover his cheeks.

"You've got to quit doing that, son." Mom's hazel-colored

eyes looked perky this morning, and Noah was glad she seemed to be feeling better. Yesterday she'd looked tired and acted kind of shakylike.

His mother shuffled over to their gas-operated refrigerator, withdrew a slab of bacon, and handed it to Noah. "Some of your daed's best."

He chuckled. "All of Pop's hogs are the best. At least he thinks so."

Mom's head bobbed up and down, and a few brown hairs sprinkled with gray peeked out from the bun she wore under her small, white head covering. "My Levi would sure enough say so."

"You're right about that. Pop gets up early every morning, rain or shine, and heads out to feed his pigs. Truth is, I think he enjoys talking to the old sows more than he does me."

Mom's forehead wrinkled as she set three plates on the table. "Now don't start with that, Noah. It's not your daed's fault that you don't share his interest in raising hogs."

"That's not the problem, Mom, and you know it." Noah grabbed a butcher knife from the wooden block on the cupboard and cut several slices of bacon; then he slapped them into the frying pan. The trouble between him and Pop went back to when Noah was a young boy. He was pretty sure his father thought he was a sissy because he liked to cook and help Mom with some of the inside chores. That was really dumb, as far as Noah was concerned. Would a sissy work up a sweat planting a bunch of trees? Would a sissy wear calluses on his hands from pruning, shaping, and cutting the Christmas pines English people in the area bought every December?

Mom took out a container of fresh goat's milk from the refrigerator. "Let's talk about something else, shall we? Your daed will be in soon from doing his chores, and I don't want you all riled up when he gets here."

Noah grunted and flipped the sizzling bacon. "I'm not riled, Mom. Just stating facts as I see 'em."

"Jah, well, you have a right to your opinion."

"Glad you think so. Now if you want to hear more about what I think—"

"Your daed loves you, Noah, and that's the truth of it."

Noah nodded. "I know, and I love him, too. I also realize that Pop doesn't like it because I'd rather be in the kitchen than out slopping hogs with him, so I'm trying to accept things as they are."

Mom sighed. "None of my boys ever enjoyed the pigs the way that husband of mine does."

Noah realized it was past time for a change of subject. "I baked a couple of lemon sponge cakes while you and Pop went to town yesterday. One with sugar and one without."

"Are you planning to give one away or set both out on the table at the meal after our preaching service?"

Noah pushed the bacon around in the pan, trying to get it to brown up evenly. "The cake I made with a sugar substitute is for us to have here at home. I figured I would give the one made with sugar to someone who might need a special touch today."

"Guess God will show you who when the time is right."

"Jah. That's how it usually goes."

"I just hope you don't develop baker's asthma from working around flour so much."

Noah snickered. "I don't think you have to worry none.

That usually only happens to those who work in bakeries and such. One would have to be around flour a lot more than me to develop baker's asthma."

Pop entered the kitchen just as Noah was dishing up the bacon and scrambled eggs. Noah's father had dark brown hair, with close-set eyes that matched his hair color, but his beard had been nearly gray since his late fifties. Now Pop was starting to show his age in other areas, too. His summer-tanned face was creased with wrinkles, he had several dark splotches on his hands and arms, and he walked with a slower gait these days.

"Something smells mighty good this morning," Pop said, sniffing the air. "Must have made some bacon."

Noah's mother pointed to the platter full of bacon and eggs. "Our son has outdone himself again, Levi. He made sticky buns, too." She nodded toward the plate in the center of the table, piled high with rolls. Noah had learned to make many sweet treats using a sugar substitute so Mom could enjoy them without affecting her diabetes, and he knew how much she appreciated it.

"You taking the leftover sticky buns to church?" his father asked after he'd washed his hands at the sink.

"Guess I could." Noah smiled. "I also made a sugar-free lemon sponge cake." Noah made no mention of the cake that he planned to give away. Pop liked lemon so well, he might want that one, too.

Pop smacked his lips. "Sounds good to me."

Noah smiled to himself. His dad might not like him spending so much time in the kitchen, but he sure did enjoy the fruits of Noah's labor. And Pop hadn't said one word about Noah not helping out with the hogs. Maybe it was a good sign. This might be the beginning of a great day.

"I can't believe how much our two boys are growing," Barbara Zook said to her husband, David, as they headed down the road in his open buggy toward Isaac and Ellen Troyer's home. She glanced over her shoulder at their two young sons. "I made a pair of trousers for Aaron but two months ago, and already they're too short for his long legs."

David smiled and nodded. "Jah, it won't be long and both our boys will be grown, married, and on their own. Someday we'll be retired, and Aaron can take over the harness shop."

She reached across the seat and gently pinched his arm. "Don't you be saying such things. I want to keep our kinner little for as long as I can."

He shook his head. "Now, Barbara, you know that's not possible, so you may as well accept the changes as they come."

She released a sigh. "I can accept some changes, but others aren't so easy."

"Are you thinking of anything in particular?"

"Jah. I was thinking about my old friend Faith. This morning as I was looking through the bottom drawer of my dresser, I came across a handkerchief Faith had given me on my twelfth birthday. The sight of it made me feel kind of sad." Barbara blinked a couple of times as the remembrance of her friend saying good-bye washed over her like a harsh, stinging rain. "I haven't heard from Faith in a good many years, but I still remember to pray for her every day."

David reached for Barbara's hand and gave her fingers a

gentle squeeze. "Prayer is the key to each new day and the lock for every night, *jah*?"

"That's right, and I'll keep praying for my friend whether I hear from her again or not."

David smiled. "I feel blessed to have married someone as caring as you."

Barbara leaned her head on his shoulder. "I'm the one who's been blessed, husband."

Faith felt as fidgety as a bumblebee on a hot summer day. She hadn't been this nervous since the first time she had performed one of her comedy routines in front of a bunch of strangers. She and Melinda sat in the back of her parents' open buggy, along with young Susie. Faith's sisters, Grace Ann and Esther, had ridden to church with their brothers John and Brian.

Faith reached up and touched her head covering to be sure it was firmly in place. She'd been in such a hurry this morning, having to get herself dressed in one of Grace Ann's plain dresses and Melinda in one of Susie's, that she hadn't taken the time to do up her hair properly. Rather than being parted down the middle, twisted, and pulled back in a bun, she'd brushed her hair straight back and quickly secured it in a bun, then hurried downstairs to help with breakfast. She would be meeting others in their congregation today, not to mention facing Bishop Martin again.

Thinking about the bishop caused Faith to reflect on her conversation with him. She'd left the bishop, as well as her family, with the impression that she had come home to stay and had given no hint that she planned to go back to her life as an entertainer.

You won't have your daughter with you, her conscience reminded. *Can you ever be truly happy without Melinda?* Faith shook her head as though the action might clear away the troubling thoughts. She wouldn't think about that now. She would deal with leaving Melinda when the time came. For now, Faith's only need was to make everyone in her Amish community believe she had come home to stay.

Soon they were pulling into the Troyers' yard, and Faith looked around in amazement. Isaac Troyer's house and barn were enormous, and a huge herd of dairy cows grazed in the pasture nearby. Papa had mentioned something about the Troyers' dairy farm doing well, but she'd had no idea it would be so big.

Faith let her mind wander back to the days when she had attended the one-room schoolhouse not far down the road. Isaac Troyer, her brother John, and Noah Hertzler had all been friends. She remembered Noah as being the shy one of the group. Faith could still see his face turning as red as a radish over something one of the scholars at school had said. He'd hardly spoken more than a few words, and then it was only if someone talked to him first. Noah hadn't been outspoken or full of wisecracks the way Faith had always been, that was for sure. She would have to watch her mouth now that she was back at home. Her jokes and fooling around wouldn't be appreciated.

I wonder if Noah's still around, and if so, is the poor man as shy as he used to be?

"You getting out or what?"

Faith jerked her head at the sound of her father's deep voice. He leaned against the buggy, his dark eyes looking ever so serious. He was a hard worker, and he could be equally hard when it came to his family. As a little girl, Faith had always been a bit afraid of him. She wasn't sure if it was his booming voice or his penetrating eyes. One thing for sure, Faith knew Papa would take no guff from any of his children. The way he looked at her right now made her wonder if he could tell what was on her mind. Did he know how much she dreaded going to church?

Faith stepped down from the buggy and turned to help Melinda and Susie out. Chattering like magpies, the little girls ran toward the Troyers' house. Faith was left to walk alone, and as she headed toward the Troyers' house, she shuddered, overcome by the feeling that she was marching into a den of hungry lions. What if she and Melinda weren't accepted? What if either one of them said or did something wrong today?

Faith drew in a deep breath and glanced down at her un-adorned, dark green dress. It felt strange to be wearing Plain clothes again, and she wondered if she looked as phony on the outside as she was on the inside. Melinda hadn't seemed to mind putting on one of her aunt Susie's simple dresses. She'd even made some comment about it being fun to play dress-up.

Oh, to be young again. I hope Melinda keeps her cheerful attitude in the days ahead. Faith kept her gaze downward, being mindful of the uneven ground and sharp stones in the Troyers' driveway. She had taken only a few steps when she bumped into someone. Lifting her head, Faith found herself staring into a pair of brown eyes that were so dark they almost looked black. She shifted her body quickly to the right, but the man with thick chestnut-brown hair moved to his left at the same time. With a nervous laugh, she swung to the left, just as he transferred his body to the right.

"Sorry. We seem to be going the same way," he mumbled. There was a small scar in the middle of his chin, and for a moment, Faith thought she recognized him. Noah Hertzler had been left with that kind of a scar from a fall on the school playground many years ago. But this mature-looking man couldn't be the same scrawny boy who had fallen from the swings.

"I–I don't believe we've met," the man said. "My name's Noah Hertzler."

"I'm Faith Andrews. . .used to be Stutzman."

Noah's jaw dropped open, and at the same time, Faith felt as if the air had been sucked from her lungs. The man who stood before her was no longer the red-faced kid afraid of his own shadow, but a tall, muscular fellow who was looking at her in a most peculiar way.

"Faith Andrews, the comedian who can yodel?" he asked, lifting his dark eyebrows in obvious surprise.

She nodded and tucked a stray hair behind one ear. "One and the same."

Chapter 5

Noah could hardly believe Faith Stutzman, rebellious Amish teenager turned comedian, was standing in front of him dressed like all the other Plain women who had come to church this morning. Only Faith was different. Not only had her last name changed, but she didn't have the same humble, submissive appearance most Amish women had. Her eyes were the clearest blue, like fresh water flowing from a mountain stream. There was something about the way those eyes flashed—the way she held her head. She seemed proud and maybe a bit defiant.

"What are you doing here?"

"You know about me being a comedian?"

They'd spoken at the same time, and Noah chuckled, feeling the heat of embarrassment flood his cheeks. He hated how easily he blushed. "You go first."

She lifted her chin. "No, you."

Noah acceded to her request. "I–I'm surprised to see you. How long have you been home?"

"We arrived yesterday afternoon."

"We?" Noah glanced around, thinking maybe Faith had a husband who had accompanied her.

"My daughter, Melinda, is with me," Faith explained. "My husband died six months ago."

Noah sucked in his breath as he allowed himself to feel her pain. "I'm sorry for your loss."

She stared down at her black shoes. "Thank you."

He wouldn't press her for details. Maybe another time—when they got to know each other better. "It's your turn now," he said quietly.

Her head came up. "Huh?"

"You started to ask a question a few minutes ago. About me knowing you were a comedian."

"Oh, yeah. I'm surprised you knew. I obviously didn't become a professional entertainer while I was still Amish." Faith pursed her perfectly shaped lips, and he forced himself not to stare at them. "I didn't figure you would know about my new profession."

"My boss is an English man. He often plays tapes, or we listen to his portable radio while we work, and I heard an interview you did on the air once." Noah paused. "You yodeled a bit and told a few jokes, too."

She tipped her head to one side. "And you lived to tell about it?"

He nodded. "As I remember, the jokes you told were real funny."

"You really think so?"

"Sure. When I was a boy and came over to your place to spend time with John, your silliness and joke telling used to crack me up."

Faith stared up at him. "Really? You never said anything."

He kicked at the small stones beneath his feet. "I was kind of shy and awkward back then, and I guess I still am sometimes."

"Do you really believe I have a talent to make people laugh?" she asked, making no comment about his shyness.

"Jah, sure." He shifted his weight from one foot to the other. "So. . .uh. . .what brought you back to Webster County?"

She stood straighter, pushing her shoulders back. "I've returned to my birthplace so my daughter can have a real home."

"Not because you missed your family and friends?"

She shrugged. "Sure, that, too."

Noah had a feeling Faith wasn't being completely honest with him. Her tone of voice told him she might be hiding something. He didn't think now was the time or place to be asking her a bunch of personal questions, though. Maybe he would have that chance later on. He glanced around and noticed his friend Isaac watching him from near the barn. Noah figured Isaac would probably expect him to give a full account of all he and Faith had said to each other.

"I'd better go since church will be starting soon. It's. . .uh. . . nice to see you again," Noah said. "I hope it works out for you and your daughter."

"Things are a little strained for us right now. It's going to be a difficult adjustment, I'm sure."

"Soon it will go better."

"I hope so."

Faith walked off toward the house, and Noah headed over to see Isaac. He knew if he didn't, the nosy fellow would most likely seek him out.

"Who was that woman you were talking to?" Isaac asked as soon as Noah stepped up beside him. "You two looked pretty cozylike, but I didn't recognize her."

"It was Faith Stutzman, and we weren't being cozy."

Isaac's dark eyebrows shot up. "Faith Stutzman? Menno and Wilma's wayward daughter?"

"Jah. Her husband died awhile ago, and she and her daughter have moved back home. Her last name's Andrews now."

Isaac reached up to scratch the back of his head. In the process, he nearly knocked his black felt hat to the ground, but he righted it in time. "So how'd you happen to strike up a conversation with her?"

"We sort of bumped into each other."

"Did you get all tongue-tied and turn red in the face?"

Noah clenched his teeth. "To tell you the truth, I didn't feel quite as nervous or shy in Faith's presence as I usually do when I'm talking to a young, single woman."

"Right. And pigs can fly," Isaac said with a snicker. He motioned toward the house, where several people were filing in through the open doorway. "Guess we'd better get in there now."

As Noah and his friend moved toward the house, Noah made a decision. He knew now who should get that lemon sponge cake he had brought today. The scripture verse he'd attached was about having faith in God, so it seemed appropriate to give it to a woman whose name was Faith. It would be like a welcome-home gift to someone who reminded him of the prodigal son in the Bible.

As Wilma approached a group of women who had gathered outside the Troyers' home to visit, she glanced across the yard and noticed Faith standing under a leafy maple tree by herself. Faith's arms were folded, her shoulders were slumped, and she stared at the ground as though she might be looking at something.

There's no mistaking it, Wilma thought ruefully. *My daughter isn't happy about being here today. Is it because she doesn't want to be home, or could she be feeling nervous about seeing all the people from our community and having to explain why she's come back to Webster County with her daughter?*

"I hear your oldest daughter has come home," Annie Yoder, one of the minister's wives, said as she stepped up to Wilma.

Wilma nodded, realizing how fast the news of Faith's arrival must have traveled. Maybe Bishop Martin had spread the news as he'd gone from house to house last night, letting everyone know about the change in plans concerning where church would be held today. "Yesterday evening, Faith arrived home with her daughter, Melinda," Wilma said, trying to make her voice sound casual.

"Is she here for a visit, or is she planning to stay?"

"Her husband recently died, and she says she's home for good." Even as the words slipped from Wilma's tongue, she wondered if they were true. Did Faith plan to give up her modern ways and join the Amish church, or would she soon tire of things and head back on the road?

No matter how hard Faith tried, she couldn't find a comfortable position. She'd forgotten how hard the backless wooden benches the people sat on during church could be. She glanced at Melinda, who sat on a bench beside Susie and some other young girls about their age. How well would her daughter manage during the long service, most of which was spoken in a language she couldn't understand? Faith was glad she had thought to bring a basket filled with some snack foods along, in case her daughter got hungry.

As the service continued, Faith's mind began to wander, taking her back in time, back to when she was a little girl trying not to fidget during one of the bishop's long sermons, and she found herself becoming more restless. Every few minutes she glanced out the living-room window, wishing for the freedom to be outside where she could enjoy the pleasant summer day. She knew they would be going outdoors for their noon meal after the service, but that was still a ways off. Besides, she would be expected to help serve the men before she could relax and enjoy her meal.

Faith's thoughts drove her on, down a not-so-pleasant memory lane. She had struggled on her own the first years after she'd left home and had ended up waiting tables and performing on a makeshift stage for a time. Then Greg had come along and swept Faith off her feet. He'd said she was talented and could go far in the world of entertainment. Greg's whispered honeyed words and promises had been like music to her ears, and it hadn't taken her long to succumb to his charms.

During the early years of their marriage, Faith had thought she was in love with Greg, and she'd believed the feeling was returned. Maybe it had been at first, but then Greg began to use her to gain riches. The more successful she became as an entertainer, the more of her money he spent on alcohol and gambling. She suspected he thought she didn't know what he was up to, but Faith was no dummy. She knew exactly why Greg often sank into depression or became hostile toward her. Never Melinda, though. Thankfully, Greg had always been kind to their child.

Of course, he might not have remained docile toward Melinda if he had lived and kept on drinking the way he was, Faith reminded herself. *If he could smack me around, then what's to say he wouldn't have eventually taken his frustrations out on our daughter?*

"As many of you may already know, one of our own who has lived among the English for the last several years returned home yesterday. We welcome Faith Stutzman Andrews and her daughter, Melinda, to our worship service this morning."

Faith sat up a bit straighter as Bishop Martin's comment drove her thoughts aside. She glanced around the room, feeling an urgency to escape but knowing she couldn't. All eyes seemed to be focused on her. Many nodded their heads, some smiled, and others merely looked at her with curious stares. What were they thinking? Did everyone see her as a wayward woman who had come crawling home because she had no other place to go? Well, it was true in a sense. She had nowhere else to go. At least no place she wanted to take Melinda. If she had kept the child on the road with her, it would have been only a matter of time before her innocent daughter fell prey to some gold digger like her father had been. Faith desired better things for her little girl. She wanted Melinda to know that when she woke up every morning, there would be food on the table and a warm fire to greet her. She needed her precious child to go to bed at night feeling a sense of belonging and knowing she was nurtured and loved.

You had all those things when you were growing up, but you left them, the voice in her head reminded. Faith shook the thoughts aside as she forced herself to concentrate on the bishop's closing prayer. Better to focus on his words than to think of all she'd given up when she left home. She hadn't really wanted to leave, but she'd done it to prove to herself and to her family that she was her own person and had been blessed with a talent for yodeling and joke telling.

A rustle of skirts and the murmur of voices made Faith realize the service was over. She glanced around. Everyone was exiting the room.

Faith saw to it that Melinda was in Esther's care, since she was also overseeing Susie. Then Faith excused herself to go to the kitchen, where several women and teenage girls scurried about, trying to get the meal served as quickly as possible.

"What can I do to help?" she asked her mother, who stood at the cupboard piling slices of bread onto a plate.

Before Mama could respond, Ellen Troyer spoke up. "Why don't you help David Zook's wife serve coffee to the menfolk out in the barn, where tables have been set up?" She handed Faith a pot of coffee. "It's good to have you back among the people. You've been missed."

Nodding at Ellen, Faith accepted the coffeepot and turned and headed out the back door.

When Faith entered the barn a few minutes later, she noticed a dark-haired woman serving coffee at one of the tables. *That must be David Zook's wife.*

She approached the woman, whose back was to her, and asked, "Which tables are yet to be served?"

The woman turned around, and a slow smile spread across her face. "*Ach,* Faith! It was a surprise to see you in church, and I'm so glad you're back home."

Faith squinted as she looked more closely at the woman. "Barbara? Barbara Raber?"

"Jah, only it's Zook now. I've been married to David for close to five years." Barbara smiled, revealing two deep dimples in her round cheeks. "Remember David? He was a year ahead of us in school."

Faith wasn't sure what to say. She and Barbara had been friends while growing up, but the truth was, she barely remembered a fellow named David Zook.

"It–it's nice to see you again." Faith's voice sounded formal and strained. She couldn't help it; she felt formal and strained around everyone here today. Everyone except for Noah Hertzler. She'd actually enjoyed their brief conversation and had felt more at ease with him than she felt with Barbara right now. It made no sense. She hadn't known Noah all that well when they were growing up, as he was four years younger than her. Noah had been John's friend, not hers. He'd also been so shy back then that he hadn't said more than a few words to anyone in their family except John. Today, however, Noah seemed easy to talk to, and there had only been a hint of shyness on his part.

"Faith? Did you hear what I said?"

Barbara's soft-spoken voice and gentle nudge drove Faith's thoughts aside.

"What was that?"

"I said I'm glad you've come home."

Faith nodded.

"Now about the tables needing to be served—you can take those four." Barbara motioned to the ones on her left.

"Okay." Faith moved away, thinking how much her friend had changed. Barbara Raber had been as slender as a reed when they were teenagers. Barbara Zook was slightly plump, especially around the middle. The mischief that could be seen in young Barbara's eyes had been replaced with a look of peace and contentment. For that, Faith felt a twinge of envy. In all her twenty-eight years, she'd never known true peace or contentment. She had always wanted something she couldn't have. Something more—something better.

Faith avoided eye contact as she served the men, but as she poured coffee into the last cup at the table, she felt gentle but calloused fingers touch her arm. *"Danki."*

"You're welcome," she murmured, daring to seek out the man's face. It was Noah Hertzler, and his tender expression was nearly her undoing.

"I have something for you," he said quietly. "It's in the Troyers' house."

She tipped her head in question. *Why would Noah have anything for me? He hardly knows me, and I'm sure he didn't know I would be here today.*

"Will you be heading back to the kitchen soon?" he asked.

She nodded.

"Okay. I'll meet you there in a few minutes."

Faith nodded mutely and moved away. She walked back to the house a few minutes later, feeling like a marionette with no control over its movements.

Relief swept over Faith when she stepped into the kitchen and realized that no one else was there. She figured the other women must have gone to the barn to eat their meal after the men were done.

Faith pulled out one of the mismatched wooden chairs and sat down. When she placed her hands on the table, she noticed that they were shaking. *What's wrong with me? I've faced tougher crowds than the one here today and didn't feel half as intimidated. I used to make an audience howl and beg for more, even when I was dying on the inside because of the way things were with Greg and me. Yet here, among my own people, I can barely crack a smile.*

Faith squeezed her eyes shut, wishing she remembered how to pray. If she could, she would ask God to calm her spirit.

When the back door creaked open, Faith jumped. She turned her head to the right.

Noah stood in the doorway with an easygoing grin on his face.

She swallowed hard. What did he have for her? What did he want in return?

Noah closed the door and strolled over to the cupboard across the room. He opened one of the doors and took out a cake carrier, which he set on the table in front of Faith. "This is for you."

"You're giving me a whole cake?"

Noah nodded. "It's a lemon sponge cake, and I made it with the idea of giving it away today."

"Why me?"

His face flooded with color. "Just call it a welcome-home gift." He pushed the plastic container toward her. "Sure hope you like lemon."

She nodded. "It's one of my favorite flavors."

"That's good. I hope you'll enjoy every bite, as well as the verse of scripture," he said.

Verse of scripture? Faith's gaze went to the little card attached to the side of the pan, and her heart clenched. She would take the cake, but she had no desire to read the scripture.

Chapter 6

W hat have you got there?" Mama asked as Faith climbed down from the buggy behind Melinda and Susie.

Faith looked down at the cake Noah had given her, hoping it hadn't spoiled. She had placed a small bag of ice she'd found in the Troyers' refrigerator on top of the plastic container, taken it out to the buggy earlier, and slipped it under the backseat. She still wondered why Noah had chosen her to be the recipient of his luscious-looking dessert.

"Faith? Did you hear what I asked?"

Clutching the cake in her hands, she faced her mother. "Uh. . .it's a lemon sponge cake."

Mama's eyebrows arched upward. "Where'd you get it?"

Faith drew in a deep breath. She may as well get the inquisition over with, because she was sure her mother wouldn't be satisfied until she'd heard all the details. "Noah Hertzler gave it to me."

Mama chuckled softly. "I thought as much. That young fellow is always handing out his baked goods to someone in our community. Ida Hertzler is one lucky mamm to have him for a son; he's right handy in the kitchen."

"Is that so?"

"Jah. From what Ida's told me, Noah's been helping out with the cooking and baking ever since he was a kinner."

Faith hadn't known that. The only thing she knew about Noah was that he used to be shy and seemed to be kind of awkward.

"Noah's not married, you know," Mama said as they headed for the house.

Faith figured as much since she hadn't seen him with a woman and he wasn't wearing a beard, which meant he wasn't married. It didn't concern her, however, so she made no response to her mother's comment.

"Maybe after you've settled in here and have joined the church, you and Noah might hit it off."

Faith whirled around to face her mother. "Mama, Greg's only been dead a short while. It wouldn't be proper for me to think about another man right now, in case that's what you're insinuating." She sniffed. "Besides, I'm not planning to remarry—ever."

Mama gave her a curious look, but Faith hurried to the house before the confused-looking woman could say anything more. She didn't want to talk about her disastrous marriage to Greg or the plans she had for the future.

Barbara Zook collapsed onto the sofa in her living room with a sigh. She'd just put her boys to bed and needed a little time to herself.

"Mind if I join you?" her husband asked, as he stepped into the room.

She patted the cushion beside her and smiled. "Not at all. I'd be happy for the company of someone old enough to carry on adult conversation."

David grinned as he seated himself on the sofa and scooted close to her. "You visited with some of the women from church today. Wasn't that adult conversation?"

Barbara nodded. "Jah, but that was some time ago. I've spent the last couple of hours feeding our boys, listening to their endless chatter, and getting them ready for bed." She took hold of his hand. "Now I'm ready for some quiet time."

"You just said you wanted some adult conversation. If you need quiet time, then maybe I'd better sit here and keep my mouth shut."

She chuckled and squeezed his fingers. "I'm sure you know what I meant."

"Jah." David leaned his headful of thick, dark hair on her shoulder and closed his eyes. "This does feel good."

They sat in companionable silence until Barbara decided to ask him a question. "What did you think when you saw Faith at church today?"

David lifted his head and opened his eyes. "It was a surprise to me, as I'm sure it was to most. She's been gone a long time, and I didn't figure she would ever come back. How about you? What were your thoughts about seeing your old friend again?"

Barbara frowned. "It was strange, David. . .very strange."

"In what way?"

"Faith was dressed in Amish clothes, so she looked sort of the same, but her personality has changed."

"How so?"

She released a groan. "Faith isn't the same person I used to know. Even after only a few minutes of talking with her, I could tell that she's unhappy."

"Well, of course she would be. Her husband died recently, isn't that what you heard?"

"That's true," Barbara said with a nod, "but I have a feeling that Faith's unhappiness goes much deeper. Truth be told, I think Faith's misery goes back to her childhood. I suspect she carried that sadness and sense of bitterness along with her when she left home ten years ago."

"You think it's because her folks disapproved of her yodeling and joke telling?"

"Not the yodeling, exactly—or the joke telling, either. There are others in our community who like to yodel and tell funny stories."

"That's true," he said with a nod. "*Mer yodel laut, awwer net gut.*"

She nodded. "We do yodel loudly but not well. But I think what the Stutzmans disapproved of was Faith cutting up all the time when she should have been getting her chores done."

Deep lines etched David's forehead. "I can't imagine what it must have been like for her to get up onstage in front of a bunch of people and put on an act. It goes against everything we've been taught to show off like that."

"I don't believe Faith saw it as showing off, David. I think she only ran away and became an entertainer because she didn't feel what she enjoyed doing the most was accepted at home."

"Sure hope none of our kinner ever feels that way. I don't know what I'd do if one of them were to up and leave home."

"Sell kann ich mir gaar net eibilde." She patted his hand and repeated, "I can't conceive of that at all. I'm sure neither of our boys will do something like that as long as they know we appreciate their abilities and God-given talents."

David leaned over and kissed Barbara's cheek. "You're a *schmaert* woman, you know that?"

She nodded and stroked his bristly, dark beard. "I had to be smart to find a good husband like you."

"Church was good today, jah?" Noah's mother asked as she handed Noah and his father each a cup of coffee, then took a seat at the table across from Noah.

Noah nodded. "It's always good."

"Seemed a little strange to see Faith Stutzman back and with a little girl she said was her daughter, no less," Noah's father put in from his seat at the head of the table.

Mom smiled. "It's nice that she's come home and wants to be Amish again."

Noah stared into his cup of coffee as he pondered things.

After his short visit with Faith this morning before church and then again after church was over, he wasn't sure she wanted to be Amish. He had a hunch the only reason Faith had come home was to find a place for her daughter to live, and if that meant Faith having to give up her life as an entertainer, then she would do it. It was obvious by the look he'd seen on Faith's face when she spoke of her child that she loved Melinda and would do most anything for her. He just wished she hadn't looked so disinterested when he'd given her the cake with the scripture verse attached. Hopefully, she would take the time to read and absorb what it said.

"You're looking kind of thoughtful there, son," Mom said, breaking into Noah's thoughts. "Is everything all right?"

"Jah, sure." He picked up his cup and took a drink of coffee. "I was just thinking is all."

"So, Noah, who'd you give the cake you made to?" Pop asked.

"Gave it to Faith, figuring she might need some encouragement today."

"That makes sense to me," Mom put in. "Faith's a nice-looking woman, wouldn't you say?"

Noah shrugged. "I suppose she does look pretty good in the face."

"So do some of my baby pigs, but looks ain't everything." Pop thumped his chest a few times. "It's what's in here that counts, and I have a hunch that wayward woman isn't as pretty on the inside as she is on the outside." He grunted. "Let's hope she's learned her lesson about chasing after the things of the world and has come home to stay."

Noah could hardly believe his father would compare Faith's

beauty to one of his pigs, but the thing that really riled him was Pop's comment about Faith not being pretty inside.

He sat there a moment, trying to decide how best to say what was on his mind. Pop could be stubborn and rather opinionated at times, and Noah wasn't looking for an argument. Still, he felt the need to defend Faith.

"I think we need to pray for Faith, don't you? Pray that she'll find peace and contentment here in Webster County, and that her relationship with God will be strengthened by her friends and family."

Pop's forehead wrinkled, and he opened his mouth as if to reply, but Mom spoke first. "Noah's right. What Faith needs is encouragement and prayer." She smiled at Noah and patted his arm. "I'm glad you gave her that cake, and I'm sure she'll enjoy eating it as much as we do whenever you bake something for us."

Noah chuckled. "Was that a hint that I should do more baking soon?"

She nodded and took a bite of the sugar-free cake Noah had made especially for her.

"I'll probably do more baking after I get home from work tomorrow evening," Noah said.

Pop snorted. "You ought to quit that foolish job at the tree farm and come back to work for me."

Noah shook his head. "No thanks. I had enough dealings with smelly hogs when I was a boy and we were raising them to put food on our own table. You're better off having Abel Yoder working for you. Ever since he and his family moved here from Pennsylvania, he's been most happy to help with your hogs. "

"That's because raising hogs is good, honest work, and Abel

knows it." Pop leveled Noah with an icy stare, making Noah wish he'd kept his comments to himself.

"What Noah does for a living is honest work, too," Mom defended.

"Jah, well, it may be honest, but Christmas trees aren't part of the Amish way, and if Noah's not careful, he might be led astray from working with that English fellow who likes to listen to country music all the time."

Noah's mouth dropped open. He'd never said anything to either of his folks about Hank playing country music, and he couldn't figure out how Pop knew about it.

"News travels fast in these parts," Pop said before Noah could voice the question. "You'd better be careful what you say and do."

"I'm sure our son hasn't gotten caught up in the world's music," Mom was quick to say. "And just because his boss chooses to listen to country music, that doesn't make him a bad person."

Noah smiled. He couldn't have said it better himself.

Pop set his cup down so hard on the table that some of the coffee spilled out. "Jah, well, just don't let anything Hank says or does that's worldly rub off on you, Noah."

"Like I would," Noah mumbled as he turned away. Why was it that Pop always looked for the negative in things—especially when it came to Noah?

Chapter 7

In the days that followed, Faith and Melinda settled into a routine. Faith got up early every morning to help with breakfast, milk the cows, and feed the chickens. She labored from sunup to sunset, taking time out only for meals and to help Melinda learn the traditional Pennsylvania Dutch language of the Amish.

The child had also been assigned several chores to do, and even though she seemed all right with the idea of wearing her aunt Susie's Plain clothes, she wasn't used to having so many responsibilities placed on her shoulders. Nor was she accustomed to being taught a foreign language. Amish children grew up speaking their native tongue and learning English when they entered school in the first grade. Since Melinda would be starting school in the fall and already spoke English, her task was to learn Pennsylvania Dutch.

"I don't like it here, Mama," Melinda said one morning as she handed Faith a freshly laundered towel to be hung on the clothesline next to the house. "When can we go home?"

Faith flinched. Home? They really had no home. Hotels and motels in whatever city Faith was performing in—those were the only homes Melinda had ever known.

She clipped the towel in place and patted the top of her daughter's head. "This is your home now, sweet girl."

"You mean, *our* home, don't you, Mama?"

"Oh, yes," Faith said quickly. "And soon you'll get used to the way things are."

Melinda lifted her chin and frowned. "Grandma Stutzman makes me work hard."

Faith wasn't used to manual labor either, and every muscle in her body ached. In the past few weeks, she had pulled so many weeds from the garden that her fingers felt stiff and unyielding. Heaps of clothes had been washed and ironed, and she'd helped with the cooking and cleaning and done numerous other chores she was no longer accustomed to doing. It wasn't the hard work that bothered Faith, though. It was the suffocating feeling that she couldn't be herself. She desperately wanted to sit on the porch in the evenings and yodel to her heart's content. She would enjoy telling some jokes or humorous stories and have her family appreciate them, but that was impossible.

"Mama, are you thinking about what I said?"

Melinda's question caught Faith's attention. "Everyone in the family has a job to do," she said patiently. "In time you'll get used to it."

Faith could see by the child's scowl that she wasn't happy.

"How would you like to eat lunch down by the pond today?" Faith asked, hoping to cheer up Melinda.

Melinda's blue eyes seemed to light right up. "Can Aunt Susie come, too?"

"If Grandma says it's all right."

"Can we bring our dolls along?"

"If you want to."

As Melinda handed Faith a pair of Grandpa Stutzman's trousers to hang on the line, she asked, "How come only the men wear pants here?"

"Grandpa and Grandma belong to the Amish faith, and the church believes only men and boys should wear pants."

Melinda's forehead wrinkled. "Does that mean I ain't never gonna wear jeans again?"

"I'm not ever," Faith corrected.

Melinda nodded soberly. "You and me ain't never gonna wear jeans."

Faith bit back a chuckle as she knelt on the grass and touched the hem of Melinda's plain blue cotton dress. "I thought you liked wearing dresses."

"I do, but I also like to wear jeans."

"You'll get used to wearing only dresses." Even as the words slipped off her tongue, Faith wondered if her prediction would come true. Melinda had worn fancy dresses, blue jeans, and shorts ever since she'd been a baby, and wearing Plain dresses all the time would be a difficult transition.

"Here's the last towel, Mama. Now can I go swing?"

"Maybe after lunch." Faith was relieved that Melinda had quickly changed the subject. Maybe the child would adjust after all. She seemed to enjoy many things on the farm—spending time with Aunt Susie, playing with the barn cats, helping Grandpa milk the cows, swinging on the same wooden swing Faith had used when she was a little girl. In time, she hoped Melinda would learn to be content with everything about her new life as an Amish girl. In the meantime, Faith would try to make her daughter feel as secure as possible and show her some of the good things about being Plain.

Faith was determined to make this work for Melinda and equally determined to get back on the road as soon as possible. Mama was already pressing her about taking classes so she could be baptized and join the church. Faith didn't know how much longer she could put it off, but for now she had convinced her mother that she needed more time to adjust to the Amish way of life. She'd been gone a long time and couldn't be expected to change overnight. Not that she planned to change. Whenever Faith had a few moments alone, she practiced her yodeling skills and told a few jokes to whatever animal she might be feeding. Soon she would be onstage again, wearing her hillbilly costume and entertaining an approving audience. Around here, no one seemed to appreciate anything that wasn't related to hard work.

Faith hung the last article of clothing on the line, picked up the wicker basket, and took hold of Melinda's hand. As much as Faith wanted to go back on the road, she had to stay awhile longer—to be sure Melinda was accepted and had adjusted well enough to her new surroundings. Besides, despite several phone calls Faith had managed to make from town, she hadn't found an agent to represent her yet. Without an agent, her career would go nowhere. On her own, all Faith could hope for were one-night stands and programs in small theaters that didn't pay nearly as well as the bigger ones.

"Let's go to the kitchen and see what we can make for our picnic lunch, shall we?" Faith suggested to Melinda, knowing she needed to get her mind on something else.

The child nodded eagerly, and the soft *ma-a-a* of a nearby goat caused them both to laugh as they skipped along the path leading to the house. On the way, they tromped through a mud puddle made by the rain that had fallen during the night. Faith felt the grimy mud ooze between her bare toes. She'd almost forgotten what it was like to go barefoot every summer. It wasn't such a bad thing, really. Especially on the grass, so soft and cushy. It was good to laugh and spend time with her daughter like this. No telling how many more weeks she would have with Melinda.

When Faith and Melinda entered the kitchen a few minutes later, they were greeted with a look of disapproval from Faith's mother. "Ach, my! Your feet are all muddy. Can't you see that I just cleaned the floor?"

Faith looked down at the grubby footprints they had created. "Sorry, Mama. We'll go back outside and clean the dirt off our feet." She grabbed a towel from the counter, took Melinda's hand, and scooted her out the door.

"Grandma Stutzman's mean," Melinda said tearfully. "She's always hollering about something or other."

"It might seem so, but Grandma just wants to keep her kitchen clean." Faith led her daughter over to the pump. She washed their feet and dried them.

"Can we still take our lunch down by the pond?" Melinda questioned.

"Sure we can."

"And Susie can come, too?"

"If Grandma says it's all right."

Melinda's lower lip protruded. "She'll probably say no 'cause she's in a bad mood about us trackin' in the mud on her clean floor."

"I don't think she'll make Susie pay for our transgressions."

"Our what?"

"Transgressions. It means doing wrong things."

Melinda hung her head. "I always seem to be doing wrong things around here. I must be very bad."

Faith knelt on the ground and pulled her daughter into her arms. "You're not bad. You just don't understand all the rules yet."

"Will I ever understand them, Mama?"

Faith gently stroked the child's cheek. "Of course you will. It's just going to take a little more time."

"But I want to wear blue jeans and watch TV, and I can't do either of those things here."

Guilt found its way into Faith's heart and put down roots so deep she thought she might choke. Had she done the right thing in taking Melinda out of the modern world she was used to and expecting her to adjust to the Amish way of doing things? Faith had never accepted all the rules when she was growing up. She had experimented with modern things whenever she'd had the chance. Had it really been all those rules that had driven her away, or was it the simple fact that she'd never felt truly loved and acknowledged by her family?

Noah whistled in response to the call of a finch as he knelt in front of a newly planted pine tree. It was still scrawny compared to those around it, and the seedling appeared to be struggling to survive.

"A little more time and attention are what you're needing," he whispered, resolving to save the fledgling. He wanted to see it thrive and someday find its way to one of the local Christmas tree lots or be purchased by some Englishers who would come to the farm to choose their own holiday tree.

The sound of country-western music blared in Noah's ear, and he figured his boss, Hank Osborn, must be nearby. Hank enjoyed listening to the radio while he worked, and Noah had discovered that he rather liked it, too. Of course, he wouldn't let his folks or anyone from their community know that, and he sure wouldn't buy a radio or listen to music on his own at home. But here at work, it was kind of nice. Besides, this was his boss's radio, and Noah had no control over whether it was played.

The man singing on the radio at the moment also did a bit of yodeling. It made Noah think of Faith and how she had given up her entertaining career and moved back home. He wondered if she had enjoyed the cake he'd given her and what she thought about the verse of scripture he'd attached to it. Had it spoken to her heart, the way God's Word was supposed to? He hoped so, for Faith seemed to be in need of something, and Noah couldn't think of anything more nourishing to the soul than the words found within the Bible.

"Did you bring any of your baked goods in your lunch today?"

Noah turned his head at the sound of his boss's voice. He hadn't realized Hank had moved over to his row of trees. "I made some oatmeal bread last night," Noah said. "Brought you and your wife a loaf of it."

Hank lowered the volume, set his portable radio on the ground, and hunkered down beside Noah. "You're the best! Sure hope your mama knows how lucky she is to have you still living at home."

Noah snickered. "I think she appreciates my help in the kitchen, but I'm not sure how lucky she is."

"A fellow like you ought to be married and raising babies, like those nine brothers of yours have done. Between your cooking and baking skills and the concern you show over a weak little tree, I'd say you would make one fine husband and daddy." Hank nodded toward the struggling pine Noah had been studying before he let his thoughts carry him away.

Noah felt a flush of heat climb up the back of his neck and spread to his cheeks. He hated how easily he blushed.

"Didn't mean to embarrass you. I'm glad to have someone as caring as you working here at Osborns' Christmas Tree Farm." Hank clasped Noah's shoulder. "Besides that, you're easy to talk to."

"Sure hope so." It was then that Noah noticed his boss's wrinkled forehead. "Is there something wrong, Hank? You look so thoughtful."

Hank ran his fingers through his thick, auburn-colored hair. "To tell you the truth, something's bothering me."

Noah got to his feet, and Hank did the same. "Is there a problem with your business? Are you concerned that you won't sell as many trees this year as you have before?"

"It's got nothing to do with business. It's about me and Sandy."

"What's the problem?" Noah kicked a clump of grass with the toe of his boot. "Or would you rather not talk about it?"

Hank shook his head. "I don't mind telling you. In fact, it might do me some good to get this off my chest."

Concern for his boss welled in Noah's soul, and he clasped Hank's shoulder. "Whatever you say will remain between the two of us; you can be sure of that."

"Thanks. I appreciate it." Hank drew in a breath and let it out with a huff. "The thing is. . .Sandy and I have been trying to have a baby for the last couple of years, and yesterday afternoon we went to see a specialist in Springfield and found out that Sandy's unable to conceive."

"I'm sorry to hear that. I'm sure you would both make good parents."

"We've wanted children ever since we got married ten years ago, but we were waiting to start our family until I got my business going good." Hank sighed. "Now that we can finally afford to have a baby, we get hit with the news that Sandy is barren."

Noah wasn't sure how to respond. Among his people, folks didn't wait until they were financially ready to have a baby. Children came in God's time, whether a couple felt ready or not.

"After we left the doctor's office, Sandy acted real depressed and would barely speak to me. I have to admit, I was pretty upset when I heard the news, too." Hank grunted. "Then last night when we were getting ready for bed, she said, 'I think you don't love me anymore because I can't give you children.' "

"What'd you say to that?"

"I tried to convince her that I do love her, but she wouldn't listen to me."

Noah rubbed his chin thoughtfully as he contemplated his reply. "She probably needs time to adjust to things, and if you let her know through your kind words and actions, she'll soon realize that your love isn't conditional."

"You're right. It's not. I would love Sandy no matter what. Even though it would be nice to have a baby of our own, it's not nearly as important to me as having Sandy as my wife."

"Maybe if you keep telling her that, she'll begin to realize it's true."

"Yeah, I hope so."

Noah didn't know why he was telling Hank all this; he was sure no expert on the subject of marriage. Even so, he felt he had to say something that might help his boss feel better about things.

"Have you thought about taking in a foster child or adopting a baby?" Noah asked.

Hank shook his head. "Oh, I don't know. . . . I don't think Sandy would go for that idea."

"Why not?"

"Because she wants her own child. She said so many times during the two years we tried to have a baby."

"She might change her mind now that she knows she's unable to have children of her own."

"I—I suppose she could, but she's so upset right now. I don't think it's a good time to talk about adoption." Hank stared at the ground.

"Maybe not, but it's something to consider." Noah paused and reflected on his next words, knowing that Hank wasn't a particularly religious man. "I want you to know that I'll be praying for you."

"Thanks." Hank looked up and clasped Noah's shoulder. "You're a good man, and I count it a privilege to have you as my employee and my friend."

"Same goes for me." Noah smiled. "And I really enjoy working with all these," he added, motioning to the trees surrounding them.

"You might not say that come fall when things get really busy."

"I made it through last year and lived to tell about it," Noah said with a laugh. The month or so before Christmas was always hectic at the tree farm. In early November, trees were cut, netted, and bundled for pickup by various lots. Many people in the area came to the Osborns' to choose and cut their own trees, as well. Some folks dropped by as early as the first of October to reserve their pine.

Hank's wife ran the gift shop, located in one section of the barn. She took in a lot of items on consignment from the local people, including several who were Amish. Everything from homemade peanut brittle to pinecone-decorated wreaths was sold at the gift store, and Sandy always served her customers a treat before they left the rustic-looking building Hank had built for her a few years ago. Last year Noah had contributed some baked goods, and his desserts had been well received. He hoped things would work out for Sandy and Hank, because they were both nice people.

"I appreciate you listening to my tale of woe, but now I guess I'd better move on to the next row and see how Fred and Bob are doing," Hank said, breaking into Noah's thoughts. "Want me to leave the radio with you?"

Noah shook his head. "No, thanks. The melody the birds are making is all the music I need."

Hank thumped Noah lightly on the back. "All right, then. See you up at the barn at lunchtime."

"Sure thing." Noah moved on down the row of pines to check several more seedlings. As a father would tend his child, he took special care with each struggling tree. He figured that like everything else the good Lord created, these future Christmas trees needed tender, loving care.

As Noah thought about Hank's comment concerning him making a good husband and father, an uninvited image of Faith Andrews popped into his mind. He could see her look of confusion when he'd given her the cake.

"Now why am I thinking about her again?" he muttered. No question about it—Faith was a fine-looking woman. From what he remembered of the way Faith used to be, she could be a lot of fun. But Noah was sure there was no hope of her ever being interested in someone like him.

I'm shy; she's outgoing. I'm plain; she's beautiful. I'm twenty-four; she's twenty-eight. I'm firmly committed to the Amish faith, and she's— what exactly is Faith committed to? Noah determined to find that out as soon as he got to know her better.

Chapter 8

Noah stood on the front porch of his folks' rambling, two-story farmhouse, leaning against the railing and gazing into the yard. Pop had built this place shortly after he and Mom moved to Missouri from the state of Indiana. Twenty-three other families had joined them in establishing the first Amish community on the outskirts of the small town of Seymour. Now, nearly two hundred Plain families lived in the area. Some had moved here from other parts of the country, while others came about from marriages and children being born to those who had chosen to stay and make their home in the area.

Noah and his brothers were some of those born and raised in Webster County, and Noah had never traveled any farther than the town of Springfield. He had no desire to see the world like some folks did. He loved it here and was content to stay near those he cared about so deeply.

His brothers Chester, Jonas, and Harvey had moved to northern Missouri with their wives and children. Lloyd, Lyle, Rube, and Henry now lived in Illinois. Only William, Peter, and Noah had chosen to stay in the area. Each had his own farm, although some had opened businesses to supplement their income.

Noah's thoughts darted ahead to his plans for the next day. Church was held every other Sunday, and since tomorrow was a preaching Sunday, Noah planned to speak with Faith. He wanted to find out if she had enjoyed his lemon sponge cake and see what she thought of the verse he'd attached. He contemplated the idea of taking her another one of his baked goods but decided she might think he was being pushy. From the few minutes they'd spent together, Noah guessed Faith felt uncomfortable and probably needed a friend. Maybe he could be her friend, if she would let him.

He gulped in a deep breath of the evening air and flopped into Pop's wooden rocking chair. It smelled as if rain was coming, and with the oppressing heat they'd been having lately, the land could surely use a good dousing.

A short time later, a streak of lightning shot across the sky, followed by a thunderous roar that shook the whole house.

"Jah, a summer storm's definitely coming," he murmured. "Guess I'd best be getting to bed, or I'll be tempted to sit out here and watch it all night." Noah had enjoyed watching thunderstorms ever since he was a boy. Something fascinated him about the way lightning zigzagged across the sky as the rain pelted the earth. It made Noah realize the awesomeness of God's power. Everything on earth was under the Master's hand, and Noah never ceased to marvel at the majesty of it all.

He rose from his chair just as the rain started to fall. It fell lightly at first but soon began to pummel the ground. He gazed up at the dismal, gray sky. "Keep us all safe this night, Lord."

Faith shuddered and pulled the sides of her pillow around her ears as she tried to drown out the sound of the storm brewing outside her bedroom window. She'd been afraid of storms since she was a child and had often been teased by her older brothers about being a scaredy-cat. But she couldn't help it. Everyone had something they were afraid of, didn't they?

"Mama, I heard an awful boom," Melinda said as she crept into Faith's room, wearing one of Susie's long white nightgowns and holding the vinyl doll her father had given her on the Christmas before he'd been killed.

Faith motioned Melinda over to the bed. "It's just some thunder rumbling," she said, hoping she sounded braver than she felt.

"I don't like the thunder, and I've got a tummy ache. Can I sleep with you?"

"Is Susie awake, too?"

"Nope. She's sound asleep. Didn't even budge when I got out of bed."

"Okay, come on in." Faith pulled the covers aside and scooted over.

Another clap of thunder sounded, and Melinda hopped

into bed with a yelp. Faith figured her own fear of storms must be hereditary. No wonder Melinda had a stomachache. Seeing the way the windows rattled and hearing the terrible boom of the thunder was enough to make anyone feel sick.

"I hope Susie won't be too disappointed when she wakes up in the morning and discovers you're not in her room," Faith said as Melinda snuggled against her arm.

"Why would she be disappointed?"

Faith swallowed a couple of times as she thought of the best way to say what was on her mind. She wanted Melinda to bond with Susie and the rest of the family so that, when Faith headed back on the road, Melinda would feel like she belonged here. "I've. . .uh. . .seen how well you and Susie have been getting along since we came here, and I'm hoping the two of you can always be friends."

"You're my friend, too, Mama," Melinda said as her voice took on a sleepy tone. "Always and forever." The child's eyes drifted shut, and her breathing became heavy as she drifted off to sleep.

Another rumble of thunder sounded, and Faith turned her head toward the window. "Dear God, give me the strength to leave when it's time to go," she murmured. It was her first prayer in a long time. "Now where did that come from?" For many years, Faith had done everything in her own strength, and she'd come to believe that she didn't need anyone's help, not even God's. So why had she prayed out loud like that? And why, as she snuggled against her daughter, did she find herself wishing she didn't have to leave Webster County? If she stayed, she would have to give up yodeling and telling jokes, and she didn't think she could endure the somber life her folks would expect her to live. No, she had to go.

Noah sat up with a start. He'd been having a strange dream about Pop's squealing pigs when something awakened him. *Strange,* he thought as he slipped out of bed. *I don't even like my daed's smelly critters, so it makes no sense that I'd be dreaming about them.*

It was still raining. Noah could hear the heavy drops falling on their metal roof and the wind whipping against his upstairs bedroom window, rattling the glass until he feared it might break.

Noah padded across the wooden floor in his bare feet and lifted the dark shade from the windowpane. He gasped at the sight before him.

Flames of red and orange shot out of the barn in all directions, as billows of smoke drifted toward the sky.

Noah threw on his clothes and dashed down the stairs. He pounded on his parents' bedroom door, shouting, "Pop, get up! *Schnell!* The barn's on fire! Hurry!"

The next couple of hours went by in a blur as Noah, his father, and several neighbors, including Noah's brothers William and Peter, tried unsuccessfully to save the Hertzlers' barn. Only by a miracle were the animals rescued, although they lost one aged sow, and several other pigs seemed to be affected by the smoke.

One of their English neighbors had phoned the Seymour Fire Department, but they hadn't arrived in time to save the barn. Noah felt sick at heart as he and his folks stood in the yard, surveying the damage. From the slump of his father's shoulders and his downcast eyes, Noah knew Pop felt even worse than he did. "I'm sorry about your barn," Noah said with a catch in his voice. "If I'd only been awake when it was struck by lightning, maybe we could've caught it in time to keep the whole place from burning."

"It's not your fault," his father said hoarsely, reaching up to wipe away the soot on his cheeks. "Trouble comes to all, and at least no human lives were taken."

Mom slipped an arm around Pop's waist. "We can have a new barn raised as soon as this mess is cleaned up."

Noah nodded. "And I'm sure we'll have plenty of help." Folks in their community always rallied whenever anyone lost a barn or needed major work done on a house.

"There's nothing more we can do here," Mom said. "I say we go on back to bed and try to get a few more hours' sleep before we have to get up for preaching."

Pop nodded and took hold of her hand; then the two of them shuffled off toward the house.

"You coming, son?" Mom called over her shoulder.

"I'll be in after a bit."

Noah heard the back door click shut behind his folks, but he just stood on the grass. The huge white barn he had played in as a child was gone. Its remains were nothing more than a pile of charred lumber and a heap of grimy ashes. Soon there would be a new barn in its place. At least that was something to be thankful for.

Faith awoke on Sunday morning feeling groggy and disoriented.

She'd spent most of the night caring for Melinda, who had come down with the flu. The child was running a temperature and had vomited several times. It was no wonder she'd complained of a stomachache.

Faith glanced over at her daughter, now sleeping peacefully on the other side of the bed. She would let the child sleep while she went downstairs for a bite of breakfast, then she'd come straight back to her room.

Faith slipped out from under the covers and plucked her lightweight robe off the wall peg. A short time later, she found her mother and three sisters in the kitchen, scurrying about to get the table set and breakfast on. The tantalizing aroma of eggs cooking on the stove made her stomach rumble. Until this moment she hadn't realized she was hungry.

"You're not dressed," Mama said, scowling at Faith and pointing to her nightgown. "And where's Melinda? The two of you are going to make us late for preaching if you don't get a move on."

"Melinda came down with the flu during the night." Faith reached for the teakettle near the back of the stove. "We'll be staying home from church today."

"I'm sorry to hear that," Mama said.

"Sorry to hear Melinda's sick or that we won't be going to church?" Faith knew her voice sounded harsh, but she didn't like the feeling that her mother disapproved of her staying home from church in order to care for Melinda.

"I don't appreciate the tone you're using," Mama said, pushing her glasses to the bridge of her nose. "I'm sorry to hear Melinda is sick, and I understand why you won't be going to preaching today."

A sense of guilt stabbed Faith's conscience. In times past,

Mama had seemed so judgmental, and Faith had assumed nothing had changed. Apparently she'd been wrong. Maybe Mama did care about Melinda being sick.

"Sorry for snapping," Faith mumbled. "Guess I'm a mite edgy this morning. Between that awful storm and Melinda getting sick, neither of us got much sleep last night."

"I'm sorry if I sounded irritable, too," her mother said.

"Am I gonna get sick, too, Mama?" Susie spoke up. She'd been setting the table but had stopped what she was doing when Faith mentioned that Melinda had come down with the flu.

"I hope not," Faith said. "That's why I kept Melinda in my room all night."

"If the child stays in your room while she's got the bug, maybe none of us will get it," Mama added.

"What about Faith?" Esther's pale blue eyes narrowed with obvious concern. She handed her mother two more eggs. "If Melinda's been sleeping with Faith, hasn't she already been exposed? Won't she likely get the flu?"

"Guess that all depends on how strong her immune system is," Mama replied. She broke one egg into the pan and reached for another.

"That's right," Grace Ann put in as she retrieved a jug of milk from the refrigerator and set it on the table. "Some people can be exposed to all kinds of things and never get sick. Maybe our big sister's one of those healthy people."

Faith could hardly believe the way her sisters and mother were discussing her as though she weren't even in the room. Irritated with their lack of manners and feeling the need to say something on her own behalf, she said, "I hardly ever become ill, but have no fear. If I do come down with the bug, I'll be sure to stay put in my room." Faith grabbed a stash of napkins and added them to the silverware Susie had set next to each plate.

"If anyone else should get sick, we'll deal with it as it comes," Mama said with a nod. "Your daed and the brothers will be in soon, so right now the only thing we should concern ourselves with is getting breakfast on the table."

Grace Ann and Faith exchanged glances, but neither said a word, and Faith was glad the discussion was over. All she wanted to do was eat a little breakfast, fix a cup of mint tea for Melinda, and head back upstairs to her room.

Once breakfast was over and Faith had gone upstairs to check on Melinda, Wilma began washing the dishes while Susie dried them. Grace Ann swept the floor, and Esther wiped off the stove and countertops.

"I don't understand why Faith gets upset so easily," Esther said as she handed her mother the wet rag she'd been using.

"She did seem a mite testy," Wilma agreed.

"It didn't sound like she got much sleep last night," Grace Ann put. "I can understand that, because I'm always cranky whenever I don't get enough sleep."

"Ha!" Esther grunted. "You're cranky every morning, no matter how much sleep you've had the night before."

"I am not."

"Are so."

"Am not."

"Girls," Wilma said with a frown, "you're acting like a couple of ornery old hens, not two young women who should know better than to carry on in such a way."

"*Bawk! Bawk!*" Susie flapped her arms and waved the dish towel. "My sisters are a couple of fat red hens."

"I didn't say your sisters were fat," Wilma corrected. "And I'll thank you to tend to your own business or you might end up making a visit to the woodshed this morning."

Susie dropped her gaze to the floor and turned toward the plates waiting to be dried on the plastic dish drainer. Wilma went back to washing the rest of the dishes. It was good to have Faith home again, but her presence had created a few problems. Her three younger sisters had become a bit disagreeable since Faith's appearance, and young Susie was much more vocal than she used to be.

"I wonder what it must have been like for Faith living in the English world and entertaining folks on a stage somewhere," Esther said as she leaned against the counter near the sink with a dreamy look on her face.

"That's not for us to know, so don't go asking Faith about it," Wilma said with a shake of her head.

"I'd like to see one of those shows sometime," Esther went on to say. "Just so I'd know what it must have been like for Faith."

Wilma dropped her rag into the dishwater with a splash, sending several bubbles floating to the ceiling. "There'll be no more talk like that in this house. It was hard enough to lose one daughter to the world, and I'll not lose another." She paused and shook her finger. "So you'd better think twice about such foolish notions."

Esther nodded solemnly and moved away from the sink, just as John entered the house and announced that the horses and buggies were ready to go. "Papa said for me to tell you womenfolk that it's time to leave for church," he added.

"We're coming," Wilma said as she dried her hands on the clean towel she'd pulled from a cupboard drawer.

John looked around the room. "Where are Faith and Melinda? Aren't they going to church today?"

Wilma lifted her gaze toward the ceiling. "Where were you during breakfast this morning?"

"At the table, same as you."

"Then you must have heard Faith tell us that Melinda took sick during the night, and that she'd be staying home in order to care for the child."

John shrugged and gave a noncommittal grunt. "Jah, okay. See you outside in the buggy."

As Wilma followed her daughters out the door, she offered a silent prayer for all her brood.

Late that afternoon, Faith stepped outside to the front porch. She'd spent the early part of the day resting and caring for Melinda and was glad the child was feeling somewhat better and had eaten a bowl of chicken broth around noon. Melinda was napping now, so Faith decided to spend a few minutes on the porch swing where she could enjoy the fresh, rain-washed scent still permeating the air after last night's storm. It had been a nasty one, and even if Melinda hadn't kept Faith up all night, the wind and rain surely would have. A bolt of lightning could do a lot of damage, and so could the howling winds. Buildings might catch on fire, roofs could be blown off, and flash floods often occurred. Any of those tragedies meant lots of hard work.

When a ball of white fur jumped up beside Faith, she shifted on the swing and stroked the top of the cat's fluffy white head. "You needed to get away from your hungry babies for a while, didn't you, Snowball?"

The cat meowed in response, curled into a tight ball, and began to purr.

Faith smiled. Oh, to live the life of a cat, whose only concern was licking its paws, batting at bugs, and chasing down some defenseless bird or mouse once in a while. Cats didn't have to answer to anyone. They could pretty much do as they pleased.

She leaned her head against the back of the swing and closed her eyes. It was so peaceful here, where the birds chirped happily and no one competed with anyone else to get ahead. Nothing like Faith's life on the road had been. There were so many demands and pressures that went along with being an entertainer. Days and nights spent in travel, hours of practicing for shows, and the burden of trying to please an audience had taken their toll on Faith. Still, she would gladly put up with the discomforts in order to do what she liked best. *If only my folks would have accepted my humor when I was a girl. Was it really so wrong to tell jokes and yodel whenever I felt like it?*

Had her family's disapproval been the reason for Faith's lack of faith? Or had it come about when she'd married Greg and been mistreated by him? Faith believed in God—had since she was a girl. But God had never seemed real to her in a personal way.

Faith's eyes snapped open, and she bolted upright when she heard the thudding of horses' hooves and the rumble of buggy wheels pulling into the yard. Her family was home from church. As John led the horses to the barn, everyone else came streaming up the path toward the house, talking a mile a minute.

"You were missed at preaching today," Mama said as she stepped onto the porch. "Noah Hertzler asked about you."

Faith nodded.

"The Hertzlers' barn burned to the ground last night," her brother Brian said, his dark eyes looking ever so serious. "There's gonna be a barn raising later this week."

"Sorry to hear about their misfortune. Was the barn hit by lightning?"

"It would seem so," Papa said as he came up behind Mama. "Sure hope everybody in this house is well by Friday, because all hands will be needed at the Hertzlers' that day."

All hands? Did that mean Faith and Melinda would be expected to go and help out?

"The little ones will remain at home," Mama said before Faith could voice the question. "Esther can stay with them, so Grace Ann, Faith, and I will be able to help with the meals for the men."

Faith clenched her teeth. She wanted to stand up to Mama and say that she was treating her like a child, and that she could decide for herself if she was going to help at the barn raising. She remained silent, however. No point in getting Mama all riled. Faith needed to keep the peace as long as she chose to stay here; it would help ensure her daughter's future. Besides, she did feel bad for the Hertzlers. Nobody should have to lose their barn.

Chapter 9

By eight o'clock on Friday morning, the air was already hot, sticky, and devoid of any breeze. It would be a long, grueling day as the men worked on the Hertzlers' new barn. Faith didn't envy them having to labor under the sweltering sun. At least she and the other women who had come to help serve the men could escape the blistering heat now and then. Their work wouldn't be nearly as difficult, either.

When Faith entered the Hertzlers' kitchen along with her mother and Grace Ann, she saw several other Amish women scurrying around, getting coffee and lemonade ready to serve the men when they became thirsty or needed a break.

Already the kitchen was warm and stuffy, making Faith long to be anywhere else but there. A dip in a swimming pool would surely be nice.

Faith leaned against the wall and thought about the last time she'd gone swimming with Melinda and Greg. It had been at a hotel pool in Memphis, Tennessee. Greg was in good spirits that Sunday afternoon, probably because he'd won big at a poker table the night before.

When Faith closed her eyes, she saw an image of Greg carrying Melinda on his shoulders. Tall and slender, his jet black hair and aqua-colored eyes made Faith think he was the most handsome man she'd ever met. The three of them had stayed in the water for over an hour that day, laughing, splashing around the pool like a model, loving family.

Only we weren't model, and Greg may have been handsome and charming, but his love was conditional. Faith blinked away the stinging tears threatening to escape her lashes. *Why didn't Greg love me the way a man should love his wife? Why couldn't we be a happy family?*

"It's good to see you," Barbara said, jolting Faith away from her memories. "I was hoping you'd be here today. It'll give us a chance to get reacquainted and catch up on one another's lives."

Faith nodded. Truth was she couldn't allow herself to re-establish what she and Barbara once had, because she knew she wouldn't be staying around long enough to develop any close ties—not even with family members. It would make it easier to say good-bye when it was time for Faith to leave.

"Are you okay?" Barbara asked with a note of concern. "You look kind of sad today."

"I'm fine." Faith nibbled on her lower lip. "Just standing here waiting to be told what I should do."

Barbara looked a little uncertain, but she handed Faith a pitcher of lemonade and grabbed one for herself. "Let's take these outside to the menfolk. Then we can sit a spell and visit before it's time to start the noon meal."

Faith followed Barbara out the door. They placed their pitchers on a wooden table beside a huge pot of coffee. As warm as it was today, Faith didn't see how anyone could drink the hot beverage, but then she remembered something her father used to say: *"If I'm warm on the inside when it's hot outside, then my body believes it's cold."*

That made no sense to Faith, and she was pretty sure it was just Dad's excuse to drink more than his share of the muddy-looking brew. She had never acquired a taste for coffee and planned to keep it that way.

"Let's sit over there," Barbara said, motioning to a couple of wicker chairs under a shady maple tree.

Faith flopped into one of the seats and fanned her face with her hands. "Sure is warm out already. I can only imagine how hot and muggy it'll be by the end of the day."

Barbara nodded. "Pity the poor men working on that barn."

Faith's gaze drifted across the yard to where the Hertzlers' barn was already taking shape. Rising higher than the family's two-story house, the framing of the new structure looked enormous. Men and older boys armed with saws, hammers, and planes were positioned in various sections of the barn. It would be a lot of work, but they would probably have most of it done by the end of the day.

"An English barn is built using all modern equipment, but it doesn't come together in twice the time it takes for an Amish barn raising," Faith noted.

"That's because we all pull together when there's a need. I

wouldn't be happy living anywhere but here among my people."

If Barbara's comment was meant to be a jab at Faith and her wayward ways, she chose to ignore it. "No, I don't suppose you would be."

"Tell me what it's like out there in the world of entertaining," Barbara said, redirecting their conversation. "Is it all you had hoped it would be?"

"It's different—and exciting. At least it was for me."

"Do you miss it?"

Faith swallowed hard. How could she tell Barbara how much she missed entertaining without letting on that she didn't plan to stay in Webster County indefinitely? She moistened her lips with the tip of her tongue as she searched for the right words. "I miss certain things about it."

"Such as?"

"The response of an appreciative audience to one of my jokes or the joy of yodeling and not having anyone looking down their nose because I'm doing something different that they think is wrong." Faith hadn't planned to say so much, but the words slipped off her tongue before she could stop them.

"You think that's how your family acted?"

Faith nodded.

"Do you believe they saw your joke telling and yodeling as wrong?"

Faith could hardly believe her friend had forgotten all the times she'd told her about her folks' disapproval. Maybe Barbara had become so caught up in her adult life that she didn't remember much about their younger days when they had confided in one another and been almost as close as sisters. The truth was, Barbara had gotten after Faith a few times. Not for her joke telling and sense of humor, but for her discontent and her tendency to fool around.

"Papa used to holler at me for wasting time when I should've been working. He thought my yodeling sounded like a croaking frog, and many times he said I was too silly for my own good." Faith's voice was edged with bitterness, but she didn't care. It was the truth, plain and simple.

"There are a few others in the area who like to yodel," Barbara reminded. "As you know, yodeling is part of the Swiss-German heritage of some who live here, and it's been passed from one generation to the next."

"That may be true, but Papa has never liked me doing it, and it took English audiences to appreciate my talent."

Barbara's raised eyebrows revealed her apparent surprise. "Did you enjoy being English?"

Faith wasn't sure how to respond, so she merely nodded in reply.

"Then why'd you come back?"

"I—I thought it was best for Melinda."

"Your mamm tells me you've been widowed for several months."

"That's right. My husband stepped out into traffic and was hit by a car."

Barbara slowly shook her head. "Such a shame it is. I'm real sorry for you, Faith. I can't imagine life without my David. We work so well together in the harness shop, and he's such a good father to our boys, Aaron and Joseph. I don't think I could stand it if something happened to David. It's hard enough to lose a parent or grandparent, but losing a husband? That would be unbearable pain." She glanced over at Faith and offered a half smile. "Might be a good thing for you and your daughter if you found another husband. Don't you think?"

Faith felt her fingers go numb from clutching the folds in her dress so tightly. She had no intention of finding another husband. Not now. Not ever.

"How old are your sons?" Faith asked, hoping to steer their conversation in another direction. She didn't want to talk about her dysfunctional marriage to Greg, his untimely death, or the idea of marrying again. Remembering was easy; forgetting was the hard part. Thinking about a relationship with another man was impossible.

"Aaron's four, and Joseph just turned two." Barbara patted her belly and grinned. "We're hoping to have another *boppli* soon. Maybe a girl this time around."

"You're pregnant?" Faith couldn't imagine having two little ones to care for, plus a baby on the way.

"Not yet, but soon, I hope. I love being a mamm."

Faith enjoyed motherhood, too, and she had hoped to have more children someday. But with the way things were between her and Greg, she was glad it hadn't happened. His unreliability and quick temper were reason enough not to want to bring any more children into their unhappy marriage, not to mention his drinking and gambling habits. Now that Faith was widowed and had no plans of remarrying, she was certain Melinda would be her only child.

Faith shifted in her chair. *At least Melinda will have her aunt Susie to grow up with. That's almost like having a sister.*

"You'll have to excuse me a minute," Barbara said as she stood. "David's waving at me. He must want something to drink."

Faith stood, too. "Guess I'll go on back to the house and see what needs to be done for the noon meal."

Just before Faith and Barbara parted ways, Barbara touched Faith's arm and said, "I always enjoyed your joke telling."

"Thanks." Faith headed around the back side of the Hertzlers' place, not feeling a whole lot better about things. Barbara's compliment was appreciated, but it didn't replace the approval of Faith's parents. That's what she longed for but was sure she would never have.

She was almost to the porch when she spotted Noah coming out the door. He carried a jug of water and lifted the container when he saw her. "It's getting mighty hot out there. Thought some of the men would rather have cold water to quench their thirst."

Faith's cheeks warmed. "Sorry," she mumbled. "I should have realized not everyone would want coffee or lemonade."

Noah tromped down the stairs, his black work boots thumping against each wooden step. He stopped when he reached Faith. "I haven't had a chance to talk to you since I gave you that lemon sponge cake after church a few weeks ago. I was wondering how you liked it."

"It was very good."

"Glad you liked it," he said with a friendly grin. "What'd you think about the verse of scripture?"

Faith sucked in her breath, searching for words that wouldn't be an outright lie. "Well, I. . .uh. . .I think it may have gotten thrown out before I had a chance to read it."

Noah's forehead wrinkled. "I'm sorry to hear that. It was a good verse. One about faith, in fact."

"There's a verse in the Bible about *me*?" Faith giggled and winked at him, hoping he wasn't one who had a dislike for the funny side of life.

A slow smile spread across Noah's face, and he chuckled. "You do still have a sense of humor. You seemed so solemn when we last talked, and I couldn't help but wonder if you'd left your joke telling back in the English world."

She shrugged. "What can I say? Once a comedian, always a comedian." So much for being careful to watch her tongue and keep her silliness locked away.

"Do you miss it?" This was the second time today that Faith had been asked the question, and she wondered what Noah's reaction to her response would be.

"Sometimes," Faith admitted. "But I'm afraid there's no place for my joke telling here in Webster County."

"You don't have to set your humor aside just because you're not getting paid or standing in front of a huge audience anymore."

She pulled in her lower lip as she inhaled deeply and then released her breath with a groan. "It's kind of hard to be funny when everyone around you is so serious."

Noah took a seat on the porch step and motioned for Faith to do the same. "We're not all a bunch of sourpusses sucking on tart grapes, you know. In case you haven't noticed, many among us like to have fun." He nodded toward two young men who stood across the yard. They'd been drinking lemonade a few minutes ago but were now sprinting across the grass, grabbing for one another's straw hats.

Faith smiled, realizing Noah had made his point.

"Now back to that verse of scripture."

Oh, no. Here it comes. I think I'm about to receive a sermon from this man.

"It was from Hebrews, chapter eleven, verse six."

"And it's about faith, right?"

He nodded. " 'But without faith it is impossible to please him: for he that cometh to God must believe that he is, and that he is a rewarder of them that diligently seek him.' "

She contemplated his words. "If it's impossible to please God without having faith, then I must be a terrible disappointment to Him."

Noah tilted his head to one side. "Now why would you say something like that?"

"Because my faith is weak. It's almost nonexistent."

"Faith isn't faith until it's all you're holding on to. Some folks get the idea that faith is making God do what we want Him to do." He shook his head. "Not so. Faith is the substance of things not seen."

"Hmm."

"Abraham was the father of faith. When he heard God's voice telling him to leave and go to a new land, he went—not even knowing where he was going."

Faith could relate to that part a little. When she'd first left home to strike out on her own, she hadn't had a clue where she was going. She had ended up waiting tables at a restaurant in Springfield for a time.

"Faith's like a muscle you've got to develop. It takes time and patience." Noah grinned at her. "Guess that's a little more than you were hoping to hear, jah?"

She shrugged, then nodded. "Just a bit."

"Oh, and one more thing."

"What's that?"

"Your name is Faith, so I think that means you've got to have faith."

"No, it doesn't." She jumped up and dashed for the house before he had a chance to say anything more.

Chapter 10

One Saturday morning a few weeks after the Hertzlers' barn raising, Faith decided to take Melinda into Seymour to check out the farmers' market. It would give the two of them some quality time together, which they hadn't had much of since they'd arrived in Webster County. Faith knew she'd be leaving soon. She'd driven one of her father's buggies into town last week and phoned the talent agency in Memphis again. This time she was told that one of their agents, Brad Olsen, was interested in representing her as soon as she was ready to go back on the road. He asked that she contact him at her earliest convenience, and Faith planned to do so as soon as she could leave.

Faith felt a need to speak to Melinda in private today, encouraging her in the ways of her Amish family and helping her adjust to their new lifestyle. Besides, getting away from the farm for the day would allow Faith to do something fun—something she was sure she would be criticized for if she did it at home. It would give Faith a chance to make another phone call, too. She needed to check in with the agency and make sure they knew she was still interested in being represented by Mr. Olsen.

After they finished browsing the market, Faith had every intention of taking Melinda to one of the local restaurants where they could listen to some country-western music. Baldy's Café had been one of her favorite places to go when she was a teenager, so she thought about taking Melinda there. Not only did they serve succulent country fried steak, tasty pork chops, and smothered chicken, but lively country music was played on the radio.

Gathering the reins in her hands and waving good-bye to her mother, who stood watching them from the front porch, Faith guided the horse down the gravel driveway and onto the paved road in front of their farm. It was another hot, sticky day, and the breeze blowing against her face was a welcome relief. There was something to be said for riding in an open buggy on a sultry summer day.

"Too bad it's such a pain in the wintertime," she muttered.

"What's a pain, Mama?" Melinda questioned.

Faith sucked in her breath. She hadn't realized she'd spoken her thoughts out loud. The last thing she needed was for Melinda to hear negative comments about living as the Amish.

"It's nothing to worry about." Faith reached across the seat and patted her daughter's knee. "Mama was just thinking out loud."

"What were you thinking about?"

"It's not important." Faith smiled at Melinda. "Are you excited about our day together?"

Melinda nodded. "Sure wish Susie could have come, too."

"Maybe some other time. Today I want to spend time alone with you."

"Will we buy something good to eat at the market?"

"We should find plenty of tasty things there, but I think we'll have lunch at one of the local restaurants."

"Can I have a hot dog with lots of ketchup and relish?"

"Sure," Faith said with a nod. "You can have anything you want."

Melinda's lower lip protruded. "Grandma Stutzman makes me eat things I don't like. She says I have to eat green beans and icky beets whenever they're on the table. How come she's so mean?"

Faith's heart clenched. How could she leave Melinda with her parents if the child felt she was being mistreated? "Vegetables are good for you," she replied.

"I still don't like 'em."

"Maybe someday you will."

Melinda shrugged.

"Are you still missing TV and other modern things?"

"Not so much. I'd rather be out in the barn helping Grandpa with the animals than watching TV."

"I'm glad to hear it."

"Mama, are you ever gonna get married again?"

Melinda's unexpected question took Faith by surprise, and she answered it without even thinking. "No!"

"How come?"

Faith thought before replying this time. She couldn't tell Melinda she was against marriage because she was bitter and angry over the way Greg had treated her. The child loved her father and had no idea what had gone on behind closed doors when she'd been sound asleep. Faith had managed to keep Greg's abusiveness hidden from their precious child, and she wouldn't take away the pleasant memories Melinda had of her father.

"Mama, how come you don't want to get married again?" Melinda persisted.

Faith reached for her daughter's hand and gave it a gentle squeeze. "Because you're all I need."

Melinda seemed satisfied with that answer, for she smiled, leaned her head against the seat, and closed her eyes. "Wake me when we get there, okay?"

Faith smiled and clucked to the horse to get him moving a bit faster. "I will, sweet girl."

"That Melinda sure has a way with animals," Menno said as he joined his wife at the table for a cup of coffee. "You should have seen how easily she picked up on milking the cows." He took a drink from his cup and set it down on the table. "I think she's going to be a real big help to me when it comes to any of the farm chores that involve working with animals."

Wilma grunted. "Jah, well. . .don't get too attached to that idea. Melinda might not be around much longer."

"Why's that?"

"Faith might leave again—you said so yourself, remember?"

"True, but Melinda is settling in pretty well, and I really enjoy being around her." He smiled. "So I'm hoping they'll stay."

"I hope so, too, but the way Faith has been acting makes me think she might not be happy living here, and if she leaves, who knows if we'll ever see her or Melinda again?"

"You really think she's going to leave us again?"

"Can't say for sure, but she's as restless as a cat walking on a hot metal roof, and I have a hunch it's because she's not happy here."

He groaned. *"Mir lewe uff hoffning."*

"I know we live on hope, but we also need to face facts. And the fact is our daughter left home once because she wasn't happy being Amish, so what's to say she won't do it again?"

He shrugged. Wilma was right; Faith had always had a mind of her own, and the truth was, he'd never quite gotten over her leaving home when she eighteen, nor had he completely forgiven her. He'd not said the words out loud, but he'd missed her something awful when she was away, and if she left home again, he would not only miss Faith, but her daughter, as well. "What can we do to keep them here?" he asked, reaching over to touch Wilma's arm.

"Don't guess there's a whole lot we can do other than pray that she won't leave."

"Maybe she would stay if she knew how much her daughter liked it here." His head bobbed up and down. "Jah, that could be all it would take. I'll keep letting Melinda help me in the barn with the animals, and she'll like it so much she'll convince her mamm that living here is the best place for them to be."

"Or maybe," Wilma said as a slow smile spread across her face, "Faith needs to find a good Amish man and settle down to marriage like she should have done in the first place."

"What are you saying?"

"I'm saying that if our daughter married an Amish man, she'd have to join the church and would have no reason to leave the faith."

He picked up his cup again and took a long, slow drink. "And I suppose you have an idea as to who that prospective husband might be?"

Wilma toyed with the ribbons on her head covering. "I might."

"Mind if I ask who?"

"Well. . .I was thinking Noah might be a good catch."

Menno lifted one eyebrow. "Noah Hertzler?"

"Jah. He's single, not too bad-looking, seems to be kind and helpful to his folks, and he's a real good cook."

Menno coughed and nearly choked on the coffee he'd put in his mouth, spitting some onto his shirt. "You're going to try and get Faith and Noah together?"

"Maybe just give them a bit of a nudge."

He reached for a napkin and swiped at the coffee that had dribbled onto his chin and shirt. "My advice is for you to mind your own business and let Faith do her own husband picking."

Faith couldn't believe how many Amish folks were at the farmers' market. When she was a teenager, only a few from her community had attended. Now several Amish families had booths and were selling fresh produce, quilts, and homemade craft items. Others, Faith noticed, were there merely to look, the same as she and Melinda.

Melinda pointed to a booth where an English woman was selling peanut brittle. "That looks yummy. Can we buy some, Mama?"

"I might get a box, but it will be for later—after we've had our lunch."

"You like peanut brittle?" asked a deep voice from behind.

Faith whirled around. Noah Hertzler stood directly behind her, holding his straw hat in his hands and smiling in that easygoing way of his.

"Noah. I'm surprised to see you. Are you selling some of your baked goods here today?" Faith asked.

Noah twisted the brim of his hat and shuffled his feet a couple of times. "Naw, I just came to look around."

"We're looking around, too," Melinda piped up. "And Mama's gonna take me to lunch soon."

Noah grinned at the child. "I was fixin' to do that, as well." He glanced over at Faith. "Would you two care to join me?"

The rhythm of Faith's heartbeat picked up, and she drew in a deep breath, hoping to still the racing. She wasn't sure whether it was Noah's crooked grin or his penetrating dark eyes that made her feel so strange. No Amish man had ever affected her this way, and she found it a bit disconcerting.

Melinda tugged her hand. "Can we, Mama? Can we eat lunch with Mr. Noah?"

"Noah's his first name, Melinda. Hertzler's his last name."

The child looked up at Faith with an expectant expression. "Can we have lunch with Noah?"

Faith was surprised to see her daughter's enthusiasm over the possibility of sharing a meal with Noah. Was it because she missed her father so much, or had she taken a liking to Noah?

If Noah had been this friendly when I was a teenager, I might have taken a liking to him myself. She popped a knuckle on her right hand. *Now where did that thought come from? Noah's four years younger than me, so even if he had been friendly and kind to me back then, I wouldn't have given him a second glance. Besides, his kindness could just be an act. Greg had acted kind and caring for a while, too, and look how that turned out.*

"I had planned to take Melinda to Baldy's Café," Faith said, pushing her troubling thoughts aside and turning to face Noah. "It was one of my favorite places to eat when I was a teenager."

Noah waggled his dark eyebrows. "That's one of my favorite places, too. They have some finger-lickin' good chicken there, not to mention those yummy corn dogs."

Melinda jumped up and down. "Yippee! We're going to Baldy's Café!"

Sitting across the table from Faith and her daughter, Noah felt strangely uncomfortable. Faith had seemed friendly enough at the farmers' market, but she'd become quiet all of a sudden and would barely make eye contact with him. Melinda, on the other hand, had been talking nonstop ever since they'd entered the restaurant.

He smiled at the child, who had a splotch of ketchup smeared on her chin from the hot dog she'd eaten. "Did you get enough to eat, Melinda?" he asked.

She bobbed her head up and down. "But I left room in my tummy for some ice cream."

Noah chuckled and was surprised when Faith laughed, too. "I think I'll have my ice cream on top of a huge piece of blackberry cobbler," he announced. "How about you, Faith? Do you like cobbler?"

She smiled at Noah, and he felt a strange stirring in his heart. "Sure. Most anybody raised in these parts has a taste for that delicious dessert." Faith swiped a napkin across her daughter's face. "You look a mess, you know that?"

Melinda scrunched up her nose. "I don't care. It ain't no fun eatin' a hot dog unless you make a mess."

"*Isn't* any fun," Faith corrected.

"Isn't," the child repeated. "Anyway, can I have some ice cream now?"

"Sure, why not?" Noah blurted out before Faith had a chance to respond. "That is, if it's okay with your mamm," he quickly amended.

Faith nodded. "I guess it would be all right."

When the waitress returned to their table, they placed an order for one bowl of strawberry ice cream for Melinda and two blackberry cobblers topped with vanilla ice cream for Faith and Noah.

While they waited for their desserts, Noah listened to the blaring country music and watched with interest as Faith tapped her fingers along the edge of the checkered tablecloth, keeping perfect time to the beat.

The woman who was singing on the radio also yodeled, and Noah marveled at her ability to make her voice warble in such a pleasant way. "Oh–le–ee–Oh–le–dee–ee–Oh–de–lay-dee–" Faster and faster the song went, until Noah could no longer keep up with the intriguing sounds.

He glanced over at Faith and noticed her staring out the window. She appeared to be a million miles away. Maybe in her mind she was back onstage, telling jokes or yodeling like the woman on the radio.

"You really do miss it, jah?"

"What?"

"Entertaining."

Melinda, who had been twisting her straw into funny shapes, spoke up. "Mama don't tell jokes no more. She gave that up when we came here to become Amish."

"Is that so?"

Melinda nodded, but Faith shrugged her shoulders.

The waitress showed up with their desserts just then, and the conversation was put on hold.

When Noah finished his cobbler several minutes later, he leaned his elbows on the table and studied Faith. She seemed so somber. It was hard to believe she had ever been a comedian. Didn't the woman realize she could still tell jokes and have fun, even though she was no longer an entertainer?

She looked at him and frowned. "You're staring at me, and it makes me nervous."

His face grew warm. "Sorry. Didn't mean to stare."

"I'll bet you were lookin' at her 'cause she's so pretty."

Melinda's candid statement must have taken Faith by surprise, for her mouth fell open and her blue eyes widened. "Really, Melinda—you shouldn't try to put words in Noah's mouth."

"She doesn't have to," he said. "Your daughter's right. You're a fine-looking woman."

Faith stared at the table. After a few seconds, she looked over at Melinda and said, "Did you hear about the restaurant that just opened on the moon?"

Melinda's eyebrows lifted. "Really, Mama?"

Faith nodded as she looked over at Noah and winked.

"Tell us about it," he said, deciding to play along.

"Well, they have lots of good food there, but there's absolutely no atmosphere."

Noah chuckled.

"See, I do still have some humor left in me," Faith said with a lift of her chin.

He nodded. "I'm glad."

"Tell us another joke, Mama."

"Not now." Faith looked back at Noah. "Why don't you share something about yourself?"

He plunked his elbows on the table and rested his hands under his chin. "What would you like to know?"

"Do you farm with your dad, or have you found some other kind of work to keep you busy?"

"Actually Pop doesn't farm much anymore. He's been raising hogs for the last nine years." Noah rubbed his hands briskly together. "I work at a nearby Christmas tree farm, and I truly like it."

Melinda's eyes seemed to light right up. "A Christmas tree farm? Does Santa Claus live there?"

He snickered as he shook his head. "No, but it's sure a great place to visit. In fact, I think you would enjoy seeing all the pine trees that are grown especially for English people at Christmastime."

Melinda licked the last bit of strawberry ice cream off her spoon and turned to face her mother. "Could we go to Noah's work and see the Christmas trees?"

"Well, I—"

"That's a great idea," Noah cut in. "I'll talk to my boss next week and see what we can arrange." He glanced over at Faith. "That is, if you're in agreement."

She deliberated a few seconds and finally nodded. "Sure, that sounds like fun."

"I'll let you know as soon as I get it set up."

As they traveled home that afternoon, Faith thought about Noah and how at ease he had seemed with her and Melinda during their meal at Baldy's. He wasn't the same shy boy she'd known when they were growing up. Faith had enjoyed Noah's company today and had actually felt relaxed. Noah's gentle way had settled over her like a soft, warm quilt.

She shook the reins, and the horse began to trot. *Makes me wonder why the man's never married. It seems like he would make a good father.* In the years Faith and Greg had been married, he'd never looked at her, or even Melinda, with the tenderness she'd seen on Noah's face today. Was it merely an act, or did Noah have the heart of a kind, considerate man? Should she have agreed to his invitation to take them to the tree farm?

She glanced over at her daughter, whose head lolled against

the seat as her eyes closed. Melinda seemed excited about the idea, and it would certainly be a nice change from all the work Faith had been expected to do since she'd come home. A visit to the tree farm would be fun for Melinda and maybe for Faith, too. It might be the only fun thing she would get to do while she was here in Webster County.

Faith grimaced as her thoughts moved in a different direction. *Oh, no. I got so caught up in the enjoyment of the day that I forgot to call the talent agency in Memphis again.*

Chapter 11

I t's nice we could have this time to visit," Wilma said to Noah's mother, Ida, as the two of them sat at Ida's kitchen table. "We've both been so busy lately, and it's been awhile since we've had a chance to get caught up on each other's lives." She lifted her glass. "This iced tea sure hits the spot on such a warm day."

Ida nodded and handed Wilma a plate of ginger cookies. "Please, help yourself. Noah made these last night, and they're sugar free."

"Danki," she said as she plucked a cookie off the plate then took a bite.

"How are things at your house?" Ida asked, as she also reached for a cookie. "Are your *dochder* and *grossdochder* adjusting fairly well?"

"My granddaughter's doing well, but with Faith, I'm not so sure."

Ida's eyebrows lifted slightly. "How's that?"

"Faith has seemed so despondent since she's returned home—hardly cracks a smile and doesn't say much unless she's spoken to."

"That's too bad. You think she'll stick around this time?"

"I don't know, but if it's within my power to keep her, I surely will."

"How are you going to do that? It's not like Faith is a little girl and you can order her to do as you say."

Wilma sighed. "How well I know that. If I'd been able to make her listen to me when she was a teenager, she wouldn't have left home in the first place."

Ida reached for another cookie. "I'm glad none of my kinner ever got the notion of leaving the Amish faith. Don't think I could stand it if they did."

Wilma stared at the table. "I'll never forget the shock of awakening one morning and discovering a note from Faith saying she was running off to find a new life—one where she could yodel and tell jokes."

"She could have done that here, couldn't she?" Ida asked. "I mean, there are some in our community who like to yodel."

"That's true, but Faith had it in her mind that her yodeling wasn't appreciated. Of course, that's partly her daed's fault; he never did like to hear her yodel. Said it sounded like a bunch of croaking frogs or like she had something caught in her throat." Wilma grimaced. "I'm sure I didn't help things any when I got after her for acting so silly all the time. Seemed like she never had a serious word and was always playing some kind of prank on her brothers and sisters. Now Faith barely cracks a smile, much less tells any jokes."

"If she's unhappy, then she might leave. Isn't that what you're thinking?"

"Exactly."

"What if Faith married someone from our community? Then you'd be assured of her sticking around."

Wilma nodded. "That thought did cross my mind."

Ida snapped her fingers. "I think I've got the perfect solution."

"What might that be?"

Ida leaned closer to Wilma, and her voice lowered to a whisper, which Wilma thought was kind of silly, since they were the only ones in Ida's kitchen. "Levi and I have been hoping Noah will find a good woman and settle down to marriage, and I'm thinking if we got our two together, it could be an answer to prayer for both our families."

Wilma's lips curved into a smile. "You know, that's exactly what I've been thinking."

When Noah stepped into the kitchen and found Faith's mother sitting at the table, visiting with his mom, he halted. He'd just arrived home from work and hadn't expected any guests.

Wilma looked up at Noah and smiled.

"It's good to see you, Wilma. What brings you out our way on this hot afternoon?" he asked.

"Just came by for a little chitchat with your mamm."

Noah took down a glass from the cupboard and got himself a drink of water at the sink. "Want me to make myself scarce so you two can talk?"

"That's okay; I think we're pretty much talked out," Wilma responded.

Noah shrugged and gulped down the glass of water.

"So, Noah, how are you doing these days?" Wilma asked.

He wiped his mouth with the back of his hand. "Pretty good. And you?"

"Oh, fair to middlin'."

"Glad to hear it. How's the rest of the family?"

"Most are doing okay. Grace Ann is still working at Graber's General Store, and Esther's helping out at the Lapps' place now. Sally Lapp had triplets awhile back, you know."

Noah nodded and went to the refrigerator. "What did you have planned for supper, Mom?"

"That can wait awhile. It's too hot to do any cooking, so I might fix cold sandwiches."

"Okay. Maybe I'll go out for a walk then." He gave his mother's shoulder a gentle squeeze. "You look tired. Are you feeling all right?"

"I'm fine." Mom fanned her face with the corner of her apron. "Just feeling the heat is all."

"Is there anything I can do for you before I take my walk?"

She shook her head. "But I appreciate the offer."

Noah headed back to the sink to get another drink of water.

"That's a good boy you've got there, Ida," Wilma said.

"I think so, too."

"It's good that you know how to cook," Wilma said to Noah.

"Most women would appreciate a man who can cook."

Noah grunted. He wasn't used to getting such praise.

"Faith has never liked to cook that much," Wilma went on to say. "But when I told her I was running a few errands and would probably be stopping here to see your mamm, she said she'd have supper waiting when I got home."

Noah's ears perked up at the mention of Faith's name, but he tried not to appear too interested. No point in giving Wilma or Mom the wrong idea.

"Even if Faith's not the best of cooks, she does seem to be a good *mudder*." Ida nodded at Wilma. "After all, she gave up her worldly ways and brought her daughter home."

"That's true," Noah said as he made his way over to the table to get a cookie.

"I just hope Faith isn't planning to leave again." Wilma's tone sounded resentful, and when Noah took a sideways glance, he saw her mouth quiver.

"What makes you think she's aiming to leave? Have you come right out and asked if that's what she's planning to do?" Noah asked before he even had time to think.

Both women turned to look at him, and Noah's face heated up. He scrubbed his hand across his chin, realizing he'd forgotten to shave that morning. "Sorry for butting into a conversation that was none of my business."

"It makes no never mind," Wilma said. "To answer one of your questions—I haven't asked her outright because I'm afraid of what the answer will be."

"But what makes you think she has leaving on her mind?" Noah persisted.

"I've caught her yodeling a few times when she didn't think anyone was around."

"But as we said earlier, others in our community yodel," Noah's mother said.

"True, but Faith knows her daed doesn't like it, and besides, she's been acting real strange since she and Melinda came to our place."

"Strange? In what way?" Noah asked.

"She won't make a decision to be baptized and join the church. Not even after talking with the bishop. And she doesn't seem the least bit interested in reading her Bible." Wilma drew in a deep breath and released it with a groan. "A smart mamm knows when her daughter's trying to pull the wool over her eyes."

Noah felt as if his heart had sunk clear to his toes. He was just beginning to get acquainted with Faith and had hoped she'd be sticking around.

"I think what Faith needs is a little encouragement—a reason to want to stay in Webster County. Don't you think so, Noah?" Mom asked as she reached for her iced tea.

Noah nodded, then glanced over at Faith's mother. "Would it help if I had a talk with Faith—maybe tried to become her friend?"

Wilma smiled, and so did Mom. "That'd be real good," they said at the same time.

In that moment, Noah made a decision. If Faith had any thoughts of leaving and had no plans to join the church, then he would do all he could to help her see the need for God as well as her family. He was glad he'd spoken to Hank this morning about taking Faith and Melinda to see the tree farm on Saturday.

"Guess I'll go out for that walk now," he said, turning to face his mother. "So I might be late getting home for supper."

"No problem," she replied. "Take all the time you need, and if you're not back in time for supper, your daed and I will just have a sandwich."

As Faith stood in front of the stove, stirring a pot of chicken broth, she thought about her lack of cooking skills and hoped the meal she was making would turn out all right. She'd been left in charge of fixing supper while Mama ran some errands. Grace Ann and Esther were in the garden picking peas, which would be added to the steaming broth. The dumpling dough had already been mixed, and Melinda and Susie were busy setting the table.

A knock at the door startled Faith, and she nearly dropped the wooden spoon into the broth.

"I'll get it," Melinda offered.

A few seconds later, Faith heard the back door creak open. When she turned from the stove, she was surprised to see Noah holding his straw hat in one hand.

"Look who came to visit, Mama," Melinda motioned to Noah.

"If you came to see Papa or one of the brothers, they're out in the barn." Susie placed a glass on the table and moved over to where Noah and Melinda stood near the kitchen door.

"Actually it's you I'm here to see," Noah said, patting Melinda on top of her head. "You and your mamm." His gaze shifted to Faith.

"What do you need to see me and my daughter about?"

Noah took a few steps toward her. "I—uh—wanted to tell you that I arranged with my boss to give you and Melinda a tour of the Christmas tree farm this Saturday. Would you be able to go then?"

Melinda bounced up and down. "Yes! Yes! The Christmas tree farm! Can we go, Mama? Can we, please?"

"Well, I—"

"Me, too?" Susie begged. "I've never been to the tree farm before."

Noah looked down at Susie and smiled. "You, too, if it's okay with your mamm."

"Oh, I'm sure it will be. I'll go outside and see if she's home yet." Susie raced out the back door.

"How about it, Faith?" Noah asked. "Can I come by on Saturday morning around ten o'clock?"

Faith pursed her lips, uncertain how to reply. She didn't want to disappoint Melinda or Susie. But did she really want to spend several hours in the company of a man who confused her thinking and made her hands feel clammy every time he came near? She'd been through all those giddy feelings with Greg and wasn't about to set herself up for that again. She didn't need a man. She'd had one before, and look how that had turned out. Sure, Greg had gotten her plenty of shows, but it had been for his own selfish gain, not because he loved Faith and wanted her to succeed.

"We could take along a picnic lunch and have a meal at one of the tables under the maple tree in front of Sandy's Gift Shop," Noah suggested.

"Who's Sandy?" Faith questioned, as she brought her thoughts back to the present.

"Hank's wife. She runs a little store in one half of their barn, and she sells everything from peanut brittle to pot holders."

"Sounds like an interesting place. If it had been there when I was a girl, I'm sure I would have wanted to visit."

He grinned. "Popping into the gift store from time to time is an added bonus to working at the tree farm. I've even donated some of my baked goods for Sandy to share with her customers." Noah grabbed a handful of napkins from the wicker basket in the center of the table and folded each one, then placed them beside the plates.

Is this man for real? Greg was never so helpful. Faith shook her head and mentally scolded herself for comparing Noah to her deceased husband. It was pointless to do so. She would be leaving soon, and besides, she didn't know if Noah was merely putting on an act.

The back door collided with the wall as Susie raced into the room, her forehead glistening with sweat and her cheeks flushed like ripe cherries. "Mama just got home, and she says I can go with you to the tree farm on Saturday."

"Yippee!" Melinda grabbed her aunt's hands, and the girls jumped up and down like a couple of hopping toads.

"Now hold on a minute," Noah said, shaking his head. "Faith hasn't agreed to go yet."

The children stopped their exuberant jumping and stared up at Faith with expectant expressions. She lifted one hand in defeat. "Okay. We'll go to the Christmas tree farm."

"Yeah!" Melinda grabbed Susie and gave her a hug.

"You'd better get busy and fill those water glasses." Faith pointed to the table.

Noah turned toward the door. "Guess I'd best be getting on home."

"Why don't you stay for supper?" Faith asked, without thinking. She wasn't sure she wanted Noah, the good cook, to sample anything she had made. But she had extended the invitation, so she couldn't take it back now.

Noah pivoted around to face her, a smile as wide as the Missouri River spreading across his face. "It's nice of you to offer, and since my mamm's only planning to make sandwiches for supper, I'm sure she won't miss me." With that, Noah plunked his hat on a wall peg, rolled up his shirt-sleeves, and sauntered back across the room. "What can I do to help?"

Faith pointed to the salad fixings on the counter. "Guess you can whip up a green salad if you've a mind to."

"It would be my pleasure," he said with a nod.

Faith turned back to the stove. She had a feeling tonight's meal would be better than most.

As Noah sat at the Stutzmans' table a short time later, he was glad he'd decided to stop by their place. He was being treated to some fine chicken and dumplings, not to mention such good company. Eating with Mom and Pop every night was all right, but Noah really enjoyed the fellowship of the Stutzmans—from Menno right down to Melinda, the youngest child present. It made him wonder what it might be like if he had a wife and children of his own. Of course, that was nothing but a foolish dream. He didn't think any woman would want a shy man with a big nose who liked to cook. At least, that's what Noah's brother Rube had told him many times. Mom said Rube was only kidding, but truth be told, Noah figured his older brother was probably right.

"Noah, would you like to join me out in the living room for a game of checkers?"

Menno's question pulled Noah from his musings, and he pushed away from the table. "I might take you up on that after I help with the dishes."

Menno's forehead creased as he shook his head. "Are you daft? Nobody volunteers to do dishes."

Noah glanced at Faith, who sat to his left, and said, "I just ate a tasty supper, so it's only right that I show my appreciation by helping out."

"You already helped by fixing the salad and setting the table," Faith reminded him.

He shrugged. "I help my mamm do the dishes most every night."

Faith slid her chair back and stood. "Okay. I'll wash, and you dry."

"It's good Noah was able to join us for dinner, jah?" Menno said to Wilma, as he set up the checkerboard in the living room and she lit a few of their kerosene lamps.

She nodded and smiled. "Couldn't have planned it better myself."

"Want me to plant a few ideas in Noah's head while we're playing checkers?"

"What kind of ideas?"

He lifted a folding chair from behind the sofa and snapped it open. "You know—about him getting together with Faith."

Wilma shook her head. "I don't think you want to be that obvious, husband."

"Why not? I don't see any point in beating around the shrubbery, do you?"

She lifted her gaze toward the ceiling. "Maybe you could just mention how nice it is to have Faith home and how we're hoping she'll get baptized and join the church real soon."

His eyebrows scrunched together. "How's that gonna get 'em together?"

"It probably won't, but it's a start." Wilma lit the lamp closest to the table where he'd set out the checkerboard. "Would you like me to stay in the room and direct your conversation?"

Menno grunted. "No way! I'll be better off on my own with this. Besides, if you're in the room talking to Noah and asking a bunch of questions, it'll throw my concentration off, and he might win the game."

Wilma pinched his arm and turned toward the door leading to their bedroom. "I'll be in our room reading a book in case you need me." She hurried from the room before he could respond.

A few minutes later, Noah showed up with his shirtsleeves rolled up to his elbows.

"How'd everything go in the kitchen?" Menno asked, motioning for Noah to take a seat in the folding chair opposite him.

"It went fine. Got the dishes washed, dried, and put away."

"I still don't see why you'd want to get your hands all wrinkled in soapy dishwater."

Noah seated himself. "I've been helping my mamm in the kitchen since I was a kinner, and I'm used to having dishpan hands."

"Whatever you say." Menno nodded toward the checkerboard. "You go first."

"I don't mind if you'd like to start the game."

Menno shook his head. "That's okay. I'm the champion of checkers, so I'd better give you the edge by letting you begin."

"Okay," Noah said with a shrug.

They played in silence for a time as each of them racked up a few kings. About halfway through the game, Menno leaned back in his chair with his hands clasped behind his head and said, "Say, I've been wondering something."

"What's that?" Noah asked, as he studied the board.

"How come a nice fellow like you, who likes to cook and do other things in the kitchen, isn't married and raising a passel of kinner by now?"

Noah's eyebrows shot up. "Well, I. . ." He jumped one of Menno's checkers and then another. "To tell you the truth, I've never found a woman who showed much interest in me."

"Is that so?"

Noah nodded. "It's your turn, Menno."

Menno contemplated his next move as he thought about what he should say. This conversation wasn't going nearly as well as he had hoped. "I should think with your kitchen skills that all the single women in our community would be chasing after you like hound dogs in pursuit of a rabbit," he said as he moved his checker piece.

Noah took his turn again, this time jumping three of Menno's checkers. "That's it! That's the end of this game!"

Menno stared dumbfounded at the checkerboard. He didn't know how Noah had done it, but he'd managed to skunk him real good. "I. . .uh. . .guess I didn't have my mind on the game," he mumbled. "That's what I get for trying to. . ." His voice trailed off. He'd almost blurted out that he was trying to help Wilma get Noah and Faith together.

"Trying to what?" Noah asked with a puzzled expression.

"Nothing. Nope, it was nothing at all." Menno pushed a stack of checkers in Noah's direction. "You take the red ones this time." He gritted his teeth. *And from now on, Wilma can do her own matchmaking.*

Chapter 12

Faith didn't know why she felt so nervous, but the idea that Noah was coming by soon to take them to the Christmas tree farm had her feeling as jittery as a cat with a bad case of fleas. She'd been pacing the kitchen floor for the last ten minutes, periodically going to the window to see if he had arrived.

"It was nice of Noah to invite you out for the day. It'll be good for you and the kinner to have some fun."

Faith whirled around at the sound of her mother's voice. She hadn't realized anyone had come into the kitchen. "I-I'm sure the girls will enjoy themselves."

Mama's eyebrows furrowed. "And what about you, daughter? Won't you have a good time, as well?"

"I suppose I will."

"Noah's a nice man, don't you think?"

Faith shrugged. "It will be interesting to see how Christmas trees are grown," she said. No use giving Mama any ideas about her and Noah becoming an item.

Her mother grunted and helped herself to a cup of the herbal tea she'd brewed a few minutes earlier. "It wonders me the way our English neighbors put so much emphasis on bringing a tree into the house at Christmas, then throwing all sorts of fancy decorations and bright lights onto the branches. Why not just enjoy the trees outdoors, the way God intended us to?"

Faith didn't bother to answer. Mama had never approved of Faith showing an interest in modern things, and if she gave her opinion now, it might be misconstrued as Faith wanting to have a tree in the house. She helped herself to a glass of water at the sink and headed for the back door. "Think I'll wait outside with the girls," she said over her shoulder. "See you when we get home."

Out on the porch, Faith took a seat in one of the wicker chairs and watched Melinda and Susie as they took turns pushing each other on the old wooden swing hanging from one of their maple trees.

"I remember the days when I was that carefree," she murmured, closing her eyes and imagining herself as a child again. Faith and her sisters used to play on the swing whenever they had a free moment. Sometimes when Barbara came to visit, she and Faith would take turns, just as Melinda and Susie were doing now. Those were untroubled days, when Faith was more content with her life—always joking and playing tricks on her siblings. She'd actually enjoyed much of her early childhood. It wasn't until Faith became a teenager that she had decided she wasn't happy being Amish. Mama and Papa had seemed more critical, saying things like, "Why don't you grow up and start acting your age?" and "Quit playing around and get to work."

Faith remembered the time she and Dan Miller had hitch-hiked into Springfield and gone to the movies. When she returned home in the evening, she'd gotten into trouble for that little stunt. Papa had shouted at her something awful, saying if she were a few years younger she'd have been hauled to the woodshed for a sound *bletsching*. He said she was rebellious and irresponsible for taking off without telling them where she was going. When it came out that they'd hitchhiked and gone to see a show, Papa blew up and gave Faith double chores for a whole month. He said what she and Dan had done was not only worldly but dangerous. What if some maniac had been the one to give them a ride? They could have been beaten, robbed, or worse. Faith couldn't believe Dan had spilled the beans. It was a good thing he and his family had moved to Illinois, or she might tell him what she thought about all that even now.

Mama, who had also been quite upset, had made Faith learn a whole list of scripture verses over the next several weeks. Faith had used that as an excuse for not reading her Bible after that.

The *clip-clop* of a horse's hooves drew Faith's musings to a halt, and she opened her eyes. Noah had arrived. She drew in a deep breath, smoothed the wrinkles in her dark blue cotton dress, and stood. "Come on, girls," she called to Melinda and Susie. "Noah's here, and it's time to go."

Noah was glad to see Faith waiting on the front porch, and he chuckled as the girls surrounded him, both begging, "Hurry up and let's go."

Soon he had the children loaded into the back of his open buggy and Faith settled on the front seat beside him.

"Sure is a nice day," Noah said, glancing over at Faith with a grin.

She nodded.

"I hope the girls like the tree farm."

"I'm sure they will."

"Hank's wife has been looking forward to your coming. She really likes kinner."

"That's nice."

"Hank has a couple of beagle hounds, Amos and Griggs. I'm guessing the girls will enjoy playing with them."

"Could be."

Noah grimaced. Couldn't Faith respond to anything he said with more than a few words? Didn't she want to go to the tree farm, or was she just being quiet because the girls were chattering so loudly in the seat behind them that it was hard to make conversation over their voices?

Deciding it might be best to keep quiet for the rest of the trip, Noah concentrated on guiding the horse down the highway. A short time later, he pulled into the driveway of Osborns' Christmas Tree Farm. He stopped in front of the hitching post Hank had built for Noah, got out, and headed around back to help the girls out. When they were safely on the ground, he turned to Faith, but she'd already climbed down.

He led the way, taking them into the area where the rows of Scotch and white pines had recently been sheared and shaped.

"Look at all the trees!" Melinda shouted as she ran down the lane. "I wish we could see them decorated for Christmas."

"You can," Noah called. "My boss's wife, Sandy, has some artificial trees in her gift shop. We'll stop in there after we've seen the real trees, and you can take a look."

For the next hour, Noah showed Faith and the girls around the farm, explaining the procedure that began in the late winter months and continued up to harvest, shortly before Christmas the following year. From late December until early June, dead trees were cut down, and new ones were planted in their place. From the first of April all the way through summer, the grass around the seedlings had to be kept mowed. The larger trees were sheared and shaped during the summer months, and by fall, certain trees were selected to be sold to local lots and shipped to other markets farther away.

"By the first of November, we start cutting the trees; then they're netted, packed, and ready for pickup on Thanksgiving weekend. The Christmas tree lots are usually open for business on the Friday after Thanksgiving," Noah explained.

"Do all Englishers buy their trees from the lots?" Susie questioned.

Noah shook his head. "Some come out here and reserve their trees as soon as October, rather than going to a lot to pick out a tree." He motioned to a group of nearby pines. "This place is really busy during the month of December, and many folks come back year after year to get a tree. Hank keeps his business operating on weekends until Thanksgiving; then it's open daily for folks to come and get their trees and browse through the gift shop."

"We put up a small tree in our hotel room last Christmas. Ain't that right, Mama?" Melinda asked, giving the edge of her mother's apron a tug.

"Yes, that's right. We did have a tree." Faith tweaked her daughter's nose. "And it's *isn't*, not *ain't*."

"Mama told me yesterday there won't be a tree in Grandma and Grandpa Stutzman's house," Melinda continued, making no mention of her mother's grammatical correction.

"That's right, Melinda. The Amish don't celebrate Christmas by bringing a decorated tree into the house." Noah motioned to the rustic barn nearby. "Now that we've seen the trees, we can go into the gift shop and take a look at all the things Sandy has for sale. After that, we'll eat our picnic lunch."

"Yippee!" the girls chorused.

Faith looked over at Noah. "I think you've made their day."

"I hope you're enjoying yourself, as well."

She nodded. "It's been quite interesting."

When they entered the gift shop a few minutes later, they were greeted by both Hank and his wife, Sandy, a petite red-haired woman with brown eyes.

"Would you all like something to drink?" Sandy asked, once the introductions had been made.

"Maybe in a bit," Noah replied. He turned to Faith. "How about you?"

"I'm fine for now, too."

The girls, who seemed mesmerized by the artificial trees

decorated with white twinkling lights, red balls, and brightly colored ornaments, darted around the room, checking each one out, while the adults found seats near the unlit, wood-burning stove.

"Did Noah explain how I run things here, while he showed you around the tree farm?" Hank asked, looking at Faith.

Faith nodded and bent to pet the Osborns' two beagle hounds, Amos and Griggs. Griggs licked her hand, while Amos nudged her foot with a rubber ball he'd taken from a wicker basket near the front door. "It's all quite impressive," she said, tossing the ball for Amos while she continued to pet Griggs.

"I'm sure glad Noah came to work for me," Hank continued. "He's one of the best workers I've ever had."

Noah's face heated with embarrassment. "I enjoy working with the trees almost as much as I like baking," he mumbled.

"And you're as good a baker as you are a tree farmer." Sandy smiled at Faith. "Noah often bakes some of his goodies for the customers who come into my shop. One of the things folks like best is his lemon sponge cake."

Faith nodded but made no comment. It was obvious that her focus was on the dogs.

Hank stood and placed his hand on Noah's shoulder. "If you'd like to come out to my workshop with me, I'll show you my latest woodworking project."

Noah nodded. "That'd be fine." He glanced over at Faith to get her reaction, but she shrugged and threw the ball for Amos again.

"We'll probably be ready for some apple cider and a few cookies when we get back," Hank said, nodding at his wife.

"They'll be ready whenever you are," she replied.

As Noah followed Hank outside, he smiled at Melinda and Susie, who played under the trees with the other hound dog.

"Are you sure you wouldn't like something to eat or drink?" Sandy asked Faith.

"No, thanks, I'm fine." Faith glanced around the shop, noticing all the gift items as well as the artificial trees. "This place must keep you plenty busy."

"It does fill the lonely hours." There was a tone of sadness in Sandy's voice, and her downcast eyes revealed sorrow.

"Isn't your husband around quite a bit? I would think with his business being near where you live, you would see him a lot."

"Not really. Whenever Hank's not working with his trees, he's in his woodworking shop, making all sorts of things."

"Things like the items you sell here?" Faith asked, gesturing with her hand to one of the birdhouses on a nearby shelf.

Sandy nodded. "He does make quite a few of the things, and I make peanut brittle, but others from the community keep me supplied with their homemade items, as well."

"Do you get a lot of customers?"

"At certain times I do. Mostly around holidays like Mother's Day and Valentine's Day. Of course, Christmastime is especially busy, too."

"I imagine it would be."

"Do you make anything you might consider selling here in the store? I'm always looking for new items," Sandy said.

"The only thing I'm good at is telling jokes and yodeling. Mama's the expert baker and quilter in our house."

"Yes, I knew you yodeled, because Hank and I were at one of your shows in Branson. The day Noah asked Hank if he could bring you and your daughter by our place, he mentioned that you'd given up your career and moved back home." Sandy's forehead wrinkled. "I was really surprised to hear that."

Faith's mouth went dry. She felt guilty every time someone mentioned her quitting her life as an entertainer and returning home. She didn't feel at liberty to tell anyone that she was planning to leave again.

"When I was an entertainer, I dressed in a hillbilly costume," she said, hoping to avoid the subject of why she'd returned home.

"That's right, you were wearing a hillbilly costume the night we saw you."

A vision of her performances flashed onto the screen of Faith's mind. She saw herself onstage, dressed in a tattered blue skirt and a white peasant blouse. A straw hat, bent out of shape, was perched on top of her head, and she'd worn a pair of black tennis shoes with holes in the toes. The audience seemed to like her corny routine, for they'd laughed, cheered, and hollered for more.

"Yodeling sounds like fun. Is it hard to learn?" Sandy asked.

Faith shrugged. "Not for me it wasn't. Ever since I was a little girl, I could whistle like a bird and trill my voice. When I went to town one day, I heard a woman yodeling on the radio at Baldy's Café. After I got home, I headed straight for my secret place in the barn, where I knew I wasn't likely to be disturbed."

"Did you actually try to yodel right then, with no teacher?"

"I did, and much to my amazement, I didn't sound half bad. After that, I practiced on my own every chance I got, but hearing the yodeler on the radio wasn't my only contact with yodeling."

"Oh?"

"A few others in our Swiss-Amish community like to yodel, but not to the extent that I do." Faith bit down on her lower lip. "And no one but me has ever gone off and become an entertainer."

"I'm surprised your family had no objections to your leaving home like that."

"They objected all right. Even before I'd made my decision to leave home, they were always after me for acting silly and sneaking off to listen to country-western music." Faith shook her head. "Papa called my yodeling 'downright stupid' and said it sounded like I was gargling or that I had something caught in my throat."

Sandy reached over and patted Faith's arm in a motherly fashion. "I guess it's safe to say that with most parents, something about their children gets their dander up." She glanced over her shoulder, and Faith did the same. Melinda and Susie were lying on the floor, with both dogs lying on their backs and getting their bellies rubbed. "I used to think that if I ever became a mother, I'd try to accept my kids just as they are." She stared down at her hands. "Hank and I have been married almost ten years, and we recently found out that we can't have any children. So I'll never have the opportunity to try out my mothering skills."

"I'm sorry to hear that. Have you thought of adopting?"

Sandy shook her head. "Hank was pretty upset when he learned that I couldn't give him any babies, and I doubt he would want to adopt."

Faith was trying to think of what she could say to offer

comfort, when the men returned to the gift shop.

"We're ready for some refreshments now," Hank said, smiling at Sandy.

She pushed her chair aside and stood. "I'll have something served up in a jiffy."

"I'll help you." Faith started to get up, but Sandy waved her aside. "I can manage. Why don't you stay put and relax?"

Faith didn't know whether to argue or take Sandy up on her suggestion, but when the hound dog Amos trotted over to her with the ball in his mouth, she decided to stay put.

Chapter 13

*S*he *likes pets, and so does her daughter,* Noah thought, as he watched Faith chuck the ball across the room for Amos, while Melinda stroked Griggs behind his ear.

Sandy returned to the room a few minutes later with a tray of cookies, some of her peanut brittle, and a pitcher of cold apple cider. When she placed the tray down on a small table, the girls scampered over with expectant expressions.

"Are you two hungry?" Hank asked with a chuckle.

"Jah," they said at the same time.

"Just don't eat too much." Faith shook her head. "Or you'll spoil your appetites for the meal Noah's made us."

Susie grinned. "I'm always hungry, so it won't matter how many cookies I eat."

"Just the same, I don't want you filling up on cookies when

there's a meal to be eaten."

The girls each took two cookies and a glass of cider and then settled themselves on the floor again.

After visiting with Hank and his wife awhile and sampling some of Sandy's delicious peanut brittle, Noah finally ushered his guests outside to one of the picnic tables. He opened the small cooler he'd packed that morning and spread the contents on the table. He had invited Hank and Sandy to join them, but they'd declined because of work they had to do.

"How do you expect us to eat all this food?" Faith asked when he placed a plate of golden fried chicken in front of her.

"Just eat what you can." He added a jar of pickles, a plastic container full of coleslaw, a loaf of brown bread, and some baked beans.

They paused for silent prayer and then dug right in. Melinda and Susie ate two drumsticks apiece, and Faith devoured a thigh plus a large hunk of white meat. Noah was glad to see her eating so well. She was far too skinny to his way of thinking. He was also pleased to see how much Faith had relaxed. Either she was feeling more comfortable in his presence or her playtime with Hank's hounds had done the trick. Noah figured he'd made some headway in befriending Faith. Now if he could only think of something to say that might give him an indication of whether she was planning to go back on the road again. He debated about asking her outright but decided that might put a sour note on the day. Besides, what if it wasn't true? Maybe Faith's mother had been wrong.

When the meal was over, Susie looked for wildflowers, while Melinda played with Amos and Griggs. Noah suggested that he and Faith sit on a quilt under a cluster of shady maples, as the afternoon had become hot and humid.

Faith leaned back on her elbows and stared up at the sky. "Sure is peaceful, isn't it? I can see why you enjoy coming to work here every day."

Noah nodded. "Working with the pine trees gives me much satisfaction."

"How come you're not married and raising a family by now?" she asked suddenly.

Noah's ears burned, and the heat quickly spread to his face. "I. . .uh. . .don't think I'm much of a catch."

"I wasn't much of a catch, either, but Greg married me." Faith grimaced. "Of course, he never really loved me."

"What makes you think that?"

"Greg only wanted me because he thought I could make him rich."

"And did you?"

"Not even close. I was doing pretty well for a while, but Greg spent most of our money on alcohol, and he gambled some." Faith's eyebrows furrowed, and she looked away. "I don't know why I blurted all that out. I sure didn't plan on it."

"It's not good to keep things bottled up." He reached out to touch her arm, but she flinched and pulled away.

"Sorry. I didn't mean to startle you."

"I—I get a little jumpy whenever someone touches me un-expectedly." As Faith looked at Noah, he noticed tears in her eyes. "Greg had a mean streak and often took out his frustrations on me, but I've never admitted it to anyone until now."

Noah's eyebrows lifted in surprise. "You mean he was abusive?"

She nodded. "A few times he hit me but usually in places where it didn't show."

"I'm sorry to hear that. No man should ever strike a woman; it's just not right." Noah's heart went out to Faith. He'd had no idea what life had been like for her in the English world.

"Greg did get me some good shows, and I felt that I needed him as my agent." She squinted. "It's not easy to find a good agent, you know."

"Why would you want to go back to that way of living if it was so hard?"

"Who says I want to go back?"

Noah felt like slapping himself. He hadn't meant to say that, and he surely couldn't tell Faith what her mother had told his mother.

"I. . .uh. . .kind of got that impression by some of the things you've said about life as an entertainer. You mentioned that you missed it and all."

Faith shrugged.

Noah decided to change the subject. "Remember that scripture verse I attached to the lemon sponge cake I gave you awhile back?"

She nodded slowly. "It had something to do with faith, right?"

"That's correct."

"Faith might give some people high expectations when things are messed up in their lives, but to me, it's nothing more than false hope."

Noah couldn't believe his ears. His own faith had grown so much over the last couple of years. He couldn't imagine that anyone who had been taught to believe in God would think faith wasn't real. "As I told you the other day at Baldy's, faith is like a muscle, and it needs to be exercised in order to become strong."

Faith looked uncomfortable as she shifted on the quilt, so Noah suggested they talk about something else.

"Okay." She moistened her lips with the tip of her tongue. "Say, did you hear about the elderly man who moved to a retirement home and hoped to make lots of new friends there?"

He shook his head. "Can't say that I have."

"The man met a lady, and they spent a lot of time together. Soon he realized he was in love with her, so he proposed marriage. But the day after the man proposed, he woke up and couldn't remember what the woman's answer was."

"So what'd he do?"

"He went to her and said, 'I'm so embarrassed. I proposed to you last night, but I can't remember if you said yes or no.' " Faith tapped her fingers against her chin and rolled her eyes from side to side. " 'Oh, now I remember,' the old woman quipped. 'I said yes, but I couldn't remember who asked me.' "

Noah chuckled. Faith was beginning to use her sense of humor again, which was a good thing. "That was a great story. Have you got another?" he asked.

She jiggled her eyebrows up and down. "Do bats fly at night?"

He grinned.

"Okay, here goes." Faith drew in a deep breath. "You know, I never got used to driving a car when I lived among the English those ten years I was gone. Especially after I discovered what a motorist really is."

"And what would that be?"

"A person who, after seeing a wreck, drives carefully for the next several blocks."

Noah grinned. Faith could be a lot of fun when she had a mind to. He hoped they would have more opportunities to spend days like this.

"Tell me how you learned to bake such delicious goodies," Faith said, changing the subject again. "I sure ate my share today."

"It's no big secret. I just started baking when I was a young fellow, found that I enjoyed it, and I've been doing it ever since."

"I see."

"Even though I did plenty of outside chores when I was a kinner, Pop and my nine brothers thought I was a bit strange because I didn't mind helping in the kitchen."

Faith grimaced as she shook her head. "My family thinks I'm odd because I can't cook so well."

"The chicken and dumplings you made the other night were good."

"Maybe so, but that dish is one of the few things I can fix well. I can't bake like you do, that's for sure." Faith took a bite from one of the brownies he'd brought along. "Mmm. . .now this is really good."

"Practice makes perfect," he said with a grin. "I didn't always bake well, but I had fun learning."

"I think I need a lot more than practice." Faith held up the brownie. "I doubt I could ever make anything as good as this."

"Sure you could. Where's your faith?"

"I don't have much faith in anything these days." She looked away. "I told you before—my faith has diminished over the years."

"Have you read your Bible regularly?"

She shook her head.

"That's the only way you can strengthen your faith—that and spending time with the Lord in prayer."

Impulsively, Noah touched her hand and noticed how soft it felt. He was glad she hadn't flinched when he'd touched her this time. "I've been praying for you, Faith," he whispered.

"You—you have?"

"Jah, and I'll keep on praying that your faith will grow so strong that you'll feel God walking right beside you every day."

She stared down at her hands, clasped tightly in her lap.

"I suppose we should gather up the girls and start for home," she murmured a few seconds later.

Noah nodded. "Jah, I guess we should."

During the first half of the ride home, the girls chattered again, but suddenly, their voices died out. When Noah glanced over his shoulder, he saw the two of them leaning their heads together, eyes shut and cheeks flushed.

Faith was quiet, too, as she stared at the passing scenery and spoke only whenever Noah posed a question. Was she thinking about the things they had discussed after their picnic lunch? Could she be mulling over the idea of exercising her faith? He hoped so, for it was obvious that the woman sitting beside him needed a renewed faith in God. He thought she needed the kind of peace that would fill her life with so much happiness she would have no desire for the things the world had to offer. She'd proven by her joke telling today that she could be joyful and funny, even when not on some stage entertaining.

Thinking about Faith and the girls in the backseat, suddenly Noah was overcome with the need for a wife and children. He'd never missed it much until lately, and he wondered if it had anything to do with Faith's return. Noah was sure from some of Faith's comments that she didn't believe in or accept the same kinds of spiritual things he did. He knew he could never take a wife who didn't share his love for and belief in Jesus.

Even though I can't allow myself to become romantically involved with Faith, I'll still try to be her friend, Noah decided.

He glanced over at Faith. "I enjoyed the day. Thanks for agreeing to come."

"I had fun, too. I'm glad you invited us to see where you work."

"Maybe we can get together some other time this summer. I'd like to hire a driver and go to Springfield to see that big sportsmen's store."

"You mean the Bass Pro Shops?"

"Jah, I've never been there, but I hear it's really something to see."

"It's billed as the world's greatest sporting goods store, and there's even a wildlife museum."

"You've been there then?"

She nodded. "A few times."

"Sounds like the place to be," Noah said, feeling his enthusiasm rise. "I'd also like to visit Fantastic Caverns, just outside of Springfield."

Her pale eyebrows wiggled slightly. "Noah Hertzler, you're a man full of surprises."

"I'm not sure I get your meaning."

"You used to be so shy when we were children, and now you seem to have such a zest for life. I feel as if I'm getting to know a whole different side of you."

He reached under his straw hat and scratched the side of his head. "I guess maybe I have changed some." *Especially since you came back to Webster County. You bring out the best in me, Faith. You just don't know it.*

Chapter 14

As Faith took a seat in a booth at Baldy's Café, her heart started to hammer. When she'd phoned the talent agency in Memphis the last time, they had informed her that Brad Olsen, the agent who'd chosen to represent her, would be in Springfield over the weekend and would like to meet with her. Faith knew she wouldn't be able to get away for that long or come up with a good excuse as to why she wanted to go to Springfield, so she asked if the agent could meet her at Baldy's Café on Monday morning. The meeting had been agreed upon, so here she sat, picking at the salad she'd ordered and waiting for Mr. Olsen to arrive. She hoped he would be here soon, because she'd told her mother she was going shopping in Seymour and that she would be back by late afternoon.

"Are you Faith Andrews?" a deep male voice asked, halting Faith's thoughts.

She looked up and saw a tall, thin man with ebony-colored hair.

"Yes, I'm Faith Andrews."

He extended his hand. "I'm Brad Olsen from the agency in Memphis."

When she reached over and shook his hand, his eyebrows lifted slightly. "I recognized your face from the pictures I've seen of you, but those clothes you've got on really threw me. When did you decide to start wearing an Amish costume?"

"Oh, this isn't a costume." Faith gestured to the bench on the other side of her table. "If you'd like to have a seat, I'll explain my situation."

"Sure thing."

During the next half hour, Faith gave Brad Olsen the details as to why she had temporarily given up her profession and come to Webster County, and she ended by saying, "So as soon as my daughter has adjusted well enough, I'll be ready to return to the stage."

"I see," he said, as he scribbled some notes on the tablet he'd pulled from his briefcase. "Do you have any idea how much longer that will be?"

Faith shrugged. "Hopefully, not long. Melinda's doing fairly well, but I can't leave until I know for sure that she's accepted the Amish way of life."

Brad's eyebrows drew together as he motioned to her plain cotton dress. "Looks to me like you've accepted it pretty well yourself."

Faith's cheeks heated up as she shook her head. "I'm only going through the motions of being Amish so none of my family will question things. It wouldn't be right for me to take off without seeing that my little girl is completely settled in."

"You need to get back in circulation as soon as possible. The longer you're away from performing, the further your name will be from people's minds." He tapped the end of his pen along the edge of the table. "Not to mention that in order for you to keep on top of your skills as an entertainer, you'll need to practice."

"I practice my yodeling whenever I get the chance to be alone, and I tell jokes to whoever's willing to listen." Faith thought about the meal she and Melinda had shared with Noah not long ago and how she'd been able to make Noah laugh.

"Well, I think that about does it for now," Brad said as he slipped his notebook into his briefcase and stood. He handed her a business card. "I'd like you to call me once a week and let me know how things are going so I'll know when to schedule you for a show."

"I'll do that," Faith promised as she followed him to the checkout counter.

They were about to head for the door when Faith caught sight of Noah sitting in a booth near the back of the restaurant. She hadn't noticed him earlier and didn't know if he'd come in during her visit with Brad Olsen or if he'd been there the whole time. She squinted and stared when she realized someone was in the booth with him—a young Amish woman with medium brown hair. Faith didn't recognize her as anyone from their community, and she wondered if the woman could be from a neighboring community and had come to Seymour to meet Noah. Was she Noah's girlfriend? They were sitting side by side, with their heads close together as though in deep concentration.

Faith considered going over to say hello but thought better of it. It might raise questions as to why she was at Baldy's, and if Noah saw her with the talent agent, he would have questions she didn't want to answer. With a quick glance over her shoulder, Faith slipped out the door.

Noah craned his neck as he watched Faith leave the café with a tall English man. He'd seen the couple walk over to the checkout counter together a few minutes ago and had wondered who the man was. Did Faith have a boyfriend—maybe a fellow entertainer? That's sure what it looked like when they'd been standing near the counter with their heads together.

"Noah, did you hear what I said?"

The soft-spoken voice pulled his attention back to his cousin Mary, who sat on the bench beside him and had been pouring out her heart about the way she'd been jilted by her boyfriend, Mark. Mary and her folks lived near Jamesport, and Mark lived in Webster County with his family. They'd been courting for several months, but two weeks ago, Mary had received a letter from Mark saying he wanted to break up with her and that he would be moving to Illinois to work with his brother who owned a dairy farm there. Mary had caught a bus to Seymour, hoping to talk Mark into changing his mind, but by the time she'd arrived, Mark had already left for Illinois. Heartbroken, Mary had asked Noah to give her a ride back to Seymour so she could catch the bus home.

Noah gave Mary's arm a gentle squeeze. "What was that you said?"

"I was telling you that I'm going to try real hard to forget about Mark and move on with my life. No point in crying over spilled honey, as my mamm likes to say."

"That's good. Glad to hear it."

"Noah, are you okay? You look like you're a thousand miles away."

"It's nothing. I saw someone I know, and I was wondering what she was doing here."

Mary's eyebrows lifted high on her forehead. "You've found yourself an *aldi?*"

"No, no," he sputtered. "It's nothing like that. The woman I saw is just a friend."

"Is she someone I know?"

"I don't think so. She's been gone from home for ten years, and you and your folks have been living in Jamesport longer than that, so— "

"Oh, my. . .look at the time!" Mary pointed to the clock hanging on the wall above the checkout counter. "If we don't get a move on, I'm going to miss my bus."

Noah nodded. "You're right. We'd better get over to Lazy Lee's Gas Station right away."

As they left their booth, Noah wondered if he should ask Faith about the English fellow he'd seen her with. *Probably not,* he decided. *Whatever Faith does is her business, not mine.*

As Faith stood at the kitchen sink that afternoon, getting a drink of water, she thought about the young woman she'd seen Noah with. Should she say something to him about it? Probably not. It was none of her business who Noah saw in private. Besides, if she brought it up to Noah, she might have to tell him why she'd been at Baldy's. If Noah knew she had hired an agent, he would realize she planned to leave, and then her folks would find out.

Faith hated to admit it, but she was attracted to Noah, and that scared her a lot. Spending time with him had made her feel different than she'd ever felt in the company of a man. Maybe it was because Noah seemed nothing like other men she'd met during her years of living among the English. He was soft-spoken, seemed to be kind, and had taken an interest in her and Melinda. Could it be an act? Was Noah too good to be true?

Faith had been looking forward to making a trip to Springfield with Noah to see the Bass Pro Shops and Fantastic Caverns, but now that she'd seen him with that woman in town, she was sure those plans had changed. It was probably for the best. She couldn't afford to begin a relationship with a man who was wholly committed to being Amish, even if he did seem to be one of the nicest fellows she'd ever met.

Faith heard shrill laughter coming from outside, and she glanced out the window. Melinda and Susie ran back and forth through a puddle of water in their bare feet, giggling and waving their hands.

"Maybe after supper I should tell Mama and Papa that I'll be leaving soon. There's no point in prolonging it," Faith murmured. "But first, I should tell Melinda."

Faith went out the back door and made her way across the lawn toward the frolicking children. She would take her daughter aside, explain everything to her, and then tell the folks. She hoped Melinda would understand that she was doing this for her own good. Faith would promise to visit as often as she could—whenever she was in the area doing a show or she had time off. Melinda might not care for the arrangement, but someday she would realize her mother had her best interests at heart.

Faith had just approached the girls when she heard a shrill scream near the house. She whirled around but saw nothing out of the ordinary.

"Help! Somebody, help me!"

That sounds like Mama. Faith rushed to the cellar steps and peered down. Her mother lay at the bottom, moaning and holding her leg.

Faith ran down the steps. "Mama, what happened?"

"I—I was going down here to get a jar of green beans, and I must have tripped." Mama winced when Faith touched her leg. "I think it's broken."

"I'd better call Papa and tell him we're going to have to get one of our neighbors to drive you to the hospital." Faith hated to leave her mother lying on the cold, hard concrete, but she had no other choice. "Hang on, Mama. I'll be right back."

She rushed out to the fields, where her father and brothers had been working on broken fences. When she caught sight of them, she began frantically waving her hands.

"What's wrong, daughter?" Papa called with a worried frown. "Has that cantankerous bull been chasing you?"

"It's not the bull. Mama's fallen down the cellar steps, and I think her leg is broken. We need to get one of our neighbors to drive her to the hospital right away."

Papa dropped his wire cutters, and the brothers let go of the shovels they'd been using. "Son," Papa said, motioning to Brian, "you run over to the Jenkinses' place and see if they can give us a ride." He turned to John. "Come with me to see about your mamm."

Brian scampered off toward the neighbors', and Faith followed Papa and John across the field, through the pasture, and into the backyard. Papa dashed down the basement stairs and gathered Mama into his arms. "What happened, Wilma? How did this happen?"

"Clumsy me. I wasn't watching where I was going, and I must have slipped on a step." Mama's lips quivered, and Faith could see the anguish on her mother's face. "Sorry to be such a bother."

"You're no bother," Papa said as he and John made a chair with their interlinked arms and carried Mama up the steps and into the house. Faith followed, and so did Susie and Melinda. After the men placed Mama on the sofa in the living room, Faith put two pillows under her mother's head.

"Is Mama gonna be okay?" Susie's eyes were huge as saucers.

"I'll be fine, daughter," Mama said, although she was gritting her teeth.

"I wonder what's taking so long for our ride to get here," Papa said as he peered out the window. "I thought Brian would have been back by now."

Faith shook her head. "Papa, it's only been ten minutes or so since you sent Brian. I'm sure Mama's ride to the hospital will be here soon, so in the meantime, you need to relax."

He whirled around and leveled her with a look of irritation. "Don't you be tellin' me what to do."

She flinched and drew back as if she'd been stung by a bee. This was exactly the way her father had treated her when she was a girl. "I wasn't trying to tell you what to do. I just thought if you relaxed, the time would pass quicker."

"Our daughter's right, Menno," Mama put in. "Pacing and fretting won't bring us help any quicker."

He grunted and stood in front of her. "You need anything, Wilma? Maybe some ice for the swelling?"

She looked down at her swollen leg. "Jah, that might be a good idea."

"I'll get it." Faith scooted for the kitchen and returned a few minutes later with an ice bag, which she carefully placed on her mother's leg.

"Danki. You're a good daughter."

Tears stung the backs of Faith's eyes. She couldn't remember the last time her mother had said anything that nice to her.

A horn honked, and John, who had been watching out the window, rushed to the door. "Lester Jenkins and his wife are here!"

The rest of the day went by in a blur. Papa, Brian, and Faith rode with Mama to the hospital, while Elaine Jenkins, Lester's wife, stayed at the Stutzmans' house with Melinda and Susie. After X-rays were taken of Mama's leg, the doctor explained that the swelling needed to go down some before the cast was put on, so Mama was kept overnight. Papa decided to stay with her, but Faith and her brothers returned home to do their chores and wait for their sisters to get home.

As Faith prepared for bed that night, she thought about the events of the day. No way could she leave Webster County now. Esther and Grace Ann had jobs outside the home, so they couldn't be counted on to take care of Mama or run the house while her leg was healing. Faith would have to stick around until her mother's cast came off and she could resume her regular chores. It was a good thing Faith hadn't said anything about leaving yet.

The following afternoon, Mama came home from the hospital, and Papa and John helped her into her bedroom. Faith thought it was a good thing her folks' room was downstairs, because with Mama having to rely on crutches for weeks, it would have been difficult for her to navigate the stairs safely.

Once Mama was situated, Faith herded Melinda and Susie into the kitchen and instructed them to set the table while she made supper. She'd no more than taken a package of meat from the refrigerator when a knock sounded at the back door.

"I'll get it!" Melinda hollered. She scurried across the room and flung open the door.

A few seconds later, Noah entered the kitchen, holding a loaf of gingerbread in one hand and his straw hat in the other.

"I heard about your mamm's broken leg, and I thought she might like this." He handed the bread to Faith.

"That was nice of you. Would you care to join us for supper?" she asked.

"I appreciate the offer, but I can't stay that long. Mom isn't feeling well today, so I promised I'd get right home to make supper." Noah smiled. "Guess I could stay long enough to have a glass of iced tea, though."

Noah took a seat at the table, and Faith handed him some iced tea. "This sure hits the spot," he said after taking a drink.

"Can Susie and I go out back and play now?" Melinda asked her mother.

Faith nodded her consent, and the girls raced for the back door, giggling all the way.

"Must be nice to be young and full of energy, don't you think?" Noah asked when Faith took the seat across from him.

"I'd give up dessert for a whole week to be able to carry on the way those two do. Even with chores to do, they still find time for fun and games."

"That's the way it should be. We adults need pleasure and laughter in our lives, too." Noah pulled a slip of paper from the pocket of his trousers and held it up.

Faith seemed interested as she leaned across the table. "What have you got there?"

"A scripture verse. I read it this morning before I left for work, and I copied it down."

Faith sat back in her chair with a look of indifference. "Oh, I see."

Noah couldn't understand why she acted so remote whenever he brought up the Bible. It worried him. Her disinterest could mean she would never get baptized and join the church, which pointed to the fact that she wasn't happy here and wanted to return to the English way of life. And if that English fellow Noah had seen Faith with at Baldy's was her boyfriend, then she might be planning to leave home.

"Don't you want to know what the verse says?" he prompted. She shrugged.

"It's Philippians 4:4: 'Rejoice in the Lord always: and again I say, Rejoice.' "

When she made no comment, Noah added, "The Bible also says in the book of Proverbs, 'A merry heart doeth good like a medicine.' I think everyone needs a bit of God's merry medicine, don't you?"

"I'm a comedian, so it's my job to try to make everyone laugh when I'm onstage."

He shook his head. "I'm not talking about entertaining, Faith. I'm referring to good, old-fashioned, God-given humor."

"I used to get into trouble with my folks for acting silly and playing tricks on my siblings."

Noah lifted his eyebrows. "Acting silly isn't so bad, but playing tricks is another matter."

"You're too good for your own good, do you know that, Noah Hertzler?"

"I don't think my daed would agree. He took me to the woodshed for my fair share of bletchings when I was a boy."

Faith shook her head. "You're such a nice man; I find that hard to believe."

"It's true."

"Well, be that as it may, I think you're a do-gooder."

"Is that a bad thing?"

"No, of course not."

Noah fought the temptation to tell Faith that he'd seen her at Baldy's Café, but he decided it was best not to mention it. Faith had enough on her mind right now, and being put on the spot about the Englisher he'd seen her with might only upset her.

Swallowing the last of his iced tea, Noah pushed his chair back and stood. "Guess I'd better head for home."

Faith scooted her chair away from the table. "Thanks for stopping by with the gingerbread. I'm sure Mama will appreciate it."

She followed him to the door, and just before he exited, Noah handed her the scrap of paper with the Bible verse. "I'd like to leave this with you as a reminder that it's okay to have fun and tell jokes."

Faith took the paper and placed it on the counter but made no comment.

"Let me know if there's anything I can do to help out while your mamm's recuperating."

"Thanks, I will."

Noah bounded down the porch steps, waved to the girls, and climbed into his buggy.

Faith watched until Noah drove out of sight. He really did seem like a nice man. Just not the right man for her. Besides, she was fairly sure Noah already had a girlfriend.

She turned to the stove, where she added the potatoes she'd peeled to the pot of stew, and when she turned back to the counter to cut up some carrots, she spotted the verse Noah had given her. Did God really find pleasure in hearing people laugh and rejoice? Was Noah all he seemed to be? Faith's head swam with so many unanswered questions. "I have to leave Webster County before I go crazy with a desire for something I can't have. I'll go as soon as Mama's back on her feet."

"Go where?"

Faith whirled around. "Nowhere! I—I didn't know you were here, Grace Ann."

"Jah. Got home from work a few minutes ago." Grace Ann headed over to the kitchen sink. "When I was putting my horse away, I saw Papa out in the barn, and he said Mama came home from the hospital."

Faith nodded. "She's in her bedroom resting."

"Is she in much pain?"

"Probably would be, but the doctor gave her some medication, so I think she's fairly comfortable."

"That's good to hear." Grace Ann looked around the room. "Where's the rest of the family?"

"The boys are doing their chores, and the girls are outside playing."

"Esther's not home yet?"

"Nope."

"Would you mind if I slip into Mama's room and say hello before I help you with supper?"

Faith shrugged. "Go ahead. The stew won't be done for another half hour or so anyway."

When Grace Ann left the room, Faith turned back to the stove. Her thoughts, however, returned to Noah.

Chapter 15

The next several weeks were difficult, with Faith working from sunup to sunset. Everything in the garden seemed to come ripe at the same time, and much of it had to be canned. Mama did all she could from a sitting position, the girls helped with the simpler tasks, and a few Amish women from their community dropped by to offer assistance. Faith gladly accepted everyone's help—even Noah's. He'd come over a few times on his way home from work and had helped Faith fix supper and do some outside chores. Last Saturday Noah had worked in the garden, helped with the canning, and done some baking, as well. It was hard to believe, but he was as much help in the kitchen as he was outdoors.

Faith hated to admit it, but she liked having Noah around. His cheerful disposition as he helped with the chores made her workload seem a bit lighter. Even so, she felt trapped like a mouse caught between a cat's paws. Would she ever be able to go back on the road? It was beginning to seem as if the time would never come.

On this Saturday, Noah had come over to help. He was out in the garden picking tomatoes. Faith had helped him earlier, but she'd gone into the house to get them some water.

When Faith stepped inside the kitchen, Melinda and Susie, who were making a batch of lemonade, greeted her. She chuckled at the sight. Two little girls squeezed lemons into a glass pitcher, but more juice was running down their arms than was making it into the container.

"Need any help?" she asked as she stepped up to the table.

"We can do this," Susie said, a look of determination on her youthful face. "Mama told us how."

"That's right, and we wanted to surprise you and Noah with a glass of lemonade," Melinda added.

"Then surprise us you shall." Faith gave her daughter a smile, then turned on her heel. "You can bring the lemonade outside when you're finished."

Faith was still smiling when she stepped outside. Melinda was adjusting so well. School would be starting in a few weeks, and as soon as Melinda was settled into that routine and Mama was back on her feet, Faith planned to leave.

"That Noah's sure a nice man," Melinda said to Susie, as they scurried over to the refrigerator to get out some more lemons.

"Jah, he sure is," Wilma answered before Susie could respond. She'd been sitting at the table, reading the latest issue of *The Budget* and couldn't help hearing Melinda's comment.

"Noah's a lot of fun, and he's real smart, too." Melinda fairly beamed as she carried a handful of lemons back to the counter across the room.

"That's right," Susie agreed. "With all the help he's given you, you'll be the smartest scholar in the first grade."

Melinda's cheeks turned pink. "I might not be the smartest, but I'm doing a lot better now that Noah's been working with me."

Wilma tipped her head and studied Melinda. Oh, how she hoped Faith would never leave and take the child away. She'd grown attached to the girl, and from the looks of Melinda's exuberant smile, she had a hunch the child was happy to be living here, too.

"Say, Melinda," Wilma asked, "do you think your mamm's happy living here?"

"Sometimes, when she's laughing and playing silly games with me, she seems happy, but other times, she acts kind of sad." Melinda squinted as she turned to face Wilma. "I think she misses my daddy, and it makes me wish Mama would get married again."

Susie plunked a sack of sugar on the counter next to the lemons. "Maybe she'll marry Noah. He seems to like her, and truth be told, I think she likes him, too."

Wilma smiled. If that were true, then she and Noah's mother wouldn't have to work so hard at getting Noah and Faith together. Maybe the young couple would begin courting on their own.

Just then, Grace Ann stepped into the kitchen. "Whew, it sure is hot out there," she said, wiping the perspiration from her forehead. "I don't know how Faith and Noah can keep working in the heat of the sun like that."

Wilma motioned to the girls. "If you'd like something to drink, some lemonade is in the making."

"Sounds good. Need any help?" Grace Ann asked, stepping up to the counter.

Susie shook her head. "We can do this by ourselves, can't we, Melinda?"

Melinda nodded. "Course we can."

Grace Ann chuckled and took a seat at the table beside her mother. "How's that leg feeling, Mama?"

"It's getting better every day," Wilma replied.

"Glad to hear it. I'm sure you'll be relieved when the cast comes off and you can get back to walking without your crutches."

"That's for sure."

Wilma and Grace Ann chatted about everyday things, while Melinda and Susie finished making the lemonade. When the girls took the pitcher of lemonade outside, Grace Ann leaned closer to Wilma and whispered, "I've been wanting to tell you something, but there never seemed to be a good time."

"What's that?"

"The day you came back from the hospital, I overheard Faith mumbling something to herself about leaving."

Wilma's eyebrows drew together. "Leave here?"

"I think so," Grace Ann said with a nod. "She was fixing stew for supper, and I heard her say, 'I'll go as soon as Mama's back on her feet.' "

Wilma's heart clenched. It was as she'd suspected. Faith wasn't happy here, and she had no intention of staying. That meant she probably wasn't as interested in Noah as Susie thought, either. "Danki for sharing that with me," she said. "You haven't told anyone else, have you?"

Grace Ann shook her head.

"Good. I think it'd be best if you didn't."

"How come?"

"Because if Faith thinks we're talking about her, it might make her want to leave all the more." Wilma patted her daughter's arm. "The best thing we can do for Faith is think of some way to make her like it here well enough to stay."

"How are we going to do that?"

"I'm working on that," Wilma said with a nod.

When Barbara pulled her rig into the Stutzmans' yard, she spotted Faith sitting on the porch with her daughter and Susie. Noah was also there, which gave Barbara a little hope that things might be getting serious between Noah and Faith.

Susie waved to Barbara and called, "Come join us for some lemonade."

Barbara tied her horse to the hitching rail and hurried toward the house. "It's plenty hot today, so something cold to drink will surely hit the spot," she said as she stepped onto the porch.

"This is real tasty, too." Noah lifted his glass in the air. "Susie and Melinda made it."

"Did they now?" Barbara patted both girls' shoulders and took a seat in the empty chair beside Faith.

Faith poured some lemonade into one of the empty glasses

sitting on the small table nearby. "See for yourself how good it tastes," she said, handing the glass to Barbara.

Barbara lifted it to her lips and took a sip. "Umm. . .you're right, this is *gut* lemonade."

Both girls beamed, and then Susie said, "Maybe we should go inside and see if there's any cookies we can have."

"Good idea." Melinda jumped up, and the two girls disappeared into the house.

"Where are your boys today?" Faith asked, turning to face Barbara.

"They're home with my mamm. David thought I needed some time to myself, so he said I should leave the shop for a while and go somewhere on my own."

"Sounds like a good man to me," Noah said.

"Jah, he's the best." Barbara smiled at Noah. "What brings you over here today?"

"Came to help Faith work in the garden."

"How thoughtful of you." Barbara had to bite her tongue to keep from saying what she was thinking. Noah would make the perfect husband for Faith, and if Faith was courted by someone as nice as Noah, it might help her smile more, the way she used to do when they were children.

Noah lifted himself from the chair. "This has been a nice break, but I think I'll get back to work and let you two women visit."

"Is there anything going on between you and Noah?" Barbara asked once Noah was out of earshot.

Faith's mouth dropped open. "Why would you ask such a question?"

"I couldn't help but notice the way he looked at you—like he thinks you're something special."

"No way! Noah and I are just friends; nothing more."

"But I heard he's been coming around here a lot lately, and—"

Faith held up her hand. "Noah's been coming over to help out since Mama broke her leg, but there's nothing special between us. Fact is, Noah already has a girlfriend."

"He does?"

Faith nodded.

"Who is she?"

"I don't know her name, but I saw Noah sitting with her at Baldy's Café sometime back. I didn't recognize her as anyone from our community."

"Hmm. . ."

"Has Noah ever said anything to you about having a girlfriend?"

Barbara shook her head. "But then, most courting couples don't broadcast their intentions until they're ready to get married."

"You think he's planning to marry this woman?"

"I have no idea. Want me to ask him?"

"No!" Faith's face heated up. "He might not like it if you started prying into his business." She shrugged. "Besides, what Noah does is his business. I sure don't care."

Barbara was tempted to say more on the subject but decided to keep quiet.

"So, how are things going in the harness shop?" Faith asked.

"Real well. David and I enjoy working together."

Faith grunted. "I still can't believe you're helping him make and repair harnesses and other leather items. That seems like hard work for a delicate woman."

Barbara patted her stomach. "After having two kinner, I'm afraid I'm not so delicate anymore."

Faith stared out at the garden, where Noah worked.

"I guess I should get going and let you get back to work," Barbara said as she rose from her seat.

Faith stood, too. "Yes, I should probably help Noah."

Impulsively, Barbara gave Faith a hug. "It's sure good to have you back in Webster County. I missed you."

"Thanks."

Barbara stepped off the porch and headed across the yard. She stopped at the garden to say good-bye to Noah, then climbed into her buggy, whispering a prayer for her childhood friend.

Noah looked up as Faith joined him at the row of beans he'd been weeding. "Did you and Barbara have a nice visit?"

"It was okay."

"Just okay? I thought the two of you used to be good friends."

"*Used to be* is the correct term. I was away from home a long time, and we barely know each other anymore."

Using the back of his hand, Noah wiped the sweat rolling down his forehead. "She cared enough to come over and see how you're doing. To me that says she wants to be your friend."

Faith shrugged. "Maybe so."

"I'd like to be your friend, too."

To his surprise, she smiled. "I'd say you've already proven that by the acts of kindness you've shown me and my family."

Noah wanted to tell Faith that he was interested in her as a woman, not just as a friend who needed his help, but he held himself in check. If there was any hope of them having a relationship, he needed to take it slow and easy with Faith. He also needed to accept the fact that she might never be romantically interested in him—especially if she was involved with an English man.

Should I come right out and ask her? Noah thumped the side of his head. *I need to quit thinking such thoughts and just be her friend.*

Chapter 16

Faith didn't know where the summer had gone. But here it was nearing the end of August, and today was the first day of school for Melinda and Susie. They'd been so busy they still hadn't made it to Springfield with Noah to see Fantastic Caverns or the Bass Pro Shops. The only trips Faith had made were into Seymour for groceries and to phone her agent.

"Maybe next spring," Noah had said a few days ago, but Faith knew otherwise. By spring she would be gone.

It's just as well, Faith decided as she hung a freshly washed towel on the clothesline. *Thanks to Mama's accident and Noah coming over to help so often, I've already seen him more than I should have. Each time we're together it makes me long for...*

She grabbed another towel from the wicker basket and gave it a good shake. *I long to be back onstage entertaining—that's what*

I long for. I won't let anything stand in my way once Mama's up and around and able to resume her chores. I plan to be on a bus heading for my next performance by the end of September.

A short time later, Faith hitched her favorite horse to one of Papa's buggies and drove Melinda and Susie to school. The one-room schoolhouse was only a half mile down the road, but this was Melinda's first time in school, and Faith figured her little girl might need some moral support. At least it made Faith feel better to see that her daughter was dropped safely off at school on her first day.

"Do I have to go to school today, Mama?" Melinda asked from her seat behind Faith. "Can't I stay home and let you be my teacher?"

Faith glanced over her shoulder and grimaced when she saw the look of despair on her daughter's face.

"She'll be okay once we get there," Susie said before Faith could respond. "I was *naerfich* last year when it was my first day, too."

Melinda's lower lip quivered. "Were you really nervous?"

"Jah." Susie tapped Faith on the shoulder. "See how well Melinda's learning Pennsylvania Dutch? She knows what *naerfich* means."

"Good job, Melinda." Faith smiled. "Susie, why don't you tell Melinda what school is like? Maybe give her an idea of what to expect."

"Well," Susie began, "the first thing we do when we get to school, after we've taken a seat behind one of the desks, is to listen to our teacher, Sarah Wagler, read some verses from the Bible. Then we all say the Lord's Prayer, and after that we sing a few songs."

"That seems easy enough," Melinda said, her voice sounding much brighter. "What happens after the songs?"

"Then it's time for lessons to begin." Susie paused, and Faith wondered if her little sister was finished sharing the details of school or trying to think of what to say next. "Sarah usually gives the older ones their arithmetic lesson, and then she or her helper, Nona Shemly, works with the younger ones who need to learn English," Susie continued.

"But I already know how to speak English."

"Then you'll be given some other assignment."

Melinda released a little grunt, and Faith figured the child was probably mulling things over. Hopefully, she would come to grips with the idea of school and get along fine.

When Faith pulled the buggy into the school's graveled parking lot a short time later, she handed the girls their lunch pails, waved a cheery good-bye, and drove away with a lump lodged in her throat. *My baby is growing up, and soon I'll be saying good-bye for much longer than just the few hours she'll be in school every day.*

The thought of leaving Melinda behind was always painful, but nothing good could come from Faith staying in Webster County. Nor could any good come from hauling her child all over the countryside while they lived out of a suitcase in some stuffy hotel room. Melinda would be better off with her Amish grandparents.

But she won't have her mother, Faith's conscience reminded her. She pushed the thought aside and concentrated on the pleasant weather. Breathing deeply, she filled her lungs with the fresh, crisp air. Soon the leaves on the maple trees would transform into beautiful autumn colors. As colder weather and winds crept in, the leaves would drop from the trees, making a vibrant carpet of color.

She had never had much time to enjoy the beauty of nature when she was entertaining. Sometimes she did two or three shows a day, and when she wasn't performing, she was practicing or sleeping. The only quality time she'd had with Melinda was on her days off. Greg had been responsible for their daughter the rest of the time, and he sometimes hired a babysitter so he could be free to do his own thing.

There was no doubt in Faith's mind—it was better for Melinda to stay in Webster County. For as long as Faith was here, she planned to enjoy every minute spent with her daughter. And she needed to make another trip to town to call her agent and let him know how things were going. While she was there, she'd pick up a few groceries, too.

Noah wasn't glad Wilma Stutzman had broken her leg, but he was grateful for the extra time it had given him to be with Faith. Not only was he doing something he enjoyed, but the hours they'd spent together seemed to be strengthening their friendship. At least he thought so. Faith always acted friendly whenever he came by to help out, and Noah took that as a good sign. She hadn't told him to stop quoting scripture or talking about God, either. *Maybe it's just wishful thinking,* he told himself as he headed down the road after leaving work for the day. *Might could be that the strong feelings I'm having for Faith have clouded my thinking. It's not good for me to be so attracted to her when I'm not*

sure if her relationship with God has grown. Besides, I still don't know if that man I saw her with at Baldy's plays a part in her life. I need to ask, but I'm afraid of her answer.

Noah's thoughts came to a halt as he approached the Amish schoolhouse and noticed Faith's horse and buggy pulling into the lot. On impulse, he did the same. It would be nice to say hello and see how Melinda had fared on her first day of school.

Faith apparently hadn't seen him, and she hopped out of the buggy and sprinted toward the school without a glance in his direction. The children were filing out the front door, and Noah sat in his buggy, watching. He would wait and speak to Faith as soon as she had Melinda and Susie in tow.

A few seconds later, Susie came out and climbed into the buggy, but there was no sign of Faith or her daughter. He figured she was probably talking to the teacher—maybe checking to see if Melinda had any homework to do.

Susie turned in her seat and waved at Noah. He lifted his hand in response. Then, deciding that Faith's little sister might like some company, he hopped down from his buggy, secured the horse to the hitching rail, and ambled over to Faith's carriage.

"Hi, Noah," Susie said. "You're not married and you've got no kinner, so how come you're here at school?"

Noah leaned against the side of the buggy and grinned at the little girl. She was cute and spunky like her big sister. "I saw your rig and thought I'd drop by and say hello to Faith," he said.

The skin around the corners of Susie's coffee-colored eyes crinkled, and she leveled him with a knowing look. "You're sweet on my sister, aren't ya?"

The child's pointed question took Noah by surprise. When

it came to owning up to his feelings for Faith, he couldn't deny them to himself, but he surely wasn't going to admit such a thing to young Susie. She would most likely blab. If word got out that he was interested in Faith, Noah would not only be the target of teasing by friends such as Isaac Troyer, but he was sure Faith would find out, as well. If that happened and she didn't return his feelings, Noah wouldn't be able to stand the humiliation.

"Do you care for Faith or not?" Susie pried.

"Of course I care for her," Noah said, carefully choosing his words. "She's a friend, and I care about all my friends."

Susie snickered. "That's not what I meant."

Noah was busy thinking up some kind of a sensible comeback when he caught sight of Faith and Melinda leaving the schoolhouse. As they drew closer, he noticed Faith's furrowed brows and puckered lips. She looked downright flustered. He was tempted to rush over and see what was wrong but waited at the buggy until they arrived.

"It's good to see you, Faith," he said.

She nodded, and her frown deepened.

"What's the trouble? You look upset."

"Sarah Wagler. She's the trouble."

"What's the problem between you and the schoolteacher?"

Faith helped Melinda into the buggy and then turned to face Noah. "That woman had the nerve to say that my daughter seems spoiled and didn't show any interest in learning how to read." Her blue eyes narrowed, and she clamped both hands against her hips. "Can you believe that?"

Noah opened his mouth to respond, but Faith cut him off.

"Sarah insisted that Melinda is behind for her age, and she

even said I was being defensive when I assured her that my little girl is as smart as any child in her class." Faith pulled her hands away from her hips and popped the knuckles on her left hand.

Noah took a step toward Faith. "I've been around Melinda a fair amount, and I can tell how smart she is. I think she'll catch on quickly to book learning if she's encouraged to keep trying. I know you've got your hands full caring for your mamm, so I'd be happy to drop by on my way home from work a few nights a week or on Saturdays to help Melinda learn to read."

"It's kind of you to offer, but—"

"I really would like to do this."

"You've already done so much, and I don't feel right about asking you to do more."

"Please, Mama? I want Noah to help me." Melinda's tone was pleading.

"Oh, all right," Faith finally conceded. "Noah can help you study."

"Great," Noah said, clapping his hands together. "We can get started Saturday afternoon."

Chapter 17

When Noah showed up on Saturday afternoon, he held a small box in his hand. "I made some chocolate chip cookies this morning," he said, leaning his head over and sniffing the box.

Melinda, who had been sitting at the table with her reading book, jumped up and dashed across the room. "Yippee! I love chocolate chip!"

"Not until your homework is finished," Faith said with a shake of her head.

"Your mamm's right." Noah placed the box of cookies on the counter. "You can have some when your lessons are done."

Faith watched Noah take a seat at the table next to Melinda, with Melinda's early reader placed between them, and as Faith finished washing their lunch dishes, Noah read from the book, pointing to each word and asking Melinda to repeat what he'd read.

"I'll be in the next room helping my mother with some mending," Faith said when the dishes were done. "Give a holler if you need me for anything."

Noah nodded and smiled. "Jah, okay. When we're finished, I'll let you know. Maybe you'd like to have a few cookies with us."

"Sounds good. Susie's outside helping Esther and Grace Ann dig potatoes. They'd probably like to have some cookies, as well."

"I brought three dozen. Should be plenty for everyone."

"Okay."

Faith headed for the living room and found her mother sitting in the rocker. Her leg, which was still encased in a heavy cast, was propped on a wooden footstool.

"Was that Noah I heard come in?" Mama asked, looking up from her needlework.

Faith nodded. "He's here to help Melinda with her reading, and he brought along some freshly baked cookies. When they're done, we'll have some. Would you care to join us?"

Mama patted her stomach. "I'd better not. Since I broke my leg and have had to sit around so much, I think I've put on a few extra pounds."

Faith took a seat on the sofa across from her mother and gathered up the sewing basket sitting on the end table. "I hardly think one or two cookies will make you fat, Mama."

"Maybe not, but with me not getting much exercise these days, everything I eat goes right here." She thumped her midsection again.

Faith shrugged. "Whatever you think best."

For the next hour, Faith and her mother darned socks, patched holes in the men's trousers, and hemmed school dresses for the younger girls. Faith had just finished hemming a dress for Melinda when Noah emerged from the kitchen. "We're done with our studies. Anyone ready for some cookies?"

"I am. I need a break from all this sewing," Faith was quick to say.

"None for me, danki," Mama said with a smile.

Faith rose from her chair. "Is it all right if we help ourselves to some goat's milk to go along with the cookies?"

Mama's glasses had slipped to the middle of her nose, and she pushed them back in place. "It's fine by me. The goats are producing heavily right now, so we've got plenty of milk to go around." She nodded at Noah. "Would you like to stay for supper?"

"That offer's tempting, but I really should get home soon. Preaching is at our place tomorrow, and even though my two sisters-in-law have been helping my mamm get the house ready, I think she'll have a few things she wants me to do yet today."

Mama looked disappointed. She'd obviously been hoping Noah would stay for supper. "I hope Ida knows how fortunate she is to have a son like you," she said. "My boys are all hard workers when it comes to outside things, but I can't get them to do much inside the house."

"My daed's the same way." Noah smiled. "I like doing many outside chores, but kitchen duty doesn't make me the least bit nervous."

Faith followed Noah through the kitchen doorway just as Melinda darted for the back door. "Where are you going?" she called after her daughter. "Don't you want some cookies and milk?"

"I'll have some later. Right now, I'm going out to the barn to see the baby goat that was born this morning. Grandpa told us about it during lunch, remember?"

Faith nodded. "And I said you'd have to wait to see it until your studies were done."

"They're done now; just ask Noah." Melinda bounded out the door before Faith could respond.

"That girl," she muttered. "Anything that pertains to an animal captures her attention. I hope she becomes that conscientious where her schoolwork is concerned."

Noah grinned as he scooped Melinda's book off the table. "If she had stayed living in the English world, she might have grown up to be a veterinarian."

Faith shrugged. Had she done the right thing bringing Melinda here to be raised? Would the child have been better off in the English world, where she could further her education and become a vet or whatever else she wanted to be? She shook her head, as though it might get her thinking straight again. If she had kept Melinda in the English world while she entertained, the child might have ended up becoming an entertainer and would never have had the opportunity to be with so many farm animals. Melinda seemed happy here, and Faith was sure she had been right to have her daughter be raised by her Amish family. She glanced over at Noah and was surprised to see him wiping a spot on the cupboard where some sticky syrup must have dripped from that morning's breakfast. She still couldn't get over how helpful the man was. For one moment, she let the silliest notion take root in her mind. *What would it be like to be married to someone as kind and ready to lend a hand as Noah?*

"I'll get the milk while you set out the cookies," Faith said.

Noah grunted as he bit back a chuckle. "You like bossin' me around?"

She halted her steps and turned to face him. "Is that how I come across—like I'm bossy?"

He shook his head. "Not really, but just now you sounded a lot like my mamm."

Faith grimaced. "I didn't mean for it to seem as if I was trying to tell you what to do."

Noah shrugged. "It's not a big thing. I'm more than willing to set out the cookies."

"Okay." Faith got out a bottle of goat's milk, and Noah piled a stack of chocolate chip cookies on a plate, then placed it on the table.

"We could take a few of these to your mamm if you think she might change her mind and have some," he said.

Faith shook her head. "When Mom says no to something, she means it."

Noah noticed the bitter tone in Faith's voice. Obviously, Faith and her mother still had problems. Should he say something about it. . .maybe offer a listening ear if Faith wanted to talk? "I. . .uh. . . sense some bitterness in the way you spoke of your mamm," he said hesitantly. "Would you like to talk about it?"

"No!" She set the bottle of milk down on the table with such force Noah feared it might break.

"Sorry. I didn't mean to upset you," he apologized.

Faith's hands shook as she took two glasses from the cupboard. "The problem between me and my folks goes back to when I was a kinner, and I don't think talking about it will change a thing."

Noah was tempted to argue the point but thought better of it. No point in upsetting her further. "If you ever change your mind and need a listening ear," he said, moving to stand beside her, "I'd be more than willing."

She gave a brief nod, then hurried across the room with the glasses.

A short time later after Noah had gone home, Faith decided to take a walk out to the barn to see what Melinda was up to, as she still hadn't come back to the house. She found her daughter hanging over one of the stall doors, staring at a baby goat while talking to Faith's father, who stood beside her.

"Look at Tiny, Mama," Melinda said when Faith stepped up to them. "Isn't he cute?"

Faith nodded. "So you've named him already, huh?"

"Sure did. Grandpa said I could pick the name, and I chose Tiny because the goat's so small."

Papa chuckled. "He won't be so tiny once he's grown."

"Did you forget about coming to the house for cookies and milk?" Faith asked, tapping Melinda on the shoulder.

The child looked up at her and grinned. "Guess I got so

busy watching the baby goat and talking with Grandpa that my stomach forgot it wanted cookies."

Faith smiled. It was good to see her daughter so happy and satisfied. It made her wish she could have been that content when she was a child. If only she'd been more accepted. If only. . .

"How's your mamm doing?" Papa asked, breaking into Faith's thoughts. "Has she been resting that leg like she's supposed to?"

"As far as I know, she's still in the living room doing some mending," Faith replied.

Papa lifted one eyebrow. "I wouldn't call that resting."

"She had her foot propped on a footstool and was sitting comfortably in the rocker with the mending in her lap, so I'm sure it didn't cause any discomfort to her leg."

"Are you trying to be *gchpassich?*" her father asked in a clipped tone.

Faith gritted her teeth as she struggled with the desire to defend herself. *Here we go again. . .being accused of trying to be funny when I was merely trying to explain something. Why is it that everything I say to him seems to be taken wrong?*

"Are you going to answer my question or not?" her father persisted. "Were you trying to be gchpassich?"

"Mama's good at being funny," Melinda interjected before Faith could respond. "Telling funny stories used to be her job before we moved here, you know." When she looked up at Faith, a look of pride shone in her eyes.

Faith figured if her father saw that look, he would accuse Melinda of being filled with *hochmut*, and then she would be in for a lecture the way Faith used to be whenever she'd said or done anything that could have been considered proud.

Much to Faith's surprise, however, Papa made no comment about what Melinda had said. Instead, he took hold of the child's hand and steered her toward the barn door. "How's about you and me going up to the house for some of those cookies you missed out on?"

Melinda nodded eagerly. "Are you coming, Mama?" she called over her shoulder.

"In a minute."

When the barn door clicked shut, Faith dropped to a bale of straw near the goat's stall. She sat there a few minutes, staring at the mother goat and her baby. Then she let her head fall forward in her hands, and she wept. She needed to get away from this place as soon as possible.

Chapter 18

The day finally came when Mama's cast was removed. Faith wasn't sure who was more relieved—she or Mama. The cumbersome cast must have been heavy, not to mention hot and sweaty during the warm days in late summer. The only trouble was, Mama's leg, though healed, was now stiff and shriveled from being stuck inside the cast and not used for six weeks. The doctor had told Mama that she would need physical therapy to regain strength in her leg. That meant more expense for Faith's folks, and it also doomed Faith to stick around a few more weeks. It wouldn't be right to leave when Mama wasn't able to function at 100 percent.

Faith had agreed to go to Springfield with her mother once a week for her therapy treatments, as her father and brothers were busy with the beginning of harvest, and Grace Ann and Esther were working at their jobs all day. Faith hired one of their

English neighbors to drive them.

On the day of the first appointment, Faith hurried to make the girls their lunches, sent them off to school with a reminder not to dawdle, and rushed around to clean up the kitchen. She'd begun to wipe off the table when she noticed one of Melinda's reading books. She hurried outside, calling, "Melinda, come back! You forgot something!"

The children were already halfway down the driveway, but Melinda must have heard, for she spun around and cupped her hands around her mouth. "What'd I forget?"

Faith held up the book. "Come back and get it!"

Seconds later, Melinda had the book and was running down the driveway to catch up to Susie. Faith clicked her tongue against the roof of her mouth as she headed back to the house. At least one good thing had happened over the last few weeks. Noah had been able to teach Melinda enough to make Sarah Wagler happy. The teacher said she was pleased with Melinda's progress and that the child seemed a bit more sure of herself.

Faith knew her daughter liked Noah a lot. She often talked about him, saying she wished he could be her new daddy. Faith tried to dissuade Melinda, reminding her that Noah had his parents to care for, and she and Melinda had Grandpa and Grandma Stutzman to help out. No point getting her daughter's hopes up over something that was never going to happen.

When Faith entered the kitchen a few minutes later, she found her mother limping around the room, putting clean dishes in the cupboard.

"Why don't you take a seat at the table and have a cup of tea?" Faith suggested. "I'll finish up here, and we'll be ready and waiting when Doris Moore comes to pick us up."

Mama's eyebrows were pinched as she sat down. "I'm beginning to wonder if I'll ever get the strength back in my leg."

"I'm sure with some therapy you'll be good as new."

"I hope so, because I'm getting awful tired of sitting around trying to do things with one leg propped up." Mama heaved a sigh and took a sip of tea. "Will Noah be coming over this afternoon when he gets off work?" she asked with a hopeful expression.

Faith shook her head as she slipped a stack of clean plates into one of the cupboards. "When I saw Noah at church yesterday, I told him we were going to Springfield this morning for your therapy. Since I didn't know what time we might get home, I suggested he wait until Tuesday to work with Melinda."

"I guess that makes sense." Mama smiled. "That man sure does have the patience of Job, don't you think? I can't get over what a good cook he is, either."

"You're right—Noah is a good cook, and he does seem to have more patience than most men." Faith's thoughts went immediately to Greg. He'd been so short-tempered. Especially when it came to Faith. He'd expected more than she could possibly give. He'd always pushed her to do multiple shows and reprimanded her whenever she wanted to take time off. And he'd let his temper loose on Faith more times than she cared to think about.

She rubbed her hand along the side of her face, thinking about how hard he had hit her one night shortly before his death. It had left a black-and-blue mark, but she'd hid it under a layer of heavy makeup.

"Susie thinks Noah might be sweet on you," Mama said, pulling Faith out of her disconcerting thoughts. "I'm wondering if the feelings might be mutual."

Faith clenched her teeth. *Not this again.* "Susie should mind her own business." She slammed the cupboard door with more force than she meant to, and it rattled the dishes. She jerked it open again and checked to be sure nothing had broken. To her relief, all the dishes were intact.

"Faith, did you hear what I asked?"

Faith whirled around. "I heard you, Mama. I just don't have anything to say."

"Oh, I see."

Maybe now was the time to tell Mama her plans. Faith opened her mouth, but the words stuck in her throat like a glob of gooey peanut butter. Maybe this wasn't the right time. Not with Mama's leg still trying to heal.

She popped two knuckles and frowned. *Shouldn't be doing that either, I guess.*

"Faith, what's wrong? You seem kind of agitated," Mama said softly. "Why don't you come over here and have a cup of tea with me while we wait for Doris?"

Faith moved back to the counter, where a stack of clean plates waited on the sideboard to be put away. "I–I'm fine, Mama, and I really do need to get the rest of these dishes put away." *Chicken. You're afraid to tell her what's troubling you.*

"All right, then. Guess we can visit while you work and I sip my tea."

For the next several minutes, they talked about the weather, who in their community was expecting a baby, how the girls were doing in school—anything but the one thing that weighed heavily on Faith's mind. If only she felt free to tell Mama the truth: that she'd come home only so Melinda would have a place to stay while Faith was on the road entertaining, and that she felt ready to leave now, knowing Melinda had adjusted to being Amish, but she didn't want to leave Mama in the lurch.

"Your teacup is empty," Faith said after turning from the sink and glancing at her mother's cup. "Would you like me to pour you some more?"

"Jah, sure, that'd be nice."

Faith dried her hands and got the simmering teakettle. She had just finished pouring hot water into her mother's cup when someone tapped on the back door.

"I wonder if that could be Doris," Mama said. "I didn't hear a car pull into the yard, did you?"

"No, I didn't." When Faith opened the door, she was surprised to see Barbara standing on the porch.

"*Wie geht's?*" Barbara asked.

"I'm all right. How about you?"

"Fine and dandy."

"Would you like to come in and have a cup of tea? Mama's having some while we wait for Doris to give us a ride to Springfield for Mama's first therapy session, and I'm finishing up the dishes." Faith held the door open.

With an eager expression, Barbara nodded. "I always enjoy a good cup of tea."

Faith led the way to the kitchen and pulled out a chair for Barbara. "Have a seat, and I'll get another cup."

"Wie geht's, Wilma?" Barbara asked, smiling at Faith's mother.

"I'm doing all right," Mama replied. "The bone in my leg's

healed, although I do need some therapy." She smiled at Barbara. "My oldest daughter's been taking real good care of me."

"Glad to hear it." Barbara sat down, and Faith scurried to get tea and cups for both herself and her friend. Then she joined the women at the table.

"What brings you over our way, and where's your horse and buggy? We never heard you pull in," Mama said, looking at Barbara.

"I walked over today. Thought I could use the exercise." Barbara patted her thick hips. "The reason for my visit, Wilma, is to invite you and your daughters to an all-day quilting bee at my house next Thursday."

"That sounds like fun," Mama said. "I'd like to come, but Esther and Grace Ann will both be working, so they won't be able to make it." She glanced over at Faith. "How about you? Would you like to go to the quilting bee?"

"How can you host a quilting bee when you work at the harness shop with your husband?" Faith asked Barbara.

"We're fairly well caught up on things right now." Barbara took a sip of tea. "So David suggested that I take a few days off and do something fun with my friends. He said I'm in the shop too much and need to fellowship more." She rested her hand on Faith's arm. "Please say you'll come."

Faith felt like a helpless fly trapped in a spider's web. The last thing she wanted to do was spend the day with a bunch of somber women who could sew better than she could and whose idea of fun was to talk about the weather, who'd been sick in their family, or who'd recently had a birthday. But she hated to say no, since Mama wanted to go and would need someone to drive her there. "Jah, okay," she finally said. "Mama and I will be at your quilting bee."

"I was wondering something, Mama," Faith said after Barbara left for home.

"What's that?"

"How did you and Papa meet, and how'd you know he was the one you should marry?"

Wilma smiled as she stared across the room, allowing herself to remember the past. "Well, as you know, your daed's two years older than me."

Faith nodded.

"All through our school days, I had an interest in him, but he never gave me more than a second glance." She took a sip of tea. "Anyway, when I went to my first young people's singing, I made up my mind I was going to get your daed to notice me one way or another."

"What happened?"

"Menno—your daed—had taken off his straw hat and laid it on a bale of straw in the Millers' barn. When he wasn't looking, I snatched the thing up and hid it behind some old milk cans."

Faith leaned her elbows on the table and cupped her chin in the palms of her hands. "Then what?"

"Well, your daed spent the next half hour searching for his hat, and in the meantime, my two brothers, Henry and Levi, decided to head for home. Only thing is, they left without me." She snickered. "I think they did it on purpose because they knew how much I cared for your daed."

Faith added more water to her teacup. "I can't believe you would do such a thing, Mama. It doesn't sound like you at all."

Wilma slowly shook her head. "I'm not perfect, Faith. Never claimed to be, neither. Besides, I had to do something to get that man to look my way."

"I assume he did, since you're married to him now."

"After I discovered my brothers had run off without me, I conveniently found your daed's hat. When I gave it to him, I just happened to mention that Henry and Levi had gone home and I had no ride."

"Of course, Papa volunteered to give you a lift in his buggy."

"He sure did." Wilma grinned. "Not only did he drive me home, but when he dropped me off, he let it be known that he thought I was pretty cute. Even said he might like to give me a ride in his buggy after the next singing."

Faith opened her mouth as if to comment, but the tooting of a car horn closed the subject. "Guess that must be Doris."

"We'd better not keep her waiting," Wilma said. "Wouldn't be good for me to be late to my first appointment."

Noah whistled as he flagged a group of six-foot pine trees with white plastic ribbon. The ones that were six and a half feet would get green and white ribbons. The trees he selected would be sold to wholesale Christmas tree lots. Amos and Griggs were at his side, vying for attention.

"Go play somewhere else, fellows," Noah scolded. "Can't

you see that I'm a busy man?"

The hound dogs responded with a noisy bark and a couple of tail wags; then they bounded away.

A short time later, Hank showed up, offering Noah a bottle of cold water. Noah took it gratefully, as it had turned out to be a rather warm day.

"Thanks. With the weather being so hot, one would never guess it's fall. Sure hope it cools off some before folks start coming to choose their trees."

"That won't be long," Hank said as he flopped onto the grass between the rows of trees where Noah had been working. Noah followed suit, and the two of them took long drinks from their bottles, then leaned back on their elbows.

"I brought you and Sandy one of my lemon sponge cakes," Noah said. "Dropped it off at the house before I started work."

Hank licked his lips. "Umm. . .sounds good. Maybe we can have a piece after we eat the noon meal."

Whenever Noah made lemon sponge cake, he thought about Faith and the cake he'd given her that first Sunday after she'd returned. He'd gotten to know her better since then, and the more time he spent with her, the more he cared about her. He hadn't heard any more from either his mother or Wilma about Faith leaving Webster County, so he hoped she might have given up on the idea. Either that or she'd never planned to go in the first place. Could be that Wilma Stutzman had misread her daughter's intentions. Maybe Noah had, as well, for Faith certainly seemed to have settled into the Amish way of life again, except for not being baptized and joining the church. Noah saw Faith's staying as an answer to prayer and figured in time she would make things permanent by joining the church—if she wasn't involved with that English fellow he'd seen her with, that is. Oh, how he wished he could get up his nerve to ask about that, but he'd let it go so long now that it might seem odd to Faith if he questioned her about it.

"So what's new in your life?" Hank asked, pulling Noah's thoughts aside.

"Not so much."

"Are you still helping that little Amish girl with her reading?"

Noah nodded. "Melinda's doing better in school, but I've had such a good time helping her that I think I'll keep going over awhile longer."

Hank shot him a knowing look. "You sure it's not the child's mother you're going to see?"

"As I've said before, Faith and I are just friends." Noah's face heated up. Hank was right. Even though Noah enjoyed helping Melinda with her studies, the real reason he wanted to keep going over to the Stutzmans' place was to see Faith. He took another swig of water and clambered to his feet. "Guess I'd best get back to work. These trees won't flag themselves."

Hank stood, as well. "If you don't want to talk about your love life, it's fine by me." He winked at Noah. "Just be sure I get an invitation to the wedding."

Noah nearly choked on the last bit of water he'd put in his mouth. Was the idea of marriage to Faith a possibility? He doubted it, but it sure was a nice thought. "Changing the subject," he said, "I was wondering how things are going with you and Sandy these days."

Hank shrugged and reached up to rub the back of his neck. "About the same, I guess. She keeps busy with her things, and I keep busy with mine. We don't talk much unless there's something that needs to be said."

"Have you thought any more about adopting a baby?"

"Nope. I've been afraid to bring it up for fear she'll say no."

"I'll continue to pray for you," Noah said. "But if you want my opinion, I think you should come right out and tell Sandy you'd like to adopt."

"I'll give it some thought." Hank gave Noah's shoulder a squeeze. "Thanks for being such a good friend." He started to walk away but turned back. "Oh, and if you ever decide to start courting that woman you're *not* interested in, you can count on me for some good advice."

Chapter 19

As Faith and her mother headed down the road in their buggy toward the Zooks' house the following week, Faith found herself dreading the day ahead. Spending time with Barbara made her think about the past, something she would rather forget. But Mama had been insistent about them going to the quilting bee, and since they'd been getting along pretty well of late, Faith didn't want to do anything to upset the applecart. Soon enough, she would tell her folks about her plans to leave Webster County, and she wanted the time they had together to be free of disagreements.

"I've sure been looking forward to the quilting bee," Mama said, glancing over at Faith and smiling. "I've been cooped up so much since I broke my leg that I like any reason to get out."

"Does that include going to physical therapy?" Faith asked.

"Jah. Even that."

"Did the last session hurt much?"

"Some, but the therapist said it'll get better as time goes on."

"Then I'm sure it will."

They rode in silence for a while. Mama pointed to the school-house as they drove by and said, "It's good that Melinda's doing better in school."

Faith nodded. "That's mostly because of the help Noah has given her."

"Noah's a good man," Mama said, reaching over to touch Faith's arm. "He's kind, trustworthy, and can cook better than most women I know. I think he'll make a fine husband and father some day."

"I'm sure he will." Faith thought about the young woman she'd seen Noah with some time ago and wondered if she might be his future wife.

"I was wondering. . ."

"What were you wondering, Mama?"

"I was wondering if you're feeling ready to take classes to prepare for church membership and baptism yet."

Here it goes again. Faith's teeth snapped together with an audible *click.* Maybe if she didn't respond, Mama would drop the subject.

"Faith, did you hear what I said?"

"Yes, I heard; and no, Mama, I'm not ready."

"Oh."

They rode along in silence awhile longer; then Mama spoke again. "Melinda seems to like Noah a lot."

"Uh-huh."

"And I believe the feeling's mutual."

"You're probably right."

"How do you feel about Noah?"

Faith shook the reins to get the horse moving faster but gave no reply.

"Faith, are you listening to me?"

"I heard you, Mama. Just didn't know how to respond, so figured it was best not to say anything."

"You don't know how you feel about Noah?"

Faith released a sigh and squinted as she looked over at her mother. "Noah seems like a nice enough man, but I don't feel any particular way about him."

Mama grunted. "Have you tried?"

"What's that supposed to mean?"

"It means, have you allowed yourself to get to know Noah well enough so you can tell whether you might have a future with him?"

Faith's hands shook as she pulled back on the reins and guided the horse and buggy to the side of the road.

"Why are we stopping?"

"So I can concentrate on what I'm saying to you without worrying about driving off the road because I'm feeling so upset."

Mama's eyebrows furrowed. "Now why would you be upset?"

Faith curled her fingers into the palms of her hands as she resisted the temptation to pop her knuckles. "I'm upset because you keep bringing up Noah and listing his many virtues."

Mama opened her mouth as if to comment, but Faith rushed on. "I'm not interested in a relationship with Noah or any other man, so please stop trying to match me up with him."

Mama blinked a couple of times. "I—I just thought—"

"I know what you thought." Faith drew in a deep breath to steady her nerves. "My husband abused me, Mama," she blurted out. "And I—I don't think I could ever get married again."

Mama's mouth dropped open, and her eyes widened. "He—he abused you?"

Faith nodded. "Greg had a terrible temper, and whenever he drank, he became mean and physically abusive."

"Did he hurt Melinda?"

"No, just me. But I was worried that if she ever said or did the wrong thing, he might take his anger out on her, too." Faith swallowed hard. "Our marriage was not a happy one, but Greg was a good agent, and he got me lots of shows."

Mama touched Faith's hand. "I'm real sorry. I had no idea you had been through so much."

Faith took up the reins again. "I'd rather not talk about this anymore. It's too painful, and the past is in the past."

"Oh. Okay."

In silence, Faith guided the horse onto the road again.

A short time later, she found herself sitting in the Zooks' living room, surrounded by eight other women. Besides her and Mama; Barbara, and her mother, Alice; Noah's mom, Ida; and four other women from the community attended.

The women enjoyed lots of friendly banter as they worked with needle and thread, bent over a quilting frame, making hundreds of tiny stitches that would hold the top of the Double Wedding Ring quilt together. Barbara's mother, who was a left-handed quilter, sat at the corner of the frame. "I imagine it's been awhile since you did any kind of quilting," she said, looking over at Faith.

Faith nodded. "That's true, but even when I helped my mother work on quilts during my younger days, I never did so well."

"Quilting's like anything else one wants to do well—it takes practice and patience," Ida put in. "I've always enjoyed the challenge of working on a circular design such as this, but I didn't learn to quilt overnight, that's for sure."

"One thing I like about this pattern is that the pieces are small so we can use a lot of scraps," Barbara said.

"So true," Faith's mother agreed. She released a dreamy-sounding sigh. "I can still remember the five quilts I received for my wedding. Three were from my mamm, and the other two came from Menno's family. Those quilts have been used on my family's beds for a good many years now, even though some are getting pretty worn."

Faith began to relax, and before she knew it, she was drawn into the conversation by telling a few jokes.

"Has anyone heard about the English man who met his wife at a travel agency?" she asked.

"Can't say as I have," Barbara said. "Tell us about it."

"Well, he was looking for a vacation, and she was the last resort."

To Faith's surprise, most everyone laughed—except for her mother. She gave Mama a sidelong glance. *Just accept my silliness. Can't you understand who I really am?*

"Tell us another joke," said Ellen Troyer.

"Let's see. . . . An English man approached the gate of an Amish farmhouse one day and was about to enter when he noticed a large dog lying under a bush. The dog seemed to be eyeing him in an unfriendly way, so the man called out to see if anyone was at home." Faith leaned slightly forward, making sure she had the women's full attention. "Now, both the Amish man and his wife came to the front door. 'Come in,' said the woman. 'But what about the dog?' asked the Englisher. 'Will he be apt to bite me?' 'Don't rightly know,' said the Amish man. 'We just got him yesterday, and we're eager to find out.' "

Barbara howled at this joke, and Faith quickly launched into another tale.

"The same English man visited another Amish farm, and he was shocked to see yellow bundles of feathers zooming all around the yard. They were going so fast he couldn't see them clearly. 'What are those things?' the man asked the Amish farmer who lived there. 'Oh, those are my four-legged chickens. They're pretty quick, don't ya think?' The man replied, 'I'd say so, but why do you want four-legged chickens?' The Amish man pointed to his wife, who stood on the front porch. 'Me, Nancy, and our two kinner all cotton to the drumstick. Now whenever we have fried chicken, there'll be a leg for each of us.' The Englisher pondered the Amish man's words a few minutes; then with a nod, he said, 'So does it taste like normal fried chicken?' 'Don't know yet,' the Amish man answered. 'We haven't been able to catch any.' "

Barbara's mother almost doubled over with laughter at the end of that joke, and Faith smiled triumphantly. This was the first time she remembered feeling so accepted or appreciated among those in her community.

Barbara nudged Faith's arm with her elbow. "Have you got any more jokes to tell?"

Faith nodded, as her confidence soared. "Does anyone know the sure sign that the honeymoon is over for a new bride and groom?"

"What's the sign?" asked Barbara's sister-in-law, Margaret Hilty, as she leaned closer to Faith.

"When the husband no longer smiles as he scrapes the edges of his burnt toast."

More snickers and chuckles filled the room.

"I know one that's true but not so funny," Barbara piped up. All heads turned toward her, but she kept her focus on Faith. "It's been proven that having a mate is healthy. Single people die sooner than married folks. So if you're looking for a long life, then you'd best get married!"

Faith squinted at her so-called friend. *Not another hint at me finding a mate? Won't Barbara ever let up?*

"Speaking of marriage, it won't be long now until we have a few fall weddings," Noah's mother commented. "I'm thinking maybe my son Noah might be a candidate for marriage."

Faith's ears perked up. Noah was getting married? He hadn't said anything to her. Could he have become betrothed to that woman she'd seen him with at Baldy's Café?

The fun Faith had been having with the women drifted away like a leaf on the wind. She didn't know why, but she felt a sense of loss. Noah had become a good friend, and if he married, everything between them would change.

It shouldn't matter to me. I'll be leaving soon, and what Noah does is his own business. I have no say in it, nor do I wish to have any. Even as the words popped into Faith's head, she knew they weren't true. She did care, and that's what scared her. She cared too much.

As Faith and Wilma traveled home from Barbara's, Wilma determined to keep the conversation light and cheery, the way it had been during the quilting bee. It had been wonderful to see the way Faith had opened up, laughed, joked, and shared stories with the other women. If only Faith could be that joyful at home, instead of acting so serious all the time. Of course, at home, Faith had responsibilities that kept her busy, especially since Wilma had broken her leg, making even more chores for Faith and the others to do.

"I'm curious about some of those jokes you told today," Wilma said, glancing over at Faith.

"What about them?"

"Were those the kind of jokes you told when you entertained onstage?"

"Yes, and I have a bunch more up here," Faith said, tapping the side of her head.

Wilma pushed her weight against the seat. She wished Faith wouldn't look so wistful whenever she talked about her days as an entertainer. If Faith enjoyed being in the limelight too much, she might become dissatisfied with her life and head out on her own again.

Faith lifted one hand from the reins and held up her index finger. "I don't know how many times I pricked my finger today, but I did better at sewing than I figured I would," she said.

Wilma smiled. A change of subject—that was better. "Jah," she said with a nod. "Your stitches were nice and even."

"Not like when I was a girl and all my sewing projects turned out bad."

"Guess you had your mind set on other things besides sewing."

Faith nodded. "I always preferred to be out in the barn talking to the animals and yodeling."

"Melinda likes to hang out there, too. Have you taught her how to yodel?"

"Not really. I figured if she learned how, she might want to. . ." Faith's voice trailed off.

"Want to what?"

"Never mind. It's not important."

"Are you worried that Melinda might want to follow in your footsteps and take to the stage?"

"Maybe so, but that won't happen, because she's here with you now."

Wilma was tempted to mention that Faith had been here once, too, and that hadn't stopped her from running off to chase after her dreams in the English world. She thought better of bringing it up, not wishing to have any unpleasant moments on the trip home.

When Faith guided the horse and buggy up the driveway a short time later, Menno stepped out of the barn. As soon as Faith stopped the buggy, he began to unhitch the horse. "If you don't mind putting old Ben away," he said, nodding at Faith, "I'll help your mamm into the house."

"That's fine with me." Faith grabbed the horse's bridle and led him to the barn.

"She had a good time today," Wilma said as Menno assisted

her into the house. "Fact is, our eldest daughter was the life of the party."

He quirked an eyebrow. "Is that so?"

"Jah. Faith was real talkative, and she ended up telling one joke after another. Had everyone in stitches, she did."

Menno frowned. "She didn't try to entertain you with that awful yodeling, I hope."

Wilma shook her head. "No, but she sure told some funny stories. At one point, Alice Raber almost fell off her chair, she was laughing so hard."

"Oh, great," Menno said with a groan. "Faith was showing off her worldly ways then, huh?"

"I don't think so. I believe she just got caught up in having a good time, but I was kind of worried that all that joke telling might make her dissatisfied about not being able to be onstage entertaining English folks."

"Did you discourage her from telling those jokes?"

"Well, no, but I didn't laugh at them, either." Wilma snickered. "Although it was hard not to when she was saying such funny things and had everyone else in stitches."

"Guess no harm was done," Menno said. "As long as she doesn't start with that yodeling stuff when I'm around, I won't complain."

They entered the house, and Wilma took a seat on the sofa in the living room. "Whew! I'm all done in. Didn't realize a whole day like that would wear me out so."

"Why don't you stretch out on the sofa and rest awhile?" Menno suggested.

She shook her head. "I've got to get supper going."

"The girls can do that. Faith's here, Grace Ann and Esther will be home from their jobs soon, and Susie and Melinda will be home from school shortly, I expect. There's no reason they can't get supper on without any help from you."

She smiled up at him. "You're right. We've got four capable daughters and one granddaughter to prepare the meal, so I think I will rest my eyes for a bit."

"And your leg, too," he said, helping her to lie down and placing a pillow under her leg.

"Danki, Menno. You're a good man."

He grunted. "Too bad our oldest daughter doesn't think so."

Wilma took hold of his arm. "Things have been strained between you and Faith since she came home, but after seeing how she was today, I think given some time, she's bound to come around."

Menno shrugged and headed for the door. "We'll have to wait and see how it goes."

Chapter 20

It wasn't until the end of October that Faith's mother finished her physical therapy. Only then was she able to get around well enough on her leg so that Faith felt Mama could handle things on her own.

As Faith got ready for bed one night, she made a decision. In the morning, she would tell Melinda and then her folks that she would be leaving at the end of the week. She had put it off long enough, and there was no good reason to stay now that Mama was better and Melinda had adjusted so well to Amish life. All she needed to do was contact the agent in Memphis and let him know she was available. Until the agent got her a show, she would probably have to launch out on her own, doing one-night stands wherever she could find work. She'd done it before Greg came into her life, and if necessary, she could do it again.

As Faith glanced at the calendar on the wall, her thoughts went to Noah. November was almost here. He would probably be getting married soon. After church last week, she had overheard Noah's mother telling his friend Isaac that Noah was interested in someone—probably the woman he'd had lunch with at Baldy's. Faith had wanted to ask Noah about it, but she'd lost her nerve. Besides, it was none of her business. She had her career to think about, and Noah's life was here in Webster County with his family and friends.

Faith stared out her open bedroom window at the night sky overflowing with thousands of twinkling stars. She drew in a deep breath, filling her lungs with fresh air. It had rained earlier in the day, and everything smelled so clean. She blinked away sudden tears. *If only my soul felt as pure as this air. If I just didn't feel so confused about things.*

The following morning, Faith busied herself at the stove, helping Mama fix pancakes and sausage for breakfast, while Melinda and Faith's three sisters set the table.

Who should I tell first about my plans to leave? Faith had intended to give her daughter some advance notice, but now she wondered if it might not be best to lay out her plans in front of everyone at once. Or maybe she should tell her mother first and get her reaction. If Mama didn't shy from the idea of caring for Melinda in Faith's absence, then Faith would inform the child.

Faith moved closer to Mama. "There's something I need to tell you," she whispered.

"What's that? I can't hear you, Faith."

"I was wondering if. . ." She gripped the spatula in her hand. Why was it so difficult to say what was on her mind? "I've. . . uh. . .made a decision."

Her mother's eyebrows lifted high on her forehead. "What sort of decision?"

"I think it would be best if I—"

The back door swung open and Papa rushed into the kitchen. His face was flushed, and his eyes looked huge as silver dollars.

Mama left the stove and hurried to his side. "Menno, what's wrong?"

He tried to catch his breath. When Mama handed him a glass of water, he shook his head and pushed it away. "Always trouble somewhere."

"What kind of trouble?" she asked in a tone of concern.

"Old Ben's dead. Found him lying on the floor in his stall this morning."

Mama gasped, and everyone else stood like statues.

"I blame myself for this." Papa clasped his hands together. "I've been using that horse in the fields every day this week, and I think I must have worked the poor creature to death."

Mama touched Papa's arm. "Menno, think about what you're saying. You've had Ben for nigh onto twenty-five years. A year ago, you tried to put him out to pasture, but he wasn't content. He liked to work with the other horses and was bound to die sooner or later." She sighed deeply. "At least the horse perished doing what he liked to do best."

Papa blinked a couple of times, and Faith wondered if he was struggling not to cry. "Mama's right," she agreed. "You shouldn't blame yourself for this."

He stared past her as though he hadn't heard her. "The boys and I are in the middle of harvest, so I need that animal. Jeb and Buck can't do the work of three horses, and I can't afford to buy another one just now."

Mama pushed the skillet of pancakes to the rear of the stove, and she dropped into a seat at the table with a moan. Grace Ann and Esther went immediately to her side, each of them patting her on the back. Melinda and Susie, obviously uncomfortable, scooted quickly out of the room. Faith, unable to think of anything more to say, stood off to the side with her arms folded.

"If you hadn't had to spend most of our savings on doctor bills and physical therapy because of my leg, we'd have the money we need to buy a new horse," Mama said with a shake of her head.

"It's not your fault, Wilma. Falling down the cellar stairs was an accident, plain and simple." Papa took a seat across from Mama and let his head fall forward into his hands. "Guess I could ask some of our church members to help out, but others have needs, too, and I hate to be asking for more money."

Faith moved to the side of the table and placed her hand on her father's shoulder as she made a painful decision. "I have some money saved up from when I was entertaining. I'll give it to you so you can buy a new horse."

Papa sat up straight and turned in his chair to look at Faith. His beard jiggled as a muscle in his jaw quivered. "You–you'd be willing to do that?"

Faith didn't understand why he was so surprised. Amish family members and friends helped each other all the time. Of course, most offers didn't come from wayward daughters returning home with money they'd made entertaining worldly English folks. Faith had been holding on to this money so she could start over when she left Webster County. If she gave her father the cash, she would be staying here even longer. Even so, this was a chance to prove that she wasn't such a bad daughter, after all—maybe even show Papa she cared about the welfare of her family. "I want you to use the money," she insisted.

He sat silently and then finally nodded. "Jah, okay, but I plan to pay the money back as soon as I'm able."

"*Der Herr sie gedankt,*" Mama said with a catch in her voice.

Faith swallowed hard in an attempt to push down the lump that had formed in her throat as she heard her mother thank God. She was happy to be helping her folks in their moment of need, but at the same time, she felt a sense of sadness. She had no idea how long it would take for Papa to pay her back. Certainly not until the harvest was over and he'd been paid for his crops. At the rate things were going, would she ever see the bright stage lights or hear the roar of the audience's laughter again?

Chapter 21

Noah shifted on the backless wooden bench as he glanced over at the women's side of the room and spotted Faith. Ever since the preaching service had begun this morning, he'd had a hard time concentrating on anything other than her. He hoped he might be able to speak with Faith after the noon meal, and he had brought an apple crumb pie to give her with Romans 5:1-2 attached to it: "Therefore being justified by faith, we have peace with God through our Lord Jesus Christ: by whom also we have access by faith into this grace wherein we stand, and rejoice in hope of the glory of God."

Noah wasn't trying to be pushy, but as Faith's friend, it was his Christian duty to help strengthen her faith. Truth be told, he was beginning to see her as more than a friend, and if there was any chance for them to have a permanent relationship, he had to be sure she had an interest in him and most of all that she was secure in her faith in God. But how would he know if there was another man in her life or if her faith had grown unless he came right out and asked? Did he dare take the chance? What if she got angry and turned away from him? What if because he questioned her, she decided to leave? He didn't want to be responsible for Faith leaving Webster County.

Noah squeezed his eyes shut and offered a silent prayer. *Dear Lord, please help Faith be receptive to the scripture verses I plan to give her today. And I'm hoping she will be receptive to the questions I have for her, as well.*

When Faith finished eating her meal and had taken a seat under the weeping willow tree on the south side of Jacob Raber's house, she spotted Noah heading her way. He held a pie in his hands, and she licked her lips in anticipation. As far as she was concerned, Noah was the best baker in Webster County, and she hoped the pie was for her.

"Would you like to have a seat?" Faith asked as Noah approached the quilt she'd spread on the ground.

"Jah, sure." He sat down beside her and placed the pie pan in her lap. "This is for you. It's an apple crumb pie."

"Thanks. I needed something to cheer me up today."

The wrinkles in Noah's forehead showed his obvious concern. "What's wrong? Is your mamm's leg acting up again?"

Faith shook her head. "It's not Mama this time. One of my dad's workhorses died yesterday, and now he's faced with buying a new one." She chose not to mention that she'd offered to loan him the money. No point making it seem as though she was bragging. Faith was well aware of the stand her people took on hochmut. She also wasn't about to share her disappointment in not being able to return to entertaining.

"That's a shame about the horse. With this being harvesttime and all, everyone needs all the help they can get. That includes the assistance of their horses and mules." He offered her a sympathetic smile. "Once the word gets out, others in the community will help—either with the loan of a horse or some money."

"That won't be necessary. It's been taken care of."

"That's good. Glad to hear it."

Faith popped a couple of knuckles, then clasped her hand tightly to keep from doing the rest. If Papa found her habit annoying, Noah might, too. She was glad he hadn't asked who had provided the money. "My family has sure had their share of problems lately. It doesn't seem fair, and it worries me that something else might happen."

"The rain falls on the just, same as it does the unjust," Noah reminded.

Faith had heard that verse before, but it didn't make it any easier to deal with things when they went wrong. Besides, she wasn't sure she was one of the "just." If Noah or her family had any idea she was planning to return to the English world, they might see her as a sinner.

"All these problems don't do much to strengthen my faith," she muttered.

Noah motioned to the pie. "I attached another verse. Maybe that will help."

She groaned inwardly. *Another reminder of the error of my ways. Just what I don't need this afternoon.* Maybe what she needed was to change the subject.

"I've been wanting to ask you something, Noah, but I wasn't sure if I should."

He tipped his head. "What's that?"

"I overheard your mother talking to my mother awhile back, and then she said something to Isaac Troyer."

"About what?"

Faith moistened her lips with the tip of her tongue. "Well, I got the impression that you might be planning to be married in November."

Noah's face flamed, and he looked away. Was he too embarrassed to talk about it? "I probably shouldn't have brought it up," she murmured. "It's none of my business anyway."

"I don't know where my mamm got the impression I'm about to be married."

"Then it's not true?"

He shook his head.

"But what about that woman I saw you with at Baldy's Café a few months ago?"

"Huh?"

"I saw you sitting in a booth, having lunch with a young Amish woman, and I assumed it was—"

"Oh, you must mean Mary. She's my cousin, and she had come down from Jamesport to speak with her boyfriend, who'd jilted her. He'd left for Illinois before she got here. Then she asked if I would give her a ride to the gas station so she could catch a bus home, but we had lunch at Baldy's first."

Faith inhaled deeply, feeling as if the breath had been squeezed clean out of her lungs. All this time she'd thought Noah had a girlfriend, when he'd just been having lunch with his cousin. She toyed with the strings on her prayer kapp. "But if you don't have a girlfriend, then why would your mother think you were seeing someone?"

A deep shade of red spread across Noah's cheeks. "Well—uh—she knows I've been seeing you."

"Me?" Faith's heart began to hammer. Surely Noah didn't see her in any light other than friendship.

He nodded. "We went to see Hank's Christmas tree farm, and I've gone over to your place several times to help with Melinda's studies and to give you a hand with some chores." He snatched up a blade of grass and bit off the end. "Guess maybe Mom could have assumed *we* were courting."

If Noah's mother thought that, did others, as well? While Faith felt a sense of unexplained relief to hear Noah wasn't courting anyone, she didn't think it was good if others had linked her and Noah together as a couple. No telling what rumors might be flying around.

"It would probably be good if you made sure your mother knows the truth," Faith said after a long pause. "So she doesn't tell others there's going to be a wedding come November."

Noah chewed on the blade of grass and looked at Faith in such a tender way it made her stomach do little somersaults. "Uh, Faith, there's something more I'd like to say. A question I want to ask you."

"What's that?"

"The day I was with my cousin at Baldy's, I saw you there

with a tall English man."

Faith grimaced. *Oh, great. How am I going to explain things to Noah without telling him I was talking to my future agent?*

"Was that fellow your boyfriend, Faith?"

"What? Oh, no, definitely not," she sputtered. "He was just. . . uh. . .an acquaintance from the entertainment business, nothing more."

A look of relief flooded Noah's face, but Faith barely noticed. All she wanted to do was nip this thing in the bud about her and Noah being an item.

Holding on to the pie, she clambered to her feet. "I–I'd better get going." She wasn't sure what he planned to say, but she knew it was important for her to let folks know they weren't courting. She would start with Barbara, who was sitting on the Rabers' porch, blowing bubbles with her two young sons.

"Thanks for the pie," she called over her shoulder.

Faith made a beeline for the house, where she put the pie in the refrigerator. Then she headed for the front porch.

Barbara turned when Faith stepped outside. "Hey! Want to join us in some fun?" She lifted a bubble wand in the air and waved it about.

"Actually, I'd like to have a little heart-to-heart talk, if you don't mind."

Barbara scooted over, making room for Faith on the step. "Have a seat, and tell me what's on your mind."

Faith sat down and cleared her throat a couple of times. "I'd kind of hoped we could talk in private."

"Oh, sure. No problem at all." Barbara leaned over and said to her boys, "Why don't you two go find Susie and Melinda? They'd probably like to blow a few bubbles, too."

Aaron and Joseph nodded, grabbed their bottles of bubbles, and bounded away.

Barbara turned back to Faith. "Now, what did you want to talk to me about?"

"Noah and me."

Barbara smiled. "Ah, so you two *are* an item. I've been hearing some rumors to that effect, and—"

Faith held up one hand, as her forehead wrinkled. "Noah and I are *not* an item."

"But Ida Hertzler told my mamm that—"

"It's not true. None of it."

Barbara tapped the toe of her black leather shoe against the step below her. "I was hoping those stories had some merit."

"What stories have you heard?"

"Just that you two went out to Osborns' Christmas Tree Farm awhile back, and—"

"We took Melinda and Susie along, so it wasn't a date."

"What about all the times Noah's been over to your folks' place? Wasn't he going there to see you?"

"Noah dropped by to help after Mama broke her leg, and he came over to assist Melinda with her studies. That's all there is to it—nothing more."

Barbara pursed her lips. "I'm sorry to hear that. As I've told you before, I think it would be good for both you and Melinda if you found another husband."

"I've been down that road, and it only brought heartaches."

"You mean because your husband was killed?"

"That and other things."

"Such as?"

"There was no joy in my marriage, Barbara." Faith's jaw snapped shut with an audible *click.* "My husband was an alcoholic who liked to gamble and smack me around whenever he wasn't happy. You get the picture?"

Barbara flinched, feeling as if she'd been slapped. "Ach! I—I didn't know."

"No one did. I never want Melinda to know what her father was really like." Faith blinked, and a few tears trickled onto her cheeks. "There's nothing good in marriage. Not for me, anyway."

Barbara slowly shook her head. "Don't say that, Faith. Never give up on the idea of marriage or God's will for your life. There's certainly a lot of joy in marriage if you have the right man."

Faith grunted. "That's easy for you to say. I'll bet you've never been slapped around by your husband."

"That's true. David has been nothing but kind since we first got married. I've always felt loved and safe with him."

"With Greg, I felt about as safe as a mouse trapped between a cat's paws." Faith's tone was one of bitterness, and her eyes narrowed into tiny slits.

Barbara touched her friend's arm in what she hoped would be seen as a comforting gesture. "There's joy all around, if you only look for it."

"Maybe for some, but not for me." Faith stood. "Noah and I are only friends, and we won't be finding any joy with one another." She walked away without another word.

Barbara bowed her head. *Heavenly Father, my friend is hurting and is probably confused about some things. Please give her a sense of joy that only You can bring.*

Chapter 22

As Faith stood on the front porch, staring across a yard covered with a blanket of freshly fallen snow, she thought about Noah and how she had tried to avoid him these last couple of weeks. The way he had looked at her that day under Jacob Raber's willow tree had made her suspicious that he might be romantically interested in her. She couldn't let Noah think their relationship could go beyond friendship, even though she was beginning to have strong feelings for him. She would be leaving soon, so any kind of permanent relationship was impossible.

Faith drew in a deep breath. While she wanted to return to her life in the English world, the idea of leaving home didn't hold nearly as much appeal as it had when she'd first returned. She would miss Melinda terribly, even with occasional visits, and now there was another reason to stay. These last few months, she'd found comfort and security being with family. Life as an entertainer could be lonely, and she felt as if a war raged within her. She needed to go yet wanted to stay. Maybe she could postpone leaving until after the holidays. A few more weeks wouldn't matter. It might be better if she waited until after Christmas to head back on the road.

Faith was glad she and Barbara had talked. At least now Barbara wouldn't be expecting a wedding for Faith and Noah. If others saw them together, more rumors would float around the community, and Faith sure didn't need that. But she'd promised Melinda and Susie they could go one more time to the Christmas tree farm. Noah had said he wanted to show them Sandy's Gift Shop when it was decorated for the holidays. Faith figured it would probably be her and Noah's last time together, and since the girls would be there, no one could accuse them of courting.

Her thoughts shifted gears. The harvest was over. Papa said he was pleased that Sam, the horse he'd bought with Faith's money, was a hardworking animal and had done his fair share of the pulling as they cut and baled the hay. She'd felt relief when Papa came to her a few days ago and returned the money he'd borrowed. Now, except for her shifting emotions, nothing stood in the way of her going back to the life she had made for herself in the English world.

"What are you doing out here in the cold?" Wilma asked as she stepped up to the porch railing where Faith stood staring out at the yard.

Faith smiled. "Watching Melinda and Susie play in the snow while we wait for Noah to pick us up to visit Hank Osborn's tree farm."

Wilma grunted. "I'm glad you're seeing Noah, but I don't see why you want to take the girls back there again."

Faith's smile faded. "Why must you always throw cold water on everything I want to do?"

"I'm not, but those fancy Christmas trees are worldly, and—"

"And you think I'm trying to convince Melinda and Susie that having a Christmas tree in the house is a good thing to do?"

"It's not that. I just don't want Susie exposed to anything that might make her dissatisfied with our way of life."

Faith's eyes blazed with anger. "So she won't turn out like me? Isn't that what you're saying, Mama?"

Wilma could have bitten her tongue. She shouldn't have mentioned her concerns about the girls visiting the tree farm. After all, she had given her consent, so it was too late to go back on her word. Bringing it up had obviously upset Faith, and the last thing Wilma needed was to put distance between her and Faith.

"I'm sorry. I shouldn't have said anything." Wilma touched Faith's arm. "I hope you'll have a good time today."

Faith's face softened some. "You mean it?"

"Jah." Wilma swallowed around the lump in her throat. She did want them to have a good time, and she didn't want to make an issue of how she really felt, so she would say nothing more on the subject. She would be praying, however, that neither of the girls came home wanting to put up a Christmas tree.

When Noah showed up at the Stutzmans' place, he wasn't the least bit surprised to see Melinda and Susie playing outside in the snow. What he hadn't expected was to see Faith and her mother standing on the front porch, with Wilma wearing no coat. He'd no more than climbed down from the buggy, when the girls dashed over to him, wearing huge smiles on their rosy faces.

"Yippee! We're going to the tree farm!" Melinda shouted as she hopped up and down.

Susie nodded in agreement. "I can't wait to see them all decorated."

"Only the ones inside Sandy's Gift Shop will be decorated," Noah said as he rapped his knuckles on the tops of the girls' black bonnets.

Melinda giggled and smiled up at him. "Maybe Sandy will serve us some cookies and hot chocolate."

"I wouldn't be a bit surprised." Noah nodded toward the house. "Shall we see if your mamm's ready to go?"

"Oh, she's ready," Susie put in. "She's been standing on the porch for some time."

Noah smiled. The thought that Faith had been waiting gave him a good feeling. Maybe she looked forward to spending the day together as much as he did. He'd been relieved to learn that she didn't have a boyfriend, and as much as he'd fought against it, he found himself wanting to be with her more all the time.

"Looks like the girls are ready to go; how about you?" he asked, stepping onto the porch and smiling at Faith.

She nodded but didn't return his smile.

He looked over at Wilma and noticed that she wasn't smiling, either. "You're welcome to join us if you like."

Wilma shook her head. "I appreciate the offer, but I've got housework and baking to finish." She glanced down at Susie, who stood beside Melinda. "Be good now, daughter, and do whatever Faith says."

"I will, Mama."

Noah clapped his hands together. "All right, then. Let's be off."

The girls bounded down the steps, and as Wilma turned to go inside the house, Noah followed Faith out to his buggy. She seemed so quiet and reserved, and he wondered what could have happened to make her cool off toward him. Until that day he'd given her the apple crumb pie with the scripture verse attached, he had thought they'd been drawing closer. Had he been too pushy in trying to help strengthen her faith? Or had it been their discussion about his mother believing them to be a courting couple? Maybe he could get Faith to open up to him today. Then again, it might be better if he backed off and kept his distance—instead of him trying to meddle and make things happen the way he wanted them to, let the Lord work in Faith's life.

As they headed down the country road in the open buggy, Noah continued to scold himself. Mom had told him time and again that he had a habit of taking things into his own hands. He hoped he hadn't botched it up where Faith was concerned—with their friendship or with her relationship with Christ. He would try to keep their conversation light and casual today and not mention anything spiritual. And he had to be careful not to let Faith know he was romantically interested in her.

"Looks like winter's got a mind to come early this year," Noah said, directing his comment to Faith.

"It would appear so," she answered with a slight nod.

"You warm enough? I could see if there's another quilt underneath the seat."

"I'm fine."

"You girls doing okay back there?" Noah called over his shoulder.

"Jah, sure," Susie shouted into the wind. "This is fun!"

Noah got the horse moving a bit faster, and soon they were pulling into the driveway leading to the tree farm. Amos and Griggs bounded up to the buggy, yapping excitedly and wagging their tails.

"The trees look like they're wearing white gowns," Melinda said, pointing to the stately pines that lined the driveway and were covered with snow.

"You're right about that," Noah agreed.

Hank and his wife stepped outside just as Noah helped Faith and the girls down from the buggy. The hounds ran around in circles, and the children squealed with delight while they romped in the snow.

"Come inside and get warm," Sandy said, motioning toward her rustic-looking store.

Everyone but the dogs followed, and soon squeals of delight could be heard as the girls ran up and down the aisles, oohing and aahing over the brightly decorated Christmas trees. Sandy took hold of Faith's arm and led her toward the side of the store where the crafts were located. Noah figured they wanted to have a little woman-to-woman talk, so he moved over to the wood-burning stove where Hank stood. Soon they both had a mug of hot coffee in their hands and were warming themselves by the crackling fire.

Noah glanced around the room. "I'm glad we got here before the rush of customers."

"You're right. By noontime, this place will probably be swarming with people," Hank said. "Usually is, right after Thanksgiving."

When Noah looked over at Faith, he wondered if she would miss having a Christmas tree with colored lights and all the trimmings. An Amish Christmas was a simple affair compared to the way most Englishers celebrated the holiday, yet it was just as special—at least he thought so. A Christmas program would be presented at the schoolhouse a few weeks before Christmas, and all the relatives of the scholars would be invited. Then on Christmas Day, families would gather for a big meal, and a few gifts would be exchanged. The emphasis would be on spending time with family and friends and remembering the birth of Jesus, not on acquiring material things or looking at tinsel and fancy colored lights decorating a tree.

"Yep, this is a busy time of the year," Hank said, nudging Noah with his elbow and bringing his mind back to the conversation.

Noah nodded. "I was in Seymour yesterday after work, and the tree lot there was doing a booming business, as well."

"That's usually the case," Hank said. He turned away from the fire and looked at Noah, his hazel-colored eyes ever so serious.

"I know this is probably none of my concern, and if you want me to mind my own business, just say so."

Noah waited silently for his boss to continue.

"You seem kind of down in the mouth today, and I'm wondering if there's something wrong at home."

"Except for Mom's bouts with her diabetes, everything's fine."

Hank took a sip of coffee. "Your sullen attitude couldn't have anything to do with one pretty little blond, could it?"

Heat flooded Noah's ears and quickly spread to his cheeks. "I'm afraid I might have ruined my friendship with Faith," he muttered.

"How so?"

Noah lowered his voice. "I've been trying to help strengthen her faith in the Lord, and I've attempted to make her my friend."

"Nothing wrong with that."

"The thing is I'm worried that I might have pushed too far and scared Faith off, because she seems to be keeping her distance and didn't say much on the way over here." Noah leaned closer to Hank, to be sure what he said wouldn't be overhead. "She might move further from me and the Lord if she thinks I'm trying to force things on her."

"Give her some time and a bit of space," Hank said. "If Faith's anything like Sandy, she doesn't want anyone telling her what to think or do."

Noah snickered. He had heard Hank's wife speak on her own behalf a time or two and knew Hank was telling the truth. "I came to that conclusion, and I've decided to back off and let God do His work in Faith's life instead of me trying to do it for Him."

Hank tapped Noah on the back. "Smart man."

"How are things with you and Sandy these days?"

"About the same. We talk but only when there's something to say." He grunted. "Every time Sandy sees a baby, I notice a look of sadness on her face."

"And you haven't brought up the subject of adoption yet?"

"No, but I'm thinking about it."

"That's good to hear." Noah gave Hank's arm a squeeze. "You're still in my prayers."

"I appreciate that, and even though I don't talk much about my religious convictions, I do believe in God, and I'll say a prayer for you and Faith, too."

Noah grinned. "Thanks. I appreciate that."

Faith couldn't believe how many items Sandy had for sale in her store. She saw three times as much stuff as when they'd visited earlier in the year. "I know you make the peanut brittle you sell," she commented, "but who provides all these wonderful quilts, crafts, and collectibles?"

"I buy a few from out of state, but most are made by local people," Sandy explained. "As I'm sure you can guess, the quilts are made by Amish women here in Webster County. English folks—especially tourists—are willing to pay a good price for a bedcovering made by one of the Plain People."

Faith fingered the edge of a beige quilt with a red and green dahlia pattern. "They are beautiful, aren't they?"

"Yes, they certainly are." Sandy released a gusty sigh. "The other day when I was shopping in Springfield, I found a store that sells baby quilts, and it made me wish all the more that I could have a baby."

Faith wasn't sure how to respond. She knew from what Sandy had said before that she and Hank were unable to have any children of their own. Seeing how much Sandy wanted a baby made Faith appreciate the fact that she had Melinda. "Have you thought any more about the idea of adoption?" she asked.

"I have been thinking about it, but I haven't mentioned it to Hank because I'm sure he'll say no."

"How can you be certain?"

Sandy shrugged. "I'm pretty sure he wouldn't want a child that wasn't his own flesh and blood."

"You'll never know until you ask."

"That's true, and I will think about it some more."

Faith opened her mouth to comment, but Sandy turned the topic of conversation. "I've been wondering about something."

"What's that?"

"How old were you when you left home, and what did your folks have to say about it?"

"I left the day I turned eighteen, and since I hadn't been baptized or joined the church, I knew they wouldn't officially shun me. But earlier when I'd discussed the idea of being an entertainer with my parents, they let it be known that they didn't want me to go. Papa even said if I did, I'd better not come back unless I was willing to give up the English ways and join the church." She groaned. "I took the coward's way out and left a note on the kitchen table, letting them know I had gone."

"Oh?" Sandy's raised eyebrows and pursed lips let Faith know that she probably thought Faith was horrible for leaving in such a manner. What would she think if she knew Faith was planning to leave again?

"But you're here now," Sandy said. "I never got the chance to ask when you were here the last time, but I'm wondering what happened to bring you home again."

"Didn't Noah tell you?"

"Not really. He only mentioned that you'd been gone a long time and had returned home this summer with your daughter. He also said your husband was killed when he was hit by a car."

Faith nodded. "I tried life on my own for six months after Greg's death, but it was hard to find a babysitter for Melinda. And being on the road full-time isn't the best way to raise a child."

"So you decided to give up being an entertainer and move back home where you knew both you and Melinda would find love and a good home?"

"Uh, something like that."

"Have you joined the church since you returned?"

Faith shook her head. She could hardly tell Hank's wife her plans were to leave Melinda with her grandparents while she went back to the life of an entertainer. Sandy obviously wanted children, and she'd probably see Faith as an unfit mother—someone who could abandon her child as easily as a frog leaps into a pond. "I. . .um. . .haven't felt ready to be baptized and join the church yet."

Sandy motioned to a couple of chairs sitting at one end of

the store. "Why don't we take a seat? In another hour or so, this place will be swamped with customers, and I probably won't have the chance to sit down the rest of the day."

Faith followed Sandy across the room, and they seated themselves in the wicker chairs.

"Would you care for a cup of coffee or some hot apple cider?"

"Not just now, thanks."

"Looks like the girls are winding down." Sandy nodded toward Melinda and Susie, who reclined on the floor under one of the taller decorated trees.

"Those kids are like two peas in a pod," Faith said. "I think living here in Webster County has been good for Melinda."

"And you, Faith? Has coming home been good for you?"

"In some ways, I suppose." Faith didn't want to say more. She might let her plans slip; then Sandy would tell Hank, who would in turn let Noah know. Sometime between Christmas and New Year's Day, Faith would tell her folks about her plans to leave, and she didn't want them finding out before.

Sandy smiled. "Noah has spoken of you and Melinda several times. I think he's grown quite fond of you both."

"Noah's a kind man." Faith stared down at her hands, which she'd folded in her lap to keep from popping her knuckles. "Noah's good with children and even helped Melinda with her studies when she first started school."

"He mentioned that." Sandy touched Faith's arm. "I think Noah would make some lucky woman a fine husband. He'd be a good father, too. Don't you think?"

"I'm sure he would. He just has to find the right woman."

"Maybe he already has."

Faith was about to ask Sandy what she meant, when Melinda and Susie crawled out from under the tree and bounded up to them.

"Mama, Susie says we aren't gonna get to have a tree in the house," Melinda said, her lower lip jutting out. "Is that true?"

Faith nodded. "I've told you before that the Amish don't believe in bringing a tree into the house, but there will be a Christmas program at school, and that will be lots of fun."

"What about presents? Will we still have those?"

"Oh, jah. . .we always exchange presents," Susie said. "Last year I got a new faceless doll and some puzzles."

"We'll have a big family dinner at Grandma and Grandpa's house, too," Faith added. She hoped Melinda wouldn't be too disappointed if she didn't get a lot of gifts.

"Mama always fixes plenty of good food," Susie spoke up.

"Speaking of food, I'm feeling kind of hungry right now," Melinda announced.

Faith wagged her finger. "Where are your manners? You had enough to eat at breakfast for three little girls."

"Aw, but that was a long time ago."

"I think I have just the thing that will make your stomach happy." Sandy stood and extended her hands to both girls. "Come with me, and we'll get some gingerbread cookies and a pitcher of cold apple cider."

The children didn't have to be asked twice, and they skipped off with Sandy to the back of the store.

Faith turned toward the wood-burning stove where Noah and Hank stood. A lock of dark hair fell across Noah's forehead as he propped his foot on the hearth. *Noah may not believe he's good-looking, but I think he's pretty cute.*

Faith drew in a shaky breath as the truth hit her squarely in the chest. No man had ever affected her the way Noah had, and she was tumbling into a well of emotions that could only spell trouble. There was just one way to stop it, and it would have to be done soon.

Chapter 23

Faith couldn't believe how many family members had come to see their scholars put on the Christmas program. The schoolhouse was filled to capacity. As Faith took a seat behind Melinda's desk and waited for the program to begin, her thoughts took her on a trip to the past. She had spent eight years as a student in this same schoolhouse and taken part in many programs. Faith remembered one program in particular, where she'd forgotten what she was supposed to say. She'd made up something silly to keep the audience from knowing she'd forgotten her lines, but afterward, she'd been scolded by her parents for acting childish and not paying attention to the part she'd been given. In that moment, Faith decided that when she was old enough, she would leave home and find a job that would allow her to say and do all the silly things she wanted. Bitterness had taken root in her soul.

Faith was pulled back to the present when Barbara took a seat at a nearby desk and leaned across the aisle. "Is Melinda nervous about being in her first school Christmas program?" she asked.

Faith nodded. "A bit, but I'm sure she'll do fine. Melinda seems to do well with everything she tries. Not like me, that's for sure," she added with a frown.

Barbara's brows puckered. "What are you talking about, Faith? You do lots of things well."

"Name me one."

Barbara held up one finger. "You yodel better than anyone I know." She lifted a second finger. "And you can tell jokes and funny stories so well that it brings tears to my eyes because I'm laughing so hard."

"That may be true, but not everyone appreciates those abilities."

"The women who came to my quilting bee awhile back thought you were funny."

Faith was about to mention that her mother hadn't thought she was so funny, when Melinda's teacher announced that the program was about to begin. It was just as well; Barbara didn't need to hear Faith's negative comment.

A few seconds later, several of the smaller children, including Melinda and Susie, formed a line and sang two Christmas songs. Faith's mouth dropped open when Melinda started to sway a bit, as though keeping time to the words they were singing. Faith wondered what her parents, who sat a few desks behind, thought of their worldly granddaughter's behavior. Faith caught

Melinda's attention and shook her head. She was relieved that the child stopped swaying.

Am I making a mistake leaving Melinda with my folks? Would she be better off on the road with me? Faith gripped the edge of the desk. *No, I want a more stable environment for my little girl. As long as Melinda continues to like it here, she'll stay.*

On Christmas Day, the Stutzmans' house bustled with activity. The entire family had gathered for dinner, including Faith's older brothers, James and Philip, along with their wives, Katie and Margaret, and their four children. Since both families lived up by Jamesport, they'd hired a driver to bring them home. Everyone seemed in good spirits, and the vast array of food being set on the table looked delicious. Even though Faith didn't consider herself much of a baker, she'd made three apple pies using a recipe Noah had given her. She hadn't tasted them yet, but as far as she could tell, they'd turned out fairly well, and she hoped they were as good as they looked.

"It's nice to have you home again," James said as he took a seat beside Faith at the table.

"Jah, I agree," Philip put in.

Faith forced a smile. If her brothers only knew the truth, they wouldn't be smiling at her.

As all heads bowed for silent prayer, Faith found herself thinking about Noah and wondering how his Christmas was going. Noah seemed so content with his life, and he obviously had a close relationship with God. Otherwise, he wouldn't attach scripture verses to the baked goods he gave away, and he wouldn't offer to pray for people as she'd heard him do for Hank Osborn when they'd gone there to look at Christmas trees last month.

"Mama, you can open your eyes now 'cause the prayer's over," Melinda said, nudging Faith with her elbow.

Faith's eyes snapped open. She'd been so preoccupied thinking about Noah that she hadn't heard her father clear his throat, the way he always did when his prayer ended.

"If everything tastes as good as it looks, then I think we're in for a real treat," James said, reaching for the bowl of mashed potatoes.

"Jah." Papa looked over at Mama and smiled. "My Wilma has outdone herself with this meal."

"I wasn't the only one working in the kitchen," Mama said with a shake of her head. "Our three oldest daughters worked plenty hard helping me, and Faith made several of the pies, which I'm sure will taste delicious."

Faith felt the heat of a blush cascade over her cheeks. She wasn't used to her mother offering such compliments, at least not directed at her. "After eating this big meal, maybe no one will have room for a taste of my pies," she mumbled.

"I'll eat a hunk of pie no matter how full I am." Brian grinned at Faith before helping himself to a piece of turkey from the platter being passed around.

"I believe you will," Papa said with a snicker, "and I'll be right behind you."

Faith began to relax. It felt good to be with her family for Christmas. She had spent too many lonely holidays before she'd met Greg, and after they were married, he'd never been much fun to be with on Christmas or any other day that should have been special. Greg was more interested in watching some sports event on TV or drinking himself into oblivion than he was spending quality time with Faith. He never complimented Faith on anything—just pointed out all the things she'd done wrong. After Faith left Webster County to return to the stage, maybe she could plan her schedule so she would be free to come home for Christmas and other holidays.

As they continued to eat their meal, Faith found herself sharing a couple of jokes with her family. "You know, the way food prices are going up," she said, "soon it will be cheaper to eat the money."

Much to Faith's surprise, all her siblings laughed, and then, after Faith shared a couple more jokes, James's wife, Katie, jumped in by saying that she'd been on a garlic diet lately.

"How did that work?" Esther asked. "Did you lose any weight?"

Katie shook her head. "No, but I sure lost some friends."

Faith chuckled. She would have to remember that joke for one of her routines. It was surprising to see the way everyone seemed to enjoy all the corny jokes that had been told. Even Mama and Papa wore smiles. *It's probably not because of anything funny I said,* Faith thought regrettably. *More than likely, they're in good spirits because the whole family is together today.*

She glanced around the table at each family member, hoping to memorize their faces and knowing that if her folks didn't allow her to leave Melinda with them, this could very well be the last Christmas they would all spend together.

Noah leaned back in his chair and patted his stomach. He'd eaten too much turkey, and now he had no room for the pumpkin or apple pies he had made. He slid his chair away from the table. "As soon as I'm done helping with the dishes, I think I'll go for a buggy ride. Anyone care to join me?"

"Not me." Pop leaned back in his chair and yawned noisily. "I'm going to the living room to rest my eyes for a bit."

"I'm kind of tired, too," Mom said. "After we're done with the dishes, I think I'd better take a nap."

"Jah, okay." Since none of Noah's brothers had been able to join them for dinner today, it was just him and his folks, so Noah figured he'd either have to go alone or simply take a nap, too. If only he felt comfortable with the idea of going over to see Faith today. But it wouldn't be right to barge in unannounced, knowing the Stutzmans had company. Besides, Faith might not want to be with him. She hadn't been all that friendly the last time he'd seen her, and he didn't want to do anything that might push her further away.

Noah reached for his jacket and headed out the door, determining once more that unless Faith had a change of heart about her relationship with God, the two of them could never be more than friends.

A short time later, Noah found himself on the road leading to Osborns' Christmas Tree Farm, and he directed the horse and buggy up the lane leading to Hank and Sandy's two-story house. He didn't see any cars parked out front except for Hank's, so he figured the Osborns probably didn't have company.

Noah tied his horse to the hitching rail near the barn, tromped through the snow, and as he stepped onto the front porch, Amos and Griggs bounded up, wagging their tails. He bent over and gave them both a couple of pats, then lifted his hand to knock, but the door opened before his knuckles connected with the wood.

"I heard your horse whinny," Hank said with a grin. "So I figured you'd be knocking on the door anytime."

Noah chuckled. "Just came by to say Merry Christmas to you and Sandy."

"Merry Christmas to you, as well." Hank opened the door wider. "Come on in and have a piece of pumpkin pie and a cup of coffee with us."

"Are you sure? I'm not interrupting anything, am I?"

"No way." Hank motioned Noah inside, and the dogs slipped in, too.

"Sandy and I didn't go see her folks in Florida this year because they went on a cruise for the holidays. And my folks are spending Christmas with my brother in Montana this year, so we're just having a quiet Christmas alone," Hank said. His smile stretched from ear to ear, and Noah had to wonder what was going on. The last time he'd seen Hank and Sandy together, they were barely speaking.

"It's good to see you, Noah," Sandy said. "Merry Christmas." She was grinning pretty good, too.

"Merry Christmas," he responded.

"Drape your coat over a chair and have a seat." Hank motioned to the recliner across from the sofa where Sandy sat.

Noah did as Hank suggested, and Hank sat on the sofa next to his wife.

"Did you get everything you wanted for Christmas this year?" Hank asked, nodding at Noah.

"I guess so," Noah said with a shrug. The truth was, what he wanted most was a permanent relationship with Faith, but he figured that was nigh unto impossible.

The two beagles rested at Noah's feet, and absently, he bent over and began to rub their ears. "How about you and Sandy? Did you both get lots of presents?"

Hank draped his arm over Sandy's shoulder, and she looked at him with such a tender expression that it made Noah squirm. What he wouldn't give for Faith to look at him in that manner.

"Are you going to tell him or shall I?" Sandy asked, patting Hank's knee.

Hank's smile widened as he turned to face Noah. "Sandy and I are going to adopt a baby."

"Really?"

Sandy nodded. "We had a long talk about it the other day and found out that there had been a misunderstanding."

"Oh?"

Hank nodded. "Yeah. I thought Sandy didn't want to adopt, and she thought the same of me, but once we talked it through, we discovered we both wanted the same thing."

"That's great. Really great." Noah stopped petting the dogs and leaned back in his chair as a vision of Faith flashed into his head. Was it possible that they both wanted the same thing? If he knew that Faith had the least bit of interest in him. . .

Noah gripped the arms of the chair as he came to his senses. Unless Faith got right with the Lord and joined the church, there was no way he could ever ask her to marry him.

Chapter 24

As Faith stood at her bedroom window one evening toward the end of December, she gazed at the carpet of snow below and thought about each family member. Christmas was only a pleasant memory, but Faith knew in the days ahead she would bask in the recollection of the wonderful time she had shared with her family—a family she would soon be telling good-bye. She'd be leaving friends like Noah and Barbara, too. Faith would miss everyone after she was gone—most of all Melinda.

So much for keeping emotional distance from family and friends. Faith grimaced as her thoughts spiraled further. She thought about the jokes she had shared with the family on Christmas Day and how surprised she'd been when they were well received. No matter how enjoyable the holidays had been, she was sure things would soon go back to the way they had been when she was a teenager. It was only a matter of time before her folks started reprimanding her for being too silly or started prodding her to take classes so she could get baptized and join the church. Worse than that, Faith had done something really stupid—she'd allowed herself to fall in love.

She gripped the window ledge so hard her fingers turned numb. *The time has come for me to leave Webster County, and nothing will stop me this time.*

When Faith awoke the following day, her throat felt scratchy. A pounding headache and achy body let her know she wasn't well.

Forcing herself out of bed, she lumbered over to the dresser. The vision that greeted her in the mirror caused her to gasp. Little pink blotches covered her face. She pushed up the sleeves of her flannel nightgown and groaned at the sight. "Oh, no, it just can't be."

"What can't be?" Grace Ann asked, sticking her head through the open doorway of Faith's room.

Faith motioned her sister into the room. "Come look at me. I'm covered with little bumps."

Grace Ann's dark eyes grew huge as she studied Faith. "It looks like you've got the chicken pox."

Faith turned toward the mirror and stuck out her tongue. It was bright red, and so was the back of her throat. "I thought I had the chicken pox when I was a child."

"Maybe not. You'd better check with Mama."

"Has anyone we know had the pox lately?"

Grace Ann nodded. "Philip's daughter, Sarah Jane, but she seemed well enough to travel so they brought her here for Christmas anyway." She shrugged. "Probably thought she was no longer contagious or that we'd all had them."

Faith slipped into her robe. "Guess I'd better go downstairs and have a talk with Mama."

"Want me to send her up? You look kind of peaked, so you might want to crawl back in bed."

The idea of going back to bed did sound appealing, but Faith had never given into sickness before. All during her marriage to Greg, she'd performed even when she thought she might be coming down with a cold or the flu. She really had to be sick before she took to her bed.

A short time later, with a determined spirit, Faith made her way down the stairs. She found Mama, Grace Ann, and Esther in the kitchen getting breakfast started. The pungent odor of Mama's strong coffee made Faith's stomach lurch, and she dropped into a seat at the table with a moan.

"Faith, do you want to make the toast this morning, or would you rather be in charge of squeezing oranges for juice?" Mama asked, apparently unaware of Faith's condition.

Faith could only groan in response.

"She isn't feeling well this morning, Mama," Grace Ann said as she stepped in front of Faith and laid a hand on her forehead. "She's got herself a fever, and from the looks of her arms and face, I'd say she's contracted a nasty case of chicken pox."

"Chicken pox?" Esther and Mama said in unison.

Mama hurried over to the table. "Let me have a look-see."

Faith lifted her face for her mother's inspection, and Mama's grimace told her all she needed to know. She had come down with the pox, and that meant she wouldn't be going anywhere for the next couple of weeks. Faith had to wonder if someone was trying to tell her something. If so, would she be willing to listen?

"Didn't I have the pox when I was a girl?"

"You were the only one of my kinner who didn't get it," Mama said. "I figured you must be immune to the disease."

Faith dropped her head to the table. "I can't believe this is happening to me now."

"What do you mean 'now'?" Grace Ann asked.

"Well, I had planned to. . . ." Faith's voice trailed off. She was sick and wouldn't be going anywhere until her health returned, so there was no point revealing her plans just yet.

"Whatever plans you've made, they'll have to wait. You'd best get on back to bed," Mama instructed.

"Okay. Could someone please bring me a cup of tea?"

"One of your sisters will be right up," Mama called as Faith exited the room.

A short time later, Faith was snuggled beneath her covers with a cup of mint tea in her hands. If she weren't feeling so sick, it might have been nice to be pampered like this. Under the circumstances, though, Faith would sooner be outside chopping wood than stuck here in bed.

Faith spent the next several days in her room with one of her sisters or Mama waiting on her hand and foot. To Faith's amazement, Melinda didn't get sick. Maybe she was immune to the chicken pox, or maybe she would get them later. Either way, Faith was glad her precious child didn't have to suffer with the intense itching she'd been going through. It was enough to make her downright irritable.

One morning after the girls had left for school, Faith made her way down to the kitchen. She felt better today and decided it might do her some good to be up awhile. She found her mother sitting at the kitchen table with a cup of tea and an open Bible. Mama looked up when Faith took the seat across from her. "You're up. Does that mean you're feeling better?"

"Some, although I have to keep reminding myself not to scratch the pockmarks." Faith helped herself to the pot of tea sitting in the center of the table. Several clean cups were stacked beside it, so she poured some tea into one and took a sip.

"Sure was a good Christmas we had this year, don't you think?" Mama asked.

Faith nodded. "It was a lot of fun."

"First time in years the whole family has been together."

Faith's breath caught in her throat. Was Mama going to give her a lecture about how she'd run away from home ten years ago and left a hole in the family? Was the pleasant camaraderie they'd shared here of late about to be shattered?

"You're awful quiet," Mama commented.

"Just thinking is all."

"About family?"

Instinctively Faith grasped the fingers on her right hand and popped two knuckles at the same time.

"Wish you wouldn't do that." Mama slowly shook her head. "It's a bad habit, and—"

Faith held up her hands. "I'm not a little girl anymore, and as you can see, my knuckles aren't big because I've popped them for so many years." As soon as Faith saw her mother's downcast eyes and wrinkled forehead, she wished she could take back her biting words. "Sorry. I didn't mean to be so testy."

Mama reached across the table and touched Faith's hand. "I did get after you a lot when you were a kinner, didn't I?"

Faith could only nod, for tears clogged her throat. She opened her mouth to tell Mama of her plans to leave again, but she stopped herself in time. Now was not the time to be telling her plans. She would wait until she was feeling better.

Faith took another sip of tea. "This sure hits the spot."

"Always did enjoy a good cup of tea on a cold winter morning." Mama touched her Bible. "Tea warms the stomach, but God's Word warms the soul."

Not knowing how to respond, Faith only nodded.

"Take this verse, for example," Mama continued. "Psalm 46:10 says, 'Be still, and know that I am God.' If that doesn't warm one's soul, I don't know what will."

Faith let the words sink in. *"Be still."* She'd been very still these past few days during her bout with the chicken pox. *"And know that I am God."*

She closed her eyes. *If You're real, God, then would You please reveal Your will to me?*

A knock on the door drew Faith's thoughts aside. Mama rose to her feet. "Must be someone come a-calling. Your daed and the boys are out in the barn, and they surely wouldn't be knocking, now would they?"

Faith watched the back door as her mother made her way across the room. When Mama opened it, a gust of cold wind blew in, followed by Noah Hertzler carrying a small wicker basket in one hand.

"Noah, what are you doing here?" Faith asked. "Shouldn't you be at work?"

He followed Mama over to the table. "Things are kind of slow at the Christmas tree farm right now, so Hank gave me and the other fellows a few days off. This is for you," he said, placing the basket in front of Faith. "I hope it will make you feel better."

"Aren't you worried about getting the chicken pox?" she asked. "I could still be contagious, you know."

He shook his head. "I had them already—when I was five years old."

"Oh, okay." Faith pulled the piece of cloth back and smiled when she saw a batch of frosted brownies nestled inside the basket. "Chocolate—my weakness. Thank you, Noah."

"You're welcome, and it's good to see you up." Noah pulled out a chair and sat down next to Faith. "The last couple of times I've dropped by, you've been in your room, too sick for visitors."

"Someone in the family has always delivered the goodies you brought me," she said.

Noah chuckled. "Sure glad to hear that. Knowing those brothers of yours, I wouldn't have been surprised to hear if John and Brian had helped themselves to some of the desserts."

"They did try," Mama cut in. She handed Noah a cup of tea. "Why don't you take off your jacket and stay awhile?"

"I think I will." Noah set the cup down on the table, slipped off his jacket, and draped it over the back of the chair.

"If you young people will excuse me, I have some laundry that needs to be done." Mama grabbed a couple of soiled hand towels off the metal rack by the sink and quickly left the room.

Faith had to wonder if her mother had left her alone with Noah on purpose. The comments she'd made lately about how much she liked Noah and how he would make a fine husband for some lucky woman made Faith think Mama and Barbara might be in cahoots.

"How come you didn't attach a scripture verse to any of the desserts you've given me lately?" Faith asked.

His face flamed. "I. . .uh. . .thought maybe I was getting too pushy. Didn't want you to think I was trying to cram the Bible down your throat."

Faith stared at the tablecloth. "Guess I probably have needed a bit of encouraging."

When Noah reached over and placed his hand on top of hers, she felt a warm tingle travel all the way up her arm. Not the kind that felt like fireworks, but a comfortable, cozy feeling. "I'm still praying for you, Faith," he said quietly. "Just thought you should know."

"I appreciate that because I need all the prayers I can get."

"Speaking of prayers. . ." Noah smiled. "I had one answered for me on Christmas Day."

Faith lifted her gaze. "What prayer was that?"

"I stopped to see Hank and Sandy to say Merry Christmas, and they told me that they're planning to adopt a baby."

"That's wonderful. They seem to like children, so I'm sure they'll make good parents."

He nodded. "I think so, too."

Faith was happy for Hank and Sandy, but an ache settled over her heart when she thought about her own life. If she never married, she wouldn't have any more children, and Faith knew that once she left home and returned to the world of entertainment, the closeness she and Melinda had now would be diminished. Even so, returning to the world of entertainment was the only way she would ever find what she'd been longing for all these years.

Chapter 25

By the following week, Faith felt much better. The pock marks had dried up, her sore throat and headache were gone, and her energy was nearly back to normal.

On Saturday morning after the kitchen chores were done, she decided to have that talk with Mama she'd been putting off far too long. Melinda and Susie were in the barn playing. Esther, Grace Ann, and Brian had gone to Seymour with Papa. John was over at his girlfriend's house. This was the perfect chance to speak with Mama alone. When that conversation was out of the way, she would do the hardest part—tell Melinda she was planning to leave.

Faith glanced over at her mother, who sat in front of the treadle sewing machine in the kitchen. "Mama, before you get too involved with your sewing, I wondered if we could talk awhile."

Mama looked up at Faith. "Is this just a friendly little chitchat, or have you got something serious on your mind?"

"Why do you ask?"

"I figure if it's just going to be some easy banter, I'll keep sewing as we talk."

Faith leaned on the cupboard. "I'm afraid it's serious."

Mama slid her chair back and stood. "Shall we sit at the kitchen table, or would you rather go to the living room?"

"Let's go in there. We'll be less apt to be disturbed should the girls come inside before we're done talking."

Mama nodded, and Faith followed her into the next room. They both sat on the sofa in front of the fireplace. The heat from the flames licking at the logs did nothing to warm Faith. Goose bumps had erupted all over her arms.

"What's wrong, Faith? Are you cold?"

"No, I–"

"Why don't you run upstairs and get a sweater?"

Faith shook her head and rubbed her hands briskly over her arms. "I'll be okay as soon as I say what's on my mind."

"You look so solemn. What's this all about?"

"It–it's about me–and Melinda."

Mama leaned forward, and her glasses slipped down her nose. "What about you?"

"I. . .uh. . .plan to go back to my life as an entertainer, and I hope to be on a bus for Memphis by Monday morning to meet with the agent I've hired." There, it was out. Faith should have felt better, but she didn't. The sorrowful look on Mama's face was nearly her undoing.

"I knew it was too good to be true, you coming home and

all." Mama squeezed her eyes shut, and when she opened them again, Faith noticed there were tears.

"I never meant to hurt you, Mama. I hope you know that."

"The only thing I know for sure is that my prodigal daughter finally returned home; only now she's about to leave again." Mama wrapped her arms around her middle, as though she were hugging herself. "No wonder you've put off baptism and joining the church. You've been planning this all along, haven't you?"

Faith nodded solemnly. "I would have told you sooner, but things kept getting in the way of my leaving."

Mama stood and moved toward the fireplace. "Why'd you come home if you were planning to leave?"

"I—I wanted to—"

"You were down on your luck and needed a place to stay for a while, isn't that it?"

"No, it's not."

"You allowed us to get close to Melinda, and now you're taking her away?"

Faith jumped up and hurried to her mother's side. "I'd like Melinda to stay here if that's okay with you and Papa. She needs a home where she'll be well cared for and loved. It's not good for a child to be raised by a single parent who lives out of a suitcase and has no place to call home."

Mama turned to face Faith. The tears that had gathered in her eyes moments ago were now rolling down her cheeks. "Melinda can stay if that's your wish. But I'd like you to think long and hard about something before you go."

"What's that?"

"If Melinda needs a good home where she'll be loved and

cared for, then what about her mamm? What's she needing these days?"

Faith nearly choked on the tears clogging her throat. She was afraid if she said one more word she would break down and sob. She had made her decision and felt certain it was the best thing for both her and Melinda.

"Oh, and one more thing. . ."

"What's that, Mama?"

"If you leave again, then you're not welcome to come home."

"But what about Melinda? I'll need to be with her for holidays and special occasions."

Mama shook her head vigorously. "If you go and Melinda stays, it wouldn't be good for her to have you showing up whenever you have a whim. It would only confuse the girl. Might make her want to go back to the English world with you."

Faith's mouth dropped open. She couldn't believe Mama was putting stipulations on leaving Melinda with them. The thought of never seeing her daughter again was almost too much to bear. Faith needed to think more about this. She had to spend some time alone and figure out what to do.

Giving no thought to the cold, she dashed out the front door and into the chilly morning air.

A few minutes later, a blast of warm air greeted her as she entered the barn. Papa had obviously stoked up the stove before he and the others left for Seymour.

Figuring Melinda and Susie were probably on the other side of the barn, Faith headed in that direction. She came to a halt when she heard her daughter's sweet voice singing and yodeling.

Surprised by the sound, Faith tiptoed across the wooden floor until she spotted Melinda. The child knelt in the hay with three black-and-white kittens curled in her lap. Susie sat off to one side, holding two other kittens.

"Oddle—lay—oddle—lay—oddle—lay—dee—tee—my mama was an old cowhand, and she taught me how to yodel before I could stand. Yo—le—tee—yo—le—tee—hi—ho!"

Faith sucked in her breath. She had no idea Melinda could yodel or that she knew the cute little song Faith had sung so many times onstage. Apparently the child had been listening whenever Faith practiced. Melinda actually had some of the yodeling skills mastered quite well.

When Melinda finished her song, she looked over at Susie and smiled. "When I grow up, I'm gonna be just like my mamm. I'll travel around the country, singing, telling jokes, and yodeling. Oh—lee—dee—tee—tee—oh!"

Faith's heart sank all the way to her toes. She'd never dreamed Melinda was entertaining such thoughts. She'd been so sure the child was settling in here and would grow up happy and content to be Amish.

The way you were? a little voice in her head asked. Faith wanted better things for her daughter than to spend the rest of her life traipsing all over the countryside, hoping to succeed in the world of music or comedy and seeking after riches and fame.

Feeling as though she'd been struck by a bolt of lightning, Faith realized those were the very things she had spent ten years of her life trying to accomplish. She wasn't rich. She wasn't famous. Had any of it brought her true happiness? Traveling from town to town, performing at one theater after another was a lonely existence. At least for Faith it had been. Being married to Greg hadn't given Faith the fulfillment she'd been searching for, either. Their tumultuous marriage had only furthered her frustrations.

I brought it on myself by marrying an unbeliever. Faith remembered what the Bible said about being unequally yoked with unbelievers. Of course, she hadn't exactly been living the life of a believer during her entertaining years.

She blinked back the tears threatening to spill over. *It's just as Mama said—the very thing I've been wanting for Melinda is exactly what I need. How could I have been so blind? I don't need fame or fortune. I've been selfish, always wanting my own way. My truest desire is fellowship with good friends, the love of a caring family, and a close relationship with God.*

Faith knew without a shadow of a doubt that if Melinda was ever to settle completely into the Amish way of life, she must see by her mother's example that it was a good life. Faith would need to stay in Webster County. It was either that or say goodbye to Melinda and spend the rest of her life wishing she had stayed.

But do I have enough faith in God to live by His rules? Staying Amish would never work unless she strengthened her faith. She must rely wholly on the Lord to meet her needs. No amount of money or recognition could fill the void in a person's heart the way Jesus' love did. The scripture verses Noah had shared over the last few months had told her that much.

It's time to come home, Faith.

She leaned against the wooden beam closest to her and closed her eyes. *Heavenly Father, I need Your help. I know now that I want to remain here with my people, and I want to draw closer to You. Forgive my sins, and please give me wisdom in raising my daughter so she will want to serve You and not seek after the things in this world.*

When Faith opened her eyes, Melinda and Susie were gone. They'd apparently left the barn, seeking out new pleasures found only on a farm. The kittens were with their mother again, just as Faith's child would be with her in the days ahead.

Faith left the barn and found the girls playing in the snow. On impulse, she scooped up a handful of the powdery stuff and gave it a toss. It hit the mark and landed squarely on Melinda's arm.

The child squealed with laughter and retaliated. Her aim wasn't as good as Faith's, and the snowball ended up on Faith's foot. She laughed and grabbed another clump of snow. For the next half hour, she, Melinda, and Susie frolicked in the snow, laughing, making snow angels, and yodeling. Faith hadn't had this much fun since she was a young child.

When it got too cold, Faith suggested they go inside for a cup of hot chocolate and some of the frosted brownies Noah had brought over. The children were quick to agree, and soon they were all seated at the kitchen table.

Melinda took a bite of brownie and smacked her lips. "Noah sure does bake good, don't ya think?"

"Jah, he does."

"I really like him, don't you, Mama?"

Faith nodded.

"I think I'd like to have Noah for my new *daadi*."

"When and if the Lord wants you to have a new daddy, He will let us know."

Melinda's forehead wrinkled. "I'm wondering if my daadi went away so Noah could come."

"Oh, Melinda, you shouldn't be talking that way."

"Why not?"

"Jah, Faith. Why not?" Susie chimed in.

A vision of Noah's face popped into Faith's mind. She did care for him, but was that enough? Could she trust him not to hurt her the way Greg had? Did Noah care about her in any way other than friendship? There were so many unanswered questions.

For a while, Faith had thought Noah might have some romantic interest in her, but here of late, he'd pulled back. She figured he must have some reservations about becoming involved with a woman who didn't share his strong faith in God. Or maybe it was their age difference that bothered him.

Faith shook her head, trying to clear away the troubling thoughts. From what she'd come to know about Noah, she doubted he would see the few years between them as a problem. It was probably her lack of faith that concerned him the most. As tears clogged her throat, she reached over and pulled Melinda into her arms.

"What's wrong, Mama? How come you're crying?"

"Mine are the good kind of tears. Tears of joy."

"What are you so happy about?" Susie questioned.

Faith hugged both little girls. "I'm thankful to God for giving me you two. I'm also happy to be back here in Webster County, and this is where I plan to stay." She turned toward the living room. "Now I must speak to Grandma Stutzman. She needs to know what I've decided."

Chapter 26

As Wilma sat in her favorite chair, rocking back and forth with her eyes closed, she thought about her conversation with Faith and grieved over the thought of her oldest daughter leaving home again. Wasn't it bad enough that Faith had left home once? Did she have to put her family through that horrible pain again? And what of Melinda? How did Faith think her daughter would understand her own mother leaving her with grandparents she barely knew while she went out into the world to seek her fortune and fame?

Father in heaven, she silently prayed, *please show me what I might say or do to persuade Faith to stay. I know I'm not the perfect mother, but I love my daughter and can't bear to think of her going away again.*

A chill shot through Wilma's body as she realized for the first time what her part had been in driving Faith away. If she'd only been more accepting when Faith wanted to tell silly jokes and yodel, the girl might never have left home in the first place.

I need to apologize—make things right between us. Even if Faith does leave home again, I can't let her go with bad feelings between us.

Wilma's eyes snapped open when she heard the floorboards creak, and she blinked a couple of times when she saw Faith standing near the front door. "What are you doing here?" she croaked. "I thought you'd gone outside to tell Melinda that you'll be leaving soon."

"I—I did see Melinda."

"How'd she take the news? Does she want to stay here with us or go away with you?"

"Melinda will be staying here."

A sense of relief flooded Wilma's soul. At least they wouldn't be losing their granddaughter. "I'm glad she won't be leaving. I've come to care a great deal for that child," she said, choking back the tears clogging her throat. "And I want you to know that—" Wilma's voice caught on a sob. She needed to tell Faith what was on her mind, but she couldn't seem to get the words out.

Faith took a seat on one end of the sofa as she shook her head. "I didn't tell Melinda my plans because I've changed my mind. I won't be leaving Webster County, after all."

Wilma's mouth dropped open. "You won't?"

"No, I've decided that my place is here—with Melinda and my family."

Wilma let Faith's words sink in. Finally, she stood and rushed to the sofa, where she dropped to her knees and hugged her daughter tightly. Tears of joy burst forth and dribbled onto her cheeks. "Oh, thank the Lord. This is such an answer to prayer."

Faith nodded and leaned her head on Wilma's shoulder, as her own tears wet Wilma's dress.

"I should've been more understanding. Maybe if I'd taken time to enjoy your humor and had looked for the good in you, things would have gone better," Wilma murmured.

Tears rolled down Faith's cheeks, and she shuddered. "You might feel bad for driving me away, but Papa sure doesn't. In all the time I've been home, he's never once said he was glad I came back or that he hoped I would stay." She shook her head. "I'm sure he would never take any of the blame for me leaving, but to be honest, I know it's as much my fault as it was yours and Papa's."

"What do you mean?" Mama asked.

"It was selfish of me to want my own way and desire recognition for talents." Faith sniffed deeply. "I'm sorry for all I put you and Papa through when I left home."

Wilma stroked Faith's back as they held each other and wept.

"Your mamm and I are both at fault for you leaving."

Faith's head came up as Menno stepped into the room and placed his hand on her shoulder. "Papa," she murmured. "I—I didn't know you'd come in. I'm so sorry for everything I put you and Mama through. Can you ever forgive me?"

He nodded slowly. "I owe you an apology, too, daughter. I should have been more accepting of your jokes and even your frog-croaking yodeling."

Faith laughed, hiccupped, and then started to cry again.

"I promise you that I'm going to be more accepting from

now on," Menno said as he pulled Faith to her feet and gave her a hug.

"And I'll try not to act silly at inopportune times," she said between sniffs.

Wilma reached for a tissue from the box on the table near the sofa and handed it to Faith. "So Melinda doesn't know you were planning to leave?"

Faith shook her head. "I saw no reason to tell her since I'll be staying."

"You're right. You're right. There's no reason for her to know. It might upset her even though you're not leaving after all," Menno said.

"Jah, I agree." Faith nodded. "God has shown me that my place is here."

The next day during church, Noah couldn't help noticing Faith, who sat across the room on the women's side. Something about her expectant expression made him wonder what was going on with her. She sat up straighter than usual and seemed to be listening to everything Bishop Martin said. Every once in a while, she blew her nose or dabbed the corners of her eyes with her handkerchief. Noah couldn't wait for the service to end so he could talk to her.

When church was over, tables were set up in the barn for the men and boys to eat their meal. Noah was disappointed when Faith wasn't one of the servers at his table, but he hoped he would get the chance to speak with her after he ate.

He hurried through the meal and was about to head for the house, when his father showed up saying Mom had taken ill.

"Sorry to hear that," Noah said. "Is her blood sugar out of whack?"

Pop shrugged. "I'm not sure. She's feeling weak and shaky, so it could just be the flu, but I think it would be best if we went home now."

Since Noah had ridden to church with his folks that morning, he felt he had no choice but to leave when they did. "Okay, Pop," he said with a nod. "I'll get the horse hitched to our buggy right away."

As Noah headed toward the corral, he spotted Faith talking to Barbara Zook on the front porch. He started that way, thinking he would at least say hello, but halted when he heard Barbara say, "What's that big smile all about, Faith?"

"I'm smiling because I'm so happy," Faith replied.

"Happy about what?"

"Well, I've been planning to leave Webster County for some time—ever since I brought Melinda here, and—"

Faith's voice was drowned out when Barbara's two boys dashed up, hollering that they wanted to play ball but the older boys wouldn't let them join the game.

"Noah, have you got the horse yet?" Pop called out. "Your mamm's feeling really light-headed."

"I'm coming, Pop." With a heavy heart, Noah moved on to the corral. He'd feared the day would come when Faith would leave Webster County, and he had been a fool to allow himself to fall in love with her. If only he could do something to make her stay. He didn't understand why God hadn't answered his prayers concerning Faith, but he knew it wasn't for him to question God's ways.

"I'm sorry for the interruption," Barbara said to Faith once she'd gotten her boys calmed down and sent them inside to get a piece of cake. "Now what was that you were saying?"

"I've been planning to leave Webster County ever since I brought Melinda here."

Barbara's heart began to pound. "You're going to leave again?"

"Oh, no. I had planned to go back on the road and leave Melinda with my folks so she would be raised in a stable home and not have to be hauled around the country while I entertained." Faith shook her head. "But I changed my mind—or I should say that God changed it for me."

"What happened?" Barbara questioned. "Why did you change your mind?"

"I heard Melinda talking to Susie about growing up to be an entertainer someday, and I realized that I didn't want that for my girl. I knew in my heart, and have known it for some time, that what I really wanted was here all the time—my family and friends."

"Oh, Faith, I'm so glad to hear that." Barbara wrapped her arms around Faith and gave her a squeeze. "Jah, I truly am."

Faith touched her chest. "I've changed, Barbara. God's changed me from the inside out, and for the first time, being in church today seemed so right to me. I've finally come to realize how much I need my family—and most of all, how much I need God."

Chapter 27

Since his mother's bout with the flu had gone on for several days and had affected her blood sugar, Noah had gone straight home after work to cook, clean, and help his father with some of the outside chores. But Mom was doing better today, and since it was Saturday and Noah didn't have to work at the tree farm, he decided to head over to the Stutzmans' and have a talk with Faith while Mom took an afternoon nap. Pop was visiting his friend Vernon, the buggy maker, so it would be the perfect time for Noah to slip away. He'd been praying about things and had decided that, before Faith left Webster County, he needed to be honest with her about the way he felt. He just hoped he wasn't too late.

As Noah hitched his horse to one of their open buggies and climbed into the driver's seat, he prayed for the right words to say to Faith and for God's will to be done.

Noah directed the horse down the driveway and drew in a deep breath. It was a fine winter afternoon, and even though the air was frosty and several inches of snow covered the ground, the sky was blue and clear.

Noah glanced at the cake sitting on the seat beside him. He remembered the conversation he'd heard Faith and Barbara having after church last Sunday and hoped with all his heart that he would find Faith at home and that they would be given the chance to talk in private. The words he had in his heart were for her ears alone.

Faith couldn't believe she and Melinda had the whole house to themselves. Her folks had gone to Seymour for the day, and they'd taken Grace Ann, Esther, and Susie with them. John and Brian were over at their friend Andy's house, so it was a good opportunity for Faith to work on her baking skills.

She'd thought Melinda might enjoy helping her make a lemon sponge cake, but the child had acted sleepy after eating their noon meal and had gone to the living room to take a nap on the sofa.

"It's probably just as well," Faith murmured as she got out the ingredients. Melinda had stayed up later than usual last night, and Faith figured a nap would do the child more good than playing in dusty flour and lemon juice.

If the cake turned out well, Faith planned to give it to Noah. He had given her so many special treats over the last few months;

it was the least she could do to reciprocate. He'd been kind in other ways, too—helping out when it was needed and sharing God's Word with her on several occasions.

Faith was sure those scripture verses had taken root in her soul, but it wasn't until the day she'd discovered Melinda yodeling in the barn that she'd really given her heart to Jesus.

As Faith mixed the cake, she smiled at the remembrance of telling her folks she had changed her mind about leaving and how they'd responded. Everything was better at home now, but she still had some unfinished business with Noah.

Faith halted her thoughts and focused on putting the cake together, but when it was ready to bake, she discovered that the oven wasn't hot enough. During the summer months, the Stutzmans used their propane-operated stove, but in the wintertime, Mama insisted on the woodburning stove because it gave off more heat that circulated throughout much of the house.

Faith slipped the cake pan onto the oven rack and opened the firebox door. Then she grabbed two pieces of wood from the wood box and tossed them in. One of the burning logs inside the stove rolled out and landed on the floor.

Faith gasped as she watched the braided throw rug ignite and flames shoot out in every direction. She'd never dealt with a situation like this and wasn't sure what to do. She ran to the sink, filled a jug with water, and flung it on the burning rug. Then she opened the back door and kicked the rug with the hunk of wood outside. By this time, the room was filled with smoke.

"Melinda!" Faith shouted. She rushed into the living room, scooped Melinda off the sofa, and bounded out the door into the frosty afternoon air.

By this time, Melinda was wide awake. "Mama, what's going on? Why are we outside with no coats?"

Faith seated her daughter on a bench at the picnic table and drew in a deep breath to steady her nerves.

"I caught the rug in the kitchen on fire, and I need to get the smoke out of the room. You stay here, and I'll be right back."

"Mama, where are you going?"

"Just stay put!"

When Noah pulled into the Stutzmans' driveway, his heart gave a lurch. Melinda sat at the picnic table with her arms wrapped tightly around her middle. What was Faith thinking, letting her daughter play out in the cold with no coat?

He grabbed the lemon sponge cake, hopped down from the buggy, and was heading for Melinda when he noticed a chunk of smoldering wood and what looked like the remains of a throw rug lying in the snow several feet from the house.

Melinda jumped up and raced over to Noah. "It's good you're here. I'm worried about Mama."

Noah's heart began to pound, and then he saw it—smoke drifting out the back door of the Stutzmans' home. "Where is everyone, Melinda? Where's the rest of your family?"

"Everyone except for me and Mama are gone today." The child pointed toward the house, her lower lip quivering like a leaf blowing in the breeze. "Mama's in there."

The reality of what the smoldering log and burned throw rug

meant caused Noah to shudder. "Stay here, Melinda." He handed her the cake. "I'm going inside to help your mamm."

Noah took the steps two at a time, and when he bounded into the smoke-filled kitchen, he was thankful he saw no flames. "Faith! Where are you?"

Through the haze of smoke, Noah noticed a moving shadow, and he reached for it. What he got was a wet towel slapped against his arm. "Hey! What's going on?"

"Noah, is that you?" Faith stepped through the stifling haze, waving the towel in front of her.

Relieved to see that Faith was all right and with barely a thought for what he was doing, Noah grabbed her around the waist. "Are you okay? What happened in here?"

Faith coughed several times. "I was trying to bake, and the oven wasn't hot enough. When I opened the firebox, a log rolled out and caught the rug on fire." She leaned on him as though she needed support.

Noah's heart clenched at the thought of what could have happened if Faith hadn't thought quickly enough. The whole house might have burned to the ground, the way Pop's barn had when it was struck by lightning.

"Melinda told me that you're the only ones at home today," he said, stroking Faith's trembling shoulders.

She coughed again and pulled slowly away, leaving him with a sense of disappointment. "That's right, and I was trying to bake you a lemon sponge cake." Her voice quavered, and she gasped. "Oh, no! My cake! It must be burned to a crisp."

She jerked the oven door open and withdrew the cake. Even in the smoky room, Noah could see it was ruined.

Faith groaned and set the blackened dessert on the counter. "I can't believe what a mess I've made of things. It seems I can never do anything right."

"It's okay," he said. "It's the thought that counts. Besides, I brought you a lemon sponge cake I made this morning. I left it outside with Melinda." Now it was Noah's turn to cough. Between the firebox being left open and the burned cake, the smoke was dense, and he was worried about Faith breathing in the fumes. "We need to get this room cleared out. Let's open some windows and head outside."

Soon they had the doors and windows open, and Noah took Melinda and Faith to the barn, where it was warmer. He noticed Faith's eyes brimming with tears and wondered if it was from the acrid smoke or because she was upset over the frightening incident. *Probably a little of both,* he decided.

Relief flooded 'his soul as he stared down at Faith, sitting beside her daughter on a bale of straw with a horse blanket draped over their shoulders. His chest rose and fell in a deep sigh as he fought the temptation to kiss her.

From the look of desire Faith saw in Noah's dark eyes, she was fairly certain he wanted to kiss her. She leaned forward slightly, inviting him to do so, but to her disappointment, he moved away. Had she misread his intentions? This was the man she had come to love. She could hardly bear the thought that he might not love her in return.

"Mama, I'm warmed up now. Can I play with the kittens?"

Melinda asked, pulling Faith's thoughts aside.

Faith nodded. "Jah, sure, go ahead."

Melinda scampered off toward the pile of hay across the room where a mother cat and five fluffy kittens were sleeping.

Faith looked up at Noah and rubbed her hands briskly over her arms as she tried to calm her racing heart. "I could have burned the house down today, but the Lord was watching out for me—for all of us really."

"I believe you're right about that, but I'm surprised to hear you say so."

"I'm not an unbeliever, Noah," she murmured. "I recently asked God to forgive my sins, and I believe He will strengthen my faith as time goes on."

A slow smile spread across Noah's face. "Really, Faith?"

She nodded.

"That's *wunderbaar*." His smile faded.

"What's wrong?"

"I heard you were planning to leave Webster County, and the reason I came here was to try and talk you out of going."

"I'm not leaving," she said with a catch in her voice.

"But I heard you tell Barbara you were."

She nodded soberly. "I was, until God changed my mind."

"I've suspected for some time that you were thinking about going, but I was afraid if I said too much or pushed too hard it might drive you further from God—and me."

Faith dropped her gaze to the floor. "From the beginning, I'd planned to leave Melinda with my folks and head back on the road again."

"You were gonna leave me here?"

Faith spun around at the sound of her daughter's voice. She hadn't realized Melinda had returned. What had she been thinking? She hadn't wanted Melinda to know.

She swept the child into her arms. "I'm so sorry. I thought it would be best for you, but God kept causing things to happen so I'd have to stay put."

Melinda sniffed deeply. "You're not leaving then?"

"No, I'm certainly not. My place is here with you."

"And you won't be telling jokes and yodeling no more?"

Before Faith had a chance to answer, Noah cut in. "I think it would be fine if your mamm told funny stories and jokes right here with her family, don't you?"

Melinda nodded and swiped at the tears rolling down her cheeks. "Will you still be able to yodel, Mama? I love it when you do, and I want to yodel, too."

Faith smiled through her tears. "Most folks in our community don't see yodeling as wrong, but I probably won't do it when Grandpa Stutzman's around. He says it bothers his ears."

Noah chuckled and motioned to Faith. "Well, he's not here now, so why don't you do a little yodeling for your own private audience?"

Faith squeezed Melinda's hand. "How about if you help me yodel?"

Melinda leaned her head back and opened her mouth. "Oh–lee–dee-ee–oh–lee–dee–tee!"

Noah did his best to join them, but he finally gave up. Suddenly, his expression turned serious, and Faith wondered if something was wrong.

"What is it, Noah?"

He leaned over and looked deeply into her eyes. "I love you, Faith Andrews, and if you think you could learn to love me, I'd like the chance to court you."

Melinda jumped up and down. "Yippee! I knew it!"

Faith swallowed and squeezed her eyes shut. "Oh, Noah, I don't have to *learn* to love you, for I already do. Thanks to God's love and to Him showing me what's really important, I know I can have the best of both worlds—the love of a wonderful man; my family and friends; and most of all, a closeness to my heavenly Father that I've never had before."

Epilogue

Two years later

Faith brushed Noah's arm with her elbow as she squeezed past him to get to the stove. Two more lemon sponge cakes were ready to take from the oven. These would be given to Barbara and David Zook in honor of their son, Zachary, who had been born the week before.

"I can't believe we've been doing this for almost two years," Noah said as he nuzzled Faith's neck with the tip of his nose.

Faith glanced down at the floor, where their one-year-old son, Isaiah, was being entertained by his big sister, Melinda. "God has been good and blessed our marriage," she said.

"That's so true."

"What scripture verse have you decided to use?"

"I was thinking maybe Luke 16:10: 'He that is faithful in that which is least is faithful also in much.'"

"Sounds like a good one." Faith grabbed a pen and paper off the counter. "I think I'll add a couple of funny quips on one side, and you can put the Bible verse on the other."

Noah nodded. "We make a good team, *fraa*. I'm sure glad you decided to marry me."

Faith wrapped her arms around Noah's neck and kissed his cheek. A few tears slipped under her lashes and splashed onto Noah's blue cotton shirt. "I thank the Lord for bringing me back here to Webster County. Home is where my heart is. Home is where I belong."

RECIPE FOR NOAH'S LEMON SPONGE CAKE

Ingredients:
- 1 cup sifted cake flour
- 1 teaspoon baking powder
- ½ teaspoon salt
- ½ cup cold water
- 2 teaspoons grated lemon rind
- 2 egg yolks, beaten
- ¾ cup plus 2 tablespoons sugar
- 2 eggs whites, beaten
- 1 teaspoon lemon juice

Preheat oven to 350°. Sift the flour, baking powder, and salt together four times. In a separate bowl, add the water and lemon rind to the egg yolks and beat them until they are lemon-colored. Add ¾ cup of sugar a little at a time, beating after each addition. Then add the sifted ingredients, slowly stirring to blend them in. In a separate bowl, beat the eggs whites until they form peaks, then add the lemon juice and 2 tablespoons of sugar, beating until they are well blended. Fold this mixture into the rest of the batter, and pour into an ungreased tube pan. Bake for 1 hour. Remove from oven. Turn pan upside down with tube over the neck of a funnel or bottle. Cool thoroughly; remove from pan.

On Her Own

DEDICATION/ACKNOWLEDGMENTS

To my friends Holly Stoolfire, Sandy Fisher,
and Marge Schaper, who were on their own for a time
and learned to rely on God for their strength and support.

Two are better than one;
because they have a good reward for their labour.
For if they fall, the one will lift up his fellow:
but woe to him that is alone when he falleth;
for he hath not another to help him up.
ECCLESIASTES 4:9-10

Chapter 1

Cradling the precious infant she had given birth to a short time ago, Barbara Zook lay exhausted, her head resting on the damp pillow.

"We have four sons now, David," she murmured into the stillness of her room. "I wish you were here to see our *boppli*. I'm planning to name him after you." Unbidden tears sprang to Barbara's eyes as she struggled against the memory of what had happened almost eight months ago. If she lived to be one hundred, she would never forget the unsuspecting moment when her world fell apart.

Barbara squeezed her eyes shut as her mind drove her unwillingly back to that Saturday afternoon when she'd been happy and secure in her marriage—when she'd been full of hope for the future.

Barbara sat in the wicker rocking chair on the front porch, watching her three young boys play in the yard and waiting for her husband's return. It was their tenth wedding anniversary, and David had taken their horse and buggy to Seymour to pick up her gift. He'd said it was something Barbara both wanted and needed.

She patted her stomach and drew in a deep breath as the rocking chair creaked beneath her weight. "When David gets home, I'll give him my gift—the news that I'm pregnant again," she whispered. Barbara had known for a couple of weeks that she was carrying David's child, but she had wanted it to be a surprise. She was sure her husband would be happy about having another baby, and she was hopeful that this time it would be a girl.

She planned to share her good news the moment David arrived. He had been gone several hours, and she couldn't imagine what could be keeping him.

Barbara's stomach rumbled as she noticed that the sun had begun to drop behind the thick pine trees on the other side of the field. It was almost time to start supper. She had just decided to head for the kitchen when the sheriff's car rumbled up the driveway.

She stood and leaned against the porch railing while Sheriff Anderson and his deputy got out of the vehicle and strode toward her.

Barbara shuddered. Something was wrong. She could feel it in every fiber of her being. "M–may I help you, Sheriff?" she asked as the two men stepped onto the porch. Her voice cracked, and she swallowed a couple of times.

"Mrs. Zook," the sheriff said, moving closer to her, "I'm sorry to be telling you this, but there's been an accident."

"An accident?"

He nodded. "It happened about a mile out of Seymour."

Barbara's heart thudded in her chest. "Is it. . .David?"

"I'm afraid so. We were called to the scene by one of your English neighbors who'd been heading down Highway C and witnessed the accident. He identified your husband's body."

My husband's body? The words echoed in Barbara's mind. *It's not true. It can't be. David's alive. Today is our anniversary. He'll be home soon with the surprise he promised me. David's always been so dependable. He won't let me down.*

"I'm sorry," Deputy Harris said, "but a logging truck pulled out of a side road and hit your husband's buggy. The stove that was tied on the back flew forward and hit David in the head, killing him instantly."

The porch swayed in an eerie sort of way, and Barbara gripped the railing until her fingers turned numb. *David's dead. He bought me a stove. David can't be dead. Today's our anniversary.*

The wail of an infant's cries pushed Barbara's thoughts to the back of her mind, and her eyes snapped open. Her nose burned with unshed tears as she focused on the joy of having a new baby in her arms. Little David needed her. So did Zachary, Joseph, and Aaron.

"I'll do whatever I need to in order to provide for my boys," she murmured.

A knock sounded at the bedroom door, and Barbara called, "Come in."

The door creaked open, and David's mother, Mavis, stuck her head through the opening. "How are you doing? Are you ready for some company?"

Barbara glanced down at her son, who was now enjoying the first taste of his mother's milk. She nodded at her dark-haired mother-in-law. "You're welcome to come say hello to your new grandson, David."

Mavis entered the room and closed the door. "Alice told me it was a boy and you'd named him David." She moved closer to the bed and sniffed deeply, her brown eyes filling with tears. "My son would be real pleased to know he had a child named after him."

Barbara swallowed around the fiery lump in her throat. "David never knew I was pregnant. He died before I could share our surprise." She stared down at her infant son. "It breaks my heart to know this tiny fellow will never know his *daed*."

Mavis reached out to touch the baby's downy, dark head. "If I could do something to help, I surely would."

"You already have, Mavis. You and Jeremiah have helped us aplenty, same as my folks."

Mavis nodded. "Your *mamm* has been real good about watching your *kinner* so you could keep working in the harness shop, and your daed's been willing to help there despite the arthritis in his hands."

"That's true." Barbara thought about how determined her

husband had been to open his own business here in Webster County, Missouri. Because of it, they had made enough money to put food on the table and pay the bills. The truth was Barbara actually enjoyed working in the shop. To her, the smell of leather was a sweet perfume. These days she found the aroma even more comforting because it reminded her of David.

"This is a day of beginnings for David Zook Jr., and it's a day of endings for our friend Dan Hilty."

Mavis's statement jolted Barbara to the core. "Has something happened to Dan?"

Her mother-in-law nodded soberly. "You didn't know?"

Barbara shook her head.

"I thought Alice might have told you."

"Mom didn't say anything. What happened to Dan?"

Mavis took a seat on the chair next to the bed. "He died of a heart attack early this morning."

"*Ach!* How terrible. My heart goes out to Margaret and the rest of the Hilty family." Barbara felt the pain of Dan's widow as if it were her own. It seemed as if she were living David's death all over again. Giving birth to her husband's namesake was bittersweet, and hearing of someone else's loss was a reminder of her own suffering.

"Death comes to all," Mavis said in a hushed tone. "It was Dan's time to go."

Barbara had heard the bishop and others in their Amish community say the same thing when someone passed away. Some said that if the person hadn't died one way, he or she would have died another. "When your time's up, it's up," someone had told Barbara on the day of David's funeral. She wasn't sure she could accept that concept. Accidents happened, true enough, but they were brought on because someone was careless or in the wrong place at the wrong time. If David hadn't gone to town the morning of their anniversary, she felt sure he would be alive today.

Barbara saw no point, however, in telling David's mother how she felt about these things. She'd probably end up arguing with her. "When is the funeral?" she asked instead.

"In a few days. As soon as Dan's brother, Paul, gets here." Mavis patted Barbara's shoulder. "You'll not be expected to go since you've just given birth and need rest."

Barbara nodded. Rest. Yes, that's what she needed. She closed her eyes as the desire for sleep overtook her. "Tell my boys they can see their little *bruder* soon. After Davey and I have ourselves a little nap."

When Barbara heard a familiar *creak*, she knew Mavis had risen from the chair. The last thing she remembered was hearing the bedroom door click shut.

Alice Raber sat at the table where her three grandsons were drawing on tablets. "Your mamm just gave birth to a boppli," she said. "You have a new little bruder."

"What'd Mama name him?" Aaron, who was almost nine, asked as he looked up from his drawing.

"David."

"That was Papa's name," said Joseph, who would soon be turning six.

Alice nodded. "That's right. Your mamm wanted to name the baby after your daed."

"Nobody will ever take Papa's place," Aaron mumbled.

She touched his shoulder. "Of course not. Your mamm just thought it would be nice to give your little bruder your daed's name so you could remember him."

Aaron grunted. "I'll always remember Papa, no matter what. Me and him used to go fishin' together, and he promised to give me his harness business some day."

"When can we see our little bruder?" Joseph asked.

"After your mamm and the boppli have had a chance to rest awhile."

"Are they tired?"

Aaron punched Joseph's shoulder. "You ask too many questions, you know that?"

"Do not."

"*Jah*, you do."

"Let's not quarrel," Alice said as she reached over and scooped Barbara's youngest boy, Zachary, off his chair and into her lap. The little guy had been the baby of the family for three and a half years. She figured he would need some extra attention now that a new baby had come on the scene. Maybe the other boys would, too.

"Are Mama and little David tired?" Joseph asked again.

"*Jah*." Alice patted his arm. "It takes a lot of work for a little one to get born. And it was very tiring for your mamm to do her part so the little one could come into the world."

"How come?"

"Just does." Aaron grunted and nudged Joseph's elbow.

"Now quit askin' Grandma so many questions."

"Who would like some cookies?" Alice hoped a snack might put Aaron in a better mood.

Joseph bobbed his head up and down with an eager expression. "I would."

Alice placed Zachary back in his chair, then retrieved the cookie jar from the cupboard. She had just set a plate of cookies on the table when Barbara's mother-in-law entered the room.

"How's my daughter doing?" Alice asked. "Are she and the boppli sleeping?"

"She was looking pretty drowsy when I left her room. I imagine she's dozed off by now." Mavis took a seat at the table.

"I'll take the boys up to see their bruder as soon as she wakes up." Alice pushed the plate toward Mavis. "Would you like a cookie?"

"Don't mind if I do."

Mavis selected a cookie and was about to take a bite, when Joseph nudged her arm. "Want some milk for dunkin'?"

She glanced over at him and smiled. "Where's your milk?"

He shrugged. "Grandma didn't give me none. Figured if she gave you some, she might give me some, too."

Mavis chuckled, and so did Alice. "I'll see to it right away." She looked at Aaron. "Do you want some milk?"

"Jah, okay."

"I'll get all three of you some—Mavis, too, if she'd like."

Mavis nodded. "Jah, sure. Why not?"

After their snack, Alice asked the boys to play in the living room. As soon as the boys left the room, Alice turned to Mavis and said, "I'm worried about Barbara."

"I thought the birth went okay. Was there a problem I don't know about?"

Alice shook her head. "The birth went fine. It's after Barbara is back on her feet that has me worried."

"What do you mean?"

"She wants to return to work at the harness shop, and I'm not sure she should."

"That shop was my David's joy." Mavis pursed her lips. "It's my understanding that Barbara likes it, too, so it's only natural that—"

Alice shook her head. "She might like it, but it's hard work. Too hard for a woman to be doing all by herself."

"Samuel helps out. Isn't that right?"

Mavis nodded. "But his arthritis bothers him more all the time, and I don't know how much longer he'll be able to continue helping her."

"Maybe she can hire someone."

"Like who? Do you know anyone in these parts who does harness work?"

"No, but—"

"I'm wondering if she should sell the shop and live off the profits until she finds another husband."

"Another husband?" Mavis flinched. "Ach, David's not been gone quite a year. How can you even talk of Barbara marrying again?"

Alice sighed. "I'm not suggesting she get married right away. But if the right man comes along, I think she would do well to think about marrying him." She smiled at Mavis and patted her arm. "David was a fine man, and I'm sure Barbara will always carry love for him in her heart. But now she has four sons to raise, and that will be difficult to do alone, even with the help of her family."

Mavis dabbed the corners of her eyes with a napkin. "I guess we need to be praying about this, *jah*?"

Alice nodded. "That's exactly what we need to do."

Paul Hilty's hand shook as he left the phone shed outside his cousin Andy's harness shop, where he worked. He still couldn't believe the message on the answering machine that Dan, his oldest brother, was dead.

Dazed, Paul meandered back into the shop. "I've got to go home. My brother passed away this morning," he said when he found his cousin working at his desk.

Andy looked up from the pile of invoices lying in front of him. "Which brother?"

"Dan. I went out to the phone shed to make a call and discovered that Pop had left a message on your answering machine. Dan died of a heart attack early this morning."

"I'm sorry to hear that. He was helping your *daed* on the farm, isn't that right?"

Paul nodded. "Him, Monroe, and Elam. Now it'll just be Pop and my two younger brothers." He grimaced. "No doubt my *daed* will be after me to come back to Missouri so I can help him work in the fields."

"You'll be leaving Pennsylvania, then?"

"Not if I can help it." Paul swallowed hard. "I will need to go back for Dan's funeral, though. I'd like to leave right away if I can get a bus ticket."

"Of course. No problem." Andy grunted. "I'd close the shop and go with you, but I just got in several new orders, and I'd get really behind if we were both gone. Having just hired Dennis Yoder, I can't expect him to take over the shop and know what to do in my absence."

Paul shook his head. "That's okay. You're needed here. I'm sure the folks will understand."

"Please give Dan's widow my condolences."

"I will." Paul turned toward the door.

Faith Hertzler had just stepped onto the back porch to shake one of her braided rugs when she spotted her mother's horse and buggy coming up the driveway.

"Wie geht's?" she asked as Mom stepped onto the porch moments later.

"I'm doing all right, but Margaret Hilty's not holding up so well this morning." Mom's face looked flushed.

Faith draped the rug over the porch railing. "What's wrong with Margaret? Is she *grank?*"

"She's not sick physically, but in here she surely is." Mom placed one hand against her chest. "Dan had a heart attack this morning and died."

"Ach! That's *baremlich!*"

Mom nodded, and her blue eyes darkened. "I know it's terrible. Poor Margaret is just beside herself."

Faith drew in her bottom lip. "I can only imagine. Dan's always seemed healthy. I guess one never knows when their time will be up, so we should always be prepared."

"Jah. Always ready to meet our Maker."

Faith opened the screen door. "Won't you come in and have a cup of tea?"

"Don't mind if I do." Mom's glasses had slipped to the middle of her nose, and she pushed them back in place before entering the house.

The women took seats at the table, and Faith poured some tea. "Would you like some cookies or a slice of cake? Noah made some lemon sponge cake last night, and we still have a few pieces."

Mom gave her stomach a couple of pats. "I'd better pass on the cake. It'll be time for lunch soon, and I don't want to fill up on sweets."

Faith blew on her tea, then took a sip. "Will Dan's brother, Paul, be coming home for the funeral?"

Mom shrugged. "I don't know, but I expect he will."

"I'll try to see Margaret later today. Maybe I'll take her one of Noah's baked goods with a verse of scripture attached."

"That'd be good. Margaret's going to need all the support she can get in the days ahead."

The back door flew open, and Noah's mother, Ida, stepped into the room. "I just talked to Mavis Zook, and she told me that Barbara gave birth to a healthy little *buwe* this morning."

"Another boy?" Mom asked.

Ida nodded. "She's already tired enough trying to run the harness shop and deal with three energetic boys. Now she'll really have her hands full."

"I guess I'd better get over to see Barbara soon," Faith said. "Even though the birth of her son must be a happy time for her, she's probably feeling a bit sad because David isn't here."

The bus ride to Missouri gave Paul plenty of time to think. How was Dan's widow holding up? What kind of reception would he receive from his family? How long would he be expected to stay after the funeral?

Paul thought about that day four years ago when he'd decided to leave home. He had been farming with his dad and brothers since he'd finished the eighth grade—first when they lived in Pennsylvania, where Paul had been born, and later when Pop moved his family to Missouri. Paul had never enjoyed farming. He'd wanted to learn a trade—preferably harness making. But there was already one harness shop in the area, owned by David Zook. Paul didn't figure their small community needed another one, and he was sure David wouldn't hire him, because his wife, Barbara, already worked in the shop.

When Paul's cousin Andy, who ran a harness shop in Lancaster County, Pennsylvania, had invited Paul to come work for him, Paul had jumped at the chance. Paul's mother had said she could understand why he wanted to leave, although she would miss him terribly, but Paul's father had shouted at Paul, calling him a *glotzkeppich naar*.

I may be stubborn, but I'm sure no fool, Paul thought as he gripped the armrest of his seat on the bus. *I like my job, and I'm much happier living in Pennsylvania than I was in Missouri.*

Guilt stabbed Paul's conscience. He liked his work at Andy's harness shop, but he wasn't really happy. Something was missing, but he couldn't figure out what it was. Andy kept telling Paul he needed to find a good wife and have a passel of kinner. Andy had been married to Sharon for five years, and they had three children already. He often said how much joy he found in being a husband and father.

Paul didn't think he would ever get married. He was thirty years old and had never had a serious relationship with a woman. Truth was, Paul was afraid of marriage, because with marriage usually came children, and since Paul had so little patience with kids, he feared he wouldn't make a good father. He figured his dislike of children went two ways, because most of the kids he'd known had avoided him like he had a case of chicken pox.

Paul's thoughts shifted to his brother's untimely death. Dan's passing was only eight months after David Zook died. Mom had written to Paul about the accident that killed David, leaving his wife to raise their three sons and manage the harness shop on her own.

I wonder how Barbara's getting along. Did she hire someone to help in the shop, or could she have sold David's business by now? If she hasn't sold the place yet, maybe she's looking for someone to buy her out.

Paul stared out the bus window, barely noticing the passing scenery. *Don't get any dumb ideas. You're going back to Pennsylvania as soon as Dan's funeral is over.*

Chapter 2

There's no reason for you to stay here with me," Barbara said to her mother, who stood just inside the kitchen doorway. "You and Dad should both go to the funeral."

Mom shook her head vigorously. "And leave you here in a weakened condition with three little ones and a new boppli? I would never do that, daughter."

There was no arguing with her mother once she'd made up her mind about something. Barbara pushed a wayward strand of hair away from her face and grimaced. She hadn't done a good job of putting up her bun this morning. For that matter, she didn't feel as if she had done much of anything right since she'd gotten out of bed. She had yelled at Joseph and Zachary for being too loud, scolded Aaron for picking on his younger brothers, and dropped a carton of eggs in the middle of the kitchen floor. Maybe her weakened condition caused her to have no control over her emotions. Or perhaps it was the fact that Dan Hilty's death had opened up the wounds of losing her husband. In either case, Barbara couldn't go to Dan's funeral. And as much as she didn't want to admit it, she needed her mother's help.

She took a seat at the table. "You're right, Mom. I do need help. Would you be willing to watch the buwe at your house while I tend to the boppli?" She was glad her folks lived next door, making it easy for her to go over for lunch with the boys. She didn't want them to think she had abandoned them now that there was a baby brother in the house.

Mom sat in the chair opposite Barbara and poured some tea. "I'd be happy to look out for your boys." She handed a cup to Barbara. "Your daed's got them out helping with chores. After breakfast, I'll take the boys over to my place and find something to keep everyone occupied so you can rest awhile. You look all done in."

Barbara released a drawn-out sigh. "I'll sure be glad when little David starts sleeping more and eating less often. He woke me every couple of hours last night."

Her mother's blue eyes held a note of sympathy. "All the more reason you should rest during the day whenever possible."

The wooden chair groaned as Barbara leaned against the back. "It's not just the lack of sleep that has me feeling so down."

"What else is bothering you?"

"I'm worried about the harness shop. I appreciate that Dad's been helping me since David died, but he can't run it alone. As you know, his arthritic fingers don't work so good, and there's too much for just one person to do."

Mom tapped her fingernails along the edge of the table. "Maybe you could hire someone to help while you're getting your strength back."

"Who would I hire? No one in our community does harness work, and Dad doesn't know enough about it to teach them." Barbara sniffed. "Dad barely manages when I'm not there to oversee things."

"That's true. Maybe keeping the shop isn't such a good idea." Mom leaned slightly forward. "Have you thought about running an ad in *The Budget* to try and sell off the supplies?"

"I don't think I could part with David's harness shop. It meant too much to him." Barbara stared down at the table as a familiar lump formed in her throat. "And it means a lot to me. I enjoy working there, Mom. Can you understand that?"

"What I understand is that my daughter's been working hard in that shop ever since her husband died—even throughout most of her pregnancy." Mom released a long sigh. "I know you want to prove you can support yourself and the buwe, but you can't do it alone. Your daed will help in the shop as long as he's able, and I'm sure David's folks will help with finances if needed."

Barbara stood. "I won't have you and Dad, or my husband's parents, taking care of us until the boys are raised. That's my job, and I'll do it." She started across the room but turned back around. "I hope you know that I appreciate your concerns and all the help you've offered."

Mom nodded. "I know you do."

"I'm going upstairs to check on the boppli, but I'll be back before Dad and the kinner come in for breakfast."

Barbara was almost to the kitchen door when her mother said, "Say, I just thought of something."

"What's that?"

"I spoke with Faith Hertzler yesterday morning, and she said she'd seen Dan's brother, Paul. Guess he came home for the funeral."

Barbara faced her mother. "I suppose he would."

"Paul's been living in Pennsylvania these last four years. . . working at his cousin's harness shop."

"So I heard."

"Maybe Paul would be willing to stick around awhile and work at your shop. Would you like me to ask your daed to talk with him about it today?"

Barbara shook her head. "Not at his brother's funeral. It wouldn't be proper to discuss anything like that there."

"You're right, of course. How about tomorrow, then?"

"Maybe. Let me think on it awhile."

"You think, and let's both be praying."

Barbara smiled at her mother's exuberance. "Thanks for the reminder, Mom."

"I hope Margaret holds up during the funeral," Faith said to her husband, Noah, who stood at the kitchen counter mixing a batch of pancake batter.

"Margaret's a strong woman. I'm sure she'll do fine with the support of her family." Noah turned to Faith and smiled. His dark eyes matched the thick crop of hair on his head. "When you took the lemon sponge cake over to her the other day, did she read the copy of Isaiah 66:13 that I attached?"

Faith nodded. "She said it was a comfort and that she would save the paper so she would be reminded that the Lord says, 'As one whom his mother comforteth, so will I comfort you.' "

"I always wonder how folks who don't know the Lord make it through difficult times without His comfort," Noah said, reaching for the bottle of fresh goat's milk.

"I know, and that's why we must always pray for others." Faith removed a jug of syrup from the cupboard. "I still haven't made it over to see Barbara, but I'm hoping to do that yet this week. I spoke with Barbara's mamm yesterday, and she said Barbara's been pretty tired since the boppli was born. I guess she won't be going to the funeral today."

"I'm sure Margaret will understand," Noah said as he lit their propane stove and placed a griddle on one of the burners. "If Barbara plans to return to work anytime soon, she'll need to rest and get her strength back."

Faith grunted. "I wish she would sell that harness shop. It's hard work, and I don't think she's up to doing it on her own while she tries to raise four boys."

"Samuel still helps her, right?"

"Jah. He started running the shop by himself the last few weeks of Barbara's pregnancy, and now he'll have to continue running it by himself until she's able to return to work." Faith stroked her chin thoughtfully. "Unless. . ."

Noah quirked an eyebrow. "What are you thinking, Faith?"

"Paul Hilty came home for Dan's funeral. He does harness work in Pennsylvania, so maybe he could stay awhile and help out at Zook's Harness Shop."

Noah pursed his lips while he poured some pancake batter onto the sizzling griddle. "If he's already got a job in Pennsylvania, he'll probably have to get right back to it after the funeral."

"Maybe not. He might have taken several weeks off so he could spend some time with his family." Faith touched Noah's arm. "Would you talk to him about it?"

His eyebrows drew together. "Why me? It was your idea."

"I think it would be more appropriate if you spoke to him, don't you?"

Noah opened his mouth, but their two children, Melinda and Isaiah, scurried into the room, interrupting the conversation.

"Is breakfast ready yet, Papa Noah?" eleven-year-old Melinda asked, sniffing the air. "I'm hungry as a bear."

Noah turned and smiled at her. "What would you know of bears? You've never even seen a bear."

Before Melinda could respond, four-year-old Isaiah spoke up. "Uh-huh. She's seen one in that big book of hers."

"You must mean the one she bought with her birthday money when we visited Bass Pro Shop in Springfield," Faith said.

"That's the one." Melinda smiled, revealing two large dimples in her cheeks. "Can we go to that place again soon, Papa Noah? I sure liked it there."

Noah patted the top of Melinda's blond head. "We'll see, daughter."

Paul left the confines of his folks' house, full of people who had come to the meal following Dan's funeral and graveside service. Some milled about the living room, while others stood outside on the lawn, visiting and offering their condolences.

Paul felt as out of place as a bullfrog in a chicken coop. Mom, his sisters Rebekah and Susan, and his brothers Monroe and Elam had been friendly enough. Pop was a different story. He'd been as cold as a block of ice, and Paul knew why. Pop still resented the fact that Paul had given up farming and had moved back to Pennsylvania to learn a new trade. Since Pop had raised all four of his sons to be farmers, he seemed to think they should farm for the rest of their lives—even if they had other ideas about the kind of work that would make them happy. It wasn't fair. Shouldn't Paul have the right to work at the trade of his choice? Why should Pop expect all of his sons to be farmers just because he had chosen to be one?

Paul hurried past the tables that had been set up on the lawn, where many of the older people sat visiting, and headed straight for the barn. He had to be by himself for a while. He needed time to think. Time to breathe.

As soon as Paul opened the barn door, the familiar aroma of sweaty horses, sweet-smelling hay, and fresh manure assaulted his senses. His ears perked up at the gentle sound of a horse's whinny, and his eyes feasted on the place where he and his siblings used to play.

He glanced at the wooden rafters overhead. The rope swing still hung from one of the beams. So many times his brothers and sisters had argued over who would get the first turn on the swing that transported them from the hayloft to the pile of straw where they would drop at will. Not Paul. He had no desire to dangle from any rope suspended so high.

Paul moved away from the old swing and was about to enter one of the horses' stalls when he heard the barn door squeak open and click shut. He whirled around.

"Hope I didn't startle you," Noah Hertzler said, holding his black felt hat in one hand. "I saw you come into the barn and wanted to offer my condolences on the loss of your brother. Dan will surely be missed. I'm real sorry about his passing."

Paul reached out to clasp Noah's hand. "*Danki.* I appreciate your kind words."

"How have you been?" Noah asked.

"I was doing okay until I got the news that my brother had died."

Noah nodded. "I understand. My grandma passed on a year ago. I still miss her a lot."

Paul swallowed hard. "It's never easy to lose a loved one."

"No, it's not."

A few minutes of silence passed between them; then Noah changed the subject. "Do you like Pennsylvania? Has it changed much since you were a boy?"

"I like it well enough. But the Lancaster area is a lot more crowded than it was when I was growing up." Paul shrugged. "I put up with all the tourists so I can do what I like best."

"You mean harness making and repair?"

Paul nodded. "Andy also sells and fixes leather shoes and boots."

"I'm sure you must've heard about David Zook passing on," Noah said.

"Jah. Such a shame. How's his wife faring? Does she have

anyone to help her in the harness shop?"

Noah shook his head. "Just her daed, and his fingers don't work so good, what with his arthritis and all."

"So it's just Barbara and Samuel?"

"Right now it's only him. Barbara won't be back to work until her strength returns and the new boppli's a bit bigger."

Paul's mouth dropped open. "She's got another child? Mom never mentioned that in any of her letters."

Noah took a seat on a bale of straw, and Paul joined him. "Barbara gave birth to son number four the same day your brother died. David never knew she was in a family way." Noah shook his head. "Barbara's mother-in-law, Mavis, told Faith that Barbara's feeling real tired. That's why she's not here today."

"Wouldn't expect her to be under the circumstances."

Noah cleared his throat. "I. . .uh. . .well, Faith and I were wondering if you might want to stick around awhile. Maybe see about working at Zook's Harness Shop."

Paul felt a rush of adrenaline course through his body. Why couldn't he have been given that opportunity four years ago? "If I did offer my services, it would only be until Barbara gets back on her feet," he said.

"Does that mean you'd never consider moving back to Webster County?"

Paul shook his head. "I doubt it. I only came home for Dan's funeral. Figured I might stay a week or two so I could visit family and friends. My sisters live in Jamesport now, and they're planning to stay here a week. I'll probably stick around that long, too, and then catch a bus back to Pennsylvania."

Noah nodded, and his dark eyes revealed the depth of his

understanding. "Before Faith and I were married, she came home not planning to stay, either."

Paul opened his mouth to say something, but Noah cut him off. "After a time, Faith realized her home was here, and she knew she was supposed to stay." He smiled. "Of course, marrying me was part of the deal."

"Faith didn't have a daed who wanted her to do something she didn't want to do," Paul mumbled. "My daed wants me to farm, and if I stick around too long, he'll start pressing me on the issue."

"As I'm sure you know, Faith was away from home for ten years, telling jokes and yodeling in the English world."

"I remember."

"She and her daed didn't see eye to eye on her yodeling, but he's come to terms with it."

Paul grunted. "Even if Pop and I could mend our fences, I still wouldn't stay here."

"Why not?"

"I like working on harnesses, and there isn't room for two harness shops in this small community."

"Maybe you could work for Barbara indefinitely."

Paul's face heated up. He wasn't about to spend the rest of his life working for Barbara Zook. She shouldn't even be running the harness shop. That was men's work, plain and simple. "Unless Barbara decides to sell out, I won't be staying in Webster County." He moved toward the door, and Noah followed. "I will drop by and see Barbara, though. I need to offer my condolences on the loss of her husband."

Chapter 3

Barbara was napping on the sofa when a knock at the back door wakened her. "Come in!" she called. "I'm in the living room, Mom!"

Moments later, a tall, blond-haired man entered the room. He wore a straw hat, short-sleeved cotton shirt, and dark trousers held up by tan suspenders. "I'm not your mamm, but you did invite me to come in," he said, removing his hat.

Barbara's mouth hung open. "Paul Hilty?"

"Jah, it's me." He shifted his long legs and shuffled his black boots against the hardwood floor. "Sorry if I startled you."

Barbara's hand went instinctively to her hair, as she checked to be sure her *kapp* was in place. She had planned on a short rest and ended up falling into a deep sleep. The baby was sleeping in his crib upstairs, and the boys were at her folks' place. It had been the perfect time to rest. The last thing Barbara expected when she woke up was to see a man standing in her living room. "No, no, that's okay. I mean—it's good to see you."

"And you, as well."

Barbara's cheeks grew warm as she stood and smoothed the wrinkles in her long dress. "I'm sorry I couldn't make it to Dan's funeral yesterday. I had a boppli a few days ago and haven't gotten my strength back yet."

A look of concern clouded Paul's deeply set blue eyes. "I heard that. I also heard about David's death. I came by to tell you how sorry I am."

Barbara sank back to the couch. "It's been a rough eight months," she admitted.

Paul took a couple of steps forward. "I can imagine."

"I'm sorry to hear about your brother, too. It's never easy to lose a loved one."

He shook his head. "No. No, it's not."

"How's Margaret holding up?"

"It was a shock to have Dan die so suddenly, but Margaret's doing as well as can be expected." The sorrowful look on Paul's face showed the depth of his sadness. "As you know, her six kinner are raised and out on their own, but I hope one of them will take her in to live with them. It'll probably be her daughter Karen and her husband, Jake, since they live the closest."

Barbara nodded and swallowed around the lump in her throat. It was hard not to feel sorry for herself. Just thinking about David's and Dan's deaths made her feel weepy.

"Have a seat," she said, finally remembering her manners.

He seated himself in the rocker close to the sofa, looking more uncomfortable by the minute. Barbara hadn't known Paul when they were children, and then he'd moved back to Pennsylvania to work with his cousin. Barbara had heard the move was against his dad's wishes, but she couldn't fault Paul for wanting to work where he felt comfortable. She would do most anything to keep working in David's harness shop.

Only the soft ticking of the mantel clock broke the quiet in the room. Barbara sat with her hands folded in her lap. Paul moved slowly back and forth in the rocker.

Finally, she spoke again. "How have you been? Are you happy living in Lancaster County?"

He stopped rocking and sat straight as a board. "I like working at my cousin's harness shop, but Lancaster's getting a bit overcrowded for my taste."

She was tempted to ask why he stayed but figured it probably had to do with the job he enjoyed. "I hear there's plenty of English and that tourists come by the thousands to get a look at the Plain folks living there."

Paul nodded. "Not like here, where so few tourists seem to know about us."

"They probably wouldn't care anyway, since we're such a small community."

"I suppose you're right about that."

"How long will you be staying in Webster County?" Barbara asked. Should she bring up the harness shop—see if he might be interested in working for her awhile?

He twisted the edge of his hat. "Guess that all depends."

"On what?"

"I had only intended on staying a week or so, but I could stay longer if there was a need."

"You mean if your daed needed you to help on his farm?"

He shook his head. "No way! I gave up farming when I moved, and I'm not about to go back to it again."

"I see."

Paul rubbed the bridge of his nose and leaned forward. "Since David's gone and you're not able to work in the harness shop right now, I thought maybe you might be thinking of selling it."

She shook her head vigorously. "I need to keep it open as long as I'm able."

He nodded. "So would you be needing someone to run the place for you right now?"

Barbara drew in a deep breath as she thought about the verse from Ecclesiastes 4 she'd read the night before: *"Two are better than one; because they have a good reward for their labour. For if they fall, the one will lift up his fellow: but woe to him that is alone when he falleth; for he hath not another to help him up."* She wondered if Paul's showing up was a sign from God that she was supposed to accept his help.

"I could use some help in the harness shop," she reluctantly admitted. "Dad's working, but his fingers won't let him do a lot, and it's going to be a few more weeks before I can return to work."

"That's what I figured."

"What about your job? Can your cousin get by without your help for a few weeks?"

He shrugged. "Don't see why not. When I called from Seymour to let him know I'd gotten here okay, he said he'd just hired on another part-time man. Unless things get busier than they have been, I'm sure Andy won't mind if I stay here awhile and help in David's shop."

"It's my shop now," Barbara corrected.

"Right. I understand, and I—"

The sound of a baby's cry halted Paul's words.

Barbara jumped up. "That's little David. I should tend to him."

Paul stood. "I can come back some other time."

She waved her hand. "That's okay. Why don't you make yourself comfortable while I tend to the boppli? When I'm done, we can talk more about the possibility of you working in the harness shop."

He sat down again. "Sounds fine to me."

Barbara started for the stairs but turned back. "If you'd like some coffee, go on out to the kitchen and help yourself to a cup. I think there's still some in the pot on the stove." She hurried from the room before he had a chance to respond, glad for the opportunity to think more about Paul's offer.

Paul remained in his chair for several minutes after Barbara went upstairs. The baby's crying had stopped, so he figured she must have things under control.

He couldn't believe how much Barbara had changed since he'd seen her four years ago. She used to be kind of plump, but now she was much thinner—almost too thin to his way of thinking. Had the years of working in the harness shop taken their toll, or had she lost the weight after David died? He'd heard of people nearly starving themselves to death when a mate had been taken, but Barbara was a new mother. It seemed to Paul that she should weigh a lot more than she did.

One more reason I need to stick around for a while and help out. She probably doesn't eat right because she worries about the harness shop and how she'll provide for her family.

Paul stood in front of the unlit fireplace. It was late spring, getting too warm for any fires.

Barbara's a fine-looking woman. Funny I never paid much attention to her before. He shook his head, trying to get himself thinking straight again. Of course he wouldn't have eyed Barbara before. She had been married to David Zook, and it wouldn't have been right for him to pay special attention to her. David and Barbara had already been courting by the time Paul and his family moved to Webster County. Even if Paul had noticed Barbara when she was still a Raber, it wouldn't have done him any good. She'd been David's girl from the very beginning. If he had taken an interest in her back then, their courtship would have ended before either of them had a chance to get serious. That's how it had always been with the women Paul had courted. Maybe it was because they knew he was leery of marriage. Besides, Barbara was two years older than Paul and probably wouldn't have given him a second glance during their teen years.

Might as well get myself a cup of coffee, he decided. *It will give me something to do until she gets back, and hopefully it'll keep me from all this crazy thinking.*

In the kitchen, Paul found a pot of coffee warming on the stove. He located a man-sized mug and had just poured himself some coffee when he heard the back door swing open and bang against the wall.

When he turned, a young boy with brunette hair and dark eyes like Barbara's faced him.

"Who are you, and what are ya doin' with my pa's coffee mug?" The child planted his hands on his hips.

Paul forced a smile. He didn't like the way the boy was staring at him. "I'm Paul Hilty. You must be one of Barbara's boys."

The lad thrust out his chin and pushed back his shoulders, but he didn't return Paul's smile. "My name's Aaron. I'm her oldest son."

Paul opened his mouth to reply, but Aaron cut him off. "When I grow up, I plan to take over Pa's harness shop." He stared down at Paul's black boots. "My mom'll be old by then and probably won't wanna work on harnesses no more."

Paul chuckled. Aaron scowled at him. "What's so funny?"

"Nothing. I mean, it seems odd that a young fellow like you would be talking about your mamm getting old and you taking her place in the shop."

"I don't think it's funny a'tall."

Paul took a sip of coffee and seated himself at the table, but the boy didn't budge.

"You still haven't said why you're in my mamm's kitchen, usin' my daed's mug."

Paul eyed the cup in question, then nodded toward the empty chair to his left. "Sit down, and I'll tell you."

Aaron flopped into a chair.

"I came over to see how your mamm was doing, and then the boppli started fussing. So your mamm said I should help myself to some coffee while she took care of your little bruder."

"But you shouldn't be usin' Pa's cup," the child persisted.

Paul was tempted to remind Aaron that his father was dead and it shouldn't matter who drank from his cup, but he thought better of it. No use getting the boy riled, especially if Barbara decided to hire Paul in the harness shop. Aaron undoubtedly still missed his father. The idea of someone using his mug could be a powerful reminder of the boy's loss.

Paul went to the cupboard and got out a different mug; then he placed David's mug in the kitchen sink. "Better?" he asked as he returned to his seat.

The boy nodded.

For several minutes, they sat in silence. Unable to tolerate the boy staring at him, Paul finally asked, "How old are you, Aaron?"

"Almost nine."

"Guess it won't be long until you can begin helping your mamm in the shop."

The child shrugged. "Used to help my daed some when I wasn't in school."

"What grade are you in?"

"Second."

"You have six more years, then."

"Jah."

Paul took another swig of coffee, wishing Barbara would return so he'd have another adult to talk to. His uneasiness around children was intensified with Aaron looking at him so strangely.

"Want some cookies to dunk in your coffee?"

Aaron's question took Paul by surprise, and he jumped.

"What's the matter? You got a fly on your nose?"

"Huh?"

"You're kind of jumpy, wouldn't ya say?"

Paul cleared his throat. "I'm fine. Just a bit restless is all."

"Some cookies might help."

Paul studied the boy's round face. He was pretty sure the subject of cookies had come up because Aaron wanted some, not because he thought Paul needed something to dunk in his coffee.

"You're right. A few cookies would be nice." Paul glanced around the room. "You know where there might be some?"

Aaron dashed across the room. He returned with a green ceramic jar. "These are chocolate chip." He set the container on the table and headed for the refrigerator. "Think I'll have some milk so's I can dunk."

Paul remembered how he had enjoyed cookies and cold goat's milk when he was a boy. Peanut butter with raisins had been his favorite, and his mother used to make them often. He watched Aaron fill a tall glass with milk, dip his cookie up and down a couple of times, then chomp it down in two bites.

"This is sure good. Grandma made these just for me."

"Your grandparents live next door, don't they?"

Aaron grabbed another cookie. "Jah. Grandma Raber keeps an eye on me and my little *brieder* during the day. Grandma and Grandpa Zook live a couple miles down the road."

"Where are your brothers right now?"

"Still at Grandma's."

"Does your grandma know where you are?" Paul questioned.

"Of course. Told her I was comin' over here to see if Mama needed me for anything." Aaron licked a glob of chocolate off his fingertips. "Sure never expected to find a stranger sittin' in our kitchen, though."

"I'm not really a stranger," Paul said. "I used to live in Webster County. I've known your folks for some time."

"It's your bruder who died last week, ain't it?"

"Jah, my brother Dan. His funeral was yesterday."

"When you said your last name, I put two and two together."

"I see." *Aaron's not only feisty, but he seems to be a right smart little fellow.*

"What'd ya come over to see Mama about?"

"He's coming to work for me starting Saturday."

Paul turned his head. He hadn't realized Barbara had entered the room. She held a baby in her arms, and her face was slightly flushed.

Aaron glared at Paul; then he turned to face his mother and gave her an imploring look. "Why do you need him, Mama?"

"Because I'm not able to work right now."

"What about Grandpa? He's still workin' in the harness shop, right?"

Barbara nodded. "But your *grossdaadi* isn't able to handle things on his own so well."

Aaron puffed out his chest. "I could help him."

"I'm sure you could help with a few things, but not nearly enough, son."

Feeling the need to make a quick escape, Paul pushed back his chair and stood. "I should head to Seymour and call my cousin to let him know that I'll be staying awhile longer." He glanced down at Aaron, then back at Barbara. "I'll be at the harness shop bright and early."

She gave him a weary-looking smile and nodded. "Danki."

Paul had just stepped onto the front porch when a horse and buggy pulled into the yard.

As John Frey stepped down from his buggy, he spotted Paul Hilty leaving Barbara's house. "I wonder what he's doing here," he mumbled.

"What was that, Papa?"

John glanced over at his fourteen-year-old daughter, Nadine, who had followed him out of the buggy. He'd dropped Hannah and Mary, his two younger girls, off at one of their neighbors' so they could play with their friend Maddie. And since Betty, his oldest daughter, was working and he didn't want to make his calls alone, he had invited Nadine to join him. "I just wondered what Paul Hilty is doing here," he said.

"Probably came by to pay his respects to Barbara since he wasn't here when her husband died." Nadine smiled sweetly. "I can hardly wait to see Barbara's new boppli. Maybe she'll let me hold him awhile."

John smiled in response. He had enjoyed holding his four girls when they were babies, but they were all older now, ranging in ages from ten to sixteen. He missed having a baby around. He also needed a mother for his daughters and hoped Barbara Zook might be willing to marry him. She was still young and could provide him with more children, as well as take charge of his household and give proper womanly instruction to his girls, so he figured she was the perfect choice. John had been widowed six months and Barbara for nearly a year. It was time for them to find new mates. Besides, he didn't think Barbara could keep working in the harness shop now that she had a new baby to care for. She needed a husband to support her and the boys.

"*Guder mariye*, Bishop Frey," Paul said, as he passed John on the way to his buggy.

"Good morning to you, too." John was on the verge of asking the reason for Paul's visit, but Paul gave a quick wave and sprinted to his buggy.

John shrugged and hurried after Nadine, who was already on the porch. Moments later, Barbara opened the door.

"Bishop John," she said. "What brings you out our way?"

"Came to see how you're getting along." He motioned to Nadine. "And Nadine would like to get a look at your boppli, if that's all right."

"Jah, sure." Barbara opened the door wider and bid them in. "I just put Davey in his cradle, but he's wide awake."

John and Nadine followed Barbara to the living room, and John took a seat on the sofa while Nadine rushed over to the wooden cradle sitting near the rocking chair.

"He's so *siess*," Nadine said dreamily.

"I think he's pretty sweet, too." Barbara smiled. "Would you like to hold him?"

"Oh, jah," Nadine replied with an eager nod. She took a seat in the rocking chair, and Barbara placed the baby in her arms.

"He feels so good. I can't wait until I'm married and have some *bopplin* of my own."

"Babies are a lot of work, but they bring many joys," Barbara said as she took a seat on the opposite end of the sofa from John.

John cleared his throat a couple of times. "We missed you at Dan Hilty's funeral. How have you been getting along?" he asked.

"I'm still feeling kind of tired, but I'm doing okay."

"Would you like me to send one of my girls over to help out? Betty's taken a job at the general store, but I'm sure either Hannah or Nadine would be glad to help you."

"I appreciate the offer, but I'm managing with the help of my mamm."

"How's Samuel doing in the harness shop? Is he able to keep up with the work now that you're not there to help?"

Barbara shook her head. "Due to Dad's arthritis, he struggles to get many things done. Paul Hilty's going to be helping in the shop for a while, so between the two of them, they'll be able to keep things going until I'm able to work again."

John's eyebrows drew together. "Are you sure you ought to return to work?"

Barbara nodded. "I enjoy working in the harness shop."

"That may be so, but it's hard work."

Barbara simply watched Nadine rock the baby.

"Have you considered selling the shop?"

She shook her head. "As long as I'm able to keep it open, I won't sell the place."

Unsure of what to say, John leaned against the sofa, folded his arms, and listened to the steady *tick-tock* of the clock mingling with the rhythmic *creak-creak* of the rocking chair. Finally, John rose to his feet. "Guess we should get going. I want to pay a call on Margaret Hilty and see how she's doing."

"I was sorry to hear of her loss," Barbara said as she stood.

"Will she be moving in with her daughter and son-in-law?"

John shook his head. "From what I've heard, Karen and Jake plan to rent their house out and move in with Margaret. It'll be easier for her if she's not alone, and I don't think she wants to leave her home right now."

"I can understand that." When the baby started squirming, Barbara leaned over and took him from Nadine. "I think he's about ready to be fed."

Nadine cast a furtive glance in John's direction. "I wish we didn't have to leave so soon."

"I think we'd better," he said, moving toward the door.

Barbara walked with them, and John was about to step onto the porch when an idea struck him. "You know, Margaret could use some encouragement, and since you lost your husband and know what it feels like to be left alone, maybe you could be helpful to Margaret."

"Helpful how?"

"Well, I know you can't get out much right now, with having a new boppli and all, but would it be all right if I encourage Margaret to come by and visit?"

"Certainly."

"Margaret's really good with flowers, so maybe she'd even be willing to help weed your garden. I'll make mention of it when I get over to her house."

"Well, I—"

"I'll be back to see you again soon." John smiled, gave Nadine a little nudge, and headed for his buggy. If things went as he hoped, in a few months he'd have a new wife, and then Barbara wouldn't have to work at the harness shop anymore.

Chapter 4

Paul was about to enter Zook's Harness Shop Saturday morning, but he slowed his pace, still unsure if he had made the right decision. *Maybe it won't be so bad. Barbara did say she would be staying at the house to do paperwork and tend to her children.* He would pretty much be in charge of things since Samuel Raber had arthritis and, according to Barbara, didn't know a great deal about the business.

As Paul opened the door and stepped into the shop, he drew in a deep breath. The smell of raw leather, savory neat's-foot oil, and pungent dye hung in the air. He glanced around. Several harnesses and bridles were looped from ceiling hooks. Enormous sheets of loosely rolled leather, looking like cinnamon sticks, poured out of shelves along one side of the shop. Hundreds of snaps, rings, buckles, and rivets nestled in open boxes lined neatly along one wall. Piled on the cement floor were bits of leather scraps, resembling spaghetti noodles. It was a comfortable feeling to be inside the harness shop. He'd only been gone from his cousin's place a few days, and already he missed it. But Andy and his part-time helpers were doing okay without him, and Andy didn't seem to mind if Paul stayed to help Barbara in her hour of need.

Paul saw no sign of Samuel, so he headed toward the back of the building. Two oversized sewing machines run by an air compressor sat side by side on a heavy table. A row of tools spilled out of round wooden holders on the wide workbench nearby. "Hello," he called. "Anybody here?"

Barbara's father stepped out of the back room, limping slightly as he ambled toward him. When Samuel clasped Paul's shoulder, Paul took notice of the older man's red, arthritic fingers.

Paul cleared his throat. "I. . .uh. . . assume Barbara told you I'd be working here awhile."

Samuel smiled through the reddish beard that matched his hair. "It'll be good to have you helping." He held up his hands. "These fingers don't work so good anymore. And to tell you the truth, when Barbara's not here to show me what to do, I often flounder."

Paul nodded. "I'll do whatever I can to help."

Samuel made a sweeping gesture. "Assembling a harness can be complicated. It involves dozens of snaps, straps, and buckles, all connected in a particular way." He grinned, and his cheeks flamed. "Guess you already know that, what with working at a harness shop in Pennsylvania and all."

"Jah, I've been working for my cousin Andy."

"You like it better there?"

Paul shrugged. "It's okay. But Lancaster County has become awful crowded."

Samuel frowned. "I guess some folks don't mind crowded areas, but I'd never want to live anyplace but here. There's nothing like the quiet, peaceful life; that's what I've got to say."

"So what jobs are needing to be done right now?" Paul asked.

Samuel motioned toward the desk near the front door. "There's a folder with all the job orders over there, and I'm way behind."

Paul rolled up his cotton shirtsleeves, eager to get busy. "I'll take a look-see."

Alice released a weary sigh as she placed a kettle of water on the stove to heat. Zachary and Joseph were playing in the living room, but ever since the boys had arrived, Aaron had just sat at the kitchen table and doodled on a piece of paper.

"Aaron, why don't you take your brothers and go outside for a while," Alice suggested. "It's a nice day, and the fresh air and sunshine will do you all some good."

"Don't feel like playing."

"What do you feel like doing?"

Aaron shrugged.

"Would you like to help me bake some cookies?"

"Bakin' is women's work."

Alice sat down beside him. "That's not true, Aaron. Look at

Noah Hertzler; he's always helping his wife in the kitchen, and he bakes lots of tasty treats that he shares with others."

Aaron grunted. "I don't care about bakin'."

"But you enjoy eating the cookies I make."

He nodded, and his eyes brightened some. "You got any oatmeal cookies, Grandma?"

She chuckled and patted his arm. "No, but I can surely make some."

"That'd be good."

"Are you sure you wouldn't like to help?"

"Naw."

"Why don't you go out to the harness shop and see if you can help your grossdaadi and Paul?"

Aaron's nose wrinkled like some foul odor had come into the room. "If it was just Grandpa workin' in the shop, I might, but not with Paul Hilty there."

Alice frowned. "What have you got against Paul?"

Aaron shrugged.

"You know your mamm's not able to work in the harness shop right now," Alice said. "So she's hired Paul to take her place until she gets her strength back."

"Couldn't she have found someone else?"

"No one in these parts knows much about harness making, and Paul works in a harness shop in Pennsylvania."

Aaron made little circles on the paper with his pencil. Finally, he pushed back his chair and stood. "Guess I'll go see what Joseph and Zachary are up to."

"Okay. I'll call you when I've got some cookies baked."

Aaron strolled out of the kitchen, and Alice got out a box of tea for the water she'd heated. She was worried enough about Barbara these days. Now with Aaron acting so moody, she had one more thing to be concerned about.

Barbara glanced at the battery-operated clock above the refrigerator as she poured herself a cup of tea. It was eight fifteen, and she'd sent the boys over to her mother's. She hadn't slept well because the baby had been fussy and demanded several feedings. She wished she could go back to bed, but she had some bills to pay, as well as a stack of paperwork that needed attention.

Barbara yawned and moved over to the window. An open buggy sat next to the harness shop. She figured it must be Paul's. Most of their customers didn't show up this early.

Barbara felt a sense of relief knowing her father would have help in the shop, but part of her bristled at the thought of anyone taking her place. She so missed working with leather.

"I need to eat enough, rest more, and get my strength back so I can work in the shop again," she murmured as she took a seat at the table. "Then Paul will be free to return to Pennsylvania."

Barbara's hand trembled as she set down her cup. She'd been much weaker since Davey's birth than she had been after her other boys were born. Maybe she'd done too much during her pregnancy. Perhaps she'd lost more blood with this delivery and that had left her feeling so tired. Or maybe she was emotionally drained, having had to go through the ordeal without her husband by her side.

She massaged her temples, trying to keep the threatening

tears at bay. Feeling sorry for herself wouldn't help a thing. She was on her own to care for her family, and because she was so weak, she needed Paul's help.

Barbara stood. "What I need to do is go upstairs and check on the boppli. Then I'll get busy with those bills."

Paul stood at the workbench, focused on the job at hand. Connecting the breast strap of a harness to a huge, three-way snap required some fancy looping. His hand wove in and out, neatly tacking the strap at the end.

"That's some fine work," Samuel said as he peered over Paul's shoulder. "It's clear you know exactly what you're doing."

Paul shrugged. "Took me awhile to get the hang of it when I first started, but I've done this type of thing many times."

Samuel stepped over a pile of dirty leather straps and buckles. "Always got lots of harnesses people bring in to get cleaned and repaired." He grunted. "If they'd take better care of 'em, they'd pretty well last forever."

"You're right about that," Paul agreed. "Folks need to bring their harnesses in for cleaning and oiling at least once a year, but unfortunately, many don't."

Samuel bent down and picked up a leather strap. "With my arthritic hands, cleaning things like this is about the only thing I do well here in the shop. I put the dirty ones in a tub of warm water with saddle soap, then scrub 'em real good."

Paul was about to comment, but a truck rumbled into the yard and stopped in front of the shop. A middle-aged English man ambled in, lugging a worn-out saddle, which he dropped on the floor. "Need to have this gone over. Can you do that for me, Sam?"

"If it's just a good cleaning you're after, I can manage it fine. But if the saddle needs a lot of fixing, then here's your man." Samuel motioned to Paul. "Paul Hilty, meet Frank Henderson. He lives up near Springfield."

"It's nice to meet you," Paul said, extending his hand.

"Howdy." As Frank returned the handshake, he looked a bit perplexed. "Where's Barbara? Isn't she working here anymore?"

"My daughter had a baby a few days ago, so she's taking some time away from the shop. Paul's from Pennsylvania. He came here for his brother's funeral and has agreed to help out until she's able to handle things again."

Paul squatted down and studied the worn-looking saddle. It needed more than soap and water, but he was sure it could be salvaged. "We'll give it a good going-over." He looked up at Samuel. "You want to write up the work order, or should I?"

Samuel shrugged. "Makes no never mind to me. Until Barbara returns, you're the boss."

Paul thought about Barbara and how pale and thin she appeared. As far as he was concerned, a delicate woman like her ought to be at home caring for her kinner, not trying to run a business—especially one that often required heavy lifting.

"Why don't you write up the order?" Paul said to Samuel. "I'll get back to work on that breast strap." He nodded at Frank. "Nice to meet you. We'll drop a card in the mail when your saddle is done."

"Appreciate that."

Paul turned back to his job.

Two more customers showed up that morning. Paul took time out to meet them and see what they needed, but he left the paperwork to Barbara's father.

A bit later, Samuel touched his shoulder. "Aaron just popped by to say that there's food on the table. Are you coming up to the house for the noon meal?"

Paul had been so caught up in his work that he hadn't realized it was lunchtime. "How come the boy's home from school today?" he asked.

"It's Saturday. No school until Monday, and then only a few weeks until the kinner will be out for the summer."

"Oh." Paul had been out of school for so long that he'd forgotten the summer break began in early May.

"So you comin' up to the house or not?"

"I. . .uh. . .brought my lunch pail along. Figured I'd eat out here."

Samuel shook his head. "No way. You been working hard all morning and need a hot meal. Alice has probably got a place set for you at the table. Believe me when I say you don't want to disappoint that wife of mine."

"Well, I—"

"Barbara and the boys will be joining us, and I'm sure she'd like to hear how your first day has been going."

"Guess I'd better say jah, then."

Samuel grinned. "Glad to hear it."

Chapter 5

"How come such a big meal today?" Barbara asked when she saw all the food sitting out in her mother's kitchen.

Mom placed a platter of ham in the center of the table and smiled. "I figured your daed would be bringing Paul Hilty up to the house for lunch, and I know how hungry those men can be after working all morning."

An image of David popped into Barbara's head. She remembered him saying many times that the noon meal needed to be the heartiest of the day. *"Fuels the body after working all morning and gives one strength for the afternoon,"* he used to say.

Barbara's mother touched her arm. "You still look tired. Didn't you get a nap this morning?"

"Every time I tried to lie down, Davey started to fuss. Now the little fellow's fast asleep in the portable crib we set up in your spare bedroom."

Mom clucked her tongue. "Isn't that the way? As a baby, your sister Clara was always wide awake when she should have been sleeping."

"You had five daughters with completely different personalities, and I've been blessed with four boys who are equally different." Barbara sighed. "I wish my sisters still lived nearby."

"I miss them, too," Mom agreed. "But I'm glad you're close by."

Barbara smiled. "What can I do to help with the meal?"

Mom shook her head. "Everything's about ready, so sit down and relax until the *mannsleit* and buwe come inside."

"Speaking of the boys, where are my other three? Haven't seen or heard from them all morning."

"A few minutes ago, I sent Aaron to the harness shop to tell the menfolk lunch was ready. The two younger ones have been playing on the back porch."

Barbara sat down. "I hope Aaron does what you asked. He used to help his daed with little things in the shop, but since David's death, he seems to have lost interest." She sighed. "Now I can barely get him to go in the shop at all."

Mom placed a bowl of coleslaw on the table. "The boy probably misses his daed, and being in the shop is a reminder that David's gone."

"Maybe so." Tears sprang to Barbara's eyes. "Aaron reminds me of David in so many ways. He enjoys working with his hands, and he's got his daed's determined spirit."

"Maybe someday, when you're ready to give up the shop, he'll take it over."

Barbara nodded. "He's not old enough to do a whole lot out

there yet, but after he finishes eighth grade and is ready to learn a trade, we'll see if he has any interest in the harness business."

Her mother smiled. "If he takes after his mamm, he surely will."

When Paul entered the Rabers' kitchen, the first person he saw was Barbara. She sat at the table, holding the baby in her arms. He halted inside the door and stared. The sight of her kissing the infant's downy, dark head brought a lump to his throat. He'd seen plenty of women with babies, but never had it affected him like this. It made him long to be a husband—but a father? No way! He didn't have the patience for that.

What's the matter with me? I shouldn't even be thinking about marriage or children. Maybe I worked too hard this morning and it addled my brain.

"Hello, Paul," Barbara said. "How'd it go in the shop?"

He hung his straw hat on the closest wall peg. "Everything went fine. There's a lot to be done out there, that's for sure."

She nodded. "With me not being able to work for the few weeks before the baby came, we really got behind."

"We'll catch up quick with this man minding the shop," Samuel said, following Paul into the kitchen. "I've never seen anyone work as hard as him."

Paul's ears burned, and he reached up to rub them, hoping to hide his embarrassment.

"I–I'm glad to hear it." Barbara's voice wavered when she spoke, and she stared down at her baby.

Alice Raber lumbered across the room, her generous frame pushing at the seams of her long blue dress. "If you men have already washed, then sit yourselves down at the table, and I'll call the boys inside."

"We cleaned up in the harness shop," Samuel said, "so we're ready to eat."

"I'll be right back," his wife said and went out the door.

Samuel sat down at the head of the table, then motioned for Paul to take a seat.

Paul complied but shifted uncomfortably in his chair. He felt out of place.

Barbara seemed equally ill at ease. She kept her attention on the baby.

The tantalizing aroma of sugar-cured ham tickled Paul's nose and made his stomach rumble. This meal was bound to taste better than the cold sandwich and apple he'd brought to work. Struggling to come up with something intelligent to say, Paul felt relief when Alice returned with three young boys in tow.

"Paul, these are Barbara's boys," she said, tapping each one on the shoulder. "This is Aaron—he's close to nine. Joseph's nearly six, and Zachary is three and a half."

Paul nodded as the boys took their seats. "I met Aaron the other day. It's nice to meet the rest of you."

The two younger ones giggled, and Joseph nudged Aaron. Paul didn't know what they found so amusing. Could they be laughing at him? Maybe so. He remembered one of the young English boys who'd come into Andy's harness shop not long ago had laughed at him, saying he was so tall he looked like a beanpole.

As soon as Alice sat down, Samuel cleared his throat, pulling

Paul's thoughts aside. Everyone at the table bowed their heads for silent prayer. When Samuel cleared his throat a second time, it was time to eat.

"Why don't you let me put the boppli in the crib?" Barbara's mother suggested. "That way you'll have both hands free to eat."

"I'm good at doing things with one hand." Barbara glanced at Paul and caught him staring at her. *Does he think I'm overly protective?* She looked away and reached for her glass of water.

"You're not going to let me put the boppli down?" Mom persisted.

Barbara lifted the infant and placed him across her shoulder. "He's fine, and so am I."

Mom shrugged.

Barbara speared a piece of ham with her fork and realized as soon as it touched her plate that it would be difficult to cut with only one hand. Little David was almost asleep; she could feel the warmth of his head against her neck and hear his even breathing. A weary sigh escaped her lips. "Maybe I will put him down."

She sensed Paul's eyes upon her again as she stood and slipped out of the room.

When she returned a few minutes later, Dad and Paul were engaged in conversation, while Mom looked content overseeing the boys. Barbara lingered in the kitchen doorway. Everyone seemed to be enjoying the meal and the camaraderie. She knew it was silly, but Barbara felt out of place. Since she wasn't working in the harness shop, she had nothing to contribute to the conversation the men were having.

A sudden wave of dizziness hit Barbara with the force of a strong wind, and a need to sit swept over her. She had to eat something, even if her appetite was gone.

She moved slowly to the table and sat down.

"Did you get the little one settled?" her mother asked as she poured a glass of milk for Zachary.

Barbara took a sip of water, hoping to dispel the feeling of nausea she felt every time she looked at food. This was worse than morning sickness. "Jah, he's fast asleep. It's his second nap this morning," she said with a weary sigh.

Mom studied Barbara intently. "I can see by the dark circles under your eyes that you're not getting enough sleep. Would it help if I started keeping the older boys at our place during the night?"

Barbara took a bite of coleslaw, but it could have been shreds of straw for all the enjoyment she got from it. She knew why she was tired but didn't understand the depression she'd been plagued with or her lack of interest in food. It wasn't good for her or the baby.

"Daughter, did you hear what I said about keeping the boys overnight?"

"The older ones aren't keeping me awake."

Mom reached across the table and patted Barbara's hand. "This boppli sleeps less than the others did, jah?"

Barbara nodded. "I wouldn't mind being up half the night if I could make up for it during the day. But I'm way behind paying the bills and sending out orders for supplies needed at the shop."

Paul spoke up. "Is there anything I can do to help? I'd be

glad to send out the orders for you."

Barbara bristled. *He's already doing my job in the shop, and now he wants to take over the paperwork, too?* She forced a polite smile while she shook her head. "Danki for the offer, but I can manage."

Paul shrugged and took another piece of ham.

Barbara pursed her lips. Did he think she was unappreciative? Didn't the man realize how badly she needed to take part in her own business? She cut her meat. *If only I wasn't so weak. If I could work in the harness shop, I might not feel so useless.* She felt like bursting into tears for no good reason as she swallowed the ham and washed it down with a gulp of water. *Am I experiencing postpartum depression, still missing David, or just out of sorts because I'm feeling so drained?*

"Grandpa, can I help in the harness shop this afternoon?" Aaron asked.

"I reckon it would be all right, if your mamm has no objections." Barbara's dad swung his gaze over to Paul. "And if it's okay with Paul."

A muscle along the side of Paul's cheek twitched.

Barbara was happy to hear that her oldest boy had an interest in the shop again, but Paul seemed uncomfortable with the idea. "Aaron, maybe you should wait for another Saturday when I'm back working in the shop," she suggested.

The boy's forehead wrinkled. "But that might take a long time. Grandma says you're real tired, and the boppli's gonna need you for a while."

Barbara couldn't deny it. She might not be able to return to work for several weeks. She glanced at Paul again to gauge his reaction. He looked as uncomfortable as when he'd first entered the room. "If Grandpa and Paul are both okay with it, then you can help a few hours this afternoon."

Paul reached up and rubbed his jaw. "I guess we could use some help cleaning up the place."

"Is that all?" Aaron scrunched up his nose. "I'll bet if my daed was still alive, he'd let me do some fun stuff. Always did before."

"We're out there to work, not have fun," Paul said with a frown.

Barbara stiffened. "You don't have to be so harsh with the boy. He meant no disrespect."

Paul's face turned bright red. "I was just stating facts."

"I think working in the harness shop is fun," she asserted.

Mom's head bobbed up and down. "That's right. Why, I can't tell you how many times I've heard Barbara say how much fun she has in the shop. Of course, that's not to say I agree with her. Personally, I think harness making is too hard for a woman, and I've told my daughter so many times."

Obviously, neither Paul nor her mother saw things the way Barbara did. She grabbed a deviled egg and bit into it, determined to get her strength back. As soon as she was on her feet again, she would be ready to take over the shop. Then Paul Hilty could hightail it right back to Pennsylvania.

"I think I hear Davey, so I'd better go check on him." She rushed out of the room.

Alice stared at her daughter's retreating form. Why was Barbara being so unfriendly? She seemed almost rude to Paul. Didn't she appreciate that he had agreed to take over the harness shop until she could return to work? And why did Paul seem so testy with Aaron? It was no wonder the boy shied away from him.

"So, what's for dessert?" Samuel asked, smiling over at Alice.

"I made a fresh batch of oatmeal cookies this morning, and we've got some applesauce to go with them."

"I'll have some," Samuel said with a nod.

"Me, too," Joseph put in.

Alice looked at Aaron, but he only shrugged. She turned to Paul and said, "What about you?"

"Dessert sounds good, but I think I should get back to work. Danki for inviting me to join you for the meal. It was very good." He pushed his chair away from the table, grabbed his hat, and headed out the door.

Alice looked at Samuel. "Do you want to take your dessert with you so you can get back to work?"

Samuel shook his head. "Paul's real capable. I think he can manage without my help awhile."

He looked over at Aaron. "You comin' out to the shop with me, boy?"

"Huh-uh."

"Why not? I thought you wanted to help."

Aaron shook his head. "Not today, Grandpa."

Samuel shrugged, glanced at Alice, and lifted his eyebrows. He was probably thinking the same thing she was—that it would be great when Barbara got her strength back and things returned to normal.

Chapter 6

I'm glad Mom could watch the kinner this afternoon so we could make this trip," Faith said to Noah as they traveled down the road in their open buggy toward Barbara Zook's place. "I really need to check on Barbara."

"And I need to visit the harness shop." Noah smiled. "So it works out well for both of us."

They rode in silence awhile; then Faith spoke again. "I'm worried about Barbara."

"Why's that?"

"I talked with Alice the other day, and she said Barbara is awfully tired and acting depressed. She thinks this baby drained Barbara's strength more than the other three did and wonders if she's feeling down because it might be some time before she's up to working at the harness shop again."

"Maybe she shouldn't return to work at all. Maybe she should sell the harness shop and concentrate on raising her boys."

"I've thought the same thing." Faith sighed. "I think my good friend needs a husband."

Noah raised his brows. "Have you got anyone in mind?"

"Not really, but—"

He reached for her hand. "Now don't go trying to play matchmaker, Faith."

"Of course not. I don't know of any available men here in our community other than Bishop John. And he's much older than Barbara, so I doubt she'd be interested in him."

Noah squinted. "Do you really think age matters so much?"

"Well, no, I suppose not." She poked his arm playfully. "After all, I'm a few years older than you."

"Jah, but only a few."

"Since I don't know who would be right for Barbara, I promise I won't try to play matchmaker, but I can sure pray about the matter. She needs a husband, and her boys certainly need a daed."

Noah nodded. "Speaking of a daed, my boss, Hank, is a lot happier since he and Sandy adopted little Johnny.

She smiled, remembering how, soon after she'd returned to Webster County, she had talked to Hank's wife about her inability to have children and how pleased Sandy had been once she and Hank had decided to adopt.

Faith placed both hands across her stomach and struggled with her swirling emotions. Despite the fact that she'd been blessed with two special children, she longed to have more. But that was not to be.

For the last few weeks, Barbara had kept pretty much to herself. She was tempted to go out to the harness shop to see how things were going but didn't want Paul to think she was checking up on him. Besides, she felt uncomfortable and defensive around him.

Barbara stared out the kitchen window. Two Amish buggies and a truck were parked in front of the harness shop. Business was obviously picking up. If Paul weren't helping out, they would probably have to turn customers away.

A knock at the front door halted her thoughts. "Now who would be using that door?" she muttered.

When Barbara opened the door, her friend Faith Hertzler stood on the porch. "Guder mariye, Barbara. I brought you one of Noah's lemon sponge cakes."

"Good morning to you, too. The cake looks delicious."

Faith smiled, and her blue eyes fairly twinkled as she stepped into the living room. "I thought it might fatten you up a bit. You're looking awful skinny."

Barbara took the cake and motioned Faith to take a seat on the couch. "I'll put this in the kitchen and bring us a cup of tea," she said.

"Sounds good. Oh, and Noah attached a verse of scripture to the cake. I added a little joke on the back side of the paper."

Barbara nodded and smiled. "That doesn't surprise me at all."

A few minutes later, she returned with two cups of hot tea.

She handed one to Faith and took a seat in the rocker across from her. "How come you used the front door?"

"Noah's out in the harness shop seeing about having some new bridles made. As I was heading up to your house, I spotted your three boys playing in the front yard and went to visit with them a few minutes." Faith chuckled. "I was too lazy to walk around back after the kinner and I finished chatting."

Barbara frowned. "Aaron's home from school already? I didn't realize it was that late."

"School let out early today. It's the last day of school, you know."

"Oh, that's right." Barbara thumped the side of her head. She didn't know why she hadn't remembered. It made her feel as if she were losing control when she forgot something. "Where are your kinner? Are they outside playing with my three?"

Faith shook her head. "We left them with my folks. Noah and I are going to Seymour to shop; then he's taking me to Baldy's Café for some barbecued ribs."

"That sounds nice."

"It's been awhile since we did anything without our two young'uns along."

"Uh-huh."

"Noah left Osborn's Tree Farm a little early today, since things are a bit slow there right now."

"I see."

"Melinda was real happy about going over to her grandma and grandpa Stutzman's," Faith continued. "Her aunt Susie's cat just had a litter of kittens."

"Is Melinda still taking in every stray animal that comes

along?" Barbara asked, realizing that she wasn't contributing much to the conversation.

"Oh, jah. That girl would turn our place into a zoo if we'd let her."

"She's never been one to sit around and play with dolls, has she?"

"No, only the one her real daed gave her before he died. She hung on to that doll until I married Noah; then she finally put it away in a drawer." Faith shrugged. "I tried to get her to play with the faceless doll my mamm made when I was a girl, but she stuck that away, too."

Barbara sipped her tea. "I guess some girls would rather do other things than play little *mudder*."

"Like me—the girl who grew up telling jokes and yodeling and couldn't have cared less about domestic things." Faith smiled. "How's the baby? I can't wait to hold him."

"Davey's fine. He's sleeping in his crib."

Faith leaned forward and set her cup on the coffee table. "I'm glad he's doing well, but I don't think you are."

Barbara felt her defenses rise. Had her friend come over to lecture her? "I'll get my weight back as soon as my appetite improves," she said through tight lips.

"You've got to eat enough for both you and little David. Nursing mothers need plenty of nourishment, you know."

"I'm fine. Still a little weak, but that's getting better. And I make myself eat even if I'm not hungry."

Faith clasped her hands around her knees. "How's your mental health?"

Barbara blinked. "What are you getting at?"

"You're depressed. I can see it in your eyes and the way your shoulders are slumped."

Heat flooded Barbara's face. Faith knew her so well, but she hated to admit the way she felt. She thought it was a sign of weakness to be depressed. Up until David died, she had always been so strong. Even after his death, she had managed to avoid depression by keeping busy in the harness shop.

"It might help to talk about it," Faith prompted.

Barbara shuddered as tears clouded her vision. It wasn't like her to lose control. "Talking won't change a thing," she muttered.

"Maybe not, but it might make you feel better." Faith patted the sofa cushion. "Come sit by me and pour out your heart."

Barbara sighed and placed her cup on the small table to her left. Faith wouldn't let up until she got what she came for, and Barbara was pretty sure the woman's goal was to make her break down. Faith had said many times that God gave people tear ducts for a good reason, and folks shouldn't be too stubborn to use them.

When Barbara sat beside her friend, she clenched her fingers and willed herself not to cry.

"Is it postpartum depression?" Faith questioned.

"Maybe." Barbara felt her neck spasm as despair gripped her like a vise. "I think it's a combination of things."

"Such as?"

"Missing David, feeling bad because our youngest son will never know his daed, wanting to be out at the harness shop but knowing I'm too weak to do much more than care for myself and the boppli right now."

"Your mamm's looking after the other three, right?"

Barbara nodded.

"And Paul Hilty's helping in the shop, so that gives you time to rest up and get your strength back."

"Jah."

"I don't mean to lecture, but you should be grateful for all the help."

Barbara crossed her arms to dispel the sudden chill she felt. A tear seeped out from under her lashes. "I am grateful, but I feel so guilty."

"Guilty for what?"

"Because I–I'm useless."

Faith reached over and gripped Barbara's hand. "How can you say that? The boppli needs you to care for him and be strong."

"I know if I get plenty of rest and eat right, I'll regain strength physically. But I'm weak emotionally, and I don't know if I'll ever be strong again." A sob escaped Barbara's lips, and she clamped her mouth shut to keep from breaking down in front of her friend.

Faith patted Barbara gently on the back. "Go ahead and get it out. Let the cleansing tears come."

"Why do I feel guilty when I'm sad?" Barbara wailed.

"Maybe because you're used to being in control of things, and this is something you can't control."

Barbara couldn't deny that she liked to be in charge. Even when she was a girl, she'd tried to tell her sisters what to do. Not that any of them appreciated it or did all she asked, but it had given her a sense of being in control to make plans and try to get them to follow her suggestions. "I wasn't feeling sad like this before little Davey was born," she said with a sniff.

"Until now, you didn't have time to be depressed. Since you've been forced to slow down, your feelings are rising to the surface."

"Jah, maybe so."

"Did you see the verse that Noah attached to the cake?"

"I didn't take the time to look at it."

"The verse reminds us that there is a time for laughter and a time for tears."

Faith's comment unleashed the dam. Barbara wept for all she was worth. When her sobs finally tapered to sniffling hiccups, she reached for a tissue from the box on the coffee table and blew her nose. "Sorry for blubbering like that."

"It's all right. God knows your pain, and you have every right to cry."

Barbara's gaze darted to the Bible, also on the coffee table. "My faith isn't so strong anymore. Not the way yours seems to be."

Faith shook her head. "My faith wasn't always strong. It used to be almost nonexistent. Remember how I was when I came home after living among the English, thinking I wanted to be famous and make lots of money as an entertainer?"

Barbara nodded. But her friend was a different person now, and God had blessed her in many ways. Noah was a wonderful, loving husband, and they had two beautiful, healthy children. Would Faith be as secure in her beliefs if she'd lost the man she loved? It was easy to talk about having faith in God when things were going well.

"I know it's wrong for me to feel this way, but I'm jealous of you, Faith," Barbara admitted.

"Why? What have you to be jealous of?"

"Your husband is alive, and everything's going great in your life."

Faith stared at the floor. "Noah and I have our share of troubles, too."

Regret as strong as a Missouri king snake coiled around Barbara's middle. She'd been wallowing in self-pity, and here was her friend going through problems she didn't even know about. "What's wrong, Faith? What kind of problems are you and Noah having?"

Faith smiled, but her soulful blue eyes revealed the depth of her pain. "The doctor gave us some disappointing news at my last appointment. We can't have any more children."

Barbara's heart clenched. She knew how much her friend loved children and had hoped for another baby. "I'm awful sorry, Faith," she murmured.

"I've come to terms with it. At least I have Melinda and Isaiah, and I love them both very much."

"I know you do."

"If it were God's will for us to have more kinner, He would not have closed up my womb."

Barbara couldn't believe how matter-of-fact Faith was being. It reminded her of what Bishop John had said on the day of David's funeral. *"Our faith teaches that when our time on earth is over, God will call us home no matter what. We just need to accept His will and move on with life."*

"You've come a long way from the rebellious teenager I used to know," Barbara said. "Your strong faith and positive attitude amaze me."

Faith gave Barbara a hug. "Your friendship is one of the things that helped me grow. I want you to know that I'm here for you."

Barbara dabbed at the corners of her eyes. "Danki. I appreciate that. But once I return to work, I'll be able to make it on my own again."

"It's good to have you back in Webster County," Noah Hertzler said, returning the strip of leather for the bridles he wanted.

Paul placed it on the workbench. "I'm not here for good, you know. Just working at the harness shop until Barbara's up to taking over again." He shook his head. "It amazes me that any woman would want to do this kind of work."

Noah snickered. "I think some of the women in our community are cut from a different cloth than most."

"How so?"

"Take my wife, for instance. She loves to yodel and tell funny stories."

Paul nodded. "So I've heard."

"Not the everyday thing you'd expect from an Amish woman, mind you. But that's what makes Faith so special." Noah grinned. "Then there's my stepdaughter, Melinda. That girl takes in every stray critter that comes near our place, and some I think she goes looking for."

Paul leaned against the workbench and laughed. "Sounds like you've got your hands full."

Noah smiled. "Jah, but in a good way."

Paul could tell by the gleam in Noah's eyes that he was a happy man. He had a wife he obviously loved, a stepdaughter whose whims he catered to, a son to carry on his name, and a job that he thoroughly enjoyed. All Paul had was a job in Lancaster County, with little hope of ever owning his own business. He had no wife or children, and he wasn't getting any younger. He'd turned thirty a few months ago, and most men his age were already married with three or four children living under their roofs.

"Are you enjoying the time with your folks?" Noah asked, pulling Paul's thought aside.

Paul shrugged. "It's good to see them, of course, but Pop and I haven't seen eye to eye since I refused to follow in his footsteps as a farmer. Fact is, we can barely be in the same room without one of us snapping at the other."

"I know what you mean. My daed has never understood why I'd rather work at the tree farm than slop hogs with him." Noah folded his arms across his chest. "He's never understood my interest in baking, either. But I've come to realize that some things probably won't change, so it's best to try and ignore them."

"Guess you're right," Paul said with a nod. "If I let Pop's grumbling get to me, I'd be on the next bus bound for Pennsylvania. But I wouldn't feel right about running out on Barbara when she needs help."

"I'm glad you're here for her, because Samuel can't carry the load alone." Noah glanced around. "Hey, where is Samuel today?"

"He hired a driver to take him to Springfield for a doctor's appointment. I've been on my own all afternoon, and as you might have noticed when you first came in, the customers have kept me quite busy."

Noah nodded. "That's why I waited until the others left to start yakkin'."

Paul pointed to the stack of papers on the desk. "I work fast, but there's no way I can keep up with the orders we have right now."

"If I knew anything about what you're doing here, I'd offer to help in my spare time, but I'd only be in the way."

"That's okay. I'll be fine. Just need to keep my nose to the leather, as my cousin Andy likes to say."

Noah chuckled and turned toward the door. "Faith went up to the house to visit Barbara. Guess I'd better see if she's ready to head for Seymour. I'm taking my wife to eat supper at her favorite place—Baldy's Café."

"Have fun. I'll let you know when your bridles are ready."

"Danki."

When the door clicked shut behind Noah, Paul turned back to the workbench, wishing he had a wife to take out to supper. "What's wrong with you, Paul Hilty? Get yourself busy and quit thinking such unlikely thoughts!"

Chapter 7

"Where are we going, Papa?" John's youngest daughter, Mary, asked as they headed down Highway C in their open buggy.

"I'm paying a call on Barbara Zook."

The ten-year-old's lower lip jutted out. "But I thought after you picked me and Hannah up from school, we'd go straight home so we could play."

"Jah, Papa." Twelve-year-old Hannah spoke up from the backseat. "This morning, you said since this was the last day of school, me and Mary could spend our afternoon playing at the creek."

"You can do that when we get home from Barbara's."

Mary nudged his shoulder. "But why do we have to go?"

"To see how she's getting along, that's why."

"Getting along with what?"

John gritted his teeth in frustration. "Why must you ask so many questions?"

She leaned away from him. "I—I just wanna know why we have to go over to Barbara's."

"She had a boppli not long ago. Don't you want to see how the little fellow's doing?"

"I'd rather play in the creek," Hannah said.

"If you don't stop complaining, you won't be playing at all today. Instead, when we get home, I'll find some work for you to do."

John glanced over his shoulder and noticed that both girls sat with their arms folded and their mouths clamped shut. Maybe now he could spend the rest of the ride in peace.

When Barbara stepped onto the back porch, prepared to air out the quilt from her bed, she spotted John Frey's buggy pulling into the yard. His two youngest daughters were with him. John pulled up to the hitching rail close to the house.

"Wie geht's?" he called as he and the girls climbed down from the buggy.

"I'm doing all right. What brings you out our way?"

He and the girls joined Barbara on the porch. "We're calling on a few folks today, so I decided to stop and check on you." He tipped his straw hat and grinned at her in a most disconcerting way. "How are things in the harness shop?"

"Paul Hilty's helping out. As far as I know, everything's going okay."

"Will he be staying long?"

Her fingers curled around the edges of the quilt she held. "Just until I feel up to working again."

"That's good." The bishop squinted against the sun while offering Barbara another lopsided smile.

Barbara draped the quilt over the porch rail. An uncomfortable feeling settled over her. She didn't like the way John Frey was looking at her. The man was a widower nearly fifteen years her senior with four daughters to raise, and two of them were teenagers. When Jacob Martin had passed on a year and a half ago, John had taken over as the bishop for their district. Then six months ago, John's wife, Peggy, had died of cancer, leaving him to raise their girls on his own. Barbara hoped John didn't plan on her being his new wife. She had no desire to marry again. Besides, she couldn't imagine having to deal with four more children. She had her hands full taking care of her boys.

"You're looking a mite peaked," the bishop said. "If you're needing some help with the boppli, I could send one of the girls over. Betty has a job, but I'm sure either Hannah or Nadine could come." He nudged Hannah's arm. "Isn't that right, daughter?"

Her head bobbed up and down. "Sure, Papa. I'll do whatever you say."

"I appreciate the offer," Barbara said, "but my mamm's been helping with the three older boys, and I'm managing okay with the boppli."

"Looks like you could use some help outside." John glanced around the yard. "I'll mention it to Margaret Hilty the next time I see her. I'm sure she and some of the other ladies would be glad to give you a hand."

Barbara couldn't argue with the fact that her yard looked a mess. Since David had died and her responsibilities had increased, the lawn and flower beds had been dreadfully neglected. Dad wasn't able to keep up with yard work and help in the harness shop, too, so the lawn only got cut when he felt up to it and had the time. Mom had a weak back, which meant Barbara couldn't count on her help with yard work, either.

"I must admit, it is difficult to keep up with everything around here," she mumbled, feeling a knot form in her stomach. "If some of the ladies want to help, I'd appreciate it."

"I'll see that it's done real soon." John leaned against the railing opposite the quilt, apparently in no hurry to leave. "I was wondering if you and your boys would like to go on a picnic with me and the girls Saturday afternoon."

The knot in Barbara's stomach tightened, and she gritted her teeth as she concentrated on the patterns of light dappling the porch floor. "I. . .uh. . .appreciate the offer, but I don't think the boppli's ready for that kind of outing."

"Couldn't you leave him with your mamm?"

Barbara's face grew warm. She could hardly remind the bishop that she had to stay close to Davey because she was nursing.

As if by divine intervention, the little guy started to fuss. "I've got to go inside now. The boppli's crying." She turned toward the door. "It was kind of you to drop by."

"What about the picnic?"

When Barbara glanced over her shoulder, the scrutiny she saw on the bishop's face made her feel even more uncomfortable. She forced her lips into what she hoped was a polite smile. "I appreciate the offer, but it's really not possible. Good day,

Bishop John." She nodded at the girls. "It was nice seeing you, Mary and Hannah."

They nodded in return.

Barbara hurried into the house and lifted the baby from the cradle she kept for him in the living room. "The bishop probably thought I was rude, but I couldn't let you keep crying," she murmured against the infant's downy, dark head. "Besides, I'm not about to give that man any hope of my becoming his wife."

As Alice stepped away from the kitchen window, where she'd been watching Barbara talk to John Frey, she sighed. The bishop seemed to be coming around a lot lately, and Alice was pretty sure he had more on his mind than checking on Barbara's physical status. She had a hunch the bishop had set his cap for Barbara—probably because he needed a mother for his girls. She couldn't fault him for that, but she didn't think her daughter should be that wife. Barbara had enough on her shoulders, trying to raise four boys and run the harness shop. If she took on the responsibility of John's girls, too, she would never get any rest.

Alice took a seat at the table. She really hoped that Barbara and Paul might get together. According to Samuel, Paul was a hard worker and knew a lot about repairing harnesses and saddles. And the boys, except for Aaron, seemed quite smitten with the man. Truth be told, Alice thought Barbara could develop an interest in Paul, too, if she'd give the man half a chance.

God knows what my daughter needs better than anyone else, she thought as she closed her eyes and offered up a heartfelt prayer.

Heavenly Father, if it's Your will for Barbara to marry again, then let it be at the right time to the right man.

"This isn't the way to our house," Hannah said as John directed their horse and buggy farther down Highway C.

"I know. I'm making a call on Margaret Hilty, and then we'll go home," he replied.

"But I thought you were just gonna make the one call on Barbara Zook." Hannah leaned over the front seat and grunted. "Now we'll get home even later and probably won't have time to do any wading."

"If you don't get to the creek today, you can go tomorrow." John gripped the reins tightly as a car zipped past, tooting its horn. "Sure wish the Englishers wouldn't drive so fast on this narrow road," he muttered. "No wonder there have been so many accidents along here."

"I'm hungry," Mary complained. "I was hoping Barbara might give us something to eat, but she didn't offer a thing."

"And we never got to see the boppli, either," Hannah complained.

"Barbara's tired, and she's probably not feeling up to baking," John said. "Maybe she needs a couple of girls to help her."

"You volunteered me or Nadine," Hannah reminded him. "But Barbara said she was getting along fine."

He nodded. "That's true, but I don't think Barbara knows what she needs right now."

Mary nudged his shoulder. "What do you mean, Papa?"

He glanced back at her and smiled. "I believe she could use some girls of her own."

Mary's eyebrows furrowed. "But she's gotta have a husband for that, doesn't she?"

"Jah, and I've been thinking. . . ." John's voice trailed off. Should he tell the girls that he was hoping to give them a mother and him a wife, and that he hoped that wife and mother would be Barbara Zook? *Better wait awhile,* he decided. *In the meantime, I'll keep visiting Barbara and trying to gain her approval.*

"What are you thinking, Papa?" Hannah asked.

"Nothing important."

John pulled into Margaret Hilty's place a short time later.

"Can we wait in the buggy?" Hannah asked when John came around to help them down.

He shook his head. "I think it would be better if you came up to the house with me."

"How come, Papa?" Mary wanted to know.

"Because it wouldn't be proper for me to call on a recently widowed woman alone."

Mary opened her mouth as if she might argue, but he shook his head.

Both girls trudged up the path leading to the home Margaret now shared with her daughter and son-in-law, and John followed. When they stepped onto the porch, Margaret came out the back door dressed in her black mourning clothes.

"Wie geht's, Bishop John?" she asked.

"I'm doing all right."

"What brings you out my way on this warm afternoon?"

"We came to see how you're doing." He motioned first to

Hannah and then to Mary. "Isn't that right, girls?"

"Jah," they said in unison.

John smiled at Margaret. "How are you getting along?"

"Oh, fair to middlin'." She yawned. "I miss Dan something awful, and I'm still not sleeping so well, but I'm grateful that Karen and Jacob were willing to move in here with me. Otherwise, I'd be even lonelier."

"I understand. If I didn't have my girls to keep me company, I'd miss Peggy a lot more than I do."

John shifted from one foot to the other. "Say, I was wondering if I might make a suggestion."

"What's that?"

"We were over at Barbara Zook's a short time ago, and I noticed how overgrown her garden's become."

"I suppose with a new boppli and three young buwe to look after, she doesn't have much time for gardening," Margaret said.

He nodded. "I was thinking it might be good if a group of ladies got together and went over to Barbara's to work on her flower beds."

"I'm sure she would appreciate that."

He turned toward Margaret's garden and made a sweeping gesture with his hand. "Since you've done such a fine job with your own yard, I was thinking you'd be the perfect one to help Barbara get her yard looking good again."

"I do need something to keep my hands and mind busy, and there's only so much work I can do here." She nodded. "I'd be happy to help Barbara."

"That's good. I'll speak to a few other women and see what day would work best for them, and then I'll let Barbara know there's going to be a work frolic in her garden plot soon."

Margaret looked at the girls. "Would you two care for some peanut brittle? My daughter Karen and I made a big batch earlier this afternoon."

Mary and Hannah both nodded enthusiastically. "That'd be real nice," Mary said, licking her lips.

A short time later, John and his girls were headed back up Highway C toward home.

"Say, Papa, I've been wondering about something," Hannah said as they neared their farm.

"What's that, daughter?"

"How come you didn't invite Margaret to go on a picnic with us the way you did Barbara?"

"Well, I—"

"Margaret seems lonely. Maybe she would've enjoyed a day at the pond."

John's face heated up. "I. . .uh. . .as you know, Barbara has kinner, so I figured you girls would enjoy playing with her boys."

"Except for Aaron, Barbara's boys are a lot younger than us," Hannah reminded him.

"Right," he said with a nod. "And for that reason, I figure they'd be fun for you to play little mudder with."

Mary opened her mouth as if to reply, but he held up his hand and said, "Just eat your peanut brittle."

Paul hated to bother Barbara, but he needed several orders to be sent, and she'd made it clear when she hired him that she would place all the orders. He'd thought about asking Barbara's dad to take the paperwork up to the house, but Samuel had left for another doctor's appointment. Since there were no customers at the moment, Paul decided to take the information up to Barbara. He put the CLOSED sign in the shop window with a note saying they would open again after lunch and headed out the door.

Paul stepped onto the back porch of Barbara's house, and as he lifted his hand to the door, he heard a child say, "Whatcha doin'?"

Paul whirled around. Barbara's six-year-old son, Joseph, stood beside a bush near the porch, holding a metal bubble wand in his hand.

"I. . .uh. . .need to see your mamm about something," Paul stammered. He didn't know why he always felt so tongue-tied around children.

"She's in the house."

Paul nodded. "I figured she might be."

"You come over for lunch?" Joseph asked, his blue eyes looking ever so serious.

"No. I'm here on business."

Joseph stepped onto the porch. "Mama's harness business?"

"Jah."

The boy turned the doorknob and called through the open doorway, "Mama, the harness man's here to see you!"

Paul felt as though he would be intruding to step into the house without an invitation, so he waited on the porch until Barbara showed up. "Is there a problem at the shop?" she asked.

"No problem. I just wanted to give you these." Paul handed her the folder full of supply orders.

"Danki. I'll get everything sent out right away."

Joseph tossed the bubble wand onto a small table on the porch and yanked on the hem of his mother's apron. "Can the harness man stay for lunch? We've got plenty, right?"

Barbara's face flamed. "His name is Paul, and I'm sure he's busy."

Joseph shook his head. "No, he ain't. There's no cars or buggies parked in front of the shop."

A trickle of sweat rolled down Paul's forehead, and he wiped it away.

"If you haven't already eaten, you're welcome to join us," Barbara said, much to Paul's surprise.

Whatever she was cooking in the kitchen smelled mighty good. His stomach rumbled. "Well, I—"

"Mama's fixin' chicken noodle soup," Joseph said, smacking his lips. "It tastes awful good, and it smells *wunderbaar*."

Paul smiled at the boy's enthusiasm. "I'd be happy to join you for lunch if you're sure it's no trouble," he said to Barbara. "Maybe we could talk about business while we eat."

Barbara nodded. "Sounds fine to me."

Paul stepped inside. "Was that Bishop Frey I saw here earlier?" Paul asked as he followed her into the kitchen.

Barbara nodded. "He came by with two of his daughters to see how I was doing."

"Guess that's part of the man's duties."

"Jah." Barbara motioned to the table. "Why don't you have a seat? If David doesn't wake from his nap right away, I'll have the soup ready in no time."

"Is there something I can do to help?" Paul offered. Anything would be better than watching the woman bustle around the kitchen. Every time Paul saw Barbara Zook, he thought she was prettier than the time before. Gone were the dark circles under her eyes, and if he weren't mistaken, she'd put on a few needed pounds.

He sucked in his breath. *I shouldn't be thinking about her like this. She's a widowed woman with four boys, and I'm going back to Pennsylvania.*

"I suppose you could go out back and call my other two boys in for lunch. Aaron's pushing Zachary on the swing behind the barn," Barbara said, halting his disconcerting thoughts.

"I can get 'em, Mama," Joseph offered.

"If I send you, Aaron will only argue, or you'll end up getting sidetracked."

"The boys aren't over at your folks' place today?" Paul asked.

Barbara shook her head. "Mom went to Springfield with Dad." She chuckled. "I think my mamm asks that doctor more questions than my daed ever does. He tends to go along with whatever the doctor says and never thinks to voice any concerns."

"I think most men are like that," Paul said, opening the back door. "I'll go get your boys."

He'd only gone as far as the barn when he noticed Joseph trudging along beside him. "I thought you were inside with your mamm."

"Wanted to be with you."

Paul wasn't sure how to respond, so he just kept walking. Until recently, no child had ever shown an interest in him. Truth be told, it felt kind of nice—though he would never admit it to anyone.

Squeals of laughter drew his attention. Aaron was pushing his little brother on the swing.

"Your mamm wants you to come up to the house," Paul said. "She's got lunch about ready."

Aaron stopped pushing the younger boy and whirled around to face Paul. "How come she sent you?"

"The harness man's stayin' for lunch," Joseph announced with a wide grin.

Paul felt Aaron's icy stare all the way to his toes. Clearly, the boy didn't like him, though he wasn't sure why. He figured it had to be for the same reason other kids avoided him—they obviously knew he didn't care much for kids, at least not until now. Aaron had dropped by the shop a couple of times, but he only came around when his grandfather was there. When Paul was minding the shop alone, the boy stayed away. It was just as well. Paul had too much work to spend time babysitting or dealing with Aaron's nasty attitude.

Guess I'm sort of babysitting right now, he thought as he looked at Joseph, who stared up at him with eager blue eyes. *Maybe I need to reach out to Aaron, no matter how awkward it makes me feel.*

"Come on, Zachary," Aaron said as he helped his little brother off the swing. "It's time to eat." He grabbed the boy's hand, and the two scampered toward the house.

Joseph reached for Paul's hand, and they followed the other boys. Was Aaron missing his father? Could that be the problem?

"Say, Aaron," Paul said as he and Joseph stepped onto the porch. "How would you like to come out to the harness shop after lunch and help me?"

"Doin' what?" he asked without looking back. "Sweepin' the floor, I'll bet."

When Paul touched the boy's shoulder, he halted and turned around. "Thought you might like to fasten some buckles on a couple of leather straps, or maybe you could dye the edges."

A flicker of interest sparked in Aaron's eyes, but when he blinked, it disappeared. "We'll see," he mumbled.

When they entered the kitchen, lunch was ready. Barbara motioned to the chair at the head of the table. "Have a seat, Paul."

"But that's Pa's place," Aaron was quick to say. "Nobody should sit there 'cept Pa."

"Aaron, your daed's gone, and—"

Paul shook his head. "It's all right, Barbara. I can sit someplace else." He waited until Aaron and Joseph had taken their seats and Barbara had put Zachary on a high stool. After she was seated, Paul took the empty chair across from her.

All heads bowed. When the silent prayer was over, Barbara passed Paul a basket of rolls.

"These look good. Did you make them?" he asked.

"My mamm did. I haven't had the energy to do much baking since the boppli was born," Barbara said.

Paul took a roll and slathered it with butter. "You'll get your strength back soon. Already you're looking better than the day I first dropped by."

She smiled. "I'm anxious to get back to the harness shop. I surely do miss it."

Paul was tempted to ask why she felt the need to do men's work, but he thought better of it. He would be going back to

Pennsylvania soon, and what Barbara did was her own business. Besides, she needed a way to support herself, and according to her dad, she was very good at her trade.

He dipped his spoon into the soup and took a mouthful. "Mmm. . .this is mighty good."

"Danki."

Joseph smacked his lips. "Mama's the best cook in all of Webster County."

Barbara snickered. "Jah, sure."

Paul glanced at Aaron, who sat to his mother's left. The boy had his head down and seemed to be playing with his soup, stirring it over and over with his spoon.

"Aaron, you'd best eat and quit dawdling," Barbara scolded. The child picked up his bowl and slurped his soup.

"Mind your manners and use your spoon." Barbara handed a roll to young Zachary, and he promptly dipped it in his soup.

"Would it be all right if Aaron comes out to the shop after lunch?" Paul asked. "With your daed being gone today, I could use some help."

Barbara's look of concern made him wish he hadn't said anything. "Are you getting further behind?"

He shook his head. "Just thought an extra pair of hands would be nice."

Barbara turned to face Aaron. "Would you like to help Paul this afternoon?"

He gave a slight shrug.

"I think you should give it a try. But you must do everything Paul says. Is that clear?"

"Jah."

Paul gripped his spoon. *I may regret asking the boy to help as much as I wish I hadn't accepted Barbara's invitation to lunch.* He knew it was silly, but being this close to her made him long for something he'd probably never have. He decided to forgo talking about the harness business over lunch. *As soon as I finish this bowl of soup, I'm going to hightail it right back to work.*

Chapter 8

Barbara curled up on her bed, glad that the baby, Zachary, and Joseph were taking naps. Since Aaron was out at the harness shop with Paul, she could rest. She'd felt exhausted by the time they'd finished eating lunch. Paul had offered to help her with the dishes, but since she knew he needed to get back to the shop, she'd declined, saying she could manage. She had left the dishes soaking in the sink, deciding she could do them later, when she hopefully would have a little more energy.

As Barbara burrowed into the pillow, a vision of Paul popped into her head. She had been avoiding him lately because he made her feel so uncomfortable. Today at lunch, however, she'd actually enjoyed his company.

Joseph sure seemed taken with him, she mused. The boy hung on Paul's every word.

"It's not fair, Mama," Joseph had wailed when Barbara said he needed a nap. *"If Aaron gets to help in the harness shop, I should, too."*

Barbara grinned. Joseph was nearly six but not old enough to help in the shop. She didn't think Aaron was all that thrilled about helping Paul, but it might be good for the boy to spend time alone with a man other than his grandpa.

Aaron misses his daed, but he can learn from Paul the way he did David. She rolled onto her other side. *If I'm feeling up to it after my nap, maybe I'll bundle up the baby and take a walk out there so I can see how things are going.*

David had enjoyed running the harness shop so much. He'd said many times that their firstborn would take over the business someday. Even when Aaron was a toddler, David had invited the boy out there just to let him hold the leather straps and "get the feel of things."

Tears welled in Barbara's eyes. How she missed working in the shop with her beloved husband. She missed their long talks after the children were put to bed, and she pined for the physical touch of the man she had loved since she was a teenager. Would she ever know love like that again? Probably not. Her focus needed to be on running the harness shop and raising her boys.

"I don't think I could ever feel for any man what I felt for David," she whispered against the Wedding Ring quilt covering her bed. It had been a gift from her mother when she and David married, and it always brought her comfort.

Heavy with the need for sleep, Barbara's eyelids closed. As she started to drift off, David's image was replaced with that of Paul Hilty. The way he'd smiled at her during lunch made her heart feel lighter than it had in weeks, and that confused her. A chunk of blond hair kept falling onto Paul's forehead, and she had to resist the temptation to push it back in place the way she often did with one of her boys. The last thing Barbara saw as she succumbed to sleep was the vision of Aaron and Paul walking side by side toward the harness shop.

Paul peered over Aaron's shoulder as the boy reached for a buckle. "Not that one, Aaron. It's too big for the strap you're working on."

The boy grabbed another buckle. As he fumbled with the clasp and tried to fasten it to the leather strap, it slipped and fell on the floor.

"Be careful now." Paul stooped to retrieve the buckle.

"It was slippery," Aaron complained.

"Maybe you've got neat's-foot oil on your hands from when you were oiling that saddle earlier."

"Nope. I washed 'em."

"Could be you didn't wash them well enough. Might be a good idea to do it again, son."

Aaron spun around, his dark eyes smoldering. "You ain't my daed."

The tips of Paul's ears warmed. " 'Course not. Never said I was."

"But you called me 'son.' "

Paul shrugged. "It was just a figure of speech."

"And you've been tellin' me what to do ever since we came out to my daed's shop."

"If you're going to be my helper, then I have the right to tell you what to do."

Aaron frowned. Then he headed for the sink at the back of the shop.

Paul shook his head. *Maybe asking the boy to help out wasn't such a good idea. Might be best if I sent him back to the house.* Paul opened his mouth to say so, but the front door swung open. Noah Hertzler stepped into the shop.

"I got off work early today and was passing by on my way home," Noah said. "Thought I'd stop and see how you're coming along with those bridles I ordered."

"They should be ready by next week," Paul answered.

Noah motioned to the back of the building. "I see you've got yourself a helper today."

Paul grimaced. "I believe he likes being in the shop, but I don't think he cottons to me so well."

"Give him time. He'll come around."

"Did he help his daed much?"

Noah nodded. "He followed David around like he was his shadow, though I'm not sure how much help he was in the shop. Never seen a father and son so close as those two seemed to be."

"Wish I could say the same for me and my daed."

"Still having problems?"

"Jah. Just last night we got into a disagreement over my returning to Pennsylvania."

Noah's eyebrows furrowed. "Will you be leaving soon?"

Paul shook his head. "Not until Barbara's back working again."

"You think it'll be much longer?"

"Don't rightly know. She invited me to eat lunch with her and the boys today, and she seemed to be doing okay." He frowned. "Come to think of it, she did look kind of tired by the time we were done."

"She's been through a lot."

Paul nodded.

"Guess your brother's widow must still be grieving, too."

"Jah. Margaret's taking Dan's death pretty hard, although she's trying to keep busy so she doesn't miss him so much."

"We've had several deaths in our community lately." Noah stuffed his hands into his pants pockets. "John Frey lost his wife six months ago."

"I heard that."

Noah's voice lowered a notch. "Word has it that he's looking for another wife already."

Paul leaned against the workbench and crossed his arms. "Is that so?"

"Jah. He's got four daughters who need a woman's guiding hand."

"I suppose they would."

"Faith thinks the bishop has set his cap for Barbara."

Paul's mouth dropped. That would explain John Frey's visit earlier in the day. Apparently, the man had more on his mind than seeing how Barbara was doing.

"You look surprised," Noah said. "It's pretty common for a widower with kinner to remarry soon after his wife's passing. Truth be told, I'm surprised Barbara hasn't remarried by now, what with her having three young'uns and a boppli to raise."

Paul gave a slight shrug. The thought of Barbara marrying

Bishop Frey made his stomach churn. She was too young and full of life to be married to a man whose hair and beard had more gray than brown. As he opened his mouth to say something, Aaron sauntered up, holding his hands out for inspection. "See, no oil."

"That's good. Why don't you get back to work on those buckles, then."

Aaron glanced up at Noah. "Did you bring any cookies today?"

"Not this time." Noah motioned toward the workbench. "Want to show me what you've been working on?"

"It's nothin' much, but if you wanna see, it's all right by me."

Noah winked at Paul. Aaron led Noah over to the bench while Paul went to work at the riveting machine. He was thankful Noah had dropped by. Aaron seemed much more comfortable with him.

When Barbara awoke from her nap, Joseph and Zachary were playing in their room. Aaron was nowhere to be found, so she assumed he was still at the shop with Paul. David was awake but not fussy. She would change his diaper and see if he wanted to nurse; then the four of them would go check on Aaron.

Half an hour later, Barbara headed to the harness shop. She held the baby in her arms while Zachary and Joseph traipsed alongside her.

"Do I get to help in the harness shop like Aaron's doin'?" Joseph asked.

She shook her head. "You're not old enough for that yet, son."

Joseph halted and dragged his bare foot through the dirt, making little circles with his big toe. "How come Aaron gets to have all the fun?"

"Working in the harness shop isn't like playing a game," Barbara said patiently. "You'll find that out in a few years when you're able to start helping there."

Joseph shrugged and started walking again.

Barbara smiled. Joseph was her most easygoing child. He would get over his disappointment quickly.

When they entered the harness shop a few minutes later, the sight that greeted Barbara sent a shock through her middle. Aaron's hands were completely black, and he had dark smudges on his face and shirt. He held on to a strap, which he'd obviously been staining, but the child had more dye on himself than anyplace else. She looked around for Paul and spotted him in front of the riveting machine, humming and working away as if he didn't have a care in the world. Didn't the man realize what a mess Aaron had made? He'd obviously not been watching the boy closely enough. Maybe Barbara had made a mistake agreeing to let Aaron help Paul. Maybe she shouldn't have hired Paul to work for her in the first place.

"What's wrong, Mama?" Aaron asked. "You look kind of grank."

Barbara moved swiftly to his side. "I'm not sick, Aaron, just a bit put out."

"How come?"

"Look at your hands."

"Jah, they're black as coal," Joseph put in.

"Black as coal," Zachary parroted.

Aaron wrinkled his nose. "Stay out of this, you two."

"There's no reason for you to be talking to your brothers like that." Barbara shifted the baby to her other arm and nodded at Aaron. "I want you to march on back to the sink and scrub your hands and face."

"But, Mama, I'm not done yet. Paul said if I finished this job by four o'clock, he'd pay me a dollar."

Barbara didn't want to say anything that might cause Aaron to dislike working in the harness shop. "All right, then. But try to be more careful. You're supposed to be staining the leather ends, not your hands and clothes."

"I'll do my best."

She moved toward Paul, but the two younger boys stayed near Aaron. That was just as well. She didn't think they should hear what she had to say.

"Did you come to see how Aaron's doing?" Paul asked when she stood beside him at the riveting machine.

Barbara nodded. "I'm not too pleased to see the mess he's making with that dye you're letting him use."

"Dying leather's a messy job."

"True, but his hands are all black, and he ended up getting dye on his shirt and face, too."

Paul kept working.

"Did you show him the right way to hold the brush and cover the edges of the leather with stain?"

"Of course."

When the baby hiccuped, Barbara put him over her shoulder and patted his back. "There's a right way and a wrong way to hold the paintbrush," she said. "The right way keeps the stain on the leather and not so much on the hands."

Paul's pale eyebrows drew together. "Are you questioning my ability to teach your son?"

She clamped her lips together, afraid she might spew some unkind words. Who did Paul Hilty think he was? He acted as if this were *his* shop.

"Well, are you questioning my ability?" he persisted.

Barbara drew in a deep breath and blew it out quickly. "I'm not questioning your ability. But I think you need to remember that this is *my* shop and Aaron is *my* son." She paused long enough to grab another quick breath. "Not only that, but I'm the one who will have to spend time trying to get the dye off his hands and face before Sunday. I sure wouldn't want him going to preaching like that."

Paul chuckled. "No, that would never do."

Barbara bit her bottom lip hard. "Are you laughing at me?"

"Not really. I was just thinking how different you look when you're mad."

Her face heated up. "I am not mad."

"You're not mad, huh? Then how come your cheeks are so pink?"

Barbara mentally counted to ten. Was he trying to goad her into an argument? "I'm upset because you haven't been watching Aaron closely enough."

"I have been watching him, and the boy's doing fine, Barbara. I know he made a mess with the dye, but how is he supposed to learn if he doesn't try?"

In her heart, Barbara knew Paul was right. Aaron would

learn best by doing, even if he did make a mess. She still felt defensive. This was her shop, and she had a certain way of doing things. That included how she would teach her son to dye leather straps.

"I'm thinking sometime next week I might come to the shop and work awhile," she blurted out.

Paul's eyebrows lifted. "You really think that's wise? It's only been a few weeks since you had the baby."

Her heart began to pound. Did he think he knew what was best for her, too? "I'm not planning to work full-time. I thought it would be good to try a few hours and see how it goes."

"What about the kinner?"

"I'm sure my mamm will watch them."

"Even the boppli? Doesn't he need to be fed regularly?"

She nodded. "I can plan my time in the shop around his feeding schedule. If he needs me, Mom can send one of the boys out to let me know."

Paul shrugged and grabbed another metal rivet. "Whatever you think best. You're the boss."

Chapter 9

Sunday dawned with a cloudless sky, and for the first time since little David was born, Barbara would be going to church. In some ways, she looked forward to it. She had missed fellowshipping with other believers. But in another way, she looked on it with dread. Paul would be there, and after their confrontation at the harness shop, she wasn't sure she could face him.

She stared out at her overgrown lawn. *He probably thinks I'm rude and controlling, but he has to understand the way things are. I own the harness shop, and that gives me the right to say how things should be done. I'm also Aaron's mother, and regardless of what Paul may think, I know what's best for my son.*

A vision of her oldest boy's dirty black hands popped into Barbara's mind. When Aaron had come home from the shop that day, she'd scrubbed for nearly an hour, trying to get the black stain off. Three days later, Aaron's hands were a dingy gray.

When Barbara's three boys came running into the kitchen, she looked away from the window.

"Is breakfast ready yet, Mama?" Joseph asked. "I'm hungry!"

She smiled. "I made blueberry pancakes."

"Yum. Those are my favorite," Aaron said as he pulled out a chair.

"Did you wash your hands?" Barbara asked.

"Didn't think I needed to this morning."

"Oh? And why's that?"

Aaron held up his hands. "Been washed so many times, there ain't much skin left."

"Don't exaggerate." Barbara nodded toward the sink. "You'd better get it done."

Aaron grunted but did as he was told.

"Me and Zachary washed our hands," Joseph said.

"That's good to hear. Now scoot up to the table." Barbara lifted Zachary onto his stool while Joseph sat in a chair. At least two of her boys were compliant. *I wonder how little David will be when he's older,* she mused. *Will he be even-tempered like these two, or will the boppli take after his oldest brother and be stubborn as a mule?*

"Margaret's yard sure looks nice," Faith commented as Noah pulled their buggy into the Hiltys' yard. "She's obviously been busy weeding."

"It probably does her good to keep busy."

Faith nodded. "Jah. It's only been a few weeks since Dan died." She looked over at Noah and smiled. "While you're getting the horse unhitched, I'll see if I can speak with her before preaching service starts."

"Okay. See you later."

Faith herded their two children toward the house and stopped to say a quick hello to her mother.

Mom smiled at the children. "Susie's out back playing on the swings with some of the other kinner. Why don't the two of you join them?"

The children didn't have to be asked twice, and as they scampered off, Faith went inside to speak with Margaret. She found her in the kitchen getting a glass of water.

"Wie geht's, Margaret?" she asked, stepping up beside the woman.

Margaret smiled, although there was no sparkle in her blue eyes. "I'm getting by. . .taking one day at a time."

"I was admiring your garden as we drove in," Faith said, glancing out the window. "Looks like you've been busy. I didn't see a single weed."

"I enjoy spending time in the garden. It makes me feel closer to God, and it keeps my hands and mind occupied."

"Speaking of gardens, did you know there's going to be a work frolic at Barbara Zook's place next week?"

"Jah. Bishop John told me. He asked if I'd be willing to go and help out since I know a thing or two about gardening."

"Are you planning to go?"

Margaret nodded. "May as well. It'll give me something meaningful to do."

Faith gave Margaret a hug. "I lost my first husband, so I know a little of what you're going through. Of course, Greg and I were never as close as you and Dan." Faith wouldn't have admitted it to Margaret, but back when she'd been living in the English world and Greg had been killed after stepping into traffic during one of his drunken stupors, she'd had mixed feelings. Greg had been harsh and abusive with her almost the whole time they were married. He'd gambled and drunk excessively and, as her agent, had forced her to do more performances than she had cared to. But Faith had been in love with Greg when they first got married, and he had been a decent father to Melinda. For that reason, Faith had grieved when he'd been killed. How grateful she was that God had brought Noah into her life and given her a second chance at being a godly wife and a good mother to her two precious children.

"I spoke with Paul the other day, and he said he's enjoying the work he does in Barbara's harness shop," Margaret said, pulling Faith's reflections back to the present.

Faith smiled. "That's what he told Noah not long ago, too."

"Do you think it'll be long before Barbara takes over the harness shop again?"

"I don't know, but I just may ask her." Faith pointed out the window. "Looks like her daed's rig pulling into your yard now."

"Well, I'll let you go so you can visit with her before preaching service begins." Margaret set her glass in the sink. "I should speak with Dan's mother."

Faith gave Margaret's arm a gentle squeeze. "I'll see you at the work frolic next week."

"You can count on it."

Faith scurried out the back door and made it to Samuel's buggy moments after he halted it near the barn. "It's good to see you this morning," she said as she helped Barbara climb down with the baby in her arms. The boys had already run off toward a group of children.

Barbara smiled. "It feels good to be out again."

Faith held out her hands. "Mind if I hold the boppli? It's been awhile since I had a newborn in my arms."

Barbara handed her son over to Faith. "I believe he's put on a few pounds since you last saw him."

"That's good." Faith scrutinized Barbara. "Looks like you've gained some weight, too."

Barbara nodded. "I believe I have. My appetite's slowly returning."

"Glad to hear it. How's the depression?"

"It comes and goes. But I'm sure it'll be gone once I'm able to work in the harness shop again."

"How long do you think it will be before that happens?" Faith asked as they walked toward the house.

"I'm hoping to work a few hours next week."

Faith's eyebrows rose. "So soon?"

Barbara shrugged. "I get bored sitting around the house."

Faith kissed the top of Davey's head. "But you have this little guy to keep you busy. Not to mention your three active boys." She motioned to the maple tree where the children awaited their turn on the swing.

"I love caring for my kinner, but I also like working in the shop. Besides, somebody's got to earn the money to support my brood."

"According to Noah, Paul's managing the harness shop just fine."

"He probably is, but he won't be here forever. I'm sure he's anxious to return to Pennsylvania." Barbara nibbled on her lower lip. "Until I'm working full-time, I doubt he'll feel free to go."

"Shows what kind of man he is, don't you think?" Faith took a seat in the rocking chair on the porch and rocked the baby.

Barbara sat in the wicker chair next to her. "Paul seems conscientious and hardworking."

"Is that all?"

"What are you getting at?"

Faith tipped her head. "I merely wondered what you think of him as a man, that's all."

"I just told you."

"Does he appeal to you?"

Barbara's mouth dropped open. "It's not proper for a newly widowed woman to think such things, and you know it."

"Barbara, it's been almost a year since David died. I've known several widows and widowers who married within the first year."

Barbara's body stiffened. "I'm not looking for a husband."

"Maybe not. But I'm pretty sure there's one looking for you." Faith nodded toward Bishop Frey. "I hear tell he's got marrying on his mind, and word has it you're the man's first choice."

John stepped onto the porch. "Guder mariye, ladies," he said with a nod in Barbara's direction.

"Morning, Bishop Frey," the women said in unison.

He gave his beard a quick tug. "You're looking tired today, Barbara. Are you sure you don't want me to send one of my girls over to your place to help out?"

She smiled, but it appeared to be forced. "I'm managing, but I'll let you know if I should need anything."

"All right, then. I'll be around to call on you again soon." He took a few steps closer to Barbara. "Oh, by the way, I spoke to Margaret Hilty the other day, and she said she'd be happy to help with your garden. She and some other women will come over next week to help."

"I appreciate that."

John shifted his weight from one foot to the other while clearing his throat. After a few awkward moments, he glanced over at Faith. "How are things with you and Noah these days?"

"We're doing fine. Noah's keeping busy with his job, and I keep busy with things at home."

"It's always good to be busy. Jah, real good." He shuffled his feet a few more times, then looked back at Barbara. "Well, I'd best be getting inside now. Service will be starting soon." With a quick nod, he left.

From where Paul sat on the men's side of the room, he had a perfect view of Barbara Zook. She looked serene, sitting on the bench, cradling her infant son. A deep yearning welled up in Paul's chest, just as it had that afternoon in Barbara's kitchen. Had he made a mistake thinking marriage wasn't for him? Should he look for a wife when he returned to Pennsylvania? Only problem was, he wasn't interested in anyone back there. No other woman had affected him the way Barbara had, yet his attraction to her made no sense. Whenever they were in the same room, he either felt uncomfortable or irritated with her criticism.

Paul forced his gaze away from Barbara and tried to focus on Bishop Frey's sermon.

" 'Lo, children are an heritage of the Lord: and the fruit of the womb is his reward. As arrows are in the hand of a mighty man; so are children of the youth. Happy is the man that hath his quiver full of them: they shall not be ashamed, but they shall speak with the enemies in the gate.' Psalm 127:3–5," the bishop read from the Bible he held. "And chapter 128, verse 1, says, 'Blessed is every one that feareth the Lord; that walketh in his ways.' " He smiled. "Be fruitful and multiply and be blessed."

Paul shifted uncomfortably. Were the bishop's words directed at him? Was God speaking through John Frey, telling Paul he should get married and raise a family and that by so doing, he would be blessed? He thought about his conversation with Noah Hertzler the other day. Noah had mentioned the bishop's interest in Barbara. Maybe the man's sermon was directed at himself. Could be that John thought if he took another wife and had more children, he would be twice blessed. That wife could turn out to be Barbara Zook.

I've got to quit thinking about this, Paul reprimanded himself. *If the bishop should marry Barbara, it's none of my business. She has the right to choose whomever she pleases.* He shuddered. *Then why does the idea of her becoming the bishop's wife make me feel so miserable?*

After the noon meal, Barbara put the baby and Zachary down for naps. She stared at her youngest son, sleeping peacefully on his side, and a lump formed in her throat. She knew she was more protective of him than she had been with her other three. Maybe it was because this little guy would never know the wonderful man for whom he'd been named. Or maybe her own insecurities caused her to feel overly protective. Ever since David had been snatched away so suddenly, Barbara had been a little paranoid. What if something bad happened to one of her children? What if she died and left them with no mother? Sure, her folks would step in and raise the boys, but because they were getting up in years, it would be difficult for them to take on such a big responsibility. Her four married sisters might be willing to take the boys, but two of them lived near Sweet Springs, and the other two had moved to Minnesota. It would be hard for the boys to move from the only home they'd ever known.

Try not to worry, she admonished herself. *As the book of Matthew states: " 'Which of you by taking thought can add one cubit unto his stature?' "*

Barbara turned away from Davey's crib and tiptoed out of the room. She needed to turn the future of her sons over to God. She decided to go outside and enjoy the rest of the day.

As soon as Barbara stepped onto the front porch, she spotted Paul sitting under a maple tree with Joseph nestled in his lap. Her heart nearly melted at the sight. He looked so natural holding her son, and Joseph appeared as content as a cat lying in a patch of sun.

I need to speak with Paul, she told herself. *I need to apologize for my abruptness the other day.*

Barbara walked swiftly across the lawn before she lost her nerve.

"Hi, Mama," Joseph said with a wide smile. "Me and the harness man—I mean, Paul—we're plannin' a fishin' trip."

Paul's ears turned pink, and he gave Barbara a sheepish-looking grin. "Guilty as charged. I thought maybe next Saturday after I close the shop in the afternoon."

Before Barbara could respond, Joseph thumped the spot beside him. "Have a seat, and we'll tell ya all about it."

Barbara knelt on the grass next to her son. "I'm all ears."

"I heard there's some pretty nice catfish in the pond over by Ben Swartley's place," Paul said. "I thought it might be fun to take the boys fishing." He motioned to Barbara. "You're welcome to come along if you like."

The thought of going fishing was like honey in Barbara's mouth. She hadn't been on such an outing in over a year. Not since David had taken her and the boys to the pond for a picnic a few weeks before his death.

"It sounds like fun," she murmured. "But I couldn't leave Davey that long."

"You wouldn't have to," Paul said. "You could bring the baby along."

Joseph nodded enthusiastically. "Jah, Mama. The boppli can come, too."

Barbara shook her head. "He can't be in the sun all day."

387

"We could put up a little tent," Paul suggested. "We'll set his baby carriage inside, and he'll be just fine."

Barbara had some netting in her sewing cabinet. Maybe she could drape it over the carriage to keep the bugs away, and if she put the carriage under the shade of a tree, it might work out okay. It would be nice to get away and do something fun. But did she really want to spend several hours alone with Paul? *Of course,* she reasoned, *I wouldn't really be alone with him. The boys will be there, too.*

"Can we go, Mama? Please?"

She patted her son's shoulder. "I'll think on it. In the meantime, I'd like you to go find Aaron."

"What for? He don't wanna play with me; he said so."

"Tell him I want to head for home soon."

Joseph's lower lip protruded. "Aw, do we have to?"

"Jah. I'm going back to the house to get Zachary and Davey in a few minutes, and I'd like you and Aaron to be ready to go."

The boy stood and squeezed Paul around the neck. It was obvious that he'd taken a liking to the man. And from the way Paul responded by grinning and patting Joseph on the back, Barbara was fairly sure the feeling was returned.

As Joseph skipped away, Barbara searched for the necessary words. "I. . .uh. . .owe you an apology for the other day."

Paul's eyebrows rose.

"I shouldn't have been so testy about Aaron's black hands, and I didn't mean to question your judgment. I hope you'll accept my apology."

A slow smile spread across his face, and a familiar longing

crept into her heart. *David used to look at me like that. Oh, I surely do miss him.*

"No apology needed," Paul said. "Aaron's your son, and you had a right to be concerned."

"I appreciate your understanding."

He plucked a blade of grass and stuck it between his teeth. "I hope you'll consider the fishing trip."

Barbara was taken aback by the stark emotion she saw in Paul's eyes. What did it mean? Was he missing someone, too? Maybe Paul had a girlfriend back in Pennsylvania. Barbara had never thought to ask. Should she say something now? No, she'd better not; it might embarrass Paul.

"I'll give it some thought," she finally murmured.

"While you're thinking on it, I hope you'll remember how much Joseph wants to go fishing." He leaned back on his elbows and smiled. "For that matter, from the look I saw on your face when the fishing trip was mentioned, I'd say it's something you might be looking forward to, as well."

Barbara rose to her feet and hurried toward the house with her heart beating an irregular rhythm.

Chapter 10

On Wednesday morning, a group of women including
Margaret Hilty and Faith showed up to work in Barbara's yard.
Barbara felt torn between helping them and going to the harness
shop. She knew it could only be for an hour or two, as she didn't
have the energy to work a full day yet. Her plan was to wait
until lunch was over and then take the three younger boys to her
folks' place so her mom could watch them. She figured Aaron
might like to help in the shop, too.

"I feel like I should be helping you with the yard work," Barbara said when Faith came up to the house to get a jug of iced tea
for the women. "But I'm planning to work in the harness shop
a few hours this afternoon, and if I work in the garden this morning, I won't have the energy to work in the shop after lunch."

Faith shook her head. "We don't expect you to help us in the garden." She touched Barbara's arm. "If you want my opinion, you shouldn't be working in the harness shop yet, either."

"Why not?"

"Have you looked in a mirror this morning? You've got dark circles under your eyes, and your face looks pale and drawn." Faith nodded toward the steps leading to the upstairs bedrooms. "What you should do after lunch is take a nap."

"I don't need a nap, and I don't need any lectures." Barbara gritted her teeth, and her hand shook as she pushed a strand of hair back into her bun. She wished people would stop telling her what to do.

Faith drew back like she'd been stung by a bee. "Sorry. I didn't mean to upset you."

Barbara's face relaxed some. "It's me who should apologize. I don't know why I'm so testy lately."

"You're tired and no doubt feeling a bit stressed with all the responsibilities you have."

"That's true, but it's no excuse for me being rude. Will you forgive me?"

Faith nodded and gave Barbara a hug. "Of course. And I'll keep praying for you, too."

"Danki. I appreciate that."

"Well, I'd best head back to the garden so the women can have a cold drink." Faith made a beeline for the yard, and Barbara hurried upstairs to check on little David.

"Looks like a group of women have converged on Barbara's yard today," Samuel said to Paul as he glanced out the window of the harness shop.

Paul stepped up beside Samuel. "I see that. I wonder what they're all doing."

"From what Alice told me, they came to weed the garden and get Barbara's yard in shape."

Paul craned his neck as he watched several women bent over the garden with hoes and rakes. "Looks like my sister-in-law Margaret is here."

Samuel nodded. "Alice heard that John Frey invited Margaret, thinking it would give her something meaningful to do that might take her mind off her grief."

Paul cringed at the mention of the bishop's name. He didn't care for the way that man looked at Barbara. . .like he owned her. He turned away from the window and grabbed a hunk of leather that needed to be trimmed. *Maybe I'm overreacting. Bishop John might not have a personal interest in Barbara at all. He may just be doing his job as head minister of this community when he pays her a call, same as he's been doing with Margaret.*

"Did Barbara tell you she plans to come out to the shop this afternoon?" Samuel asked.

Paul shook his head. "She never said a word. I guess it's her right to drop in and check on things, since this is her shop."

Samuel glanced out the window again as the rumble of buggy wheels could be heard coming up the driveway.

"Guess there must be more women coming to the work frolic, huh?"

Samuel shook his head. "Nope. It's John Frey's rig, and he doesn't seem to be headed to the harness shop, so he must be planning to pay another call on Barbara. Or maybe he came by to see how the yard work is coming along."

Paul clamped his teeth together. *More than likely the bishop's here to see Barbara.*

Knowing the three older boys were playing in the barn, Barbara opened the door and stepped outside to call them in for lunch.

"There's a buggy comin', Mama," Aaron said as he, Joseph, and Zachary hurried across the lawn.

She shielded her eyes against the harsh glare of the sun and noticed Bishop Frey's rig heading toward the house. Instinctively, she reached up to straighten her kapp.

"Wie geht's?" the bishop called as he stepped down from the buggy.

"I'm fine, and you?"

"Hot and thirsty." He swiped his hand across his forehead. "It's a real scorcher."

"It sure is," she agreed. "It makes me feel guilty to see how hard the women are working in my yard."

Bishop John glanced over his shoulder. "Have they been working long?"

"A few hours, but they'll be stopping soon for lunch. My mamm made some sandwiches, so I'll be calling them in to eat in a few minutes." Barbara nodded toward the porch swing. "If you'd like to have a seat, I'll get you a glass of iced tea."

He grinned and seated himself on the swing. "I'd be much obliged."

Barbara wasn't sure whether to leave her boys with Bishop John or take them inside with her. Seeing how much fun Zachary was having as he raced back and forth on the lawn, chasing after Joseph, she decided to leave things as they were. "I'll be right back," she said before hurrying inside.

A few minutes later, she returned with a glass of iced tea for the bishop and some crackers for her boys. She figured it would tide them over until lunch and maybe keep their mouths too busy to talk. Joseph could be quite chatty, and the last thing she needed was for him to tell John Frey any of their personal business.

She called the boys over to the porch, gave them the crackers, and instructed them to go back to the barn and play.

"How come, Mama?" Aaron asked. "You just called us out of the barn, and now you want us to go back?"

"I know I did, but I want you to play awhile longer so I can speak with Bishop John."

Joseph didn't have to be asked twice. He grabbed hold of Zachary's hand, and the two scampered off. But not Aaron. He glanced at the bishop with a strange expression, then stared at the porch floor, scuffing the toe of his boot along the wooden planks.

"Go on now," Barbara instructed. "Get on out to the barn with your brothers."

Aaron grunted and finally ambled off.

"Won't you sit with me and visit awhile?" the bishop asked.

Barbara's skin prickled as she sensed it was more than a casual visit, since he hadn't brought any of his daughters along. She sat in the wicker chair on the other side of the porch.

"I don't bite, you know," he said with a slanted grin.

She forced a smile in return. "I'm sure you don't. But I want to be close to the back door so I can hear the boppli if he starts to cry."

He shrugged and removed his straw hat, using it to fan his face. "Whew! Sure hope it cools down some. It's only the beginning of June, and already it's hotter than an oven turned on high."

She nodded. "Jah, hot and sticky."

The bishop cleared his throat. "I've been thinking about the two of us."

The speed of Barbara's heartbeat picked up. "What about us?"

"You've been widowed almost a year now, and it's been six months since my wife died." He paused and licked his lips. "The book of Ecclesiastes says, 'Two are better than one; because they have a good reward for their labour.' "

She nodded politely.

"I figure you've got young ones who need a daed, and I have four daughters who certainly could use a mother's hand. Since two are better than one, I was wondering how you'd feel about marrying me."

Barbara's mouth fell open. She'd suspected John Frey had marriage on his mind, but she hadn't expected him to be quite so direct. This proposal, if she could call it that, was much too sudden and abrupt. They hadn't courted or done anything of a social nature together, and she doubted they had much in common.

"Your silence makes me wonder if you find the idea of marriage to me objectionable." His forehead wrinkled. "Is it the thought of being a bishop's wife that bothers you, or is it our age difference?"

Barbara twisted her hands in her lap. How could she put her feelings into words and not sound as if she were being too particular or unappreciative of his offer? "There is a good fifteen years between us," she admitted. "Though I know many folks who have married people much older or younger and things worked out fine."

His lips turned upward. "That's how I see it, too."

"As far as being a bishop's wife, I don't think that's reason enough to keep someone from marrying another, either."

He jumped up and moved quickly to stand beside her. "Does that mean you'd be willing to marry me?"

Barbara cringed. She was making a mess of things and had to fix it before she ended up betrothed to this man for whom she felt nothing but respect as her bishop. "I'm not ready to commit to marriage again," she said, carefully choosing her words. "And if I should ever marry, I would want it to be for love, not merely for the sake of convenience."

A pained expression crossed his face, and she was sure she had hurt his feelings.

"You're saying you don't find me appealing, isn't that right?" The poor man looked as if he'd taken a whiff of vinegar.

"That's not it at all." Barbara sucked in her lower lip. "It's just that I'm not over the loss of David yet, and it wouldn't seem right to take another husband until the pain subsides."

The bishop paced the length of the porch several times. After a few minutes, he stopped and faced her again. "Both of us will always have love in our hearts for the ones we married in our youth. But that shouldn't stop us from starting a new relationship. Fact is, getting married again might help heal our pain."

Even if the bishop was right, Barbara didn't want or need a husband right now. She had her hands full making sure her business didn't fail. "I truly do appreciate the offer, John, but—"

He held up one hand. "I want to take care of you, Barbara. I'd like to offer you a home and provide for you and your boys."

The man sounded sincere, but what he'd said caused her spine to go rigid. "I've got my job at the harness shop, and it supports us well enough."

"I understand that, but wouldn't you prefer not to have to work in order to take care of your boys?"

"I enjoy working with leather."

"But keeping the harness shop is becoming harder for you to do now that your daed's arthritis is getting worse and you have to rely on your mamm to care for the boys. Isn't that right?"

She nodded.

John reached out his hand like he might touch her, but he pulled it back and smiled instead. "You don't have to give me your answer this minute. Just promise you'll think about marrying me, okay?"

Not wishing to hurt the man's feelings, Barbara nodded.

"I'll give you a few more months to make up your mind."

"I. . .uh. . .appreciate that," she mumbled.

He handed her his empty glass. "I think we could both benefit if we were to marry, and I believe our kinner would gain something from our union, too."

Barbara's hand shook as she lifted it to touch her flushed

face. "If you'll excuse me, I need to get my boys. It's past their lunchtime."

"I can call them for you, since I'll be headed that way to my buggy," he offered.

"That would be fine." Barbara scurried into the house. Maybe she would feel better after she'd had some lunch. She was determined to do a little work in the harness shop, no matter how drained she felt.

When John poked his head into the barn, he discovered Zachary and Joseph sitting on a pile of straw playing with two kittens. The oldest boy, Aaron, sat on a wooden stool, fiddling with an old wooden yo-yo. "Your mamm wanted me to tell you that she's got lunch ready," John said, smiling at the boys.

Zachary and Joseph set the kittens down and scampered out. But Aaron just sat twisting the string of the yo-yo around his finger.

Deciding to take advantage of the situation, John stepped up to Aaron and touched his shoulder. "I was thinking it might be kind of fun to go on a picnic and maybe do some fishing sometime. What do you think of that idea, huh?"

Aaron looked up, and his eyebrows lifted slightly. "Just you and me?"

John shook his head. "I was planning to ask your mamm and brieder to go along."

"Mama and my brothers might want to go, but I'm not interested."

"How come?"

"Just don't wanna go, that's all." Aaron shrugged. "Paul Hilty asked Mama to go fishing with him on Saturday, but if she goes, only my brothers are goin'."

John stiffened. Was Paul planning to stay in Webster County for good? Did he have his cap set for Barbara? He grimaced. Maybe the man was after Barbara's harness shop and figured the best way to get it was to marry the woman.

Well, it's not going to happen. I'll keep after Barbara until she marries me. It's my job as her bishop to see that no one takes advantage of her.

Chapter 11

Paul glanced at the clock. It was almost one, and he'd just finished eating his lunch. His mother had outdone herself when she'd packed him leftover meat loaf, tangy potato salad, and zesty baked beans. The food had gone down a lot better than two hunks of bread with a slice of ham sandwiched between, which was what he usually fixed.

As Paul slipped his lunch pail under the counter, he thought about the day he'd been invited to join Barbara and her boys for their noon meal. It had been simple fare, just soup and rolls, but he had enjoyed it immensely. The food wasn't the only thing Paul had taken pleasure in. He actually liked being around Barbara's boys. All but Aaron. He wasn't sure he and the boy would ever see eye to eye, but he hoped they could at least come to an understanding, especially if Aaron continued to help in the harness shop.

Paul was preparing to cut a piece of leather when the shop door opened and Barbara and Aaron stepped into the room. His heartbeat quickened. Every time he was around the woman, he felt more drawn to her. That scared him.

"We thought we'd help out for a few hours," Barbara said. "That is, if you don't mind."

He shook his head. "It's your shop; you can do whatever you like." Paul could have bitten his tongue. He hadn't meant for his words to come out so clipped. "Sorry," he mumbled. "I just meant—"

"Anything in particular you're needing help with?" she asked.

He nodded toward the back of the shop. "Your daed's trimming the edges of some leather. When he's done, they'll need to be dyed."

Barbara's forehead creased. "More black hands for Aaron?"

Paul shrugged. "Maybe you can show him a better way or find some rubber gloves he could wear."

Barbara nodded. "I think I may have a pair somewhere that will fit him." She moved away, and Aaron followed.

Paul went back to work on the leather strap he was planning to cut, feeling a sense of irritation he didn't fully understand. Was it the fact that this was Barbara's shop and not his that bothered him so much? Maybe his irritation stemmed from her thinking she knew more about dying leather than he did. Well, if she had a better way of doing it that wouldn't stain the boy's hands, then she was more than welcome to show him.

Paul gripped the piece of leather in his hands as the truth behind his agitation surfaced and threatened to boil over. Every time Barbara came out to the shop, even for a short visit, it was a reminder to him that she would soon be back working full-time, taking over *her* shop again. When that happened, there would be no reason for Paul to stay in Webster County. Unless, of course, he could convince Barbara to sell the shop to him. If she married John Frey, she might be willing to.

Paul dropped the hunk of leather on the workbench with a thud. *But I don't want Barbara to marry the bishop. I want—*

What did he want, anyway?

With a grunt of determination, Paul resumed his work. If he kept focused on the job at hand, he wouldn't have so much time to think about other things. Things he had no right to be thinking about.

A short time later, Barbara returned to the front of the shop. "I think Aaron can manage on his own now," she said. "So I'm available to help with whatever else needs to be done."

Paul thought. He didn't want her doing anything too strenuous, yet he was sure she wanted to feel needed. "How about pressing some grooves into the edges of the straps that have been cut and dyed?"

Barbara nodded. "I can do that. I haven't worked the pressing machine in some time, but it should feel good to get back at it."

Paul watched as she moved to the machine and took up her work. He could see by the smile on her face that she loved working in the harness shop. *And who am I to say otherwise? Just because I don't think this is the kind of work a woman should do doesn't mean it's not right for Barbara. Besides, the sooner she gets back to work full-time, the sooner I can return to Pennsylvania.*

Paul shook his head. Who was he kidding? He liked it

here and wished he could stay. He forced his gaze away from Barbara and on to the job at hand. This kind of thinking was dangerous.

Barbara straightened with a weary sigh, easing the kinks out of her back. She'd only been working an hour, and already she felt as if the strength had been drained from her body. *Maybe I wasn't ready to come back yet, not even for a short time.* Tears flooded her eyes, and she willed them away. She loved being in the shop, where the subtle smell of leather mixed with the tangy aroma of linseed and neat's-foot oil. *Just take it slow,* she told herself. *If you work a few hours each week, soon you'll be up to working full-time again.*

"Are you okay, daughter?"

Barbara whirled around. She hadn't realized her father had come up behind her. "I–I'm a bit tired," she admitted. "Maybe I should call it a day."

He nodded soberly. "I should think so. You're paler than a bucket of fresh milk. And look at your hands—they're shaking."

Barbara clasped her fingers tightly together.

"I can't believe you're out here today," he said with a frown. "You ought to be up at the house, taking care of that new boppli of yours."

Barbara's cheeks warmed. "Dad, I'm a grown woman, and I know my limitations. Mom's watching Joseph, Zachary, and Davey, and if the boppli needs me, she will send Joseph straightaway." Barbara's voice quavered, but she hoped her father wouldn't notice.

Paul stepped up beside them. "Is everything all right?"

Barbara opened her mouth to respond, but her father cut her off. "She's not ready for this yet. Just look at the way she's trembling like a baby tree in the midst of a storm."

Paul frowned. "I should have been watching closer. Sorry about that, Samuel."

Barbara stomped her foot. "I am not a little girl who needs to be pampered. No one has to watch me or tell me when I should quit working."

The men stood silently, apparently dumbfounded by her outburst.

"Your daed's right about how tired you look," Paul finally said. "But if you want to continue working, it's your right to do so. After all, this is *your* shop, and *you're* the boss."

Not this again, Barbara fumed. *Why does he feel the need to keep reminding me that I'm the boss?*

She drew in a deep breath. "Actually, I should probably check on the boppli. So if I'm not needed for anything else, I'll go on up to the house."

"I'm sure we can manage," Paul said, glancing at Barbara's father.

"Jah, with Aaron's help, we'll do just fine."

"All right."

As Barbara headed for the door, Paul tapped her on the shoulder. "Can I speak with you a minute, outside?"

Barbara nodded.

When they stood outside the shop, she asked, "What is it?"

Paul stared at the ground and pushed the toe of his boot around, making little circles in the dirt. Barbara listened to the soft swooshing sound and wondered when or if he was going to tell her what was on his mind.

"I was wondering if you've thought anymore about Saturday," he mumbled.

"Saturday?"

"Jah, my invitation to take you and the boys to the pond for a picnic and some fishing."

Barbara hated to disappoint the boys, and she didn't want to send the three oldest ones with Paul while she stayed home with the baby. What if one of them fell in the water and he didn't see him in time? A lot could happen with three little boys.

"It will be a lot of fun," he prompted.

"Jah, okay. We'll go."

His lips lifted at the corners. "That's. . .uh. . .great. I'll check with my brother and see if he has a pole I can borrow."

Barbara thought about loaning him David's pole, but that idea didn't sit well with her. It wouldn't seem right to see someone else using her husband's fishing rod. "See you Saturday if not before," she said with a nod.

He turned back to the shop. "You can count on it."

Chapter 12

Barbara didn't go out to the harness shop the rest of the week. She needed to rest as much as possible if she was going to feel up to going on the picnic. Despite her misgivings about spending time with Paul outside the harness shop, she looked forward to taking the boys to the pond. She had packed some food they would eat for supper. Paul had promised to come by the house as soon as he closed the harness shop at three.

Barbara glanced at the kitchen clock, and a sense of apprehension crept up her spine. Should she have accepted Paul's invitation? She'd gone to bed early the night before, but she was exhausted. Maybe a little time spent at the pond would do her good. She used to like going there when David was alive. The children deserved to have a little fun at the pond, and maybe she did, too.

She opened the back door and spotted Aaron and Joseph sitting on the top porch step with a jar full of ladybugs. "You two need to go out to the barn and look for your fishing poles," she said.

Joseph jumped up, but Aaron sat unmoving.

"Aaron, did you hear what I said?"

"I don't wanna go fishing."

"Why not? You love to fish."

"Only with Pa when he was alive." Aaron's shoulders trembled.

She took a seat on the step beside him. "Grandpa's busy today, and Paul was nice enough to invite us. Don't you think you should go?"

He shook his head.

"It might hurt Paul's feelings if you don't come."

"I don't care."

"But you can't stay home alone."

"I can go over to Grandma and Grandpa's."

She took hold of his hand. "You'd rather be with them than fishing?"

"Jah," he said with a sober nod.

"We won't get home until after supper."

Aaron shrugged.

Barbara gave a weary sigh. "All right, then. If it's okay with Grandma and Grandpa, you can stay at their place."

Paul couldn't remember the last time he'd been this enthused about going fishing. Was it the anticipation of catching a mess of catfish, or was it the idea of spending time with Barbara and her boys? *A little of both,* he admitted as he shut down the gas lantern hanging above his workbench.

He reached under the bench and grabbed the fishing pole his brother Monroe had loaned him, then headed out the door.

When Paul reached the house, Zachary and Joseph were sitting on the porch, each holding a small fishing pole. He grinned at their enthusiasm. *Those two must like fishing as much as I do.*

"We've been waitin' for you," Joseph said eagerly. "Want me to call Mama?"

Paul stepped around them and onto the porch. "Sure, if you don't mind."

"Don't mind a'tall." Joseph jumped up, leaned his pole against the porch railing, and scurried into the house. A few minutes later he returned, lugging a wicker picnic basket. Barbara followed, holding the baby.

"Are you sure you don't mind me bringing David along?" she asked. "I just fed him, so he could be left with my mamm for a few hours."

Paul shook his head. "I think he'll be fine under the makeshift tent I've got stashed in my buggy. Besides, if you bring the boppli along, we won't have to hurry back if the fish are biting real good."

She smiled. "That's true, and I appreciate your making a little tent for the carriage." She nodded at the baby carriage on one end of the porch.

Paul reached down and scooped up the carriage, then glanced around. "Say, where's Aaron?"

"He ain't comin'," Joseph announced.

Paul glanced at Barbara.

"He said he'd rather stay with his *grossmudder* today," she said.

"Ich wolle mir fische geh," Zachary said, looking up at Paul with wide eyes.

Paul smiled and started for the buggy. "I'm glad you want to go fishing, Zachary." If Aaron didn't want to go, Paul couldn't do much about it.

He loaded the carriage and Barbara's two boys into the backseat. Then he helped Barbara and the baby get settled up front with him.

As they pulled out of the yard, Paul caught a glimpse of Aaron heading for the barn. Barbara waved, but the boy didn't look their way.

"Aaron's missing his daed," she said. "They used to go fishing together every chance they got."

He nodded. "I figured as much."

"I guess going to the pond today would be a painful reminder that his daed's not here anymore."

"He'll come around in time." Even as the words slipped off Paul's tongue, he wondered if they were true. Aaron might never completely get over his father's death, and he would probably never take a liking to Paul.

Barbara kissed the top of her baby's head. "At least Aaron will have some memories of David, which is more than this little guy will have." She glanced over her shoulder. "For that matter, Zachary probably won't remember his daed at all. I'm not even sure about Joseph."

Paul wished he could say or do something to ease the pain

on Barbara's face. It wasn't fair that she had to bear the loss of her husband and try to raise four boys on her own. It didn't seem right for Margaret, his brother's widow, to go through life on her own, either. At least Margaret and Dan's four children were grown, so she didn't have the responsibility of caring for little ones. Even so, Margaret must be lonely without Dan.

Paul's thoughts turned to John Frey. Had the man considered Margaret as a candidate for marriage? She was closer to his age than Barbara. But she'd only been a widow a few weeks. It wouldn't seem proper for the bishop to court a newly widowed woman. Would the man consider someone else in this small Amish community for a wife?

When Barbara's baby gurgled, Paul set his thoughts aside. He glanced over at Barbara. "Is the little fellow doing okay?"

She nodded. "I think he's enjoying the ride."

Paul looked over his shoulder. "The boys in the back must be, too. They're fast asleep."

Barbara chuckled. "As soon as we pull up to the pond, they'll be wide awake and raring to go."

"I sure hope the fish are biting today," he said. "Wouldn't want to disappoint the kinner."

"Zachary's not old enough to do much fishing yet, so I doubt he would care whether or not they were biting."

"Joseph might, though."

"Maybe. But he's so taken with you, he'd probably be happy just sitting on the grass by your side."

"Sure don't know why. I've never been that comfortable with little ones. I think most of 'em feel the same way about me."

"What makes you think that?"

"Don't rightly know, but I am sure of the reason I'm leery of them."

"Why's that?"

"I dropped my brother Elam when he was a boppli, and it left him with a fat lip and a lump on his forehead." He blew out his breath. "I was afraid of holding any bopplin after that."

"That must have been scary for both of you. But you were only a boy, and what happened was just an accident."

"Jah, well, I still get *naerfich* around kinner—especially little ones. I never know what to say to them." He grunted. "Take your boy Aaron, for example. He doesn't like me; that's obvious enough."

"Don't take anything Aaron says or does personally, Paul. He's still struggling with his daed's death."

He shrugged. "Guess you might be right about that. Even so—"

"I believe Joseph sees something you don't," she said, reaching over to touch his arm.

The feel of Barbara's slender fingers on his bare skin made Paul's arm tingle. He inhaled deeply, searching for something else to talk about. "We're getting close to the pond. I can smell it. Can you?" he asked as she pulled her hand away.

"Jah, I believe I can."

A short time later, they pulled onto a grassy spot. Paul had no sooner secured the horse to a tree than the boys woke up and clambered out of the buggy. "Here, let me help you down," Paul said, offering Barbara his hand.

She leaned forward and gave him the baby. "If you'll take Davey, I can get out of the buggy a little easier."

"After what I said about dropping my little bruder, are you sure you trust me to hold him?"

She nodded. "I'm sure you'll do fine."

Reluctantly, Paul took the infant. He'd never held a baby this young before and wasn't sure if he was doing it right. He laid the baby against his shoulder, then patted the little fellow's back, feeling more awkward and nervous by the minute.

As soon as Barbara stepped down, she took her son. Paul felt a rush of relief. He'd seen many fathers hold their babies and look perfectly comfortable, but he doubted he ever would if he became a father.

Paul reached under the front seat and grabbed an old quilt. He handed it to Barbara. "If you and the boys want to get settled, I'll get the rest of the stuff unloaded."

"Joseph can help," she said.

Paul nodded toward the shoreline. The boys were already romping back and forth, throwing rocks into the water. "Let him play. I can manage."

"All right." Cradling little David, Barbara headed for a grassy area not far from the water.

In short order, Paul had a little tent set up for the baby carriage. Barbara put the infant inside and draped the piece of netting she'd brought over the sides. After Paul got the boys' fishing poles ready, he baited Barbara's hook and handed her the pole.

"Danki." She placed it on the ground and took a seat on the grass. "I'm not used to having someone wait on me, you know."

He grinned and sat next to her, noticing that she looked more rested. "It feels nice to be taking the time to go fishing."

She nodded, then leaned forward and cupped her hands around her mouth. "Joseph, Paul has your pole ready! Bring Zachary over here, and let's do some fishing."

The boys came running, and soon all four of them had their lines in the water. The sound of the children's laughter rippled over Paul like a bubbling brook, and he was amazed at how comfortable he felt. Savoring the moment, Paul closed his eyes and allowed himself to fully relax.

"Would you like to have some cookies and milk?" Alice asked Aaron when she opened the back door and found him sitting on the top porch step with his shoulders slumped and his head down.

"Naw. I ain't hungry."

She resisted the urge to correct his English and instead seated herself beside him. "Are you wishing you'd gone to the pond with your mamm and brieder?"

He shook his head vigorously. "Paul's there, too, and I don't want to do anything with him."

"Not even help in the harness shop?"

"I only go there 'cause it's my daed's shop, and he promised it'll be mine someday. Otherwise, I'd never go anywhere near Paul Hilty."

"What have you got against Paul?"

Aaron shrugged.

"Your grandpa says Paul knows a lot about harness making. I'm sure he could teach you plenty of things."

"Mama can teach me when she starts workin' full-time again."

"Even so, it's good for you to be around a man," Alice said.

"I'm around Grandpa a lot. At least he doesn't think he knows everything."

Alice placed her hand on Aaron's knee. "I'm sure Paul doesn't think he knows everything."

"Jah, he does. He acts like he's the boss of me and everything in my daed's harness shop." Aaron grunted. "You should see the way Joseph and Zachary hang all over him—like he's somethin' real special."

"They like Paul. He seems to like them, too."

"Humph!" Aaron folded his arms and stared straight ahead. "I think he's only pretendin' to like 'em."

"Why would he want to do that?"

A horse and buggy rolled into the yard just then, interrupting their conversation.

"That looks like Faith Hertzler's rig," Alice said. "She must be looking for your mamm."

Aaron stood. "Think I'll go out to the barn awhile and see what Grandpa's doin'."

"If you change your mind about having some milk and cookies, give a holler."

As Faith stepped down from her buggy, she noticed Barbara's oldest boy dart into the barn. She glanced up and saw Alice standing on the porch.

"I came to see how Barbara's doing. Is she at home?" Faith called.

Alice shook her head. "She and the three younger ones went to the pond with Paul Hilty for a picnic and to do some fishing."

"Really?" Faith asked as she joined Alice on the porch.

"Jah. I was surprised that she agreed to go, but I'm glad she did. My daughter needs to get out more. Maybe some fresh air and sunshine will perk her up a bit."

"I totally agree." Faith glanced at the barn. "How come Aaron didn't go?"

"That boy's been acting moody as all get-out ever since Paul began working for Barbara. He was invited to go fishing, but he didn't want to go."

"That's too bad. I'm sure he would have enjoyed spending the evening at the pond with a fishing pole in his hand. I know Isaiah sure would have." Faith chuckled. "For that matter, Melinda would rather be at the pond or in the woods than doing anything at home."

Alice smiled. "Is she still taking in every critter that comes along?"

"Jah, as many as we'll allow."

"At least she has something that holds her interest. That's more than I can say for Aaron these days. All he seems to want to do is sit around and mope." Alice motioned to the wicker chairs sitting near the front door. "Would you like to have a seat and visit awhile?"

"I don't mind if I do." Faith sank into one of the chairs with a weary sigh. "I spent most of the day helping Noah bake, and my feet are tired from standing so long."

"That man of yours is a wonder to me," Alice said. "Most men don't go near the kitchen unless it's to fill their bellies with food, but he actually enjoys being there."

"That's true. According to Noah's mamm, he started helping her in the kitchen when he was just a boy. I feel fortunate to have him."

"I hope Barbara finds another husband someday. She deserves to be happy, and it's getting harder for her to run that harness shop by herself." Alice gave a gusty sigh. "Of course, she thinks she can do everything on her own."

"Has she started working in the shop again?"

"Just a couple of hours here and there, but as soon as she regains her strength, she'll be back working full-time. Then Paul Hilty will probably be on his way back to Pennsylvania."

"Paul seems like a nice man," Faith said. "From what Noah's told me, Paul's real good at what he does, too."

Alice nodded. "I don't think he would have left Missouri if he'd been able to do harness work here."

Faith popped a couple of knuckles as she contemplated the best way to say what was on her mind. "I was wondering. . . ."

"What's that?"

"If Paul invited Barbara and her boys to go to the pond with him, do you think he might be interested in Barbara?"

Alice blinked. "Is that what you think?"

Faith's face heated with embarrassment. "I didn't say that. I just meant—"

Alice waved her hand. "It's all right. To tell you the truth, I'm hoping things work out so Barbara and Paul can be together.

After all, they both enjoy the harness business, and Barbara's boys—all but Aaron—seem to like Paul a lot."

"Maybe in time, Aaron will come around." Faith smiled. "Now we just have to hope and pray that Barbara will see that she needs another man, and that if it's meant to be Paul, they'll both realize it before Bishop John convinces her to marry him."

Barbara couldn't get over how relaxed she felt as she fixed her gaze on Paul. For one crazy moment, she was hurled into a whirlwind of conflicting emotions as she wondered what it would be like if Paul were to stay in Missouri and—

Barbara shook her head. She couldn't allow herself the luxury of thinking about Paul as anything other than her temporary employee. She had a business to run, not to mention four boys to raise. There wasn't time for romantic notions or even a close friendship with someone who would be leaving Webster County soon.

She nibbled on her lower lip. *Even if I did feel free to begin a relationship with Paul, and I knew he wanted one, he's never been married. He wouldn't want to take on the responsibility of raising another man's children, especially when one of them doesn't seem to like him much.*

"Hey! I've got me a bite!" Joseph hollered, pulling Barbara's musings aside. "I think it's a big one!"

"Hold on tight," Paul instructed as he sprang to his feet. "Would ya help me reel him in?"

Paul grabbed Joseph's pole and held it steady.

"Don't let him get away, okay?"

"I won't." After several tugs, a nice big catfish lay flopping at the boy's feet.

Zachary squealed and jumped up and down. *"Fisch! Fisch!"*

Barbara laughed. It felt nice to see her boys having such a good time.

Joseph pointed to his trophy. *"Es bescht,"* he said with a wide grin.

Paul nodded. "Jah, the best." He removed the hook, then placed the catfish in a bucket of water.

For the next hour, they continued fishing. With Paul's help, they each caught at least one fish. The boys vied for Paul's attention, plopping down beside him and taking turns crawling into his lap. It pleased Barbara to see them so happy and carefree. If only Aaron hadn't been too stubborn to come. He would have enjoyed himself as much as his younger brothers.

After a while, the baby woke up and started to howl.

Zachary and Joseph covered their ears. "Make him quit, Mama," they pleaded in unison.

"There's only one way to stop his crying," Barbara said. "I'll need to feed him." Feeling the heat of a blush cover her cheeks, she looked over at Paul. "Would you mind if I take the boppli to your buggy?"

Paul shook his head, and she noticed the blotch of red covering his face. "Sure, go ahead. Maybe when you're done, we can eat our picnic supper," he said.

A short time later, the baby was fed and settled back in his carriage. Barbara spread the contents of their picnic basket on the quilt, and they bowed for silent prayer. Following the prayer, they dug into the fried chicken, baked beans, carrot sticks, and rolls. Paul brought out a batch of peanut butter cookies Noah had given him.

"Everything tastes great," Paul said, smacking his lips. "Especially the chicken."

"It's a recipe my mamm and her mamm used to make," she said with a smile. "I call it Webster County Fried Chicken, and it used to be David's favorite meal."

Paul smacked his lips again. "I can see why. It's *appeditlich*."

She smiled and pushed the container of chicken closer to him. "Since you think it's delicious, would you like to have some more?"

"Don't mind if I do," he said, reaching for another drumstick.

"Have you gone on many picnics in Lancaster County?" Barbara asked.

He shrugged. "I've gone on a few with my cousin's family."

"How about a girlfriend?"

He shook his head. "Don't have one of those right now."

"Oh, I see." Barbara handed Paul a glass of lemonade, and when their fingers touched briefly, a strange sense of warmth crept through her body. She hadn't felt this giddy since her courting days with David. It was more than a bit disconcerting.

Paul smiled. "Danki, Barbara."

She returned his smile, realizing that despite her best intentions a special kind of friendship was taking root in her heart. She didn't need love or romance to enjoy the company of a man—especially this man.

Chapter 13

Paul was glad to have an off Sunday, when there would be no church. It wasn't that he disliked the services. He just wanted some time alone. After yesterday's trip to the pond with Barbara and three of her boys, he needed to think and pray. He'd had a good time. *Too good, maybe,* Paul thought as he headed for his folks' barn. Since he wouldn't be doing any work that wasn't absolutely necessary on this day of rest, a little getaway might do him some good.

As soon as Paul entered the rustic building, he took a seat on a bale of straw. He had come here countless times when he was a boy, and it had always been a good place to think and pray.

Heavenly Father, I don't know why I'm so drawn to Barbara, he prayed. *Mom told me how hard Barbara mourned when David was killed, and I have an inkling she might still be grieving.*

A vision of Barbara's pretty face popped into his head. *Despite my attraction to her, Lord, I know it's not likely she would ever be interested in me. She's got the bishop after her, and I suspect she'll consider marrying him.*

The barn door creaked, and Paul's eyes snapped open. "Paul?"

"Jah, Pop, I'm over here."

His father removed his straw hat, revealing a thick crop of nearly gray hair, and plopped the hat over a nail protruding from a nearby beam. "What are you doing in here?"

"Just sitting, thinking, and praying."

"Always did like to hide out in the barn, didn't you?"

"Jah."

"I would like to talk to you for a minute if you're done praying."

"Sure, what's up?"

Pop leaned against a wooden beam as he studied Paul. "Your brothers and I could use some help in the fields next week. We were hoping we could count on you."

Paul shifted uneasily on the bale of hay. "Sorry, but I can't."

"Why not?"

"I can't leave Barbara in the lurch."

Pop squinted his pale blue eyes. "She's not back to work yet?"

Paul shook his head.

"When will she be?"

"I don't rightly know. She tried working a few hours one day last week, but I think it took its toll on her."

Pop crossed his arms. "Your mamm tells me Barbara and a couple of her kinner went fishing with you yesterday afternoon.

Doesn't sound to me like she's feeling so weak if she can fish all afternoon."

Paul's defenses rose as his face heated up. "Sitting on a grassy bank with a fishing pole is relaxing. It's not hard work like the things we do in the harness shop."

His father's face contorted. "Jah, well, it makes me wonder if there isn't more going on with you and Barbara than just you working for her."

Paul clenched his fists. Pop had no right to be saying such things, but there had been too many harsh words between them in the past. He didn't want to respond disrespectfully.

"There's nothing going on between me and Barbara," Paul said slowly. "I promised to help her until she's back on her feet, and I aim to do just that."

Pop grunted. "And then what?"

"Then I'll be on my way back to Lancaster County to work in Andy's harness shop. Fact is, I went to Seymour the other day and phoned Andy to see if my job's still waiting."

"And?"

"He's got a couple of fellows working there now, but he said my job will be waiting for me when I go back to Pennsylvania."

"Didn't figure it would be any different." Pop grabbed his hat and stalked out of the barn, letting the door slam shut behind him.

Paul shook his head. "I guess some things will never change."

Barbara stood on the front porch of her house. As she watched her three boys play in the yard, her thoughts took her back to the pond, where she had enjoyed herself so much yesterday. Paul had shown a side of himself she hadn't known existed. Usually serious, he had joked with her, frolicked with Zachary and Joseph, and seemed genuinely relaxed. He'd even commented on how much the baby was growing and said he was a cute little guy. As long as they stayed away from the topic of the harness shop, Barbara and Paul got along quite well.

"Mama, Aaron's bein' mean."

Barbara whirled around at the sound of Joseph's voice. "What's the problem, son?" she asked, leaning over and wiping away the tears glistening on his cheeks.

"Aaron says Paul's tryin' to be our new daed."

Barbara's mouth dropped open. "Where did he get such a notion?"

"I was tellin' him how much fun we had at the pond yesterday and how Paul said he wished he had a son like me." Joseph's lower lip quivered slightly. "Aaron said Paul was just tryin' to butter me up. He said that Paul's a mean man."

"And what has Paul done to make Aaron think he's mean?"

Joseph sniffed. "He says Paul's real bossy and is always givin' him crummy jobs in the harness shop."

Barbara pursed her lips. Paul had given Aaron menial jobs to do. But her son was too young to do anything complicated or that required heavy lifting. She also knew the child wanted to help in the shop and figured he would appreciate any job, no matter how small. Aaron had never complained when his father had given him easy chores to do. Barbara suspected Aaron's dislike of Paul had more to do with not wanting anyone to take his father's place.

She tousled Joseph's curly, blond hair and gave him a hug. "I'll speak to Aaron about his attitude. In the meantime, why don't you take Zachary inside? There's a jar of chocolate chip cookies that Grandma made yesterday on the cupboard. You two can have some with a glass of milk, if you like."

Joseph smiled, and his blue eyes brightened considerably. "Okay. I'll climb up on a stool and get us some." He turned around and motioned for Zachary. "Come inside and have some cookies and milk."

Zachary darted across the grass like a colt kicking up its heels and bounded onto the porch. When Joseph jerked the screen door open, both boys scampered into the house.

Barbara glanced across the yard. Aaron was seated on the swing hanging from the maple tree, kicking at a clump of grass with his bare toes.

Lord, please give me the right words, Barbara prayed as she headed for the swing.

Aaron looked up. "I suppose that tattletale Joseph told you we was sayin' things about Paul Hilty," he said with a lift of his chin.

She nodded. "Did you tell your brother that Paul was mean and trying to butter him up?"

He nodded. "Jah, and I meant it, too."

"That wasn't nice, and it's not true."

He grunted. "You haven't seen the way that bossy fellow treats me whenever I'm in the harness shop. He acts like I'm *dumm* or something."

"I'm sure Paul doesn't think you're stupid, Aaron."

"Jah, he does."

"Are the jobs Paul has given you any different from the ones you did for your daed?"

He dropped his gaze to the ground. "Not really, but—"

"Then why do you think Paul's treating you differently?"

He shrugged.

"You're still young, Aaron, and Paul's giving you jobs you're able to do. If you keep doing them well, I'm sure Paul will give you other jobs as he sees that you're capable of doing them."

Aaron stared straight ahead.

"You need to give Paul a chance to get to know you better," Barbara said. "Maybe you should have gone fishing with us. Then you'd have seen for yourself that he's not mean."

"Humph! All Joseph's been talkin' about since Saturday is that dumb old fishin' trip and how much fun he had with Paul." Aaron wrinkled his nose. "Paul favors my little brothers—that's for certain sure."

Barbara knelt and touched Aaron's knee. "That isn't true, son. Paul has reached out to Joseph and Zachary, but they'd also reached out to him. If you would give the man half a chance, you and he could become friends, too."

Aaron started pumping the swing. "I don't care if he takes 'em fishin' every day of the week. I'm never gonna like him!"

Barbara wanted to say more, but the words wouldn't come. It wasn't likely anything she had to say would change Aaron's mind. That would have to come from Paul, and since he wouldn't be staying around Webster County much longer, she doubted there could be a resolution. All the more reason she had to get back to work as soon as possible. If Aaron helped her instead of Paul, he would be more agreeable.

"Your brothers are having cookies and milk up at the house," she said. "If you've a mind to join them, I'm sure there's plenty left."

Aaron kept swinging. Barbara walked away with a sick feeling. Her oldest boy was becoming more belligerent all the time. If he didn't come to grips with his father's death soon, would he carry the resentment clear into his adult life? She had to find some way to help him. Maybe if she spoke to her father, he could get through to Aaron.

Barbara headed for the house. When she stepped into the kitchen, she was greeted with a mess. Joseph and Zachary sat at the table with chocolate all over their faces and crumbs covering their light blue cotton shirts. The cookie jar was nearly empty, and an empty bottle of milk sat beside it. The milk was on the floor.

"What happened?" Barbara yelled. "Just look at the disaster you two have caused!"

Joseph gave her a sheepish look. Zachary continued to munch on his cookie.

"Sorry, Mama," Joseph said. "The milk spilled on the floor."

Barbara grabbed a sponge from the kitchen sink. So much for the quiet Sunday morning she'd hoped to have. First Aaron's impossible attitude, and now this!

The baby started to howl from the crib in the next room.

"The boppli's awake," Joseph announced.

"I can hear him." Barbara tossed the sponge onto the kitchen table. "Here, Joseph. Please get things cleaned up while I tend to Davey." She marched out of the room before he had a chance to respond. Tomorrow she would work in the harness shop no matter how tired she felt. At least that might bring some sense of normalcy to her life.

Chapter 14

For the next several weeks, Barbara forced herself to get out of bed early, feed the boys, and send them to her folks' house. With a renewed sense of determination, she worked in the harness shop three days a week, taking breaks only for lunch and to feed the baby. On the days her father had physical therapy, she took Aaron to the shop so he could help. Dad's hands had become stiffer, but the therapy and wax treatments seemed to help some.

At Barbara's request, her father had spoken to Aaron about his attitude. The boy wouldn't open up to his grandpa, but he seemed a little more compliant while working at the shop. Barbara suspected it might be because she was there, too.

As Barbara cleared the breakfast table, she noticed for the first time in many weeks that her energy level was actually up.

Maybe it's because my appetite's back, she mused. *Or it could be because I'm back doing what I love best—making and repairing leather items. Maybe I can start working full-time soon.*

She placed a stack of dishes in the sink and ran water over them. It wasn't easy being a full-time mother and running a business, but she enjoyed the work and it did support her family.

"I'm ready to go when you are, Mama."

Barbara turned at the sound of Aaron's voice. "I've still got to feed the boppli. Why don't you head out to the shop. Zachary and Joseph are already at Grandma's, so I'll be along shortly."

Aaron's dark eyebrows drew together. "I'd rather wait for you."

"But Paul might need you for something."

Aaron stared at the floor. "Do I have to go now?"

"Jah."

Aaron huffed and turned toward the door. "Don't be too long, okay?"

"If I can get your wee bruder to cooperate, I shouldn't be more than half an hour or so." Barbara's heart went out to her melancholy son. "*Naemlich do,* Aaron," she called.

"I love you, too."

The door clicked shut, and Barbara hurried into the next room to get the baby. She prayed things would go all right between Aaron and Paul today. She prayed that her full strength would return soon, too.

"Here's that bread you wanted, Papa," Nadine said, as she handed John a loaf of bread with an overly browned crust.

He grimaced. "What happened? Did you forget to check on it while it was baking?"

"Papa, I—"

"You're fourteen years old, daughter. You ought to be able to bake a loaf of bread without burning it."

Nadine's chin quivered, and her blue eyes filled with tears. "I'll make another batch, and I promise I won't leave the kitchen until it's done baking."

He shook his head. "Never mind. I need to call on Barbara Zook so I can get back to work here." He held up the bread and studied it intently. "Only the crust is overly brown; I'm sure it'll taste okay."

"Papa's right," Betty put in as she put away the orange juice. "Some of the bread I've made has been overly brown, but it tasted fine and dandy just the same."

"How come you're calling on Barbara again?" Nadine asked. "Didn't you, Mary, and Hannah go there not long ago?"

"That's right, we did," Mary said as she washed dishes. "Doesn't Barbara have time to make bread?"

"I—I don't know if she's had time for baking or not," John sputtered. "She's got her hands full taking care of the boppli right now, and she's still looking pretty tired, so I'm sure she would appreciate the bread." He took a seat at the table. *Maybe now's the time for me to tell the girls what's on my mind.*

"How come you're sitting down, Papa?" Nadine asked. "I thought you were in a hurry to get to Barbara's."

"I am in a hurry, but it can wait a few minutes." He motioned to the four empty chairs across from him. "Why don't you all have a seat? I'd like to say something to you."

"But I'll be late for work," Betty said as she reached for her lunch pail sitting on the counter near the door.

"This will only take a minute."

Betty and Nadine took a seat, and the two youngest girls dried their hands and did the same.

John cleared his throat a couple of times.

"What's wrong, Papa? Have you got something caught in your throat?" Mary questioned with a worried frown.

"Do you need a drink of water?" Nadine asked.

He shook his head. "I'm fine. Just trying to think of the best way to say what's on my mind."

The girls stared at him with curious expressions.

He drew in a sharp breath and released it quickly. "The thing is. . .your mamm's been gone over half a year now, and things have been kind of confused around here without her."

The girls nodded soberly.

"And I've concluded that I need another wife—someone who'll make a good mudder for all of you."

Betty's eyebrows shot up, Nadine's mouth dropped open, and the two youngest girls stared at him with wide-eyed expressions. Betty spoke up. "I don't think we need a new mother, Papa. Me and the sisters are getting along just fine."

The other three girls nodded.

"No one could ever take our mamm's place," Nadine put in.

John gripped the edge of the table. He was botching things up badly and needed to think of something to say that would smooth things over with his girls. "Of course no one could ever take your mamm's place. She was a loving mudder and a faithful *fraa*. Your mamm will always be with us in here," he said,

431

touching his chest with the palm of his hand.

The girls' heads bobbed up and down in agreement.

"Even so," he continued, "I think it would do well for me and be good for you if I got married again."

Betty leaned forward, her elbows on the table, as she gazed at him. "Have you got someone in mind?"

He nodded. "Barbara Zook."

"What?" Betty and Nadine said in unison.

"I said—"

"But, Papa, Barbara's a lot younger than you, and—"

John held up his hand to halt Betty's words. "Your mamm wanted to give me more kinner, but that didn't happen because we lost her to cancer." He drew in another quick breath. "Barbara's still in the childbearing years, and she's got four kinner of her own, so she would not only be a suitable wife, but she could give me those kinner your mamm wanted me to have."

The girls' mouths dropped open, and they stared at him as if he'd taken leave of his senses.

He shifted in his chair. The air had become so thick he thought he could have sliced right through it if he'd had a knife in his hands. Maybe he'd said too much. It might have been better just to state the obvious—that he needed a wife and they needed a mother.

"Have you already asked Barbara to marry you?" Nadine questioned.

His face heated up. "Well, I did make mention of it."

Betty's pale eyebrows drew together. "Don't you think we should have some say in this?"

He puffed out his cheeks. "That's why we're talking about it now."

Betty shook her head. "But we're not really talking about it, Papa. You're telling us what we need and saying you've already spoken to Barbara about marrying you. It doesn't sound to me like our opinion matters much at all."

John opened his mouth to reply, but Hannah cut him off. "Has Barbara agreed to marry you?"

He shook his head. "She said she'd think on it, that's all."

"Do her boys know about this?" The question came from Mary.

"I don't think so. . .unless Barbara decided to mention it to them after I left her place the other day." John reached out and touched the plastic wrap surrounding the loaf of bread sitting in front of him. "Barbara's been trying to run her husband's harness shop for nearly a year now—ever since he died. And it's getting harder for her to keep up with things, which is why she had to hire Paul Hilty to help out. What Barbara needs is a husband to care for her and the boys. She needs someone to protect her from. . ." His voice trailed off, and he turned to look at the clock on the far wall. It was past time for Betty to leave for work. He needed to wrap this conversation up so both he and she could be on their way.

"Protect her from what, Papa?" Nadine asked.

"From anyone who might want to take advantage of her." John pushed away from the table and stood, snatching up the loaf of bread. "I'd better get going, and so should Betty. If Barbara has an answer for me today, then tonight I'll let you all know what she said."

Paul had just entered the back room and was looking over an old saddle when he heard the front door of the shop creak open and then click shut.

"I'm back here, Barbara," he called.

A few seconds later, Aaron came into the room. "It's me, not my mamm," he said with a frown.

"Guder mariye," Paul responded, hoping the greeting would wipe the scowl off the boy's face.

"Mornin'," Aaron mumbled.

"Where's your mamm?"

"Had to feed the baby. Said she'd be here soon."

Paul reached for a clean rag and handed it to Aaron. "Why don't you rub this saddle down with some neat's-foot oil while I take care of a few other things?"

Aaron responded with a muffled grunt, but he did take the rag.

"If you need me, I'll be up front at my desk looking over some work orders."

"It ain't *your* desk," Aaron muttered. "It belonged to my daed."

Paul blew out an exasperated breath. Wouldn't the boy ever lower his defenses? Couldn't he see that Paul wasn't his enemy?

"I know it's not my desk," Paul said. "It was just a figure of speech."

No reply.

Paul stood there a few seconds; then he shrugged and went

to the desk. *I sure hope Barbara gets here soon. Then she can deal with Aaron.*

Forty-five minutes later, Barbara finally showed up. "Sorry I'm late," she said breathlessly. "I got the boppli fed okay, but then he wouldn't burp."

"No problem," Paul replied, barely looking up from the papers on the desk.

"Is everything going okay?"

"I guess so."

"What have you got Aaron doing?"

"Oiling a saddle in the other room." Paul craned his neck in that direction. "It sure is taking him awhile to get it done, though."

"Maybe he finished up and found something else to do."

"I didn't give him any other chores."

"Would you like me to check on him?" Barbara asked.

"Sure."

She took a step toward the back room but turned around and leaned over the desk. "Are there any new work orders I should know about?"

When Paul brought his head up, it connected with Barbara's.

"Ouch!" they said in unison.

"Sorry." Paul rubbed his forehead; then instinctively, he placed his fingers against her head. "Are you okay?"

"I think so."

"I don't feel a lump anywhere," he said, swallowing hard. Being this close to Barbara made his heart pound and his hands sweat.

She stared at him with an anxious expression; then she

reached out and touched his forehead. "You, on the other hand, do have a little bump."

Barbara's fingers felt cool, and Paul's heart pounded even harder when he noticed the tender look in her eyes. An unexpected flame ignited in his chest, and he fought against the sudden urge to kiss her. "I. . .uh. . .it's nothing to worry about," he mumbled.

Barbara pulled her hand away, but her touch lingered in his mind. His arms ached to hold her. His lips yearned for the touch of hers. This wasn't good. Not good at all.

Paul grabbed a work order off the top of the pile. "This one's the most recent," he said, handing the piece of paper to Barbara and hoping his trembling hands wouldn't betray his feelings.

She pursed her lips as she studied it. "Is this one for the saddle Aaron's working on?"

He nodded.

Her eyebrows drew together. "But this says Harold Shaw wants the saddle repaired, not oiled or cleaned. Haven't you got Aaron doing something completely unnecessary?"

Paul sat up straight as the feelings of tenderness he'd had for Barbara dissolved like a block of ice left sitting in the sun. What right did she have to question him like this? Didn't the woman realize it was good business to clean and oil a saddle that had been brought in for repair? He opened his mouth to say so, but she spoke first.

"David always asked the customers if they wanted something cleaned or oiled. If they did, he wrote it on the work order so I would know. If not, then we didn't do it." She blinked a couple of times. "I don't see any point in doing something not asked for when there's lots of other work to be done."

A muscle in Paul's cheek quivered, and he reached up to massage the spot.

Barbara placed her hand on her hip and stared at him. "Your silence makes me wonder if you disagree with that practice."

He shrugged. "This is *your* harness shop. Who am I to say anything about the way you do business?"

She tipped her head. "After working together these past few weeks, I think we know each other well enough to be honest. I'd like it if we could express our thoughts and concerns, not clam up or become defensive."

He pushed the chair away from the desk and stood. "I'd say you've expressed your thoughts clear enough for the both of us."

When he started to walk away, she stepped in front of him. "I think we need to talk about this."

"I don't think there's much to be said." He grunted. "You see things one way, and I see them another. You're the boss. I'm just helping out until you're back working full-time."

"I would like to hear your reason for oiling the saddle without Harold having asked to have it done."

Paul reached up to rub his forehead. That bump from their heads colliding hurt more than he realized. Either that or he was getting a headache caused by stress.

"Paul?"

"Jah?"

"Are you going to share your thoughts on this or not?"

"I don't see how it'll do much good."

"Please."

He motioned for her to sit in the chair at the desk. When she complied, he leaned over and pointed to the stack of work orders. "If you'll look through these, you'll see that some of them are from customers who have returned more than once since I started working here."

"And?"

"After their first order, they found other things for me to do. Things they said they'd originally planned to do themselves."

"Then why didn't they?"

"Some said I had done such a thorough job on their previous order, they decided to bring in a second or third item."

She turned in her chair and nodded slowly. "I see what you mean."

"My cousin Andy taught me that doing a little something extra for a customer makes for good business."

"I guess you're right. I should have realized that." Barbara's dark eyes took on a faraway look. "I'm sure David tried to please our customers. But sometimes, when we got real busy, he might not have thought to do the little extra things."

Paul smiled, feeling somewhat better. "I'm sure David was good at his job. He and you made this business succeed."

She returned his smile. "Danki."

Paul touched her shoulder. "Barbara, I—"

His words were cut off when the front door opened and in walked Bishop John Frey.

"Guder mariye, John," Barbara said when the bishop entered her shop. "What brings you here today? Did you need a new harness made, or do you have one that needs to be repaired?"

Paul stepped aside as the bishop walked up to the desk and offered Barbara a wide smile. "Came to see about getting a new bridle for one of my driving horses." He held out the paper sack he had in his hand. "Also wanted to give you this."

Barbara took the sack and peered inside at a loaf of bread that appeared to have a very dark crust. She guessed it must have been baked too long. Certainly not the kind of baked goods she was used to getting from Noah Hertzler.

"Betty made it," John said with a crooked grin. "I figured with you back here working again, you probably wouldn't have much time for baking."

"I'm managing with my mamm's help, but I appreciate the gesture. Tell your daughter I said danki."

Paul cleared his throat, and she turned toward him.

"Why don't you check on Aaron?" she suggested.

"You're the boss." He gave the bishop a quick nod and headed for the back of the shop.

Barbara set the bread aside, pulled out her order pad, and grabbed a pencil. "Let's see now. . . . You said you wanted a new bridle?"

"Jah, that's right."

"It shouldn't be a problem." Barbara scrawled the bishop's name at the top of the page and wrote down the order. "Do you want it to be black or brown?"

"Black. And nothing fancy added." He shook his head. "Wouldn't do for the bishop to be driving around using a worldly-looking bridle on his buggy horse."

"No, of course not."

When Barbara finished writing up the order, she tore off the top sheet and handed it to John, placing the carbon copy in the metal basket with their other orders. "If you'd like to drop by in a few weeks, we'll have the bridle ready for you."

His forehead wrinkled. "I was kind of hoping to come by sooner than that."

She tapped the tip of the pencil against the desk. "I don't think we can have it ready any sooner."

He grunted. "That's not what I meant."

"Oh?"

"I was planning to come calling on you. Maybe take you and the boys for a drive or on a picnic."

Barbara gulped and tried to keep her composure. If the bishop had heard she'd gone fishing and shared a picnic supper with Paul a few weeks ago, there was no way she could tell him she wasn't up to such an outing yet. Besides, it would be a lie, and her conscience wouldn't let her knowingly tell an untruth.

"How about it, Barbara? Can I come by on Saturday and pick you and the boys up?"

She nibbled on the inside of her cheek, searching for the right words. She didn't want to offend the man, but she didn't want to lead him on, either. "Well, I. . .uh. . .appreciate the offer, but—"

"She's made other plans."

Barbara dropped the pencil and whirled around in her chair. Paul stood slightly behind her, off to one side. She opened her mouth to ask what other plans she had for Saturday, but the bishop cut her off.

"Is that so? What kind of plans?"

"She and the boys are going fishing with me." The look of

determination on Paul's face made Barbara wonder what was going on. He hadn't said a word to her about going fishing again, but the idea did sound rather appealing, especially if it gave her an excuse to turn down the bishop's invitation.

A warm rush spread through Barbara. She struggled to hide the unexpected pleasure of knowing Paul had spoken on her behalf.

John took a few steps in Paul's direction and scowled at him. "I hear from your daed that you're planning to return to Pennsylvania soon."

Paul shrugged. "When Barbara doesn't need me anymore."

The bishop turned his gaze on Barbara. "How long will that be?"

Her face heated up, and she pressed both hands against her cheeks, hoping to cool them. "Really, Bishop John, I don't think—"

Before Barbara could finish her sentence, Paul jumped in. "We haven't set a date for my leaving, but since you're so interested, I'll be sure to let you know when it's time for me to go."

Barbara couldn't believe Paul's boldness or the way his eyes flashed when he spoke to John. What was he thinking, speaking to their bishop that way? *Of course, he's not Paul's bishop,* she reasoned.

John shook his finger in Paul's face. "I'll have you know, I've asked Barbara to be my wife. Has she told you that?"

A vein on the side of Paul's neck bulged. Violence went against their teachings, yet Barbara worried he might be about to punch the bishop right in the nose.

"Mama, are you gonna marry the bishop?"

Barbara whirled around. She hadn't realized Aaron had come onto the scene.

She reached for her son's hand. "I've made no promises to marry anyone. I only said I would think on it."

Aaron stared up at the bishop. "My mamm doesn't need another husband. She's got me to help out." Then he looked at Paul. "Someday this harness shop will be mine, and then nobody can tell me what to do!" Aaron rushed out the door. Barbara just sat there, too stunned to say a word.

Chapter 15

"I still don't see why I have to go fishing," Aaron complained when Paul pulled up in his buggy on Saturday. "You let me stay home with Grandma and Grandpa before. Why can't I stay with them again?"

"Because Grandma's going to visit her friend Ada, and Grandpa's got a cold and needs to rest." Barbara ruffled his hair. "Besides, a day of fishing will be good for you."

He gave a muffled grunt as he climbed into Paul's buggy behind his brothers.

"Looks like a good day for fishing," Paul said after he'd helped Barbara and the baby into the front seat.

She smiled. "Jah, there's plenty of sunshine."

As they traveled down the road, Barbara couldn't believe she had let Paul talk her into going fishing again—this time with all four boys in tow. She hoped today would be as pleasant as their other fishing trip had been.

It's strange, she thought as she cast a sidelong glance at Paul. *We get along fine at certain times, but other times, we're at odds with each other.*

She wished she understood what attracted her to him. Other than their love for harness making and their commitment to God, they were as different as north from south. Of course, they did both enjoy fishing.

"I do love it here in Webster County, especially the warm days of summer," she said, lifting her face toward the sun.

Paul grunted. "I'm not really partial to hot, muggy weather."

"Doesn't it get humid in Pennsylvania?"

"Jah."

"But you still like it there?"

"I like my job."

"Wasn't it hard to leave your family and friends and move so far away?"

"It was, but I didn't want to farm. I wanted to work in a harness shop. Since you and David owned the shop here, I didn't see a need for a second one in our small community. So going to Pennsylvania to help my cousin was the only way I could do what I wanted."

Barbara could see by the wistful expression on Paul's face that he would have preferred to open a harness shop here rather than move to Pennsylvania. A sense of guilt stabbed her, but she realized it wasn't her fault Paul had chosen to move. If he'd wanted to work in a harness shop that badly, he could have talked to David about working for him. Maybe Barbara never would have become interested in working with leather if her husband had hired a helper.

"Did you ever talk to David about going to work for him?" she asked.

"By the time I figured out what I wanted to do, you were already his partner, and I didn't think he'd need anyone else in the shop."

"He could have used you part-time."

He shook his head. "I didn't want to work part-time. Pop would have expected me to farm when I wasn't helping David."

She could understand why he felt forced to leave Webster County. But from the tone of Paul's voice, Barbara sensed bitterness in his heart toward his dad.

"I sure hope the fish are biting today," he said. "I'd like to catch some nice big bass."

"I think my boys would agree." Barbara shifted the sleeping baby in her arms and glanced over her shoulder. Joseph and Zachary were drawing on their tablets. Aaron sat with his arms folded, looking straight ahead. She hoped that once they got to the pond and he saw how much fun the others were having, his attitude would improve.

A few minutes later, Zachary leaned over the seat and tapped her on the shoulder. "Mama, I'm hungry."

"We'll eat when we get there." She touched Paul's arm lightly. "Would you mind if we have supper before we fish?"

He patted his stomach. "That's fine by me. I'm always ready for good food."

When they pulled into the grassy area by the pond, Barbara noticed another open buggy parked there. She thought she recognized it, and her suspicions were confirmed when she saw Bishop John sitting on a large rock holding a fishing pole.

"What's he doing here?" Paul mumbled. "I'll bet he only came because he knew we were coming."

"He has as much right to be here as we do," Barbara reminded him. "Why would you care, anyway?"

"I just do, that's all." When Paul came around to help Barbara and the boys down from the buggy, Barbara noticed deep furrows in his forehead. He was obviously not happy about having to share their fishing spot.

"It might be better if we go to the other side of the pond," Paul said with a frown. "Wouldn't want to scare away any fish the bishop might want to catch."

Before Barbara could reply, her three boys took off on a run, heading straight for the area where the bishop sat.

"Yippee!" Zachary shouted. "Fisch! Fisch!"

"I hope I get me some big ol' bass!" Joseph hollered.

Barbara grasped Paul's arm. "So much for not disturbing the bishop."

Paul's skin prickled under his short-sleeved cotton shirt. Every time he and Barbara made physical contact, his insides turned to mush.

If I had a lick of sense, I'd catch the next bus heading for Pennsylvania and let Barbara marry the bishop. Paul grimaced. *Of course, she might become the man's wife even if I were to stick around.*

"Would you mind holding the boppli while I get the picnic

basket out of the buggy?" Barbara asked.

He blinked. "Huh?"

"I said—"

"I heard what you said, but don't you think it would be better if I got the basket and you kept the boppli held securely in your arms?"

She grinned at him, and his heart did a little flip-flop. "Davey won't bite, you know. He has no teeth yet."

Paul's face heated up. What if the little guy started to howl or spit up all over him? What if he dropped the baby?

"I think you're blushing, Paul Hilty," Barbara said with a smirk. "A big man like you isn't afraid of a baby, I hope."

Regaining his composure, Paul held out his hands. "I'm not afraid of much. Leastways, not a little scrap of a guy like Davey."

She chuckled and reached into the buggy to grab a quilt, which she tucked under Paul's arm. "Why don't you ask Aaron to spread this on the grass? You and Davey can have a seat, and I'll be there soon with our picnic supper."

"What about the boppli's carriage?"

"We can get it later."

"Okay." Paul glanced over at Aaron and forced a smile. "Are you looking forward to putting your line in the water, Aaron?" he asked, hoping the idea of fishing might put a smile on the boy's face.

Aaron grunted.

"You've been grunting an awful lot lately," Paul said as they strode to the pond. "I'm wondering if you're spending too much time with your grandpa's pigs, because you're beginning to sound like one of them."

"I ain't no pig," Aaron said with a frown.

Paul bit back a chuckle. "Let's get that quilt put on the ground like your mamm asked us to do."

The boy complied, but not without first giving Paul another disgruntled look. To make matters worse, he placed the blanket not three feet from where the bishop sat fishing.

"Good day to you, Paul," John said with a slight nod. "Looks like you've got your hands full."

Paul's face flooded with warmth again. "How's the fishing?" he asked.

"Got myself a couple bass and a nice fat catfish." The man nodded toward his cooler sitting nearby. " 'Course, with the way Barbara's boys are running around hollering like that, it'll be harder to lure the fish now."

If the bishop was looking for an apology, or even an offer to move, Paul wasn't about to provide him with one. He was pretty sure the man had come here on purpose. Well, two could play that game. If Bishop John wanted to marry Barbara, he'd have to earn the right. But the man hadn't won Barbara's hand or her heart yet. At least not as far as Paul knew.

The baby started to cry, and Paul shifted uneasily on the quilt. *Sure hope Barbara shows up soon, or the bishop will have one more thing to razz me about.*

Paul watched in horror as Zachary picked up a flat rock and pitched it into the pond—right in front of John's fishing line. *Splat!* Drops of water splattered everywhere, some landing on the man's shirt and trousers. A few even made it to the quilt Paul sat on. At least he and the baby hadn't gotten wet.

"Hey, watch what you're doing!" The bishop's face turned

red, and a vein on the side of his neck stuck out like a noodle boiling in a pot.

"What's going on here?"

Paul cranked his head. Barbara stood nearby, holding the picnic basket and tapping her foot.

"Your boy Zachary is throwing rocks into the pond," John said before Paul could open his mouth.

Barbara's brows furrowed. "Is that so, Zachary?"

"He only threw one," Paul said in the boy's defense.

"Jah, and it splashed water all over me." The bishop held up his arm, but there was barely a sign of the water droplets left.

Barbara took a step toward her son. "Zachary, tell Bishop John you're sorry."

The boy's lower lip quivered, and he stared down at the grass. "S–sorry, Bishop."

"Jah, well, don't let it happen again." The bishop smiled up at Barbara. "It's good to see you. Even though your boy tried to drown me."

She nodded but didn't return his smile. Paul felt a sense of relief.

"Come now, boys," Barbara said, grabbing Zachary's hand. "Let's see about eating our supper."

Aaron, Joseph, and Zachary followed her to the quilt, and in short order, she had the food set out.

"Yum, this looks good," Joseph said, licking his lips.

"Let's pray, and then we'll eat," Paul said, handing Barbara the baby.

She turned to face the bishop, who was watching them like a hungry cat ready to pounce on its unsuspecting prey. "Would you care to join us, John? That is, if you haven't already eaten."

"Haven't had anything since lunch, so I'd be much obliged." John quickly reeled in his line and set the fishing pole aside. Then he took a seat beside Barbara.

Paul gritted his teeth. It didn't surprise him when the bishop accepted her invitation, but did he have to plunk down right beside Barbara, as though he was the one who'd brought her and the boys to the pond?

The bishop cleared his throat. "Shall we pray?"

All heads bowed. When he cleared his throat a second time, they opened their eyes.

"Everything looks mighty good," the older man said as he reached for a piece of Barbara's fried chicken.

"I hope it tastes as good as it looks." Barbara handed the container to Paul, who took a drumstick. Then he passed it to each of her boys.

"Want me to get the boppli's carriage from the buggy so you can eat with both hands?" Paul asked, looking at Barbara.

She nodded. "That would be nice."

Paul set the drumstick on his paper plate and stood. When he returned a few minutes later, he set up the carriage and took the baby from her. After the little guy was settled, he draped the netting across the top and sides of the carriage. He sat back down and was about to reach for his piece of chicken when he noticed Aaron's plate still had most of his food on it.

He tapped the boy on the shoulder. "You haven't eaten very much."

Aaron shrugged. "I ain't all that hungry."

"Well, I sure am. Guess a few hours of fishing gave me a

hearty appetite." John chomped down the last hunk of white meat he'd taken and licked his fingers. "Your mamm is one fine cook, Aaron." He turned to Barbara. "Got any corn bread or baked beans?"

"As a matter of fact, I do." Barbara handed the man the bowl of baked beans, followed by the basket of corn bread.

"Danki."

"You're welcome."

It was all Paul could do to keep from telling the bishop what he thought. He had wanted to spend the evening with Barbara and her boys, do a little fishing, and hopefully work on his relationship with Aaron. Instead, he was being forced to sit here and watch the bishop eat the choicest pieces of meat, listen to the man praise Barbara for her cooking skills, and worst of all, watch John make cow eyes at her. Paul was beginning to wish he had never suggested this outing.

He gritted his teeth. *It's only natural that Barbara would be interested in a man like the bishop. He has the respect of those in the community, he plans to stay in Webster County, and he has the smarts to outwit me.*

Paul leaned back on one elbow and took a bite of chicken. *Might as well make the most of the evening, because if John has his way, this will probably be the last time I take Barbara and her kinner anywhere.*

John studied Paul as he ate his chicken. He couldn't figure out why the man would be showing such an interest in Barbara and her boys when he didn't plan to stay in Webster County—unless Paul planned on staying with the hope of marrying Barbara and taking over her harness shop. If Barbara accepted John's proposal, then Paul would know he didn't have a chance and would soon be back in Pennsylvania, where he belonged.

"How's Margaret doing these days?" Barbara asked, looking over at John. "I've only seen her at church since the day she came to help with my yard work, and we haven't had much chance to talk."

"She's getting along all right, but of course, she still misses Dan." He smiled. "I think it did her some good to help with the work frolic, so maybe if you've got more work that needs to be done, you might see if she's free to help."

"I'll be going back to work in the harness shop full-time soon, I hope," Barbara said. "It'll be even harder for me to keep up with things around the house and yard, so I might have to ask for more help."

John was tempted to tell Barbara that if she married him she'd have all the help she needed from his daughters and that she wouldn't have to work in the harness shop at all because he would suggest that she sell it. But it would be out of place to mention his marriage proposal in front of Paul, so he merely nodded and said, "Anytime you need some help, just let me know, and I'll spread the word."

"Danki." Barbara lifted the container of chicken and held it out to him. "Would you care for another piece of chicken?"

He nodded and licked his lips. "Don't mind if I do."

Chapter 16

On Sunday morning, Barbara awoke with a headache. Church would be held at her in-laws', and as much as she enjoyed visiting with Mavis, she dreaded going. It wasn't merely the constant pounding in her head that made her want to stay home in bed. After yesterday's picnic supper and fishing, she wasn't looking forward to seeing either Paul or Bishop John. They had acted like a couple of little boys the whole time, causing Barbara to wonder if they both might be vying for her attention.

Barbara swung her legs over the edge of the bed and rubbed her temples. She knew the bishop wanted to marry her, if only to help raise his girls. But why would Paul try to gain her attention? He would be going back to Pennsylvania soon and surely had no interest in her. So why had he seemed irritated because the bishop had been at the pond?

She padded across the room to check on the baby. *Maybe I'm imagining things. It could be that Paul was just worried the bishop would take all the good fish, like I'd suspected in the first place. Paul is a strange man—sometimes friendly and relaxed, other times distant and uptight. I wish I could figure him out.*

Barbara stared down at her son sleeping peacefully in his crib and thought about the baby's father. "Oh, David, why did you have to die and leave me with four boys to raise and a business to run on my own? I feel so helpless and confused. I miss you so much. If only you were here to tell me what to do."

Barbara glanced around the room she had shared with her husband for ten years. Everything looked the same—their double bed and matching dresser made by David's father, the sturdy cedar chest at the foot of the bed given to Barbara by her parents when she'd turned sixteen, and the beautiful Wedding Ring quilt her mother had made as a wedding present.

Her gaze came to rest on the Bible lying on top of the dresser. It had been David's, and she always found a measure of comfort by simply holding it in her hands. Not because it was God's Word, but because it had belonged to her husband and she knew how much the Bible had meant to him. Truth was, Barbara had been neglecting her Bible reading lately. She was too busy during the day and too tired at night.

Barbara left the crib and made her way across the room. As she picked up David's Bible, tears coursed down her cheeks. The feel of the leather cover made her think about the harness shop. Should she sell the business and hope to make enough money so they could live off it? She certainly couldn't rely on her folks to support her and the boys. It was all Dad could do to help part-time in the shop. But the wages she gave him were a much-needed supplement to the meager income he and Mom made selling some of their garden produce and the quilts Mom made. Dad's arthritis had kept him from farming for quite a spell, and even though Barbara's sisters sent money to their folks whenever they could, Barbara still felt the need to assist her parents as much as possible.

"Of course, I could sell the shop and marry the bishop," she said with a weary sigh as she sat on the edge of her bed. "Maybe Paul would be interested in buying it." She opened the Bible to a place marked with a slip of paper. In the book of James, David had underlined the fifth verse of chapter one. " 'If any of you lack wisdom, let him ask of God, that giveth to all men liberally, and upbraideth not; and it shall be given him,' " she read aloud.

Setting the Bible aside, Barbara closed her eyes. "I'm so confused, Lord. I need the wisdom of Your words found in this *Biwel*. I need to know what to do about the bishop's offer of marriage, the harness shop, and my befuddled feelings toward Paul."

She released a sigh as she thought about the verse from Ecclesiastes that John had quoted to her awhile back, about two being better than one. Maybe she did need someone to share her life with. But could she ever be truly happy married to the bishop, for whom she felt no love? Could she take on the responsibility of raising the bishop's four girls plus her boys? She would have to give up the harness shop unless she could count on the girls to watch the boys.

Barbara rubbed the bridge of her nose. There was so much

to think about—so many conflicting thoughts whirling around in her head. Truth be told, she was falling in love with Paul, but she couldn't let him know that. If they were meant to be together, he would have to make the first move and let her know he felt the same way.

With another long sigh, she stood. It was time to set her thoughts aside and turn things over to God. She needed to wake the boys up, start breakfast, and get ready for church. "I'm going to pray for wisdom and leave my future in God's hands, just as David always did. And I'm not going to let a little old headache keep me from worshipping the Lord today."

Paul had a hard time keeping his thoughts on the preaching service and not on Barbara, who sat directly across from him on the women's side of the room, holding her baby. On one side of Barbara sat her mother. The bishop's oldest daughter, Betty, occupied the other spot. Paul wondered if it was merely a coincidence or if John Frey might have asked Betty to sit beside the woman he hoped to marry.

It was all Paul could do to keep from staring at Barbara's dimpled cheeks, which were slightly pink, no doubt from the heat of this warm summer morning. He wished he were free to fall in love with her and stay in Webster County. But there were too many complications to prevent them from having a relationship—his insecurities about becoming a husband, her possible marriage to the bishop.

Paul thought about yesterday's trip to the pond. Despite

his irritation over the bishop's presence, he had enjoyed being with Barbara and her boys. With the exception of Aaron, who'd remained aloof all day, Barbara's children had really warmed up to him. Even the baby had seemed content when Paul held him, and the little guy sure was soft and cuddly. When the infant had nestled against Paul's chest, it made him feel loved and appreciated. It had also caused him to wish for something he felt sure he would never have.

The bishop's booming voice drove Paul's thoughts to the back of his mind. "The Bible says, 'For the Lord God will help me; therefore shall I not be confounded: therefore have I set my face like a flint, and I know that I shall not be ashamed.' Isaiah chapter fifty, verse seven."

John Frey was preaching on challenges, and Paul wondered if the verse he'd just quoted was an announcement of the man's personal challenge to win Barbara's hand in marriage.

At the moment, Bishop Frey's face looked like it was set in flint. He pursed his lips and held the Bible in front of him as though it were a weapon.

Paul stared at the floor. *Maybe his message is directed at me. Could be he wants me to realize how determined he is to make Barbara his wife.*

He grimaced. It didn't seem likely that the bishop would bring his personal life into the sermon. But the man was only human. And he obviously needed a wife to help him raise his four girls.

Paul was pretty sure John had God on his side, him being a spiritual leader and all. Still, that shouldn't give him an edge with Barbara, at least not to Paul's way of thinking.

Forcing his thoughts aside so he could concentrate on the rest of the service, Paul reminded himself that he needed to keep his focus on God.

When church was over, Paul headed quickly for the door. It was stuffy inside the house, and he needed some fresh air.

"I still don't understand why you're chasing after Barbara Zook, Papa," Betty said, stepping up to John as he headed toward the barn.

He halted his footsteps and turned to face her. "What are you talking about, girl?"

"I saw the way you were looking at Barbara when she was helping the other women serve lunch. It was probably obvious to all the other men sitting at your table."

"I am trying to find you and your sisters a mudder," her father said impatiently. "Barbara would make a good mother, don't you think?"

"Maybe so, but as far as I can tell, we've been getting along fine since Mama died."

"You might believe that to be so, but the truth is, things aren't done around the house the same as your mamm used to do them."

She tipped her head and stared at him as if he didn't have a lick of sense. "What makes you think Barbara would do things the way Mama used to do them?"

He shrugged. "Maybe she wouldn't, but I'm sure things would go better than us trying to fend for ourselves."

"I think we're doing all right on our own."

He folded his arms and stared hard at her. "Oh, jah, right. . . overly done bread, tasteless stew, and arguments over who does what chores and when. Does that sound like you girls are doing all right on your own?"

"Things might go better if my sisters would listen to what I tell them." Betty grunted. "And don't you think adding four boys to the family would make things more hectic and stressful?"

"I rather like the idea of having a couple of buwe around," he said with a nod. "It would be kind of nice to have a few sets of strong hands in a couple years to do some of the harder chores. I could use some help with my business, too."

Betty cleared her throat. "Papa, I just want to know one thing."

"What's that?"

"Do you love Barbara?"

"Well, I—"

"You don't love her, do you?"

"There's a lot more involved in marriage than a bunch of romantic nonsense. Besides, love can be learned."

"Did you love Mama?"

"Of course I did. Loved her from the first moment I laid eyes on her."

There was a brief pause before Betty spoke again. "Papa, I hope you do remarry someday. But it needs to be for love, not convenience, or even to have a mudder for me and my sisters."

"Guess I'll have to think on that awhile." He started walking again, hoping she would take the hint and realize the subject was over. Being the oldest, Betty had begun to act a bit bossy toward her sisters since Peggy had died, and there were times, like now, when she said more than she should to her father.

"Where are you going?" she asked.

"Out to the barn to visit with some of the men."

"Oh, okay." Betty turned toward the house, and John breathed a sigh of relief. Obviously, Betty didn't want him to remarry. He hoped if he did talk Barbara into marrying him, all four of his girls would accept it and be kind to Barbara and her boys.

When John entered the barn a few minutes later, he discovered Barbara's father petting one of the horses. Deciding to take this opportunity to speak with Samuel about Barbara, he stepped up to the man.

"Wie geht's, Samuel?"

Samuel offered John a smile. "Except for the pain and stiffness of my arthritis, I'm doing all right. How about you?"

John shrugged. "Can't complain, I guess."

"Are you keeping busy with your seed and garden supply business?"

"Jah. That and making calls on people in our community who are sick or hurting."

"I heard you've been by to see Barbara a few times since the boppli was born."

"That's right," John said with a nod. "I saw her and the boys at the pond the other day, too."

"Heard that, as well. Guess they went there with Paul for some fishing and a picnic."

John cleared his throat a couple of times, searching for the right words to say what was on his mind. "I'm. . .uh. . .concerned for Barbara's welfare."

"You mean because she's been so tired since the boppli was born?"

"That and a few other things."

Samuel tipped his head. "Such as?"

"Well, for one thing. . .I think she needs to consider selling the harness shop. It's too much for her to run on her own, and I know you're not able to help as much as you'd like."

"That's true, but Paul's there helping out now, and he does the work of two good men."

John held up one hand. "Which brings me to my next point."

"And that would be?"

"Paul Hilty."

"What about Paul?"

"I don't trust the man." John lowered his voice. "I think he's out to get the harness shop any way he can."

A muscle on the side of Samuel's cheek quivered. "What's that supposed to mean?"

"It means, I think Paul might be trying to woo Barbara so she'll marry him." John grunted. "As her husband, he would have full run of the harness shop, you know."

Deep creases formed in Samuel's forehead. "I don't know what would make you think such a thing, but I'm sure it's not true. Fact is, I've been working with Paul for several weeks now, and he's been nothing but helpful and hardworking."

"That doesn't prove he's not trying to gain control of the harness shop without having to buy it."

Samuel turned his hands palm up. "Doesn't prove he's trying to get it, either."

John pulled his fingers through the ends of his beard and grimaced. "If you would have seen the way he acted around Barbara when they were at the pond the other day, you might understand what I'm saying."

"How'd he act?"

"He said some goofy things and looked at her like a horse eyeing a tree full of ripe apples."

Samuel chuckled. "Are you sure it wasn't all that good food Barbara prepared that he was eyeing?"

John shook his head. "You can laugh all you want, but I'm sure of one thing—Paul's trying to win Barbara's heart, and I think he's using her boys to do it!"

Samuel's eyebrows rose. "How so?"

"He's got those boys—well, two of them, anyway—wrapped around his long fingers."

"I've seen the way Paul acts around Zachary and Joseph, and I don't think he's using them to get to my daughter." Samuel pursed his lips. "What I think is that Barbara's boys, with the exception of Aaron, enjoy spending time with Paul because they see the good in him."

John opened his mouth to respond but was interrupted when Moses, Paul's dad, showed up.

"Are you two talking about something private, or can anyone join the conversation?" the man asked.

"We weren't discussing anything important," Samuel said with a shrug. "Matter of fact, I was just petting one of the horses when John showed up."

Moses smiled. "How are things going in the harness shop these days? Is my son Paul really as much help to you as he says?"

Samuel nodded vigorously. "Oh, jah. Paul does the work of two men. His cousin must have taught him well, because he really seems to know what he's doing."

John ground his teeth together. The way Samuel talked, one would think Paul was some kind of a saint. He was good with Barbara's boys, he did the work of two men, and he knew a lot about the harness business.

Moses gave his left earlobe a quick pull. "Paul used to help me and the boys in the fields until he got it into his head to move to Pennsylvania and learn the harness trade from Andy. Now all he talks about is leather straps, silver rivets, and the smooth feel of a well-made harness." He grunted. "If there wasn't already a harness shop in Webster County, I believe he'd open one of his own."

Hmm... John folded his arms and contemplated Moses's statement. If Paul wanted to open his own harness shop, maybe his suspicions about the man wanting to get his hands on Barbara's shop weren't so far-fetched, after all. Now John was even more determined to get Barbara to marry him. She needed someone to watch out for her and protect her interests.

Soon after lunch, Barbara left the baby with her mother-in-law and allowed the three boys to play with their friends. When Barbara spotted her friend Faith on the other side of the yard, she headed that way.

"You're looking a bit down in the mouth today," Faith said as she and Barbara took a seat on the grass under the shade of a hickory tree. "Are you still feeling *hundsiwwel?*"

"No, I think I'm done with the postpartum depression."

"Then why the long face?"

"I'm struggling with several issues," Barbara admitted. "Things I really need to talk about if you're willing to listen."

Faith nodded. "Of course I'll listen. What issues are you struggling with?"

"Bishop John and Paul."

"What about them?"

"John wants me to marry him."

"Ah, I suspected as much."

"He's been over to my house a couple of times, asking me to go places with him, but I've always turned him down."

"So he knows you're not interested?"

"I'm not sure, but John was at the pond yesterday when Paul and I arrived with the boys, and he acted like a jealous little boy."

Faith's mouth dropped open. "You went there with Paul again?"

"Jah."

"I should have guessed what was going on."

"What's that supposed to mean?"

"I can see by the look on your face that you're smitten with the man."

"Paul and I don't see eye to eye on some things concerning the harness shop," Barbara said. "But I must admit I'm attracted to him, though I can't figure out why."

Faith leaned her head back and laughed.

"What's so funny?"

"Don't try to figure out love, my friend. When two people

fall for each other, they can be as different as sandpaper and polished cotton—yet the feelings are there, and you can't do a thing to stop them."

Barbara moaned. "I don't know how Paul feels about me."

"He's invited you to go fishing with him twice. I'd say that says something about his interest."

"It's really strange, but there are times when Paul acts friendly and nice, and other times when he seems distant and almost as if he's angry about something. I think he wants to do things his own way in the harness shop, and he gets irritated when I want things done my way." Barbara frowned. "To tell you the truth, I don't think he likes me very much."

Faith clicked her tongue. "Ever since Adam met Eve, there has been trouble between men and women. Just because Paul doesn't always see things the same as you doesn't mean he dislikes you."

Barbara shrugged. "I think he believes my place is in the house with the kinner, not running a harness shop."

A ruckus on the lawn interrupted their conversation, and Barbara turned to see what was going on. She was taken by surprise when she heard Joseph hollering and saw him running after Faith's son, Isaiah, with a squirt gun.

"Now, where in the world did he get that?" she muttered as she scrambled to her feet.

"Guess we'd better put our conversation on hold and see about our boys before one of them ends up crying." Faith shook her head. "Most likely it'll be Isaiah unless his big sister comes to the rescue."

Barbara marched across the yard, planted herself in front of

Joseph, and reached for the squirt gun.

Swish! A spurt of water hit her right in the face.

"Give me that!" she ordered. "What's gotten into you? And where did you get this squirt gun?"

Joseph's brows furrowed, and he pointed across the yard. "Paul Hilty gave it to me."

Barbara hurried across the lawn to where Paul stood talking to Faith's husband. "Excuse me, Noah," she said, "but I need to speak with Paul."

"No problem." Noah smiled and moved off in the direction of his wife.

"What's up?" Paul asked with raised eyebrows.

She handed him the item in question. "Would you mind telling me why you gave my son a squirt gun?"

He shoved the toy inside his shirt pocket and looked at her as though she were daft. "Didn't see any harm in it. The boy said he was hot, so I got the squirt gun out of my buggy, figuring it would help cool him off."

"What were you doing with a squirt gun in your buggy?"

"It was mine when I was a kinner, and I found it in my daed's barn the other day. So I decided to bring it today to see if one of your boys might want it."

Barbara wrinkled her nose. "I don't cotton to the idea of my boys pointing a gun at anyone—not even a toy one."

Paul's ears turned bright red. "Sorry," he mumbled. "At least this time you're not chewing me out for something related to the harness shop."

His statement caught Barbara off guard. Was she always chewing him out? Did Paul think all she ever did was nag? She had to admit that she had been pretty testy of late, but he seemed to know just how to get under her skin.

Unable to look him in the eye, she lowered her gaze. "I–I'm sorry for snapping. It's just that I would have preferred it if you'd checked with me about the squirt gun. Then I could have explained my reasons."

"You're right. I shouldn't have given Joseph the toy without first asking you."

Shivers shimmied up Barbara's spine as Paul stared intently at her. Did he really agree with her on this, or was he merely giving in to avoid an argument?

"Mama?"

Barbara glanced down when she felt a tug on her dress. Aaron stared up at her with a curious expression. "Is it all right if I spend the night at Gabe Schwartz's?" he asked. "Gabe's daed has hired a driver to take 'em to Springfield tomorrow morning. They're going to Bass Pro Shop, and I think they plan to do some other fun stuff, too."

"Oh, I don't know, Aaron. Paul might need you in the harness shop tomorrow."

Paul shook his head. "Your daed said he's free to help in the morning, so I think we can manage okay without Aaron."

Barbara deliberated a few seconds. Her oldest child had been moody and sad ever since David died. This was the first spark of the old Aaron she'd seen in a long time. Maybe she should let the boy have a good time with his friend.

Finally, she nodded. "Jah, okay. You can go."

Aaron clasped her hand. "Danki. I'll ask Gabe's daed to stop by our house when they head for home today so I can get a change of clothes."

Barbara smiled at her son's enthusiasm. "Don't forget your toothbrush and comb. I wouldn't want my boy going off to the big city looking like a ragamuffin." She bent down and gave him a hug. "You be good now, you hear?"

"I will, Mama." The child scampered off toward Gabe.

Paul smiled. "Seemed real eager, didn't he?"

Barbara nodded. "Aaron and Gabe have been good friends since they were little fellows."

"Sure wish he'd see me in a friendlier light."

"Give him time, Paul." As the words slipped out, Barbara wondered why she had bothered to say them. She would be back working full-time soon, and it would only be a matter of days before Paul would announce his intention to return to Pennsylvania. Then everything would be back to normal.

Chapter 17

On Monday morning as Barbara headed to the harness shop, she decided to tell Paul that she could manage on her own now. If she gave him the option of leaving and he took it, she would know he had no interest in developing a relationship with her. If he hesitated and said he wanted to stay, then maybe he could take Dad's place permanently.

Barbara shook her head, hoping to get herself thinking straight again. Having Paul working in the shop with her alone six days a week wouldn't seem proper when they weren't married or even related.

As Barbara drew closer to the shop, she noticed that Paul's buggy wasn't parked outside. *Strange,* she thought as she opened the front door. *He's always here early—usually before Dad or me. Surely he wouldn't have gone back to Pennsylvania without telling me first.*

When Barbara entered the shop, she spotted her father working at the riveting machine. He smiled and nodded in her direction. "Guder mariye, daughter."

"Good morning, Dad. I'm surprised to see you pressing rivets. Paul usually does that, and it's not like him to be late for work."

Dad stepped away from the machine and placed the leather he'd been holding on one of the workbenches. "Paul dropped by a little bit ago. He wanted me to let you know that he wouldn't be in today."

She wrinkled her forehead. "He's not sick, I hope."

"*Nee*. His daed fell off a ladder in their barn this morning. An ambulance had to be called to take him to the hospital, so Paul and his brothers hired a driver to take them there."

Barbara's breath caught in her throat. "How bad was Moses hurt?"

Dad shook his head. "Paul didn't have any information yet. He said he would let us know as soon as he could what the doctors had to say."

"I hope it's nothing serious." Barbara sighed. "We've had enough tragedy in our community lately."

Barbara's father patted her shoulder. "And that's why we need to pray."

Paul paced the length of the hospital waiting room, anxious for some report on his father's condition. The doctors had been running tests on him for the last couple of hours, and Paul worried that might mean something was seriously wrong.

"Won't you please stop that pacing?" his mother said from the bench where she sat. She blinked her dark eyes and patted the sides of her grayish-brown hair, which she wore parted down the middle and pulled tightly into a bun.

He came to a halt in front of the window and stared out at the cloudy sky. They might be in for some rain, which seemed fitting for an already gloomy Monday morning.

"I wonder why Monroe and Elam aren't back yet. It shouldn't take them this long to get a few cups of coffee." Mom shifted restlessly on the bench. "I sure could use some about now."

Paul clenched and unclenched his fingers. How could Mom be worried about coffee when Pop was in the emergency room and they didn't know how badly he'd been hurt? *Maybe it's just Mom's way of trying to take her mind off the situation,* he concluded. *I know how much she loves Pop.*

"Maybe you should head down the hall and see what's taking your brieder so long," she said.

Paul turned to face his mother. "I'm sure my brothers will be back in due time. They don't need me to go traipsing after them."

Mom grabbed a magazine from the table in front of her. "I just figured it would give you something to do besides wear down the soles of your boots as you pace back and forth."

A middle-aged nurse stepped into the room. "Joann Hilty?" she asked, looking at Paul's mother.

Mom nodded and stood.

"Your husband has been moved to a private room now, so if you wish to see him, please follow me."

Mom's face looked pinched, and deep lines etched her forehead. "Is Moses going to be all right? What did the tests reveal?"

The nurse offered a reassuring smile. "The doctor will fill you in on all the details."

Paul started to follow his mother, but she stopped him with a raised hand. "I think it would be better if you waited here for your brothers so they won't worry when they return."

Paul looked at the nurse. "What room is my dad in?"

"Second floor, room 202."

"Okay." Paul offered his mother what he hoped was a reassuring smile. "Monroe, Elam, and I will be up to see Pop as soon as they get back."

As soon as Alice stepped into the harness shop, she spotted Barbara bent over a huge metal tub filled with neat's-foot oil. Holding a leather strap in each hand, she dipped them up and down in the savory-smelling oil. Samuel stood in front of the riveter, punching shiny silver rivets into a leather strap. "I heard about Paul's *daed* and knew Paul wasn't helping today," Alice said, stepping up to him. "How are things going here without his help?"

"We're managing okay," Barbara said before Samuel could respond. She hung the straps overhead to dry, then stood.

"Are you sure? You looked awfully *mied*."

Barbara arched her back and rubbed a spot near her right hip. "I'm not really tired. Just feeling a little stiff is all."

Alice glanced over at Samuel to gauge his reaction. He merely shrugged.

"I've got lunch ready, so if you'd like to come up to the house, I'll put it on the table."

"Sounds good to me. I'm hungry as a mule." Samuel moved away from the riveter and toward the door.

Alice looked back at her daughter. "Are you coming?"

"I'll be there shortly," Barbara said, motioning to the pile of leather strips lying at her feet. "I want to get these oiled and hung before I eat."

Alice's forehead wrinkled. "Can't it wait until you've had some lunch?"

"I need to get this done so I can work on some orders this afternoon."

"But you need to keep up your strength, and you can't do that unless you eat," Alice argued. "Besides, the boppli will be waking from his nap soon, and you'll need to feed him, as well."

Barbara released a sigh. "There's so much work to do, and it seems there's just not enough of me to go around anymore."

"Which is exactly why you should think about giving up the harness shop."

"But the harness shop is all I have left of David."

"That's not true. You've got four of David's buwe to raise." Alice looked over at Samuel, who stood near the door with his arms folded. "Can't you talk some sense into our daughter?"

"I've tried, but she won't listen to anything I have to say concerning the shop." He held up his hands. "She knows that I'm not much help to her, what with these old gnarled hands that don't work so well. Yet she's determined to keep the shop going, and I guess I can't fault her for that." He smiled at Barbara. "So I'll continue to help as long as I can."

Barbara's chin quivered, and her eyes filled with tears. "I love working here, Mom. I love the feel of leather beneath my fingers, and I love knowing that this shop is mine and will be passed on to my oldest boy someday."

Alice moved over to Barbara and patted her gently on the back. "Be that as it may, you still need to take care of yourself. So I insist that you come up to the house with your daed and have some lunch."

Barbara blinked a couple of times, and then her lips curved into a smile. "Guess I should know better than to argue with my mamm when she's determined to make me do something."

Alice gave Barbara's arm a gentle squeeze. "Well, at least I get my way on some things."

"Papa, I don't see why Mary and I couldn't have stayed home and baked some cookies this afternoon," Hannah complained from her seat at the back of John's buggy.

John grimaced. Not this again. It seemed like all his girls ever did anymore was whine. "It's not proper for me to call on Margaret alone when she's newly widowed. I've told you that before." He glanced over his shoulder. "Besides, the last time I left you two at home alone, you ended up arguing all day."

Hannah poked Mary's arm and glared at her. "Papa wouldn't have known that if you hadn't blabbed."

"And if you hadn't been tryin' to tell me what to do, we

wouldn't have had a *dischbedaat* that lasted most of the day," Mary shot back.

John ground his teeth together. "You're having an argument now, and if you don't stop it, you'll both end up with double chores for the rest of the week."

The girls sat back in their seats and clamped their mouths shut. John breathed a sigh of relief.

At this point, he wondered if he shouldn't have left them home. Maybe it wouldn't be so bad if he called on Margaret by himself. In times past, either her daughter, son-in-law, or one of the grandchildren had been around, so they hadn't really been alone. Well, it was too late to turn back now.

When he pulled into Margaret's yard, John spotted Margaret filling one of her bird feeders from a large sack that sat near her feet. "Why don't you girls go out to the barn to play while I visit with Margaret awhile?" he suggested as they clambered out of the buggy.

"Okay," the girls said in unison. They scampered off and disappeared inside the barn before John could get the horse tied to the hitching rail.

"Hello, John. It's good to see you again," Margaret said when John stepped up to her.

"Good to see you, too. You must like feeding the birds," he said, nodding at the wooden feeder that was shaped like a covered bridge and had been nailed to a sturdy post.

She nodded and smiled. "I've enjoyed bird-watching ever since I was girl."

"Me, too." His face heated up. "I mean, since I was a boy."

Margaret chuckled, and a flash of light seemed to dance in

her pale blue eyes. It was good to hear her laughing again. She'd been so somber on John's other visits.

"Would you like to sit on the porch and have a glass of iced tea with me?" she asked. "We can watch the birds eat at the feeders."

John nodded enthusiastically. "That'd be real nice." He pointed to the sack of birdseed. "Would you like me to carry this for you?"

"Danki, I'd appreciate that. Jacob carried it out to the yard after lunch, but he had to head back to the fields. Karen took the two little ones to town to do some shopping, so I figured I'd be stuck lugging it back to the house."

John hoisted the sack into his arms and placed the birdseed on one end of the porch.

"If you'd like to have a seat, I'll run into the house and get the tea," she said, motioning to the porch swing.

"Sounds good."

She reached for the screen door handle and was about to open it when she turned back around. "I saw Mary and Hannah go into the barn. If you'd like to call them, I'd be happy to fix them each a glass of iced tea, too."

"I think I'll let them play awhile," he said, lowering himself to the swing. "It would be nice for us to visit without any interruptions."

She tipped her head in question.

"They've been arguing a lot lately and asking too many questions."

"Ah, I see. Maybe it would be best if we had our tea first; then I'll offer some to the girls." Margaret gave him another smile and disappeared into the house.

John leaned his head against the back of the swing and closed his eyes. It was peaceful here with the birds singing in the yard and a slight breeze blowing against his face. Soon fall would be upon them.

"Are you sleeping, John?"

His eyes snapped open, and he sat up straight. Margaret stood in front of the porch swing holding two glasses of iced tea. "Uh. . .no. I was just thinking, is all."

"They must have been good thoughts, because I saw a smile on your face."

"I was enjoying listening to the birds and thinking about the nice weather we've been having."

She handed him a glass and took a seat on the swing beside him. "With all the sad things that have gone on in our community the past year or so, it's nice to have something good to think about, jah?"

John nodded. "Hopefully nothing else will happen for some time. We need a break from tragedy."

Margaret's forehead wrinkled as she frowned. "Guess you haven't heard about my father-in-law's accident, then."

His eyebrows lifted. "No, I haven't heard. What happened to Moses?"

"He fell off a ladder in his barn early this morning."

"Sorry to hear that. Was he hurt badly?"

She shrugged. "I haven't had any word since he was taken to the hospital, but from what Paul told me this morning, his daed had complained that his back hurt really bad."

John slowly shook his head. "Moses sure doesn't need that

kind of thing happening to him right now. Especially with the harvest about to begin." He took a sip of his tea. "Think I'll see about hiring a driver to take me to the hospital later this afternoon so I can see how Moses is doing."

"I'm sure Moses and his family will appreciate having you there with them."

Chapter 18

Barbara had just closed up shop for the day when Paul Hilty pulled into the yard. Anxious for news of his father, she hurried out to him.

"How's your daed?" she asked when he got down from the buggy.

"He broke a couple ribs, bruised his left elbow real good, and pulled a muscle in his lower back." Paul slowly shook his head. "He'll live, but he'll probably be in traction for the next few days."

Barbara breathed a sigh of relief. At least Moses Hilty's wounds would heal, and they wouldn't have to face another death in the community right now. "I'm sorry about your daed's accident, but I'm glad it wasn't any worse."

"So am I."

"I guess he'll be laid up awhile, huh?"

Paul nodded soberly. "I'm sure Pop won't be able to farm for several weeks." He shifted his weight in an uneasy manner. "I. . . uh. . .was wondering if you'd be able to get by without my help at the harness shop. I promised Pop I'd help Monroe and Elam in the fields until he's back on his feet."

"Oh, of course, we'll get by here." Barbara hated to admit it, but she would miss Paul's help—and seeing him every day.

Paul grunted. "You know things haven't been good between my daed and me for some time, and I want to show him I care by helping out in this time of need."

"I understand. I'm feeling stronger now, so I think Dad and I can manage okay on our own."

She wondered if she should tell Paul he was free to return to Lancaster County after his father's injuries were healed. *I'd better not say anything just now,* she decided. *It can be said after Paul's done helping his brothers.*

Paul shuffled his boots and stared at the ground. "Well, I guess I'd better be going."

Barbara couldn't help but notice his forlorn expression. He was probably worried about his father and not looking forward to working in the fields.

Impulsively, she touched his arm. "How would you like to join the boys and me for supper tonight? We're planning to eat outside at the picnic table with my mamm and daed."

Paul hesitated, but only for a moment. His lips curved into a wide smile. "Sounds real nice."

Barbara motioned to the house. "Come along, then. You can relax on the porch swing with a cold drink while I go next door to my folks' place to get the kinner."

Paul leaned against the cushion on the back of the porch swing, sipping the lemonade Barbara had given him before she went next door. It felt nice to sit a spell and enjoy the cool evening breeze. He drew in a deep breath and savored the varied aromas of country air. Soon fall would be here, with its crisp fallen leaves and bonfires to enjoy. He'd always liked autumn, especially here in Webster County where life was easygoing and much more unhurried.

Paul closed his eyes and let his imagination run wild. In his mind's eye, he saw Barbara sitting in the rocking chair on her front porch. In her lap was a baby, but it wasn't Davey. The baby he envisioned was a dark-eyed little girl with shiny blond hair.

Instinctively, he reached up and touched the side of his head. *Hair just like mine. What would my life be like if I could stay right here, marry Barbara, and have a few kinner of my own?* Was it a foolish dream, or could Barbara possibly open her heart and home to him? With each passing day, Paul had fallen harder for her.

"You sleepin', Paul?"

Paul jerked upright and snapped his eyes open. He'd had no idea Joseph was standing there, and he wondered how long the boy had been watching him.

"I was resting my eyes, son," he said with a smile. "It's been a long day."

Joseph's forehead wrinkled. "I heard Mama tell Grandma you've been at the hospital with your daed."

"That's right. He fell off a ladder in the barn this morning and banged himself up pretty good."

"Sorry to hear that. I'll say a prayer for him."

"That'd be nice. I'm sure he'll appreciate all the prayers he can get."

Joseph's eyes brightened. "Mama also said you'd be joinin' us for supper tonight. I'm real glad 'bout that."

"Me, too." Paul patted the empty spot on the swing beside him. "Want to join me awhile?"

The boy scrambled onto the swing and cuddled against Paul's side.

"You miss your daed?" Paul asked.

"Jah."

"That's understandable. I'm sure your mamm and brothers miss him, too."

"I know Mama does. She cries when she's alone in her room sometimes. I think it's 'cause she's pinin' for Papa."

Paul's heart clenched. *It's a shame for Barbara to have lost her husband and for such a young boy to lose his father. But then, many things happen in life that aren't fair.* He thought about his brother dying so unexpectedly and how sad it was to see Margaret all alone and missing Dan so much.

They sat in silence awhile, Paul pumping the swing back and forth, and Joseph humming softly.

"Sure wish you were my daed now," the boy blurted out.

"That's a nice thought, but I don't know if it's possible," Paul said, giving the child's hand a squeeze. "I hope I'll always be your friend, though."

Joseph leaned away and stared up at Paul. His blue eyes were wide and his face ever so solemn. "Aaron says Bishop John is after Mama to marry him."

"And what do you think about that?"

Joseph shook his head. "Don't like it. Don't like it one little bit." He pushed his weight against Paul again. "It's you I want as my new daed. Nobody else."

A lump formed in Paul's throat. In all his grown-up years, he'd never had a kid take to him the way Joseph had. It made him long to be a father—Joseph's father, anyway.

"Can you marry my mamm and be my daed?"

Paul patted the boy's knee. "It's not that simple."

"Seems simple enough to me. You just go right up to her and ask. That wouldn't be so hard, now, would it?"

The back door of the Rabers' house opened, and Barbara stepped out, carrying the baby, with Zachary and Aaron at her side. Paul welcomed the interruption. At least he didn't have to come up with an answer for Joseph. That question had been rolling around in Paul's head for the past couple of days, and he had found no satisfactory answer.

Paul stood and followed Barbara and the boys into her house. When they entered the kitchen, Barbara placed little David in his baby carriage, instructing Zachary to push it back and forth if the infant got fussy. Aaron and Joseph were asked to haul pitchers of lemonade and iced tea out to the picnic table, while Barbara busied herself at the counter slicing thick hunks of juicy ham.

Paul's stomach rumbled. He'd spent most of the day at the hospital and hadn't taken the time for anything other than a few cups of coffee and a stale doughnut from the cafeteria. Since Mom had decided to stay at Pop's side awhile longer, Paul figured he'd have to manage on his own for supper. Barbara's invitation had been a pleasant surprise. Not only would his hunger be satisfied, but he was being offered an opportunity to spend time with Barbara again, even if they would have her parents and the boys as chaperones.

"Is there anything I can do to help?" he asked. "I'm sure you're tired after a long day at the shop."

She shook her head but kept her back to him. "Dad and I managed okay, and I'm not feeling too done in."

"Even so, I'd like to do more than stand here by the wall and watch."

"If you really want to do something, you can check the boppli's *windle*."

Paul's eyebrows shot up. Did she really expect him to change a diaper?

"Just kidding," she said with a muffled snicker. "Mom made sure Davey's diaper was clean and dry before I showed up to get the boys."

"Alice has been a big help to you since David died, huh?"

"Jah. I don't know what I'd have done without her or Dad." Barbara turned to face him. "I don't want to be dependent on their help forever, though. Sooner or later, I'll have to make it on my own."

For want of anything better to do, Paul pulled out a chair and took a seat at the table. "Guess you could always take the bishop up on his offer of marriage."

Barbara dropped the knife to the counter with a clatter and spun around. "You—you really think I should?"

Paul wanted to tell her right then that it was him she should marry, but she'd never given any indication that she cared for him that way, and unless she did. . . He pushed the thought aside and shrugged. "It's really none of my business."

Barbara studied him as if she were waiting for him to say something more. Was she hoping he would tell her that marrying the bishop wasn't a good idea? Or maybe she wanted his approval. Did his opinion matter?

She reached for her knife again and started cutting the meat.

"Are you considering it, then?" Paul had to know. If she were the least bit interested in the bishop, he would back off, plain and simple.

"Told him I'd think on it, that's all."

Paul leaned both elbows on the table. "And have you?"

"Jah."

"He's some older than you."

"That's true enough. A good fifteen years, at least."

"And being married to a bishop could put an extra burden on you."

"Maybe so."

"What of the harness shop?"

"What about it?"

"Would you sell the place if you were to marry John?"

"Guess I'd have to, seeing as how I'd be taking on the responsibility of helping raise his four daughters plus my boys."

Paul grabbed a napkin from the basket in the center of the table and wadded it into a tight ball. The thought of Barbara marrying the bishop was enough to make him lose his appetite. Still, he couldn't seem to muster the courage to speak on his own behalf. Besides, what if she rejected him?

"I thought you loved running the harness shop," he said. "How could you give up something you enjoy doing so much?"

Barbara shrugged her slim shoulders. "One does what one has to do in a time of need." She sliced the last piece of ham and placed it on the platter. "But I haven't decided yet."

Paul breathed a sigh of relief. Maybe he still had a chance with Barbara. At least he hoped he did.

As John entered Moses Hilty's hospital room, he prayed that God would give him the right words to say. He knew it had to be hard for Moses to be lying flat on his back in a hospital bed when he wanted to be at home working in the fields with his sons.

"Wie geht's?" John asked, stepping to the end of Moses's bed.

"Not so good." Moses groaned. "That fall really messed up my back. Don't know how long it'll be before I'm on my feet again and can return to farmwork."

"It's never easy to be laid up." John moved over to the side of the bed and lowered himself into a chair. "Elam and Monroe are pretty capable, though. I'm sure they'll keep things going until you're able to work again."

"Jah, but they can't do all the work alone. Thankfully, Paul's agreed to help 'em until I'm healed up."

"You mean after he gets done working at the harness shop each day?"

Moses shook his head. "He quit helping Barbara so he could help his brothers."

John's eyebrows drew together. "Does that mean he's not going back to Pennsylvania, after all?"

"Not right now, but I think he's planning to return as soon as the harvest is done."

"What about helping Barbara?"

"Don't know. But from what Paul said, she's back working full-time in her shop, so I doubt she'll be needing him from now on."

"I see." John gave his beard a couple of sharp pulls. If Paul was being kept busy in the fields and he wouldn't be returning to work for Barbara, then he would probably leave for Pennsylvania in just a few weeks. Unless, that is, he decided to stick around and try to win Barbara's hand so he could take control of the harness shop.

"You'd think you were the one in pain," Moses said.

"What makes you say that?"

"You ought to see the creases in your forehead. That worried-looking frown on your face makes me think something's wrong. Is there a problem?"

John fought the temptation to share his suspicions about Paul with Moses. No point in upsetting the man more than he already was. Besides, he might be worried for nothing. Maybe Paul would hightail it out of Missouri as soon as Moses was able to return to work. Then Barbara would be fair game. "It's nothing for you to be concerned about," he said with a smile. "I'm sure everything will work out fine—according to God's will."

Chapter 19

Paul wiped the sweat from his forehead with the back of his hand as he stopped working to catch his breath. He couldn't believe he had been helping his brothers in the dusty fields for a whole week already. Every evening, he trudged back to his folks' house, sweat-soaked, dirty from head to toe, and exhausted, while Monroe and Elam went home to their own families.

Pop had been released from the hospital three days ago, but due to the pain in his ribs and back, he was pretty much confined to bed. He was also as cranky as a mule with a tick in its backside.

Due to his father's condition, Paul tried hard to be kind and patient. However, his patience had been tested yesterday when Pop summoned him to his room and proceeded to tell Paul that if his back didn't heal up right, he might never be able to work in the fields again. That being the case, Monroe and Elam would need another pair of hands on a regular basis—namely, Paul's hands. Then he said he hoped Paul might consider giving up his job at Andy's harness shop in Pennsylvania and help on the farm permanently.

Seeing how much pain his father was in, Paul had merely said he would think on it. But after he was done working for the day, Paul was prepared to state his case before he lost his nerve. He just hoped Pop would be willing to listen.

As John pulled his rig out of Margaret's yard, his heartbeat picked up speed. He'd been calling on her ever since her husband died, and the more time he spent with her, the more he enjoyed her company. Despite the fact that Margaret was a few years older than he and her children were already grown and married, they had a lot in common. They both enjoyed looking at flowers, liked working on puzzles, took pleasure in feeding and watching birds, and had an interest in playing board games. Not only that, but John had discovered that Margaret was a kind, pleasant woman, easy to talk to, and a great cook. She'd had John and his daughters over for supper last night, and the meal had been delicious. An added benefit was that John's daughters seemed to enjoy Margaret's company, too.

"Margaret's probably past her childbearing years, so she couldn't give me any kinner," he mumbled. But that didn't seem to matter so much anymore. If only he felt free to ask her to marry him.

I might feel free if Paul Hilty were out of the picture and I knew Barbara wouldn't be in jeopardy of losing her harness shop. Maybe I need to stop and see Moses again. If I can convince him to talk Paul into going back to Pennsylvania, I'd know that Barbara wouldn't lose her harness shop and would be able to support herself and the boys if I don't marry her.

A short time later, John turned his buggy up the Hiltys' driveway. After he'd tied his horse to the hitching rail, he headed for the house.

Moses's wife, Joann, greeted John at the door. "Did you come to see Moses?" she asked with a friendly smile.

John nodded. "Is he up and about yet?"

"Only for short periods." Joann shook her head. "His back still hurts whenever he moves around too much, so he spends most of his time lying in bed complaining about his pain and mumbling that he needs to get back to work." She released a sigh. "I guess a complaining husband is better than no husband at all."

"I'm sure Margaret Hilty and Barbara Zook would agree with you on that point."

Joann motioned to the bedroom just down the hall from the living room. "Moses is in there. Do you want me to see if he feels up to coming out, or would you rather go to his room to visit?"

"I'll go to Moses." John winked at her. "No point in giving him one more thing to complain about."

"That's true enough." She smiled and turned toward the kitchen. "When you're done visiting, stop by the kitchen, and I'll have a cup of hot coffee and a hunk of apple pie waiting for you."

"Danki, I just may do that."

Joann disappeared into the kitchen, and John headed for the downstairs bedroom, where he found Moses lying on the bed, his head propped up on two thick pillows.

"It's good to see you," Moses said.

"Good to see you, too. How are you feeling these days?"

"I'm doin' some better but still not able to be working in the fields."

"Give it some time, and try to be patient." John lifted his straw hat from his head and moved closer to Moses's bed.

Moses grimaced as he pushed himself to a sitting position. "That's a lot easier said than done."

"Jah, I know."

"So how are things going with you? Are you keeping busy with your business?"

"That and making calls on ailing members of our community," John said.

Moses motioned to the chair beside his bed. "Have a seat so we can visit awhile."

"Don't mind if I do." John sat down, flopped his hat over one knee, and cleared his throat a couple of times.

"You gettin' a cold?"

"No, I was just getting ready to say something."

"What's that?"

"I was wondering if Paul's still planning to return to Pennsylvania."

Moses grimaced, and a muscle on the side of his face twitched like a cow's ear when it was being bothered by a pesky fly. "I had a talk with Paul the other day, and when I asked if he'd consider staying here and working on the farm permanently, he said he'd think on it."

John's face flamed. "But—but I thought he didn't like farmwork. That day I came to see you at the hospital, you said Paul would be going back to Pennsylvania as soon as you were on your feet again."

Moses nodded. "That is what I said, but things have changed."

"How so?"

"The day I was released from the hospital, the doctor told me that my back was weakened by the fall and that I might never be able to do any heavy lifting again." Moses released a deep moan. "Being a farmer means doing heavy work—lifting bales of hay, sacks of grain, and the like."

"Can't you hire someone to take your place?"

"I suppose I could, but—"

John touched his friend's arm. "Is it really fair to force your son to do work he'd rather not be doing? I mean, if Paul was happy working for his cousin in Pennsylvania and he stays here only as a favor to you, resentment might creep in, and then—"

"Paul's and my relationship would become even more strained than it is," Moses said, finishing John's sentence.

"Jah." John twisted the brim of his hat a couple of times. "Do you want my advice?"

Moses nodded.

"Tell Paul you'll hire someone to take your place and give him the freedom to return to Pennsylvania where he belongs."

Moses compressed his lips as he squinted. "I'll think about what you've said."

John smiled. "You should think about it and ask God what would be best for both you and Paul."

When Paul entered the kitchen, Mom turned from her place at the stove and shook her head. "You surely do look a mess. Hardly a speck of skin showing that's not covered with dust."

He nodded. "I'm heading to the bathroom to wash up now. Then I need to speak to Pop before we eat our supper."

"Take your time," she replied. "The meal won't be ready for another thirty minutes or so."

Paul left the room. After he'd cleaned off most of the field dirt, he went straight to his parents' room. Pop was sitting up in bed reading from the Bible.

"How are you feeling today?"

"How'd it go in the fields?"

They'd spoken at the same time. As Paul stepped to the side of the bed, he said, "You go first."

His dad set the Bible aside and motioned to a nearby chair. "Have a seat and tell me how your work's going."

Paul did as Pop requested. "It's coming along okay. We should be ready to harvest the hay and corn in a few more weeks." Paul clasped his hands tightly together. "How's your back doing?"

"Feels fine as long as I don't move." Pop grimaced. "I'm supposed to start physical therapy tomorrow morning. Sure don't relish that."

"It should help your muscles relax."

"Jah, well, I don't much like the idea of anyone pushing and shoving on my spine." Pop shifted on the pillow and groaned. "I have to wonder if I'll ever get back to working in the fields."

Paul felt as if a heavy weight rested on his chest. The thought of giving up work in the harness shop to farm made his heart ache. When he'd left Missouri to learn the harness business, he'd never expected to move home again, much less return to farming.

He leaned forward, resting his elbows on his knees. "I've been thinking on the things we talked about yesterday and doing some praying, too."

Pop turned his head and looked directly at Paul. "Jah?"

Paul swallowed hard. He hated to upset Pop when he was hurting, but the things that weighed heavily on his mind couldn't wait forever. There was no use getting his father's hopes built up over something that wasn't going to happen.

"I know you're not able to work right now, and I said I'd help in the fields until you're better, but—"

Pop narrowed his eyes. "Are you backing out of our agreement?"

Paul shook his head. "I'll help Monroe and Elam until we get caught up and the harvest is in. But after that, I'll be returning to Pennsylvania. I've been gone a lot longer than I'd planned, and if I don't go soon, there might not be a job waiting for me at Andy's shop."

"What about Barbara Zook?"

"What about her?"

"I thought you were needed to help in her harness shop."

"I was. But her daed's doing some better, and she's back at work full-time, so she doesn't really need me anymore." *But I would stay if she asked me to,* Paul thought. *I'd proclaim my love for her and stay on as her husband if there was any indication that she loved me and would agree to become my wife.*

Pop blew out his breath. "So you're saying you'll hang around until the harvest is done; then you plan to head back to Pennsylvania?"

"That's right."

"And nothing I can say will change your mind?"

Paul shook his head. "I enjoy working with leather and never have cottoned to farmwork."

"How well I know that," Pop agreed with a nod. "Even when you were a boy, you complained about all the dust and long hours in the fields."

"You understand the way I feel, then?"

"I recognize your desire to do what makes you happy, and after some thinking and praying of my own, I've come to the conclusion that it's not fair of me to try and force you to stay." Pop swallowed a couple of times. "If I'm not able to return to farming because of my back, then I'll hire someone to help your brothers in the fields."

Paul clasped his dad's hand as a sense of gratitude welled in his soul. The change in Pop's attitude was a miracle. An answer to prayer, that's what it was. "Danki," he murmured. "I appreciate that."

"You'll be missed when you leave Webster County," Pop added.

Paul nodded. "I'll miss you all, too."

Barbara stared out the shop window, watching Aaron and Joseph head toward the one-room schoolhouse down the road. Today was the first day back to school after summer break and Joseph's first time to attend.

"Are you worried about the boys?" her father asked as he stepped up behind her.

Barbara turned. "Just Joseph. He's so young. I hope he does okay and doesn't give Ruthie Yoder a hard time." She sighed. "I wish Sarah still taught school here. He might feel more secure having his aunt as his teacher."

"I hear tell Ruthie's done a fine job of taking over for my daughter. I'm sure Joseph will do all right." Dad chuckled. "I remember when I attended school for the first time. I didn't like first grade and didn't care much for my teacher, but I sure enjoyed playing on the teeter-totter out behind the schoolhouse during recess."

Barbara smiled. Dad was probably right; Joseph would do okay. He was an easygoing, obedient child and should get along fine with the teacher as well as with the other scholars. Aaron, however, could be a real handful at times.

He's stubborn, just like his father, she mused. *But I'm sure he'll manage okay on this first day. Leastways, I pray it's so.*

"Sure seems different around here without Paul Hilty, don't you think?"

Barbara nodded. She hated to admit it, but she missed Paul coming to work every day. She missed his friendly banter, sparkling blue eyes, and lopsided grin. He'd been a big help and knew a lot about running a harness shop, even if they didn't see eye to eye on everything. Paul must be working hard at his father's farm. She'd thought about inviting him to join them for supper one night after work but had set that idea aside, fearful he might get the impression she was interested in him. She was, of course, but didn't want him to know that since he hadn't revealed any feelings for her other than friendship.

And then there's Aaron, she thought as she turned away from the window. *He finally seems to be adjusting to his daed's death. But if Paul starts coming around when it's got nothing to do with work, Aaron might become upset again.*

Barbara wasn't sure why, but Aaron seemed to consider Paul a threat. The other children liked the man real well. In Joseph's case, maybe a little too much. The last Sunday they'd had church, the boy had hung around Paul all afternoon. Barbara had noticed him clinging to Paul's hand and enjoying the piggyback rides Paul had graciously given to both Joseph and Zachary.

Paul will make a good daed someday. But I'm afraid it's not going to be my boys he'll be fathering.

Barbara grabbed some leather and dropped it into the washtub filled with dye. "I guess it's time to get something constructive done."

"Jah," Dad agreed. "Sure won't happen on its own, no matter how much I might wish it could."

Barbara's conscience pricked her heart. She knew the harness business wasn't Dad's true calling. Fact was, he'd much rather be tending his garden or relaxing on the porch than helping her keep the place running. But with Paul gone off to help his brothers, Barbara couldn't make it on her own without Dad's help. So she would take one day at a time, thanking the Lord for each hour that her father felt well enough to lend a hand. She tried not to think about the day when he could no longer hold a piece of leather in his hands. How would she manage? Aaron would help during his breaks from school, but to be on her own all the time would be nearly impossible.

Maybe I do need to give the bishop's offer of marriage more thought. I'd better pray harder about this, she decided.

"Are you sure you don't mind me quitting work early today?" Barbara's father asked as he headed toward the shop door.

She shook her head. "I don't mind at all. I know your fingers have been aching all day, and I think you might feel better if you go home and soak your hands in some Epsom salts."

"I believe you're right." He had just reached the door when he turned back around. "Don't you work too late now, you hear?"

"I won't. It'll be time to feed Davey soon, so I'll be closing shop and coming up to the house before you know it."

"Okay." Dad stepped outside and closed the door.

Barbara had just sat down when the shop door opened. Bishop John stepped into the room. Her heart thudded in her chest. Was he here to get an answer to his proposal? Was she prepared to give him one?

Maybe I should marry him and sell the harness shop. Maybe Paul would buy it if he knew he wouldn't have to put up with me working here, telling him what to do.

"You're looking well, Barbara. How are things going now that you're back working full-time?" the bishop asked.

She smiled. "I'm pretty tired by the end of the day, but with my daed's help, I'm managing okay."

He shifted from one foot to the other and cleared his throat a couple of times. "Ahem. I was wondering—"

"Are you needing an answer to your marriage proposal? Is that why you've come by?"

"Uh. . .no. . .not exactly."

"You're here on harness business, then?"

He shook his head.

"What is the reason for your visit?"

"I've. . .uh. . .just come from seeing Margaret Hilty."

"Oh. How's she getting along?"

He smiled, and his eyes lit up like fireflies doing their summer dance. "She's doing real well, and so am I."

"I'm glad to hear it."

He leaned forward, resting the palms of his hands on her desk. "The thing is. . .I. . .uh. . .would like to ask Margaret to marry me. And I. . .uh. . .need to know if you're okay with that."

Barbara stared up at John. He wanted to ask Margaret to marry him, and he needed Barbara's approval? That made no sense at all. Besides, Margaret hadn't been widowed a year yet, and as far as Barbara knew, there was nothing going on between John and Margaret in a romantic way.

"I don't understand," she mumbled. "I thought you wanted to marry me."

"Well, I—I did," he stammered. "But it wasn't because I was in love with you." His face turned as red as a ripe tomato. "What I mean to say is, I care about your welfare."

"I appreciate that."

"And after your boppli was born and you seemed so tired, I didn't know if you'd be able to keep running the harness shop."

Barbara felt more confused than ever. "What exactly are you saying, Bishop John?"

The color in his cheeks deepened. "I had thought that if you married me, you wouldn't have to work at the harness shop anymore."

"But I love working here," she said, making a sweeping gesture of the room with her hand.

"I'm sure you do, but the kind of work you do isn't easy—not even for most men."

"It may not be easy, but it's what I want to do." She moved over to a nearby workbench and touched the piece of leather lying there. "This shop was David's, and he loved what he did." She paused and moistened her lips with the tip of her tongue. "If I can manage to keep the shop going, sometime it'll hopefully be Aaron's."

"I understand that, but I have one other concern."

"What's that?"

"I'm afraid if you marry Paul, you'll lose the shop to him, and—"

Barbara's mouth dropped open as she held up one hand. "Where did you ever get the idea that I might marry Paul?"

"I've seen the syrupy way he looks at you and butters up to

your boys." John grunted. "It's more than obvious to me that he's been after you so he can get his hands on your harness shop."

Barbara gasped. "Is that what you really think?"

He nodded. "Paul would have liked to have opened a harness shop here in Webster County some years ago, but he couldn't do it because you and David had already opened up one."

"That's true, but Paul moved to Pennsylvania to work in his cousin's harness shop. As far as I know, he's been happy working there."

John shifted his weight again. "Well, none of this is a problem now, because I spoke with Paul's daed. He's going to hire someone to take his place in the fields so Paul can go back to Pennsylvania where he belongs."

Barbara's heart sank. If Paul planned to leave, he obviously didn't have any feelings for her. It had just been wishful thinking on her part. All his friendliness to the boys must have just been an act, too. *Can what the bishop said about Paul be true?* she wondered. *Does Paul wish this shop could be his? Is it possible that he's acted like he cares for me and the boys in order to get his hands on my harness business?*

"What does all this have to do with you asking Margaret to marry you?" she asked, looking up at the bishop.

"After spending quite a bit of time with her since Dan died, I've come to realize that I love her and would like to make her my wife." He paused and swiped at the sweat rolling down his forehead. "I'm just waiting for the right time to ask Margaret to be my wife, but I didn't want to speak of marriage to her until I knew if you were okay with the idea and didn't need me to marry you."

Barbara's spine went rigid. "I don't *need* anyone to marry me. I'm doing fine on my own."

He blanched. "I—I didn't mean for it to sound as if. . ."

Her face softened as she realized she was being overly harsh. A short time ago, she had actually been considering his proposal. "I have no objections to your marrying Margaret. In fact, I wish you both well."

Bishop John released an audible sigh. "I appreciate that." He shuffled his feet, then turned toward the door. "I know you have your hands full taking care of the shop and your boys, so if there's anything I can do to help, please let me know," he called over his shoulder.

"I appreciate the offer, but I'm sure we'll be fine."

The door clicked shut behind the bishop, and Barbara let her head fall forward onto her desk. *Dear Lord, please let us be fine.*

Paul hadn't been back to Zook's Harness Shop since he'd said that he would be quitting to help on the farm. But today he needed to go there. One of their mules had busted its bridle, and it needed to be repaired right away.

Part of Paul dreaded seeing Barbara again. Being around her evoked emotions he'd rather not deal with. Yet another part of him looked forward to seeing her beautiful face and dark eyes that made him want to shout to the world that Barbara Zook had captured his heart. Of course, he would never do anything so foolish. If Barbara was considering marrying the bishop, then

Paul had no right to be thinking such thoughts about her. But if Barbara had decided not to marry John, then maybe Paul had a chance. He just needed to get up the nerve to ask her.

Paul took the time to clean up before heading over to Barbara's place. He didn't want her to see him looking like a mess or smelling like a sweaty old mule. As he pulled into the Zooks' driveway sometime later, he cringed when he saw John Frey standing beside his buggy outside Barbara's shop.

"Doesn't that man ever give up?" he muttered.

Paul pulled his buggy alongside the bishop's and climbed down. "Afternoon, Bishop," he said, hoping his voice sounded more relaxed than he felt. "You here on business?"

John gave his beard a couple of tugs. "I was, but the business has been concluded. I'm on my way home."

Good. I wasn't looking forward to watching you flirt with Barbara. Paul hurried toward the harness shop.

"See you on Sunday if not before," the bishop called.

Paul nodded as he turned the doorknob and stepped inside the building. He didn't see anyone at first and wondered if Barbara might have gone up to her folks' house to check on the boys. Even if she had, her father should be around. The shop was still open for the day.

Paul cupped his hands around his mouth. "Anyone here?"

"Be right with you."

He smiled at the sound of Barbara's voice coming from the back room. He'd really missed her, and no matter how much he tried to fight the feelings, Paul didn't think he would ever meet another woman who made him feel the way Barbara did.

A few minutes later, she headed his way, carrying a chunk of leather that looked much too weighty for her to be lugging.

Paul stepped quickly forward and held out his hands. "Here, let me help you with that."

She hesitated a moment but finally turned the bundle over to him. "Danki."

"You're welcome." Paul placed the leather on the closest workbench. "Is this okay?"

She nodded. "What brings you by this afternoon? I figured you'd still be hard at work in the fields."

He pointed to the broken bridle draped over his shoulder. "We had a little accident with the mules. This snapped right in two."

"I can try to get it fixed first thing in the morning," she said. "Will that be soon enough?"

"We really need to have it when we start work tomorrow. I was hoping you wouldn't mind if I did the repairs myself."

Her eyebrows lifted. "You mean now?"

"Jah. If it's okay with you." He paused and licked his lips, which seemed awfully dry. "I'll pay for any supplies I use, of course."

Barbara waved her hand. "Nonsense. Just help yourself to whatever you need. It's the least I can do to say thanks for helping me out in my time of need."

"But you paid me a fair wage for that," he reminded her.

She shrugged. "Even so, that doesn't make up for the fact that you stayed here helping me when you wanted to get back to your cousin's harness shop in Pennsylvania."

He was tempted to tell her that he really wasn't in a hurry to return to Pennsylvania, but what reason could he give? He couldn't just blurt out that he had fallen in love with her and wished he could stay right here in Webster County and marry her.

"How are you managing now?" he asked instead. "Is your daed able to be here all the time?"

She shrugged and released a noisy sigh. "He comes in every day but doesn't always work the whole time. His hands are bothering him again, but he keeps at it the best he's able."

Paul's heart clenched, and he felt like he was being ripped in two. Pop needed him to work in the fields, but it was obvious that Barbara could still use his help. Then there was his cousin Andy, who'd written and said he was getting really busy and wondered when Paul planned to return to Pennsylvania. Paul wasn't sure where he belonged or who needed him the most. The only thing he knew for certain was that he loved Barbara Zook. But what, if anything, should he do about it?

Chapter 20

Would you like to join us for supper?" Barbara asked as Paul was about to get into his buggy. "It'll just be me and the boys," she added with a look of uncertainty. "Mom and Dad are going into town to eat."

"I'd be happy to join you for supper," Paul said as a shiver of enthusiasm tickled his spine. This was the opportunity he'd been waiting for. With any luck, after Barbara's sons were finished eating, he'd have some time to be alone with her, to tell her how he'd come to care for her, and to hopefully discover how she felt about him. He didn't want to leave Webster County until he knew. Maybe, if his prayers were answered, he wouldn't have to leave at all.

He smiled to himself. *She must care a little, or she wouldn't have invited me to stay for supper.*

At Barbara's suggestion, Paul waited on the back porch while she went next door to get her brood. He took a seat on the top step and stared into the yard, overgrown with weeds again and direly in need of a good mowing. He figured Barbara was probably hesitant about asking some of the women to do more yard work for her, but he was surprised that the bishop hadn't thought to ask someone to do it. If Paul didn't forget, he might speak with Margaret about helping Barbara again. She was good with flowers and probably wouldn't mind helping out. Paul figured his widowed sister-in-law most likely needed something to do.

His thoughts returned to Barbara. *Lord, give me the courage to open my heart to her tonight. I need to know if she's going to marry John or whether she might have an interest in me. If it's Your will for us to be together, help her to be receptive to the idea.*

When Paul heard a door open, he glanced over at the Rabers' place. Joseph was the first to exit his grandparents' house, and he bounded across the lawn like an excited puppy.

Waving at Paul as if he hadn't seen him for several weeks, the child leaped into Paul's arms. "Mama said you're here for supper again!"

"That's right." Paul ruffled the boy's blond hair.

"I'm ever so glad." Joseph nestled against Paul's chest, and once more, Paul was filled with a strong desire to marry and raise a family. Never had he felt so much love from a child.

Barbara showed up then with Aaron, Zachary, and the baby. "Let's go inside, shall we?" she said with a smile that warmed Paul's heart.

"Sounds good to me." Paul stood, and Joseph latched onto his hand.

"How was school today, Aaron?" Paul asked as the boy tromped up the steps behind his mother.

"Okay."

"Have you been helping your mamm in the harness shop after school and on Saturdays?"

"Sometimes."

Paul sighed. So much for trying to make small talk with Barbara's oldest. It was apparent the boy wasn't near as happy to have Paul staying for supper as his younger brother seemed to be.

As soon as they entered the house, Aaron took off upstairs. Joseph pulled Paul into the kitchen and pointed to the rocking chair. "Why don't ya set a spell, and I'll sit with you?"

Paul looked at Barbara. When she nodded, he took a seat. Without invitation, Joseph crawled into his lap, and Zachary did the same. As Paul balanced the little guys on his knees, he wondered how it would feel to come home every night after work and be surrounded by his boys.

He began to rock, hoping the action would get him thinking straight again. These were Barbara's boys, not his.

Barbara placed the sleeping baby in his carriage on the other side of the room and donned her choring apron. "Would soup and sandwiches be okay? I've got some leftover bean soup in the refrigerator." When she glanced at Paul, he noticed how tired she looked—even more tired than when they'd been in the harness shop earlier. Dark circles hung beneath her eyes, her cheeks were flushed, and her shoulders drooped with obvious fatigue.

"How can I help?" he asked. "Would you like for me to set the table or make the sandwiches?"

Barbara presented Paul with a smile that let him know she was grateful for the offer. "The boys can set the table. If you've a mind to make the sandwiches, there's some barbecued beef in the refrigerator. Maybe you could get the container of leftover soup out for me, too."

"Sure, no problem."

She looked at Joseph. "Take Zachary to the bathroom and see that you both get washed up. Tell Aaron to do the same. When you're done, I'd like you to set the table."

Joseph leaned heavily against Paul's chest. "Promise you won't leave?"

Paul tweaked the boy's nose. " 'Course not."

The children climbed down and scampered out of the room.

Paul retrieved a platter of shredded beef and the bowl of bean soup from the refrigerator. After Barbara lit the propane stove, Paul poured the soup into a pot and set it on the burner. Then he grabbed the sandwich rolls and filled them with barbecued beef. He licked his lips as the tantalizing aroma of bean soup permeated the kitchen. His stomach rumbled, reminding him how hungry he was.

Should I say something to Barbara about the way I feel or wait until after supper? In spite of the sense of urgency that pulled on Paul's heart, he decided it would be better to wait until the boys were finished eating so he could speak to her without interruption.

All during supper, Barbara sensed Paul wanted to say something to her. Maybe it was something important. He seemed kind of edgy, toying with his napkin and staring at her in an odd way.

Does he care about me? Should I allow myself to have feelings for him in spite of Aaron's negative attitude? Would it be possible for us to have more than a working relationship or friendship?

Determined to set her troubling thoughts aside, Barbara finished her last bite of soup and pushed her chair away from the table.

Paul did the same, placing his empty bowl and eating utensils in the sink. "Barbara, I'd like to speak to you alone, if it's all right. Maybe we could sit outside on the porch awhile—just the two of us?"

"That sounds nice, but I need to do up the dishes first."

"Why not let Aaron and Joseph do them? They're old enough, don't you think?" He turned to face the boys, who still sat at the table. "Maybe even little Zachary could help by clearing the rest of the table."

Joseph grinned as though he considered it a compliment that Paul thought him big enough to do the dishes. Aaron, however, glared at Paul with a look of defiance glinting in his dark eyes.

"You've got no right to be tellin' me or my brieder what to do," Aaron mumbled.

Paul stepped forward and turned his palms up. "It was only a suggestion to your mamm."

Joseph grabbed his plate and scrambled out of his chair, hurrying toward the sink. "Boost me up, Mama, so I can do these dishes."

Barbara leaned over and tickled her son under the chin. "If you're going to be washing dishes, then you'll need a chair to stand on."

Joseph turned to face Aaron. "Bring me a chair, would ya please?"

Aaron folded his arms in a stubborn, unyielding pose. "Get it yourself!"

"What's gotten into you?" Barbara shook her finger and gave the boy a stern look. "Bring a chair over to the sink now, and apologize to your brother for the way you spoke to him."

Aaron stared straight ahead, not budging from his seat. Zachary kept eating his soup, apparently unaware of the tension that permeated the room.

Barbara grimaced. She'd thought her oldest boy was doing better lately, but apparently she'd been wrong. She opened her mouth to reprimand Aaron, but Paul spoke first.

"Your mother's right. You do owe your brother an apology. And you owe your mamm one, too, for not doing as she told you."

Aaron compressed his lips into a thin line as he sat in his chair, unmoving.

Paul crossed the room, pulled out a chair beside the boy, and sat down. "This is not acceptable behavior. What have you got to say for yourself?"

Aaron's shoulders slumped as he stared at the table.

Paul glanced at Barbara with a questioning look. He seemed to be asking for her permission to handle the situation.

"Go ahead, if you don't mind," she said, grabbing the closest chair and pushing it over to the sink. Joseph climbed onto the chair, and she helped him fill the dishpan with soap and water.

Silence reigned at the table, and Barbara wondered if she'd made a mistake letting Paul take charge of things. When she was certain Joseph could handle the dishes on his own, she took a seat across from Aaron.

"I don't know why you're acting this way," she said sternly, "but I will not have you disobeying or spouting off like this; is that clear?"

The boy nodded soberly.

Paul touched Aaron's arm, but he jerked it away and glared at Paul. "You ain't my daed."

Paul opened his mouth, and so did Barbara, but before either could speak, Aaron pushed his chair aside and raced out the back door.

Chapter 21

Paul stared out the kitchen window. "My mamm always said I ought to learn to keep my big mouth shut. Now I've made the boy real mad."

"It's not your fault," Barbara said, joining him at the window. "Aaron started acting moody and belligerent after David died. I thought he was getting better." She shrugged and sighed. "Guess I was wrong."

"Maybe I should go after him."

Barbara shook her head. "I think it's best if we let him be by himself awhile."

"But who's gonna help me with the dishes?" Joseph spoke up from his place at the sink.

Paul crossed the room and patted the boy's shoulder. "You wash, and I'll dry. How's that sound?"

Joseph grinned up at him. "I'd like that." He looked over at Zachary, still sitting at the table, dawdling with his bowl of soup. "Hurry up, ya slowpoke. We need them dishes."

"Let's get the ones in the sink done first," Paul suggested. "By then, maybe your little brother will be finished."

"Okay."

If only my oldest son would be so compliant, Barbara thought. *Is it Aaron's personality to be so negative and defiant, or have I failed him somehow? If David were still alive, would things be any different? Probably so, since Aaron and his father were always close, and Aaron was willing to do most anything his father asked of him.*

Just then the baby began to cry. Barbara turned her attention to the precious bundle lying in the carriage across the room. "I need to feed and change Davey," she said to Paul. "If you'll excuse me, I'll be upstairs for a while."

He nodded as he took another clean dish from Joseph. At least Barbara hoped the boy was getting them clean.

"Maybe by the time you come back to the kitchen, Aaron will have returned," Paul said in a reassuring tone.

Barbara felt his strength and kindness surround her like a warm quilt. For one wild moment, she had the crazy impulse to lean her head against his chest and feel the warmth of his embrace.

Pushing the ridiculous notion aside, she scooped the baby into her arms. "I shouldn't be gone too long."

Paul glanced at the clock on the wall above the refrigerator. It was almost seven. He really should be getting home so he could do any final chores for the day. Barbara had been gone nearly an hour, and so had Aaron. It was possible that she might have fallen asleep while feeding the baby, but why wasn't that insolent boy back yet?

"Hey, watch what you're doin'!" Joseph shouted.

Paul turned just in time to see Zachary chomp down on a piece of puzzle, leaving an obvious tooth mark on one end.

"Give me that!" Joseph reached across his little brother and snatched the puzzle piece from his mouth.

"You're not supposed to eat the puzzle," he said with a grunt.

"*Hungerich,*" Zachary whined.

"I don't care if you are hungry," Joseph grumbled. "You should have eaten more of your supper."

Zachary's lower lip quivered, and his eyes pooled with tears.

Joseph shot Paul a beseeching look. "Can he have a cookie?"

Paul shrugged. "I—I guess it would be all right. Where does your mamm keep the cookies?"

Joseph pointed to the cupboard across the room.

"Okay. I'll see if there are any." Paul made his way across the room and opened the cupboard door. Inside, he found a green ceramic jar with a matching lid. He opened it and discovered a batch of chocolate chip cookies. He set the jar on the table, dipped his hand inside, scooped out four cookies, and set two in front of each of the boys. Then he opened the back door and stepped onto the porch. He saw no sign of Aaron.

He stuck his head inside the kitchen doorway. "Joseph, I'm going to run over to your grandma and grandpa's place a minute. Will you and Zachary be all right?"

The boy's head bobbed up and down. "We'll be fine. Mama's just upstairs, ya know."

"Okay. I'll be back quick as a wink." Paul bounded off the porch and raced over to the Rabers' house. He pounded on the door several times, but no one answered. Then he remembered that Barbara had said her folks were going out for supper. They probably weren't back yet.

Paul thought about looking for Aaron in the barn or harness shop, but he didn't want to leave Zachary and Joseph alone that long.

"I'd better get back inside," he muttered, turning toward Barbara's house. "No telling what those two little boys are up to."

When he entered the kitchen again, Paul discovered the children had helped themselves to more cookies and a glass of milk. Joseph had a white mustache on his upper lip, and Zachary's face was dotted with chocolate. Cookie crumbs were strewn all over the table, and a puddle of milk lay under Zachary's chair.

Paul grabbed a dishrag from the kitchen sink and tossed it to Joseph. "You'd better get this mess cleaned up before your mamm comes downstairs."

While Joseph sopped up the milk, Zachary continued to nibble on his cookie.

Paul pulled a towel off the rack under the sink, dampened it with water, and sponged off the younger boy's face. He'd just finished when Barbara entered the kitchen.

"The boppli's asleep in his crib, and—" She halted and stared at her sons. "Looks like you've had yourselves a little party while I was gone."

"*Kichlin,*" Zachary announced, licking his fingers.

"Jah, I see you've been eating some cookies."

"I gave them two apiece when Zachary said he was hungry, and I made the mistake of leaving the cookie jar on the table while I went outside to see if Aaron had gone over to your folks' place," Paul explained. "Guess they must have helped themselves to a few more after I left the house."

Barbara glanced around the room. "Aaron's not back yet?" A look of alarm showed clearly on her face.

Paul took the dishrag and towel back to the sink and turned to face her. "I thought about going out to the barn or harness shop to look for Aaron, but I didn't want to leave the younger ones alone that long."

Barbara's gaze went to the window. "I'm worried."

"Tell me where his favorite places are, and I'll see if I can find him," Paul said. His chores could wait. Right now, finding the boy was more important.

"Let's see. . . . He likes to play in the barn." Barbara massaged her forehead, making little circles with the tips of her fingers. "He enjoys being in the harness shop, of course."

"I'll look around the yard real good, head out to the shop, and then check the barn." Paul moved toward the back door. "Try not to worry. I'm sure he's fine."

As Paul made his way across the yard, he thought about his plan to speak with Barbara about their relationship. It didn't look like he was going to get that chance. Not tonight, anyway.

Barbara had been pacing the kitchen floor for the last half hour.

Where was Aaron, and why wasn't Paul back with a report? She was tempted to gather up the boys and go looking herself, but the baby was asleep, and the other two needed to be put to bed, as well.

She glanced out the window one more time. It was getting dark, and since no gas lamps glowed in any of her folks' windows, she assumed they still weren't back from town. She had been watching for them, hoping her father could join Paul in the search for Aaron. Or maybe Mom could stay with the children while Barbara helped the men look.

Barbara closed her eyes and clasped her hands tightly together. *Please, Lord, let my boy be okay.*

"Mama, Zachary's hidin' pieces of puzzle on me," Joseph whined.

"Nee," Zachary retorted.

"Jah, you are so."

"Nee."

"Uh-huh. I seen you slip one onto your chair. And you tried to eat a puzzle piece awhile ago."

Zachary shook his head.

"Jah, you sure did. Ya left a tooth mark in it, too."

Zachary opened his mouth and let out an ear-piercing screech.

"Stop it!" Barbara's hands shook. She forced herself to breathe deeply and count to ten. No good could come from yelling at the boys just because she was upset over Aaron's disappearance.

This is my fault, she thought miserably. *I should have sent Aaron to his room as soon as he started mouthing off. I'll never forgive myself if anything bad has happened to him.*

Paul closed the door of the harness shop. Aaron wasn't in the shop, and as far as he could tell, the boy wasn't anywhere in the yard. Paul had checked every conceivable hiding spot outdoors, so he decided that his next stop would be the barn. If Aaron wasn't there, he didn't know where else to look.

Maybe he wandered off the property and headed down the road to his friend Gabe's. If he's not in the barn, I'd better hitch my horse to the buggy and go there.

Paul entered the barn. It was dark and smelled of hay and animals. He cupped his hands around his mouth. "Aaron, are you in here?"

The only response was the gentle nicker from the buggy horses.

Paul located a lantern and struck a match. A circle of light encompassed the area where he stood. He held the lantern overhead and moved slowly about the building. "Aaron!" he called several times.

No answer.

As he continued to circle the barn, looking in every nook and cranny, Paul noticed the door to the silo was open. On a hunch, he stepped through the opening.

"Anybody here?" he hollered.

"Help!"

Paul cocked his head and listened.

"Help me, please!"

"Aaron, is that you?"

"Jah. I'm up here."

Paul held the light overhead and looked up into the empty silo. His heart nearly stopped beating when he saw Aaron standing on the top rung of the ladder.

"What are you doing up there? Don't you know how dangerous that is?"

"I climbed up to be by myself, but I got scared and couldn't get back down."

Paul gulped as a familiar feeling of terror swept over him. He hated high places—had ever since he was a boy and had gotten himself stuck in a tree. He hadn't been able to talk any of his brothers into helping him down and had ended up falling and breaking his leg.

"C-can you help me get down?" Aaron pleaded.

His heart hammering in his chest, Paul drew in a deep breath and hung the lantern on a nearby nail. "I'm coming, Aaron. Just, please, hang on."

Chapter 22

Paul's hands turned sweaty, and his legs trembled like a newborn foal's as he drew in a deep breath, grabbed hold of the ladder, and slowly ascended it. *Don't think about where you are. Don't look down. Take one rung at a time. Lord, please ease my fears and help me do this.*

"I–I'm really scared," Aaron cried from above. "My hands hurt from holdin' on so tight. I feel like I'm gonna fall."

A chill rippled through Paul. What if the child let go? If Aaron fell from that height, it could kill him. "Be still, Aaron. I'm almost there." Paul didn't want to admit it, but he figured he was probably more afraid than the boy. Philippians 4:13 floated through Paul's mind: *"I can do all things through Christ which strengtheneth me."*

Paul sent up a silent prayer. *With Your help, Lord, I can get Aaron back down this ladder and safely into his mother's arms.*

When Paul reached the rung directly below Aaron, he wrapped his arms around the boy and held him tightly for a few seconds. Aaron stiffened at first but finally relaxed. Paul did the same.

The child sniffed. "H–how are you gonna get me down?"

"We'll go the same way we came up—one rung at a time." Paul kept one arm around Aaron's waist and grabbed hold of a rung.

"D–don't let me go." Aaron's voice shook with emotion, and Paul's fears for himself abated. Aaron was his first priority. All that mattered was getting Barbara's son safely to the ground.

"I'm going to hold you around the middle with one arm, and we'll inch our way down the ladder together. Are you ready?"

"I–I think so."

"Step with your left foot until you feel it touch the rung below. And whatever you do, don't look down."

Paul was relieved when Aaron did as he was told.

Slowly, rung by rung, the two descended the ladder. All the while, Paul kept one arm around Aaron's waist and whispered comforting words in his ear. "We're going to make it, son. Almost there. Just a few more rungs to go."

When Paul's feet touched the ground, he lifted Aaron with both hands, turning the child to face him.

Aaron threw his arms around Paul's neck and clung to him tearfully. "I ain't never goin' up there again—that's for certain sure."

Paul patted Aaron's back as the boy's tears dampened his shirt. "It's okay now. You're going to be all right."

"I shouldn't have run off like I did. Shouldn't have climbed the silo ladder, either." Aaron hiccuped. "I'm sorry for spoutin' off back at the house."

"All's forgiven. It's behind us now."

When Aaron's tears subsided, Paul set him on the ground. "You know what?"

"What?"

"I've been afraid of heights ever since I was a boy. Climbing up that ladder had me scared half to death."

Aaron's dark eyes grew large. "Really?"

"Jah. I prayed and asked God to help us through it, though. "

"You're not just sayin' that to make me feel better?"

"Nope. It's the truth, plain and simple."

"Then why'd you do it?"

"Because I care about you, son." The words came surprisingly easy, and Paul paused as he thought about what to say next. This was the chance he'd been waiting for with Aaron, and he didn't want to mess it up by saying the wrong thing. "I know I can never take your daed's place, and I'm not trying to," he assured the boy. "All I want is for us to be friends."

Aaron's lower lip quivered. "It was brave of you to climb up and rescue me. I'll never forget it, neither. Danki, Paul."

"You're welcome." Paul gave Aaron's shoulder a squeeze. "I think we'd better head back to the house, don't you?"

"I guess. But I'll probably be in big trouble for bein' gone so long and all."

"Your mamm has been worried about you."

"You think she'll be real mad?"

Paul shrugged. "That's hard to say. When I was a boy and did something my mamm disapproved of, I always knew she loved me, even if I ended up getting a *bletsching*."

Aaron's eyes were wide. "You think Mama's gonna use the paddle on my backside?"

"I doubt it. Seems to me she'll just be glad to see you're okay."

"Guess I'd better take my chances, huh?"

Paul ruffled the boy's sweat-soaked hair. No telling how long he'd been up on that ladder, too scared to move a muscle. "It's going to be fine—you'll see."

"Jah, okay. Let's go."

Paul breathed a sigh of relief, shut the door leading to the silo, and sent up another prayer. *Thank You, God, for giving me the courage to climb that ladder and for mending fences between Aaron and me. Maybe now he'll allow me to be his friend.*

Barbara finally put the boys to bed, and hoping to calm her nerves, she decided to fix herself a cup of chamomile tea. She had just put the kettle on to heat when the back door swung open. Her heart leaped as Aaron stepped into the room, followed by Paul.

"Thank the Lord, you found him!" she cried.

Aaron rushed to his mother's side and wrapped his arms around her waist. "I'm sorry for sayin' such ugly things before and running out of the house that way. It was wrong, and I know it."

"Your apology is accepted." Barbara leaned down and kissed her son's damp cheek. His eyes were red and puffy, moist with lingering tears. She looked up at Paul. "Where'd you find him?"

Before he could respond, Aaron blurted out, "Way up on the silo ladder. Scared silly, I was, too."

"What?" She gasped. "Oh, Aaron, you know you're not supposed to play in there. It's dangerous. What if you'd fallen? What if—"

"He's okay, Barbara," Paul interrupted. "No harm came to the boy."

Aaron nodded. "Paul climbed up, even though he was scared, and he saved me, Mama. Him and me are gonna be friends from now on." He grinned at Paul. "Ain't that right?"

Paul nodded. "It sure is."

Barbara blinked back sudden tears. This change in Aaron's attitude was an answer to prayer. "I'm so glad, son—about you being safe and Paul becoming your friend." Her gaze went to Paul. "Danki."

"You're welcome."

Barbara glanced at Aaron again. "Your hands are dirty. You'd better wash up at the sink."

He did as he was told, and Barbara turned back to Paul. "Would you like to sit a spell and have a cup of tea?"

Paul shook his head. "I appreciate the offer, but I'd better get home. I'm sure some chores still need to be done." He chuckled. "Besides, knowing Mom, she's probably fretting by now. When I left the house earlier, I only told her I was bringing that busted bridle over, so she's most likely wondering what's taken me so long."

"I hope she didn't hold supper on your account."

"Naw, Mom knows if I'm not home when it's time to eat, I must have found someplace else to take my meal. That's how it's been ever since I was a boy."

Barbara smiled as she walked Paul to the door. "Thanks again for rescuing Aaron. I guess we'll see you at church on Sunday."

"You can count on it." He turned and waved at Aaron, who was drying his hands on a towel. "Good-bye, son."

"Bye, Paul."

On the drive home, Paul replayed the events of the evening in his mind. Even though he hadn't been able to tell Barbara what was on his heart, two good things had happened. He had conquered his fear of heights, and he'd finally made friends with Barbara's oldest son.

"Now, that's a step in the right direction," Paul murmured into the darkness. Maybe tonight wasn't the time to tell Barbara how he'd come to feel about her, anyhow. It might be best to wait until he and Aaron had developed a stronger relationship before he told Barbara that he'd fallen in love with her.

Paul clicked his tongue and jiggled the reins to prompt his horse into moving a bit faster. Maybe sticking around Webster County until the harvest was done wouldn't be such a bad thing after all.

When he arrived home, he was still smiling over his encounter with Aaron. If things went well, he might have a chance with Barbara. If she didn't marry the bishop, that is.

"Where have you been so long?" Paul's mother asked when he walked in the door. "Your daed and I were getting worried."

"I went over to Barbara's to get the bridle fixed and ended

up staying for supper," he replied.

"I told your mamm that's probably what happened," Pop said with a wink in Paul's direction.

"I would have been home sooner, but Aaron got stuck on the top rung of the silo ladder, and I had to rescue the boy."

Mom's mouth dropped open. "But you're afraid of heights."

Paul nodded. "I know, but I couldn't let the little fellow fall just because I was scared to go up the ladder. But after tonight, I think I could climb up there again and not be afraid."

"I'm glad to hear you've conquered your fear," Mom said.

"Jah, me, too," Paul responded. "It was only because I prayed and God helped me through it, though."

"It's good that we can call on Him through prayer whenever we need to."

Paul nodded.

"How are things at the harness shop?" Pop asked, taking their conversation in another direction. "Is Barbara getting along okay?"

"She's managing, I guess. But Samuel's arthritis had been acting up again, and Barbara told me she's getting further behind."

"Harvesting will be done soon," Pop said. "I was wondering if you might consider speaking to Barbara about the possibility of buying into her shop. Sure would make your mamm and me glad if you stayed here instead of going back to Pennsylvania."

"I'll give the matter some consideration." Paul wanted to stay in Webster County and work at Zook's Harness Shop. Whether he did that as Barbara's business partner and friend or as her husband remained to be seen.

Chapter 23

On Sunday, the preaching service was held at Samuel Raber's house. When Bishop John pulled his horse and buggy up to the barn, he was pleased to see Moses Hilty climbing down from his own rig. "Wie geht's?" he asked. "How's your back feeling today?"

"It's doing some better," Moses said, "but I still have to be careful with it."

"That's probably a good idea. Don't want to risk reinjuring it."

"Nope, that's for certain sure." John waited until Moses's wife had headed to the house; then he moved closer to Moses and said, "Have you decided whether to hire someone to take your place in the fields, or does Paul plan to stick around and keep farming for you?"

Moses shook his head. "He won't be staying once the harvest is done, and I already spoke with Enos Miller about working for me. He's looking for a job right now, so it should work well for both of us."

"That's good to hear. Jah, real good." John squeezed Moses's shoulder. "Guess I'd better go inside and get ready for church. Take care of that back, now, you hear?"

Moses nodded. "I'm doin' my best."

As John headed for the Rabers' house, he was filled with a sense of hope. Paul would be moving back to Pennsylvania, Barbara was content to run her harness shop on her own, and Moses would soon have a new helper. Now he just needed to get up the nerve to ask Margaret to marry him. If she said yes, everything would be perfect.

Paul shifted on the hard bench where he sat on the men's side of the room. He was having a hard time keeping his mind on the church service. All he could think about was Barbara. He hadn't been able to speak with her since the night Aaron had climbed up the silo ladder, but he hoped he might get the chance later today. He wasn't sure what he was going to say now that he'd had more time to think about things. Maybe it would be best if he kept his feelings for her to himself and waited to see how things went between Barbara and the bishop. In the meantime, he needed to work on strengthening his relationship with Aaron.

Paul glanced across the room and spotted Barbara sitting beside her mother and cradling little Davey. His heart clenched when she leaned down and kissed the baby's downy head. Paternal feelings he'd never felt before had surfaced unexpectedly since he had spent time with Barbara and her children. If only those boys were his. If only he and Barbara. . .

Paul jerked his attention to the front of the room when Bishop John began reading from Ecclesiastes 4:9–10. " 'Two are better than one; because they have a good reward for their labour. For if they fall, the one will lift up his fellow: but woe to him that is alone when he falleth; for he hath not another to help him up.' "

Is the bishop preaching to himself again? Does he think he needs Barbara as his wife because two are better than one? Paul gritted his teeth. *If only I had the nerve to ask her not to marry John but to marry me instead. But even if I were to do something so bold, she would probably say no. She's given me no indication that she cares for me other than as a friend.*

Paul felt relief when church was finally over and he could be outside in the fresh air. He ate his meal quietly, sitting at one of the tables under a large maple tree in the Rabers' backyard. As he ate, he tried to decide exactly what he should say whenever he spoke with Barbara again.

After everyone had finished eating, Paul decided to seek Barbara out. He wandered around the yard but didn't see any sign of her. He figured she was probably still inside, either visiting with the women or taking care of the baby.

From Paul's vantage near the barn, he noticed Aaron across the yard, watching a group of older children play a game of baseball. It wouldn't be long before the weather turned too cold for baseball.

He pushed his thoughts aside as he approached Barbara's

oldest son. "Hey, Aaron, how are you doing?" he asked, clasping the boy's shoulder.

"I'm doin' okay, but I sure wish the older kids would let me play with 'em."

"Won't be any time at all until you'll be included with the older ones," Paul said, hoping to make Aaron feel better about things. "Why, I think you've grown a couple inches since I first came home."

Aaron smiled, and his face turned a little pink. "You really think so?"

"Sure do." Paul hesitated a moment; then he decided to plunge ahead. "Say, I've been thinking—"

Aaron looked up at him expectantly. "Jah?"

"I'm planning to go fishing next Saturday afternoon, and I was wondering if your mamm might give her permission for you to join me. That is, if you'd like to go."

"Only you and me? Not Mama and my brothers?"

Paul shook his head. "Just the two of us."

Aaron's lips turned upward, and his dark eyes glistened with anticipation. "I'd like that. Jah, I really would."

"Great. I'll speak to your mamm as soon as I find her."

The boy pointed to the house. "I think she went inside to feed the boppli."

"Okay, then. Guess I'll just wait until she comes outside again."

Barbara sat in the rocker and leaned her head back as she fed her hungry baby. She was glad church had been held at her folks' place today. When Davey got fussy, all she had to do was walk a few steps to nurse him in the privacy of her own bedroom.

Feeling kind of drowsy, she let her eyes drift shut, enjoying this special time of being alone with her infant son. *Oh, David, how I wish you could be here to see your namesake—to hold him—talk to him—watch him grow into a man.*

She thought about her other three sons. Zachary had been so young when David died that he would never remember his father. Joseph might not, either. Aaron was the only one who would, and he was the one who had been promised the harness shop someday.

If I sell the shop, it will never be Aaron's. Yet, if I keep it, I'll have to keep relying on Dad's help until Aaron's old enough to take his place. She groaned. *Dad's arthritis isn't getting any better, and it's not really fair to expect him to keep working for me when his hands are stiff and everything he does causes him pain.*

Barbara drew in a deep breath and tried to relax. She knew she needed to quit worrying, stop being so indecisive, and place the matter in God's hands. He knew what was best for her and the children. For now, the best thing she could do was pray and wait on Him to give her clear direction.

As Barbara was putting Davey into his crib, a soft knock sounded on the door.

"Come in," she called.

The door creaked open, and Faith stepped into the room. "Is he asleep?" she whispered.

"Jah."

"I wanted to talk with you, but I guess we'd better do it

downstairs so we don't wake the little guy."

Barbara moved over to the bed, took a seat on one end, and patted the spot beside her. "It's okay. Davey's like his daed—he could sleep through a thunderstorm."

Faith chuckled and sat down.

"What did you want to talk about?"

"Noah said he was by your shop the other day and that your daed had mentioned how far behind you're getting."

"It's true. We've got more work than the two of us can manage."

Faith's blue eyes revealed her concern. "Your daed's arthritis really slows him down, doesn't it?"

Barbara nodded. "I wish I didn't have to rely on his help. But no matter how hard I try, I simply can't do all the work on my own."

"Is Paul planning to come back to the harness shop to help you after the harvest is over?"

"As far as I know, he'll be returning to Pennsylvania." Barbara swallowed around the lump in her throat. She hated the idea of Paul leaving but didn't know what she could do to stop him from going.

"I thought the bishop had asked you to marry him. Whatever happened with that?"

Barbara shrugged. "He changed his mind." She couldn't very well tell her friend that the bishop had taken an interest in Margaret. Not when he'd told her he hadn't asked Margaret to marry him yet. Besides, it was his place to do the telling, not hers.

"You're in love with him, aren't you?"

"The bishop?"

"No, silly. Paul."

"What?" Faith's direct question jarred Barbara clear down to her toes.

"Don't try to deny it. I've seen the look of love written all over your face every time Paul's name is mentioned."

Barbara dropped her gaze to the floor. "I can't allow myself to have feelings for him."

"Why not?"

"I don't want to forget David or let go of what we once had."

Faith slipped her arm around Barbara's shoulders. "Romans 7:2 tells us, 'For the woman which hath an husband is bound by the law to her husband so long as he liveth; but if the husband be dead, she is loosed from the law of her husband.' "

Barbara sniffed as tears formed in her eyes. "I know that verse. But part of me will always love David."

"And well you should. He was a wunderbaar husband and a good daed. However, I'm sure David wouldn't want you to spend the rest of your life pining for him. He'd want you to find love and happiness again." Faith picked up the handkerchief lying on the bedside table and handed it to Barbara. "Dry your eyes and tell me how you feel about Paul Hilty."

Barbara blotted her eyes with the hanky. Then she lifted her head and looked directly at Faith. "You're bound and determined to make me say it, aren't you?"

Faith chuckled. "As you may recall, you were pretty determined that I see my need for Noah after I returned to Webster County a few years ago."

Barbara forced a smile. "I knew your place was here with your family and friends, not on the road trying to make a name for yourself. I also knew Noah could make you happy."

"You were right about that." Faith patted Barbara's hand. "I believe Paul can make you happy, as well."

"But I don't know how he feels about me. One minute I think we're getting close, and the next minute he pulls away. It's almost as if he's afraid of something."

"Maybe he is. Have you asked him?"

Tears hung on Barbara's lashes. "I can't. It wouldn't be right. It would be too bold."

"Humph! You know how I feel about that notion."

Barbara smiled despite her tears. "I think your time of living among the English made you see things in a different light than most people in our community do."

Faith nodded. "I guess you're right about that, but at least I'm not a rebellious daughter anymore, and I know how good I've got it right here with my family and friends." She grimaced. "Back in the days when I wasn't following the Lord, I was silly enough to believe the fifth commandment was to humor my father and mother rather than honor them. Only then, my folks never thought anything I said or did was funny."

"That's all changed, though."

"Right. Often I'll tell a joke, and my daed will laugh so hard he'll have tears running down his cheeks."

"Anything in particular you've told him lately?" Barbara asked, eager for a joke to lighten the mood.

"Oh, sure. I told him the story about the Amish man who went to visit his friend right after a bad storm."

"What happened?" Barbara asked.

"The man said, 'Did you lose much in that tornado?' His

friend nodded and replied, 'Jah. I lost the henhouse and all my chickens. But that was fine with me, 'cause I ended up with four new cows and somebody's horse and buggy!' "

Barbara laughed. "You sure haven't lost your sense of humor."

Faith smiled, but then she sobered. "There's one thing I did not learn while I was living in the English world. It's something I grew up knowing but didn't come to recognize until I moved back to Webster County."

"What was that?"

"The importance of committing every situation to God. I think it's time for the two of us to pray that the Lord will direct you and Paul." Faith squeezed Barbara's fingers. "Keep an open mind and trust Jesus. If you're supposed to be with Paul, it will all work out."

Barbara drew in a deep breath and sighed. "I surely hope so."

Barbara opened the front screen door and discovered Paul and Aaron seated on the porch step. She smiled at the way they had their heads together, talking as though they were the best of friends.

Both of them looked up when Barbara stepped out the door.

"Hey, Mama," Aaron said with a lopsided grin.

"Hey, Aaron. Where are your little brothers?"

"They went for a walk with Grandpa." He grinned up at Paul. "We've just been sitting here talkin' about the fishin' trip he wants to take me on this Saturday."

Paul looked kind of sheepish, and his ears turned pink. "I was planning to ask you first, of course," he said, nodding at Barbara.

Barbara noticed Aaron's hopeful expression. "Would it just be him and you?" she asked, looking back at Paul.

He nodded. "I thought it would give us a chance to get better acquainted."

Barbara stared at the wooden planks beneath her feet as she contemplated the idea. *If he wants to spend more time with Aaron, does that mean Paul doesn't plan to leave Webster County right away? Maybe he's given up on the idea of returning to Pennsylvania.*

"Can I go fishin' with Paul, Mama. . .please?"

She smiled. "Jah, I think it's a good idea."

"Danki, Mama."

"You're welcome," she said, patting her son's arm.

Paul stood. "Well, I'd best be going."

Aaron jumped up, too. "Where to?"

"I've developed a headache and am feeling kind of tired, so I think I'd better go home and take a nap." Paul's long, lanky legs took him quickly down the steps. When he got to the bottom, he looked back over his shoulder. "I'll be by for Aaron on Saturday around one, if that's okay with you."

"One sounds fine."

"And if you have the time, I'd like to discuss something with you then," he added.

"I'll make the time," she replied in a shaky voice. Was Paul going to tell her that he'd decided to return to Pennsylvania? Or could he have something else on his mind?

Chapter 24

John's hands trembled as he tied his horse to the hitching rail near Margaret Hilty's barn. Last night, he'd told his girls of his intention to marry Margaret and was pleased that they'd actually approved. Mary had spoken up right away and said she hoped Margaret would say yes because she was surely a good cook. And when John had explained that he'd fallen in love with Margaret, Betty had said she was glad he'd decided to marry for love and not merely for convenience. John had assured his daughters that he would always love their mother, and they'd said they knew that. Nadine had even told him that she thought he deserved to be happy again.

When John had gotten up this morning, he'd decided this was the day he would ask Margaret to marry him. He prayed she would be receptive to the idea and wouldn't take offense because she hadn't been widowed a year yet.

John found Margaret bent over one of her flower beds, pulling weeds. "Wie geht's?" he asked.

"I'm doing fairly well, thanks to the love and support of all my family and friends." She straightened and offered him a sincere smile. "I saw your buggy come in and wondered if you'd come by to see me or my son-in-law, Jake.

"Came to see you." John shifted from one foot to the other while he raked his fingers through the back of his hair. "I've been wanting to talk to you about something important."

"Oh? What's that? Is Barbara needing more help in her yard?"

"She probably does, but that's not the reason I came by today. Could we find a place to sit while we talk?" he asked, as his stomach did a little flip-flop when she smiled at him again.

"Jah, sure. I'm in need of a break anyhow, so let's have a seat over there." Margaret took off her work gloves and pointed to a spot on her back porch where several wicker chairs sat.

"Sounds good to me." John followed Margaret across the yard, and after she was seated, he lowered himself into the chair next to hers.

"Would you like something to drink?" she asked. "A cup of coffee or something cold?"

"Maybe a cup of coffee, but not until I've said what's on my mind."

Margaret's pale eyebrows puckered. "You look so serious, John. Is there something wrong?"

He shook his head. "Not wrong, really. But there is. . .uh. . . something I need to ask you."

"What is it?"

John swiped his tongue over his lower lip, wishing now he had taken her up on the offer of something to drink. But he needed to get this said before he lost his nerve. "I. . .uh. . .well, during the time we've spent visiting these past few months, I've come to realize that we have much in common."

She nodded slowly.

He leaned slightly forward and stared at the porch floor, unable to make eye contact with her. "I've become quite fond of you, Margaret, and I've enjoyed the time we've spent together."

"I've enjoyed being with you, as well."

He lifted his gaze and turned to face her. "Enough to become my wife?"

Margaret's mouth dropped open, and her eyes widened in obvious surprise. "You—you want to marry me?"

He nodded. "I know it hasn't been a year yet since Dan died, but I'm willing to wait until the proper time if you feel it's too soon."

Margaret's cheeks turned pink, and she placed both hands against them. "Ach, my! This is such a surprise. I never expected—"

He held up one hand. "I'm sorry if I've been too bold—too presumptuous. Maybe I'm out of line in thinking—"

She shook her head. "It's not that. It's just that I'm a few years older than you, and I—well, I thought you were interested in Barbara Zook."

"You did?"

"Jah. In fact, someone mentioned not long ago that you had asked Barbara to marry you. So I just assumed—"

He lifted his hand again. "I can't deny it. I did ask Barbara to marry me, but not because I'm in love with her."

"Why, then?"

"I thought she needed someone to protect her."

Margaret tipped her head as she pursed her lips. "Protect her from what?"

John swallowed hard. He couldn't come right out and tell Margaret that he thought her brother-in-law was out to get Barbara's harness shop. On the other hand, he couldn't think of any sensible reply.

"What do you think Barbara needs protecting from?" Margaret persisted.

"I. . .uh. . .well, she's been so tired since her boppli was born, and it's getting harder for her to run the harness shop. I felt it was my duty as her bishop, and as David's friend, to see that she and her boys were cared for and that no one came along and took advantage of her." He reached up to swipe at the sweat rolling down his forehead. He decided it wouldn't be right to tell Margaret that he had originally been looking for a younger wife who could give him more children. "I've come to realize that it wouldn't be right for me to marry Barbara when it's you I love."

Margaret stared at her hands, clasped tightly in her lap. After several seconds, she turned to face him and smiled. "When the proper time has elapsed for me to set aside my mourning clothes, I would be honored to marry you, John Frey."

"I would be equally honored." He reached over and took hold of her hand. "Now, if that offer of something to drink is still open, I think I'll take a glass of cold water."

On Saturday afternoon, Barbara was about to begin working on a new harness for Noah Hertzler when she spotted John Frey's rig coming up the driveway. Since her father was in the back room taking stock of their supplies, she knew she would have to be the one to wait on the bishop.

A few minutes later, John entered the harness shop wearing a grin as wide as the Missouri River. "Just came by to share my good news," he said, removing his hat.

"What news is that?"

John looked around, as though worried that someone might hear them. "Are we alone?"

"Dad's here, but he's in the back room right now."

"I have some news I wanted to share with you, but for now, I'd rather not tell anyone else. I would ask that you not mention it to anyone, either."

"Whatever you say won't leave this room," Barbara promised.

"I've just come from seeing Margaret Hilty, and she's agreed to become my wife."

Barbara smiled. "That's good news. The last time we talked, you said you wanted to marry her."

"Jah, I was just waiting for the right time to ask." He twisted the brim of his straw hat in his hands. "We won't marry until Margaret's set her mourning clothes aside, of course." He took a step closer to Barbara. "Are you going to be okay here on your own? If I thought for one minute that you—"

She shook her head. "There's no need for you to worry about

me, Bishop John. I'm praying about what God would have me do with the harness shop, and I'm confident that He'll show me the way."

He patted her arm in a fatherly fashion. "Jah, I'm sure He will."

Paul was glad the hay had finally been harvested and that his dad had no problem with Paul taking off to go fishing with Aaron.

"It sure is a nice day for fishing," Pop said as Paul hitched the horse to his buggy. "Bet they'll be bitin' real good, too. Won't be long before the weather will be turning cold."

"How about you and me going fishing sometime next week?" Paul asked.

"Sounds good. I'll be looking forward to it." Pop gave him a nod. "I hope you and Aaron enjoy your day."

Paul grinned and hopped into the open buggy. "I'm sure we will."

Fifteen minutes later, he pulled into the Zooks' yard, eager to take Aaron fishing and anxious to see the boy's mother. Much to Paul's chagrin, he noticed Bishop Frey standing outside the harness shop talking to Barbara. As far as Paul was concerned, the older man stood much too close to the woman Paul wanted to make his own.

He clamped his teeth together and jumped down from the buggy.

Trying not to appear as though he were eavesdropping, Paul stroked his horse behind the ear and strained to hear what the two of them were saying.

"I'm glad you agree," John said, giving Barbara a wide smile. "I think we'll be very happy together."

Barbara nodded in return. "I think so, too."

A knot formed in Paul's stomach, and he nearly doubled over from the pain. Apparently, Barbara had decided to accept the bishop's marriage proposal. Paul felt like climbing back into his buggy and heading straight for home, but just then, Aaron rushed across the yard waving his fishing pole and grinning from ear to ear. Even though Paul wasn't in the mood to go fishing now, he had promised the boy, so he would see it through. When he brought Aaron home, however, he planned to tell Barbara he was leaving Webster County for good. He'd come back home planning to stay only a few weeks but had ended up staying several months. There was no point in him staying any longer.

With a sigh of resignation, Paul helped Aaron into the buggy, gave a halfhearted wave to Barbara, and pulled out of the yard.

"Sure have been lookin' forward to this day," Aaron said, nudging Paul's arm.

Paul nodded. "Me, too."

As they rode in companionable silence, Paul relished the sounds of birds singing from the trees lining the road and the steady *clip-clop* of the horse's hooves against the pavement. It was quiet and peaceful on this stretch of road. For that matter, all of Webster County was quiet compared to the area he'd left back in Pennsylvania. Paul would miss all of this, and he sure wished he could stay. But it would be hard to stick around and watch Barbara become the bishop's wife. Of course, if she married John, she would probably decide to sell the harness shop. Paul could offer to buy the place, and that would mean he could stay here and live near his folks. But owning the harness shop didn't hold nearly the appeal anymore. Not without Barbara at his side. No, the best thing he could do was return to Pennsylvania and try to forget he'd ever allowed himself to foolishly fall in love with Barbara.

Aaron poked Paul's arm again, pulling him out of his musings. "Sure can't wait to catch me some big old fish today."

Paul smiled. "I hope they're biting real good."

A short time later, they pulled up by the pond. Paul hopped down and secured his horse to a tree while Aaron ran off toward the water.

They spent the next few hours sitting on a large rock, visiting and fishing. Paul was pleased that they'd each hooked a couple of big catfish. It would give Aaron something to take home to show his mother, and Paul would have some fish to contribute to his meal at home tonight.

"Guess it's time for us to head for home," Paul finally said, reeling in his line.

"Do we have to go so soon? It seems like we just got here."

"It's getting close to supper," Paul said, ruffling the boy's hair. "And I don't want your mamm to worry about you."

"Aw, she won't worry 'cause she knows I'm with you."

"Even so, I think it's time for us to go."

"You gotta catch me first!" Aaron hopped up and started running along the banks of the pond.

Paul set his pole aside and quickly followed. He'd almost caught up to Aaron, when the boy's foot slipped on a rock, and he fell toward the pond. Paul reached out his long arm and grabbed Aaron just in time. "Got you!"

Aaron looked up at Paul, his dark eyes wide and his mouth hanging slightly open. "You did it again, Paul. That's the second time you've saved my life."

"I don't really think your life was in danger this time, Aaron. I just saved you from a chilly dunking, that's all," Paul said, his voice thick with emotion.

"I hope you stay in Webster County forever." Aaron clung to Paul's arm. " 'Cause I sure do need you."

Paul swallowed around the lump lodged in his throat. He knew he would be leaving soon, but he sure didn't want to go.

Paul and Aaron didn't return home until nearly five o'clock, so Barbara figured they'd had a good time. She couldn't wait to hear about their fishing trip and find out what Paul wanted to discuss with her. He hadn't said anything before they left, but she'd been busy talking with John Frey. Paul must have decided the matter could wait until he'd brought Aaron home this evening.

When Paul halted the horse, Barbara stepped up to the buggy. "Did you two have a good time?"

Aaron jumped down holding a plastic sack with a couple of fish tails sticking out. "We each caught two nice catfish, and I almost fell in the pond."

Barbara's gaze went immediately to Paul. "What happened?"

He shrugged. "Aaron was running along the edge of the pond, and he slipped. He nearly fell in, but I caught him before he hit the water."

Aaron's dark eyes shone like two shiny pennies. "That's the second time Paul's saved me now."

A lump formed in Barbara's throat. It was wonderful to see Aaron enjoying Paul's company and appreciating him so much. "I'm glad you're okay and didn't get wet." She smiled at Paul. "Danki, Paul."

He nodded.

"Are you two hungry?" she asked.

Aaron's head bobbed up and down. "Jah, sure. I could eat a mule."

Barbara chuckled. "I'm afraid your grandpa might have something to say if you go after one of his mules." She looked at Paul. "Would you like to stay for supper? I've made a big pot of beans and some corn bread."

A shadow crossed Paul's face, and he avoided her gaze. "I appreciate the offer, but I'd best be getting home."

"Aw, can't you stay awhile?" Aaron asked with a pout. "I know my little brothers would like to see you."

"Sorry." Paul leaned over and handed the boy his fishing pole. "I promised my mamm I'd be home early tonight, so I'd better be on my way." He climbed into his buggy and quickly gathered up the reins.

"What about the talk we were supposed to have?" Barbara asked. "I thought you had something you wanted to discuss with me."

"It was nothing important. I just wanted to let you know that I'll be leaving for Pennsylvania early next week." Paul stared at her with a strange expression. "I hope you have a good life, Barbara." Before she could respond, he drove swiftly out of the yard.

"Sure wish he could've stayed to eat with us," Aaron said dejectedly.

Barbara nodded slowly. She wished Paul would have stayed, too. "Maybe some other time, son."

"But you heard him, Mama. Paul said he'll be leaving soon." Aaron's lower lip trembled, and his eyes filled with tears. "And just when we were becoming good friends."

Barbara gave Aaron a hug as she fought to control her own emotions. "I'm awful sorry. I guess some things just aren't meant to be."

"Are you coming to bed?" Noah asked as Faith stood in front of their bedroom window, staring at the night sky.

She turned to face the bed, where he sat holding his Bible. "I'm not sure I can sleep."

A look of concern flashed across his face. "What's wrong? Are you worried about one of the kinner?"

Faith shook her head and sat down beside him. "I spoke with Margaret Hilty today, and she gave me some surprising news."

"What?"

"Margaret told me that John Frey asked her to marry him."

Noah's eyebrows shot up. "That's sure a surprise. What'd she tell him?"

"She said yes. But they won't be getting married for a few more months. Not until she has set her mourning clothes aside."

"I guess that makes sense."

"I knew the bishop had been making calls on Margaret, but

until today, I had no idea they had developed such a personal relationship or that he'd proposed marriage." Faith's forehead wrinkled. "At one point, the bishop was after Barbara to marry him. But the last time I spoke with Barbara, she told me John had changed his mind about marrying her, and she was glad because she's not in love with him." She grunted. "My good friend never said a word about John proposing marriage to Margaret, though. It makes me wonder what happened to change his mind."

Noah reached for Faith's hand. "After spending so much time with Margaret, John probably realized he'd fallen in love with her."

Faith nodded as she pursed her lips. "I wonder. . . ."

"What's going on in your head?"

"Since Barbara won't be marrying John, I wonder if Paul will ask her to marry him."

Noah squeezed Faith's fingers. "Now, fraa, don't you be trying to play little matchmaker. If it's meant for Paul and Barbara to be together, then you'd best let the Lord work things out between them."

She nodded and kissed him on the cheek. "I promise not to meddle, but I can sure pray."

Barbara sat straight up in bed. She was drenched with perspiration from having tossed and turned most of the night. She'd seen David in one of her dreams, kissing her good-bye before he headed to town to pick up her anniversary present. John Frey had been in another dream, calmly telling her of his plans for the future. The last dream had Paul Hilty in it, driving away from her house and out of her life forever.

Barbara slipped out of bed and padded across the room to the dresser. She massaged her temples a few seconds, then leaned over the basin of water on top of the dresser. As the cool water hit Barbara's face, she allowed her anxieties to fully surface.

"I've got to sell the harness shop," she moaned. "There's no way I can keep running it on my own." She had prayed long and hard about this matter and, under the circumstances, felt it was the only thing she could do.

Barbara dried her face on the nearby towel and grimaced. *If Paul leaves Webster County, who will I find to sell the place to? Nobody else in our community does harness work. And without a harness shop, people will have to go to another town to get their work done.*

She sighed as she glanced at her infant son sleeping peacefully in his crib. *At least someone in the room isn't feeling the burdens of life.* She moved over to the window and lifted the dark shade. A light rain fell, dropping more leaves from the trees in her yard and matching the tears Barbara felt on her cheeks.

She drew in a deep breath. *Paul has to buy the shop. I should have spoken up yesterday when he was here and asked if he'd be interested.*

She reflected on Paul's announcement that he'd be leaving in a few days. *I should have been more prepared for that news, but it caught me off guard. Paul has seemed so settled here of late.* Ever since he had helped Aaron down from the silo, he had acted like he cared about the boy and wanted to be his friend. *That will never happen if he leaves.*

Barbara paced the room in quick, nervous steps. There was

only one thing she could do, and that was to ask Paul outright not to go. Maybe when he heard her offer to sell him the harness shop, he would decide to stay.

"But I'd better move fast," she murmured.

Chapter 25

Where you going, son?" Paul's mother asked.

"Thought I'd take a ride. Since I'll be leaving in a few days, I'd like to see the countryside one last time."

Mom frowned. "I still can't get over the announcement you made last night. I don't see why you have to go and leave us again. Don't you know how much your daed and I will miss you?"

Paul nodded. "I know, and I'll miss you, too. But with Barbara getting. . ." His voice trailed off.

"With Barbara getting what?"

"Oh, never mind." He grasped the doorknob.

"Will you be back in time for the noon meal?"

"I don't know."

"We're having Margaret over, along with your brothers and

their families." She paused. "And there'll be a couple other guests, as well."

Paul did want to see his sister-in-law again, if just to see how she'd been getting along and to tell her good-bye. "I'll try to be back by noon."

"That's good," she responded. "This might be the last time our family can all be together for some time."

"Okay, Mom."

As Paul trudged across the yard toward his buggy, he felt the weight of the world on his shoulders. All his plans and dreams had gone out the window in one brief moment when he'd overheard Barbara and the bishop speaking about their upcoming marriage.

He stepped into his buggy and grabbed the reins. Maybe some time alone with the wind blowing in his face and the smell of crisp autumn leaves tickling his nose might calm his anxieties. He could also do some serious praying.

"Giddyap there, boy," he called to the horse. "You and me have got some riding to do."

As Paul headed down the road, anxious thoughts tumbled around in his mind. He loved Barbara, but she was going to marry Bishop John. He'd come to care for her boys, but they could never be his. He enjoyed being in Webster County, but he didn't belong anymore. He loved working in the harness shop but would probably never own one of his own.

Sometime later, the smell of sweaty horseflesh drifted up to Paul's nose, and he grimaced when he realized that he'd been making his poor gelding trot for the last several miles. He had thought this buggy ride would make him feel better, but by the time he returned home, he was even more agitated than when he'd headed out. He didn't want to leave his friends and family again, but he didn't want to stay and see Barbara marry the bishop, either.

In a brief moment of desperation, Paul had considered driving straight over to Barbara's and begging her to marry him instead of John Frey. But he'd quickly decided that it was a dumb idea. *She's already chosen him. I'd only make myself look like a fool if I barged in and declared my love.* The best thing he could do was to get back to Pennsylvania as quickly as he could and hope he'd be able to forget about Barbara and her boys.

Paul took his time unhitching the horse and putting him in the barn. He dreaded the meal with all his family present. Good-byes would be hard, especially with Mom and Pop so set against him leaving.

When Paul headed around the back of the house, he was surprised to see Bishop Frey sitting in a chair on the porch. Beside him sat Dan's widow, Margaret.

What's he doing here? Paul fumed.

Gritting his teeth, Paul stepped onto the porch.

"Wie geht's?" the bishop asked.

Paul forced a smile. "I'm fine, and you?"

"Good. Real good."

Paul looked over at Margaret. "Are you doing okay?"

"I'm fine and dandy." She grinned up at Paul, and he noticed for the first time since Dan's death that Margaret looked quite relaxed. Maybe she'd been counseling with the bishop and Paul had interrupted. Best he should make a fast exit.

He grabbed the handle on the screen door and was about

to open it when the bishop said, "Your mamm tells me you're planning to go back to Pennsylvania sometime this week."

Paul gave a curt nod. "I'll probably see about getting a bus ticket tomorrow morning."

"That's too bad," the older man said. "We were hoping you'd be here for the wedding."

Paul's body became rigid. What was the bishop trying to do—rub salt in his wounds? "I didn't think there was any need for me to see you and Barbara get married," he said stiffly.

Margaret gave a little gasp, and John's bushy eyebrows drew together.

"I'm not marrying Barbara Zook," John said with a shake of his head.

Confusion settled around Paul like a thick fog rolling in. "But I thought—"

"It's me John is planning to marry," Margaret said, her face turning crimson.

Paul felt as if the air had been squeezed right out of his lungs. He grabbed the porch railing for support. "When? How?" he stammered.

"We've been seeing each other for a few months now," the bishop replied. "And last week, Margaret agreed to become my wife. After the proper time for her mourning to be finished, of course."

"But—but I saw you at Barbara's harness shop yesterday. I overheard you saying—"

"I was telling her about Margaret accepting my proposal."

Paul continued to lean heavily against the rail. If John was going to marry Margaret and not Barbara, that meant Paul still had a chance. At least, he hoped he did.

Drawing in a deep breath, Paul said, "I'm happy for the both of you." He started for the steps. "Would you tell Mom I have an errand to run and won't be able to join the family for lunch after all?"

"She'll surely be disappointed," his sister-in-law said.

He turned to look at Margaret, whose pale blue eyes held a note of concern. "I'll try to be back in time for dessert." Paul hopped off the porch and raced for the barn.

As Paul's buggy sped out of the yard, John looked over at Margaret and frowned. "Now, I wonder what's gotten into him? As soon as we told him of our plans, he hightailed it right on out of here."

She shrugged. "I don't know, but he did seem to be in a hurry to go somewhere."

"Do you think he might be upset because I'm going to marry you?"

"I can't imagine why he would be," she replied.

"Well, it *was* Paul's brother you were married to. Maybe he thinks it's too soon for you to find another husband. Or maybe he doesn't think I'm good enough for his sister-in-law."

"He said he was happy for us, remember?"

John nodded slowly. "Even so, he's never been all that friendly toward me, and it could be that he doesn't want you to marry a bishop."

Margaret reached for his hand and gave his fingers a gentle

squeeze. "I don't care what anyone thinks. You're exactly what I need."

John smiled, relishing in the warmth of her hand and delighting in the look of love he saw on her sweet face. "You're just what I need, too."

Barbara felt relieved when her mother agreed to watch the boys. Mom was always so good about it, but Barbara didn't want to take advantage of her mother's willingness to help. Mom assured her she enjoyed spending time with the children. Today, when Barbara said she wanted to take a buggy ride and be by herself awhile, Mom had readily agreed.

As Barbara guided her horse down the lane, she was glad she hadn't told her mother the real reason for this buggy ride. She didn't want to tell either of her folks that she was planning to sell the harness shop until she had a buyer. Dad had said many times that he didn't mind helping out, even though he wasn't able to do a lot. He knew how important the shop was to her and said he'd do whatever he could to see that it kept running. And Mom, even though she often reprimanded Barbara for working too hard, had often said that she knew Barbara enjoyed her job and needed to keep working in order to support her family. Even so, she was sure they would support her decision to sell the place.

Barbara glanced at the darkening sky. "Looks like it could rain some more," she muttered. She was glad she'd thought to bring an umbrella along. An open buggy offered little protection from the unpredictable fall weather.

She'd only made it halfway to the Hiltys' home when the wind picked up and droplets of water splashed against her face. As she reached for her umbrella under the seat, Barbara spotted another buggy coming from the opposite direction.

Barbara snapped the umbrella open as the buggy approached. She recognized the driver immediately. It was Paul, and from the way his horse trotted down the road, she figured he must be in a hurry to get somewhere.

She slowed the buggy and waved at him. Paul slowed his rig, too, and motioned for her to pull over to the side of the road.

They stopped under a nearby tree. Paul tied his horse to a sturdy branch, then came around to the passenger side of Barbara's buggy and climbed in.

Barbara scooted over so they could share the umbrella. "The rain sure hit quickly, didn't it?" she asked, feeling suddenly nervous and unsure of herself.

Paul nodded. "I just spoke to Bishop Frey over at my folks' place. He informed me that he plans to marry my sister-in-law Margaret."

"That's what he told me yesterday afternoon, about the time you were picking Aaron up for the fishing trip." She smiled. "I'm glad for them. I think they'll be good for each other."

"Jah." Paul cleared his throat. "I. . .uh. . .wanted to speak with you yesterday, but after hearing what the bishop said, I figured it was pointless."

"What does the bishop marrying Margaret have to do with your talking to me?"

"I thought it was you he planned to marry. And since I only

heard part of your conversation, I got the impression you had agreed to become his wife."

Barbara shook her head. "He told me several weeks ago that he wanted to marry Margaret and that he didn't love me." She smiled. "I felt relief hearing that, because even though I have great respect for our bishop, I'm not in love with him. I loved David very much, and the truth is, unless love was involved, I could never marry another man."

Paul sat, looking perplexed. "I totally agree with that, Barbara."

"So what did you want to say to me yesterday?"

"I had a business proposition to discuss. But now that I've had time to think it over, I've decided it's not such a good idea."

She tipped her head. "Funny thing. I had a business proposition for you, too."

His eyebrows lifted. "Really? What was it?"

"After much prayer and thought, I've come to the conclusion that I can no longer run the harness shop on my own."

Paul leaned closer. So close that Barbara could feel his warm breath against her face. "Maybe you won't have to," he murmured.

"That's the deduction I came to, as well." Barbara bit her bottom lip, hoping she wouldn't give in to the tears pushing against her eyelids. "I have decided to sell the business, and I was wondering if you might be interested in buying it."

Paul shook his head. "I could never do that. I had thought I could at one time, but not now."

"Why not? Is it because you prefer living in Pennsylvania?"

Paul lifted Barbara's chin with his finger and stared into her eyes. "I'd rather stay here with you and your boys."

She swallowed hard. What was he getting at? Could he possibly mean. . . "If you want to stay in Webster County, then why not buy my business?"

He inched his head closer. "If I stay and work at the harness shop, it would have to be on one condition."

"What's that?"

"That it be as your husband." There was a pause as he took her hand. "I'm in love with you, Barbara."

The shock of Paul's words sent a shiver up Barbara's spine, and she let the umbrella drop to the floor behind them. "Are— are you asking me to marry you?"

"Jah, if you'll have me."

Barbara thought about the verses from Ecclesiastes that talked about two being better than one. She thought about the feelings Paul evoked in her whenever he was around and about how much her boys liked being with him.

She swallowed again. "I can hardly believe the way God has answered my prayers."

He raised one eyebrow. "A prayer to keep your shop open, or a prayer to find love again?"

She touched the side of his face. "Both. But mostly to find love again. I do love you, Paul Hilty, but I've been afraid to admit it."

"Why?"

"Because I was scared to open my heart to love again. And I didn't know if you felt the same way toward me."

"Does this put your fears at rest?" Paul's lips sought hers in a kiss so gentle and sweet she felt as if she could drown in it.

"Oh, jah," she murmured as she stared at his handsome

features. "I don't want to be on my own anymore. I need some-one to share my life with—the joys and the sorrows, the present and the future. I want that someone to be you, Paul."

"Does that mean you'll marry me?"

She nodded slowly. "I want you to be my life partner as well as my business partner. . .for as long as we both shall live."

Epilogue

Eighteen months later

I can hardly believe our first wedding anniversary is next week," Paul said as he cut a hunk of leather and handed it to Barbara.

She smiled and reached up to stroke his beard. "Would you mind very much if I give you my gift now?"

"A whole week early?"

"I can't wait a moment longer."

"Sure, go ahead." Paul chuckled and set the leather aside. "I always did have a hard time waiting for things."

She grasped his hands and placed them against her stomach, her heart hammering like a stampede of horses. "My gift to you is a son or daughter of your own."

His eyes grew large. "A boppli?"

She nodded. "Are you happy about that?"

Paul wrapped his arms around Barbara and pulled her close. "Oh, jah. I'm very happy."

"Does that mean I'm gonna be a big bruder again?"

Barbara and Paul turned at the same time. Aaron stood off to one side, his arms folded and a strange look on his face. Barbara hadn't realized he'd come into the harness shop. "That's exactly what it means," she said, praying he wouldn't react negatively.

Paul moved toward the boy. "I hope you know that the boppli coming won't change anything between you and me or affect the way I feel about Joseph, Zachary, or Davey."

Aaron grinned up at him. "I know. You've been my new daed for almost a year already, and I won't let nothin' change that—not ever."

Paul gave Aaron a hug, and Barbara joined him. "Now we need to tell our other three sons," she said, blinking against tears of joy.

Paul nodded and gave her a kiss.

"Aw, do you have to do all that mushy stuff?" Aaron asked, shaking his head.

"You'll be doing the same thing someday when God brings the right woman into your life." Paul chuckled and boxed the boy playfully on the shoulder. "And if you're really lucky, she'll be able to make Webster County Fried Chicken as good as your mamm's."

Aaron grabbed a chunk of leather and headed for the back room. "I ain't never gettin' married," he called over his shoulder.

Barbara smiled at Paul.

He winked, then kissed her again. "When the time comes, I hope our boy finds someone as wunderbaar as his mamm."

She smiled and nodded. "No one should spend their whole life on their own. I'm glad I finally realized that I couldn't do everything on my own. And that I trusted God enough and made the decision to spend the rest of my days with you, for two really are better than one."

Recipe for Barbara's Webster County Fried Chicken

1 cut-up frying chicken
1 cup sifted flour
2 teaspoons salt
½ teaspoon pepper
Shortening

Combine flour, salt, and pepper. Sprinkle some additional salt over the chicken. Roll the pieces of chicken in the flour mixture. Melt a few tablespoons of shortening in a heavy frying pan. Add the chicken and brown on both sides. Then cover the pan, turn the heat to low, and continue to cook until the chicken can easily be pierced with a fork.

Dear to Me

DEDICATION/ACKNOWLEDGMENTS

To my dear friends Diane and Phil Allen,
whose love for the wildlife that come into their yard
prompted me to write this story.

Be ye therefore followers of God, as dear children.
EPHESIANS 5:1

Chapter 1

Melinda Andrews hurried across the grass, eager to arrive at her favorite spot. Just a few more steps, and there it was—dappled canopies of maple, hickory, cedar, and pine towering over a carpet of lush green leaves and fragrant needles. She drew in a deep breath, relishing the woodsy scent. The sun had tried all morning to overcome the low-hanging clouds. It had finally made an appearance, and Melinda planned to enjoy each moment she could spend here.

She slowed her pace and crept through the forest, being careful not to snag her long, dark blue dress or matching apron on any low-hanging branches. After awhile, she came to a clearing with several downed trees. "This looks like the perfect place for me to sit and draw," she murmured.

Taking a seat on a nearby log, Melinda pulled her drawing

tablet and pencil from the canvas tote she'd brought along. "Where are you, deer friends?"

The only movement was the flitter of leaves as the wind blew softly against the trees.

Melinda spotted a cluster of wild yellow crocuses peeking through a clump of grass. Spring was her favorite time of the year, with new life bursting forth everywhere. She lifted her pencil, ready to sketch a tan-colored rabbit that had hopped onto the scene, when two does stepped into the clearing.

"You're so beautiful," she whispered.

The does lifted their heads in curiosity as a hawk soared high overhead.

Melinda watched the deer nibble on leaves while she sketched their picture. Her stomach rumbled, which caused her to think about the lemon sponge cake Papa Noah had made last night. She'd had a sliver of it for breakfast this morning, and it had been delicious. She thought her stepfather was the best cook in all of Webster County, Missouri.

Melinda had been six years old when her real father had been hit by a car and killed. Shortly after his death, her mother had given up her career of telling jokes and yodeling among the English. She and Melinda had caught the bus from Branson to Seymour and come to live with Grandpa and Grandma Stutzman in the Amish community where Melinda's mother had been raised.

Even though Melinda had been young back then, she remembered many things about their arrival in Webster County. She especially recalled meeting her aunt, Susie Stutzman, for the first time. Susie was Grandma's youngest child, and she was a year older than Melinda. Melinda and Susie had become friends right away and had remained so ever since.

Melinda smiled at the memory of seeing her aunt dressed in a long blue dress with a small white *kapp* perched on top of her head. "Plain clothes" is what Mama had told Melinda. "My folks follow the customs and rules of the Amish church, and they live differently than we're used to living."

Melinda hadn't minded wearing the unusual clothes, for it seemed as if she were playing dress-up at first. The strange rules and numerous jobs Grandma Stutzman had expected her to do were the hardest part. She remembered, too, that Mama hadn't seemed too happy when they first came home—not until Noah Hertzler had started hanging around, taking an interest in her. Melinda had figured Noah would be her new daddy even before Mama had said she loved him. She'd been real pleased when they'd decided to get married.

Melinda lifted her face to the sun as thoughts of marriage made her think of Gabe Swartz, who had begun courting her a few months ago. Gabe had hazel-colored eyes with little green specks and brown hair that curled around his ears. He was tall and slender yet strong and able-bodied. Melinda had developed a crush on him when they were attending the one-room school-house down the road.

When Gabe, who'd been a year ahead of Melinda in school, graduated from eighth grade and began learning the trade of woodworking under his dad's tutelage, she missed seeing him every day and looked forward to their every-other-Sunday church services, where Gabe and his family would also be in attendance. Now Gabe, who had recently turned twenty, worked full-time at his father's woodworking shop.

When Melinda had finished school, she'd begun her vocational training at home with her mother, where she learned various household chores that would prepare her for marriage. Then a year ago, she'd begun working part-time for Dr. Franklin, the local veterinarian. At first it was just cleanup work, as well as feeding, watering, and exercising some of the animal patients. But later, when the doctor realized how much Melinda cared for the animals and noticed her special way with them, he had allowed her to assist him with minor things. Melinda had done everything from holding a dog while it received a shot or had its nails clipped, to giving flea baths and bringing animals from their cages into the operating room.

"You've been blessed with a unique gift," Dr. Franklin had told Melinda the other day while she held a nervous kitten about to receive its first shot. "Have you ever considered becoming a veterinarian's technical assistant or even a vet?"

Melinda had to admit that the thought of becoming a vet had crossed her mind, but she figured it was an impossible dream. Not only was she lacking in education, but going to college and then on to a school of veterinary medicine would mean leaving the Amish faith. Since she'd been baptized and joined the Amish church a year ago, it would affect her whole family if she left the faith and became part of the English world.

Melinda remembered several years ago, before their old bishop died and John Frey had taken his place, a young man named Abner had left home during his running-around years, and he'd ended up coming back a few months later, saying it was too hard being away from his family. As a young woman, her own mother had left the Amish faith for ten years, trying to make a name for herself in the entertainment business.

It would probably break Mama's heart if I left home the way she did when she was my age, Melinda thought. *And what would it do to my relationship with Gabe?* She shook her head. *No, becoming a vet is most likely just an impossible dream. I'll probably never leave my home here in Webster County.*

"I can't believe Melinda's not back yet." Faith placed a sack of flour on the counter and turned to face her mother and youngest sister, who sat at the kitchen table. "She said she was going for a short walk and would be here in plenty of time to help with the baking, but she must have lost track of time."

Susie, Faith's sister who had recently turned twenty, sighed. "Knowing Melinda, she's most likely off taking care of one of her critters or out in the woods sketching pictures of the deer."

Faith nodded. "You're probably right. My daughter has been taking in injured and orphaned animals ever since she was a little girl. It's not gotten any better since she became a young woman, either. Sometimes I wonder if Melinda will ever grow up."

"Just because she likes helping animals doesn't mean she's not mature," Faith's mother put in. "She wouldn't be able to work for Dr. Franklin if she wasn't grown up enough to make good decisions."

Faith wrinkled her forehead. She didn't know why her mother was sticking up for Melinda. She sure hadn't taken Faith's side of things when Faith was Melinda's age. *Of course,*

Faith reasoned, *back then I was headstrong and disobedient, running off to do my own thing in the modern world. Mama only saw me as a rebellious teenager, not as a mature woman who made good decisions.*

"Be that as it may," Faith said as she pulled out a rolling pin, "Melinda's showing her immaturity this morning by not keeping her word and being here to help us with the baking."

"Would you like me to go look for her?" Susie offered.

Faith pursed her lips and finally nodded. "That's a good idea, since she's obviously not planning to come back anytime soon of her own accord."

Susie stood. "I'll check the barn first. If she's not there, I'll head for the woods."

As Susie scurried out the door, Faith moved over to the table and took a seat across from her mother. "Since we don't have the help of either of our daughters at the moment, why don't the two of us sit and visit over another cup of tea?"

Mama smiled and pushed back her metal-framed glasses, which had slipped to the end of her nose. "Sounds good to me."

"You know, it's not just Melinda's preoccupation with her animal friends that bothers me," Faith said while pouring her mother a cup of tea.

"What else is bothering you?"

"I'm concerned because Melinda's been acting kind of strange."

Mama's eyebrows lifted as a deep wrinkle formed above her nose. "Strange in what way?"

"Besides the fact that I have to stay after Melinda to get her chores done because she's too busy tending her animal friends, she seems to be off in her own little world. It's like her thoughts are somewhere else most of the time."

"I think you need to be more patient with Melinda. From what I can tell, she and Gabe Swartz are getting serious. I think it's just a matter of time until they become betrothed." Mama smiled. "Once that happens, I'm sure Melinda will settle down and act more like the mature woman you want her to be."

Faith poured herself a cup of tea and took a sip. "I hope you're right about that, Mama. *Jah,* I surely do."

Susie had gone a short ways into the woods when she spotted Melinda sitting on a log with her drawing tablet. Susie was tempted to scold her niece for wasting time and trying to get out of work she should be doing, but she figured if she said too much, she and Melinda would probably end up arguing. Ever since Melinda had been a young girl, she had enjoyed spending time with animals. Susie used to think that once Melinda grew up, she would focus on the important things in life. But no, Melinda kept drawing and daydreaming, shirking her duties at the house, and causing her mother to send Susie after her on many occasions.

A twig snapped as Susie took a step toward the log. She halted and held her breath. Should she sneak up on Melinda and take her by surprise or make a loud noise so Melinda would know she was coming? Deciding on the latter, Susie moved closer and cleared her throat.

Melinda, engrossed in her artwork, didn't budge.

Susie held her hands above Melinda's head and clapped. "Hey!"

Melinda jumped, and the deer she'd been drawing bolted into the protection of the thick pine forest.

"Thanks a lot!" Melinda spun around and glared at Susie. "You've scared away my subjects, and they probably won't be back. Leastways not anytime soon."

"Sorry about that," Susie mumbled. She glanced at Melinda's drawing tablet and couldn't help but be impressed with what she saw. Despite the fact that Melinda drew well, was it really necessary to spend every free moment—and some time that was stolen—sketching her woodland friends?

Melinda stood and shook her finger at Susie. "I don't think you're one bit sorry. You look rather pleased with yourself, Susie Stutzman. I'll bet you clapped and hollered like that on purpose, just to scare away my subjects. Didn't you?"

Susie nodded slowly.

"Why?"

"Because your *mamm* has been looking for you, and your mamm and my mamm need our help baking pies for Sunday after church at my folks' house."

Melinda groaned and flopped down on the log.

Susie pursed her lips. "I also knew that if I just whispered in your ear that you were needed in the kitchen, the deer would have stayed put, and you'd have kept right on drawing."

Melinda pushed a wayward strand of golden blond hair away from her face and tucked it into the bun she wore at the back of her head. "How did you know where to find me, anyway?"

Susie wrinkled her nose. "You're kidding, right?"

Melinda shrugged. Her gaze traveled around the wooded area, and she said, "Just listen to the music of the birds. Isn't it the most beautiful sound you've ever heard?"

"It's nice, but there's other—"

"Do you smell that fresh pine scent from all the trees?"

Susie nodded and drew in a deep breath as the woodsy aroma filled her nostrils. "It does smell nice in the woods," she admitted.

"It's so peaceful here, don't you think?"

"Jah, but there are other things I'd rather do than sit in the woods for hours on end." Susie took a seat on the log beside Melinda. "What draws you to these woods, anyway?"

"The animals that live here, of course. Every creature God created is special, but the ones that live in the woods fascinate me more than any others."

"There's a big difference between *fascinated* and *fanatical*."

Melinda snickered. "Fanatical, is it? Since when did you start using such fancy words?"

Susie shrugged. "I've been reading a novel about a young woman who likes to solve mysteries. Her mother accuses her of being *fanatical*."

"You'd better not start shirking your duties because you're reading too much, or your mamm will become *fanatical*."

"Who's going to tell her—you?"

"Of course not. You know I'm not one to blab anyone's secret."

"No, but you sure do like to change the subject."

"What subject was that?"

"The one about animals and your love for them. Ever since you were little, you've been playing nursemaid to any stray animal

577

that came near your place." Susie shook her head. "I just don't understand it."

"Do you think me wanting to care for animals is a bad thing?"

"I suppose not, unless it's all you think about." Susie turned her head sharply, and a wisp of hair slipped out from under her kapp and fell onto her cheek.

Melinda pointed to Susie's hair. "I thought it was only me who didn't get her bun put up right."

Susie snickered. "I guess that's one thing we still have in common."

"What do you mean? There are lots of things we both like."

Susie elbowed Melinda gently in the ribs. "Jah—lemon sponge cakes, barbecued beef, and Aaron Zook's new puppy, Rufus."

"I'm wondering if it's Aaron you're interested in and not his dog."

Susie's elbow connected with Melinda's ribs a second time. "You're such a kidder."

"I wasn't kidding."

"Aaron's more like a *bruder* to me than anything."

"He's like a brother to me, too. His mamm and my mamm have been friends a long time. Her *kinner*, Isaiah, and I have grown up together, so I could never see Aaron as more than a brother." Melinda scanned the woods again. "I wish those deer would come back so I could finish sketching their picture."

Susie stared at a noisy crow circling overhead. "You and Gabe Swartz have been courting several months now, right?"

"That's true."

"Do you think you'll end up marrying him?"

"That all depends."

"On what?"

"On whether he asks, and whether I decide to—" Melinda halted her words then slipped her drawing tablet and pencil into the canvas tote at her feet. She jumped up and grabbed Susie's hand. "We'd better go. It wouldn't be good to keep our mamms waiting any longer, you know."

Gabe whistled as he swiped a piece of sandpaper across the door of a new kitchen cabinet. He was alone at the shop today. His dad had gone to Seymour to pick up some supplies he had ordered. Gabe figured it might be some time before Pap returned, because when he went to town he usually headed straight for the fast-food restaurant and bought a juicy cheeseburger and an order of fries. And he'd often drop by Lazy Lee's Gas Station and chew the fat with whoever was working that day.

Gabe smiled. He liked being alone in the shop. It gave him a chance to try his hand at making a few new things without his dad holding him back or scrutinizing every little detail.

When I'm done with this door, I think I'll start making that birdhouse I plan to give Melinda for her birthday next month. She's always feeding the birds and taking care of any that get hurt, so I'm sure she'd like to have another birdhouse—maybe a feeder, too. He rubbed his chin thoughtfully. *Maybe I should make a birdhouse with a feeding station attached. I'll bet she'd like that.*

A vision of Melinda's pretty face popped into Gabe's mind. Her golden blond hair and clear blue eyes were enough to turn any man's head. He had been interested in her since they were both children. But it wasn't just Melinda's pretty face that had made him fall in love with her. It was Melinda's spunky attitude and zest for living he found so appealing. She had always been adventurous, wanting to explore new things and eager to learn all she could about birds and animals. Gabe still remembered how nervous he had felt months ago when he'd asked her stepfather for permission to court her.

The cowbell hanging by a rope on the front door jangled, and Gabe looked up, his musings halted.

Melinda's stepfather, Noah Hertzler, entered the room. "*Wie geht's? How's business?*"

"I'm doing well, and so is the business. How's your job at the Christmas tree farm?"

"We've been keeping plenty busy." Noah looked around. "Where's your *daed*? Is he around someplace?"

"He went to Seymour to pick up some supplies. Probably won't be back for a few hours yet."

Noah chuckled. "If I know Stephen, he's having lunch at his favorite burger place."

"No doubt, but I don't know why Pap would choose fast food over barbecued ribs, baked beans, or hillbilly chili."

"I have to agree, but each to his own."

"Jah. Everyone has different likes and dislikes." Gabe moved over to the desk in the center of the room. "What can I help you with, Noah?"

"Thought I'd see if you could make a birdhouse for me to give Melinda for her nineteenth birthday next month."

Gabe inwardly groaned. There went his plans for Melinda's special birthday present. He didn't have the nerve to tell Noah that he had intended to give her a combination birdhouse-feeder. Now he would have to come up with something else to make for Melinda. Maybe he could whittle a miniature fawn, since she seemed so taken with the deer that lived in the woods behind their place.

"I'm sure I can have a birdhouse done for you in time for Melinda's birthday," Gabe said. "Is there a particular size or color you'd like it to be?"

Noah shook his head. "You're the expert; I'll leave that up to you."

Gabe smiled. He liked being called an expert. Most folks who came into their shop thought Pap was the professional woodworker, and many saw Gabe as merely his dad's apprentice. Someday, though, Gabe hoped to have his own place of business, and then nobody could think of him as an amateur in training.

Noah leaned against the desk and visited while Gabe wrote up the work order. "You think you'll take over this shop when your daed's ready to retire?" he asked.

Gabe looked up. "I'm not sure. I might want to go out on my own some day." He covered his mouth with the palm of his hand. "My daed doesn't know of my plans, so I'd appreciate it if you wouldn't say anything to him about it."

Noah shook his head. "It's not my place to do the telling."

Gabe breathed a sigh of relief. Did Melinda know how fortunate she was to have such a nice man as her stepfather? *I wouldn't mind having Noah for my father-in-law,* he mused. *That is, if I ever get up the nerve and find the right time to ask Melinda to marry me.*

Chapter 2

"How come we had to bake so many pies today?" Melinda asked her mother after Grandma Stutzman and Aunt Susie left for home. "Won't some of the other women be bringing desserts on Sunday?"

"It was your grandma's idea to have a pie social after church, and she wanted to furnish all the pies," Mama said as they finished cleaning the kitchen. She handed Melinda a sponge and pointed to the table, where streaks of flour and globs of gooey pie filling stuck to the oilcloth covering.

Melinda gave the table a thorough cleaning then dropped the mess into the garbage can under the sink. "If church is going to be at Grandpa and Grandma's, why did we do the baking over here and not at their house?"

"Melinda, weren't you listening when I told you this before?"

Mama asked in an exasperated tone.

Melinda shrugged. "I—I guess not."

"Your daed's busy with other things today, and I didn't want to leave Grandpa Hertzler alone in the *daadihaus* all day with his memory not being so good. No telling what might happen if he were left by himself for any length of time."

"That's right," Melinda's eleven-year-old brother, Isaiah, said as he came up behind their mother. "Remember the last time we left Grandpa alone in the grandfather house while we went to Bass Pro Shops in Springfield? When we got home, he wasn't there, and we found him down the road at the schoolhouse." The boy snickered. "I still can't get over seein' Grandpa on one of them swings, talkin' to Grandma like she was right there."

"Grandpa's memory loss is no laughing matter, Isaiah. Your daed and I are watching him closely, and if he gets any worse, we'll take him to see a specialist in Springfield." Mama shooed Isaiah away with the cotton dish towel she held in one hand. "Now get back outside and see that the rest of the wood is chopped before your daed gets home."

"Okay, I'm goin'." Isaiah grabbed a handful of peanut butter cookies from the ceramic jar on the cupboard then headed out the back door.

"That boy," Mama muttered as she ran water into the sink. "It'll be a miracle if I'm not fully gray by the time he's grown and married."

"If he can ever find a wife who'll put up with him." Melinda thought her young brother was a bit spoiled. The fact that Mama wasn't able to have any more children after Isaiah had been born could account for the fact that she didn't always get after the boy the way she should. At least that's how Melinda saw it.

"Isaiah's young yet," Mama said. "There's still plenty of time for him to grow into the kind of man a woman would want to marry."

Melinda's thoughts went to Gabe, the way they usually did whenever the subject of marriage came up. Was he the man she would marry? She cared deeply for him, but what would happen to their relationship if she left the Amish faith to become a veterinarian? Would he understand her desire to care for animals in a more professional way? Of course, she hadn't made up her mind yet about going English. There was a lot to think on and a good deal of planning to do if she did decide to pursue a career in veterinary medicine.

Pushing her thoughts aside, Melinda glanced at her mother, engrossed in the job of washing dishes. Mama's once shiny blond hair had turned darker, and a few streaks of gray showed through. Even so, she seemed youthful and full of energy. Mama had a zest for living, often telling jokes and yodeling whenever the mood hit. Of course, this usually happened when Grandpa Stutzman wasn't around. He found yodeling an annoyance, even though many Amish in their community liked to yodel.

I enjoy yodeling, too, Melinda thought as she wiped down the refrigerator door where some gunk had also splattered. *But I'll never yodel when I'm in the woods, because it would probably scare away the deer.*

"Did you read your Bible this morning?" Mama asked.

Melinda sucked in her lower lip, searching for words that wouldn't be a lie. She hadn't been doing her devotions regularly for sometime, even though she knew she should. "I'll do it this evening before bed," she promised.

"I have found that in order to stay close to God, I need to spend time with Him in prayer and Bible reading," Mama went on to say.

"I feel close to God when I'm out in the woods."

"That may be, but spending time in nature is not the same as reading God's Word."

"I know, and I'll read some verses tonight."

"Jah, okay. In the meantime, would you check on that last pie we've got baking?"

Melinda set the sponge on the table and went to open the oven door. When she looked inside, it appeared as if the apple crumb pie was done. Just to be certain, she poked the tip of a knife through the middle. "The apples seem tender enough, so I think it's ready," she announced. "I'm sure it won't be nearly as good as the ones Papa Noah bakes, though." She pulled two pot holders from a drawer and carefully lifted the pie from the oven. "Should I turn the propane off?"

"Go ahead. I won't need the stove again until supper time."

Melinda set the pie on top of the stove while she turned the knob on the propane tank. She was thankful her folks didn't use a woodstove for cooking the way some Amish in their community did. Wood cooking was too hot to her liking, and it could be dangerous.

Melinda remembered once when she was young how her mother had caught the kitchen rug on fire after a piece of wood fell out of the firebox. Fortunately, Mama had been able to throw the rug and the wood outside before anything else caught fire. The whole kitchen had become a smoky mess, and Mama's cake had been ruined. Melinda had been forced to sit outside in the cold until the smoke cleared.

Melinda picked up the pie again and started across the room. While it cooled on the kitchen table, she planned to go out to the barn and check on the baby goat that had been born a few days ago.

She'd only made it halfway to the table when the back door swung open and Isaiah rushed into the room, all red-faced and sweaty. "My dog broke free from his chain again, and he's chasin' chickens all over the yard!"

Before either Mama or Melinda could respond, Hector, Melinda's favorite rooster, flew into the house, squawking all the way. Isaiah's hound dog, Jericho, followed, nipping at Hector's tail feathers. The rooster screeched and flapped his wings, and the two animals darted in front of Melinda, causing her to stumble. The pie flipped out of her hands and landed upside down on the floor with a *splat*.

Jericho screeched to a halt and sniffed the apple filling. The critter must have realized it was too hot to eat, for he let out an ear-piercing howl and ducked under the table. Hector crowed raucously as he strutted around the room, and Isaiah stood howling.

"*Ach!*" Mama shouted. "Get those creatures out of my kitchen!"

Melinda didn't know whether to laugh or cry. The pie was ruined, and Hector could have gotten hurt, but the whole thing really was kind of funny. "You'd better get your dog," she told her brother. "After I clean up this mess, I'll take Hector outside and put him in the chicken coop."

"Better yet, I'll clean the floor, and you can take the rooster out now," Mama said sharply.

Melinda frowned. "It wasn't Hector's fault Jericho broke his chain and chased the poor bird."

Mama tapped her foot. "I don't care who was at fault. We have one less pie now and a big mess to clean."

Melinda bent down and scooped Hector into her arms. Isaiah grabbed his dog by the collar, and they both hurried out the door.

"As much as I like animals," Melinda muttered, "I have no use for that mutt of yours. He's dumber than dirt."

"Is not," her brother retorted. "Why, I'll have you know that the roof of Jericho's mouth is really dark, which means he's a smart one."

"That's probably just an old wives' tale you heard somewhere."

"Maybe it's not. Why don't you see what the vet has to say about it?"

Melinda shook her head. "I'm not going to bother Dr. Franklin with something so silly."

"It's not silly, and it'll prove once and for all that Jericho's not *dumm*."

"I'll think about it," Melinda muttered. Didn't her little brother realize she had a lot more on her mind than finding out if the color of a dog's mouth meant it was smart or dumb?

"What happened in here?" Noah asked when he entered the kitchen and found his wife down on her knees with a sponge and a bucket of soapy water, scrubbing away at a sticky mess on the floor.

Faith looked up at him and groaned. "My mamm and Susie were here earlier, and we baked some pies. But now, thanks to Melinda's dumm *hinkel* and Isaiah's spirited *hund*, we have one less pie to share during the social after preaching service tomorrow."

Noah hung his hat on the nearest wall peg. "Do I want to know why one of the chickens was in the house?"

"Isaiah was coming inside, and when he opened the door, the chicken ran in with Jericho right behind him. They had quite a tussle, and then they got in front of Melinda, causing her to stumble and drop one of the pies on my clean kitchen floor."

Noah bit back a chuckle. He could only imagine the disastrous scene. With all the critters Melinda had running around, something silly always seemed to be happening at their house these days.

"Do you think what happened here was funny?" Faith asked, tipping her head back and staring up at him with a pinched expression.

"What makes you think that?"

"You're smiling."

"I am?"

She nodded. "I don't see anything funny about this mess or about losing that pie."

"Would you like me to bake the replacement pie?" he asked, kneeling beside Faith. "I can make one quick as a wink."

"I know you can, and if you're sure you've got the time, I'd appreciate you doing that for me."

Noah reached out and tweaked the end of her nose. "For you, *schee fraa*, I've always got the time."

She grunted. "I'm glad you think I'm your pretty wife, but I don't feel so pretty right now."

"To me, you'll always be pretty." Noah patted her arm and rose to his feet. "Say, where are those two kinner of ours anyway?"

"Isaiah's supposed to be tying up his dog, and I assume Melinda's putting Hector back in the chicken coop like I asked her to do." Faith's pale eyebrows drew together as she frowned. "Of course, she should have been back by now, so I wouldn't be surprised if she's camped out in the barn, fooling with one of her animals."

"If she's not back by the time I get the pie put in the oven, I'll go check on her," Noah said as he grabbed one of Faith's choring aprons and tied it around his waist. No point in getting flour all over his trousers. He was just glad his dad was over at the daadihaus and wasn't here to see him wearing Faith's apron or making a pie. Even though Pop had relaxed his attitude some on men working in the kitchen, he still had no understanding of Noah's desire to cook and bake.

But he sure enjoys the fruit of my labor, Noah thought as he turned toward the cupboard to get the necessary ingredients. *Fact is, since Mom died, Pop's become almost like a child.*

"How was your day?" Melinda asked when her stepfather entered the barn and found her kneeling in the straw beside the new baby goat. "Did you get everything done that you wanted to do?"

He nodded. "I worked the first half of the day at the tree farm; then I stopped by Swartz's Woodworking Shop around noon. After that, I ran some other errands."

"Did you see Gabe?"

"Sure did. He was working alone at the shop because his daed had to go to Seymour."

Melinda was tempted to ask if Gabe had mentioned her, but she thought better of it. If Papa Noah knew how much she cared for Gabe, he'd probably tease her the way he did Mama whenever she was in one of her silly moods.

Melinda stroked the goat behind its ears as she thought about how sweet Gabe had been to her on the way home from the last young people's gathering. He'd asked if she was cold, and when she said, "Jah, just a bit," he had draped his arm around her. Melinda could almost feel the way his long fingers had gently caressed her shoulders. Even now, thinking about it caused her to shiver.

"Are you cold?" Papa Noah asked as he grabbed a brush and started grooming one of their buggy horses.

She shook her head. "Just felt a little chill is all."

"Spring has been fairly warm so far, but it does cool off in the evenings," he commented.

"That's for certain sure."

"I heard that you and your mamm did some baking today with Susie and Grandma Stutzman."

"Did you also hear what happened to one of the pies?" He nodded.

Melinda moved over to the horse's stall. "The pies turned out fine until Isaiah's dog caused me to trip and fall." She groaned.

"Now we have one less pie."

"That's not true." He reached under his straw hat to scratch the side of his head. "I just came from the kitchen, where I helped your mamm bake another pie. I don't get to bake as often as I used to, what with having so many other things to do, so it was kind of nice to spend some time in the kitchen."

Melinda smiled. She wasn't sure if Papa Noah had really enjoyed making the pie or if he was merely trying to make her feel better. "Mind if I ask you something?" she asked.

"What's that?"

"What will happen if Grandpa Hertzler's memory loss gets any worse? Will he have to move into our side of the house?"

"Maybe so."

"I wish there was something we could do to make him feel better."

Papa Noah's dark eyes clouded over. "We need to remember to pray for Grandpa and be there whenever he needs us."

"I agree."

"So, how's that little kid doing?" he asked, motioning to the baby goat. "Is she getting along all right?"

"I think so. I thought at first she might need me to bottle-feed her, but her mamm seems to be taking care of her now."

"Glad to hear it."

Melinda swatted at a bothersome fly. That was the only bad part about being in the barn—too many bugs that liked to buzz and bite. "Say, Papa Noah, I was wondering if—"

"What's that?"

"Do you think you might have time to build a few more animal cages so I can take care of more orphaned animals?"

"I'm not sure I'd have the time for that right now, but I'll bet Gabe Swartz would."

"Should I ask him?"

"Don't see why not." He winked at her. "After all, a fellow bitten by the love bug is sure to do most anything for his favorite girl."

Melinda's mouth dropped open. "You know about Gabe and me?"

"Of course. You can't fool an old man like me. I've seen the way you two look at each other."

"You're not old, Papa Noah." Melinda placed her hand on his arm and gave it a gentle squeeze. "You don't even have any gray hairs on your head."

He pulled his fingers through the end of his beard. "I've got some here, though."

She leaned closer for a better look. "Well, maybe just a few. But I still think you look plenty young."

He chuckled. "You sound just like your mamm."

"Is that a bad thing?"

"Of course not. If you were to follow in your mamm's footsteps all the way through life, it would be a good thing."

Melinda felt the heat of a blush cover her cheeks. *If Papa Noah knew what Dr. Franklin had suggested I do, he might wonder if I was preparing to follow in the footsteps Mama took when she left the Amish faith many years ago. He'd probably think Dr. Franklin was a bad influence, and he might insist that I quit my job.*

Chapter 3

Melinda hurried through her kitchen chores, eager to get outside. She planned to check on the baby goat and its mother, see that Isaiah's dog was secured for the day, and make sure all the chickens were doing okay. After yesterday's close call with Hector, she didn't want to see a repeat performance, and she was sure her mother didn't, either. Mama hadn't been happy about the loss of that pie.

"I'm going over to Grandma Stutzman's to help her clean," Mama said as Melinda passed her in the downstairs hallway. "Your daed, Grandpa Hertzler, and Isaiah loaded the pies into the buggy and will drop them over there before they head to Ben and Mary King's place to pick up the benches for tomorrow's church service."

"I'm glad Grandpa's going with Papa Noah, because I'll be

heading for work soon, and it wouldn't be good for him to be left home alone."

Mama popped a couple of her knuckles, a habit she'd had ever since Melinda could remember. "I thought it was just Mondays, Tuesdays, and Thursdays you helped out at the veterinary clinic."

"It was, but Dr. Franklin thought I could learn some new things if I spent more time there, so I may be working some Fridays and Saturdays, too."

Mama sighed. "Learn more of what, Melinda? I thought you were only hired to clean the cages and feed the animals."

"I—I was, but sometimes the doctor lets me do certain things—like give a dog its flea bath or hold on to a nervous cat while it's being examined." Melinda shrugged. "He says the *gedier* are calmer when I'm there."

"You have a way with animals. Even unruly ones like Hector."

Melinda was on the verge of defending the poor rooster and reminding her mother that the incident yesterday was Jericho's fault, but Mama grabbed her black purse off a wall peg and headed out the door. "See you this evening. Have a *gut* day."

"You have a good day, too."

Melinda stood in the doorway, watching her mother head down the driveway on foot. Since Grandpa and Grandma Stutzman lived less than a mile away, Mama often chose to walk there instead of bothering with a horse and buggy.

Melinda smiled at the way her mother held her head high, with shoulders straight back and arms swinging in perfect rhythm with the strides of her long legs. Soon Mama began to yodel. "Oh-lee-ay-tee—oh-lee-ay-tee—oh-lee-ay-tee-oh!"

Melinda cupped her hands around her mouth and echoed, "Oh-lee-ay-tee—oh-lee-ay-tee—oh-lee-ay-tee-oh."

Mama lifted her hand in a backward wave, and Melinda shut the door. She needed to get busy and clean her room before she left for the clinic. If there was enough time, she would check on the animals in the barn.

For the next half hour, Melinda dusted, shook her oval braided throw rug, pulled the colorful crazy quilt up over the four-poster bed, and swept the hardwood floor. Just as she was finishing up, she noticed her writing tablet on the dresser, and it reminded her that she'd forgotten about the note she was supposed to leave Gabe inside the old birdhouse near the front of her folks' property. She grabbed a pen from the drawer and hurriedly scrawled a message.

Dear Gabe,

I got your last letter, and I do plan on going to the young people's gathering tomorrow night. I'm looking forward to a ride home in your buggy.

I've enclosed a picture I drew of the baby raccoon Ben King found in the woods behind his place the other day. He said the critter's mother was killed, so the poor thing needs a home. I told him I would keep her, since the coon seems to have a problem with her eyes and probably wouldn't survive on her own. I've named her Reba, and I can't wait for you to see her.

I look forward to seeing you at church on Sunday morning. After the common meal, maybe we can play a game of croquet with some of our friends. Until tomorrow. . .

Yours fawnly,
Melinda

Melinda slipped the note, along with the picture of the orphaned raccoon, into an envelope and hurried out of her room. She made a quick trip to the barn and was pleased to discover that the baby goat was sleeping peacefully beside its mother. The kid's bulging tummy let a relieved Melinda know it had recently eaten. Too many times she had bottle-fed some animal because it was orphaned or its mother wouldn't take care of it. Not that she minded playing nursemaid, but it was better for the animal if its mother fed it.

"Sleep well, and I'll check on you both when I get home from work this evening," she murmured as she stroked the mother goat behind its ear.

Melinda left the goats and led Jenny, her favorite buggy horse, out of the barn then hitched her to one of their open buggies. Sometimes she wished they could drive the box-shaped, closed-in buggies most other Amish communities used, but when she and Mama first moved to Webster County, Mama had explained that the community she belonged to was more conservative than most. One of the things they did that separated them from other Amish was to drive only open buggies.

"These buggies aren't so bad in warmer weather," Melinda murmured, "but in the wintertime, it can sure get cold." She gave Jenny a quick pat, climbed into the driver's seat, and picked up the reins.

At the end of the driveway, Melinda saw the familiar gray birdhouse and halted the horse. "Just a few more minutes, Jenny, and then we'll be on our way."

Melinda hopped down and lifted the removable roof from the birdhouse. She was pleased to see that no birds had claimed it as their new home. She and Gabe had been sending each other messages this way since they'd started courting, and so far, the birds seemed to know it was off-limits.

She slipped the note inside and replaced the roof. "I just hope Gabe comes by before tomorrow and picks it up."

Melinda was about to walk away when she caught sight of a small bird in some tall grass, chirping and furiously flapping its wings. She bent for a closer look and realized it was a fledgling blackbird that apparently couldn't fly well yet.

"I can't leave you here. Some big cat or hawk might come along and make you its meal." Gently Melinda picked up the tiny bird and set him on a low branch of a nearby tree. "There you go; be safe." She smiled, content with the knowledge that she'd helped another one of God's creatures, and hurried away.

Gabe shielded his eyes from the glare of the sun and pulled his buggy to the side of the road by the Hertzlers' driveway. *I sure hope there's a note from Melinda today.*

He hopped down and lifted the lid of the weathered birdhouse. To his surprise, a few blades of grass and a piece of string lay on top of an envelope. "Some bird must have decided to make a nest here," Gabe muttered. He reached inside, pulled out the grass and string, and tossed them on the ground. "That ought to discourage those silly birds from claiming this as their new home."

Unexpectedly, a sparrow swooped down, just missing Gabe's head. He ducked. "Hey, cut that out! This is Melinda's and my message box. Go find someplace else to build your nest."

Gabe stuck his hand inside the birdhouse and retrieved Melinda's note. As soon as he had replaced the lid, he bent down, grabbed a small rock, and plugged the opening in the front. "That should keep you birds out of there."

As Gabe climbed into his buggy, he decided that, in all fairness to the birds, it wasn't right to shoo them out of a birdhouse that was built for them. He would add a separate compartment to the birdhouse he was making for Noah to give Melinda on her birthday. Then even if the birds decided to make it their home, he and Melinda would still have their secret place to hide messages—one without a hole in the front.

Gabe headed down Highway C toward Seymour, letting the horse lead while he read Melinda's note. He was pleased to discover that she planned to be at the young people's gathering on Sunday night and was looking forward to him taking her home afterward.

"I like a woman who knows what she wants," he said with a chuckle. "Especially if it's me she's wanting." Melinda's eagerness to be with Gabe made him believe she might say yes if he were to propose marriage. He just needed to find the right time and the courage to do it.

He studied the pencil drawing Melinda had made of the baby raccoon. It certainly looked like a coon, but he was concerned about her making a pet out of a wild animal. What if the critter bit or scratched her real bad? She could end up with rabies or something!

"That woman doesn't think straight when it comes to the animals she takes in," he mumbled. "She would cozy up to a bull snake if she thought it needed a friend. I think I'd better have a talk with Melinda and let her know I'm concerned."

When Susie stepped into the kitchen, she was surprised to see Faith sitting at the table having a cup of tea with their mother. "Wie geht's, Faith?" Susie asked. "I didn't know you were here."

Faith smiled. "I'm doing fine. I came over to help Mama clean house today."

"I appreciate it, too," Mama said with a nod. She took a sip from her cup. "Of course, we're not getting much done sitting here drinking tea."

"Well, you deserve a little break," Susie said as she grabbed her lunch pail off the counter and flipped it open so she could begin making her lunch. "I'd help with the cleaning if I didn't have to work at Kaulp's General Store today."

"If it makes you feel any better, Melinda won't be helping us, either, because she's working for the vet today."

"She's been working there a lot lately, jah?" Mama asked.

"A little too much, if you ask me." Faith's voice held a note of irritation, making Susie wonder if her big sister disapproved of her daughter working for the English vet.

"Why do you say that?"

Susie's ears perked up. That was something she'd like to know herself. She glanced discreetly over her shoulder and waited for Faith's response.

"All Melinda talks about anymore is either the critters she's caring for at home or the ones she helps Dr. Franklin with at his clinic." Faith set her cup down and popped a couple of knuckles, causing Susie to cringe. "Gabe Swartz and Melinda are courting, yet she spends more time with those silly animals than she does him." Faith popped a couple more knuckles. "Wouldn't you think she would want to concentrate on honing her cooking, sewing, and baking skills so she'll be ready for marriage, rather than trying to play *dokder* to a bunch of smelly creatures?"

"If I had a boyfriend, I sure wouldn't be thinking about any dumm old animals or trying to play doctor," Susie put in as she slathered two pieces of bread with butter.

"Do I detect a note of envy in your voice, daughter?"

Susie turned to face her mother. "I don't begrudge Melinda having a boyfriend; she has the right. I just wish I was being courted by someone, that's all."

"It will happen in due time," Faith put in. "Just try to be patient and wait on the Lord to bring the right fellow along."

Susie shrugged and turned back to her sandwich making. At the rate things were going, Melinda would be married with a houseful of kinner before Susie had a boyfriend. It didn't seem fair that everything always seemed to go Melinda's way. It wasn't fair at all.

Chapter 4

On Sunday morning when Melinda and her family arrived at Grandma and Grandpa Stutzman's for church, Melinda spotted Susie on the wooden two-seater swing hanging from the rafters under the Stutzmans' front porch. Papa Noah and Isaiah headed to the barn to put the horse inside, and Mama and Grandpa Hertzler went into the house right away. Melinda stopped at the swing to speak with Susie.

Susie patted the seat beside her. "Why don't you sit with me awhile before everyone else shows up?"

"Don't mind if I do." Melinda sat down and started pumping her legs to get the swing moving again. The day was warmer than most April mornings had been so far, and the breeze from the motion of the swing felt nice.

Susie glanced over at Melinda with a puckered brow. "I see

you've got dark circles under your eyes. How come?"

"I stayed up late last night caring for my animals."

"Which ones?"

"I've only got a couple I'm taking care of right now. One's a baby goat, and I've been checking to be sure the mother goat keeps feeding her little one." Melinda tapped her finger against her chin. "I also helped Papa Noah groom the horses and spent some time with my raccoon because she was acting kind of peculiar."

Susie's eyebrows shot up. "What coon? I didn't know you had a coon."

"I got her from Ben King. She's an orphan and nearly blind."

"That's too bad."

"At first, Reba wouldn't eat and kept bumping into the side of her cage. After I sat with her awhile, she finally ate a little and seemed much calmer."

Susie groaned. "I can't believe you'd lose sleep over some dumm critter or that you'd bother to name a wild animal."

"Reba's not dumb. Do you think your cat's dumb?"

"Of course not. Daisy's a good mouser. She also keeps me company and likes to cuddle."

"Well, there you go."

"Are you still planning to go to the young people's gathering at the Hiltys' place tonight?" Susie asked.

Melinda was thankful for the change in topic. She and Susie seemed to be arguing a lot lately—especially whenever they talked about Melinda's love for animals.

"Of course. I wouldn't miss it." Melinda smiled. "Gabe's giving me a ride home again. He said so in the note he left in our birdhouse the other day."

"You're sure the lucky one." Susie released a gusty sigh. "I wish I had the promise of a ride home with some cute fellow tonight."

Melinda stopped swinging and reached over to pat Susie's hand. "Your time will come. Just wait and see."

"Jah, well, I'm twenty years old. Many Amish women my age are married by now. I'll probably end up *en alt maedel*. Could be I'll spend the rest of my days working at Kaulp's and never have a husband or family of my own."

"You won't be an old maid, and I doubt you'll be working at Kaulp's General Store the rest of your life. One of these days you'll—"

Susie jumped up, jostling Melinda and nearly tossing her out of the swing. "Let's not talk about this anymore. Some more buggies have pulled into the driveway, and one of them belongs to Bishop Frey. Church will be starting soon, so we'd better get inside."

"You go on," Melinda said. "I'm going to sit here awhile and enjoy the fresh air. Once we're all in the house, it will be hot and stuffy."

"Suit yourself." Susie went in the front door, and Melinda resumed her swinging.

A few minutes later, John Frey and his wife, Margaret, stepped onto the porch. The bishop walked with a limp these days and was beginning to show his age, but he could still preach God's Word and lead the people. Melinda figured he would continue as bishop for several more years before he died.

"*Guder mariye*," Margaret said, as they approached Melinda.

"Good morning," she answered with a nod.

"Are you planning to be baptized and join the church soon?" the bishop asked.

Melinda could hardly believe the man had posed such a question. Was Bishop John's memory failing him the way Grandpa Hertzler's seemed to be? It was a shame to witness older folks forgetting so many things.

"I got baptized last year, Bishop John," she said. "It was soon after my eighteenth birthday."

The wrinkles in the bishop's forehead deepened, and he gave his long gray beard a couple of sharp pulls. Then he narrowed his eyes and stared at Melinda so hard she began to squirm. "Hmm. Well, jah, that's right, you were one of those I baptized last year."

Melinda realized the man's memory wasn't going after all. His problem was probably failing eyesight. She had felt bad when her mother began to lose her close-up vision and started wearing reading glasses, but Mama had laughed and said, "It's okay. That's what comes with getting older."

Margaret smiled and adjusted her own metal-framed glasses. Then she clasped her husband's arm and said, "Shall we go inside now, John? The service will be starting soon."

The bishop yawned noisily. "Jah, guess we'd better."

As soon as John and Margaret stepped into the house, Melinda left the swing and headed straight for the barn. If she hurried, there would be time to see the kittens Susie's cat had given birth to a few weeks ago.

Inside the barn, Melinda took a seat on a bale of straw to watch Daisy feed her six squirming babies. *All baby animals are cute. Some more than others, but I enjoy each one,* she thought dreamily.

She drew in a deep breath, relishing the sweet smell of fresh hay. A horse whinnied from one of the stalls nearby, and a pigeon cooed from the loft overhead. *It's so peaceful here. Next to being in the woods, this is my favorite place to sit and relax.*

Sometime later, Melinda left the barn, but as soon as she closed the door, she realized that the preaching service had already begun. The chantlike voices of the people singing inside her grandparents' house filtered through the open windows. She hurried in through the back door and tiptoed down the hall. Backless wooden benches filled the large living room and spilled over into the parlor. The rooms were separated by a removable wall that was taken out whenever preaching services were held in this home.

As Melinda slipped quietly into the main room, a few people looked up from their hymnbooks and glanced her way. Most, however, stayed focused on the song they were singing.

Susie motioned Melinda over to the bench where she sat. There was an empty spot on the end, and Melinda figured her aunt had been saving it for her.

"Where have you been?" Susie whispered when Melinda took a seat.

"Out in the barn with Daisy and her brood. They're sure cute little things."

Susie shook her head.

Melinda clutched the folds in her dress. *She doesn't understand. Sometimes I wonder how Susie and I can be such good friends when we don't think alike on the subject of animals.*

She glanced across the room at the men and boys who were seated opposite them. Gabe sat beside his friend Aaron, and she caught him staring at her. He'd probably seen her sneak into the room, and she wondered if he thought she was irresponsible for being late. Would he say something about it later? More than likely, she would get a lecture from Mama on the subject of tardiness. She hoped she wouldn't get one from Gabe, too.

Gabe's friendly smile and quick wink caused Melinda's heart to flutter. It was enough to let her know he wasn't judging her. She shivered at the anticipation of spending time with him that evening.

Melinda's thoughts spun faster than a windmill blade whirling in a gale. Maybe if she could think of the right way to say it, she would open her heart and tell Gabe what Dr. Franklin had suggested she do. It would be good to tell someone what had been weighing so heavily on her mind these past few weeks.

A nudge to the ribs brought Melinda's thoughts to a halt. "You're not paying attention," Susie whispered.

"I am so."

Susie leaned closer. "You're paying attention to Gabe, but that's about all."

Melinda sat up straight and folded her hands. If her aunt had noticed her preoccupation with Gabe, others might have, as well. She was thankful Mama sat three rows ahead. Maybe she hadn't noticed Melinda's late arrival.

Melinda turned her attention to the front of the room, where Preacher Kaulp had begun the first sermon of the day. He spoke from the book of Proverbs on the subject of wisdom.

Wisdom is what I need, Melinda thought. *Wisdom to know if I should do as Dr. Franklin suggested and separate myself from those I love in order to become a vet so I can properly care for sick and injured animals.*

She closed her eyes. *Dear Lord, You know that Mama and Papa Noah already think I spend too much time with my animal friends. If they knew what Dr. Franklin wanted me to do, they would probably be upset with him. Oh, Lord, what should I do?*

As soon as church was over and the women had begun serving the men their meal, Faith decided it was time to have a little talk with her daughter. She found Melinda on the porch with an empty platter in her hands. Apparently she'd just come from the barn where the men were eating.

"Hi, Mama," Melinda said with a smile. "I'm just heading back to the kitchen to get some more sandwiches."

"Before you do that, I'd like to speak with you a minute." Faith stepped in front of Melinda and blocked the door to the house.

Melinda's cheeks flamed as she stared down at her shoes. "Is it about me being late to church this morning?"

"Jah. This isn't the first time you've been late, either."

"I know." Melinda lifted her gaze. "I went to the barn to see Daisy's *busslin,* and I lost track of time."

Faith grunted. "I can't believe you would get so involved with a batch of kittens that you'd forget to come inside for church."

The color in Melinda's cheeks deepened. "Well, I—"

"You need to get your priorities straight, Melinda. Being in church is more important than spending time with some smelly animals."

"Daisy's kittens aren't smelly, Mama. They're sweet and soft as a downy chick."

"I don't care how sweet or soft they are. You should have been in church on time this morning."

"I'll try harder from now on."

Faith tapped her foot against the faded porch boards. "You're not a little girl anymore, Melinda. You need to start acting your age."

Melinda nodded.

Faith stepped aside, hoping she'd been able to get through to Melinda. This business of her fooling around with animals when she should be facing her responsibilities was getting old. "You'd better get those sandwiches now, or you'll likely get a lecture from the menfolk when you return to the barn."

"Okay, Mama." Melinda offered Faith a brief smile then hurried inside.

As Faith turned toward the porch steps, she spotted her friend Barbara heading her way with a coffeepot in her hands.

"You don't look so happy," Barbara said when she stepped onto the porch. "Is something wrong?"

Faith nodded. "I think I've failed as a *mudder*."

Barbara's eyebrows furrowed. "Ach, Faith, what would make you think that?"

"I've tried my best to raise Melinda so she'll become a mature, responsible woman, but apparently all I've taught her has fallen on deaf ears." Faith shrugged. "Either that, or I made some huge mistakes with Melinda somewhere along the line."

Barbara patted Faith's arm. "I don't think you made any mistakes. From what I've observed, both you and Noah have done a fine job raising your two kinner."

"Then how come Melinda's priorities are so messed up? And how come she's late to church so often these days?"

Barbara offered Faith a look of sympathy. "I noticed that she came in after the service had already begun, but I figured she'd been using the bathroom."

Faith shook her head. "She went to the barn."

"Why'd she go there?"

"To see a batch of busslin, of all things." Faith grimaced. "I have nothing against animals, mind you, but Melinda is consumed with them. It's getting so bad I'm beginning to think we live at the zoo."

Barbara gave Faith's arm another pat. "Is it really that bad?"

"Jah, it is. You should have seen the mess my kitchen was in yesterday after Melinda's chicken got into the house, with Isaiah's dog right on the rooster's tail feathers. Melinda ended up tripping over the dog and dropping a pie all over my clean floor."

Barbara's lips twitched, but then her face sobered. "No one ever said it would be easy to be a parent. Not even when our kinner are on the verge of leaving the nest."

"Puh!" Faith said with a wave of her hand. "At the rate Melinda's going, she'll be old and gray before she's ready to leave home and make a life of her own. For that matter, if she doesn't grow up and start acting more responsible, it's not likely she'll ever find a man who'll want to marry her."

"What about Gabe Swartz? Aren't the two of them courting?"

"Jah, but I'm not sure how serious they have become."

Barbara opened her mouth, but she closed it again.

Faith leaned closer to Barbara. "Do you know something I don't know?"

"No, not really. It's just that my boy Aaron's a good friend of Gabe's, and he's mentioned a couple of times how smitten Gabe is with Melinda."

"Well, if Gabe's really interested in my daughter, then he'd better be prepared to put up with all her critters." Faith grunted. "Either that, or he'll have to do something to make Melinda see where her priorities need to be."

Barbara lifted the coffeepot in her hands. "Let me put this in the kitchen, and then we can take a little walk. I think you need to talk about this some more."

Gabe was glad when the church service was over so he could be outside. Not that he hadn't enjoyed the sermons or time of singing, for he'd listened intently to the verse Bishop Frey had quoted near the end of his lengthy sermon. It was Proverbs 18:22: "Whoso findeth a wife findeth a good thing, and obtaineth favour of the Lord."

Those words made Gabe even more determined to make Melinda his wife, and if everything went well tonight, he might get up the nerve to propose. If Melinda accepted, he hoped they could be married sometime this fall.

From Gabe's vantage point under the shade of a walnut tree, he'd seen Melinda on the front porch awhile ago, talking to her mother, but now Faith was speaking to Barbara Hilty.

I wonder if Faith chewed out her daughter for being late to church. Melinda really ought to try harder to be on time to our services.

Gabe flopped onto the grass and leaned against the trunk of the tree. He was nearly asleep when he heard female voices nearby.

His eyes popped open, and he spotted Faith and Barbara heading his way.

"I wish I knew what to do about my daughter," Faith said.

Gabe's ears perked up. He wasn't trying to eavesdrop, but he was curious to hear what Melinda's mother was saying.

"Sometimes, raising teenagers can be just as hard as when they were kinner," Barbara said. "I guess we'll be trying to steer them in the right direction until they get married and leave home."

"Jah," Faith agreed. "I just need to keep praying for Melinda and try to give her direction without being too pushy."

"I agree," Barbara said. "You know, my Aaron claims he's never getting married. It makes me wonder if he plans to stick around home and be told what to do for the rest of his life."

As the two women strolled past the tree where Gabe sat, he yanked his straw hat down over his eyes, plucked up a blade of grass, and stuck it between his teeth, hoping to look inconspicuous. Faith and Barbara continued on their way, apparently unaware of his presence.

Gabe drew in a deep breath and said a prayer for himself and Melinda. Someday, Lord willing, they would have their own kinner to worry about.

Chapter 5

It's nice of you to drive us to the young people's gathering, but I don't see why we couldn't have walked to the Hiltys' place. It isn't that far," Melinda said to Grandpa Stutzman as she settled herself on the buggy seat between him and Susie.

He grunted. "I won't have my youngest daughter or my granddaughter out walking in the dark no matter how close we live to the Hiltys."

Melinda glanced over at her aunt to gauge her reaction. Susie shrugged.

"I'll be back to pick you both up around ten," Grandpa said with a nod.

"Oh, Melinda won't be needing a ride," Susie blurted out. "She's already been promised one from—"

Melinda poked Susie on the arm. "Hush."

"Uh—what I meant to say was, I'll be the only one needing a ride home tonight."

"How do you know some young fellow won't be asking to bring you home?" Grandpa's bushy gray eyebrows lifted clear into his hairline. "Huh?"

Susie stared at her hands. "I don't know who it would be."

Melinda's heart went out to her aunt. It wasn't right that a woman Susie's age didn't have a steady boyfriend. Especially when she was so kind and pretty.

"How about I come by a little later than ten?" Grandpa asked, smiling at his daughter. "Just in case all the young men are too shy to ask and you find yourself without a ride."

Susie gave a quick nod. "I guess that would be all right."

As much as Melinda wanted to spend time alone with Gabe, she couldn't stand the thought of Susie being picked up by her father. It was bad enough he had insisted on driving them here. "If Susie doesn't get asked, Gabe and I will bring her home."

Grandpa chuckled. "Gabe, is it? I might have known."

Melinda covered her mouth with the palm of her hand. "I—I meant to say, Susie can ride with me and my date."

"I know," Grandpa said with a grin. "And if Susie's okay with that, it's fine by me."

Susie shook her head. "I don't think it's a good idea."

"Why not?" Melinda wondered what her aunt could be thinking.

"I'm not going to be a fifth wheel on the buggy," Susie said with a shake of her head.

"It'll be fine. We'll drop you off first; then Gabe can take me home."

Susie sighed but finally nodded. "Jah, okay."

A short while later, they pulled into the Hiltys' driveway. Grandpa drove past the house and the harness shop, stopping the buggy near the barn. "Here you go. I hope you both have yourselves a real good time."

"Thanks, Papa." Susie hopped out of the buggy and sprinted toward the barn, where peals of laughter and chattering voices drifted on the night air.

Melinda turned to face her grandfather. "She'll be fine, Grandpa. You'll see."

"I know, but it sure would be nice if she found herself a beau." He picked up the reins. "Now go have some fun, and be sure to tell Gabe Swartz I said he's gettin' one fine girl."

Melinda's face warmed, and she leaned over to kiss her grandfather's wrinkled cheek. "I love you, Grandpa."

"That goes double for me."

She patted his arm then climbed out of the buggy. "See you soon."

"Jah." Grandpa Stutzman backed the horse up and headed down the driveway.

As Melinda hurried to the barn, the rhythm of her heartbeat kept time with her footsteps. She could hardly wait to see Gabe.

Gabe stood at the refreshment table, about to ladle some punch into a paper cup for Melinda, whom he'd spotted on the other side of the barn.

"Gettin' some sweets for your sweetie, are you?" Gabe's friend Aaron teased as he stepped up beside Gabe.

"What do you think?"

"I think you'd get down on your hands and knees and lap water like a dog if Melinda asked you to."

Gabe grunted and rubbed the side of his nose. "Would not. Besides, she's already got plenty of pets."

"Jah, well, she might want one more."

"Are you trying to goad me into an argument this evening?"

Aaron chuckled. "Who me? Never!"

"Jah, right." Gabe grabbed two peanut butter cookies, a handful of pretzels, and a wedge of cheese then piled them on a paper plate.

"Are you taking Melinda home tonight?"

"What do you think?"

"You sure do like to answer my questions with a question." Aaron bumped Gabe's arm, nearly knocking the plate out of his hands.

"Hey, watch it!"

"Sorry."

"Are you planning to offer anyone a ride home?" Gabe asked, hoping to get Aaron out of his teasing mode.

"No way! I'm not ready to get tied down yet."

"Who said anything about getting tied down? You can take a girl home without proposing marriage, you know." Gabe wasn't about to tell his friend that a marriage proposal was in his plans for the night. If he did spill the beans, he was sure Aaron would only taunt him that much more.

Aaron snatched one of Gabe's cookies and bit into it. "That

might be true, but as soon as you give some female a ride in your buggy, she starts thinking you want to court her. After that, the next thing on her mind is marriage." He shook his head. "I'm not ready for that. All I want is to own my daed's business."

Gabe lifted his eyebrows. "Is Paul planning to quit working at the harness shop?"

"Not yet, but someday he'll want to retire. When that time comes, I'll be ready to take it over. My real daed wanted me to have the shop he started, you know."

Gabe nodded. "I'm sure Paul does, too."

"Maybe so. Maybe not."

Gabe moved away from the table, and Aaron followed. "To tell you the truth, I think my daed still sees me as a little kid who doesn't know nearly as much as him about making things. It isn't easy being the youngest in the family, with four sisters who are all married and out on their own."

"What's that got to do with anything?" Aaron asked.

"Ever since I was little, Pap, Mom, and even my sisters have treated me like a *boppli*. I believe my daed likes being in charge of everything and telling me what to do."

"I'm not really treated like a baby, but my stepdad sure likes to order me around. The truth is I think our relationship was better when I was a boy."

"I guess in the eyes of our parents we'll never be grown up," Gabe said with a frown.

"You're probably right." Aaron bit off the end of one fingernail and spit it on the straw-covered floor.

Gabe wrinkled his nose. "That was so nasty. Where are your manners, anyhow?"

Aaron lowered his gaze and looked kind of sheepish. "Sorry. Nail biting's a bad habit that I probably should break. Least that's what my mamm thinks."

"So why don't you quit?"

"Maybe I will someday. . .when I have a good enough reason to."

"You mean when you find an *aldi*?"

Aaron shook his head vigorously. "No way! I don't need a girlfriend complicating my life."

"Well, Melinda's waiting for me, so I'd better get over there with this food," Gabe said, deciding it was time to move on.

Aaron thumped Gabe on the back a few times. "You do that, you lovesick *hundli*."

Gabe shrugged his friend's hand away. "I'm not a lovesick puppy."

"Okay then, you're a lovesick man."

Gabe swallowed a retort and headed across the room. Aaron was only funning with him, and if the tables were turned, he'd probably do the same. Right now, though, he had other things on his mind.

For the next couple of hours, Gabe relaxed and enjoyed visiting, playing games, and eating with the other young people. Shortly before things wound down, Melinda was called on to lead the group in some singing and yodeling. Her face turned red, but after some coaxing from Gabe and a few other friends, she finally agreed. While several others in attendance could yodel fairly well, nobody did it as expertly as Melinda.

Maybe that's because her mother used to be a professional yodeler, Gabe thought as he sat on a bale of straw and watched Melinda in action. She cupped her hands around her mouth as she belted out, "Oddle-lay—oddle-lay—oddle-lay—dee-tee. My mama was an old cowhand, and she taught me how to yodel before I could stand—yo-le-tee—yo-le-tee—hi-ho!"

Gabe glanced around the room and saw that all eyes were trained on his girlfriend. He figured he was the luckiest man there and that the other fellows must surely be envious.

Susie was glad when the singing was over. Watching Melinda show off her yodeling skills was enough to make her feel downright sick. She left the table where she'd been sitting and moved over to the bowl of punch sitting across the room. *Funny Melinda. Cute Melinda. Talented Melinda. No wonder Melinda has a boyfriend, and no one's interested in me. I can't yodel worth a hill of beans, and I'm not nearly as pretty as Melinda. Truth be told, I'll probably be an old maid until the day I die.*

She grabbed a paper cup and was about to ladle some punch into it when someone bumped her arm.

"Oops. Sorry about that. I hope you didn't get any punch on yourself."

Susie turned at the sound of a deep male voice and nearly dropped her cup when she saw a pair of dark brown eyes staring down at her.

The tall, blond-haired Amish man grinned, revealing two large dimples in his cheeks. "What's the matter? Is there a cat around here somewhere?"

"Huh?"

"Well, you weren't saying anything, so I figured maybe some old cat had stolen your tongue."

Susie's face heated with embarrassment.

"I'll bet you don't remember me, do you?" the young man asked as he folded his arms and continued to smile at her.

Susie swallowed a couple of times, realizing how dry her throat had suddenly become. "Jonas Byler?"

He nodded. "I'd just graduated from the eighth grade when I went to Montana to work for my uncle at his log furniture shop."

Susie ladled herself some punch and swallowed some down so she could speak. "You've changed a lot since then."

He gave a slow nod. "So have you."

Susie's cheeks burned hot under his scrutiny. Was Jonas staring at her in such a strange way because he thought she was homely as a horny toad? Of course, Susie didn't really think she was homely; just not real pretty and full of exuberance, the way Melinda was.

She took another swallow of punch. "Have you moved back to Webster County?"

Jonas shook his head. "Just came for a visit with my folks. They've come to Montana several times to see me, but this is the first time I've been home since I left ten years ago."

"Uh-huh." Susie didn't know why she felt so tongue-tied in Jonas's presence. It wasn't like she might have a chance with him or anything. Beside the fact that he was five years older than she, he would be going back to Montana again, and then it could be several more years before she would see him. He probably had a girlfriend waiting for him back in Montana, and by this time next year, he might even be married. So there was no good reason for her to be looking at him, wishing for something that wasn't going to happen. What she needed to do was grab a few cookies from the refreshment table, get back to her table, and forget she'd even spoken to Jonas Byler with the big brown eyes.

"I'll see you around," Jonas said, as he turned away from Susie.

Susie reached out a shaky hand and snatched a cookie. Then she turned and watched Jonas make his way across the room, where he took a seat beside Aaron Zook.

I wish he wasn't going back to Montana, she thought ruefully. *But then, even if he were staying here, he would never be interested in someone like me.*

She glanced over at Melinda, who sat next to Gabe, and a pang of jealousy sliced through her as sharp as a knife. Dropping the cookie back to the platter, she turned away. Her appetite was gone.

As Melinda sat beside Gabe in his open buggy, she closed her eyes and breathed in the sweet perfume given off by the trees and flowers bursting with spring buds. The temperature was just right this evening, and the full moon illuminated the road ahead to light their way.

"Are you sleeping?" Gabe asked.

She opened her eyes and smiled at him. "Just enjoying the fresh air and peaceful ride."

"It is a nice evening." He draped his arm across her shoulders, bringing them so close she could smell the pine-scented soap he must have used when he'd gotten ready for the gathering tonight. "Are you warm enough?"

"I'm fine."

They rode in silence for a while, with the only sounds being the steady *clip-clop* of the horse's hooves and an occasional *hoo-hoot* of an owl. Melinda thought about how things had gone this evening. Susie had hung around some of the other young women her age most of the evening, while Gabe stuck close to Melinda. Poor Susie never did pair off with any of the young men in attendance. Even during the time of yodeling Melinda had led and the singing of some lively songs like "Mockingbird Hill" and "Yellow Rose of Texas," Susie had appeared glum. "I Never Will Marry" seemed more like her song. Aaron's, too, for that matter, for he hadn't paired off with anyone, either.

When it came time for them to leave, Susie had informed Melinda that she'd found a ride home with Kathy and Rebecca Yoder. Melinda didn't argue, knowing once Susie made up her mind about something, she wasn't likely to budge. Besides, Melinda really did want to be alone with Gabe during the ride home.

"Say, Gabe, I was wondering if you might have the time to build me a couple more cages for my animals," she asked suddenly.

"I'd like to, Melinda, but right now Pap and I are really busy in the shop." He smiled. "I will try to squeeze it in when I have some free time, though."

"*Danki.* I'd appreciate that."

"Do you ever think about your real *daed* or find yourself wishing you and your *mamm* had stayed in the English world?"

Gabe's unexpected question startled Melinda, and she sat up straight. Did he have an inkling of what she was thinking about doing? Had Gabe spoken with Dr. Franklin recently? Could the vet have mentioned his suggestion that Melinda think about becoming a veterinarian? Surely he wouldn't have said anything, since she'd asked him not to mention the idea to anyone until she'd told her folks what she was thinking of doing.

"What would make you ask me such a question?" she asked, looking at Gabe out of the corner of her eye.

"If there's even a chance you might want to return to the English way of life, I feel I have the right to know."

Melinda drew in a quick breath. Since Gabe had brought up the subject, maybe now was the time to discuss Dr. Franklin's idea. She squeezed her eyes shut, searching for just the right words, and when she opened them again, she was shocked to see a man standing in the middle of the road up ahead. He had his back to them, but she could tell by his dark clothes and straw hat that he was Amish. "Gabe, look out!" she hollered.

He pulled sharply on the reins. "Whoa there! Steady boy."

When the horse stopped, Gabe grabbed a flashlight from under the seat, and he and Melinda jumped down from the buggy.

The man in the road turned around, and Melinda's mouth fell open. "Grandpa Hertzler?"

Grandpa didn't answer. He stood staring at Melinda as though she were a complete stranger.

"He looks confused, like he doesn't know where he is," Gabe whispered.

Melinda nodded. "We've got to get him home."

"Levi, it's Gabe and Melinda," Gabe said, gently taking hold of Grandpa's arm.

Grandpa studied him a few seconds then turned to face Melinda. Finally, a look of recognition crossed his face. "What are you doin' out here, girl?"

"Gabe was giving me a ride home from the young people's gathering. We stopped the buggy when we saw you in the middle of the road." She grabbed his other arm. "Don't you know how dangerous it is to be out walking after dark? Especially dressed in clothes that aren't brightly colored."

The confusion Melinda saw on her grandfather's face made her heart ache. He'd obviously wandered off their property and onto the road. She was sure Mama and Papa Noah had no idea where he was.

"Let's get into the buggy, and I'll drive you both home," Gabe said.

Melinda was relieved when her grandfather went willingly, but she could see by the frown on Gabe's face that he wasn't happy when Grandpa took a seat next to him, which left Melinda sitting on the outside edge.

She reached for Grandpa's hand and gave it a gentle squeeze. This buggy ride might not have been the romantic one she had hoped for, but at least Grandpa was safe. Maybe she and Gabe would have another chance to be alone soon. Maybe by then she would be better prepared to discuss her future with him.

Chapter 6

Good morning," Dr. Franklin said when Melinda stepped into the veterinary clinic one Monday morning a few weeks later. "How are you on this fine sunny day?"

"I'm fine. How are things going here?"

The middle-aged man's blue eyes twinkled. "I got a squirrel in this morning with an injured foot."

Melinda moved quickly to the counter where he stood. "How bad is it hurt? Will it be okay? What are you planning to do with it once you've doctored its foot?"

The doctor chuckled. "One question at a time, please."

"Sorry. I tend to be eager when it comes to helping suffering animals."

"I know you do, but your caring attitude is what makes you so special." He smiled as he held up one finger. "Now to answer your first question: the wound isn't real deep."

"That's good to hear. Do you know how the injury happened?"

He nodded. "I believe the squirrel had its foot stepped on."

She frowned. "Who would do something that mean?"

"I don't think it was done on purpose." Dr. Franklin reached up to scratch the side of his head, where several streaks of gray showed through his closely cropped brown hair. "Tommy Curtis brought the critter in, saying he'd found it lying beside a maple tree near his school. I have a hunch Tommy may have accidentally stepped on the squirrel."

"Will you keep it here until it's better?" she asked.

He grinned. "I thought maybe you'd like to take it home until it's ready to be set free, which should only be a few days from now, I'm guessing."

Melinda nodded eagerly. "I don't have many spare cages right now, but I did find an old one at a yard sale awhile back. I suppose I could keep him in that until his foot's healed."

"That's a good idea. I'll give you some ointment to put on the wound, and you can take the squirrel home with you this evening."

Melinda smiled as she donned her work apron. It felt good to know the doctor trusted her enough to care for the squirrel. Of course, if the animal's injuries were serious, she was sure Dr. Franklin would keep it at the clinic. "Guess I'd better get busy with the cleaning," she said.

"Before you get started, I'd like to ask you a question," Dr. Franklin said, stepping around the front of the counter.

"What is it?"

"I was wondering if you've had a chance to think over the

things we talked about a few weeks ago, concerning you becoming a vet."

She nodded. "I have thought about it, but—"

"Have you looked at the brochures I gave you on the school of veterinary medicine I attended in New Jersey?"

"I did read through the information, and I've been thinking a lot about it." Melinda pursed her lips. She had hidden the brochures under her mattress so her mother wouldn't see them, since she wasn't ready to talk to her folks about this yet. "The thought of becoming a vet is appealing," she admitted. "But it would mean getting a college education, and that doesn't fall in line with our Amish beliefs."

The doctor's eyebrows drew together. "I've lived in Seymour for several years and know most of the Amish in the area. Yet I still don't understand all their ways."

"We believe the Bible instructs us to be separate from the world," she explained. "We're not against basic education and learning from others, but our leaders feel that progressive education could lead to worldliness."

He took a step toward her. "So you're saying you've decided not to pursue a career in veterinary medicine?"

"No, that's not what I'm saying." Melinda swallowed hard. Just thinking about leaving home made her feel jittery, and talking about it with Dr. Franklin behind her parents' backs didn't seem right. "There's so much to be considered, and I haven't been able to think it all through. I haven't said anything to my folks about this yet, so I'd appreciate it if you didn't mention this to anyone."

"I understand. It's a big decision, so take your time, Melinda.

I promise I won't say a word to anyone until you've made up your mind and have told your family what you plan to do."

She nodded. "When I do finally decide, I'll let you know."

Noah opened the door of Swartz's Woodworking Shop, and the odor of freshly sanded wood tickled his nose, causing him to sneeze. He was glad the work he did at Hank's Christmas Tree Farm didn't require sanding. He stepped into the shop and discovered Gabe sanding the tops of some kitchen cabinets.

"Wie geht's?" Noah asked.

"I'm doing all right. How about you?"

"Getting along fairly well." Noah smiled. "I was heading to work and decided to stop and see if you've finished that birdhouse I want to give Melinda for her birthday."

Gabe nodded. "I finished it yesterday. It's right over there," he said, motioning to the shelf across from him.

Noah turned, and in a few strides, his long legs took him to the other side of the room, where he lifted the birdhouse from the shelf. "This is real nice," he said. "You did a fine job making it. I'm sure Melinda will be pleased."

Gabe's grin stretched from ear to ear. "I hope so. And I hope she'll like what I made for her, too."

"What might that be? Or is it a *geheemnis?*"

"It's not a secret I'd keep from you—just from Melinda until Saturday night." Gabe opened the cabinet door behind him and withdrew a small cardboard box. He reached inside and pulled out Melinda's present. "I carved this little deer and glued it to a chunk of wood, thinking maybe she could use it as a doorstop."

"I'm sure whatever my daughter does with the deer, it will be one of her most treasured gifts since it came from you." Noah couldn't help but smile when he saw how red Gabe's face had become. It was obvious the young man was in love with Melinda. "Looks like you're doing a good job with those," Noah said, pointing to the cabinets Gabe had been sanding when he'd entered the shop.

"One of our English neighbors ordered them a few weeks ago, and Pap gave me the job of finishing them up."

"Speaking of your daed, where is he this morning?"

"Still up at the house. Mom wanted him to go over the checkbook with her. I guess she found a mistake when the statement came from the bank in yesterday's mail." Gabe nodded toward the door. "I'm sure he'll be here soon if you'd like to wait around and say hello."

"I would like to, but if I don't head out now, I will be late for work." Noah moved over to the desk near the front door. "If you will get my bill, I will settle up with you and be on my way."

Gabe nodded and scurried over to the desk.

A few minutes later, with the bill paid and the birdhouse tucked inside a cardboard box, Noah headed for the door. "I'll look forward to seeing you and your folks at Melinda's party on Saturday evening."

"We'll be there right on time."

Noah chuckled under his breath as he headed for his buggy. *Oh to be young again and so much in love.* He figured it wouldn't be much longer until Gabe and Melinda would be announcing their intentions to get married.

As Gabe resumed sanding the cabinets, he thought about Melinda's upcoming birthday and hoped the week would go by quickly. He was eager to give Melinda the little fawn, which had turned out pretty well.

Sure hope I'll be able to spend a few minutes alone with her on Saturday night, Gabe thought. *We haven't been able to be by ourselves since I took her home from the gathering and we discovered her grandpa standing in the road.* At the rate things were going, Gabe wondered if he'd ever get the chance to ask Melinda to marry him.

"From the way you're swiping that sandpaper across the cabinet tops, there might not be anything left by the time you're done. I'd have to say your thoughts must be on something other than work this morning," Pap said, stepping up beside Gabe.

"I was thinking about this coming Saturday night."

"Looking forward to Melinda's birthday party, I imagine." Pap's blue eyes twinkled when he grinned at Gabe.

"Jah."

"It was nice of her folks to include your mamm and me in the invitation."

"We've known their family a long time, so I guess it's only natural that they'd want all three of us to be there."

"Probably would have asked your sisters to come if they were still living at home," Pap added.

Gabe nodded, wondering if his dad knew he and Melinda

were courting. He hadn't actually told his folks he was courting Melinda and planned to ask her to marry him, but he knew Pap was no dummy. Gabe figured his dad had probably put two and two together by now.

"Sure hope this nice weather holds out so we can have the party outside," Gabe commented.

Pap raked his fingers through the ends of his full brown beard, which was generously peppered with gray. "It's been a nice May so far. Makes me wish I had some free time to go fishing." He turned toward the rear of the shop with a shrug. "Well, time's a-wasting, so guess I'd best get back to work on that rocking chair Abe Yutzy ordered last week."

"Holler if you need any help."

"I appreciate the offer, but you'd better stick with the project you're working on now."

Gabe grimaced. "Say, Pap?"

"What is it, Gabe?"

"You think we might broaden the business to include more than just cabinets and basic furniture? I'd like the chance to work on some other things."

"I don't think so. We've got our hands full making what we do now."

Gabe gritted his teeth as his dad walked away. *Will he ever see me as capable? Will he ever let me try out some new things?*

He grabbed a fresh piece of sandpaper and gave the top of the cabinet a few more good swipes. *As soon as I get enough money saved up, I'm going to open my own woodworking business. When that happens, I plan to make a lot more things than just cabinets and a few pieces of furniture!*

When Melinda arrived home that evening with the squirrel she'd named Cinnamon, she headed straight for the barn. She set the cardboard box with the squirrel inside on a small wooden table and reached for a pair of leather gloves hanging on a nail. It wasn't tame like Reba seemed to be, and she didn't want to risk getting bitten by handling Cinnamon with her bare hands.

Melinda located the spare cage and reached inside the box to retrieve Cinnamon.

He didn't squirm or try to get away, probably because of his hurt foot. When she closed the door on the cage, she discovered that the latch was broken and wouldn't stay shut.

"I don't need you getting out, Cinnamon," Melinda muttered. "At least not until your foot is healed." She headed across the barn in search of some wire, but before she could locate it, Papa Noah stepped into the barn.

"*Gut-n-owed,*" he said with a smile. "How was your day?"

"Good evening to you, too," Melinda replied. "My day was fine until now."

"What's the trouble?"

Melinda pointed to the cage. "The latch on the cage door is broken, and I was looking for some wire to hold it shut."

Papa Noah moved over to the cage. "Where did you get the squirrel, and what happened to its foot?"

"I got him from Dr. Franklin. Some English boy in Seymour found him outside the schoolhouse, and Dr. Franklin thinks the poor critter's foot got stepped on."

"Why isn't the vet taking care of him instead of you?"

"The doctor did all he could, but he didn't want to turn Cinnamon loose until the wound had healed properly." Melinda grinned. "So he gave him to me for safekeeping."

"Couldn't the vet have kept the squirrel in a cage there at the veterinary clinic?"

"He probably would have, but all of the cages are full of other animals right now."

Papa Noah grunted as he shook his head. "If you're not careful, you're going to have so many critters around here that they'll take over the place." He motioned to the cage. "I guess if you keep him in there it will be all right, but we'll have to wire that door shut."

"That's what I was about to do, but I haven't been able to find any wire."

"I know right where it is." Papa Noah headed across the barn and flipped open the toolbox sitting on a shelf.

In short order, he had the cage door wired shut. "I didn't make it too tight, because I know you'll need to be able to undo it so you can get inside to give the squirrel food and water," he said.

"Danki. I appreciate the help."

"Should we head for the house and see what your mamm's got for supper?" he asked, nodding toward the barn door.

"You go ahead. I want to check on the raccoon and the baby goat before I come in."

He shrugged. "Okay, but don't be too long. I'm sure your mamm could use your help in the kitchen. You know how upset she gets when you spend too much time taking care of your critters."

Melinda knew all too well how Mama felt about her animal

friends. She'd never seemed to mind a couple of pets hanging around, but when Melinda had started bringing home creatures that lived in the woods, her mother had become less understanding.

"I won't be but a few minutes," she promised.

"Okay. See you at supper." Papa Noah lifted his hand and went out the door.

M elinda couldn't remember when she'd been so excited about one of her birthdays as this one. It wasn't turning nineteen that excited her so; it was knowing she would be able to spend the evening with Gabe.

"I wonder what he'll give me," she murmured as she stepped into a freshly ironed, blue cotton dress in preparation for the big event. She was sure it would be something he'd made. Gabe could take any plain piece of wood and turn it into something beautiful.

The twittering of birds outside Melinda's open window drew her attention outdoors. At least she knew that Cinnamon, the squirrel Dr. Franklin had put in her care, wasn't chasing any of the birds. This morning, she'd let the critter out of his cage for a bit and later caught him trying to eat at one of the bird feeders. After that, she'd put him back in the cage, and he would stay there until his foot was healed and she could set him free in the woods.

A warm breeze coming through Melinda's bedroom window made the dark curtains dance. She drew in a deep breath and headed downstairs, excited that her guests would be arriving soon.

Outside, she discovered Papa Noah lighting the barbecue. He'd set up two large tables with benches, and Mama had covered them with green plastic tablecloths.

"It looks like we're about ready," Melinda remarked to her stepfather.

"Now all we need is our guests," he said with a chuckle.

"They'll be here soon, I expect." Melinda took a seat on the end of the bench closest to the barbecue grill, where she could feel the heat already rising from the hot coals. "Where's Grandpa Hertzler? I thought he would be out here already."

Papa Noah blew out his breath with a puff of air that lifted the hair off his forehead. "I'm not sure what to do about him."

"You mean his forgetfulness?"

"Jah. I reminded my daed this morning about your birthday party, but when I went over to his side of the house a few minutes ago, I found him asleep in his favorite chair."

"Maybe he's just feeling tired."

"I thought that at first, but when I woke him and suggested he get ready for the party, he gave me a bewildered look. He didn't seem to have any idea what I was talking about."

Melinda frowned. "It's hard to understand why some days he seems pretty good and other days he barely knows who we are."

"Your mamm made him a doctor's appointment in Springfield. I'm hoping they'll run some tests that will help us know what's wrong."

"Sounds like a good idea."

"I hear a buggy rumbling up the driveway," Papa Noah said, glancing to the left. "Why don't you see who's the first to arrive?"

Melinda stood. "Jah, okay."

When she rounded the corner of the house, she was greeted by Gabe and his parents, Stephen and Leah Swartz.

Gabe offered her a friendly smile. "Happy birthday, Melinda."

"Happy birthday," Gabe's folks said in unison.

"Danki." Melinda motioned toward the house. "Papa Noah has the barbecue fired up, and Mama's in the kitchen. So feel free to go out back or inside, whichever you like."

"I believe I'll go in the house and see if there's anything I can do to help Faith," Leah said.

"And I'll head around back and find out what kind of meat Noah's grilling," Stephen put in.

As soon as Gabe's folks left, he stepped up beside Melinda. "You sure look pretty tonight."

Heat radiated up the back of Melinda's neck and spread quickly to her cheeks. "I don't think I look much different than the last time you saw me."

He leaned in closer until she could feel his warm breath tickle her ear. "You're the prettiest woman I know."

"Danki, Gabe."

"Do you want to open my gift now or wait until later?" he asked, lifting the paper sack he held in one hand.

"I guess it would be best to wait and open all my gifts at the same time."

"Jah, okay."

Gabe leaned closer and studied Melinda so intently her toes

curled inside her black leather shoes.

"Hey, Gabe! What are you up to?"

Melinda whirled around to face her brother. "Isaiah, you shouldn't sneak up on people like that."

"I wasn't sneakin'. I just happened to come around the house in time to see the two of you makin' eyes at each other."

Gabe ruffled Isaiah's hair. "You're right—we're caught."

"Why don't you go see if Papa Noah needs any help?" Melinda suggested.

Isaiah squinted. "I've never figured out why you call him that. Can't ya just say, 'Papa,' without addin' the Noah part?"

"I was seven years old when Mama married Papa Noah. He's been like a daed to me all these years, but he's not my real father. So I've always thought it best to call him Papa Noah, and he's never complained or asked me to call him anything else."

"Suit yourself," Isaiah said with a shrug. "Guess I'll mosey around back and see what's cookin'."

"We'll be there soon," Melinda called to his retreating form.

Gabe reached for Melinda's hand and drew her aside. "As I was saying before Isaiah came along—"

Two more buggies rolled into the yard just then, and Gabe released a moan. "Guess what I wanted to say will have to wait until later." He gave Melinda's hand a gentle squeeze. "Maybe after the party winds down, we can take a walk."

She nodded. "I'd like that."

As Susie stepped down from her parents' buggy, she spotted

Melinda and Gabe holding hands as they stood in the yard together. *Oh, how I wish I had a boyfriend*, she thought dismally. *If there was only someone to hold my hand and look at me with the tenderness I see whenever Gabe looks at Melinda.*

"Something sure smells good," Susie's dad said, sniffing the air. "I'll bet Noah's been cooking up a storm."

"Besides whatever meat he's barbecuing, it's a pretty good guess that either he or Faith has made some other tasty dishes," Mama put in.

Papa smacked his lips. "When I talked to Melinda the other day, she said there would be a batch of homemade ice cream to go with the cake Noah baked for her birthday."

"That sounds good to me," Mama said with a smile. "Don't you think it sounds good, daughter?"

Susie shrugged.

"What are you looking so glum about?" Papa asked as he un-hitched the horse from their buggy. "We're at a party—a celebration of Melinda's nineteenth birthday. You ought to be smiling, not frowning like you've got a bad toothache, for goodness' sake."

Susie forced her lips to form a smile. "Is that better?"

"Much." Mama nudged Susie with her elbow. "Let's head for the house and see if Faith needs our help with anything while your daed gets the horse put in the corral."

As they started walking toward Faith and Noah's house, Susie cast a quick glance in the birthday girl's direction. Melinda was so busy talking to Gabe that she hadn't even noticed them. Susie was tempted to stop and say a few words, but she decided Melinda might not appreciate having her conversation with Gabe interrupted. So she hurried to the house behind her mother, knowing the best thing she could do to get her jealousy under control was to keep her hands busy.

Melinda bit into a piece of moist chocolate cake and savored the moment. Her family and closest friends were here: Gabe and his folks; Grandpa and Grandma Stutzman; Susie; Barbara and Paul Hilty with their six children; and her immediate family—Mama, Papa Noah, Isaiah, and Grandpa Hertzler.

"Why don't you open your gifts now, Melinda?" Mama suggested.

Isaiah bobbed his head up and down and said, "Let's see what you got, sister."

Melinda blotted her lips on the paper napkin that had been lying in her lap. "Which one shall I open first?"

"Why don't you start with Susie's?" Grandma nudged Susie's arm. "Run on out to the buggy and get it."

Susie left the picnic table and hurried across the yard. A few minutes later, she returned carrying a small cardboard box, which she placed in Melinda's lap. "Happy birthday. I hope you like it."

Melinda opened the flaps on the box and grinned when a pair of pretty blue eyes stared up at her and a pathetic meow escaped the tiny white kitten's mouth. "She looks like a fluffy ball of snow," Melinda said as she lifted the kitten out of the box and nuzzled its little pink nose. "I think I'll call her 'Snow.' "

Susie grinned from ear to ear. It was the first genuine smile Melinda had seen her aunt give all evening. "I'm glad you like it,

Melinda. It's one of Daisy's busslin."

"Danki," Melinda said.

"I can hold the kitten while you open the rest of your gifts," Susie offered. "That way you'll have both hands free."

Melinda handed the kitten to Susie, and Susie took a seat on the bench to the left of Melinda. Gabe occupied the spot to Melinda's right. "Who wants to be next?" Melinda asked, glancing around the table.

"I will." Papa Noah placed a cardboard box on the picnic table in front of Melinda. "I had this made especially for you, and after you see what it is, you'll probably know who made it."

Melinda lifted the flaps on the box. Inside she discovered an ornate birdhouse with a little door on it. She looked at Papa Noah and smiled. "Danki. I really like it."

"I'm glad you do, and now you can thank Gabe for all his hard work."

"You made this for me?" Melinda asked, glancing over at Gabe.

He nodded and smiled, looking rather pleased with himself.

She opened the little door on the birdhouse and peered inside. "What's this?"

Gabe's smile widened. "It's a separate compartment I added so we can keep sending notes to each other and not have to worry about the birds making a nest on top of our messages."

"That's a good idea," she said.

"Why don't you open mine next?" Gabe handed Melinda a smaller cardboard box. "I hope you like it."

With mounting excitement, Melinda tore open the box. Her breath caught in her throat when she lifted out a little carved fawn that had been glued to a small piece of wood. "It's beautiful, Gabe. Danki so much."

He smiled and reached under the table to take her hand. "I attached the piece of wood to the deer, thinking you might be able to use it as a doorstop."

"That's a good idea, but it's so nice, rather than using it as a doorstop, I might decide to set it on my dresser so I can look at it every morning when I first get out of bed."

Melinda was about to open the rest of her gifts, but the wind became restless and clouds raced across the sky. Minutes later, it started to rain. Everyone grabbed something off the table and dashed for the house.

There goes my walk with Gabe. It doesn't look like we'll get any time alone tonight, Melinda thought with regret.

"Whew! What a downpour," Mama said as they entered the kitchen. "It amazes me how swiftly the weather can change during the spring."

Melinda placed her kitten on the floor, and it scurried under the stove. The older guests found seats around the kitchen table, while the younger ones went to the living room to play games. Melinda, Gabe, Susie, and Aaron headed outside to watch the storm from the safety of the front porch.

"I like watching the way the *wedderleech* zigzags across the sky," Gabe commented with a sweep of his hand.

"I've always been afraid of the *dunner,*" Susie put in.

"It's not the thunder that can hurt you," Aaron asserted. "It's those bolts of dangerous lightning you've got to worry about."

Melinda shivered and rubbed her hands briskly over her arms.

"Are you cold?" Gabe asked in a tone of concern.

"A little. Guess I should have grabbed a sweater before coming outside."

"Want me to get it for you?"

Melinda raised her voice to be heard over the thud of more thunder. "I'll be okay." She glanced nervously into the yard. "I hope all my critters are doing okay. Most animals don't like storms."

"At least we know Snow's all right," Susie put in. "She's probably curled up in someone's lap by now."

Aaron turned around. "I'm tired of watching the rain. Think I'll head back inside and see what the kinner are doing."

"Maybe I should, too," Susie said with a nod.

Melinda smiled. She figured their friends had decided to give her and Gabe some time alone. Gabe must have known also, for he reached for her hand and gave it a gentle squeeze.

As soon as Aaron and Susie entered the house, Gabe led Melinda over to the porch swing. Once they were seated, he pulled her close to his side. "Happy birthday, Melinda." He lowered his head and brushed his lips against hers.

Melinda melted into his embrace. Their first kiss was even sweeter than she had expected.

Suddenly the front door opened, and Isaiah stuck his head out. "Oh, yuck! I'll never kiss any girl 'cept Mama."

Melinda's cheeks burned hot as she shook her finger. "You say one word about what you saw here, and I'll tell Papa Noah that your dog ate out of a pie pan the other day."

"Aw, Jericho didn't hurt a thing." Isaiah wrinkled his nose. "Besides, the plate got washed."

Melinda jumped up, ready to tell her little brother what she thought of his juvenile antics, but a flash of fur darted over her foot, raced across the porch, and dove inside the open doorway.

"Cinnamon!" she shouted. "How did you get out of your cage?"

Chapter 8

Melinda dashed into the house after the runaway squirrel, and Gabe followed right on her heels. He couldn't believe the way things were going tonight. First, the rain had put a damper on their plans to take a walk. Then Melinda's younger brother had interrupted them when Gabe was on the verge of proposing. Now a silly critter had come along and ruined things.

Pandemonium broke out as soon as they entered the living room. Not only was the squirrel skittering all over the place, but Melinda's new kitten seemed to be the squirrel's prey. The two animals circled the room, darting under chairs, banging into walls, and sliding across the hardwood floor. When Snow crawled under the braided oval throw rug, Cinnamon pounced on her. The kitten sailed out and zipped to the other side of the room.

"You get the cat, and I'll corner the squirrel," Gabe shouted to Melinda as he waved his hands.

Aaron, Susie, and the children, who'd been playing games in the adjoining room, came on the scene and became part of the chase, but no one had any luck catching either animal.

"Have you got any paper sacks?" Gabe called to Isaiah.

"I think there's some in the kitchen."

"Get four of the biggest ones you can find!"

When Isaiah returned a few minutes later, the older folks were with him.

"What's going on here?" Noah asked with a look of concern. "Isaiah said something about a squirrel."

"Cinnamon got out of his cage and ended up in the house," Melinda panted. "Now he's after Snow."

"The squirrel's gonna eat the cat," five-year-old Emma hollered. When Cinnamon whizzed past the child, she jumped, squealed, and ran for cover behind her mother's long green dress.

"Settle down," Barbara said, taking hold of Emma's hand. "Let's go to the kitchen and let the others handle this."

"She needs our help."

"We're gonna have to trap 'em."

"They're just a couple of desperate critters."

"Come here, Snow."

"Easy now, Cinnamon."

Everyone spoke at once, and the animals kept circling the living room. Finally, Noah held up his hands. "Everybody, please calm down." He turned to Isaiah. "What are the paper sacks for?"

The boy shrugged. "I don't know. Gabe asked me to get 'em."

Gabe swiped at the sweat beaded on his forehead. "I figured if the four of us each took a sack, we might be able to trap Cinnamon or Snow inside one of the bags."

"I believe I have a better plan." Noah turned back to Isaiah. "Please go to the kitchen and get a broom from the utility closet."

Melinda's eyes grew huge as silver dollars as she grasped her stepfather's arm. "I hope you're not going to smack either one of my pets."

Faith spoke up. "Only one of them is a pet, Melinda, and I'm sure your daed wouldn't intentionally hurt either animal."

Grandpa Hertzler sank into the closest chair. "Would ya put that broom away? I hate housework; always did." He shook his head, and his white beard moved back and forth across his chest like the pendulum on the clock above the fireplace.

"We're not going to clean house, Pop," Noah said. "And I don't plan to do the animals any harm." He nodded at Isaiah. "Now hurry and get me that broom."

The boy shoved the paper sacks at Gabe and scurried out of the room.

Gabe handed one sack to Melinda, one to Aaron, one to Susie, and kept the one for himself. He crouched down and opened his sack, telling the others to do the same. "If either the cat or the squirrel comes your way, try to scoop it into your bag."

Noah shook his head. "I don't think that's going to work. I believe my way's better." He cupped his hands around his mouth. "Isaiah, where is that broom?"

"I'll see what's keeping him," Melinda's mother offered.

Just then, Isaiah dashed into the room, flung the broom at

his father, and scuttled off to one side with an expectant look on his face.

"Somebody, open the front door!"

Melinda rushed to do as her stepfather had commanded.

Gabe groaned. Whatever Noah had in mind, he was sure it would fail. He remained on his knees, waiting for either the squirrel or the kitten to pass his way again. A few seconds later, Cinnamon skittered across the floor in front of Gabe's paper sack, and Noah's broom swooshed past the critter's bushy tail. Cinnamon took off like a flash of lightning and zipped through the open doorway.

With a pathetic meow, the cat darted under the sofa, and no amount of coaxing on Melinda's part could bring her out.

"Just leave her be," Noah said as he headed for the kitchen with the other adults. "She'll come out when she's good and ready."

As Gabe stood, his heart went out to Melinda. She looked so dejected, sitting with her head down and her shoulders slumped. What had started out to be a nice birthday party had turned into utter mayhem.

"Come on, the excitement's over. Let's head back to the dining room and finish those games we started," Aaron said to the others.

"I'm going to the kitchen to get more cake," Isaiah announced.

The children and teens filed out of the room, but Melinda stayed in a kneeling position as she continued to call her kitten. "Here, Snow. You can come out now. The squirrel is gone."

Gabe shifted from one foot to the other, unsure of what to do. He thought about offering to go outside and look for the squirrel but knew that would be ridiculous. Cinnamon was probably halfway to Seymour by now.

For lack of anything better to do, he flopped into a chair and sat with his arms folded, staring out the window at the pouring rain and streaks of lightning while he mulled things over.

"I can't believe the way Melinda carried on just 'cause her dumm old *bussli* got chased by an *eechhaas*," Isaiah said as he dropped into a chair at the kitchen table.

Faith turned from the refrigerator, where she'd gone to get a glass of iced tea for her mother. "Your sister did overreact a bit, but if she hadn't brought that silly squirrel home in the first place, the whole incident never would have happened."

"I'm just glad nothing happened to the bussli," Faith's mother put in as she pulled out a chair and sat down. "A wild squirrel is no match for a helpless little kitten."

Isaiah grunted. "If you ask me, Melinda cares way too much about all the animals she brings home."

Faith couldn't argue with that, although it wasn't as if Melinda's squirrel had gotten into the house and caused such havoc on purpose.

"I think we'd better find another topic of conversation," she said as she started across the room with the glass of iced tea in her hand.

Isaiah pointed to the chocolate cake sitting on the counter. "Can I have another piece of that?"

Faith nodded. "Help yourself."

Isaiah grabbed a hunk of cake and headed back to the dining room to join the other children.

Faith handed her mother the glass of iced tea then took a seat in the empty chair beside Noah. "There's still plenty of cake left if anyone wants some."

Faith's mother patted her stomach. "None for me. Thanks to Noah being such a good cook, I ate way too much supper."

Noah's ears turned pink. "It was nothing special."

"Jah, it was." Gabe's mother smiled. "But then, I would enjoy eating most anything I didn't have to cook."

Everyone laughed, and Gabe's father needled her with his elbow. "If you're hoping I'll start doing the baking and cooking, you'd better think again, Leah, because I can barely boil water."

"My wife, Ida, can sure cook up a storm," Noah's dad put in. "Fact is, she makes the best rhubarb-strawberry jam around."

Faith glanced over at Noah to gauge his reaction, but his placid expression gave no indication as to what he might be thinking. Was Noah embarrassed by his dad's apparent loss of memory, or did he think it best not to make an issue of it in front of their company?

"Ida couldn't come to the party tonight," Noah's dad went on to say. "She came down with a cold last night."

Faith's mother looked over at her with a strange expression, and Gabe's mother did, too. The men just sat there with stony faces. Finally, Noah stood and moved to the other side of the table, where his father sat. "You look tired, Pop. Why don't you let me walk you home?"

With a grunt, the older man rose from his chair and shuffled out the door behind Noah.

"The poor man's memory really seems to be failing him." Faith swallowed against the lump in her throat. She hoped nothing like this ever happened to her or Noah when they got old.

"Come, Snow. Here, kitty, kitty. Come out from under the sofa." When the kitten didn't budge, Melinda looked up at Gabe, hoping he might have a suggestion.

He shrugged. "You heard what your daed said. Leave the cat be. She'll come out on her own when she's ready."

Melinda released a sigh. "That could be hours from now. Snow's really scared."

"I'll tell you what," Gabe said as he scrambled to his feet. "Why don't we go out on the porch and watch the rain? If there's no one in the living room, the cat will be more apt to come out."

"You could be right."

Gabe opened the front door, and Melinda followed him outside.

"I hope Cinnamon's okay," she murmured. "He's probably as frightened as Snow seems to be."

"Maybe so, but you need to remember that the critter's a wild animal. I'm sure he'll be fine on his own."

"I suppose. His foot's nearly healed, so he should be okay even if he ran into the woods." Melinda leaned on the porch railing and stared into the yard. "Some party this turned out to be."

Gabe slipped his arm around her waist. "It'll be one you

won't likely forget, that's for certain sure."

She nodded. "You're right about that."

"Uh—Melinda, I've been wanting to ask you a question."

Melinda turned to face him. "What did you want to ask?"

He reached up and stroked the side of her face with his finger. "I love you, Melinda. I have for a long time."

"I—I love you, too." Melinda could barely get the words out, her throat felt so dry.

"Would you marry me this fall?"

Melinda swallowed around the lump in her throat. She had to think—had to stop this roaring rush of emotions and hold on to reason. If she accepted his proposal without telling him about Dr. Franklin's suggestion that she become a vet, it would be even harder to tell him later on. *I must tell Gabe now. I shouldn't wait any longer.*

Before Melinda could get the words out, Gabe leaned down and kissed her so tenderly she almost melted into his arms. When the kiss ended, he whispered, "If you marry me, I'll be the happiest man in the world."

Her eyes filled with tears and splashed onto her cheeks. He reached up to wipe them away. "I hope those are tears of joy."

She nodded. "I do want to marry you, Gabe, but—"

"I'm glad, and I promise to be the best husband in all of Webster County." He reached for her hand. "The rain's letting up, so let's take a walk now."

As the rush of water in the drainpipes became mere drops from the eaves, Melinda's resolve to tell Gabe about Dr. Franklin's suggestion for her future melted away. All she wanted to do was enjoy the time they had together.

"Think I'll ask Aaron to be one of my attendants at the wedding," Gabe said as they headed down the driveway, hand in hand. "Will you ask Susie to be one of yours?"

Melinda nodded. "Probably so, since I have no sisters."

"We'll each need one more person to stand up for us. Maybe we could ask one of our cousins."

"There's plenty of time to decide."

"Jah."

As they walked on, Melinda noticed the misty clouds that seemed as if they were clinging to earth. On both sides of the driveway, leaves littered the ground where the wet wind had spun and stuck them in place. It almost seemed as if she were in a dream. *What would Gabe say if he knew what I was thinking of doing? Would he break our engagement as quickly as he'd proposed?*

"Did you get everything you wanted for your birthday?" Gabe asked, breaking into her thoughts. "Or is there some secret present you were hoping to get and didn't?"

"Well, I—" Melinda halted.

"What's wrong? Why'd you stop walking?"

"Don't move a muscle."

Gabe froze. "Is there a poisonous snake underfoot?" he rasped.

"Relax; it's not a snake." She nudged his arm. "Aren't they sweet?"

"What?"

"Twin fawns, to your left."

Gabe turned his head just as two young deer walked out of the bushes, not three feet away.

Melinda inched closer to the deer.

"Wh–what are you doing?"

"Shh. . ."

She took a few more steps and dropped to her knees.

One of the fawns held back, but the other deer moved closer.

Melinda held her breath. Then the most surprising thing happened. The fawn came right up to her and licked the end of her chin.

When the deer moved away and disappeared into the brush, she touched the spot on her chin where the fawn had licked. "Did you see that, Gabe?" she murmured. "The little deer gave me a birthday kiss."

Chapter 9

Over the next several weeks, Melinda's emotions swung from elation over Gabe's marriage proposal to frustration because she hadn't yet told him that she was considering leaving the Amish faith to pursue a career in veterinary medicine. She knew she needed to say something soon. Although they'd agreed not to tell anyone about their betrothal until they had set a wedding date, speculation about their courtship was bound to get around. And a few weeks before their wedding, they would be officially published during a church service; then everyone would know of their plans.

To make matters worse, Dr. Franklin had recently given Melinda another orphaned raccoon she'd named Rhoda, and every day at work, the doctor continued to tell Melinda what a God-given talent she'd been given when it came to working with animals. Melinda felt that way, too. More and more she felt the pull to become a veterinarian so she could help as many animals as possible. Yet she loved Gabe and wanted to be his wife. She also loved her family and knew how hard it would be if she decided to leave them. Sometimes Melinda felt like a rope during a game of tug-o-war, being pulled first one way and then the other.

As Melinda bent over the rhubarb patch in their garden one Friday morning in early June, she made a decision. *I must find out if Gabe would be willing to leave the Amish faith with me. If we leave together, it will be a little easier, but if I have to do it on my own, I'm not sure I can.*

"Melinda, have you got enough rhubarb yet?" Grandpa called from the back porch, where he stood with a pot holder in his hand.

Melinda smiled and waved. "Almost. I'll be there with it soon!"

Grandpa waved back at her and returned to the house. He was doing better these days, and Melinda was pleased.

Two weeks ago, Papa Noah and Mama had taken him to see a specialist in Springfield. After numerous tests had been run, it was determined that Grandpa's loss of memory was due in part to a malfunctioning thyroid. The doctor said it could be treated with medication, which was good news. Grandpa also had low blood sugar, which could be controlled by his diet. Those two things, coupled with the fact that he'd never gotten over Grandma's death, had put him in a state of depression and caused some occasional memory loss.

Melinda was sure things would be better now. Grandpa had recently begun helping Mama make jams and preserves to sell at the farmers' market, which seemed to ease his sadness. His mind appeared to be sharper already, too. It was a real surprise to see Grandpa spending time in the kitchen, though. Melinda remembered how he used to avoid doing anything related to cooking. She'd heard him tell Papa Noah how odd he thought it was that his youngest son enjoyed baking so much. But now that Grandpa was making delicious jams and jellies, he acted like he'd been interested in working in the kitchen for a good long time.

Melinda chuckled to herself. "It just goes to show, no one's ever too old to change their mind about some things."

When Melinda had picked the last stalks of rhubarb, she ran up to the house. As soon as she had deposited the rhubarb into the kitchen sink, she headed back outside to check the birdhouse Papa Noah had given her as a birthday present.

"Maybe there will be a note from Gabe," she murmured. It had been several days since she'd heard from him, and she was eager to know when they would be going on another date. Seeing him only at their every-other-week preaching services didn't give them any privacy, and they needed to talk without anyone overhearing their conversation.

When Melinda reached the double-sided birdhouse, she was pleased to hear some baby birds peeping from one end. Careful not to disturb the little sparrows, she lifted the lid on the side that was now her and Gabe's message box. She was equally pleased to see that a note was waiting for her.

Dear Melinda,
Since the weather has been so warm, I thought it would be nice to go for a drive this evening after supper. Let me know if

*you'll be free or not. I'll be back to check the message box later
this afternoon.*

Happily yours,
Gabe

Melinda reached inside the box to retrieve the pencil and
tablet they kept there and then scrawled a note in reply.

Dear Gabe,
*Tonight should be fine. Come by around seven. I'm looking
forward to our time together, as we have some important things
to talk about.*

Yours fawnly,
Melinda

"What do you think of this hunk of walnut for the gun stock I'm
planning to make?" Gabe asked as he held the item in question
out for his dad's inspection.

Pap nodded and ran his fingers over the block of wood.
"Looks like it'll work out fine. Always did like to have a hunting
gun with a well-made stock."

Gabe smiled. *Maybe this will show him I'm able to make more
than simple cabinets, birdhouses, and feeders.*

"Are you expecting to do some hunting this fall?" his father
questioned.

"Jah, and I hope to use my new gun."

"Sounds good, but any hunting you want to do will have to

be done on your day off or after the shop is closed for the day."
Pap picked up a stack of work orders and thumbed through
them quickly. "We need to get busy with these jobs. You'll have
to work on your gun stock during your free time, too."

Gabe frowned but set the piece of wood aside. If he worked
on his own projects after hours, he would have less time to court
Melinda.

He thought about the note he'd left her earlier, saying he
would be by this evening to take her for a buggy ride.

Guess I could run over to her place during lunch and leave her
another note saying I can't take her for a ride after all. Gabe pondered
the idea a moment then shook his head. *No way! Melinda comes*
first. Hunting season is several months away. I can work on the gun
stock some other time.

Melinda had just started setting the table for supper when Papa
Noah entered the kitchen wearing a worried expression on his
face.

"Where's your mamm?" he asked.

"Over at Grandpa Hertzler's side of the house. They're
finishing up with the rhubarb-strawberry jam they've been
making today."

"Do you know if we've got any hydrogen peroxide in the
house?"

"I think there's some in the cupboard above the sink. What
do you need it for?"

"That horse I bought a few days ago has a cut on her back

leg. At first, I thought I'd have to call the vet, but after checking things over real good, I realized the cut isn't too deep. I think it's something I can tend to myself."

"She didn't have a cut leg when you bought her, I hope."

He shook his head and ambled across the room to the cupboard. "I believe she may have gouged it on the fence. Probably trying to get out."

Melinda felt immediate concern. "She's not happy here? Is that what you think, Papa Noah?"

He pulled the bottle of peroxide down and turned around. "Looks like it. If I had more free time to spend with her, she might feel calmer and at home already. Between my job at the tree farm and all the chores I have to do here, there aren't enough hours in the day."

Melinda placed the last glass on the table and moved toward her stepfather. "I could doctor the wound and work with the horse to get her calmed down and more comfortable here. I'm good with animals, Papa Noah—you know that."

"Of course you are, but I don't think—"

"Please, let me try. I'll show Nellie some attention so she learns to like it here, and I'll tend that cut on her leg. She'll be good as new in no time."

Papa Noah's furrowed brows let Melinda know he was at least thinking on the idea.

"I'll squeeze it in between chores here and my job at the veterinary clinic." She clasped his arm. "Please, Papa Noah."

He finally smiled and handed her the bottle of peroxide. "Okay, then, you can start right now."

Melinda sprinted for the door. "Tell Mama I've got the

burner on the stove turned to low, and I'll be back in time to help her serve up the stew that's cooking for supper."

"Did Papa Noah tell you that I'll be tending his new horse that's got a cut on its back leg?" Melinda asked Faith as they sat at the table eating supper later that evening.

Faith grimaced and glanced over at Noah. "Don't you think you should ask the vet to take a look at the horse rather than allowing Melinda to play doctor?"

"I don't think it's anything too serious." Noah shrugged. "Besides, I know what a way Melinda has with animals, and I figured I'd let her see what she can do first."

"She'll probably end up bringing the horse into the house." Isaiah nudged Melinda in the ribs with his elbow. "First a chicken then a squirrel. I figure a horse must be next on your list."

"I have no intention of bringing Papa Noah's horse into the house." Melinda pursed her lips and squinted at Isaiah. "I think you need to eat what's on your plate and mind your own business."

Isaiah scrunched up his nose and glared at her. "You ain't my boss, sister."

"Never said I was."

"But you're always bossin' me around."

"Am not."

"Are so."

"No, I—"

Noah clapped his hands together and everyone jumped.

Noah rarely got upset, but when he did, he meant business.

"I don't want to hear any more silly bickering," he said. "I've given Melinda permission to doctor the horse, and she'll be doing it in the barn. So this whole conversation you two have been having is just plain *lecherich.*"

"I agree," Faith said with a nod. "For that matter, most arguments are ridiculous."

Isaiah gave Melinda one more scathing glare; then he grabbed his fork and popped a hunk of stew meat into his mouth.

Faith didn't know why Melinda had become so testy lately. It made her wonder if there was more going on than just the usual bickering between brother and sister. Well, now that Noah had laid down the law, maybe they could eat in peace.

Gabe whistled the whole way over to Melinda's house. He could hardly wait to spend time with her and talk about their future. The summer months would go by quickly; soon it would be time for their wedding. Of course, they hadn't set a date yet, so he didn't know exactly which month it would be.

"If I had my own business, I would feel more prepared for marriage," he mumbled. "I wonder how long I'll have to keep working for Pap before I have enough money saved up to go out on my own." Gabe had looked at a couple of places to rent, but the owners of the buildings were asking too much, and he didn't think his dad would take to the idea of him building a shop right there on the same property as his place of business.

I need to be patient and pray about this more, Gabe decided.

When Gabe pulled into the Hertzlers' front yard, he spotted Isaiah on the lawn playing with his beagle hound, Jericho. The boy had received the dog as a birthday present last year from Noah's boss, Hank Osborn, who raised hound dogs, as well as acres of pine trees. Gabe used to enjoy visiting there when he was a boy, but he hadn't gone to the Christmas tree farm in sometime.

Isaiah waved when he spotted Gabe, and Gabe lifted his hand in response. "Where's Melinda? I hope she's ready for our date."

The boy turned his palms upward. "Don't know nothin' about no date, but Melinda's out in the barn with Papa's new horse."

Gabe figured Melinda had probably gone there to pass the time while she waited for him. He guided his horse to the hitching rail and pulled on the reins. Then he jumped down, secured the animal, and sprinted for the barn.

He found Melinda inside one of the stalls on her knees next to a nice-looking gray-and-white mare. "Are you ready for our ride?" he called.

She stood and smoothed the wrinkles in her long green dress. "Oh, Gabe, I don't think I can go with you tonight."

"How come?"

"Didn't you get my two notes?"

His face warmed. "Uh—I forgot to check the birdhouse on my way in. What did your notes say?"

"The first note I wrote said I could go, but since then, something has come up, so I wrote you a second note, figuring you'd look in the birdhouse before coming up to the house."

His eyebrows drew together. "What's come up that would keep you from going for a ride with me?"

She pointed to the horse. "Nellie has a cut on her back leg. I tended it before supper. She's been acting kind of spooky and hasn't adjusted to her new surroundings yet, so after we ate, I came back to the barn to see that she remains calm and doesn't start her wound bleeding again."

Gabe folded his arms as they exchanged pointed stares. "I hope you understand," she said with a lift of her chin. "I don't."

"Have you no concern for Papa Noah's horse?"

"It's not that I don't care. I just don't see why it's your job to nursemaid the animal. Shouldn't the vet be doing that?"

"Now you sound like my mamm." Melinda stroked the horse's ears. "If the cut were deeper and needed stitches, Papa Noah would have called Dr. Franklin. But it's not bad enough for stitches, which is why he asked me to tend Nellie's leg."

"That's fine," Gabe said through tight lips, "but how is staying here going to help her?"

Melinda left the stall and moved to his side. "The horse is calmer when I'm here, and I'm just starting to gain some headway with her."

Gabe shrugged as frustration and disappointment boiled inside his chest like a kettle of hot water left unattended on the stove. "Sure, whatever. If your daed's horse is more important than me, then I guess that's just the way it is." He turned and started to walk away, but she grabbed hold of his arm.

"Please don't leave mad. You could stay and help me with the horse."

He swung around. "I can't believe you'd expect me to spend this warm summer evening cooped up in the stuffy barn with a sweaty animal that isn't even mine."

Tears gathered in the corners of Melinda's eyes, and it was nearly Gabe's undoing. He hadn't meant to make her cry. Hadn't meant to be so harsh or unwilling to help, either. One of the things that had originally attracted him to Melinda was her caring attitude and sensitivity toward hurting animals, and here he was scolding her for it.

Gabe pulled Melinda into his arms. "I'm sorry. Let's not fight, okay?"

She sniffed. "I don't want to. I want us to always be happy. But if you don't understand my desire to work with animals, then I don't see how—"

He stopped her rush of words with a kiss, and any shred of anger he'd felt earlier fell away like wood chips beneath the sander. "I love you, Melinda."

"I love you, too."

"How about tomorrow night? Will you be able to go for a buggy ride with me then?"

"I–I hope so."

Gabe motioned toward the horse's stall. "How about if I stay and help you cross tie the horse so she won't move around so much?"

She grinned up at him. "That would be *wunderbaar*."

Chapter 10

Melinda sat at the kitchen table, reading a passage from her Bible out loud. " 'Peace I leave with you, my peace I give unto you: not as the world giveth, give I unto you. Let not your heart be troubled, neither let it be afraid.' "

She closed her eyes. *In my heart there is no peace, Lord. Help me make this agonizing decision about becoming a vet, and give me the courage and opportunity to speak with Gabe about it on our buggy ride tonight. I can't decide what I should do until I know how he feels about things.*

Melinda knew she should have told Gabe last night when they'd spent time in the barn with Nellie. But after having that one disagreement, she'd been afraid to bring up anything that might cause more dissension.

"Are you about ready to help me and Grandpa make jam?"

Mama asked, pulling Melinda's thoughts aside. "He would like us to go over to his place as soon as we can."

Melinda nodded. "I'll be able to help for a while, but Dr. Franklin needs me at the clinic this afternoon."

"I'm sure we can get most of it done by noon."

Melinda had just closed her Bible when Isaiah bolted through the back door, grinning from ear to ear. "Look what I found!" he said, holding out his hands.

Mama's face turned pale, and she trembled. "Isaiah Hertzler, get that snake out of my house!"

He glanced at the reptile and frowned. "It's dead, Mama. Found it down in the root cellar, and it wasn't movin' a lick."

"So that was a reason to bring the creature in here?"

"I don't see why you're afraid of a dead garter snake. It can't hurt ya none."

"Isaiah—" Mama's tone was one of warning, and Melinda held her breath and waited to see what her little brother would do.

"All right, all right." Isaiah turned toward the door but suddenly whirled back. "I'm thirsty and need a glass of water. I'll get one real quick and be gone, okay?" Without waiting for Mama's reply, he plopped the snake on the floor, grabbed a glass from the cupboard, and headed for the kitchen sink. He had no more than turned on the faucet when Mama's shrill scream ricocheted off the walls.

Melinda's attention was immediately drawn to the creature Isaiah had dropped. Not only was the snake very much alive, but it was slithering across the linoleum toward the table.

Mama hollered again and jumped onto a chair. "You said

it was dead, Isaiah!"

"Guess it was only sleepin'." Isaiah stood there laughing until tears rolled down his cheeks.

"It's not the least bit funny," Mama said. "I want you to pick up that snake and haul it back outside where it belongs."

Isaiah took a few steps backward and shook his head. "No way! I ain't about to touch him."

"Why not?"

"He might bite me."

"You weren't worried about that when you lugged him into the house."

"I thought he was dead."

"Garter snakes aren't poisonous," Melinda put in.

"Maybe not, but its bite could still hurt," Isaiah retorted.

"If you're not going to do as I say, then go on up to your room. And don't come out until I say you can," Mama said, shaking her finger at Isaiah.

Isaiah frowned. "But that might be hours from now."

"Would you rather go to the woodshed and receive a *bletsching*?"

"No, Mama." He turned and fled from the room.

Melinda could hardly believe her brother was acting like such a baby. If she'd been Mama, she would have given him that spanking she had threatened.

"It's bad enough that we have to put up with all your critters. We sure don't need your *bruder* lugging snakes into the house." Mama squinted at Melinda. "See what kind of example you've set for Isaiah?"

Melinda cringed. Why was she being blamed for this? She

opened her mouth to ask that question, but Mama cut her off.

"Are you just going to stand there, or did you plan to help me get rid of this horrible creature?" Mama asked, pointing a shaking finger at the snake.

Melinda bent down, grabbed hold of the snake, and hurried out the door. Once outside, she set the snake on the ground and watched it slither toward the woods. *If I leave home to become a vet, Mama won't have to put up with all my critters or worry about me influencing Isaiah in the wrong way.*

She stood staring at the stately pine trees behind their place and breathing in the fresh outdoor scent. *I wish I didn't have to go back inside and help Mama and Grandpa make jam. I'd much rather spend my morning in the woods where I can draw, watch for deer, and think about my future.* Melinda sighed and turned around. Her responsibilities came first, despite her deep longings.

With a feeling of anticipation, Gabe headed down the road in his buggy toward the Hertzlers' place. He'd been busy in the shop all day and hadn't been able to get away long enough to leave Melinda a note to confirm their buggy ride.

"I hope she's not still doctoring that horse's leg," Gabe muttered.

When Gabe pulled into the Hertzlers', he jumped down from the buggy and hitched the horse to the rail near the barn. As he stood on the front porch, ready to knock on the screen door, he heard loud voices coming from inside the house.

"Melinda, how many times have we told you about bringing

your critters into the house?" Gabe recognized Noah's voice, and he sounded upset.

"Only your kitten is allowed inside," Faith chimed in. "And sometimes even she causes problems."

"I've told her that already, but then she never listens to nothin' I have to say," Melinda's little brother added.

It sounded like Melinda's folks were miffed at her. If that was the case, Gabe figured she probably wouldn't be allowed to go out with him. Would he suffer another disappointment tonight? *Maybe I should turn around and head back home.*

"Reba and Rhoda were fighting in the cage they share," Melinda said.

"Why wasn't Reba in her own cage?" her stepfather questioned.

"The latch won't stay shut, and she keeps chewing the wire and getting out, the same way the squirrel did the night of my birthday party."

Gabe drew in a deep breath and blew it out quickly. *I knew I should have had a talk with her about releasing that raccoon into the woods. I'd better see if I can help in some way.*

He lifted his hand and knocked on the screen door.

"Someone's at the door," Isaiah announced. "Want me to see who it is?"

"It's probably Gabe," Melinda said, moving in that direction. "He said he'd be coming over tonight to take me for a buggy ride."

Mama frowned. "What about the raccoon? She belongs outside."

"Can I at least answer the door?"

"Jah, sure. If it's Gabe, maybe he can help capture the critter." Papa Noah's face was red as a tomato, and a trickle of sweat rolled down his forehead. They'd all been in on the chase to catch Reba, but so far, the quick-footed raccoon had managed to escape everyone's grasp.

Melinda rushed to the door and was glad to see Gabe standing on the porch.

"I came to pick you up for our buggy ride, but I have a notion this isn't such a good time."

"We've been trying to catch one of my raccoons," she explained.

His forehead wrinkled. "Seems like every time I come over here you're either chasing some critter or tending to one."

"It has been kind of hectic lately," Melinda admitted, opening the screen door for him. "Come in. Maybe you can help us catch Reba."

"If you do catch the coon, are you planning to let it go?"

She tipped her head. "Go?"

"Release it into the woods."

"I can't do that, Gabe. Reba's half blind, and she needs to be somewhere safe."

"What about the other raccoon?"

"Rhoda's an orphan, too."

"But she's not sick or anything?"

"No."

"Then why not let her go free?"

"Because she's been keeping Reba company."

Gabe released a huff and stepped into the house just as the

raccoon darted into the living room from the door leading to the hallway. Before Melinda had time to respond, the coon snatched one of her mother's slippers, growling and shaking it like a dog would do.

Melinda bent down and grabbed one end of the slipper, tugging it free from Reba's mouth. Gabe came around behind the animal and nearly had it in his grasp when Melinda's cat showed up on the scene. Reba growled. Snow hissed. Then each of them took off in opposite directions.

Melinda watched in horror as the raccoon darted around the living room, bumping into pieces of furniture and acting disoriented.

"What's wrong with that coon?" Gabe asked, scratching the side of his head. "It's carrying on like it's been drinking hard cider or something."

"As I said before, Reba has limited vision. She does seem to be able to follow movement, though."

Gabe snapped his fingers. "That's good news. Open the front door, and I'll see if I can get the critter to follow me outside."

"I'll help you, Gabe," Papa Noah said when he entered the room, followed by Mama and Isaiah.

Melinda wasn't sure Gabe's plan would work, but she figured she should be prepared just in case. "Let me go out to the barn and get Reba's cage. If she does run out the door, I'll need to be ready for her."

"Okay, but hurry," Mama said, fanning her flushed face with her hands.

Moments later, Melinda stood on the front porch holding

the cage. She set it in front of the door and hollered, "Okay. I'm ready!"

Mama held the door open, and as Melinda watched the scene unfold, she didn't know who looked funnier—the raccoon, who continued to bump into things, or the menfolk, as they took turns diving after her.

After several more attempts, Reba was finally ushered out the door and into the cage. Relieved that the chase had ended, Melinda flopped into a chair and doubled over with laughter.

"I don't see what's so humorous," Mama grumbled. "This is the second time in a month that one of your critters has gotten into the house and caused an uproar, and I'm getting tired of it."

"Your mamm's right," Papa Noah added firmly. "This kind of commotion has got to stop."

Melinda was tempted to remind her folks that she wasn't the only one in the family responsible for bringing animals inside, but she didn't want to start anything with Isaiah. She glanced over at Gabe, hoping he would say something on her behalf, but he merely stood there with a placid look on his face. Was he on their side, too?

"Gabe and I had planned to go for a buggy ride," Melinda said. "That's why he dropped by."

Mama shook her head. "Until you can find some way to keep your animals locked in their cages and out of my home, you won't be going anywhere to socialize."

"But Mama, that's not fair—"

"And neither is tearing up the house! You're nineteen years old, Melinda, which means you should be more responsible." Papa Noah frowned. "And one more thing: As long as you're living under our roof, you'll do as we say. Is that clear?"

Melinda nodded slowly and blinked back tears. One crept from the corner of her eye and into her hairline. She wiped it away with a sniff. *Maybe I shouldn't be living under your roof.*

Chapter 11

Melinda was on her way to Seymour to deliver some of Grandpa's rhubarb-strawberry jam to the owner of the bed-and-breakfast when she decided to stop and see Gabe. She planned to ask if he would make some new locks for her cages, because as long as her animals kept getting out, her folks would be irritated and might ask her to stop taking in strays altogether. If that happened, she would feel as if she had no other choice but to leave.

When Melinda pulled up to Swartz's Woodworking Shop and hopped down from the buggy, she noticed Gabe's mother in her vegetable garden, working with a hoe.

"Nice day, isn't it?" Leah called with a friendly wave.

"Very pretty."

"Have you got a minute?"

"Jah, sure." Melinda headed up the driveway and joined Gabe's mother at the edge of her garden. "It looks like things are growing well. How are you able to keep up with all the weeds?" She knew Gabe's parents were both in their sixties and figured with no children except Gabe living at home, it would be harder to get things done.

Leah pushed a wayward strand of grayish-brown hair away from her flushed face. "My daughters Karen and Lydia often drop over with their kinner, and everyone helps me weed."

Melinda did a mental head count. Leah and Stephen Swartz had five children and twenty grandchildren. Since all of their offspring were still young enough to have more kinner, they could likely end up with several more grandchildren. She wondered if she and Gabe would be blessed with many children when they got married. *If we get married,* she corrected her thoughts. *What if he changes his mind about marrying me after I tell him about Dr. Franklin's suggestion that I become a vet?*

Melinda still struggled to make a decision, but with her folks not understanding her need to care for animals and refusing to let her go out with Gabe, she wondered if it might not be best if she did leave home and pursue a career in veterinary medicine. Truth was that the longer she worked for Dr. Franklin, the more she desired to become a vet. It would mean great sacrifice and a lot more schooling, but she'd almost convinced herself that it was God's will. Of course, she would still need to convince Gabe.

"I've got a question for you," Leah said, bringing Melinda's thoughts to a halt.

"What is it?"

"I know you work at the vet's and care for lots of animals at home."

"That's true."

"I've been having some trouble with deer getting into my garden and wondered if you had any ideas on keeping them out."

Melinda knew firsthand that the deer and other wildlife in the area could take over a garden if certain measures weren't taken. She also knew some folks used that as an excuse to shoot the deer.

"The best thing would be to build a tall fence, but we've had fairly good luck at keeping the deer out by hanging tin cans around our garden so that when the wind blows, the noise from the cans scares the deer away," Melinda said. "My mamm has also shaved some strong-smelling soap and sprinkled it around the outside of the garden. Another idea would be to put some feed out for the deer close to the edge of your property. If they're getting enough to eat, they won't be as likely to bother your garden."

Leah smiled. "I appreciate the suggestions. You're real *schmaert*, Melinda."

"I'm only smart about things pertaining to animals."

Eager to see Gabe, Melinda glanced toward the woodworking shop.

"I won't keep you any longer. I'm sure you came to visit my son," Leah said. "And if I know Gabe, he'll be pleased to see you."

Melinda nodded. "I did want to speak with him. Guess I'll head out to the shop and do that now."

"Tell Gabe I'll have lunch ready in an hour or so."

"Okay. It was nice talking to you, Leah."

"Same here."

Melinda entered the woodworking shop and spotted Gabe sanding a cabinet door. "Nice job you're doing," she said with a smile.

"Danki." He set the sandpaper aside and leaned on his workbench. "You're just the person I was hoping to see today."

She felt a warm sensation spread over her face. "That's nice to know."

"I've been planning to make new cages for your critters but haven't had the time yet." Gabe smiled. "I have been able to make a couple of new doors for the cages you already have, though. I thought if it was okay, I'd bring the doors by your house this evening and test them on your sneaky raccoons."

"That would be great," Melinda said with a burst of enthusiasm. Gabe's solution was better than her idea of getting new locks for her cages. "I'll be home all evening, so feel free to come by anytime after supper."

"Where are you headed to now? Or did you drive down this way just to see me?" he asked with a hopeful-looking smile.

She grinned in response. "I did come by to see you, but I'm also on my way to Seymour to take some of Grandpa's jam to the bed-and-breakfast. The owners will probably serve some of it to their customers, and I think they're planning to sell a few jars in their gift shop."

"I'm glad your grandpa's doing better these days and has found an outlet for his jam." Gabe motioned to the door. "My daed's outside cutting a stack of lumber that was delivered yesterday afternoon, but I think he's planning to head for Seymour soon, too. He has some finished cabinets he wants to deliver to an English woman who works for the chiropractor there."

Melinda made a sweeping gesture with her hand. "If they look anything like the ones I see here, I'm sure she'll be real pleased."

Gabe blew the sandpaper dust off the cabinet, and it trickled through the air, causing Melinda to sneeze.

"Sorry for sending all that dust in your direction," he said with a look of concern.

"I'm all right."

"I guess you'll have to get used to sandpaper dust if you're planning to marry a carpenter."

She shifted her weight from one foot to the other. "Gabe—there's—uh—something I need to tell you."

"What is it, Melinda? Are you having second thoughts about marrying me?"

"It's not that."

"What is it, then?"

She was about to reply, when Gabe's father stepped into the room. "Herman Yutzy's here to pick up the table and chairs his daed ordered," he announced. "I need your help loading them into his wagon, Gabe."

"Jah, okay." Gabe smiled at Melinda. "Duty calls."

"That's all right. I need to get going anyhow. I'll see you this evening, Gabe."

"You can count on it."

"It's good you didn't have to work today," Mama said to Susie as the two of them finished up the breakfast dishes. "Maybe the two of us can get some baking done."

Susie wiped her sweaty forehead with the back of her hand and groaned. "It's hot in here, and I don't feel much like baking."

"What do you feel like doing?"

"I don't know, but anything that will get me outside would be a welcome relief. My job at the store keeps me inside way too much, and my face is paler than goat's milk."

Mama clucked her tongue and reached for another clean dish to dry. "How you do exaggerate, girl."

"I'm not exaggerating. When I looked in the mirror this morning, I could hardly believe how pasty I looked."

"If you think you need more sun on your face, then why not spend the day weeding the garden?"

"Since Grace Ann and Faith were here last week helping you work in the garden, it's almost weed-free."

Mama nodded. "That's true. They were a big help to me that day."

Susie glanced out the window and noticed an open buggy pulling into their yard. "Looks like Melinda is here," she said, motioning toward the window with her soapy hand. "I wonder what she wants."

"Probably stopped to say hello."

A few minutes later, the back door opened, and Melinda

stepped into the kitchen. "Wie geht's?" she asked with a cheery smile.

"We're doing fine," Mama replied.

"What brings you by so early this morning?" Susie asked.

"I'm on my way to Seymour to take some jars of Grandpa's rhubarb-strawberry jam to the bed-and-breakfast," Melinda replied. "I decided to drop by here first and see if you wanted to ride along."

Susie smiled. "A trip to Seymour sounds like a fun way to spend my day off. If we stay around long enough, maybe we can go somewhere for lunch."

Melinda nodded. "I wouldn't mind getting some barbecued ribs at Baldy's Café."

Susie licked her lips. "That does sound good."

"If you're going into town, maybe you could drop by the grocery store and pick up a few things for me before you head back home," Mama said.

Susie looked over at Melinda to get her approval.

"Sure, that shouldn't be a problem." Melinda slipped one arm around her grandmother's waist and gave her a squeeze. "Would you like to go with us?"

Mama shook her head. "I appreciate the offer, but I think it would be good for the two of you to do something fun together. With Susie working at the store, and you helping out at the vet's part-time, you don't get much time together anymore."

"And when you're not working for Dr. Franklin, you're either with Gabe or taking care of some injured or orphaned critter," Susie put in as she finished the last dish and turned to face Melinda.

Melinda's forehead wrinkled. "You make it sound as if I don't have time for my family anymore."

"I never said that."

"Not in so many words, but—"

"I'm ready to go if you are," Susie said, cutting Melinda off in midsentence. She wasn't in the mood to argue this morning, and it seemed that every time she and Melinda discussed her need to be with animals, they ended up in a disagreement.

"Let's go then." Melinda opened the back door. "See you sometime this afternoon, Grandma."

"Jah, okay. Have a good time."

Susie dried her hands on a towel, grabbed her black handbag from the wall peg, and rushed out the door behind Melinda.

"Sure is a nice day, isn't it?" Melinda asked as she and Susie headed down the road in her open buggy.

Susie nodded.

"You've been awfully quiet since we left your house. Is something bothering you?"

Susie shrugged.

Melinda nudged Susie with her elbow. "There is something bothering you, isn't there?"

Susie released an extended sigh. *"Es is mir verleed."*

"Why are you discouraged?"

"Every time I find a fellow I'm interested in, he either has no interest in me, already has a girlfriend, or is going back to Montana."

Melinda glanced over at Susie as she lifted her eyebrows. "How many fellows do you know who are heading to Montana?"

"Just one. Jonas Byler."

"Ah, I see." Melinda brought her gaze back to the road and gripped the reins a little tighter as they crested the top of a small hill. "I saw Jonas at the last young people's gathering and heard someone mention that he'd come back to the area for a visit." She nudged Susie again. "I didn't know you had an interest in him, though."

"For all the good it does me." Susie grunted. "I doubt he knows I'm alive. And even if he did, he won't be sticking around Webster County long enough to spend any time with me."

"Maybe you could go to Montana and visit Jonas sometime," Melinda suggested. "It would probably be an exciting trip."

"Jah, right. Like Mama and Papa would ever give their permission for me to go off by myself like that."

"They might. I know a lot of Amish young people who like to travel around and see some sights before they get married and settle down."

Susie leaned closer to Melinda. "Say, I have an idea. Why don't the two of us plan a trip to Montana? Think how much fun it would be to catch the train or a bus and go out West to see the sights."

Melinda shook her head vigorously. "I can't go on any trips right now."

"Why not?"

"For one thing, I've got my job at the veterinary clinic."

"It's only part-time, Melinda. I'm sure Dr. Franklin would give you a few weeks off so you could go on a little vacation."

"Even if he did give me the time off, I have responsibilities at home."

"Such as?"

"Taking care of my animals."

"Couldn't someone else in your family do that in your absence?"

"No way! Mama and Papa Noah are too busy with other things, and I wouldn't trust Isaiah to feed my bussli, let alone take care of any of the orphaned animals I have in my care." Melinda drew in a deep breath and released it quickly. "And then there's Gabe."

"Oh, I see how it is," Susie said in a wistful tone. "You're in love with Gabe and don't want to leave him for a few weeks. Isn't that right?"

Melinda nodded. But while it was true that she didn't relish the idea of being away from Gabe, she wasn't about to tell her aunt that the main reason she didn't want to leave home right now was because she was on the verge of making one of the biggest decisions of her life. If she decided to prepare for a career in veterinary work, she would have to begin by taking her GED test, and for that, she needed to be at home, studying.

"So, where would you like to go after I drop off Grandpa's jam at the bed-and-breakfast?" Melinda asked, changing the subject.

"I thought we were going to have lunch at Baldy's."

"We are. But I thought maybe you'd like to do some shopping first."

"We can do that afterwards, when we pick up the groceries for my mamm."

"Oh, that's right." She looked over at Susie again. "Did she give you a list?"

Susie's eyebrows drew together. "A list?"

"A list of the groceries she wants."

Susie clamped her hand over her mouth. "Ach! I hurried out of the house so quickly, I forgot to ask what she needed."

"Maybe she'll send Grandpa after the items she needs."

"Either that, or as soon as you drop me off at home, she'll give me the list and I'll have to head right back to town."

Melinda snickered. "Oh, well. Then you'll have two good doses of sunshine and fresh air."

Chapter 12

When Melinda arrived home later that day, she was greeted with a sorrowful sight. Isaiah's dog had gone on the rampage, killing a female rabbit that had gotten out of its cage. Melinda was sure it had happened because the door wouldn't stay latched. She was heartsick when she discovered the dead rabbit's four orphaned babies, knowing they might not survive without their mother.

"I'll need to feed them," she murmured, reaching into the open cage.

"Sorry about this," Isaiah said, stepping up beside her. "Don't know what came over Jericho to do such a thing."

"If you kept him tied up like I've asked you to do, he wouldn't have had the opportunity." Melinda lifted the rabbits gently out of the cage and placed them inside a cardboard box. "I'll take them into the house where I can better care for their needs."

"Mama won't like it," Isaiah asserted. "She's gettin' sick of your critters and the messes they make."

Melinda wrinkled her nose. "You'd best let me worry about that." She hurried out of the barn before her brother could offer a retort.

When she stepped onto the back porch a few minutes later, she spotted Grandpa sitting in the wicker rocking chair outside his living quarters. He waved at her. "Did you get my jam delivered?"

She nodded. "Every last one is gone."

"Then what have you got in the box?"

"Four baby rabbits." Melinda moved closer to his chair and held out the box so he could take a look. "Isaiah's dog killed the mother. Now it's my job to save them."

Grandpa fingered his long white beard. "It doesn't surprise me that you'd be willing to do that. You're such a caring young woman."

She leaned over and kissed his wrinkled cheek. "I'd best get these little ones inside and find a way to feed them."

"I hope they make it."

"Me, too." Melinda opened the back door and stepped into the house.

When the back door opened and banged against the wall, Faith turned from her task at the kitchen sink, where she'd been peeling some carrots. She fully expected to see Isaiah standing there, but found Melinda holding a box in her hands instead.

"Mercy, daughter, can't you be a little quieter when you enter the house? And for goodness' sake, please shut the door."

Melinda placed the box on one end of the counter, turned, and closed the door with her hip. "Sorry, Mama. I was in a hurry to get the *bopplin* inside."

Faith dropped the carrot into the sink and hurried across the room. "Babies? What kind of babies have you got in that box?"

"Baby rabbits." Melinda's forehead wrinkled as she frowned. "Thanks to Isaiah's mutt, these poor little critters are orphans now."

"Jericho killed the mother rabbit?"

Melinda nodded solemnly. "So now it's my job to raise them."

"You can take care of them out in the barn, but not in here," Faith said with a shake of her head.

"How come?"

Faith blew out an exaggerated breath. "Do you really have to ask? You know how I feel about having animals in the house."

"But you allow Snow to be inside."

"That's different. Snow's a pet, not a wild animal."

Melinda peered into the box and stared at the tiny bunnies. "These little *haaslin* aren't wild, Mama. They're helpless, hungry, and without a mamm."

"Be that as it may—"

"Can't I keep them in my room? I promise they won't be any trouble to you. They'll be inside a box, so there's no chance of them running all over the house or making a mess."

Faith slipped her hands behind her back and popped two knuckles at the same time.

Melinda winced. "Are you upset with me, Mama? You always pop your knuckles whenever you're upset."

"I'm not upset. I just don't want you turning our home into a zoo."

"I'm not trying to." Melinda peered into the box again. "I only want to take care of these orphaned bunnies because they won't make it on their own."

Faith released a blustery sigh. "Oh, all right. But as soon as they start trying to get out of that box, they're to be put in a rabbit cage inside the barn. Is that clear?"

Melinda nodded and gave Faith a hug. "Danki, Mama." Then she grabbed the box and scurried out of the room.

Faith lifted her gaze to the ceiling. "Oh, Lord, please give me the wisdom of Solomon and the patience of Job."

That evening after supper, Melinda sat on the front porch swing, waiting for Gabe to show up. She had just fed the orphaned bunnies with an eyedropper and put them back inside the cardboard box.

A slight breeze came up, whisking away some of the oppressive, muggy July air that had hovered over the land most of the day. A horse and buggy trotted into the yard just then, and Melinda smiled when she saw that it was Gabe. She left the porch and hurried out to greet him.

Gabe climbed down from his buggy and retrieved two

wooden cage doors from the back. He motioned to the barn. "Let's go see how they work, shall we?"

As soon as they entered the barn, Melinda took Reba and Rhoda out of their cages and placed them inside an empty horse stall. Gabe removed the old cage doors, and a short time later, he had the new doors set in place.

"The latches can't be jimmied from the inside," he explained. "I don't think the coons will be able to escape, and as soon as I find the time, I'll make you a couple of new cages with doors just like these."

"That would be wunderbaar." Melinda retrieved Reba and Rhoda and put them in their respective cages.

Gabe closed the doors and clicked the locks shut. "I dare either of you critters to get out now," he said, squinting at the animals.

"If it keeps them in, I'll be happy, and so will my folks."

Gabe lifted Melinda's chin with his thumb and lowered his head. His lips were just inches from hers when her brother burst into the barn. "Yodel-oh-de-tee! Yodel-oh-de-tee! My mama taught me how to yodel when I sat on her knee. . . ." Isaiah halted when he saw Gabe and Melinda, and his face turned cherry red. "Oops. Didn't know anyone was here."

"And I didn't know you could yodel," Gabe said. "I thought only Melinda and your mamm were the yodelers in the family."

"He *can't* yodel." Melinda tapped her foot impatiently. "He only does that to mimic me."

Isaiah glared at her. "Do not. I came to the barn to see if Jericho was here."

"He's not." Melinda clenched her teeth. "That mutt had

better not be running free again, either."

"He can't be chained up all the time, and it's not his fault your goofy pets are always gettin' out of their cages."

"I think that problem's been solved," Gabe said. "I just put new doors with better locks on the coons' cages, and if it keeps them in, I'll be making more cages for Melinda's other animals."

Isaiah peered at Reba's cage door. "If Papa ever gets around to buildin' Jericho a dog run, maybe you can put a door like this on his cage."

Melinda poked her brother's arm. "Is that any way to ask a favor? Gabe doesn't have a lot of time on his hands and shouldn't be expected to make a cage door for your dog."

"I'll make the time for it," Gabe said with a wide smile. "Fact is I'll build the whole dog run for Jericho. It will give me a chance to build something on my own without Pap looking over my shoulder and telling me how it's done. Not only that, but it will keep your dog from hurting Melinda's critters."

"That'd be great." Isaiah gave Gabe a wide grin. "Danki, Gabe. You're a right nice fellow."

Melinda moved toward the barn door. "Come on, Gabe. Let's go tell my folks about the cage doors and see if they mind if we go for a buggy ride."

Chapter 13

Melinda drew in a deep breath and prayed for the courage to say what had been on her mind for the last several weeks. Gabe deserved to know what Dr. Franklin wanted her to do, and now was the time to tell him.

"I've been wanting to discuss something with you," she said as they headed down Highway C in his open buggy.

"What's on your mind?"

Melinda moistened her lips with the tip of her tongue. "You know how much I enjoy working with animals."

"Jah."

"And I want to help as many of the sick and hurting ones as I can."

He nodded.

"The thing is—" She paused and drew in a quick breath. This

was going to be harder than she'd expected. No wonder she had put off telling him for so long.

"The thing is what?" Gabe prompted.

"Well, Dr. Franklin says I have a special way with animals. He called it a 'God-given talent.' "

"He's right about that. Look how well your daed's horse has responded to you. And those baby bunnies are doing well under your care. Animals have a sixth sense and know when a human being cares for them."

Melinda felt relief that Gabe realized her capabilities. Maybe he would be receptive to the idea of her becoming a vet.

"I do care a lot," she admitted, "but unfortunately, I'm not able to do as much for wounded or sick animals as I would like."

"That's why Doc Franklin's available." Gabe flicked the reins, and his horse picked up speed. "When you find an ailing critter or somebody brings an animal over to your place that has more wrong with it than you can handle, you take it to the vet."

Melinda clasped her hands tightly in her lap. Her throat felt so dry all of a sudden.

"Well, if that doesn't beat all," Gabe said, pointing to the other side of the road. "It's another dead *hasch*. Probably some car or a truck ran into it."

Melinda flinched. She hated to see dead deer, whether they were lying alongside the road after being hit by a car or hanging in someone's barn during deer hunting season.

"If the deer aren't thinned enough during hunting season," Gabe said, "they overpopulate and will soon overrun our area." He glanced over his shoulder and pointed to the deer they'd just passed. "I'd rather see 'em shot for meat than go to waste that way, though. Wouldn't you?"

Melinda formulated her next words carefully. She wanted to be sure Gabe didn't take anything she said the wrong way. "To tell you the truth, I don't like to see *any* deer killed. We raise hogs, sheep, and cows for food, so why would anyone need to kill the deer?"

He shrugged. "Some folks in our community prefer the taste of deer meat, and even if we do have other animals to butcher, a change is nice."

Melinda didn't like the way this conversation was going, so she decided to get back to the subject she needed to discuss with Gabe. "Dr. Franklin thinks I have what it takes to become a vet." There, it was out, and Melinda should have felt better, but she didn't.

A muscle in Gabe's cheek quivered as he stared straight ahead. Was he mulling things over or trying to stay focused on the road? The buggy rolled along, and the horse's hooves made a steady *clip-clop, clip-clop* against the pavement, but Gabe remained quiet.

Unable to stand the silence, Melinda reached over and touched his arm. "Awhile back, the doctor gave me some information on the necessary college courses I would need to take. He told me about a couple different schools of veterinary medicine, too."

Gabe jerked on the reins and guided his horse and buggy to the side of the road. When they were stopped, he turned in his seat and stared hard at Melinda. "Just how far have you gone with all this? Have you already made up your mind to leave the Amish faith? Have you made application to a college?"

She shook her head. "No, no. I would need to get my GED first, and then—"

"So you have decided."

"Not yet, but Dr. Franklin says if I want something badly enough, I should be willing to make whatever sacrifices are necessary. Even if it means giving up those things that are dear to me in order to reach my goal."

"If you were to get the training you needed to become a vet, it would mean leaving the Amish faith and everyone you love behind." Gabe's shoulders slumped as he stared at the floor of his buggy. Apparently he thought this would mean the end of their relationship.

Melinda clasped his hand. "Would you be willing to leave here with me?"

"What?" His mouth dropped open. "How could you even suggest such a thing?"

"I—I thought if you loved me—"

A vein in Gabe's temple began to throb. "You know I love you, Melinda. But I'm happy living here, and I don't want to leave the Amish faith." He squinted as he stared at her long and hard. "I can't imagine you wanting to leave, either."

"I don't really want to leave, but in order for me to—"

"I asked you once if you ever missed the English world or thought you would want to go back to it someday, and you said you were happy being Amish."

"I—I am happy being Amish, but I can't become a veterinarian and remain part of our faith."

"So I guess that means you'll have to choose between me and the modern world."

Frustration welled in Melinda's soul as she fought to keep her emotions under control. Gabe didn't understand the way she felt at all. "It's not the modern world I'd be choosing," she said. "Becoming a vet would mean I could help so many animals."

"You're helping some now, aren't you?"

"Jah, but in such a small way."

He shrugged. "Seems to me you ought to be happy with what you can do for the animals you've taken in and quit wishing for something that goes against our beliefs."

She lowered her head. "My folks don't approve of my desire to care for animals. They're always hollering at me for spending too much time caring for animals."

Gabe grabbed both of Melinda's arms as a look of frustration crossed his face. "You've been baptized and have joined the church. You've made a vow to God to adhere to our church rules. If you left to become part of the English world, you'd be shunned. Have you thought about the seriousness of that?"

"Of course I have, and it would hurt to leave my family behind." Tears seeped out from under her lashes, and she swallowed around the constriction in her throat.

"What do your folks have to say about this? Are they letting you go with their blessings?"

Melinda shook her head. "I haven't told them yet. I wanted to discuss it with you first and see if you'd be willing to—"

"I don't want to leave the Amish faith." Gabe sat for several seconds with a pained expression; then his features softened some. "I've been working real hard and saving up money so I can start my own place of business," he said, taking hold of her hand. "I'm doing it for us so that I can make a good living and provide for the family I'd hoped that we would have someday."

Confusion swirled in Melinda's brain like a tornado spinning at full speed. She did love Gabe, but if he wouldn't leave the Amish faith, then she would be completely on her own if she decided to get the necessary schooling to become a vet. And how would she pay for her classes? College was expensive, not to mention the additional training at a veterinary school. What she made working for Dr. Franklin wasn't nearly enough, and she sure couldn't ask her folks to help out.

Melinda squeezed her eyes shut as a sense of shame washed over her. *That was a selfish thought. I'm not asking Gabe to leave the Amish faith so he can help me financially. I want him to support my decision because he loves me and wants to be with me no matter which world I choose to live in.*

She opened her eyes and looked at him. "Would you do me one favor, Gabe?"

"What's that?"

"Would you at least pray about the matter?"

His forehead wrinkled as his eyebrows drooped. "You want me to pray about you becoming a vet?"

She nodded. "And ask God what His plans for you might be, too."

Gabe gathered up the reins. "I will pray about this, but I think right now I'd best take you home. I don't feel like riding any farther tonight."

Melinda placed her hand on his shoulder. "Gabe—"

"Jah?"

"Please don't say anything to my folks or anyone else about what we've discussed this evening, okay?"

He gave a quick nod. "It's not my place to do the telling. I'll leave that up to you."

Chapter 14

Melinda's hands shook as she stood in front of the bird-house by their driveway, holding the note she had discovered from Gabe. Had he been thinking about what she'd told him concerning Dr. Franklin's suggestion that she become a vet? Had Gabe decided that he would be willing to go English with her?

She focused on the words he'd written:

Dear Melinda,

    I spoke with your daed yesterday, and he said it would be fine if I want to help Isaiah build a dog run, since he still hasn't found the time. He also said he thought I would do a much better job than he could, since I'm a carpenter and have the skills and proper tools.

*So I plan to come by after work today and begin the
project. If you don't have anything else to do, maybe you can
keep me company. If not, then I hope we can get in a few
minutes to visit when I'm done for the day.*

Always yours,
Gabe

Melinda frowned as she tucked the note inside the front of
her apron. Gabe hadn't said a word about her becoming a vet or
made any mention of whether he'd made a decision regarding
their situation or not. Maybe he planned to discuss it with her
tonight. That could be why he'd mentioned her keeping him
company and hoping to have a few minutes to visit when he was
done at the end of the day.

Melinda bent down and picked up her cat, who had been
sunning herself on the grass. "You've got life made, you know
that, Snow?"

Snow's only response was a soft *meow* as she opened one lazy
eye and snuggled against Melinda.

"I wish all I had to do was lie around and soak up the sun,"
she said as she walked toward the house.

"You wouldn't be happy, and you know it."

Melinda smiled when she heard her grandfather's deep,
mellow voice. He sat in his wicker rocking chair on the front porch
snapping green beans into a bowl wedged between his knees.

"You're right, Grandpa. I wouldn't be happy if I wasn't busy,"
she said as she stepped onto the porch and stood beside him. "I
enjoy caring for my animals too much to sit around all day and
do nothing."

"Speaking of your animals, have you let either of the coons go yet?"

She nodded and sat in the chair beside him, nestling Snow in her lap. "In all fairness to Rhoda, the healthy raccoon, I released her into the woods the other day. But Reba is really lonely without her."

"Maybe you should let her go, too."

"I can't. She's partially blind, and I'm sure she wouldn't make it in the woods on her own." Melinda stroked the cat behind its left ear. "Gabe's coming over later to help Isaiah build a dog run, so maybe once my brother's mutt is locked away, I can let Reba roam around our place whenever I'm at home and am able to keep an eye out for her."

Grandpa's bushy gray eyebrows drew together. "Do you think it's fair to confine Isaiah's dog so your raccoon can run free?"

Melinda shrugged. "I suppose not, but Jericho's been known to attack other animals, too. Don't forget the baby bunnies I'm caring for. Jericho killed their mother, you know."

"That was a shame, but the dog was only doing what comes natural to him. Maybe when Gabe's done with the dog run, he can build some other kind of pen for the coon."

"You mean something bigger than the cage I keep her in now?"

"Jah. Maybe he could make it more like the cages I've seen at the zoo." Grandpa dropped another bean into the bowl. "Some of those zoo cages are real nice—tree branches, scrub brush, and small pools of water inside."

Melinda's heart pounded as a host of ideas skittered through her mind. How wonderful it would be if she had larger cages that were similar to the animals' natural habitat. The critters would feel more at home until it was time to let them go free.

Why am I even thinking such thoughts? If I leave home to go to college, I won't be caring for any of my animal friends until I become a vet, and then it will be in a much different way. Besides, that could be several years from now.

Gabe clucked to his horse to get him moving. He was tired after a long day at the shop. Even so, he looked forward to going over to the Hertzlers' to build the dog run for Isaiah. It would be something different to work on for a change, and it would give him a chance to speak with Melinda. Maybe he could talk some sense into her—make her see more clearly what the consequences would be if she left the Amish faith.

He thought about his own plans to open a woodworking shop where he could make a variety of things. What would be the point in doing that if Melinda left and he stayed behind? Without her by his side, nothing would ever be the same. He felt sure he could never be happy if he left the Amish faith, because he was Amish through and through. For Melinda, though, it might be different because she had been born into the modern world and her father had been English. Maybe Melinda didn't have the same commitment to the Amish faith as Gabe did. Maybe she could leave it behind and never look back.

He swallowed hard. *Why'd I have to go and fall in love with a woman who isn't satisfied with the plain, simple life? Why can't I set aside my feelings for her now?*

Gabe flicked the reins to get the horse moving faster. He knew the answer to that question. He loved Melinda and didn't want to lose her. But did he love her enough to give up the only way of life he'd ever known and go English?

Gabe pulled into the Hertzlers' yard sometime later and parked his buggy next to the barn. Since he would be there a few hours, he decided to unhitch the horse and put him in one of the stalls.

As Gabe led the gelding through the barn door, he spotted Melinda standing on the other side of the building in front of an animal cage with her back to him.

He hurried to get the horse situated in a stall then strolled over to where she stood. "Hey! What are you up to?"

Melinda turned, and Gabe saw that she held a raccoon in her arms.

"You shouldn't carry that coon around like that," he admonished, wishing he'd said something sooner about her taking such chances. "What if the critter bites or scratches you real bad?"

Melinda lifted her chin and looked at him as if he'd taken leave of his senses. "Reba's as tame as my cat. And for your information, she likes it when I hold her."

"Humph! She's a wild animal. You can't be sure of what she might do."

Melinda's eyes narrowed. "I don't want to argue with you, Gabe. I've been taking in wild animals since I was a young girl, and I think I know what I'm doing."

Gabe blew out his breath in a puff of air that lifted the hair off his forehead. She was right; they shouldn't be arguing.

Besides, his irritation had more to do with what she had told him about wanting to leave the Amish faith and becoming a vet than it did with the silly raccoon. He needed to handle this situation carefully so he didn't make Melinda mad. If she became angry with him, she might jump the fence and go English just to spite him. Even so, Gabe knew he'd have to tell Melinda that he didn't want her to leave; nor did he want to leave with her.

"I didn't mean to upset you," Gabe muttered.

"All's forgiven." Melinda put Reba back in her cage and turned to face him. "I was wondering if you've thought any more about what we discussed the other night."

He glanced around nervously. "Are—are we alone?"

She nodded. "Papa Noah's still at work, Mama and Grandpa are inside the house, and the last time I saw Isaiah, he was digging in the dirt out behind the barn."

Gabe plunked down on a bale of straw, and Melinda seated herself beside him. "In answer to your question," he said, "I have thought more about what we discussed the other night, and I've also been praying."

"Have you made a decision?"

"I'm hoping you'll change your mind and decide to be content with being Amish."

"As I told you before, I am content being Amish. I'm just not content being unable to properly care for any animals I find that are hurt." She frowned. "And I'm sure not content with always being scolded by my folks for helping my animal friends."

"So what it boils down to is that one of us has to give up something we feel is important in order for us to be together." He hurried on before he lost his nerve. "If you left home to get the schooling you would need to become a vet, and I went with you, then I'd be giving up a way of life I love and respect."

She nodded slowly.

"And if you stayed Amish to please me, then you'd be giving up your desire to care for more animals than you're doing now."

She nodded again. "That's true, but if I leave home, I'll also be giving up my family and the way of life I've become accustomed to, same as you. Sacrifices would have to be made on both our parts if we decided to go English."

Gabe massaged the bridge of his nose as he contemplated their problem. As far as he was concerned, it was a no-win situation. No matter how it turned out, one of them would be unhappy. Truth be told, he figured if they left the Amish faith together, they both would be unhappy. Melinda might think being a vet was what she wanted, but he knew one thing for sure—if they went English, Melinda's relationship with her family would be greatly affected.

"We don't have to make a decision right now," Melinda said, touching his arm. "However, I need to get registered for classes at the college in Springfield before the end of August. In the meantime, I'm going to see about getting my GED—graduate equivalency diploma."

"I know what a GED is, Melinda." He slowly shook his head. "I'll bet your folks would be upset if they knew what you were planning to do. Are you going to tell them soon?"

She grunted. "I plan to, but it needs to be said at the right time, in the right way. Maybe after I pass the GED test I'll tell them."

Gabe stood, feeling the need to end this discussion. He

didn't want Melinda to take the GED test, but he figured there was no way to stop her from doing so, since she seemed to have her mind set on it. The best thing he could do was continue to pray that she would change her mind.

"I'd best round up Isaiah so we can get busy on that dog run." Gabe took a few steps toward the door but turned back around. "Do you know where your daed had planned to build it?"

"He cemented some posts in an area to the left of the barn."

"Are you coming out to keep us company?"

"I've got a few things I need to do inside the house right now. Then some corn needs to be shucked."

"Maybe I'll see you later then." Gabe hurried out of the barn, grabbed some tools from the back of his buggy, and went to look for Melinda's brother. He hoped a few hours of hard work would get him calmed down.

Gabe found Isaiah digging in the soil just as Melinda had said. Streaks of dirt covered the boy's pale blue shirt and dark brown trousers, and several murky-looking smudges were smearing his face.

"What are you doing out here?" Gabe asked, squatting beside Isaiah.

"Lookin' for an old bone Jericho buried some time ago."

Gabe squinted. "Why would you be doing that?"

"My dog's bored and needs somethin' to do. Thought if he had a bone to chew on, he might be happier." Isaiah's mouth turned down at the corners. "Since I'm not supposed to let Jericho off his chain during the day, I figured it wouldn't be good to let him loose in order to look for the bone himself."

"Why not just give him a new bone?"

"Don't have one," Isaiah said with a shrug. "Mama hasn't made any beef soup in a while, and those are the only kind of bones Jericho likes."

Gabe chuckled as he rose to his feet. "How about you and me getting busy on that dog run, and you can worry about finding Jericho a bone later on?"

"Jah, okay." When Isaiah stood and slapped the sides of his trousers, dirt blew everywhere. Gabe stepped quickly aside, and the boy sneezed. He pulled a dusty hanky from his pocket and blew his nose. "You think Jericho will be happier once he has a pen of his own?"

"I believe so."

"It's important for dogs to be happy, same as people, jah?"

"I suppose." Gabe clenched his fingers. *I'd be happy if I had my own business, stayed right here in Webster County, and married Melinda. I've got to figure out some way to make her see how foolish it would be to leave the Amish faith. Doesn't she realize how many people will be hurt if she goes English? Me, most of all.*

"How are things going with you these days?" Noah's boss, Hank, asked as he lowered himself to the ground where Noah knelt, studying a struggling pine tree.

Noah looked over at Hank and smiled. "You mean how are things going here or at home?"

"Both."

"Here, things are going well enough, but at home I'm not so sure."

Hank pulled his fingers through the sides of his reddish-brown hair. "What's going on at home?"

"It's the same old thing. Melinda's critters stirring up trouble, and Faith getting perturbed with Melinda for shirking her duties because she's preoccupied with her animals."

Hank thumped Noah on the back. "At least you know where your daughter is, and you don't have to worry about her running all over creation in some fancy souped-up car, like some of the English kids who live in this area are doing."

"That's true. I guess we should be grateful that Melinda spends most of her time in the barn tending to some critter or working at the veterinary clinic with Dr. Franklin."

"When does she find the time to be courted? I heard that Gabe Swartz has an interest in her."

"Oh, she manages to fit that into her schedule. But whenever Faith needs something done, Melinda has a dozen excuses." Noah groaned. "Sometimes I wish Faith and I could have had more children, but then there are days when either Isaiah or Melinda does something foolish that I think maybe the Lord gave us all the children He knew we could handle."

Hank snickered. "I hear you there. When Sandy and I first decided to adopt, we talked about getting four or five kids. But after we got Cheryl, and then Ryan, we knew we were blessed and decided two children were enough to make our family complete."

"I guess God knew what each of us needed." Noah leaned closer to the fledgling pine tree and squinted. "Raising children is a lot like taking care of the trees you grow here on your Christmas tree farm."

"How so?"

"They both need lots of attention and plenty of nurturing in order to make 'em grow. I just hope I've nurtured my children enough."

Melinda sat in a wicker chair on the back porch, shucking corn and watching Gabe and Isaiah work under the sweltering sun. She could hear the steady *thump, thump, thump* as they pounded nails to hold the wire fencing that was being connected to the wooden poles Papa Noah had previously put in.

I wish I could make Gabe understand my need to become a vet. If only he loved me enough to. . .

A piercing scream halted Melinda's thoughts. Had Gabe been hurt? Was it Isaiah?

She dropped the corn, leaped off the porch, and dashed across the yard.

When Melinda arrived at the dog run a few seconds later, she discovered Isaiah holding his thumb and jumping up and down. "Ouch! Ouch!" he hollered. "Ach! That hurts me somethin' awful!"

"What happened? Are you seriously injured?"

"He smacked his thumb with the hammer," Gabe explained. "But he won't let me get a good look, so I don't know how much damage was done."

"Give me your hand," Melinda ordered, grabbing hold of her brother's arm.

"Don't touch me!"

"I need to see how bad it is."

"You'd better let her look at that," Gabe put in.

Isaiah whimpered but finally released his thumb for Melinda's inspection.

She held it gently between her fingers. The skin was red and swollen, and the nail was beginning to turn purple. "You might end up losing that nail," she said with a click of her tongue.

Isaiah sniffed, and a few tears trickled down his cheeks. "How can ya tell? You ain't no doctor."

"No, but she'd like to be."

Melinda glared at Gabe then looked quickly back at her brother. What was Gabe thinking, blurting out something like that in front of Isaiah? "What Gabe meant to say is that I've doctored enough animals to know many things. Besides, I lost a couple of nails myself when I slammed two fingers in my bedroom door when I was a girl."

Isaiah rocked back and forth on his heels, moaning like a heifer about to give birth.

"You'd best go up to the house and ask Mama to put some ice on your thumb. If it's cared for right away, the nail might not come loose," Melinda instructed.

"Guess I won't be able to help ya no more, Gabe. Sorry about that," the boy mumbled.

Gabe patted Isaiah on the shoulder. "It's okay. I'll do what I can on my own. We probably wouldn't have gotten it all done today anyway. I'll come back in a few days to finish the project."

"I can help you," Melinda volunteered after her brother had scurried away. "After I'm done shucking corn, that is."

Gabe's expression was dubious at first, but then he nodded. "I'll take any help I can get."

"Please hold still, Isaiah," Faith instructed as she dabbed some peroxide under the nail of his thumb. "I want to be sure you don't get an infection."

"It hurts like crazy, Mama." Isaiah wiggled back and forth in his chair and groaned.

"I know, son."

"Do you think I'm gonna lose my nail?"

"Time will tell." Faith reached for the ice bag lying on the table and handed it to Isaiah. "You'd better keep this on your thumb awhile. It'll help the swelling go down and should help ease the pain, too."

Isaiah positioned the bag of ice over his thumb and leaned back in his chair. "I think I might feel better if I had some of Papa's lemon sponge cake to eat while I'm sittin' here."

Faith chuckled and ruffled her son's hair. "You think that would help, huh?"

He grinned. "I surely do."

"All right then. I'll fix us a slice of cake and some cold milk to wash it down."

A few minutes later, Faith was seated at the table across from her boy, with a piece of Noah's delicious lemon sponge cake sitting before them.

"This sure is tasty," Isaiah said after he'd taken his first bite. "I think Papa's the best cook in all of Webster County."

"Melinda thinks that, too."

Isaiah's eyebrows furrowed. "Speaking of Melinda, do you

wanna know what I heard Gabe say about her?"

"Not if it's gossip."

"It ain't."

"Isn't."

"That's what I meant." Isaiah took a drink of milk and wiped his mouth with the back of his hand.

Faith reached into the wicker basket sitting in the center of the table and handed him a napkin.

Isaiah swiped it across his mouth. "As I was saying, when Melinda was lookin' at my sore thumb, and she said I might lose my fingernail, I said to her, 'How do you know? You ain't no doctor.' And then Gabe said, 'No, but she'd like to be.' "

Faith pursed her lips. "What did he mean by that?"

"Beats me. I never got the chance to ask, 'cause Melinda sent me up to the house to have you take a look at my thumb."

"Gabe probably made that comment because Melinda's always playing doctor on some sick or hurting animal."

Isaiah shrugged. "Maybe so. She does think she can fix every critter that's ailin'."

Faith reached for her glass of milk and took a sip, letting the cool liquid roll around in her mouth. *I hope that's all it meant. I don't know how I would deal with it if Melinda decided to leave the Amish faith and pursue a career in the English world the way I did when I was her age.*

Chapter 15

For the next few weeks, Melinda struggled for answers as to what she should do about becoming a vet, but no clear direction came. She'd helped Gabe finish Jericho's dog run, and Gabe had agreed to make Reba a larger cage when he found the time. But every time Melinda broached the subject of them leaving the Amish faith, they ended up in an argument. Before she left for work on Thursday morning, she had found a note from Gabe in the birdhouse. He wanted her to go with him to the farmers' market on Saturday after the woodworking shop closed at noon. She'd written him back, saying she could go because she wouldn't be working at the veterinary clinic.

Now Melinda sat on the porch swing waiting for Gabe and hoping things would go all right between them. She had to make a decision soon and needed Gabe's final answer. Thursday after work, she'd spoken with Dr. Franklin again, and he'd explained the necessary procedure for getting her GED. Without her folks' knowledge, she had gotten the information she needed in order to study for the test and was scheduled to take it at the college in Springfield in two weeks. Dr. Franklin's wife, Ellen, had agreed to drive her there.

Melinda jumped up when she heard a horse and buggy pull into the yard, figuring it must be Gabe. Instead, she recognized Harold Esh, one of their Amish neighbors.

"Wie geht's?" the elderly man called as she approached his buggy.

"I'm doing fine, and you?"

"Oh, can't complain."

"Are you here to see my daed?"

Harold shook his head and stepped down from the buggy. "Found some pheasant eggs in the field this morning, and their mamm was lyin' dead beside them." He motioned to the cardboard box in the back of his buggy. "Don't believe she'd been gone too long, because the eggs were still warm."

"What do you think happened?"

"Looked to me like she'd been shot with a pellet gun."

Melinda gasped. "It's not pheasant hunting season yet. I can't understand who would do such a thing."

He shrugged. "Probably some kid usin' the bird for target practice."

Melinda's heart clenched. To think that someone would kill a defenseless animal for the mere sport of it made her feel sick.

"I thought you might like to try and get the eggs to hatch," Harold said.

"I may be able to keep them warm under the heat of a gas lamp, but it would be better if I could get one of our hens to sit on the eggs."

Harold grunted. "I've read about such things but have never attempted it before." He reached for the box and handed it to Melinda. "With all the interest you have in animals, you'd probably make a good vet. 'Course, you'd have to be English for that, I guess."

Melinda's throat constricted. Did Harold know what she was considering? Had Gabe let it slip, or had Dr. Franklin mentioned the idea of her becoming a vet to someone?

"I'm taking some of my pencil drawings into Seymour today," she said, hoping Harold wouldn't pursue the subject of her making a good vet. "In the past, I've sold a few pictures to the gift shop at the bed-and-breakfast there, so I'm hoping they'll want to buy more."

Harold reached under the brim of his straw hat and swiped at the sweat running down his forehead. "Wouldn't think there'd be much money to be made selling artwork around these parts."

"The owner of the bed-and-breakfast told me that tourists who stay there are usually looking for things made by the Amish."

When Harold made no comment, Melinda said, "Well, I'd best get these eggs out to the chicken coop. Thanks for bringing them by, and I'll let you know how it goes."

Harold climbed into his buggy and gathered up the reins. "Have a nice time in Seymour, and drive safely."

Melinda hurried off as Harold's buggy rumbled out of the yard. Now if she could only get one of the hens to adopt the eggs he had brought her.

Gabe was glad his dad had gone to Springfield and decided to close their shop for the rest of the day. That gave him the freedom to take Melinda to the farmers' market without having to ask for time off. Pap was a hard worker and didn't close up any more often than necessary. Whenever Gabe wanted a break from work, Pap usually made some comment like, "Them that works hard eats hearty."

"I work plenty hard," Gabe mumbled as he headed for the house. He planned to grab a couple of molasses cookies his mother had made yesterday, chug down some iced tea, and be on his way to Melinda's.

Inside the kitchen, Gabe found his mother standing in front of their propane-operated stove, where a large enamel kettle sat on the back burner. Steam poured out, and the lid clattered like Pap's old supply wagon when it rumbled down the graveled driveway.

"What are you cooking, Mom?" he asked, washing his hands at the sink.

"I'm canning some beets."

He sniffed deeply of the pungent aroma. "I wondered if that was what I smelled. Some tasty beets will be real nice come winter."

Gabe poured himself some iced tea. "Sure is hot out there today."

His mother turned and wiped her damp forehead with the towel that had been lying on the counter. "It's even warmer in here. That's the only trouble with canning. It makes the whole kitchen heat up."

Gabe grabbed a molasses cookie from the cookie jar on the counter and stuffed it into his mouth. "Umm. . .this is sure good."

She smiled. "Help yourself to as many as you like. Your sister Karen is coming over tomorrow, and we plan to do more baking."

Gabe took out six cookies and wrapped them in a paper towel. "Guess I'll eat these on my way over to the Hertzlers' place."

"Going to see Melinda?"

He nodded. "I'm taking her to the farmers' market in Seymour."

"Sounds like fun. Melinda's a nice girl."

"I think so."

"She and I had a little talk one day not long ago before she stopped by the woodworking shop to see you."

He tipped his head to one side. "Was it me you were talking about?"

Mom chuckled and reached behind the kettle to turn down the burner of the stove. "I was asking her advice on how to keep the deer out of my garden."

"What'd she tell you?"

"She suggested a couple of things. One was to put some feed out for the deer along the edge of our property." Mom gestured to the pot of boiling beets. "As you can see, it worked, because I have plenty of garden produce."

"Melinda's pretty schmaert when it comes to things like

that." *She's just not so smart when it comes to making a decision that would affect the rest of her life.* Gabe glanced at his mother. *Sure wish I could talk this over with Mom. She's always full of good advice and might have some idea on how I can get Melinda to see things from my point of view.*

"Are you troubled about something, son?" his mother asked. "You look a bit *umgerennt.*"

Gabe shook his head. "I'm not upset. Just feeling kind of confused about some things."

"Do you want to talk about it?"

Of course Gabe wanted to talk about it, but he thought about his promise to Melinda not to mention her plans to anyone, and he couldn't go back on his word. "Naw, I'll figure things out in due time."

Mom smiled. "I'm sure you will. Now run along and have yourself a good day at the market."

"I will," Gabe said as he hurried out the door.

A short time later, he was headed down the road toward the Hertzlers' place. As he gave his horse the freedom to trot, he thought about Melinda and prayed she would change her mind about becoming a vet. He'd been reading his Bible every night and asking God to show him if leaving the Amish faith was the right thing for either of them to do. So far, he'd felt no direction other than to keep working toward his goal of opening his own woodworking shop. If only Melinda would be content to marry him and stay in Webster County as an Amish woman who looked after needy animals, the way she was doing now. It didn't seem right that she'd want to follow in her mother's footsteps and leave the Amish faith to pursue a strictly English career.

By the time Gabe pulled into the Hertzlers' driveway, he was feeling pretty worked up. What he really wanted to do was tell Melinda exactly how he felt about things, but he didn't want to spoil their day at the farmers' market by initiating another argument. With a firm resolve to hold his tongue, he hopped out of his buggy and secured the horse to the hitching rail near the barn. He glanced up at the house, hoping Melinda would be on the porch waiting for him, but no one was in sight. He scanned the yard, but the only thing he saw was Isaiah's dog, Jericho, pacing back and forth in his new pen.

Gabe meandered over to see Jericho, and the mutt wagged his tail while barking a friendly greeting.

"You like your pen, boy?" Gabe reached through the wire, gave the dog a pat on the head, and then headed for the house. He was almost to the back door when he heard the sound of yodeling coming from the chicken coop.

"That has to be Melinda," he said with a chuckle.

He strode toward the coop and found Melinda on her knees in front of some eggs that were nestled in a wooden box filled with straw.

"What are you doing?" Gabe asked, shutting the door behind him.

Melinda lifted her head and smiled. "I'm watching to see if one of our hens will sit on some pheasant eggs Harold Esh brought by awhile ago."

Gabe squatted beside her. "How come he brought you those?"

"The mother pheasant had been killed, and since the eggs were still warm, Harold thought I might be able to get them to hatch."

Gabe shook his head. "You may as well become a vet, because everyone in Webster County thinks they should bring their ailing, orphaned, or crippled animals to you."

Melinda looked at him pointedly. "You really think I should become a vet?"

Gabe could have bit his tongue. Of course he didn't think she should become a vet. "It was just a figure of speech," he mumbled.

"I really do like caring for animals," she said in a wistful tone.

"I know you do."

"Are you're still thinking and praying about it?"

He nodded.

"Any idea how long it will be before you give me your final answer?"

He shrugged. "Can't really say. I've got to be clear about things before I can make such a life-changing decision."

"I understand. I feel that way, too. I don't want either of us to make a hasty decision." Melinda pointed to the pheasant eggs lying in the nest of straw. "I wonder how I can coax one of the chickens to sit on these."

In one quick motion, Gabe reached out, grabbed a fat red hen, and plunked her on top of the eggs. He didn't know who was the most surprised when the chicken stayed put, him or Melinda.

"She's accepting them!" Melinda clapped her hands. "Oh, Gabe, you're so schmaert. I should have thought to do that."

Gabe took Melinda's hand as they stood. "Are you ready to go to Seymour?"

She nodded toward the hen. "I'd better wait and see how things go. She might decide not to stay on the nest."

Gabe's face heated as irritation set in. "You'd give up an afternoon at the market to stay home and babysit a bunch of pheasant eggs that may never hatch?"

She shrugged.

"If your animals are more important than me, then I guess I'll head to Seymour alone."

Melinda's eyes were filled with tears. "Please don't be mad."

Gabe hated it when she cried, and he pulled her quickly into his arms. "I'm not mad—just hurt because you'd rather be out in the chicken coop than spend the afternoon with me."

"That's not true." Her voice shook with emotion. "I do want to go to the farmers' market with you today."

He glanced at the setting hen. "Does that mean you'll go?"

She nodded. "Jah, okay. I'll check on the eggs after we get back."

"Since I don't have to work today, I thought I'd go into Seymour and check out the farmers' market," Susie said to her mother as they finished cleaning up the kitchen.

Mama turned from washing the table and smiled. "I think that's a good idea. You're always complaining that you don't get to do anything fun, but going to the market should be enjoyable."

Susie smiled. "Would you like to go along?"

"I appreciate the offer, but I've developed a headache, so I think I'll go to my room and lie down awhile."

Susie felt immediate concern. "Are you *grank?*"

"I don't think I'm sick; just have a headache is all." Mama reached up and rubbed the back of her neck. "Probably slept wrong on my neck."

"Maybe it would be best if I stayed home." Susie placed the broom she'd been using into the utility closet and shut the door. "That way if you need anything, I'll be here to see that your needs are met."

Mama shook her head. "Don't fret about me, daughter. I'll be fine once I lie down and rest my head. You go along to the market and enjoy your day." She patted Susie's arm. "I insist on it."

Susie sighed. "Oh, all right. Is there anything you'd like me to pick up while I'm in town?"

"Hmm. . ." Mama pursed her lips. "Maybe some peanut brittle if anyone's selling it at the market. I haven't had time to make your daed any for quite a while, and it's his favorite."

Susie nodded. "All right then. If I see any peanut brittle, I'll be sure to bring some home." Feeling a sense of excitement, she scurried around to clean off the kitchen counters and wipe them dry. She could hardly wait to hitch up a buggy and head for town. Maybe she would see Melinda at the market. Maybe they could go out for lunch together.

Chapter 16

When Gabe and Melinda pulled into the parking lot at the farmers' market, Melinda felt a sense of excitement. She'd always enjoyed coming here and remembered several times when she was a little girl and had spent the day with her mother. She thought about one time when she and Mama had met Papa Noah at the farmers' market, before her parents were a couple. After leaving the market that day, the three of them had gone to lunch at Baldy's Café, and Melinda had enjoyed Mama's jokes and listening to country music on the radio.

"Maybe we can eat at Baldy's today," she suggested to Gabe. "Or how about Don's Pizza Place?"

"Either one is fine, I guess," she said. "We can look around the farmers' market awhile, eat lunch, and head over to the bed-and-breakfast where they sell Grandpa's rhubarb-strawberry jam and some of my drawings. I want to see what's sold and ask if they want me to bring any more in."

"That's fine by me." Gabe jumped down to help Melinda out of the buggy. "So where shall we start first?" he asked as they walked toward the tables on the other side of the parking lot.

"Wherever you like."

He took her hand and gave it a gentle squeeze. "I like it when we're not arguing."

"Me, too."

They walked hand in hand until they came to a table where an English man had some wooden holders for trash cans for sale. They resembled a small cupboard, but the door opened from the top, and the trash can was placed inside.

Gabe seemed quite impressed and plied the man with several questions. They soon learned that he lived near Kansas City and had been heading to Branson to sell some of his wooden items to a gift shop there. He said he'd heard about the farmers' market in Seymour and decided to rent a table before he went to Branson.

"I think I could make something like those and probably sell them for a lot less money than his are going for," Gabe whispered to Melinda as they moved away from the table. "I believe I'll make one to give Mom for Christmas this year."

"Have you ever thought that you could make and sell wooden items if you lived in the English world?" Melinda blurted without thinking.

Gabe frowned so deeply his forehead was etched with wrinkles, and Melinda knew she had spoiled their day together.

Gabe gritted his teeth as he and Melinda walked away from the English man's table. Melinda had obviously not given up her idea of going English, and it seemed as if she was trying to convince him that he would be happy giving up the only way of life he had ever known. *Could I be happy living in the English world?* he wondered. *Would l have more opportunity to have a woodworking shop of my own there, and would I be successful at it if I did?* The English man who had wooden trash holders for sale was obviously doing all right. Of course, that didn't mean Gabe would do well, but it did mean there was a need for well-crafted wooden items in the English world, as well as here in his Amish community.

Gabe grimaced. *Why did Melinda suddenly have to decide she wanted to become a vet? Why couldn't she be happy with the way things were? Maybe I should go see Dr. Franklin and ask if he'll try to talk Melinda out of leaving the Amish faith.*

"Let's look over there at the table where Mary King's selling peanut brittle," Melinda suggested, nudging Gabe's arm.

"Jah, sure," he mumbled. Maybe a hunk of peanut brittle would help brighten his spirits. He sure needed something to make him feel better right now.

"Wie geht's?" Melinda asked, stepping up to Mary's table.

Mary smiled, her brown eyes looking so sincere. "I'm doing well. How are you?"

"I can't complain." Melinda scanned the table full of baked goods, candy, and fresh produce. "Are you here alone, or is the rest of your family around someplace?"

"Ben's got our two oldest boys, Harvey and Walter, helping him do chores around our place today," Mary replied. "And the younger children are with Ben's sister, Carolyn."

"Is it hard for you to be on your own here today?"

Mary shook her head. "To tell you the truth, it's kind of nice. If Dan and Sarah were here, I'd be dealing with them wanting to run around, and then I'd probably end up having to work alone at the table anyhow."

Melinda chuckled. "That's how my little brother is, too. He always wants to run around and play when he should be working."

Gabe cleared his throat a couple of times. "I thought we were going to buy some candy, Melinda."

"Of course we are." Melinda picked up a hunk of peanut brittle that had been wrapped in cellophane paper. "If we break it in two, this one should be big enough for both of us."

"Whatever," he muttered. Melinda sure wanted to be in control of things. She couldn't even let him pick the peanut brittle he wanted. Well, there were some things she couldn't control, and him going English was one of them!

As Melinda and Mary continued to visit, Gabe glanced around the market area. He spotted his friend Aaron across the way, talking to his younger brother, Joseph.

Gabe cleared his throat, hoping to get Melinda's attention, but she kept right on yakking. Finally, he nudged her arm. "I'm going over to speak with Aaron."

"Okay. I'll join you there in a few minutes."

When Susie stepped down from her buggy and secured the horse to the hitching rail, she spotted Melinda on the other side of the market talking to Mary King. She was about to head that way when she noticed another buggy pulling in. Her heart skipped a beat when she saw Jonas Byler sitting in the driver's seat.

"I'm surprised to see you," she said when he jumped down from his buggy. "I figured you'd probably gone back to Montana."

"Nope, not yet. I thought it would be good if I stayed awhile and spent some time with my family."

A sense of excitement bubbled in Susie's chest. If Jonas wasn't going back to Montana right away, maybe there was a chance he might take an interest in her. "What can you tell me about Rexford, Montana?" she asked, hoping to let him know in a subtle way that she had an interest in him.

"What do you want to know?"

"What's the weather like, how many Amish people live in the area, what do the homes look like—"

Jonas held up his hand. "Whoa! One question at a time, please."

Susie's cheeks warmed. Ever since she'd been a little girl, she'd had a habit of running off at the mouth. No wonder she still had no boyfriend. Who would want a *blappere* woman for a girlfriend?

"You don't have to be embarrassed for asking questions." Jonas leaned against his buggy and smiled. "I just can't answer more than one at a time."

Susie felt herself begin to relax. Maybe Jonas didn't think she was a blabbering woman after all. "Let's start with the weather," she suggested.

For the next several minutes, Susie listened with rapt attention as Jonas told her about the cold, snowy winters they had in Montana, and how he went deer hunting every fall. He said most of the Amish homes there were built from logs, and that many of the Amish men in the area made log furniture.

"Even though we're a small community, I still enjoy living there," he concluded.

I wish you would stay here, Susie silently cried. *If you'd only take an interest in me, I'd do my best to make you happy.*

Jonas cleared his throat a couple of times. "Guess I'll wander around the market now and see what's for sale."

Invite me to join you. Oh, if you'd only ask. Susie knew she couldn't boldly suggest such a thing, but she might be able to drop a hint. "I was about to start looking, too," she said with a smile. "It's always interesting to see what others from our community are selling."

He shuffled his feet a few times then gave his horse a pat on the neck. "Well, I'll be seeing you around." Before Susie could open her mouth, he strode off toward a group of tables.

Should I follow him? No, that might seem like I was being pushy. With a frustrated sigh, Susie headed for some tables in the opposite direction.

Melinda had just left Mary's table when she noticed Susie

heading her way. "I didn't know you were going to be here today," she said when Susie reached her.

"I didn't know I was coming until this morning." Susie glanced around. "Are you here alone?"

"I came with Gabe." Melinda pointed across the way. "He's over there talking to Aaron."

"Oh, I see. Then I guess you'll be hanging around with him the rest of the day."

Melinda nodded. "We're going somewhere for lunch soon." She gave Susie's arm a gentle squeeze. "Why don't you join us?"

Susie shook her head. "I've told you before: I don't like being the fifth wheel on a buggy."

Melinda thought a moment before responding. "Maybe Gabe could invite Aaron, too. That way there will be four of us instead of three."

"No way!"

"Why not?"

"It might seem like you're trying to match me up with Aaron, and I'm sure he wouldn't like that any more than I would."

"Don't be silly," Melinda said with a shake of her head. "Everyone knows you and Aaron are only friends."

Susie grunted. "We're not really that much. I just know him is all."

"We've both known Aaron Zook since we were kinner, so it shouldn't seem to him or anyone else as if you're a courting couple."

Susie glanced over at the table where Jonas stood talking to a man who had some wooden products for sale, and Melinda couldn't help but notice her wistful expression. "I'm surprised to see Jonas Byler here today. I thought he was going back to Montana."

"I spoke with him a few minutes ago, and he said he had decided to stick around awhile longer so he can visit with his family."

"Is that so?"

"Jah, that's what he said."

"Maybe there's another reason he hasn't gone back to Montana yet."

"What other reason could there be?"

"Maybe some pretty woman has caught his eye."

Susie frowned. "You really think so?"

Melinda nudged Susie again. "You're smitten, aren't you?"

Susie's cheeks turned bright red, and her eyes darted back and forth as if she was worried someone might be listening to their conversation. "Okay, so I do have an interest in him." Susie grimaced. "For all the good it'll do me."

"What's that supposed to mean?"

"Jonas isn't interested in me. If he was, he would have asked me to walk around the market with him instead of going off by himself."

"Maybe he's shy." Melinda smiled. "Say, I have an idea. How about if I ask Gabe to invite Jonas to join us for lunch? Then you and Jonas can spend time together, and it'll give him the chance to see how wunderbaar you are."

"Puh! I'm not wonderful, and I don't want Jonas to think he's being set up." Susie shook her head. "If it's meant for us to be together, then Jonas will come to me on his own." Before Melinda could comment, Susie turned and hurried away.

"My poor aunt Susie," Melinda mumbled. "She wants a boyfriend so badly, and I've got one who doesn't see things my way. Maybe we'll both end up being old maids."

As Gabe sat at a table across from Melinda in Baldy's Café, he struggled to find something to say. It seemed as if every time they'd been together lately they had ended up in a disagreement. He still couldn't believe that while they were at the farmers' market, Melinda had suggested he make wooden items while living as an Englisher in the modern world. Didn't she realize he was happy living here, close to his family and friends? Didn't she realize how selfish she was being, asking him to leave all he loved behind?

But you love Melinda, a little voice niggled at the back of his mind. *Would you be happy living without her if she goes English and you stay Amish?*

"What's wrong?" Melinda asked, reaching across the table to touch Gabe's hand. "You look so *verwart.*"

"I am feeling a bit perplexed," he admitted.

"About what?"

"You and me going English."

"Are you still struggling with a decision?"

He nodded. "It would be hard to leave my family and friends."

"But we'd have each other, and we can come home for visits."

Gabe shook his head. "It wouldn't be the same, and you know it. Since we've both joined the church, if we leave, our ties to the church would be broken, and it would affect our relationship with our families, too."

"I know," she said with a slow nod. "But then, there are always concessions to be made when making a major change in one's life."

Gabe reached for his glass of iced tea and took a drink. "Let's change the subject, shall we?"

"What do you want to talk about?"

He plunked his spoon into the tumbler and stirred the ice around, making it clink against the glass. There didn't seem to be much they could talk about without arguing. If they talked about him wanting to hunt, Melinda would get defensive. If they talked about her wanting to become a vet, Gabe would be upset. If they talked about her preoccupation with animals and her lack of interest in other things, they would probably go home not speaking at all.

"Let's talk about the weather," he finally said. "It seems to be the safest subject of all."

Melinda smiled, but it appeared to be forced. "Jah, sure, we can talk about the weather."

Chapter 17

Melinda lounged against a log in the woods behind their home, where she'd been sitting for the last several minutes, sketching two does eating some corn she had scattered on the ground.

She thought about the way Gabe had looked at her when he'd brought her home from Seymour earlier today—as if he'd wanted to say something but was afraid to for fear they would have another disagreement. So instead of saying what was obviously on his mind, Gabe had told Melinda good-bye without even giving her a hug or a kiss. When she'd invited him to stay for supper, he had turned her down, saying he had somewhere else to go this evening. She was sure he was using it as an excuse not to be with her.

"We can't continue on like this," Melinda murmured. "We

both need to make a decision soon, and it should be Gabe, since I've pretty much made up my mind that I'd like to become a vet."

She glanced back at the deer grazing a few feet away. They looked so peaceful, she almost envied them.

"You're too pretty for anyone to kill," she whispered.

Pow! Pow! Pow!

Melinda jumped at the sound of a gun being fired, and the deer scattered.

"*Was is letz do?* What is wrong here? It's not hunting season yet." She dropped her tablet and pencil into the canvas tote at her feet, slung it over her shoulder, and followed the repeated popping sounds.

As Melinda stepped into an open field, the sight that greeted her sent a shock wave spiraling from the top of her head all the way to her toes. There stood Gabe, holding a gun and firing continuously at a target nailed to a tree several yards away.

Melinda remained motionless, unable to think, speak, or even breathe. Gabe kept on shooting, apparently unaware of her presence. When he ran out of bullets and began to reload, she marched up to him and poked her finger in his back. "Just what do you think you're doing?"

He whirled around. "Melinda, you scared me half to death!"

"Thanks to that noisy gun of yours, you scared the deer away that I had been sketching." Melinda's voice trembled, and her ears tingled.

"Sorry about that, but I'm target practicing—getting ready for fall, when hunting season opens." Gabe's eyebrows squeezed together. As he stared at her, the silence between them was thick like cream, only not nearly as pleasant. "If I'd known you were nearby trying to draw a picture, I wouldn't have shot the gun," he finally mumbled.

Melinda's hands shook as she held them at her sides, trying to gain control of her swirling emotions. "So this is where you planned to come after you dropped me off this afternoon, huh?"

"Jah."

"Why didn't you tell me that you were going to target practice?"

His chest expanded with a deep breath then fell when he exhaled. "I didn't think you'd want to hear it."

"How come?"

"I know how you feel about hunting, Melinda. I figured we'd end up having another argument if I even mentioned using my gun."

Melinda planted both hands on her hips. "The creatures in these woods are dear to me."

"And I'm not?" Gabe's eyelids fluttered in rapid succession. "Do the deer mean more to you than me?"

Melinda stared at the toes of her sneakers. How could she make him understand? "I do love you, Gabe, but I care about the animals God created, too. That's why I want to become a—"

"God made many animals for us to eat—deer included."

"Jah, well," Melinda huffed, "I'd better not see you on my folks' property with your gun again. I'm going home right now and ask Papa Noah to post some NO HUNTING signs on our land."

Gabe's mouth dropped open. "You're kidding!"

"I'm not."

"Listen, Melinda, you can't save every deer in the woods."

"I know that, but I can save those in *our* woods."

Gabe's only response was a disgruntled groan.

"And since we're already arguing—I think it's time we both make a decision about me becoming a veterinarian and us leaving the Amish faith."

"I can't leave, Melinda."

"Can't or won't?"

He stared at the ground. "I love you, but—"

"But not enough to help me realize my dream?"

"I want you to be happy, but I don't think leaving family and friends to become a vet will bring you the happiness you're looking for."

"This isn't about happiness, Gabe. It's about helping animals—as many as I can."

"I think you're obsessed with the whole idea, and I don't believe you've thought everything through."

"For several weeks I've done nothing but think about this. I'd thought that if you were in agreement with me and were willing to start a new life in the English world, I would know it was God's will."

"But I'm not willing, so it must not be God's will. Can't you see that?"

She shook her head. "You're confusing me."

Gabe reached out his hand to her, but Melinda backed away.

"I—I need to go," she murmured.

"Please don't, Melinda. Stay, and let's talk about this some more."

She turned her hands palm up. "What else is there to say? You want to stay Amish, and I want to—no, I *need* to—leave the faith."

"But you don't need to. You can—"

Melinda pivoted away from Gabe before he could finish his sentence. Clutching tightly to the canvas bag slung over her shoulder, she fled for home.

As Gabe watched Melinda run away from him, he wondered how the day could have ended on such a sour note. There had to be some way to make Melinda aware of how much he loved her. If he could get her to realize that fact, she might change her mind about leaving the Amish faith.

Gabe dropped to a seat on a nearby log and stared at his gun. *If I gave up hunting, would that make her happy?* He shook his head. *No, that's not our main problem. Even if I were to promise never to hunt another deer, I think she would still want to leave home and become a vet. Maybe I should talk to Noah about this—let him know what his daughter is thinking of doing.*

Gabe groaned and slapped the side of his head. "That would just make Melinda mad and maybe even more determined to have her way on this."

He sat several seconds, pondering things and praying for guidance, until an idea popped into his head. He jumped up. "I'm going home right now and make Melinda a special gift— something that will let her know how much I care. Something she can't take to any old college."

Melinda had just stepped into the yard when she spotted Susie climbing down from her buggy.

"Have you been in the woods again?" Susie asked as Melinda drew near.

"Jah. I was drawing a picture of some deer. Until Gabe scared them off, that is."

Susie's forehead wrinkled. "How'd he do that?"

"He had a gun and was shooting at a target nailed to a tree."

"You'd better get used to hearing guns go off," Susie said. "Soon it will be hunting season, you know."

"I do know, and it's not me I'm worried about. My concern is for the deer."

"Many of our men hunt," Susie reminded her. "It's just the way of things."

"I know that, too. I also realize I can't save every deer in the woods." Melinda compressed her lips. "I can, however, protect those that do come onto our property."

"So if you know you can't save every deer, then don't be so hard on Gabe. I'm sure he loves you."

"Then he should prove it."

"I think he did that when he asked you to marry him."

Melinda's mouth fell open. "You—you know about his proposal?"

Susie nodded. "I heard it from Gabe's mamm when I was working at Kaulp's Store last week. She dropped by to get—"

"Gabe must have told her," Melinda interrupted with a shake of her head. "I can't believe he'd do that after we agreed to keep it quiet until we had set a date."

"I don't see what the big secret is." Susie leaned against

the buggy and folded her arms. "Even if you're not officially published, your close friends and family members should know what you're planning."

"I would have told them if things weren't so *verhuddelt*."

"What things are mixed up?"

"Things between me and Gabe." Melinda drew in a shaky breath. "I'm beginning to wonder if I made a mistake in agreeing to marry him."

"You can't mean that. I think you're just upset about Gabe hunting. You're not thinking straight right now, that's all."

"You're right, I am upset, but there's more involved than just Gabe wanting to hunt. It's a lot more than you realize." Tears trickled down Melinda's cheeks, and she swiped at them with the back of her hand.

"I realize this," Susie said in a snappish tone, "If Gabe were *my* boyfriend, I'd do everything I could to make him happy. He's a good man and will make you a fine husband."

"I know he's a good man, but he doesn't love me enough to—" Melinda's voice trailed off, and she looked away.

"To what?"

"To—to leave the Amish faith with me." Melinda almost choked on her final words.

Susie's eyebrows shot up, and her eyes widened. "Please tell me you're kidding."

Melinda shook her head. "I'm not kidding."

Susie grabbed Melinda's arm and pulled her toward the buggy. "We'd better sit down so you can tell me about this crazy notion."

Melinda took a seat beside Susie in the front of her buggy

and drew in a deep breath. This was going to be harder than she'd thought.

"Now what's all this about you wanting to leave the Amish faith?" Susie asked, nudging Melinda's arm with her elbow.

"I didn't say I *wanted* to leave."

"But you said Gabe doesn't love you enough to leave the faith with you."

Melinda swallowed hard and pulled in another quick breath. "As you know, I've been working at Dr. Franklin's clinic for some time now."

Susie nodded.

"He's been telling me for quite a spell that I've got a special way with *gediere*."

"We all know that. You've been good with animals since you were a kinner."

Melinda moistened her lips with the tip of her tongue. "Which is why Dr. Franklin thinks I would make a good vet."

Susie's mouth dropped open. "But in order to become a vet, you'd need lots of schooling. A lot more than the eight years you've had, that's for sure."

"I know, and in order to get the necessary schooling, I'd have to leave the Amish faith and go English." Melinda paused and waited for Susie's reaction, but Susie just sat with her arms folded, staring straight ahead.

"I've made plans to take my GED test, which is the first step I'll need in order to prepare for college," Melinda continued.

"And Gabe knows about this and doesn't go for the idea?"

"He hasn't exactly said he doesn't go for the idea of me becoming a vet, but in order for us to be together, he'd have to go English with me, and he says he's not willing to do that."

Susie pursed her lips and squinted at Melinda. "And you are?"

"Well, I—"

"I know Gabe loves you, Melinda, but he'll have to break up with you if you go English and he doesn't."

Melinda grimaced. "At first Gabe said he would pray about things. But then we had an argument in the woods over him target practicing so he can hunt in the fall, and he ended up telling me that he won't leave the Amish faith."

"I can't believe this. I just can't believe it," Susie mumbled with a shake of her head.

"Do you think I'm wrong for wanting to take care of animals?"

"Not wrong for wanting to take care of animals. Just wrong for wanting to leave the only life you've ever known."

"That's not true," Melinda corrected. "I lived in the English world with my mamm and my real daed until I was six years old."

"You can't tell me you remember much about that."

"I remember some things."

Susie groaned. "I can't imagine how it would be not to have you in my life, Melinda. How can you even consider leaving your family and friends?"

"This isn't an easy decision for me, and I know the sacrifices I would have to make." Melinda nibbled on the inside of her cheek. "I feel a need to care for animals, and Dr. Franklin says I can't do it properly unless I have professional training."

"What do your folks have to say about this?"

"They don't know yet."

"You haven't told them a thing?"

Melinda shook her head.

"But they know Gabe's asked you to marry him, right?"

"No. I figured I'd wait until after I passed my GED test to tell them that, too. But since Gabe's not going to leave the Amish faith, there's really no point in telling them about his marriage proposal." Melinda clasped Susie's hand. "You've got to promise you won't say anything about this to anyone. Do I have your word?"

"I still think you should tell them, but until you're ready, I'll keep quiet."

Chapter 18

On Monday morning, Melinda stopped at the birdhouse out front before she headed for work. There she discovered a note from Gabe.

Dear Melinda,

I'm sorry about our disagreement yesterday, and I hope we can figure out some way to resolve our differences. I was wondering if you would be free to go on a picnic supper with me this evening. I'll bring the food, and I'll check the birdhouse for an answer before I pick you up. If you're willing, we can leave around six o'clock.

Always yours,
Gabe

Melinda smiled. Gabe had said he was sorry. Did that mean he'd changed his mind about leaving the Amish faith with her? Did he finally understand her need to become a vet?

She removed the pencil and tablet from the birdhouse and scrawled a note in return.

Dear Gabe,

I accept your apology, and I hope we can settle things between us. A picnic supper sounds nice. I'll be waiting for you at six, and I'll bring a loaf of homemade bread and some of Grandpa's rhubarb-strawberry jam.

Yours fawnly,
Melinda

With a feeling of anticipation, Melinda slipped the note into the birdhouse and climbed back into her buggy.

Things would be better now that Gabe had apologized, and she looked forward to their date tonight. For now, though, she needed to hurry or she would be late for work.

"Melinda, can you come here a minute?" Dr. Franklin called from examining room one.

Melinda set the mop aside that she'd been using to clean another examining room. "What do you need, Dr. Franklin?" she asked when she entered the other room and found him clipping the toenails of a little black Scottie.

"Would you mind holding Sparky while I finish cutting his

toenails? He's as jittery as a june bug this morning."

"I'd be happy to help." Melinda stood on the left side of the examining table and gripped the little dog around the middle with one hand. With her other hand, she held his front paw so the doctor's hands were free to do the clipping. She had assisted Dr. Franklin several times when he had a dog's nails to trim, and the animals always seemed relaxed and calm in her presence.

"Say, Dr. Franklin, I've been wondering about something."

"What's that, Melinda?"

"Well, actually, it's more Isaiah who wants to know the answer to a question."

He glanced up at her. "What does your little brother want to know?"

"Isaiah told me one day that he'd heard that if a dog has a dark mouth, it means he's smart. But if the inside of his mouth is light, then he'll likely be dumb." She giggled, feeling self-conscious for having asked such a silly question. "I told him it was probably just an old wives' tale, but he said I should ask you about it."

The doctor continued to clip Sparky's nails. "Actually, there's some truth in what your brother told you. It's not documented that I know of, but many animal breeders take stock in the color of a dog's mouth. I've heard it said that a dark mouth means a smart dog."

"Hmm. . .that's interesting."

"Sparky's sure doing well," Dr. Franklin commented. "He's a lot more relaxed with you holding him than he was when I tried working on him alone."

Melinda smiled in response. It made her feel good to assist

the doctor, and if she could help an animal relax, it was an added bonus.

"If you were a certified vet's assistant, I'd have you helping with many other things here in the clinic," the doctor said.

"I'd like that."

"And if you ever do become a veterinarian, I might consider taking you on as my partner."

"Really?" Melinda's heart swelled with joy. How wonderful it would be to work side by side with Dr. Franklin as his partner, not just as someone who cleaned up the clinic, helped with toenail clipping, or gave flea baths to the dogs and cats that were brought in.

"I really mean it. In fact, I've been thinking that I'd like to help with your schooling."

"Help?"

"Yes. Financially."

Her mouth fell open. "You—you'd really do that for me?"

He nodded. "As you know, my wife and I have no children of our own. It would give me pleasure to help someone who has such a special way with animals. You've got real potential, Melinda, and I'd like to see you use your talents to the best of your abilities."

"And you think in order to do that I'd need to go to school and become a vet?"

"Let me just say this. If you were my daughter, I would do everything in my power to make it happen." He set the clippers aside. "There you go, Sparky. All done until next time."

"Do you want me to put him in one of the cages in the back room until his owner comes to pick him up?"

"Yes, if you don't mind."

"I don't mind at all." Melinda scooped the terrier into her arms and started for the door.

"Oh, Melinda. . .one more thing," Dr. Franklin called.

She turned back around.

"I know my wife said she would drive you to Springfield next Friday to take your GED test, but her mother, who lives in Mansfield, fell and broke her hip last week. So Ellen will be helping her mother for the next couple of weeks, which means she won't be available to drive you to Springfield after all."

Melinda forced a smile to her lips in order to hide the disappointment she felt. "That's all right. I'm sure I can find someone else to drive me that day. I'll also need to give my folks a legitimate reason for me going to Springfield."

"You're still planning to wait and tell them after you've taken the test?"

She nodded.

"I hope it works out for you."

"Me, too, Dr. Franklin. Me, too."

As Gabe entered Dr. Franklin's veterinary clinic, his face beaded with sweat. He hoped Melinda had left for the day, because he wanted to speak to Dr. Franklin without her knowing. He found the man sitting behind his desk looking at some paperwork.

"Good afternoon, Gabe. I see you don't have your dog with you today," the doctor said. "Did you need something specific, or did you just drop by for a friendly chat?"

"I was wondering if Melinda is here," Gabe said, stepping up to the desk.

Dr. Franklin shook his head. "She left half an hour ago."

A sense of relief swept over Gabe. "That's good to hear."

The doctor's eyebrows drew together as he squinted. "If you're looking for Melinda, why would you think it's good that she's not here?"

Gabe swiped the back of his hand across his damp forehead. He was already botching things and hadn't even said what was on his mind. "I'm not actually *looking* for Melinda. I wanted to talk to you, but I don't want Melinda to hear what I have to say."

Dr. Franklin leaned forward, his elbows resting on the desk. "What did you want to speak to me about?"

"Melinda and her plans to become a vet."

"Oh, I see."

"She said you were the one who gave her the idea. Is that true?"

The doctor nodded. "Melinda's got a special way with animals, and she could use her abilities much better if she furthered her education and got the right training."

"But she takes care of stray animals at her home." Gabe made a sweeping gesture of the room with one hand. "And she helps you here at the clinic."

"Not the way she could if she were to become a vet or even a certified vet's assistant."

Gabe clenched and unclenched his fingers. This conversation wasn't going well at all. He moved a little closer and placed his palms on the desk. "I was hoping you'd be willing to discourage Melinda from leaving the faith."

"Why would I do that? As I said before, I think Melinda has potential."

"But if she leaves the faith, it will mean we can't be married. It will also put space between Melinda and her family."

Dr. Franklin stacked the papers lying before him into a neat little pile, pushed his chair away from the desk, and stood. "Have you considered leaving with her? I'm sure you could find a job in the field of woodworking. From what Melinda's told me, you're an excellent craftsman."

Gabe rubbed his sweaty hands along the sides of his trousers. It was obvious that Dr. Franklin didn't understand the way things were. All the man seemed to see was his own perspective, and he obviously had no idea of the consequences involved if Melinda left home. "So, you won't discourage Melinda from becoming a vet?"

The doctor shook his head. "Sorry, but no."

"Guess I'll have to be the one to do it then," Gabe mumbled as he turned and walked out the door.

Chapter 19

When Melinda returned home from the veterinary clinic later that day, she found her mother standing in front of the kitchen sink peeling potatoes.

"How was your day?" Mama asked over her shoulder.

"It was good. Dr. Franklin had me hold a terrier so he could clip its nails. He said the animal seemed calmer with me there."

"I know how much you enjoy working at the veterinary clinic. Do you think you'll miss it after you and Gabe are married?"

Melinda sank to a seat at the table. "Who told you Gabe had asked me to marry him?"

"I heard it from Freda Kaulp when I stopped by her store earlier today. She overheard a conversation between Susie and Leah Swartz the other day." Mama sounded disappointed, and Melinda knew it wasn't that she didn't want Melinda to marry

Gabe. More than likely, Mama was hurt because Melinda hadn't told her the news herself.

"I'm sorry you had to hear it secondhand," Melinda apologized. "When Gabe proposed, we decided not to tell anyone until we had agreed on a date." She sighed. "I guess Gabe must have told his mother. How else would Freda have found out?"

Mama washed and dried her hands then joined Melinda at the table. "So, *have* the two of you set a wedding date?"

"Not yet. We've had a couple of disagreements lately, and I don't want to make any definite plans until we get some things resolved." Melinda cringed. She hated keeping secrets from her mother. It would feel so good to tell the whole story about her wanting to become a vet and Gabe being unwilling to leave the Amish faith with her. But she knew how upset her parents would be if they knew she was thinking of leaving, and until she knew for sure, she didn't see any point in revealing her secret.

Mama reached over and took Melinda's hand. "We're all human, and disagreements come up even between two people who are deeply in love."

Melinda nodded.

"Just keep God in the center of your lives, live each day to the fullest, and after you're married, never go to bed angry at one another." Mama smiled. "It's important to work through your differences and pray about things rather than harboring resentment if you don't always get your way."

"I know that, Mama, but it's not always as easy as it seems."

"I never said it would be easy. A good marriage takes work, just like anything else that's worthwhile."

Melinda fiddled with the stack of paper napkins piled in

the wicker basket on the table. Could she and Gabe be putting themselves first? Was that why they'd been having so many problems lately? "Gabe's coming by around six o'clock to take me on a picnic supper," she said. "Maybe we can talk some things through then."

"That sounds like a good idea. Will you want help filling the picnic basket?"

"The note he left in the birdhouse out front said he's going to furnish the food. But I thought it would be nice if I took a loaf of bread and some of Grandpa's delicious jam."

"I baked a batch of honey-wheat bread this morning, so help yourself to a loaf. And we have several pints of Grandpa's rhubarb-strawberry jam in the pantry." Mama popped a couple of her knuckles and smiled.

Melinda winced. "Doesn't it hurt when you do that?"

"To me it feels good. Keeps my fingers from getting stiff."

Melinda didn't think she would ever crack her knuckles, no matter how old she was or how stiff her fingers might become. She stood. "Guess I'd better get my cat's supper ready before I go upstairs to change clothes for my picnic date with Gabe." She cupped her hands around her mouth and called, "Here Snow! Come, kitty, kitty. It's time for your supper."

"That's odd," Melinda said when, after a few minutes, there was no sign of the cat. "Snow usually comes running on the first call. Have you seen her, Mama?"

"Not since early this morning when she was racing around the house like her tail was on fire. I figured she might be after a mouse or something."

"Has she been outside today?"

"Not that I know of." Mama popped two more fingers, with an audible *click, click*. "I've never known a cat that liked to hang around the house the way that one does."

Melinda frowned. "I wonder if Isaiah's playing a trick on me and has hidden her someplace."

"He's upstairs in his room. Why don't you go ask him?"

"I think I will." Melinda turned toward the door.

"I hope you find Snow. I know how much you care for that cat," Mama called.

"I care about all my animals." Melinda sprinted up the stairs, making her first stop Isaiah's bedroom, where she rapped on the door.

"Come in!"

She found her brother sprawled on the bed with a book in his hands. "Isaiah, have you seen Snow?"

"Not since last winter. Sure hope we get plenty of it this year, 'cause I plan to do lots of sledding."

Melinda shook her head. "Ha! You must get your funny bone from our mamm."

"You're right; Mama can be kind of silly at times."

"Seriously, have you seen my cat today?"

Isaiah closed his book and sat up. "No, but awhile ago I thought I heard her out in the hall."

"Upstairs or down?"

"Up here."

"You heard Snow but didn't see her?"

"Right. I heard meowing, and then it stopped. Figured if it was the cat, she'd probably gone downstairs."

Melinda made little circles with her fingertips across her

forehead, hoping to stave off the headache she felt coming on. "I didn't see any sign of Snow downstairs, and when I called, she didn't come. It's not like her to hide when it's time to eat."

"Maybe she ain't hungry."

"Always has been before. And it's *isn't*, not *ain't*." Melinda leaned against the door jamb and gritted her teeth as frustration rolled through her body like a whirling windmill. Why did her little brother have to be so difficult? "Has Snow been in the house all day?"

"Don't know. Haven't seen her at all."

Meow. Meow.

Melinda cocked her head. "Did you hear that?"

"Sounds like the cat's somewhere nearby."

"I'm going to find her." Melinda left the room and followed the meowing sounds until she came to a small hole in the wall at the end of the hallway. It seemed too little for her cat to have gone through, yet she could hear Snow's pathetic meows inside the wall.

The first thing Gabe did when he pulled into the Hertzlers' driveway was to check inside the birdhouse to see if there was a response from Melinda. Sure enough, she had left a note saying she would go on the picnic supper with him.

He grinned and glanced at the surprise he had in the back of his buggy. He hoped she would be so pleased with the gift that she would see how much he loved her and change her mind about leaving home to become a vet.

Gabe hopped back into the buggy and picked up the reins. A few minutes later, he tied his horse to the hitching rail and took the porch steps two at a time. He knocked on the door and waited. It took awhile for someone to answer, and when the door finally opened, Melinda's brother stood on the other side.

"I'm here to pick up Melinda. Is she ready to go?" Gabe asked the boy.

Isaiah shook his head. "I don't think so. She's sittin' in front of a hole in the wall upstairs."

Gabe's eyebrows lifted. "Why would she be doing that?"

"Her cat's stuck in there, and she can't figure out how to get the silly critter out. The hole's too small for Melinda to reach her hand into."

"What does your daed have to say? Can't he cut a bigger hole?"

Isaiah shrugged. "Guess he could, but Papa ain't here. He's workin' late at the tree farm and probably won't be home until it's almost dark."

"I'd better go see what I can do to help," Gabe said, stepping into the house.

Isaiah led the way, and Gabe followed him up the stairs and down the hall until they came to the place where Melinda and her mother were on their knees calling to the kitten.

Gabe cleared his throat, and Melinda looked up at him with a dismal expression. "Snow seems to have squeezed through this tiny hole, but she can't get back out."

"She was probably after a mouse," Faith put in.

"I can cut a bigger hole if you want me to," Gabe offered. "Where does Noah keep his saws?"

"Out in the barn." Faith nodded at Isaiah. "Run on out there and get one of your daed's saws, would you, son?"

"Okay." The boy scampered off.

Gabe squatted beside Melinda. "I can patch the hole I make with a piece of Sheetrock, and it'll be good as new."

"What if Snow won't come to me once the hole is bigger?" Melinda asked.

Meow! Meow!

"Does that answer your question?" Gabe smiled. "Sounds like your cat can't wait to get out of there."

"I agree," Faith said. "Once Gabe cuts a bigger hole, you can stick your hand inside. I'm sure Snow will come right away."

Isaiah showed up a few minutes later holding a small handsaw, which he handed to Gabe. It didn't take long for Gabe to make a larger opening, and he was careful not to let the blade of the saw stick too far through the other side. He knew if he cut the cat by mistake, Melinda would never forgive him. She might even see it as one more reason for her to leave home.

Once the opening was made, Melinda put her hand inside. "Here, Snow. Come, kitty, kitty."

There was a faint *meow*, and when Melinda pulled her hand out again, she had Snow by the nape of the neck.

Gabe breathed a sigh of relief. The cat was okay, and Melinda was smiling again.

"Danki, Gabe," she murmured.

"You're welcome." *Maybe now she'll realize how much she needs me. And when she sees what I have in my buggy, she's sure to know how much I love her.*

"I think I'll take Snow downstairs and feed her while you

patch the hole." Melinda stood and hurried off toward the stairs.

"If there's a scrap of Sheetrock in the barn, I can fix the hole now," Gabe said, turning to Faith. "If not, I'll bring some over later on."

"I appreciate that. It's very kind of you. It's obvious you like working with your hands," Faith said. "The little deer you carved for Melinda turned out very nice."

"Danki."

"Speaking of deer, Melinda's been spending a lot of time in the woods lately, drawing pictures of the wildlife she sees there. Has she shown you any of her pictures?"

Gabe grimaced. After the argument he and Melinda had a few days ago over him hunting, just the mention of deer made him cringe.

"You're frowning. Don't you care for Melinda's drawings?"

"It's not that," Gabe was quick to say. "It's just. . .well, she seems so protective of the deer in the woods. She doesn't even want me to go hunting."

"I've heard her complain about others who like to hunt, too. However, Melinda realizes she can't keep all the deer safe or stop everyone from hunting, but she wants to protect those that are on our property." Faith sighed. "Sometimes I worry about Melinda's preoccupation with the animals. It seems like all she wants to do is sketch pictures of those she sees in the woods and take care of those she's in contact with here and at the veterinary clinic. Sometimes she shirks her duties at home in order to care for one of her animals."

Gabe fought the temptation to tell Faith that her only

daughter was contemplating leaving the Amish faith to become a vet. It was Melinda's place to tell her folks, not his. Besides, he'd made a promise not to tell anyone until she felt ready and knew for sure what she planned to do.

"I'd better get out to the barn and see if there's any Sheetrock so I can fix this hole," Gabe said, pushing his thoughts aside.

Faith nodded. "And I'd better head back downstairs and get some sewing done."

Half an hour later, Gabe and Melinda stood in front of his open buggy. He had patched the hole with a piece of plywood he'd found in the barn and planned to come back tomorrow with a new piece of Sheetrock, tape, and the mud he would need to do the job correctly.

"See that piece of canvas I have right there?" Gabe said, motioning to the back of his buggy.

Melinda nodded.

"Pull it aside and take a look at what I made for you last night."

"Is it a trash can holder like the one we saw at the farmers' market?"

He shook his head. "It's something I hope you'll like even better."

Melinda gave the canvas a quick yank, and when a long wooden object came into view, she tipped her head in question. "What is this, Gabe?"

"It's a feeding trough—so you can feed the deer that come

into the woods bordering your place."

"That's a wunderbaar idea. If the deer come to our place to eat, they'll be safe from hunters." Unexpectedly, Melinda threw herself into Gabe's arms and squeezed him around the neck. "I'm so glad you want to care for the deer now rather than kill them."

Gabe swallowed hard. Melinda had obviously misinterpreted his gift. How could he admit to her that he had no intention of giving up hunting? He enjoyed hunting and would continue to do so. He just wouldn't do it on her folks' land.

Chapter 20

With the warm August breeze tickling her nose, Melinda leaned back on her elbows and sighed. She loved being here at the pond where birds and wildlife abounded and everything seemed so peaceful. Gabe's picnic supper of barbecued beef sandwiches, dill pickles, and potato salad had left her feeling full and satisfied. Even though he'd admitted that his mother had made most of the meal, Melinda appreciated the gesture. Gabe seemed to enjoy Mama's homemade bread, too, for he ate several pieces slathered with some of Grandpa's rhubarb-strawberry jam.

Not wishing to ruin their meal with a possible argument, Melinda hadn't asked Gabe if he had told his mother that he'd proposed. She thought it would be best to wait awhile on that. So they'd only had a pleasant chat on the drive from her house to the pond, and for the last hour, they'd been sitting on an old quilt enjoying the picnic supper and having more lighthearted conversation.

Melinda glanced over at Gabe. His eyes were closed, and his face was lifted toward the sky. He obviously enjoyed being here, too. *If I can't get him to change his mind about going English, and I have to leave on my own, I'll surely miss him. It doesn't seem fair that I'm expected to choose between those I love and the joy of caring for animals. I wish I could have both.*

As if sensing her watching him, Gabe opened his eyes. "Were you sleeping?" she asked.

"Nope." He smiled at her in such a sweet way it sent shivers up her spine. "I was just enjoying the warmth of the sun and thinking about how much I want to make you my wife."

Her cheeks warmed. "Gabe—I—"

"Whatever differences we may have, can't we just agree to disagree?"

A little crease had formed in the middle of Gabe's forehead, and Melinda reached up to rub it away. "I wish it was that simple."

"You love me, and I love you. We shouldn't allow anything to come between us."

Melinda was about to reply, but Gabe stopped her words by pulling her into his arms and kissing her. She couldn't think when she was in his arms. Nothing seemed to matter except the two of them sharing a special time of being alone together.

"Let's go for a walk," he said suddenly. "When we get back, we can have some of that apple crisp my mamm made for our dessert."

Melinda nodded, and he helped her to her feet. As they walked together among the pine trees, she knew all the wonderful moments she had shared with Gabe today would stay with her forever.

"I hate to spoil the evening," Gabe said sometime later, "but there are a few things we need to discuss."

"You're right," she agreed. "I also have a question I want to ask you."

"You can ask me anything, Melinda."

"Did you tell your mamm that you'd asked me to marry you?"

Gabe stopped walking, and so did she. "I hope you don't mind, but Mom came right out and asked how serious I was about you. So I felt she had the right to know that I'd proposed marriage."

"I see. Well, apparently, your mamm told Susie when she dropped by Kaulp's General Store, and Freda Kaulp overheard the conversation, and then she blabbed it to my mamm today." Melinda groaned. "Mama wasn't too happy hearing this news secondhand."

Gabe's forehead wrinkled. "I'm sorry she had to learn about it that way, but you really should have told your folks yourself. Don't you think?"

"I agree, but we had decided not to tell anyone until we'd set a date and had resolved things between us."

"I know, but—"

Melinda jerked her head. "Did you hear that?"

He shrugged. "I didn't hear anything except the rustle of leaves when the wind picked up."

"Listen. There it is again—a strange thrashing sound." Melinda let go of Gabe's hand and hurried off.

"Where are you going?"

"To see what that noise is."

"Not without me, you're not. It might be some wild animal."

When they came upon the source of the noise a few seconds later, Melinda was shocked to discover a young doe with its leg caught in a cruel-looking metal trap. The poor animal thrashed about pathetically, obviously trying to free itself.

"Oh no!" She rushed toward the deer, but Gabe grabbed her around the waist and held her steady.

"What are you trying to do, get yourself hurt?" he scolded.

"I need to free the deer and make sure her leg's not broken."

"Melinda, I don't think that's such a good idea."

She wiggled free and went down on her knees.

Gabe watched as Melinda crawled slowly toward the deer. He didn't like her taking chances like this but figured if he made an issue of it, she would get mad. All he wanted to do was keep her safe—locked in his heart and loved forever.

The doe lay on its belly with the trapped foot extended in front of her. Strangely enough, when Melinda approached, it stopped thrashing and twitched its ears. It was almost as if the critter knew Melinda was there to help.

I wish there was something I could do, but if I get as close to the deer as Melinda is, it will most likely spook. Except for my dog, most animals aren't as comfortable around me as they seem to be with her. Gabe held his breath as Melinda pressed the sides of the trap apart, freeing the animal's leg. An instant later, the deer jumped up and bolted into a thicket of shrubs.

"I wish I'd had the chance to check it over thoroughly," Melinda said when she returned to his side. "I'm sure the doe's leg must have been cut." She shook her head slowly. "I'll never understand why anyone would want to hurt a beautiful deer like that."

Gabe resisted the temptation to argue that hunting deer for food was perfectly acceptable to his way of thinking. But he knew they would argue if he broached that subject again. Besides, setting a trap was no way to catch a deer or any other animal, for that matter. To make the situation worse, it wasn't even hunting season yet.

Gabe checked the trap to be sure it would no longer work and then buried it in the dirt.

"See why I asked Papa Noah to post NO HUNTING signs on our property?" Melinda's eyes shimmered with unshed tears. She really was sensitive where animals were concerned. A little too sensitive to Gabe's way of thinking. After all, it wasn't as if the critters were human beings.

"Let's head back to our picnic spot and eat our dessert," he said, hoping to brighten Melinda's mood.

She shook her head vigorously. "I have no appetite for food right now. Besides, we haven't finished our conversation yet."

Melinda and Gabe had gone only a few feet, and hadn't even begun to talk about things, when she spotted a baby skunk scampering out of the bushes. "Oh, look, Gabe! Isn't it cute? I wonder if it's an orphan."

"Don't get any dumb ideas, Melinda."

She halted and held her breath, waiting to see what the little skunk would do next. If it wasn't orphaned, she was sure its mother would show up soon.

"Melinda, let's go."

She shook her head. "I need to see if the skunk's mother is around."

"If she does come on the scene, we could be in a lot of trouble." Gabe grabbed Melinda's hand and gave it a tug, but she pulled away.

"I won't go back until I know the baby's not alone."

"And if it is?"

"I'll take it back to my place so I can care for it."

"No way! I won't allow that skunk in my buggy. What if it sprays?"

"Baby skunks never spray unless they're bothered, Gabe."

"Jah, well, picking up a skunk and hauling it home in a buggy could easily be considered 'bothering.' "

Ignoring his comment, Melinda tiptoed a bit closer to the small creature, but she'd only taken a few steps when the baby's mother trotted out of the bushes. Before Melinda had the presence of mind to turn and run, the skunk lifted its tail and let loose with a disgusting spray.

"Let's get out of here!" Gabe hollered.

Melinda gasped for a breath of fresh air as she and Gabe raced toward his buggy. They were about to climb in when he stopped her with an outstretched arm.

"What's wrong? Why are you blocking my way?"

"It's bad enough that we both smell like a skunk. If we get

into my buggy, it will stink to high heavens, too."

She squinted at him. "We can't walk home, Gabe. It's too far."

"You're right, but I'm afraid my buggy will never be the same after this trip to the woods."

Melinda dropped her gaze to the ground. "I'm sorry. This was all my fault. I just wanted to be sure the skunk wasn't orphaned, and—" She stopped talking when her eyes started to water.

"Don't cry, Melinda. I hate it when you cry."

"I'm not crying. My eyes are watering because of this awful odor." She fanned her face and whirled around a few times. "Phew! Did you ever smell anything so awful?"

Gabe shook his head. "Not since we found a batch of rotten eggs out behind our henhouse." He plugged his nose. "Even that didn't smell half as bad as we do now."

"I'll help you wash down the buggy," she promised.

"We've got to get this smell off ourselves first."

She nodded. "Maybe Dr. Franklin has something we can use to get the odor out of the buggy—and us, too."

"My dog Shep got himself mixed up with a skunk once," Gabe said. "We bathed him in tomato juice."

"Did it help?"

"Some, but it took weeks before that animal smelled like a dog again."

Melinda folded her arms. "That's not exactly what I wanted to hear."

Gabe laughed, and so did she. At least it had only been a skunk that had come between them this time. And they'd been able to find some humor in it. That was a sign that things were improving in their relationship. At any rate, Melinda hoped they were, even if she and Gabe hadn't had the chance to discuss things and get everything ironed out between them.

Chapter 21

Melinda awoke on Friday morning, tingling with excitement along with a sense of apprehension. Today she would be going to Springfield to take her GED test at the college. Their English neighbor, Marsha Watts, had agreed to give her a ride, but Melinda had only told her folks that she was going to Springfield to do some shopping. It was true. She planned to shop for a few things after she'd taken her test. She would tell her folks about Dr. Franklin's suggestion that she become a vet after she passed the test.

"*If* I pass the test," she murmured as she stepped into a freshly laundered dress.

Melinda hurried from the room and headed for the kitchen to help her mother with breakfast. Usually, Mama was already up and scurrying about, but today Melinda found the kitchen empty.

"Where's Mama?" she asked Papa Noah when he came in

from doing his morning chores a short time later. "Was she outside with you?"

He shook his head. "Your mamm came down with the stomach flu during the night."

Melinda felt immediate concern. "I'm sorry to hear that. Is there anything I can do?"

"I'd appreciate it if you would cancel your trip to Springfield today," he said, hanging his straw hat on a wall peg near the door. "She can't keep anything down and is feeling as weak as a newborn kitten. I don't think it's a good idea for her to be alone today."

"What about Isaiah? Won't he be at home?"

Papa Noah shook his head. "Hank Osborn is shorthanded because a couple of his fellows also have the flu. So I'm taking Isaiah with me to help at the tree farm today."

Melinda nibbled on the inside of her cheek. "How about Grandpa? Can't he keep an eye out for Mama today?"

"He's got his own share of health problems, Melinda. I don't think it's a good idea for him to be exposed to your mamm when she's sick, do you?"

"No, of course not, but—"

"You can go shopping some other day, right?"

Melinda released a sigh. "Okay, Papa Noah. I'll run over to Marsha's house and tell her I won't need a ride to Springfield after all."

Papa Noah smiled. "You're a helpful daughter, and it puts my mind at ease to know I can go to work knowing that my wife will be in good hands today."

Melinda reached for her choring apron. *I suppose I can wait a few more weeks to take that test. Maybe by then I'll be more prepared.*

Gabe stood in front of his workbench sanding the arms of a wooden rocking chair. It was a nice change from working on cabinets, which was what Pap usually stuck him with. Even so, Gabe would rather have been working on the gun stock he'd promised to make for Aaron. After Aaron saw how nice Gabe's gun stock had turned out, he'd placed an order for one just like it. A couple of other men in their community had also asked Gabe to make them a new gun stock, which meant he had plenty of his own work to keep him busy after regular working hours.

If he kept getting orders for gun stocks, he might be able to open his own business sooner than he'd expected. If he had his own place, Melinda might understand why he didn't want to leave their Amish community and start life over in the English world.

Gabe glanced over his shoulder. His dad was working on a coffee table Bishop Frey had recently ordered for his wife's birthday.

Maybe I should tell Pap what I'm thinking of doing. Let him know I'm wanting to go out on my own. It wouldn't be right to wait and drop the news on him when the time comes.

Gabe set the sandpaper aside and moved across the room. "Say, Pap, I was wondering if I could talk to you about something."

"Sure, son. What's on your mind?"

Gabe shifted from one foot to the other, his courage beginning to waver. "I've. . .uh. . .been thinking that I'd like to have my own place of business."

"Are you saying you'd like to open another woodworking business here in our area?"

"Jah."

Pap crossed his arms and stared hard at Gabe. "Would you mind explaining why you'd want to be in competition with me?"

Gabe shook his head. "It wouldn't really be in competition. I'd be making other stuff—things like gun stocks, animal cages, birdhouses, and maybe some different kinds of household items, like the trash can holder I've made to give Mom for Christmas."

"I see."

Hope welled in Gabe's soul. Maybe Pap understood.

"Do you think you could handle a shop on your own?"

Gabe nodded.

"Guess time will tell." Pap shrugged his shoulders. "In the meanwhile, we've got a job to look at in Branson that will take a couple of weeks to finish."

"What kind of job?"

"A bed-and-breakfast needs some new furniture, and they want it to be made by an Amish carpenter."

Gabe leaned against his dad's workbench. "What part of the job will you expect me to do?"

"That all depends."

"On what?"

"On what all the customer wants made."

"Who'll we get to drive us to Branson?"

"I don't know yet. Probably Ed Wilkins. He's usually available whenever I need to go somewhere outside the area."

Gabe headed back to his own workbench. At least Pap hadn't

said he would be stuck doing the menial jobs for the bed-and-breakfast. Maybe he would let Gabe build some of the furniture and not just do finish work.

"Oh, and Gabe, there's one more thing," Pap called over his shoulder.

"What's that?"

"If it turns out you're still working for me after you and Melinda get married, I want you to know that I'll pay you enough so you can make a decent living."

Gabe sucked in his breath. Should he tell Pap that he and Melinda might not be getting married? Would Pap have some good advice if he knew what Gabe was up against right now? Or if Pap knew the whole story, would he be worried that Gabe might decide to leave their Amish community and go English with Melinda?

Gabe grabbed his piece of sandpaper and gave the arm of the chair a couple of good swipes. *I'd best not say anything yet. Better to wait until I know for sure what's what.*

When they woke up Saturday morning, Melinda's mother had said she was feeling better and suggested that she and Melinda pick some produce from their garden. They'd spent most of the morning harvesting tomatoes and green beans. Now they stood at the kitchen sink washing the bounty of produce.

"Why don't you let me finish this up?" Melinda suggested. "You were sick yesterday, and it's probably not a good idea for you to overdo."

Mama fanned her hand in front of her face. "I'm fine, dear one. It was only a twenty-four-hour bug, and I promise to rest once the produce is washed and put away." She smiled. "I appreciated your canceling your shopping trip yesterday and staying home to see to my needs. It proves what a thoughtful daughter you are."

Melinda's face heated with embarrassment. If her mother only knew that she'd planned to do more than shopping in Springfield, she wouldn't be saying such kind things.

"All these tomatoes make me think about that day a few weeks ago when the skunk sprayed you and Gabe," Mama said.

"The two of us smelled to high heavens, and you wouldn't let me come inside until I'd bathed in the galvanized tub Papa Noah had set up in the woodshed." Melinda grimaced at the memory of it. After several baths, alternating tomato juice and a mixture of hydrogen peroxide, baking soda, and liquid dishwashing soap, she had scrubbed so hard she was afraid she wouldn't have any skin left on her body.

The day after their spraying, she and Gabe had washed his buggy down with something Dr. Franklin had given her that was stronger than what she'd bathed in. Never again would Melinda knowingly go near a skunk.

Mama had just placed another batch of tomatoes on a towel to dry when Isaiah entered the room. "I'm glad I didn't have to go to work with Papa today," he muttered. "Pullin' weeds around them trees was harder than workin' in the garden."

"A little hard work never hurt anyone, and I know your daed and Hank Osborn appreciated the help." Mama smiled. "Both of my kinner sacrificed to help others yesterday, and it pleases me to know we've raised such willing workers. I don't know what

I'd do without either of my dear children."

Melinda cringed. *What will Mama say when she finds out what I'm thinking of doing? Will she understand why I feel the need to become a vet? Will I feel guilty and miserable once I leave home? Can I really give up all that I have here with my family and friends? I wish I felt free to tell Mama that I'm going to take my GED test as soon as I can reschedule a time. But if she knew, she would probably try to stop me.*

Melinda closed her eyes and leaned against the kitchen cupboard as confusion swirled in her brain like a windmill going at full speed. *Oh, Lord, please help me to know what to do.*

Chapter 22

Two weeks later as Melinda left the college in Springfield where she'd finally gone to take her GED test, a feeling of weariness settled over her like a drenching rain. The test had been difficult—much harder than she'd expected it to be. But she had studied hard and knew she had done her best. If all went well, by this time next week, she might know the results of her scores.

If I find out I've passed the test, then what? she wondered. *Do I really want to leave everyone I love and start life over in the English world?* So many conflicting thoughts swirled around in her brain. One minute, she wanted to become a vet, and the next minute, she wanted things to remain as they were. Why was it so hard to decide what was best for her? She had been thinking and praying about this for weeks. Why wasn't God giving her any clear direction?

She shook the troubling thoughts aside as she approached Marsha's car. *I'll figure this out after I get the results of my test.*

"How did it go?" Marsha asked when Melinda opened the car door and slid into the passenger's seat.

Melinda shrugged. "It was a hard test, but I think I did okay."

"When will you know the results?"

"In a week or so, I expect."

"And then will you tell your folks?"

Melinda nodded.

"Would you like to go somewhere for lunch now, or do you want to do some shopping first?" Marsha asked.

"I'm kind of hungry, so if you don't mind, I'd like to have lunch first."

"That sounds good to me." Marsha started the engine and pulled away from the curb. "When we get back to Seymour, I'd like to stop by Kaulp's General Store before I drop you off at your house. I want to buy a couple of those large wooden spoons they sell there."

"That's fine by me. Since Kaulp's isn't far from my home, I'll just walk from there." Melinda leaned against the seat and tried to relax. Oh, how she wished she knew the results of that test. She hated being deceitful, but if she had told Mama or Papa Noah the real reason she'd gone to Springfield today, they would have tried to talk her out of it. She felt grateful that Marsha had promised not to say anything.

"I'm heading out to make a delivery," Gabe's dad said as he plucked his straw hat off the counter near the front door and plunked it on his head. "Can you handle things here while I'm gone?"

"Jah, sure," Gabe mumbled. It always irked him whenever Pap asked that question. And he asked it nearly every time he left the shop. Wouldn't the man ever realize that Gabe was capable and could manage things on his own?

"I'll be back sometime before supper," Pap said as he headed out the door.

Gabe grunted and reached for a hunk of sandpaper. "I can't wait until I own my own shop," he muttered when the door clicked shut. He gritted his teeth and gave the arm of the rocking chair he'd been working on a couple of solid swipes.

Sometime later, the shop door opened, and Noah stepped into the room. "How's it going, Gabe?"

"Fine. We're keeping plenty busy these days."

"It's always good to be busy."

"Jah."

"Is your daed around, or are you on your own this afternoon?"

"It's just me. Pap had a delivery to make."

"I see." Noah leaned against the workbench closest to where Gabe was working. "I was on my way home from work and thought I'd stop and talk to you for a minute."

Gabe stood and brushed the sawdust off his trousers. "Is there a problem?"

"Not a problem, exactly." Noah shifted his weight as he cleared his throat. "I'm. . .uh. . .a bit concerned about my daughter."

"Is Melinda all right? Has something happened to her?"

Noah shook his head. "She's not sick or anything like that. In fact, she had one of our neighbors take her to Springfield for the day so she could shop for some things that aren't available in Seymour."

Gabe grimaced. If Melinda had gone to Springfield, she was probably planning to take her GED test today. Did Noah know about it? Is that why he wanted to talk to Gabe? Did Noah think Gabe had some influence over Melinda and could talk her out of going English? But what if Noah didn't know? Gabe had to be careful about what he said so he wouldn't let the cat out of the bag in case Melinda hadn't told her folks about her plans yet.

"What did you want to say to me about Melinda?" Gabe asked.

Noah drew in a quick breath and released it with a huff. "Her mamm and I think she's spending way too much time with those critters of hers. We're afraid if she doesn't find a happy medium soon, she'll end up spending the rest of her life with her priorities all mixed up."

"What's that got to do with me? As I'm sure you must know, Melinda's and my relationship isn't so solid anymore."

"I know you've had words a few times; Melinda confided that much to her mamm. Even though you don't always see eye to eye on things, I'm sure she cares for you, Gabe."

"I care for her, too."

"I'm hoping you might be able to convince her not to spend so much time with those critters of hers. She needs to spend more time helping her mamm and learning things that will help prepare her for marriage."

Gabe groaned as he pulled his fingers through the sides of his hair. "I'm not sure I'm the one you should be talking to, because I don't have that much influence where your daughter is concerned. Fact is our relationship is slipping so bad that she doesn't much care what I have to say about anything."

Noah placed his hand on Gabe's shoulder. "Do you love my daughter?"

Gabe nodded. "Guess I'll always love her."

"Do you think it would help if I put in a good word for you? Or maybe Faith could invite you and your family over for a meal sometime soon."

Gabe shook his head. "Melinda knows what it will take for our relationship to get better. I don't think a meal or a good word from you will make any difference."

"Is the problem you're having about hunting? Does Melinda expect you to give up hunting?"

Gabe rubbed his chin as he contemplated the best way to reply to Noah's question without revealing the real problem. "Let's just say that Melinda's priorities are different than mine, and unless she changes her mind about certain things, we can never have a future together."

Noah stared at Gabe with a peculiar expression. Finally, he turned toward the door, calling over his shoulder, "I'll be praying for you and Melinda."

"I appreciate that."

When the door clicked shut behind Noah, Gabe dropped to his knees and resumed sanding the rocking chair. Oh, how he hoped Melinda would come to her senses and choose him and her family over her animal friends.

Susie had just put a bolt of blue material on one of the shelves near the back of Kaulp's store when the bell above the front door jingled, signaling that a customer had entered the building. She turned and saw Melinda and Marsha Watts step up to the front counter where Freda Kaulp stood.

A few minutes later, Marsha and Freda moved over to the shelf where the kitchen items were kept, and Melinda headed in Susie's direction.

"Did you come here with your neighbor, or did you just happen to arrive at the same time?" Susie asked as Melinda joined her in front of the shelves full of fabric.

Melinda leaned close and whispered in Susie's ear. "Marsha drove me to Springfield this morning."

"That's nice, but why are you whispering?"

Melinda gave a quick glance over her shoulder then blotted the perspiration from her forehead with the corner of her apron. "I don't want Freda to know where I've been."

Susie squinted. "Why not? Lots of folks in our community hire a driver to take them to Springfield for shopping and appointments."

"Not the kind of appointment I had this morning."

"What kind of appointment did you have?"

Melinda's voice lowered even further. "I went to the college to take my GED test."

Susie swallowed hard as a sick feeling swept over her. So Melinda really was serious about leaving the Amish faith and becoming a vet. She had hoped it was only a passing fancy and that Melinda would give up the idea when she'd had a chance to pray about it.

"You don't look very happy about me taking the test."

"I'm not."

"Don't you even want to know how it went?"

Susie shrugged. "I figured you'd get around to telling me."

Melinda pursed her lips. "It was a hard test. Much harder than I expected it would be."

Susie bit the inside of her lip to keep from smiling. She'd never say it to Melinda, but she'd hoped the test would be difficult and that Melinda would fail. Flunking the test might be the only thing that would keep Melinda from making the biggest mistake of her life. At least, that's how Susie saw it.

"When will you get the results?" Susie asked.

"I–I'm not sure. I expect I should know something in a week or so."

"I see." Susie's fingers traveled over the bolts of material stacked on the shelf as she mulled things over. If Melinda passed her GED and decided to take some college courses to prepare for her veterinary training, they might never see each other again. Once Melinda moved away and pursued a career, she'd have little reason to come home except for an occasional visit. Susie figured even those times would be strained.

Melinda tapped Susie on the shoulder.

"What?"

"Ever since we were little and Mama and I moved here after she'd been an entertainer, you and I have been good friends and shared everything with each other."

Susie knew full well how close she and Melinda had been over the years. But things were tense between them now, and they would only get worse once Melinda left home. *How does Melinda expect me to be happy about this decision?* She turned to face Melinda.

"Does Gabe know you went to take the GED test today?"

Melinda shook her head. "I saw no reason to tell him."

"I'll bet you haven't told your folks yet, either. Am I right?"

"No, I haven't told them. I will, though, as soon as I receive my test scores."

"Will you tell them even if you've failed?"

"I don't know. Probably not, since there would be nothing to tell. I can't make a final decision on what I should do with my future until I've passed that test. So, until I do, mum's the word, okay?"

Susie drew in a deep breath as she slowly nodded. Oh, how she wished she didn't have to keep Melinda's secret.

Chapter 23

Clutching a basket of freshly picked tomatoes, Melinda trudged wearily from the garden to the house. It seemed as if there were no end to the ripe tomatoes, and today she and Mama planned to do up several canner-loads. Dr. Franklin had wanted Melinda to work at the clinic this afternoon, but with so many tomatoes to be harvested, she felt obligated to lend her mother a hand. It was a sacrifice, considering that Melinda would much rather be holding a dog or a cat than canning squishy tomatoes. If she became a vet, she'd have even more contact with animals than she did just working for Dr. Franklin a few days a week.

Melinda couldn't believe it had been a week already since she'd taken her GED test. She worried about when she would get the results and whether she had passed. All this week, she'd alternated her time between working at the clinic and helping

Mama can beans and tomatoes, hoping to keep busy enough that she wouldn't think about the test results.

Melinda glanced out the window at the line of trees bordering the back of their property. If she couldn't be working at the clinic, she would have enjoyed being in the woods on this Saturday morning, sketching some of the wildlife. Even being inside the chicken coop, checking on the baby pheasants that had hatched yesterday morning, would have been preferable to being here in the stuffy house. Maybe when she finished with the tomatoes, there would be time for her to make a quick trip to the woods.

Melinda had just placed the tomatoes into the sink to be washed when Isaiah entered the kitchen waving a stack of letters.

"Mail's here," he announced. "Where do you want it?"

Mama nodded toward the table. "You can put it over there, and then I'd like you to go back outside and pull some weeds in the garden. They're starting to overtake the bean plants again."

Isaiah's forehead creased, making a row of tiny wrinkles. "How come Melinda didn't pull the weeds when she was out there picking tomatoes?"

"I didn't have time for that," Melinda responded before Mama could open her mouth. "As it is, I'll be busy all afternoon helping put up the tomatoes I got picked. So the least you can do is to pull a few weeds."

"Melinda's right," Mama agreed. "So grab yourself something cold to drink and hurry out to get the job done."

Isaiah grunted, ambled over to the refrigerator, and withdrew a jug of lemonade. He poured himself a tall glass of the liquid, drank it down, and headed out the door, letting it slam shut behind him.

Mama clicked her tongue noisily. "That boy! Sometimes I think he was born in a barn."

Melinda smiled. It was kind of nice to hear Mama become riled over something Isaiah did for a change. Usually it was Melinda she was upset with. "Is it all right if I take a break to look at the mail?" Melinda asked.

"Sure. I can handle this on my own for a bit."

Melinda took a seat at the table and thumbed through the mail. Her hands trembled when she spotted an envelope with the college's return address. It had to be the results of her GED test. She was glad she'd been given the opportunity to go through the mail first, and not someone else in the family.

I probably should have had them send it to Dr. Franklin's office, she thought, glancing at her mother, who was still at the sink with her back to Melinda. *But they asked for my home address, and I didn't want to be deceitful by writing down something other than where I actually live.* She cringed as a sense of guilt washed over her. *I've already been deceitful by not telling my folks I took the test or letting them know about my plans for the future. I need to right that wrong—and soon.*

Melinda ripped open the envelope, and as she studied her scores, her heart took a nosedive. She'd failed the test.

She had passed the English part of the exam, but the math section had been much harder and she'd missed too many questions. Her only recourse was to study more then retake the test. Either that, or she would have to give up her dream of going to college and eventually on to veterinary school. Maybe it wasn't meant for her to go. Maybe. . .

"Anything interesting in the mail today?" Mama asked, breaking into Melinda's contemplations.

"What? Uh. . .I haven't looked through all of it yet." Melinda slipped the envelope with the GED results under her apron waistband. If she had passed the test, she would have told Mama her plans. But since she'd failed, she saw no point in mentioning it now.

Maybe the Lord is trying to tell me something. Could He want me to give up the idea of becoming a vet and learn to be content being an Amish housewife?

She grabbed the rest of the mail and quickly thumbed through it. *Or maybe I'm supposed to be patient and wait until I'm more prepared. Oh, Lord, please show me what I'm supposed to do.*

Gabe stared out the window of the van. He and his father had hired Ed Wilkins to drive them to Branson this morning, and after meeting with the owners of the bed-and-breakfast, Pap had signed a contract to make five new tables with matching chairs for their guest kitchen. Gabe wouldn't know until later how much of that job he would be allowed to do, but he had enjoyed his time in Branson.

As they traveled along the main street, he observed several fancy theaters with parking lots full of cars and tour buses. Melinda had told him that this was one of the towns where her mother used to perform, and he wondered if it had been in any of the theaters along this stretch of road.

What must it have been like for Faith to live here and be up on stage before an audience, yodeling and telling jokes? he wondered. *Does she ever miss it? Would Melinda want to live here if she becomes part of the English world again? I'm sure the reason she wants to leave the Amish faith has more to do with her desire to help animals than it does with the allure of the modern world.*

Gabe grimaced. They still hadn't talked things through, and the truth was Gabe had been avoiding the subject whenever he'd seen Melinda. He wanted her to stay Amish and become his wife, not run off to some fancy school and go English. As much as he wanted to be with her, the thought of leaving the Amish faith turned his stomach sour.

"Did you enjoy the lunch we had at the Country Buffet?" Pap asked, breaking into Gabe's disconcerting thoughts.

Gabe nodded and patted his stomach. "I had more than my share of peach cobbler and vanilla ice cream at the dessert bar, too."

His dad chuckled. "Same here."

"What have you got lined up for us to do after we get home this afternoon?" Gabe asked.

"A couple of doors need to be sanded. But since there won't be many hours left to work by the time we get back to the shop, I think you can take the rest of the day off."

"You mean it?"

Pap nodded. "Said so, didn't I?"

Gabe smiled. He figured if he headed straight for the woods after they got home, he'd have plenty of time to do some target practicing before Mom had supper ready.

Melinda tromped through the tall grass, making her way to the woods behind their house. She was glad to finally have some time to herself. All day as she and Mama had canned tomatoes, she'd grieved over failing her test. Maybe being in the woods awhile would help her gain some perspective.

As Melinda passed the deer feeder Gabe had made, she wondered if she could survive in the English world without him. She hadn't seen Gabe for a couple of weeks, but he'd left a note in the birdhouse yesterday saying he and his dad would be going to Branson to look at a job today. Melinda wished she could have gone with him. She hadn't been back to Branson since she was a little girl. A couple of times during her growing-up years, she'd asked about going there, but Mama always said Branson was part of her past and that she had no desire to go there again.

As Melinda stepped into the woods, her mind whirled with confusion. *English or Amish? Forget about taking another GED test or try again? Marry Gabe or become a vet?*

She shook her head, trying to clear away the troubling thoughts. Three deer—a buck and two does—showed up on the scene, and she quickly took a seat on a tree stump. Pulling her drawing tablet and pencil from the canvas bag she'd brought along, she watched in fascination as she sketched the beautiful creatures.

Pop! Pop! Pop! Melinda tipped her head. It sounded like a gun had been fired somewhere in the distance. But that was impossible. It wasn't deer season yet. Besides, Papa Noah had posted No Hunting signs on their property. Someone would have to be pretty dumb to be hunting on their land.

Pop! Pop! The noise came again, a little closer this time.

The deer bolted into the bushes, and Melinda groaned. *Just one more thing to ruin my day.*

She tossed her artwork into the canvas satchel, slung it over her shoulder, and headed toward the gunfire, keeping low and, hopefully, out of danger. Whoever was shooting was in for a good tongue-lashing.

A few minutes later, she came to a halt. Gabe stood next to her little brother, and Isaiah held a gun in his hands!

Melinda marched over to them, jerked the gun away from Isaiah, and thrust it at Gabe. "What are you doing here?"

"I'm showing Isaiah how to shoot."

Her heart pounded, and her mouth felt so dry she could barely swallow. "What would make you do such a thing?"

"Isaiah saw the gun stock I made for Aaron when he was over at the Zooks' playing with Aaron's younger brothers," Gabe explained. "When he and your daed dropped by our shop the other day, Isaiah asked if I'd teach him how to shoot."

"Did my stepdaed agree to that?" Melinda's question was directed at Gabe, but it was Isaiah who responded.

"When I asked Gabe about shootin' a gun, Papa was busy talkin' to Gabe's daed. I didn't think he'd mind since I'm twelve years old now." Isaiah looked at Melinda as though daring her to say otherwise. "I can hunt with a youth permit as long as I'm with an adult who's licensed to hunt."

Melinda's attention snapped back to Gabe. "You said you

were giving up hunting."

He frowned. "I never said that."

"You told me you were sorry about our disagreement and that—"

"I *was* sorry. Sorry we had words but not sorry for shooting my gun." His jaw clenched, and the late afternoon shadows shifted on his cheek. "I don't see anything wrong with hunting deer when it's for food, not just a trophy."

Melinda realized Gabe was right. He hadn't actually said he wouldn't hunt anymore. She'd just assumed that's what he meant when he'd apologized. And after he gave her the deer feeder he'd made, she thought he felt the same way about the forest animals as she did. She also knew that many men hunted deer for food, not just the sport of it. Even though she couldn't save every deer in the woods, the ones in these woods were hers, and she didn't want any of them hurt. She also didn't like the idea of Gabe teaching her little brother how to hunt.

"It's obvious to me," she said in a shaky voice, "that you don't care nearly as much about animals as I do, which is probably why you won't—"

Gabe held up his hand and nodded toward Isaiah.

Melinda knew it wasn't a good idea to discuss their problems in front of her little brother. In her irritation with Gabe, she'd almost forgotten Isaiah was still there.

"You'd better head for home," she told her brother.

He jutted out his chin. "You ain't my boss."

Gabe intervened. "Isaiah, I think it would be best if you did go home. Your folks might be missing you by now."

Melinda was tempted to tell Gabe he should have thought

about that before he dragged her little brother into the woods and placed a gun in his hands, but she decided to keep quiet. Enough had already been said in front of Isaiah, and she didn't want him going home and spouting off everything he'd heard her and Gabe say.

"Okay, I'll go," Isaiah mumbled. "But it's only because Gabe asked me so nice." He cast a quick glance at Melinda and wrinkled his nose.

Melinda folded her arms and said nothing.

"Maybe we can target practice some other time," Isaiah said, smiling at Gabe.

"We'll have to wait and see how it goes," Gabe replied.

"Jah, okay." Isaiah tromped off toward home.

Melinda waited until he was out of sight before she spoke again. Drawing in a deep breath to steady her nerves, she looked right at Gabe. "You don't have to worry about me leaving the Amish faith. At least not any time soon."

He blinked a couple of times as though he didn't quite believe her.

"I failed my GED test."

"You. . .you did?"

She nodded solemnly.

"So you've given up on the idea of becoming a vet?" he asked with a hopeful expression.

"Well, I—"

"It's for the best, Melinda. You'll see that once we're married."

Melinda drew back like a turtle being poked with a sharp stick. "You don't even care that I failed, do you?"

"Of course I do, but—"

"You know what I think, Gabe?"

He shook his head.

"Even if I was to stay Amish and we did get married, we would probably always be arguing."

"I don't think so, Melinda."

"Jah, we would. We'd argue about all my pets that you think are silly. We'd argue about whether it's okay for you to hunt or not. We'd argue about—" Melinda's throat felt too clogged to say anything more. All she wanted to do was run for the safety of home. And that's exactly what she did.

Chapter 24

Gabe watched Melinda's retreating form as a sense of despair washed over him. He had made such a mess of things. It seemed as though that's all he did anymore—clutter everything between him and Melinda and make her upset. "I never should have brought Isaiah into the woods to target practice," he mumbled. "Especially not without getting Noah's permission." He gathered up his gun and ammunition. "This whole thing between me and Melinda stinks about as bad as when the two of us got sprayed by a skunk!"

Gabe knew the first thing he needed to do was apologize to Melinda's stepfather. Then he had to come up with some way to patch things up with Melinda. There had to be something he could do to make her realize how much he loved her. Either that or they would have to go their separate ways, which seemed to be what she wanted. But it sure wasn't what Gabe wanted. Why couldn't Melinda just be happy with the way things were? Why would she want to give up her family and friends just to take care of some dumb old animals?

Gabe swallowed around the lump that had formed in his throat as he started walking toward the Hertzlers' place. He'd been in love with Melinda too long to let their relationship go, no matter how much they disagreed on things. No, he couldn't give up on them yet.

Melinda paced the length of the front porch, waiting for Papa Noah to show up. Usually he had Saturdays off, but he had worked at the Christmas tree farm today because Hank Osborn was shorthanded.

Melinda thought about the tree farm and how much she had enjoyed visiting there when she was a girl. It had been exciting to see the rows of various-sized pine trees that would eventually become some English person's Christmas tree. She hadn't visited Osborn's Tree Farm in several years.

I don't need to look at Christmas trees anymore. Not when I've got a whole forest full of beautiful trees I can gaze at whenever I want.

Melinda glanced at the darkening sky, knowing she needed to go inside and see if her mother needed help with supper. She was about to turn when her stepfather's buggy rolled into the yard.

Melinda bounded off the porch and sprinted out to the buggy in time to see Gabe walking across the open field between their house and the woods. She hurried to Papa Noah's side as soon as he stepped down from the buggy. "I need to tell you something," she panted.

"What is it? You look *verlegge*."

"I am troubled. I've just come from the woods, where I discovered Isaiah and Gabe. You'll never guess what they were doing."

"What was it?"

"Gabe was teaching Isaiah to shoot a gun."

Papa Noah's eyebrows furrowed. "He was?"

"Jah."

Before Papa Noah could say anything more, Gabe stepped between them, all red-faced and sweaty. "I need to speak with you, Noah."

"Is it about you teaching my son how to shoot?"

Gabe nodded. "When Isaiah asked me to teach him to shoot a gun, I figured he'd gotten your permission and that you had a youth permit for him." Gabe gave Melinda a sidelong glance, but she looked away.

"Isaiah has never said a word to me about wanting to hunt or even asked about shooting a gun," Papa Noah said with a shake of his head.

"I'm sorry. I should have asked you first. Please know that it will never happen again." Gabe's expression was somber, but Melinda couldn't help but wonder if he really was sorry. Maybe he was simply trying to keep himself out of trouble with her stepfather.

"I accept your apology, Gabe," Papa Noah said. "I appreciate the fact that you had the courage to come talk to me about this matter."

A look of relief flooded Gabe's face.

Papa Noah glanced over at Melinda. "I need to put my horse away. Would you please tell your mamm I'll be in for supper soon?"

She nodded. "I'll give her the message."

Papa Noah headed for the barn, and Melinda turned toward the house. She'd only taken a few steps when Gabe touched her shoulder. "Listen, about our disagreement—"

She halted and turned around.

"I'm sorry about your GED. I understand how much it meant to you."

Melinda shook her head. "I don't think you do understand, Gabe. If you did, you might be more willing to do some things just for me."

"Like what?"

She pointed to the gun in his hands.

"I wasn't planning to hunt on your property."

"I don't care where you had planned to hunt. You shouldn't be teaching Isaiah to hunt. He's too young."

"Not if he has a youth permit and hunts with your daed."

"Papa Noah doesn't hunt, and to my knowledge, he never has."

Gabe stared at the ground, kicking small rocks with the toe of his boot. "The truth is you don't want me to hunt at all. Isn't that right?"

"I know we need some animals for meat," she said, avoiding his question. "But the deer are special to me."

"I realize that. The deer and every other critter you want to help." He stared at her with such intensity she thought he might break down and cry. "The simple fact is you care so much about animals that you'd be willing to give up your faith, family, and friends in order to care for them the way Doc Franklin does."

"Gabe, I—"

"And you want me to give up all those things in order for us to be together."

Tears welled in Melinda's eyes. Gabe was right. She did want that. She thought if he was willing to leave the Amish faith, it would prove how much he loved her.

"Even if we both left the faith, things would never feel right between us," he said with a catch in his voice.

"What do you mean?"

"I'd be leaving family and friends, and so would you."

"I know that, and the thought of it pains me, Gabe. But we would have each other, and eventually, we'd have a family of our own."

"I'd have to give up my dream of owning my own woodworking business, too."

She shook her head. "You could do carpentry work in the English world."

He took a step toward her. "I love you, Melinda, and I always will, but it's time I face the fact that your wants and my wants don't mesh. I'd thought maybe we could work things out, but now I realize it's just not possible. So, as much as it hurts me to say this, I've come to realize that it has to be over between us." Before she could comment, Gabe swung around and bolted from the yard.

With tears coursing down her cheeks, Melinda moved slowly toward the house. Gabe was right. They both wanted different things. Even though it pained her to admit the truth, if she decided to leave the Amish faith, they would have no future together because Gabe wasn't willing to leave.

It was difficult for Melinda to attend church at the Hiltys' the next day, but she knew that unless she was sick, there was no way she could get out of going. After what had happened yesterday between her and Gabe, she didn't want to face him.

Melinda had just stepped down from the buggy when Susie rushed up to her. "Is it true, Melinda? Have you and Gabe broken up for good?"

"I can't believe the news is out already," Melinda muttered. "Who told you?"

"Gabe must have told his mamm, and then she told my mamm when they got here a few minutes ago." Susie eyed Melinda critically. "Please tell me it's not true."

Melinda quickly explained the way she'd discovered Gabe teaching Isaiah how to shoot and how they had argued, and then Gabe had broken things off.

Susie's expression was solemn. "I can't believe you'd be so *narrisch*. Don't you realize how much Gabe loves you?"

"I'm not being foolish." Melinda shrugged. "I guess Gabe doesn't love me as much as I thought."

"Maybe there's something you can say or do to make Gabe change his mind."

Melinda shook her head as tears clouded her vision. "I would have to give up caring for animals if we got back together."

Susie's eyebrows lifted. "Why would you have to do that?

You're caring for animals now, aren't you?"

Melinda didn't know how to respond. It was true—she was caring for some animals, but in a very small way. The little bit she did for the animals she rescued was nothing compared to how she would be able to help them if she became a vet. "We'd better get inside," she said, moving toward the house. "There's no point discussing this because it won't change a thing. Besides, church will be starting soon."

Susie touched Melinda's arm. "If you've broken up with Gabe, does that mean you won't be at the young people's gathering tonight?"

Melinda nodded. "I had planned on going until our breakup, but not now. It wouldn't seem right."

"But you'll miss all the fun if you don't go."

Melinda shrugged.

Susie stared at the ground. "I guess if you're not going, then I won't, either."

Melinda felt as if a heavy weight rested on her shoulders. Susie had no boyfriend to take her home from the gathering, but she'd obviously been looking forward to going. *If Susie stays home on account of me, she'll be miserable, and I'll feel guilty for days.*

Melinda forced her lips to form a smile. "Jah, okay. I'll go tonight."

"You look like you've been sucking on a bunch of sour grapes," Aaron said to Gabe as they climbed down from their buggies.

Gabe moved to the front of his buggy and started to unhitch

the horse. "Yesterday, Melinda and I broke up," he mumbled.

Aaron skirted around his own rig. "You're kidding, right?"

"No, it's the truth."

"But I thought you two were crazy in love."

Gabe grunted. "I used to think that, too."

"What happened?"

"Melinda caught me in the woods behind their place teaching her little bruder how to shoot a gun."

Aaron reached under his hat and scratched the back of his head. "That's all? She broke up with you because you were teaching her brother to shoot?"

"Actually, it was me who broke up with her, but I think she agrees that things could never work out between us." Gabe grabbed his horse's bridle and led him toward the corral, where several other horses milled about.

Aaron followed, leaving his own horse hitched to the buggy. "If you love the woman so much, why don't you fight for her?"

"Melinda's love for animals has come between us," Gabe said. "She doesn't want me to hunt, either." He was tempted to tell his friend the rest of the story but figured Aaron might blab to someone else that Melinda wanted to become a vet. Gabe felt sure it would be better for everyone if he kept that information to himself.

"I think it's ridiculous that Melinda would object to you hunting. She can't save every deer in the woods." Aaron shook his head. "If you want my opinion, Melinda's got *verhuddelt* thinking."

"It might be confused thinking to you and me, but it isn't to her."

Aaron leaned against the corral while Gabe put his horse inside. "What are you going to do about this?"

Gabe turned his hands palm up. "What can I do?" *Besides give up hunting and leave the Amish faith so Melinda can fulfill her crazy, selfish dream.*

"I know what I would do," Aaron said.

"What's that?"

"I'd tell Melinda she's verhuddelt and that she needs to come to her senses."

Gabe shook his head. "That would only make things worse. The best thing I can do at this point is to pray about our situation."

"You never know. Melinda might change her mind about you hunting. Women are prone to that, you know," Aaron said with a serious expression.

Gabe gave his horse a gentle pat and left the corral. "You'd best get your horse in here. Church will be starting soon."

"You're right." Aaron followed Gabe back to his horse and buggy. "You know, this whole ordeal you're going through with Melinda is just one more reason why I'm never getting married!"

Maybe Aaron had the right idea about marriage, Gabe thought. Maybe it would have been better if he'd never allowed himself to fall in love with Melinda.

Chapter 25

Melinda didn't know why she had let Susie talk her into attending the young people's gathering, but there she sat, alone on a bale of straw in Abe Martin's barn. It was hard to watch others engage in playing games and sharing friendly banter. Everyone but her seemed to be having a good time. How could she enjoy herself when she wasn't with Gabe and wouldn't be riding home in his buggy at the close of the evening?

It might have been easier if Gabe hadn't been here tonight, but he was standing in front of the punch bowl talking to Mattie Byler. Had he found a replacement for Melinda so soon? The thought of Gabe courting someone else made Melinda's stomach feel queasy, and unbidden tears sprang to her eyes. She sniffed and swiped them away when Susie plunked down beside her.

"Guess what?"

Susie seemed excited about something, but in Melinda's glum mood, it was all she could do to respond with a shrug.

"I can't believe it, but Jonas Byler asked if he could give me a ride home in his buggy tonight."

"Mattie's brother?"

"Jah. Jonas is five years older than me, and until now he's never given me so much as a second glance." Susie grinned. "Maybe Jonas sees me in a different light now and realizes that I'm not a little girl anymore."

"That could be."

"If Jonas decides he likes me, maybe he will stay here and not return to Montana after all."

"Maybe so."

"I hear tell many Amish folks who have moved to remote settlements like those in Montana don't stay very long." Susie popped a couple of her knuckles, the way Melinda's mother often did. "Jonas says. . ."

Melinda broke off a piece of straw and clenched it between her teeth. She really didn't care about any of this but didn't want to appear rude.

"I've never traveled much and would like the chance to see some of the states out West," Susie went on to say. "Jonas says the Amish who live in northern Montana have log homes, only they're much nicer than those the pioneers used to live in."

Melinda listened halfheartedly as her aunt droned on about Jonas and Montana. It was hard for Melinda to concentrate on anything other than Gabe and Mattie, who stood off by themselves in one corner of the barn with their heads together.

I wonder if he's doing that just to make me jealous. He probably thinks if I believe he's interested in someone else, I'll say it's okay for him to hunt and I'll stay Amish and won't try to retake my GED or become a vet. Melinda clenched her fingers into tight balls and held them firmly in her lap. "Maybe I ought to move to Montana," she muttered.

Susie nudged her arm. "What was that?"

"Oh, nothing." Melinda stood, smoothing the wrinkles in her dark blue dress. "I think I'll go outside for a breath of fresh air."

"Would you like some company?"

Melinda shook her head. "If Jonas plans to take you home tonight, you'd better stay put. I wouldn't want you to miss out on your first date with him because of me."

"I'm sure he won't leave without me. Besides, the gathering's not over yet."

"Just the same, I'd rather be alone if you don't mind."

Susie shrugged. "Suit yourself."

Melinda noticed Jonas heading their way with two glasses of punch, so she hurried off. At least Susie was having a good time this evening, and she deserved to be happy.

Outside, Melinda wandered around the yard, staring up at the sky and studying the bright, full moon and thousands of brilliant stars twinkling like fireflies in the night sky. She thought about an old yodeling song her mother had taught her a few years ago.

With arms folded and face lifted toward the night sky, she quietly sang the words of the song. "O silvery moon, I'm so lonely tonight; to stroll once again in your beautiful light. There's a fellow I adore and a longing to see, in that beautiful Yo Ho Valley. My little yodel-tee-ho—yodel-tee-ho—yodel-tee-ho—tee!

I'll sing you a song, while the moon's growing low. My little yodel-tee-ho—yodel-tee-ho in the beautiful Yo Ho Valley."

A lump formed in Melinda's throat, and she couldn't go on singing. It hurt too much to be reminded that Gabe was no longer her special fellow. *I probably shouldn't have come here tonight,* she thought regretfully as tears spilled onto her cheeks. *If only Gabe and I could work things out. If only. . .*

Philippians 2:3 popped into her mind: *"Let nothing be done through strife or vainglory; but in lowliness of mind let each esteem other better than themselves."*

More tears came, and Melinda reached up to wipe them away. She knew she hadn't put Gabe's needs ahead of hers, but shouldn't he care about her feelings, too? If Gabe really loved her, why couldn't he see how much she wanted to help hurting animals, and why wouldn't he reconsider leaving the Amish faith with her so she could do it? It would be a sacrifice on both their parts, but. . .

"How come you're out here by yourself?"

Melinda whirled around at the sound of a deep voice. In the light of the full moon, she realized it was Gabe's friend, Aaron.

"I–I'm just getting some fresh air."

He grunted. "Jah, fresh and chilly. Fall's right around the corner, and winter will be here before we know it."

"I assume winter's not your favorite time of the year?"

He shrugged. "I can take it or leave it. To tell you the truth, I prefer the warmer days of summer when I can go fishing."

Melinda rubbed her hands briskly over her arms. Aaron was right. It was kind of nippy.

"I'm sorry about you and Gabe breaking up," Aaron said.

"Seems a shame you two can't find some way to work out your differences."

Melinda swallowed hard, hoping to push down the lump in her throat that wouldn't go away. So Aaron knew, too. Probably all the young people here tonight had heard the news. "Gabe doesn't understand how I feel about things," she murmured.

"Seems to me that you don't understand him, either."

Melinda cringed. Had Gabe told Aaron all the details of their breakup? He must have, or Aaron wouldn't have said such a thing. Now everyone would soon know the truth, if they didn't already. She wasn't sure she was ready to deal with that. Especially since she still hadn't told her parents any of the details.

"Uh, Aaron, please don't say anything to anyone about me wanting to leave the faith, okay?"

"Huh?"

"I haven't told my folks I'm thinking about becoming a vet, so—"

"Whoa!" Aaron held up his hand. "You're thinking of what?"

"I thought you knew. From what you said earlier, I figured Gabe must have told you everything."

Aaron let out a low whistle. "Now I know why he seemed so upset."

"You mean he didn't tell you what I'm thinking of doing?"

He shook his head. "Just said you'd broken up because he wants to hunt and you're opposed to the idea."

Melinda grimaced, feeling like someone had punched her in the stomach. Aaron hadn't known the truth until she'd opened her mouth and blabbed the whole thing. Now he might tell others, and then things could get really sticky.

She glanced to the left and caught sight of two people walking toward one of the open buggies. Her heart plummeted when she realized it was Gabe and Mattie. When Gabe helped Mattie into the passenger's seat then climbed up beside her, Melinda's whole body trembled. It hurt to know he had gotten over her so quickly.

She turned away, unable to watch the couple drive off together.

"Sorry you had to see that," Aaron said, touching her arm.

"I'd better get used to it, because from the way things look, Gabe will probably marry someone else and I'll be—" Her voice caught on a sob. "Oh, please, Aaron, don't say anything about what I've shared with you tonight."

He shook his head. "It's not for me to say, Melinda."

"Danki. I appreciate that." She sighed. "I wish the singing was over and I could go home. Papa Noah won't be here to pick me up until ten o'clock, but I've got a headache and don't think I can make it through the rest of the evening."

"I'd be glad to give you a lift home right now," Aaron offered. "It would save your daed a trip and keep you from having to stick around here."

Melinda sniffed. "I'd hate for you to miss all the fun on account of me."

"Nah. I wasn't havin' much fun anyway."

"Are you sure? I mean, isn't there someone else you'd rather escort home?"

Aaron shook his head then chuckled as if he were embarrassed. "If I ever find a woman I'm willing to court, she'll have to be spunky like my mamm. I'd want someone who likes to fish and isn't afraid to get her hands dirty, either."

"Most Amish women I know work in their gardens. Doesn't that count as dirty work?"

"I reckon so, but that's not what I meant." Aaron led Melinda toward his buggy.

"What did you mean?"

He tipped his head to one side. "Any woman I'd even consider courting would have to be willing to do lots of outdoor stuff."

"Oh, you mean she should be a tomboy?"

Aaron shrugged. "Guess that's one way to put it, but that's not likely to happen, because there are no women around here that I'd be interested in." He released an undignified grunt. "Even if there was, I'll never get married."

"Why not?"

"Just won't; that's all."

Melinda didn't argue the point, and she found herself wondering if Aaron might not have the right attitude about staying single. If she left home to become a veterinarian, she would probably stay single unless she met and married some English fellow. That thought did nothing to make her feel better. She'd been miserable since she and Gabe had broken up, but she saw no way they could get back together unless one of them made a huge concession. Gabe would probably be better off with Mattie. She was cute and wanted to remain Amish.

"Well, Aaron Zook," Melinda said as he helped her into his buggy, "I hope you have better luck at finding love than I've had."

Susie's stomach felt as if it were filled with a bunch of swarming bees as she settled herself on the seat of Jonas's buggy and he reached for the reins. The fact that he'd asked to give her a ride home tonight was like an answer to prayer. She just hoped she didn't say anything stupid that might make him wish he hadn't asked.

"I saw you talking with Melinda earlier this evening. Are you and she still good friends?" Jonas asked as they turned out of the driveway and headed down Highway C.

Susie nodded. "Although we don't see eye to eye on much these days."

Jonas chuckled. "I guess that's true with most friends and even family. My cousins John and Jared, who live in Montana, don't always think alike, and they're identical twins."

He flicked the reins to get the horse moving faster, and Susie gripped the edge of her seat. She had hoped they could take a leisurely ride home so she could spend more time with Jonas.

"Is Melinda still drawing pictures of animals and taking in strays?"

"Jah. She works part-time for our local vet, too."

"That sounds interesting. I admire anyone who has a way with animals."

Susie's heart gave a lurch. Was Jonas interested in Melinda? Had he offered Susie a ride home only to ask about her niece? Was that why he kept asking questions about Melinda?

"I'll bet Melinda would like it where I live," Jonas continued. "There's more wildlife in Montana than you can imagine."

"Do you hunt?" Susie hoped her question might take Jonas's mind off Melinda.

"Jah. Got me a nice big buck deer last year and also a turkey."

"Some of the menfolk in our community also hunt deer. Melinda's boyfriend, Gabe, likes to hunt." Susie figured mentioning that Melinda had a boyfriend might discourage Jonas from taking an interest in her niece. She saw no reason to mention that Melinda and Gabe had recently broken up. No point in giving Jonas any hope of courting Melinda, if that's what he had on his mind.

"Say, I was wondering about something," Jonas said, breaking into Susie's disconcerting thoughts.

"What's that?"

"I'll be leaving for Montana by the end of next week, and I was wondering if it would be all right if I write to you sometimes."

Susie's heart began to hammer as hope swelled in her breast. If Jonas wanted to write her, did that mean they were courting? *No, of course it doesn't mean that,* she berated herself. *Since I acted so interested in Montana, he probably just wants to write and tell me about some of the things going on there.*

"Well, is it all right if I write to you or not?"

"I'd like that," she said, hoping the excitement she felt didn't show too much in her voice. She didn't want to appear overeager.

He smacked the reins to get the horse moving faster. "I'm kept pretty busy with my job and all, but I'll write as often as I can."

Susie smiled. "I'll write often, too."

"I appreciate you giving me a ride home," Mattie said as Gabe directed his horse onto the highway.

He nodded and forced a smile. Deep down, he felt miserable. When he'd seen Melinda talking to his so-called friend, he'd felt as if someone had punched him in the stomach. It had been only a short time since Gabe and Melinda had broken up. He couldn't believe she'd found someone to replace him so quickly. And Aaron Zook, of all people! Didn't she even care that Gabe and Aaron had been friends since they were boys? How could she have proclaimed her love just a few short weeks ago and suddenly taken an interest in someone else?

"I figured you'd be taking Melinda home tonight," Mattie said, breaking into Gabe's troubling thoughts.

"Why would you think that?"

"Since the two of you are courting, I just assumed—"

Gabe shook his head. "We're not courting. Not anymore."

Mattie's pale eyebrows furrowed. "Did you break up with her?"

"Let's just say it was a mutual decision."

"Mind if I ask why?"

Actually, Gabe did mind. He didn't want to think about his breakup with Melinda, much less talk about it. "We. . .uh. . . decided that since we both wanted different things it would be best to go our separate ways."

"That's too bad. Melinda always seemed so happy whenever the two of you were together. I figured it wouldn't be long before an announcement of your betrothal would be published in church."

"I thought that, too," Gabe mumbled. "But things don't always go the way we want. I've come to realize that some things just aren't meant to be."

Mattie reached across the seat and touched his arm. "I'm real sorry, Gabe."

He gave a brief nod. No one could be any sorrier than he.

Chapter 26

I came by to check on some kitchen cabinets I plan to give Faith for Christmas," Noah said when he stepped into Swartz's Woodworking Shop on Monday morning, two weeks after Gabe and Melinda had broken up.

Gabe leaned against his workbench and crossed his arms. "My daed's delivering some furniture right now, but I know your cabinets have been made and are waiting to be sanded and stained. I'm sure they'll be ready in time for Christmas." He thought about all the orders they had for holiday gifts and how Pap had allowed him to make some chairs and a table for the bed-and-breakfast in Branson. They'd turned out well, and Pap had said he was pleased with Gabe's work.

"I'm glad to hear the cabinets will be ready soon, because the ones in our kitchen were bought used when we built the house next to my folks' place," Noah said, jolting Gabe out of his musings. "They need to be replaced, and my wife's been wanting new ones for quite some time." Noah shifted from one foot to the other. "I. . .uh. . .wanted to tell you that I'm sorry to hear about you and Melinda breaking up. I like you, Gabe, and was looking forward to having you as my son-in-law." He handed Gabe a plate of chocolate chip cookies wrapped with cellophane. "I made these last night and thought you might like some."

"Danki. That was nice of you." Gabe placed the cookies on one end of his workbench. The truth was, he thought highly of Melinda's stepfather and figured Noah would probably make a good father-in-law.

Noah placed his palms on the workbench and leaned toward Gabe. "Melinda's been acting like a kitten with sore paws ever since you two split up. She spends most of her time with those critters of hers, and Faith is fit to be tied because she has to prod Melinda to get any work done."

Gabe pondered Noah's words before responding. "If she's so concerned about going our separate ways, then why'd she ride home from the last young people's gathering with my best friend?"

"Aaron Zook?"

"Jah, that's what I heard."

"I didn't realize that. I thought one of the girls who had no date had given Melinda a ride home that night. I was supposed to pick her up, but she arrived home way before ten." Noah looked intently at Gabe. "I'm thinking this is something you and Melinda need to discuss. I don't believe she'd like the idea of me butting in on something that's really none of my business."

"There's a lot more going on than just her riding home with Aaron."

Noah nodded. "If you're talking about her not wanting you to hunt, she explained her reasons to me, and I said I thought she was wrong."

Gabe toyed with a piece of sandpaper, pushing it back and forth across the work space in front of him, even though there was nothing there to sand. "That's not the whole issue, but it's not for me to be saying. I'm sure Melinda will tell you everything when she's ready." He drew in a deep breath and released it with a huff. "Short of a miracle, I'm afraid it's too late for anything to be resolved between Melinda and me."

Noah shook his head. "It's never too late. Not as long as you're both still free to marry." He turned toward the door, calling over his shoulder, "My daughter is worth fighting for."

The door clicked shut, and Gabe's gaze came to rest on the cookies Noah had given him. It was then that he noticed a verse of scripture had been attached to the edge of the plastic wrap. He reached for it and read the words out loud. " 'But the wisdom that is from above is first pure, then peaceable, gentle, and easy to be intreated, full of mercy and good fruits, without partiality, and without hypocrisy. And the fruit of righteousness is sown in peace of them that make peace.' "

Gabe scratched the side of his head. *What was Noah trying to tell me? Does he think I should try and make peace with Melinda?* Gabe wasn't sure there was any way they could get back to where they had been before she'd told him that she wanted to become a vet, but he would pray about the matter.

Early that morning, Melinda's mother had hired a driver and taken Grandpa to Springfield for a doctor's appointment, asking Melinda to do some cleaning before she left for work at noon. True to her promise, Melinda was now mopping the kitchen floor.

She glanced at the calendar on the opposite wall. It had been two weeks since she and Gabe had gone their separate ways, and the pain in her heart was still so raw she could barely function. Even spending time with her animal friends didn't hold the appeal it once had.

She took another look at the calendar and realized it had been one week since Jonas Byler had returned to Montana, so she figured Susie was probably also grieving.

Dear Lord, bless Gabe and give him a happy life, even if he ends up being with Mattie Byler. Give me wisdom and direction for my own life, and help me to know whether I should take another GED test. Be with Susie, and help her find someone who will love her. . . .

Loud barking in the backyard interrupted Melinda's prayer. She set the mop aside and peeked out the window, wondering what Isaiah's dog was up to. But it wasn't her brother's hound she saw in the yard. It was Gabe's German shepherd, Shep, running around in circles and barking like crazy.

Melinda opened the back door and stepped onto the porch. "What's the matter with you, Shep? You act like you've been stung by a swarm of bees."

As soon as Melinda spoke, the dog quit running and crawled toward the house on its belly.

"What's wrong, boy?" She stepped off the porch. "Are you hurt?"

Shep's only response was a pathetic whimper.

When Melinda drew closer, she realized Shep had several porcupine quills stuck in his nose. "Looks like you had a run-in with an angry critter, didn't you? We need to get those out right away."

The dog looked up at Melinda with sorrowful brown eyes. "Come on, fella. Let's go to the barn and get that taken care of." She led the way, and obediently, the dog followed.

A short time later after removing the quills with a pair of pliers, Melinda was putting antiseptic on Shep's nose when an unexpected visitor showed up. Gabe stepped into the barn, the stubble of straw crackling under his weight. "I've been looking everywhere for you, Shep." He glanced at Melinda then looked quickly away as though he was afraid to make eye contact. "The critter took off last night. I figured he'd come over here to play with Isaiah's dog, but he didn't return, and this morning I got worried." Gabe's forehead creased as he looked back at her and frowned. "What's wrong with him? Why are you doctoring my dog?"

Melinda set the bottle of peroxide back on the shelf before she answered, hoping the action would give her time to take control of her swirling emotions. Ministering to Gabe's dog and then having Gabe show up made her long for things she couldn't have—unless she was willing to set aside her dream and do what Gabe wanted her to do.

When Melinda turned to face Gabe again, her legs shook so badly she could barely stand. "I found Shep in the backyard barking and running around in circles. Then I discovered the poor dog had a bunch of porcupine quills stuck in his nose."

Gabe's face softened some as he patted his knee. "Come here, Shep. Come here, boy."

The dog went immediately to his side, wagging its tail as though nothing had ever happened.

Gabe clicked his tongue. "You silly critter. I thought you had more sense than to tangle with a porcupine."

Shep licked Gabe's hand and whined in response.

"I appreciate you looking out for him," Gabe said, lifting his gaze to meet Melinda's again. "Guess Shep was smart enough to know who to come to when he needed help."

Melinda smiled as she finally began to relax. "Animals have a sixth sense about things."

Gabe took hold of Shep's collar and led him toward the barn door. "I'd better get back home. Pap's at the shop by himself, and we've got lots of work to do."

"It's kind of chilly this morning. Would you like a cup of hot chocolate before you head out?" Melinda asked, not wanting him to go.

He licked his lips, and a slow smile spread across his face. "Hot chocolate sounds nice. If you've got a couple of marshmallows to go with it, that is."

Melinda's heart skipped a beat. Being here in the barn with Gabe felt so natural—like nothing had ever come between them. "I think there are some marshmallows in the kitchen cupboard. Why don't you put Shep in the dog run with Jericho, and I'll meet you on the back porch in a few minutes?"

"Sounds good to me."

Melinda knew there was no point in letting her thoughts run wild with things hoped for but not likely to occur, but she couldn't seem to help herself. She gave him a quick nod then hurried into the house.

Gabe's palms felt sweaty, and his throat was so dry he could barely swallow when he joined Melinda on the porch a short time later.

"Here you go," she said, handing him a cup of steaming hot chocolate.

"Danki." Gabe blew on the chocolate drink as he tried to think of something sensible to say. What he really wanted to talk about was their relationship and how they could get it back on track, but he couldn't seem to find the right words.

"How's Mattie Byler?" Melinda blurted suddenly.

Gabe nearly choked on the warm liquid in his mouth. "Huh?"

"How's Mattie Byler?"

He reached up to wipe away the chocolate that had dribbled onto his chin. "I guess she's okay. Why do you ask?"

Melinda's cheeks turned bright pink, and he didn't think it had anything to do with the chilly weather. "I saw the two of you together at the last young people's gathering."

"I didn't hang around Mattie all evening," he said defensively. "I just talked to her a few minutes after we both had some punch."

"But I saw her get into your buggy, and you were obviously driving her home."

He nodded. "That's true. Mattie told me her brother Jonas was planning to ask your aunt Susie if she'd be willing to ride in his buggy after the gathering was over."

"What's that got to do with you taking Mattie home?"

"I'm getting to that." Gabe set his empty cup on the porch floor. "Mattie mentioned that she'd come down with a headache and wanted to go home. Since Jonas wasn't going to leave until the gathering was over, Mattie had no transportation."

"So you volunteered to drive her?"

"That's right."

Melinda stared at her empty cup. "Guess I must have gotten the wrong impression."

"There's nothing going on with me and Mattie. We're just friends, and I was only doing a good deed." Gabe squinted. "While we're on the subject of rides home, I heard you rode with Aaron that night."

She nodded. "It's true."

"Are you two seeing each other now?"

She shook her head so hard the ties on her kapp came untied. "Of course not. Aaron only gave me a ride because I, too, had a headache and wanted to go. Papa Noah was supposed to pick me up at ten, but I didn't want to wait around until then."

Gabe smiled as a feeling of relief washed over him. "I'm glad to hear that."

"What? That I had a headache?"

"No, that you and Aaron aren't seeing each other."

"I'm not interested in Aaron," she said in a near whisper. "Never have been, either."

Gabe leaned a bit closer as he fought the temptation to kiss her, but a ruckus in the dog run ruined the mood. He decided that was probably a good thing, considering that he and Melinda had recently broken up.

"I hope they're not fighting over the bone I gave Jericho last night." Melinda jumped up and bounded off the porch.

Gabe followed. "I'd best get my dog and head for home."

Several minutes later, Gabe had Shep out of the pen and loaded into the back of his buggy. As he pulled out of the driveway, he waved, and Melinda lifted her hand in response. Even though things weren't back to where they should be, at least Melinda and he were speaking again.

"How'd things go with Grandpa's appointment?" Melinda asked her mother that evening as they prepared supper.

"The results of his blood tests were good," Mama replied. "The doctor was pleased with how well Grandpa seems to be doing."

Melinda smiled. "He sure has made a turnaround, especially where his memory is concerned."

Mama handed her a sack of flour. "Would you mind making some biscuits while I fry up the chicken?"

"Sure, I can do that."

Melinda and her mother worked in silence for a time. Then Mama turned down the gas burner under the pan of chicken and nodded toward the table. "Want to sit awhile and have a cup of tea while the meat cooks and the biscuit dough rises?"

"That sounds good."

"How'd your day go?" Mama asked as she poured them both a cup of lemon-mint tea.

"It was busy and kind of crazy."

Mama's eyebrows lifted. "In what way?"

"It began with me doing the cleaning you'd wanted done, and that went fairly well. But then Gabe's dog showed up with a bunch of porcupine quills stuck in his nose."

"I'll bet that hurt," Mama said.

"I'm sure it did. I removed them with a pair of pliers and put some antiseptic on his nose, and by the time Gabe took Shep home, he was acting his old spunky self."

"Did Gabe bring the dog over for you to doctor?"

"Shep came here on his own, and Gabe showed up later looking for him."

Mama took a sip of tea and blotted her lips on a napkin. "How'd that go? Did the two of you get anything resolved between you?"

Melinda shrugged. "Not really, but we didn't argue, either."

"That's a good thing. Maybe if you give yourselves a bit more time, you'll be able to settle your differences."

Snow whizzed into the room with something between her teeth.

"What's that crazy cat got now?" Mama leaned over and squinted as Snow sailed under the table. "Looks like a hunk of balled-up paper."

Melinda chuckled. "At least it's not a mouse."

"Here, kitty. Let me see what's in your mouth," Mama said, reaching for the cat.

Melinda didn't know who was more surprised, her or Mama,

when Snow dropped the wad of paper at Mama's feet.

"Well, what do you know—she listened to me for once." Mama bent down and picked up the paper, pulling it apart with her fingers and laying it flat on the table. "Now, what is this?"

Melinda froze as her gaze came to rest on the item in question. It was the results of her failed GED test.

Mama's forehead wrinkled as she studied the piece of paper; then she looked pointedly at Melinda.

"I—I can explain."

"I certainly hope so."

Melinda moistened her lips with the tip of her tongue. "Uh—as you know, Dr. Franklin thinks I have a special way with animals."

Mama nodded.

"He believes I would make a good vet or certified veterinarian's assistant."

No response.

"And. . .well, he suggested I take the GED test, which I would need in order to sign up for some college classes."

"You want to go to college and become a vet?" Mama's voice sounded calm and even, but Melinda could see by the pinched expression on her mother's face that she was having a hard time keeping her emotions under control.

"As you can see by the scores on that paper, I failed the test."

"Does that mean you've given up the idea?"

Melinda toyed with the handle on her teacup. "I–I'm not sure. I've thought about retaking the test."

Mama released a sigh. "And you've been planning all of this

behind your daed's and my back, sneaking off to take the test without ever saying a word about it?"

Melinda's eyes filled with tears as a wave of shame and regret washed over her like a drenching rain. "I was planning to tell you."

"When?"

"After I passed the GED test."

Mama grabbed two fingers on her left hand and gave them a good pop. "Have you thought about what it would mean if you went off to college and got a degree? Have you thought about how it would affect everyone in this family?"

"Of course I have, and it wouldn't be easy for me to leave." There was a tremor in Melinda's voice, and it was all she could do to look her mother in the face.

"After all the things I've told you about my life as an entertainer, I wouldn't think you would even consider becoming part of the English world—not when all your family and friends are Amish living here in Webster County." Mama sniffed deeply, and her quivering chin let Melinda know she was close to tears.

Melinda stared at her untouched cup of tea. "I—I don't really want to leave home, Mama, but becoming a vet would allow me to care for so many hurting and sick animals. If I have a special way with animals, as Dr. Franklin says I do, then wouldn't it be wasted if I didn't learn how to care for them in the best possible way?"

"I guess you'll have to choose what's more important to you—the animals you think need your help, or your family and friends who love you so much," Mama replied without really answering Melinda's question.

Melinda blinked against the tears blurring her vision but made no comment.

Mama leaned across the table and looked at Melinda long and hard. "I'm not saying these things to make you feel guilty. I just don't want you to make the same mistake I did when I left home." She slid her chair back and stood. "Please know that as much as I would hate to see you go, I won't try to stop you. It's your life, and you will have to decide."

Melinda felt as if she were in a stupor, and seeing the distressed look on her mother's face only made her feel worse. *I should have told Mama sooner—maybe even had Dr. Franklin talk to her and Papa Noah. I shouldn't have let her find out by seeing my failed GED test. That could have been avoided if I'd burned the silly thing.*

"I. . .uh . . .need to check on my animals in the barn," she mumbled, pushing away from the table.

When Mama made no reply, Melinda rushed out the back door and headed straight for the barn.

Faith let her head fall forward until it rested on the table. She'd held up well while Melinda told of her plans, but now that Faith was alone in the kitchen, she could allow herself to grieve. How could this have happened? It was like reliving the past, only this time it wasn't Faith wanting to leave home; it was her own precious daughter.

Is this my punishment for leaving my family behind while I tried to make a name for myself in the fancy, modern English world? It was bad enough that I left home and became an entertainer, but then, after I came home with Melinda, I was planning to go back on the road and leave my home again.

Stinging tears escaped Faith's lashes and dribbled onto her cheeks. "Like mother, like daughter," she murmured as a burning lump formed in her throat. "My selfish desires and wayward ways have come back to haunt me."

"Faith, what's wrong? What are you mumbling about?"

Faith's head jerked up. Noah stood staring down at her with a look of concern. She had been so caught up in her sorrow over Melinda that she hadn't heard him come in.

She rushed into his arms. "Oh, Noah, I don't know how to tell you this, but we've lost our daughter to the world!"

Noah pushed Faith gently away from him so that he was looking directly at her. "What are you talking about? How is Melinda lost to the world?"

Faith drew in a shaky breath and quickly related about Melinda taking the GED test, failing it, and wanting to leave the Amish faith and become a vet. When she finished, she gulped in a quick breath of air and collapsed into a chair at the table.

Noah took the seat beside Faith and reached for her hand. "No wonder our daughter's been acting so *fremm* lately. I'll bet she's been planning this for some time."

Faith nodded. "I thought Melinda's strange behavior was because she was upset over her and Gabe breaking up. I should have realized with her unhealthy preoccupation over animals that something more was on the wind." She sniffed deeply. "Oh, Noah, this is all my fault."

"How can it be your fault?"

"If I hadn't been so hard on Melinda, always scolding her

for spending too much time with her animal friends, maybe she wouldn't have become discontent. Maybe—"

"Don't be so hard on yourself." Noah gently squeezed her fingers. "We've both gotten after Melinda, and neither of us figured she'd ever want to leave home to become a vet."

Faith blinked against another set of tears. "What are we going to do? How can we keep Melinda from going English?"

Noah let go of her hand and slipped his arm across her shoulders. "The best thing we can do is try to be more understanding and not push Melinda to do what we want. We also need to pray that the Lord's will is done."

She nodded slowly. "Would you at least speak to her about this? The two of you have always had a special bond, even before you and I were married. If anyone can get through to our daughter, it will be you."

"I'll do what I can, but I won't press Melinda on this or try to make her feel guilty."

"I wouldn't expect you to."

Noah pushed back his chair and stood. "Whatever Melinda decides, she needs to know that we still love her."

"Of course." Faith sniffed. "I'll always love my little girl, even if she does leave home."

As Noah headed for the barn, he prayed that God would give him the right words to say to Melinda. He knew if he said the wrong thing, it could drive her further away and might make her want to leave out of rebellion, the way Faith had done when she was a teenager and thought her folks disapproved of her joke telling and yodeling. If Faith had only known back then that it wasn't her jokes or yodeling they disapproved of. It was the fact that she'd fooled around and shirked her duties so often.

Just the way Melinda's been doing here of late, he thought ruefully. *Oh, Lord, why didn't I see what was going on and do something about this sooner?*

When Noah stepped into the barn a few minutes later, he found Melinda inside one of the horse stalls brushing the mare's mane.

"Hi, Papa Noah," she said, glancing over at him as he approached the stall. "Did you just get home from work?"

He nodded. "I went into the house to say hello to your mamm first and found her sitting at the kitchen table quite upset."

Melinda dropped her gaze to the floor, and her hand shook as she set the brush on the edge of a nearby shelf. "She told you then?"

"Jah."

"Papa Noah, I—"

"Why, Melinda? Why did you keep your plans a secret from us? Wouldn't it have been better if you'd told us right away?"

"I—I didn't want to upset you or Mama. And since I haven't passed my GED test yet or made a definite decision, I saw no point in talking about what I might want to do."

Noah leaned on the stall door and groaned. "I know you have a special way with animals and would probably make a good vet, but have you thought about how your leaving would affect this family—your mamm most of all?"

Melinda nodded slowly as tears slipped from her eyes and rolled down her cheeks. "It's affected my relationship with Gabe, too. That's the main reason we're no longer a courting couple."

"Did you ask Gabe to leave the Amish faith with you?"

"Jah, but he doesn't want to." Her chin quivered. "I guess he doesn't love me enough to want to be with me."

"Maybe Gabe feels the same way about you."

Melinda lifted her gaze to meet his. "Oh, Papa Noah, I feel like my heart's being torn in two. I do love Gabe, and I love my family, but if God has blessed me with a special talent to care for sick and hurting animals, shouldn't I be using that talent to its full extent?"

Noah grimaced, unsure of how best to answer. Just as he enjoyed working with the fledgling trees at Hank's tree farm, he knew Melinda enjoyed working with the animals that came into Dr. Franklin's clinic. Even so, they were just animals, and he didn't understand why she would choose a career that would take her away from her family just to help animals who couldn't really love her in return. And to give up her Amish faith and become part of an English world she barely remembered made no sense to him at all.

He stepped inside the stall and drew Melinda into his arms, knowing a lecture was not what she needed right now. "I want you to know that your mamm and I will be praying that God will reveal His will and show you what you're supposed to do."

"I'm praying for that, too," Melinda said in a shaky voice.

Noah patted her back then stepped out of the stall. As he

left the barn, he made a decision. He would not mention the subject of Melinda leaving home again. Not until she was ready to give them her choice.

Chapter 27

On the first day of deer hunting season as the Hertzlers sat around the breakfast table, Noah instructed Melinda and Isaiah to stay out of the woods.

"But, Papa Noah, No Hunting signs are posted all over our property," Melinda reminded him.

"That's true," he said with a nod, "but there's always someone who either doesn't see the signs or refuses to take them seriously and hunts wherever he pleases."

"Your daed's right," Grandpa put in. "I remember when I was a boy someone shot a deer right out in our front yard."

Melinda gasped. "I hope the deer on our property will be okay and stay where it's safe."

Isaiah grunted. "Like you can keep all the deer safe, Melinda."

"I can sure try."

"No, you can't. The deer have a mind of their own, and—"

Noah nudged Isaiah with his elbow. "Why don't you eat your breakfast and quit being such a *baddere* to your sister?"

"I ain't bein' a bother." Isaiah wrinkled his nose. "She's just verhuddelt, that's all."

"I'm not confused," Melinda shot back. "You're the one who's verhuddelt."

Noah lifted his hands as he shook his head. "Enough of the squabbling. You two are worse than a couple of hens fighting for the same piece of corn."

Grandpa chuckled, but Isaiah and Melinda both sat frowning, staring at their bowls of oatmeal.

"Do like your daed says and eat before your food gets cold," Faith said sternly.

Melinda pushed back her chair. "I'm not hungry. If nobody has any objections, I think I'll go out to the barn and see how my animals are doing."

Noah's patience was beginning to wane, but he figured if Melinda wasn't hungry he couldn't force her to eat. "Go ahead to the barn," he said. "But be sure and come back in time to help your mamm do the breakfast dishes and clean up the kitchen."

"I will." Melinda rushed out of the kitchen without another word.

All morning as Melinda did her chores, she worried about the deer. By the time she had finished cleaning the kitchen, she was a ball of nerves.

Maybe a walk in the woods would make me feel better, she told herself as she placed the last glass in the cupboard.

"Stay out of the woods." Papa Noah's earlier warning echoed in her ears.

I'll only be there a short time. Just long enough to check on the deer.

She glanced around the room. No sign of Mama or Grandpa, and she knew Isaiah had gone fishing over at Rabers' pond. Papa Noah had left for work as soon as they were finished eating, and she figured her mother had gone next door to clean Grandpa's house.

As Melinda hung up her choring apron, she thought about how there had been no mention of her failed GED test or plans of becoming a vet since she first told her parents. She wasn't sure if they had accepted the idea of her leaving home or if it was just too painful for them to talk about. Either way, Melinda was glad there had been no mention of it. Until she took another GED test and got her scores, there wasn't much she could do about her future plans.

"I'd better leave Mama a note," Melinda murmured, "so she doesn't worry if she returns to the house and finds me gone." She grabbed a piece of paper from a nearby drawer, hurried over to the table, and scrawled a message saying that she was going for a short walk before it was time to leave for the clinic. Then she rushed out the back door and headed straight for the woods.

A short while later, Melinda stepped into the thicket of trees, wishing she had remembered to bring along her drawing tablet. *It's probably for the best. If I took the time to draw, I'd likely get carried away and be here much longer than I should.*

The sound of gunfire in the distance caused Melinda to shudder. Some poor animal had probably met its fate. At least it hadn't happened on their property. She walked deeper into the woods, savoring the distinct aroma of fall with its crisp, clean air and fresh-fallen leaves strewn all over the ground like a carpet of red and gold.

The rustle of leaves halted Melinda's footsteps. She tipped her head and listened. There it was again.

She scanned the area but saw nothing out of the ordinary. Suddenly a fawn stepped out of the bushes and stood staring at Melinda as though it needed her help.

Melinda took a step forward, then another and another, until she was right beside the little deer. That's when she saw it—a doe lying dead among a clump of bushes. "Oh no!" Her breath caught in her throat.

It didn't take Melinda long to realize that the mother deer had been shot, and this little one must be her fawn. Had someone been hunting on their property despite the signs Papa Noah had posted? Or had the doe been shot elsewhere and stumbled onto their land while it bled to death?

The fawn stood beside Melinda with its nose and ears twitching. Melinda bent down and picked it up, noting that the little deer was lightweight and couldn't have been more than a few days old. It was probably born late in the year, she decided.

She hurried from the woods and entered the barn a short time later, where she settled the fawn in an empty horse stall. "I'll need to find one of my feeding bottles and get some nourishment into you right away," she said, patting the deer on top of its head.

She stepped out of the stall and closed the door, planning to feed the deer and then head for work.

"Guess what, Dr. Franklin," Melinda said breathlessly as she entered the veterinary clinic later that day.

"I can't even begin to guess," the vet said with a crooked smile. "But if it has something to do with an animal, then I'll bet that's why you look so wide-eyed and excited."

She nodded enthusiastically. "I found a baby deer in the woods, and its mother had been killed."

"Sorry to hear that. The fawn probably won't survive without its mother."

"I'm hoping it will. I brought it back to our place and put it in an empty stall inside the barn. I plan to bottle-feed it, and—"

Dr. Franklin held up his hand. "And what, Melinda? Make a pet out of it?"

She nodded again.

He shook his head as deep wrinkles creased his forehead. "That's not a good idea."

"Why not?"

"A deer is a wild animal, and it belongs in the woods, not held captive in a barn."

"I won't keep it in the barn forever. When it's bigger, I'll have Papa Noah build a pen."

The doctor leaned forward with his elbows resting on the desk. "Do you think that's fair to the deer when it should be running free in the woods?"

"It might get shot like its mother."

"That's part of life, Melinda. You can't protect every animal from harm, you know."

"But I don't like the thought of animals being hunted for the sport of it." Melinda frowned. "Some people hunt just so they can brag to their friends about the big set of antlers they got or how good their gun is because they can shoot a deer from a long distance."

"I can see where you're coming from, Melinda. It's your sensitive spirit and caring attitude that would help you become a good vet."

She dropped her gaze to the floor. "That may never happen now."

"How come?"

"I failed my GED test."

"I'm sorry to hear that. Are you planning to take it again?"

Melinda shrugged. "I was, but my mother found my test scores, and I had to tell my folks about my plans to become a vet." She groaned. "They weren't happy about it and offered me no support, except to say they'll be praying that God will show me what I should do."

Dr. Franklin nodded. "I may not be as religious as your folks, but I do believe in God. Therefore, I have to say that your folks are right—you do need to pray about this and trust God to show you the right road to take."

"That's what I plan to do." She smiled. "In the meantime, I came here to work, so I guess I should get busy. Do you have anything in particular that needs to be done?"

He nodded toward the door behind him. "Why don't you

clean out those empty cages in the back room? After that, you can help me clip the toenails on Hank Osborn's two beagles."

Melinda gave a quick nod and scurried out of the room.

When Noah stepped into the barn after arriving home from work that evening, he was shocked by the sight that greeted him. A young fawn stood in one of the empty horse stalls, and Melinda was kneeling in the straw beside it, stroking the little deer's head.

"What's that deer doing in one of the horse's stalls?" he asked, pointing at the fawn.

Melinda looked up at him with a worried expression. "I found the poor thing in the woods earlier today, standing beside its dead mother." She groaned. "I'm sure someone must have shot it, Papa Noah."

"I thought I had made myself clear when I told you and Isaiah not to go there today." Noah clenched his teeth. Didn't Melinda ever listen? Sometimes she made it so difficult to be patient and understanding.

"I'm sorry, but if I hadn't gone, this little deer would have died."

"What if the person who shot the fawn's mother had been nearby and took another shot that might have hit you?"

"God protected me, as well as this one," she said, motioning to the fawn.

"Jah, well, don't go to the woods again. At least not until hunting season's over."

She nodded in reply.

Noah glanced around. "Where's your bruder? Was he with you when you found the deer?"

"Isaiah wasn't with me. He went fishing over at Rabers' pond soon after breakfast."

"And he's not back yet?"

"I don't think so. His pole isn't where he keeps it." She pointed to the spot on the wall where Isaiah usually hung his fishing gear.

"It'll be getting dark soon, and I don't like the idea of him being at the pond so late. Some crazy hunters could be out road hunting before dusk. That's when the deer start to move around again."

"Would you like me to go look for him?" Melinda offered. "I could take the horse and buggy."

Noah shook his head. "If he's not here within the hour, I'll go after the boy myself."

Melinda shrugged and patted the little deer's head. "Whatever you think is best."

Gabe leaned his gun against a tree and lowered himself to a log. Soon the sun would be going down; then the deer would likely show themselves.

Sure am glad I could get into the woods this afternoon, he thought, leaning his head back and savoring the last few moments of full sunlight. He had decided to hunt in the wooded area to the left of Rabers' pond, which wasn't posted.

Gabe's thoughts went to Melinda, and he wondered if

hunters were respecting the No Hunting signs her stepfather had put around their place. *I hope Melinda has the smarts to stay out of the woods until hunting season is over. No telling what could happen if someone goes onto their property and ignores those signs.*

He reached into his backpack, checking to be sure he'd brought along enough ammunition. Everything seemed to be in order. Now all he needed was a nice-sized buck to step into the clearing. He knew his folks would be pleased to have some deer meat on the table during the winter months.

A twig snapped, and Gabe leaped to attention. He was about to grab his gun when Isaiah Hertzler stepped out from behind a tree.

"What are you doing here?" Gabe asked. "Don't you know how dangerous it is to be in the woods during hunting season when you're not one of the hunters?"

Isaiah shrugged. "I was on my way home from fishin' at the pond, and I ain't scared of bein' in the woods."

"Well, you should be scared, and you should have taken the road, not cut through the woods."

"Mind if I shoot your gun again?" Isaiah asked, ignoring Gabe's reprimand and eyeing the item in question.

"Not unless we get your daed's permission. I think it'd be best if you went straight home." Gabe started to get up, but his backpack fell to the ground. He reached down to pick it up, and when he lifted his head again, he was shocked to see Isaiah holding the gun.

Before Gabe could open his mouth, the gun went off. A piercing pain shot through his left shoulder, and he toppled to his knees. As Gabe fought to remain conscious, a wave of nausea coursed through his stomach.

"Gabe! Gabe, are you all right?" Isaiah dropped down beside him, his youthful face a mask of concern. "I—I didn't mean to shoot you. I don't know how the gun went off."

"I'm bleeding really bad," Gabe said through clenched teeth. "I need something to put on the wound so I can apply pressure."

Isaiah pulled a hanky from his pants pocket and handed it to Gabe. "Will this work?"

Gabe balled it up and shoved it against his shoulder, wincing in pain. "You need to go for help, Isaiah. If I try to stand, I'll most likely pass out."

The boy blanched. "You're not gonna die on me, are you?"

Gabe moaned and tried to make his voice sound more convincing than he felt. "I—I think I'll live, but I need to go to the hospital. Run home and tell your daed what's happened. Ask him to go to the nearest phone and call for help."

"O-okay."

Gabe felt warm blood soak through the hanky and onto his fingers, and the world started to spin. "Hurry, Isaiah."

The last thing Gabe remembered was a muffled, "I'm goin'." Then everything went black.

Melinda had just stepped out of the barn when her little brother dashed into the yard, yelling and waving his arms. "I shot Gabe! I shot Gabe!"

She rushed out to meet him, her heart hammering in her

chest. "What do you mean, you shot Gabe?"

"He needs to go to the hospital. He may be bleedin' to death." Isaiah was clearly out of breath, and his cheeks were bright red and splattered with tears.

Melinda grabbed his shoulders and gave them a shake. "Slow down, take a deep breath, and tell me what happened."

"I—I was walkin' through the woods on my way back from Rabers' pond when I ran into Gabe. I asked if I could shoot his gun, but he said no."

"Then what did you do?"

"When Gabe was bent over his ammunition bag, I picked up the gun." Isaiah's lower lip trembled, and more tears spilled onto his cheeks. "The gun went off, Melinda. I didn't mean for it to, but the next thing I knew, Gabe was lyin' on the ground, and there was blood oozin' out of his shoulder somethin' awful."

"Where is Gabe now?" Melinda asked, trying to keep her voice steady and her hands from shaking.

"He's—he's in the woods. Sent me to get Papa and call for help."

As the metallic taste of fear sprang to Melinda's mouth, she grabbed Isaiah's hand and dashed for the house, pulling him with her. Once inside, she made Isaiah tell their folks what had happened.

"Isaiah can take me back to the woods to see about Gabe." Papa Noah looked over at Melinda with a worried frown. "We don't know how badly he's been hurt, but it doesn't sound good. Why don't you run over to the Johnsons' place and ask them to call an ambulance? Your mamm can head over to Gabe's house and let his family know what's happened."

"Can't I go with you?" Melinda asked as a wave of fear shot through her. What if Gabe's wound was so bad that he bled to death? She had to see Gabe. Had to let him know what was on her mind.

Papa Noah shook his head. "Someone needs to get help, and if your mamm has to go to the Johnsons' and then over to see Gabe's folks, it will take her twice as long."

Mama touched Melinda's shoulder. "Your daed's right about this."

Melinda finally nodded.

"As soon as Isaiah shows me where Gabe is, I'll send the boy back to the house to wait for the ambulance. That way he'll be able to show the paramedics where we are."

Swallowing against the burning lump in her throat, Melinda rushed out the door. She had some serious praying to do.

Chapter 28

Thankful to be alive, Gabe placed the Bible he'd been reading onto the nightstand next to his hospital bed and closed his eyes. *You were looking out for me today, Lord. Me and Isaiah both, and I thank You for that.*

He thought about what could have happened if Melinda's little brother, who obviously hadn't realized the gun was loaded, had pointed it at himself and accidentally pulled the trigger. Or this afternoon, some hunter in the woods could have shot Isaiah, mistaking him for a deer. The boy hadn't been wearing an orange vest or any bright colors.

The accident was more my fault than his. I never should have taught Isaiah how to shoot a gun. Leastways not without his folks' permission. He's only twelve years old—not really ready for hunting yet.

Gabe clenched his fists, and a shooting pain sliced through

his injured shoulder. *I shouldn't have left the safety off my gun, either. That was a careless thing to do, and it makes me wonder if I should even own a gun.*

Heavy footsteps told Gabe someone had entered the room, and his eyes snapped open. A middle-aged nurse with bright red hair strode toward his bed. "How are you feeling?" she asked.

"My arm's pretty sore, but I'm happy to be alive."

She slipped a thermometer under Gabe's tongue then wrapped his good arm with the blood pressure cuff. "You're lucky that bullet went into your shoulder and not your chest. It could have been much more serious and required lengthier surgery."

Gabe nodded.

A few minutes later, the nurse removed the blood pressure apparatus and the thermometer. "Looks like your temperature is normal, and your pressure's right where it should be."

"That's good to hear. When can I go home?"

"The doctor wants to keep you here overnight to watch for possible infection. If everything looks good by tomorrow morning, he'll probably release you then."

"Glad to hear it. I don't enjoy being in the hospital so much."

The nurse chuckled. "Few do." She nodded toward the door. "There's someone in the hall waiting to see you."

Gabe cranked his head in that direction. "Is it my folks? They were here earlier, but I told them to go home and get some sleep."

"It's not your parents. It's a young Amish woman with blond hair and pretty blue eyes."

Gabe pushed himself to a sitting position as a mixture of excitement and dread coursed through his body. He was pretty sure the nurse had described Melinda, because his sisters all had dark hair, and he couldn't think who else might be here to see him.

Maybe I shouldn't see her right now. She's most likely miffed and probably came here to give me a lecture for allowing Isaiah to handle a gun again. Gabe glanced at the door. *Of course, I never said he could touch my gun, but he might not have if I hadn't shown him how to shoot in the first place.*

"Should I show the young woman in?" the nurse asked, breaking into Gabe's deliberations.

He nodded. "Might as well get this over with."

The nurse quirked one auburn eyebrow and looked at Gabe in a curious way, but then she shrugged and scurried out of the room. A few seconds later, Melinda entered. Seeing her red face and swollen eyelids, Gabe realized she had been crying.

"Are you all right?" they said in unison.

Melinda nodded and offered him a weak smile. "I'm fine. It's you I'm worried about."

She's worried about me. Now that's a good sign. Maybe she's not here to chew me out after all. Gabe nodded toward the chair. "Come, have a seat."

Melinda moved slowly across the room, feeling as if she were in a daze. It was hard to comprehend all that had happened this afternoon, and now here was Gabe lying in a hospital bed in Springfield, recovering from surgery, during which the doctors had removed a bullet from his shoulder.

"Are you sure you're okay?" Gabe asked. "Your face is as

white as my bedsheets."

"I was just thinking how pale you looked when the ambulance took you away earlier today and how scared I was of never seeing you again." She flopped into the chair with a groan. "Oh, Gabe, I'm glad you're going to be all right, and I'm thankful God has answered my prayers."

"Me, too." He smiled at her in such a sweet way it was all Melinda could do to keep from throwing herself into his arms. But that wouldn't be a good idea, not with his injury and all. Besides, they needed to get some important issues resolved.

"Melinda, I've made a decision—"

"Gabe, I need you to know something—"

They'd both spoken at the same time again.

"You go first," she prompted.

"No, that's okay. I'd like to hear what you've got to say."

Melinda reached out and took his hand, holding it gently and stroking her thumb back and forth across his knuckles.

"You're just what the doctor ordered," he murmured. "Better than any old shot for pain, that's for certain sure."

She cleared her throat and looked directly into his eyes. "Your accident has caused me to do some serious thinking."

Gabe nodded. "Same here."

"I don't want to spend the rest of my life without you."

"That goes double for me, Melinda."

She smiled as relief flooded her soul. "I've decided that even if I can't become a vet, and even if you continue to hunt, I want us to be together."

His eyes brightened. "Does that mean you still want to marry me?"

She nodded. "While you were in surgery, I was sitting in the waiting room, praying and reading the Bible I'd brought from home. God showed me that family and friends, as well as my personal relationship with the Lord, are more important than anything else."

"I'm glad." Gabe smiled. "Now I have something I'd like to say to you."

"What is it?"

"I've been lying in this hospital bed asking God what I should do to make things right between us." He squeezed her hand. "For me, hunting should only be done whenever there's a real need—for food, I mean. I don't want to hunt just for the sport of it, the way some folks do."

"I think I could live with that, as long as you don't shoot any of the deer I'm feeding."

"I wouldn't think of doing that. But I believe you'd better hear what else I have to say."

Melinda tipped her head. "What is it?"

Gabe drew in a deep breath. "I've decided that if becoming a vet is really that important to you, then I'll jump the fence and go English with you."

Melinda's mouth dropped open. "You—you would do that for me?"

He nodded, and tears shimmered in his hazel-colored eyes. "I've been miserable since our breakup, and I can't stand the thought of going through life without you at my side. I want to be with you, Melinda, no matter what."

She shook her head. "I thought becoming a vet was what I wanted, but I've changed my mind. I can't ask you to make such a sacrifice, and I know how hard it would be on both of us to leave our family and friends."

Gabe motioned to the Bible lying on the table beside his bed. "I'd like you to read something I read earlier. I marked the page with a slip of paper."

Melinda opened the Bible to the place he had marked and read the verse out loud. " 'Be ye therefore followers of God, as dear children.' " She paused and sniffed back the tears that threatened to spill over. "Oh, Gabe, I want to follow God all of my days; that's the most important thing."

"That's true for me, as well," he said with a nod.

"As much as I enjoy caring for sick and orphaned animals, I've been wrong to put it before my relationship with the Lord and those I love." Tears coursed down Melinda's cheeks, but she didn't bother to wipe them away. "I know I must learn to be content as I seek after God and try to do His will."

"But what if you could serve God and still take care of the animals that are so dear to you?"

"How can I do that without the proper training or a decent place to keep all my animals?"

"I think I might have an idea about that."

She leaned closer. "What is it?"

"After we're married, I'd like to make you more cages—regular ones for the animals you would keep until time to let go, and larger ones, more like the critters' natural surroundings, for those who aren't able to be set free."

"Grandpa Hertzler suggested something like that sometime ago, but I never mentioned it to you."

"With the new cages, you could continue to care for animals

the way you're doing now."

"But I still won't be able to help the animals who are seriously injured."

"You can turn those over to Dr. Franklin, same as you've been doing."

She sighed. "I guess it doesn't have to be me who makes them well. Just as long as they have a place to stay while they're mending or needing a home because they're orphaned."

Gabe motioned her to come closer, and when she leaned her face near his, he kissed her tenderly. "I love you, Melinda. Will you marry me?"

She nodded. "I'd be pleased to be your wife."

Epilogue

Melinda and Gabe sat side by side at their corner table, along with their attendants Aaron, Susie, and two of their cousins. Several of their family members and friends stopped by the table to offer congratulations on their marriage, which had taken place a short time ago. Melinda had never been happier. While she hoped to spend many days ahead caring for her animal friends, her primary goal would be to care for the man she loved.

Gabe leaned over and thumped Aaron on the back. "You're the next one to be married, you know."

Aaron shook his head. "No way!"

Gabe glanced over at Melinda and winked. "That's what they all say."

Aaron's face turned bright red, but he gave no retort.

Grandpa Hertzler stepped up to the table. "I left my gift for you on the kitchen table," he said, leaning over to give Melinda a hug. "It's a box filled with jars of my homemade rhubarb-strawberry jam." He winked at Gabe. "Melinda's mamm taught her how to make it, but I think mine's much better."

Melinda and Gabe laughed, and Melinda turned to embrace Susie, who sat next to her.

"I'm glad you decided not to leave home," Susie whispered in Melinda's ear. "Although, I may be leaving."

Melinda tipped her head, as confusion swirled in her brain. "Why would you leave home?"

"I got another letter from Jonas the other day, and he wants me to come to Montana for a visit. He said he's hoping I'll like it there." Susie's grin stretched from ear to ear. "Doesn't that sound like a good sign to you?"

Melinda nodded and gave Susie's shoulder a squeeze. "It sounds to me like there might be another wedding in our family soon."

Susie shrugged. "One never knows what the future will hold." She patted Melinda's arm.

Isaiah came by next. He smiled at Melinda; then he turned to Gabe and said, "I'm sure happy you're married to my sister now. Maybe someday, when you think I'm old enough, we can go huntin' together."

Gabe glanced over at Melinda.

She nodded and said, "Just as long as neither of you does any hunting on *our* property."

"Wouldn't think of it," Isaiah and Gabe said at the same time.

Papa Noah and Mama stopped at the table, offering their congratulations. "When I was your age, I was out on my own in the English world," Mama whispered to Melinda. "I'm sure glad my daughter had more sense than me."

Melinda wiped tears from her cheeks and gave her mother a hug. "But you returned home, and because of it, you married Papa Noah. That was a very schmaert thing to do."

Mama nodded. "And now you're married to a wonderful man, which is also smart."

"It took me awhile, but I finally realized what I have right here is more important than anything the world has to offer."

Melinda's folks moved on, and Dr. Franklin and his wife, Ellen, stepped up to the corner table. "I not only wanted to say congratulations to both of you," Dr. Franklin said, shaking Gabe's hand, "but I wanted to apologize to Melinda."

Melinda tipped her head in question.

"It wasn't right for me to push you into taking your GED or try to influence you to become a vet."

Melinda gave Dr. Franklin a hug. "You were only trying to help me take better care of the animals I care so much about."

"That's true, but I should have realized how important the Amish way of life is to you, and I should have tried to help you find a way to care for your animal friends without having to leave your faith to do it."

"It's all right; that's all behind us now," Melinda said tearfully. "I want you to know that I appreciate all that you've taught me about animal care, and I'm glad you were able to find a replacement for me at the veterinary clinic."

Ellen spoke up. "Yes, my nephew, who just graduated from

high school, is quite excited about becoming my husband's new assistant." She patted her husband's arm. "Who knows, maybe Len will enjoy working at the clinic so much that he'll decide to become a vet."

"You never know how things are going to turn out." Dr. Franklin gave Gabe's hand another hearty shake, and he and his wife moved on.

Gabe's parents showed up then. Leah's eyes filled with tears as she smiled at Melinda. "Take good care of my boy, okay?"

Melinda nodded. "I will, Leah. You can count on that."

"I have a wedding present for you that couldn't be put on the gift table," Gabe's dad said.

"Is it a new buggy horse?" Gabe asked with a hopeful expression.

Stephen shook his head. "It's something I think you'll like even better."

"What is it?"

"I made an important decision the other day." He clasped Gabe's shoulder. "You are now the official owner of Swartz's Woodworking Shop."

Gabe's eyes grew large, and his mouth hung wide open. "You mean it, Pap?"

Stephen nodded. "I'm sixty-five years old, and for some time, I've been wanting to take life a little easier. I'd like to spend more of my days fishing and whittling. But of course I'll be available to help you in the shop whenever you need me."

Melinda could see by Gabe's strained expression that he was on the verge of tears. "I'll do my best to keep the place running smoothly, Pap. I'd count it a privilege to have your help anytime."

When Gabe's folks moved away, Melinda reached over to quickly touch her husband's clean-shaven cheek. Since he was now a married man and would begin growing a beard, there wouldn't be many days left to touch the smooth skin on his face. But that didn't bother her. She had always enjoyed the feel of Papa Noah's and Grandpa's fuzzy beards.

"You know what, Gabe?" she said as he stared lovingly into her eyes.

"What?"

"I've learned many things in the last few months, but one thing stands out as most important."

"What's that?"

"Like an obedient fawn follows its mother, I will always follow God, because I am his dear child. And as I follow God's leading, each day will be blessed because you'll be at my side."

Gabe pressed her fingers into the palm of his hand. "I feel the same way."

Melinda smiled and gently squeezed her husband's fingers. Today was the happiest day of her life. She glanced at Aaron and Susie talking to some other young people. She wondered what the future held for her and Gabe's two best friends. She hoped Susie and Aaron would both find someone as dear to them as Gabe was to her. And most of all, Melinda hoped she and Gabe would be blessed with a whole houseful of kinner so they could teach them the importance of God, family, and friends.

RECIPE FOR GRANDPA'S RHUBARB-STRAWBERRY JAM

Ingredients:
    8 cups of rhubarb, cut into small pieces
    4 cups of mashed strawberries
    6 cups of sugar

Wash the fruit and cut the rhubarb into ½-inch pieces. In a large kettle, cover the rhubarb with half the sugar and let it stand for 1 to 2 hours. Crush the berries and mix with the remaining sugar, then combine with the rhubarb. Place the mixture on the stove over low heat until the sugar dissolves, then boil rapidly, stirring often to prevent burning. Cook until the mixture thickens. Remove from heat, pour into sterilized canning jars, and seal while hot.

Allison's Journey

DEDICATION/ACKNOWLEDGMENTS

To Leeann Curtis,
who makes beautiful faceless Amish dolls.

And ye shall seek me, and find me,
when ye shall search for me with all your heart.
JEREMIAH 29:13

Chapter 1

With a sense of dread, Allison Troyer stepped into the kitchen. Today was her nineteenth birthday, but she was sure Aunt Catherine wouldn't make a bit of fuss over it. In the twelve years Papa's un-married sister had lived with them, she had never made much over Allison's or any of her five older brothers' birthdays. Allison figured her aunt didn't care for children and had only moved from her home in Charm, Ohio, to Bird-in-Hand, Pennsylvania, because she felt a sense of obligation to Allison's father. After Mama's untimely death, Papa had been left to raise six children, and it would have been difficult for him without his sister's help.

Allison glanced at her aunt, standing in front of their propane-operated stove. She was a lofty, large-boned woman with big hands and feet. Aunt Catherine's gray-streaked, mousy brown hair was done up tightly in a bun at the back of her head, and her stiff white *kapp* was set neatly on top.

The wooden floor creaked as Allison stepped across it, and her aunt whirled around. Her skin looked paler than normal, making her deeply set blue eyes seem more pronounced.

"*Guder mariye,*" Allison said.

"Morning," Aunt Catherine mumbled, her thin lips set in a firm line. "You want your eggs fried or scrambled?"

"Whatever's easiest."

"It's your birthday, so you choose."

"I prefer scrambled." Allison offered her aunt a faint smile. So she hadn't forgotten what day it was. Maybe this year she would bake Allison a cake. "Would you like me to set the table or make some toast?"

"I think it would be best if you set the table. Last time you made toast, it was burned on the edges." Aunt Catherine's pale eyelashes fluttered like clothes flapping on the line.

If you'd let me do more in the kitchen, I might know how to do things better. Without voicing her thoughts, Allison opened the cupboard door and removed four plates and glasses, placing them on the table.

"I thought I might make a batch of peanut brittle after the chores are done," Aunt Catherine said as she went to the refrigerator and withdrew a jug of milk. "Your brothers and their families will probably join us for supper tonight. I'm sure they would enjoy the candy."

Peanut brittle? Allison felt a keen sense of disappointment. She liked peanut brittle well enough, but it wasn't nearly as good as moist chocolate cake. At least not to her way of thinking. Sally

Mast, Allison's best friend, always had a cake on her birthday. Of course, Sally's mother, Dorothy, was still living and cared deeply for her eight children. Allison didn't think Aunt Catherine cared about anyone but herself.

Allison had just set the last fork in place when her father and her brother Peter entered the kitchen.

"*Hallich gebottsdaag,*" Papa said, giving Allison a hug.

"*Jah.* Happy birthday." Peter handed Allison a brown paper sack. "I hope you like this, sister."

Allison placed the sack on the table, reached inside, and withdrew a baseball glove. She grinned at her blond-haired, blue-eyed brother. "*Danki*, Peter. This is just what I needed."

He smiled and squeezed her arm. "Now you'll be able to catch those fly balls a lot easier."

"Fly balls—*puh!*" Aunt Catherine mumbled. "Baseball's such a waste of time."

Papa cleared his throat real loud, and Allison and Peter turned to face him. "I have something for your birthday, too." He handed Allison an envelope.

Allison smiled and quickly tore it open. If there was money inside, she planned to buy a new baseball to go with the glove, since her old ball was looking pretty worn. She pulled a piece of paper from the envelope and stared at it, unbelieving. "A bus ticket?"

Papa nodded, his brown eyes shining with obvious pleasure. "It's to Seymour, Missouri, where your aunt Mary and uncle Ben King live."

Aunt Catherine's thin lips formed a circle, but she didn't say a word.

Allison's forehead wrinkled as she studied the ticket. Why,

she was supposed to leave in two days! Tears sprang to her eyes, and she sank into the closest chair.

"Aren't you happy about this?" Papa asked, pulling his fingers through the sides of his thinning brown hair. "I figured you'd be excited about making a trip to Missouri."

"I—I had no idea you wanted to send me away."

"*Ach*, Allison," he said kindly as he took a step forward. "I'm not sending you there for good. It's just for the summer."

That bit of news gave Allison some measure of relief, but she still didn't understand why her father wanted her to be gone all summer. With the garden coming up, it was Allison's job to keep the weeds down, and it was one of the few chores she actually enjoyed and did fairly well. "Why do I have to go to Missouri for the summer? Can't I stay right here in Lancaster County?"

Papa glanced at Aunt Catherine as if he hoped she might say something, but she turned her back to them as she cracked eggs into a glass bowl.

I'll bet this was Aunt Catherine's idea. She probably asked Papa to send me to Missouri so I'd be out of her hair. Allison squeezed her eyes shut. *She doesn't like me; she never has!*

Papa touched Allison's shoulder, and her eyes snapped open. "I thought you might enjoy getting to know your *mamm*'s twin sister and her family. Mary's a fine woman; she's so much like your mamm. You probably don't remember her well, but Mary's a fine cook, and she can clean a house like nobody's business."

Allison swallowed around the tears clogging her throat.

"From the things Mary has said in her letters over the years, it's obvious that she has a way with the sewing machine, too," Papa continued.

"Not like me; that's what your *daed*'s saying," Aunt Catherine spoke up. "I've never been able to do much more than basic mending, because I. . ." Her voice trailed off, and she started beating the eggs so hard Allison feared the bowl might break.

"Because why?" Allison asked. "You've never really said why you don't do much sewing."

Aunt Catherine turned to face Allison. Her lips pressed together, deepening the harsh lines in the corners of her mouth. "Before my mamm died, she never spent much time teaching me to sew." She pinched her lips even tighter. "Used to say I was all thumbs and that she couldn't be bothered with trying to show me things on the sewing machine because I kept making mistakes."

Allison felt a stab of compassion for her aunt. Apparently, she'd had a difficult childhood. Even so, was that any reason for her to be so sharp-tongued and critical all the time?

Allison shook her thoughts aside and looked up at her father. "Are you sending me to Missouri because you think I should learn to cook and sew?"

Papa motioned to the baseball glove lying in Allison's lap. "Thanks to being raised with five older *brieder*, you've become quite a tomboy. Truth is you'd rather be outside playing ball than in the house doing womanly things."

Peter, who had wandered over to the sink to wash his hands, added his two cents' worth. "Allison always did prefer doing stuff with me and the brothers. Even when she was little and the girl cousins came around with their dolls, Allison preferred playing ball or going fishing with us."

Allison grunted, her defenses rising. "What's wrong with

that? I enjoy doing outdoor things."

"Nothing's wrong with fishing or playing ball, but if you're ever going to find a suitable mate and get married, you'll need to know how to cook, sew, and manage a house," Papa said.

"Maybe I won't get married. Maybe I'll end up an old maid like—" Allison halted her words. She knew she'd already said more than she should.

Aunt Catherine's face flamed as she stomped back to the refrigerator to put the eggs away.

The lump in Allison's throat thickened. As much as she didn't want to leave her home and spend the summer with relatives she couldn't remember, she didn't wish to seem ungrateful for Papa's unexpected birthday present. If her learning to cook and sew was important to him, then she would try to act more willing. But she doubted she would ever find a husband. Because none of the available young men in her community seemed interested in marrying a tomboy, unless she learned to be more feminine, she'd probably never catch any man's eye.

Allison forced her lips to form a smile as she looked at Papa. "I promise to make the best of my time in Missouri." *But I'll do it for you, not because I want to.*

Allison had a difficult time eating breakfast that morning. Every bite she took felt like cardboard in her mouth. All she could think about was the bus ticket lying on the counter across the room. Was Papa really sending her to Missouri so she could learn to manage a household? Or was the real reason to appease

Aunt Catherine? Allison's cranky aunt rarely had a nice thing to say, but since Papa needed his sister's help, he'd probably do most anything to keep her from leaving—even if it meant sending Allison away for the summer.

When breakfast was over and the menfolk had gone outside to clean the milking barn, Allison and Aunt Catherine began cleaning up the kitchen.

"That was some birthday gift your daed gave you, wasn't it?" Aunt Catherine asked as she carried a stack of dishes to the sink.

Allison followed with the silverware. "Jah, I wasn't expecting a bus ticket to Missouri."

Aunt Catherine placed the dishes in the sink and ran water over them. "Your daed thinks going there will turn you into a woman, but if you don't listen to your aunt Mary any better than you do me, I doubt you'll learn much of anything."

Allison winced, feeling like she'd been slapped in the face with a dishrag. "I. . .I listen to you."

"You may listen, but you don't do as I say." Aunt Catherine grunted. "You've always had a mind of your own, even when you were a young *maedel*."

Allison silently reached for a clean dish towel.

"If you want to be a woman, you can do that right here," Aunt Catherine continued. "My *bruder* shouldn't have to spend his hard-earned money on a bus ticket to send you away so you can learn from your mamm's sister what you could learn from me."

Allison bit her tongue in order to keep from saying anything negative. Maybe being gone for a few months would be good for her. She picked up a glass and poked one end of the towel inside. *It will be a welcome change to be away from Aunt Catherine's angry looks and belittling words.*

A knock sounded on the back door, and Allison hurried to answer it. She found her friend Sally on the porch, holding a package wrapped in white tissue paper.

"Hallich gebottsdaag," Sally said, handing the gift to Allison. "Has it been a good birthday so far?"

Allison swallowed against the burning lump in her throat and gave a quick nod. She couldn't let on to Sally that the day had begun so terribly. Not with Aunt Catherine standing a few feet away at the kitchen sink.

"Danki for the gift," Allison said. "Won't you come in?"

Sally smiled, her blue green eyes fairly glistening. "Of course I'll come in. I want to see if you like the gift I brought."

Allison pulled out a chair at the kitchen table and offered Sally a seat.

"Aren't you going to sit with me and open your gift?" Sally asked.

Allison glanced at her aunt to get her approval. They were supposed to be doing the dishes, and she knew better than to shirk her duties.

Aunt Catherine grunted and gave a quick nod. "I guess it'll be all right if you finish drying the dishes after you're done opening Sally's gift."

I'll bet Aunt Catherine only said that because Sally's here and she's trying to make a good impression. Any other time, she would have insisted that I finish the dishes before I did anything else.

Allison took a seat next to Sally and tore the wrapping paper off the package. She discovered a book about the Oregon Trail inside. "Danki, Sally. This is very nice."

"You're welcome." Sally smiled. "Since you've always shown an interest in history, I thought you might enjoy reading about the pioneers who traveled to the West by covered wagon."

"I'm sure I will, and it'll give me something to read on my trip."

Sally tipped her head. "What trip is that?"

"I'm going to Webster County, Missouri—just outside the town of Seymour," Allison answered. "Papa bought me a bus ticket to Seymour for my birthday."

"Why Seymour?"

"My mamm's twin sister and her family live there, and Papa thought—"

"He thought Allison could learn how to run a household better there than she can here," Aunt Catherine interrupted. Her forehead wrinkled, and she pursed her lips. "Guess my brother thinks his wife's sister can teach Allison things I'm not able to teach her. He obviously thinks Mary King is more capable than me."

"I don't think Papa believes his sister-in-law is more capable," Allison said in her father's defense. "As he mentioned before breakfast, Aunt Mary knows a lot about sewing, and—"

"She can cook and clean like nobody's business." Aunt Catherine grunted. "That's exactly what Herman said."

"How long will you be staying in Missouri?" Sally asked, touching Allison's arm. "I hope not indefinitely, because I would surely miss you."

Allison shook her head. "I'll only be gone for the summer, so you shouldn't miss me too much. Besides, you'll have my bruder to keep you company while I'm gone."

Sally's cheeks turned as red as her hair, and she stared at the table. Peter and Sally had begun courting several months ago. Allison figured it was just a matter of time before they decided to get married.

"I hope you'll write me while you're gone," Sally said.

Allison smiled. "Of course I'll write. I hope you'll write, too."

Sally's head bobbed. "I'll be looking forward to hearing about all the fun you have while you're in Missouri."

Allison swallowed around the lump in her throat. *I doubt that I'll have any fun.*

When the bell above the door to the harness shop jingled, Aaron Zook looked up from the job he'd been assigned—cutting strips of leather. His best friend, Gabe Swartz, stepped into the room, carrying a broken bridle.

"Hey, Aaron, how's business?" Gabe asked as he dropped the bridle to the workbench.

"Fair to middlin'," Aaron replied. "Business always seems to pick up in the summertime."

Gabe glanced around. His hazel-colored eyes seemed to take in the entire room. "Where's Paul? I figured he'd be up front minding the desk while you were in the back room doing all the work." He chuckled. "Isn't that how it usually is?"

Aaron grimaced. He knew Gabe was only funning with him, but the truth was Aaron's stepfather did like to be in charge of the books. There were times when Aaron's father was still alive that helping in the harness shop had seemed like fun—almost a game. But when Aaron first began helping the man who eventually became his stepfather, he'd always felt like he was stuck with the dirty work. Now working here was just plain hard work—but at least he was getting paid for it.

"Paul, Mom, and my sisters, Bessie and Emma, went to Springfield for the day," Aaron said. "Bessie had an appointment with the dentist. Paul said they'd probably do some shopping and go out to lunch while they're there."

Gabe pushed a wavy brown lock of hair off his forehead. "What about your brothers? Didn't they go along?"

"Nope. Joseph and Zachary went to the farmers' market in Seymour. Davey's visiting one of his friends."

"Which left you here at the shop by yourself all day."

"Jah. Somebody has to keep the place open." Aaron stared wistfully out the window. "I do like working here, but on a sunny morning like this, I'd rather be fishing than working."

"Me, too."

"So how are things at your place?" Aaron questioned. "Has Melinda taken in any new critters lately?"

Gabe grinned. "Almost every week she finds some animal that's either orphaned or injured. Just yesterday she found a half-starved kitten out by the road. The pathetic little critter had one of those plastic things that holds a six-pack of soda pop stuck around its neck."

"Will the kitten be okay?"

"Jah. Melinda will see to that."

Aaron fingered Gabe's broken bridle. "Guess there's never a dull moment in your life, huh?"

"That's for sure." Gabe's eyes narrowed as he stared at Aaron. "When are you going to settle down and find a nice young woman to marry?"

Aaron's ears burned. "I'm not interested in marriage. I've told you that plenty of times already."

"Wouldn't you like someone to keep you warm on cold winter nights?"

"Rufus is good at that. He likes to sleep at the foot of my bed."

"*Puh!* No flea-bitten mongrel can take the place of a flesh-and-blood woman." Gabe poked Aaron's arm and chuckled. "Besides, think how nice it would be to have someone to cook, clean, and take care of you when you're old and gray."

"It'll be a long time before I'm old and gray, and I don't need anyone to care for me."

"What about love? Don't you want to fall in love?"

Aaron stiffened. Why did Gabe keep going on about this? *Is he trying to goad me into an argument? Or does he think it's fun to watch my face turn red?*

"I know you're dead set against marriage," Gabe continued, "but if the right woman came along, would you make a move to court her even if you didn't have marriage on your mind?"

Aaron shrugged. "Maybe, but she'd need to have the same interests as me. She'd have to be someone who isn't afraid of hard work or getting her hands dirty, either."

"You mean like your mamm?"

"Jah. She and my real daed worked well together in the harness shop. She and Paul did, too."

"I wonder if your mamm misses working here now." Gabe motioned to the stack of leather piled on the floor a few feet away. "I heard her tell my mamm once that she enjoyed the smell of leather."

"It's true; she does. So did my daed. He loved everything about this harness shop." Aaron picked up the bridle and ran his fingers over the broken end. "I love the feel of leather between my fingers. I'm hoping to take this shop over someday—when Paul's ready to retire."

"Do you think that'll be anytime soon?"

Aaron shook his head. "I doubt it. He seems to enjoy working here too much."

"Maybe he'll give the shop to you, the way my daed gave the woodworking business to me after Melinda and I got married."

Aaron squinted. "Are you saying I'd have to find a wife before Paul would let me take the place over?"

"Not necessarily."

"My real daed wanted me to have this business. He told me that more than once before he was killed."

Gabe leaned against the workbench. "You were pretty young back then. I don't see how you can remember much of anything that was said."

Aaron dropped the bridle, moved over to the desk, and picked up a pen and the work-order book. "I was barely nine when my daed's buggy was hit by a truck, but I remember more than you might think."

"Like what?" Gabe asked as he followed Aaron across the room.

Aaron took a seat at the desk. "I remember how the two of us used to go fishing together. I remember him teaching me to play baseball." Before Gabe could comment, Aaron glanced back at the bridle and said, "How soon do you need your bridle?"

"No big hurry. I've got others I can use for now."

"By the end of next week?"

"Sure, that'll be fine." Gabe moved away from the desk. "Guess I should get on home. Melinda and I are planning to go to Seymour later today. We want to see if the owner of the bed-and-breakfast needs more of her drawings or some of my handcrafted wooden items for his gift shop."

"See you Sunday morning at church, then. It's to be held at the Kings' place, right?"

"Jah." Gabe started for the door. "Maybe we can get a game of baseball going after the common meal," he called over his shoulder.

Aaron nodded. "Sounds like fun."

The door clicked shut behind Gabe, and Aaron headed to the back room to dye some leather strips. After that, he had a saddle to clean. Maybe if he finished up early, he'd have time to get in a little fishing. At least that was something to look forward to—that and a good game of baseball on Sunday afternoon.

Chapter 2

Allison stared vacantly out the window at the passing scenery as the bus took her farther from home and all that was familiar. She would be gone three whole months, living with relatives she didn't really know, in a part of the country she'd never seen before—all because Papa thought she needed to learn to be more feminine while she learned domestic chores.

Allison glanced at the canvas bag by her feet. Inside was the book Sally had given her, as well as some of Aunt Catherine's peanut brittle, which she planned to give Aunt Mary and her family. Allison's faceless doll was also in the bag. She'd had it since she was a little girl. Papa said Mama had made it, but Allison didn't remember receiving the doll. All her memories of Mama were vague. She'd been only seven when Mama died. Papa said a car had hit Mama's buggy when she'd pulled out of their driveway one morning. Allison had supposedly witnessed the accident, but she had no memory of it. All these years, she'd clung to the bedraggled, faceless doll, knowing it was her only link to the mother she'd barely known. Allison had named the doll Martha, after Mama.

Allison reached down and plucked the cloth doll from the canvas satchel. Its arms had come loose long ago and had been pinned in place. Its legs hung by a couple of threads. Its blue dress and small white kapp were worn and faded. "Mama," she murmured against the doll's head. "Why did you have to leave me? If only I could remember your face."

Allison was sure if her mother were still alive, she would have mended the faceless doll. Whenever Allison had mentioned the doll to Aunt Catherine, the crotchety woman had said she was too busy to be bothered with something as unimportant as an old doll. But even if Aunt Catherine had been willing to fix the doll, she'd admitted the other day that she couldn't sew well.

As Allison continued to study her doll, she noticed a spot of dirt on its faceless face and realized that she felt as faceless and neglected as tattered old Martha. Tears blurred Allison's vision and trickled down her hot cheeks. *My life has no real purpose. I have no goals or plans for the future. I'm just drifting along like a boat with no oars. I have no mother, and Aunt Catherine doesn't love me. She doesn't care about anyone but herself.*

Allison had spent most of her life trying to stay out of Aunt Catherine's way rather than trying to learn how to run a home. Maybe a few months of separation would be good for both of them. Aunt Catherine would probably be happier with Allison gone.

More tears dribbled down Allison's cheeks. *I've never been to Missouri before. What will Aunt Mary and her family be like? Will I make any new friends there? Oh, Sally, I miss you already.*

Allison returned her doll to the satchel and reached for the book Sally had given her. If she kept her mind busy reading, maybe she wouldn't feel so sad.

"Did you get Allison put on the bus okay?" Catherine asked Herman as he stepped onto the porch. She was shelling a batch of peas from the garden.

He nodded and took a seat beside her. "It was sure hard to see her go."

"Then why'd you buy that bus ticket for her birthday?"

"You know why, Catherine. I want Allison to have the chance to know her aunt Mary better and to learn to cook, sew, and keep house."

"Humph! She could have learned those things from me if she'd been willing to listen." *Plink. Plinkety-plink.* Catherine dropped several more peas into the bowl braced between her knees.

"You don't sew very well; you said so yourself." Herman pulled at a loose thread on his shirt. "Let's face facts, Catherine. You and Allison have never hit it off. I believe that's why she hasn't learned as much as she should have under your teaching."

"And you think she'll take to her aunt Mary better than me?"

"I'm hoping she does." Herman gave his beard a quick pull. "I'm also hoping Mary relates so well to Allison that she'll want to give up her tomboy ways and become a woman."

"Jah, well, I could have related better to the girl if she hadn't been so set on doing things her own way." Catherine gave an undignified grunt. "Never did understand why Allison preferred to be outside doing chores with the boys when she should have been in the house learning to cook and clean."

"It might have helped if you'd been willing to let Allison try her hand at cooking more."

"I didn't like the messes she made." Catherine shrugged. "Besides, it's quicker and neater if I do the cooking myself."

Herman leaned heavily against the chair and closed his eyes. The morning sun felt warm and helped soothe his jangled nerves. He hadn't wanted to send Allison away. It had nearly broken his heart to see his only daughter board that bus, knowing she would be gone for three whole months and might even decide to stay in Missouri if she liked it there. But watching Allison turn into a tomboy and realizing that if she didn't learn some womanly things she would never find a man to marry had made Herman decide it was time for a change. If Allison stayed in Pennsylvania under the tutelage of his sister, she would never learn the skills of a good homemaker.

Herman grasped the arms of the chair and clenched his fingers. That was another reason he'd sent Allison to Missouri. She needed some time away from Catherine. He'd seen how frustrated she'd become the last few years, having to deal with his cantankerous sister. He'd even thought about asking Catherine to leave, but she'd been with them so long and really had no place else to go. His and Catherine's folks had been dead a good many years, and their siblings, who used to live in Ohio near Catherine, had moved to a newly established community in Wisconsin. Since Catherine had never married, Herman felt responsible for her. After his wife's death, he figured Catherine felt responsible for him and the children, too.

"Are you sleeping?"

Herman's eyes snapped open. "Uh. . .no. Just thinking, is all."

Catherine lifted the bowl of peas into her arms and stood. "Jah, well, you can sit out here and think all you like. I need to get inside and start fixing our meal."

Herman nodded. "Call me when it's ready."

With a weary sigh, Allison reached for her canvas tote and stood. It had taken a day and a half to get from Lancaster, Pennsylvania, to Springfield, Missouri. From Springfield, the bus had headed to the small town of Seymour, where someone was supposed to pick her up at Lazy Lee's Gas Station. Allison had slept some on the bus, but the seats weren't comfortable, and there wasn't much leg room. She hadn't rested nearly as well as she would have in her own bed.

Allison glanced down at her dark blue dress. It was wrinkled and in need of washing. She knew she must look a mess. Unfortunately, there was nothing she could do about that now, for the bus had just pulled into Lazy Lee's parking lot.

Allison gathered up her satchel and stepped off the bus. She spotted a young Amish man with red hair standing beside an open buggy on the other side of the building. When he started toward her, she noticed his deeply set blue eyes and face full of freckles.

"You must be Allison," he said with a lopsided grin.
She nodded. "Jah, I am."

"I'm your cousin, Harvey King." He motioned to the suitcases being taken from the luggage compartment in the side of
the bus. "Show me which one is yours, and I'll put it in the
buggy for you."

Allison pointed to a black canvas suitcase, and Harvey
hoisted it and her small satchel into the back of his open buggy.
Then he helped Allison into the passenger's side, took his own
place, and gathered up the reins.

"My mamm will sure be glad to see you," he said as they
pulled out of the parking lot. "Ever since your daed phoned
and said you were coming, she's been bustling around the house
doing all sorts of things to get ready for your arrival. She hasn't
seen you since you were a little girl. I'll bet she'll be surprised to
see how much you've grown."

Allison smiled. "Is your telephone outside in a shed?"

Harvey shook his head. "No, but they have one at the harness
shop. From what I was told, your daed and Paul Hilty know each
other from when Paul worked in his cousin's harness shop in
Pennsylvania. Since Uncle Herman knew Paul had put a phone
in at the shop, he called there and asked Paul to get the message
to us that you were coming to visit for the summer."

"Ah, I see."

"I hope you don't mind a little detour, but I need to stop
by the harness shop before we go home," Harvey said. "I would
have done it on my way to Seymour, but I got a late start and
didn't want to miss your bus."

"I don't mind stopping," Allison assured him. "I've been

sitting on that bus so long, it will feel good to get out and move around."

"I figured you'd probably just want to wait in the buggy while I ran in and picked up my daed's new harness. But if you'd like to go into the shop or walk around outside the place, that's fine by me."

She nodded. "I like the smell of leather, so I think I'll go inside with you."

Harvey cast her a sidelong glance but made no comment. He probably figured she was strange for liking the smell of leather. He'd probably think she was even stranger if he knew all the tomboy things she liked to do.

"Are you finished pressing those rivets into that harness yet, Aaron?" Paul called from the front of the shop. "Ben King said his son would be over sometime today to pick it up, and it should have been ready this morning."

Aaron frowned. Why did his stepfather always have to check up on him? Did Paul think he was incapable of getting the job done on time? He clenched his teeth to keep from offering an unkind retort. Truth was, when Paul first came to Webster County for his brother's funeral and had stayed to help Mom in the harness shop, Aaron had resented Paul. He'd been worried that Paul wanted to marry his mother and take over the harness shop. Then when Paul had rescued Aaron from the top rung of the silo ladder, he and Paul had established a pretty good relationship. Paul had eventually married Aaron's mother, and things had remained fine between them—until recently, that is. For some reason, ever since Aaron had become a man, Paul had become kind of bossy, and for the last few months, he'd started talking to Aaron like he was a child again.

"Aaron, did you hear what I said?" Paul called, pulling Aaron's thoughts aside.

"I heard. The harness is almost done."

"Good, because I see Harvey pulling up outside."

Aaron snapped the last rivet into place, picked up the harness, and headed to the front of the shop. He reached Paul's desk just as the front door opened. In walked Harvey with a young Amish woman Aaron had never seen before. Her hair was the color of dark chocolate, she was of medium height and slender build, and her nose turned up slightly on the end. Had Harvey found himself a new girlfriend? If so, she wasn't from around here. Aaron knew all the young women in their small Amish community. Maybe she was from one of the towns near Jamesport, where a good number of Amish people lived.

"Afternoon, Harvey," Paul said with a friendly smile. "Your timing is good; we just finished your daed's harness."

"Great." Harvey turned to the young woman at his side. "This is Allison Troyer. She's my cousin from Pennsylvania, and she'll be staying with us for the summer."

Paul took a step forward. "You're Herman's daughter, aren't you?"

"Jah," Allison said with a nod.

"I haven't seen you since you were a little girl."

Allison opened her mouth as if to say something but closed it again.

"You came to my cousin's harness shop with your daed a couple of times."

"I. . .I don't remember."

"You were pretty young." Paul smiled. "Anyway, I took the message when he phoned to say you were coming."

How come I didn't know about it? Aaron wondered. *I had no idea Harvey had a cousin living in Pennsylvania.*

Paul took the harness from Aaron. "Here's what you came for, Harvey. I hope it's done to your daed's liking."

"Looks fine to me," Harvey said with a nod.

"Where are my manners?" Paul motioned to Aaron. "Allison, this is my son Aaron."

Stepson, Aaron almost corrected, but he caught himself in time. "It's nice to meet you," he mumbled.

She smiled, kind of shylike. "Same here."

"Are you related to Isaac and Ellen Troyer, who live not far from here?" Aaron asked.

"No, I don't know them," she said with a shake of her head.

"Guess I'd better settle up with you and get on home." Harvey moved over to the desk. "Mom's probably pacing the floors by now, waiting for me to show up with her niece."

As Paul wrote out the invoice and Harvey leaned on the desk, Aaron ambled over to one of their workbenches and picked up a piece of leather that needed to be cut and dyed. He was surprised when Allison followed.

"It smells nice in here," she said, tilting her head and sniffing the air.

"You really think so?"

"I sure do."

"Most women don't care much for the smells inside a harness shop. Except for my mamm, that is," Aaron amended. "She used to work here with my real daed when I was a young boy. Then she took the place over by herself for a time after he died." He glanced over his shoulder at Paul. "After Mom married Paul, she kept working in the shop, but then my grandparents' health started to fail, so she had to give up working here in order to see to their needs."

"I see."

Aaron's ears burned with embarrassment. He didn't know what had possessed him to blab all that information to a woman he'd only met.

"I can see why your mamm would enjoy working here," Allison said, motioning to the pile of leather on the floor. "This looks like a fun place to be."

"Some might see it as fun, but it's a lot of work."

"I'm sure it would be." Her fingers trailed over the end of the harness. "I'd like to know more about harness making."

Aaron was about to comment when Harvey sauntered up, holding his finished harness. "Guess we'd better get going," he said, nodding at Allison.

She gave Aaron a quick smile. "Maybe I'll see you again sometime and you can tell me more about harness making."

"No maybe about it. You'll see him at church tomorrow morning." Harvey winked at Aaron, but before Aaron could think of a sensible reply, Harvey and his cousin walked out the door.

"She seemed like a nice person, didn't she?" Paul asked, as Aaron resumed his work.

"Huh?"

"Harvey's cousin, Allison. She seemed real nice."

Aaron shrugged. "I guess so."

Paul thumped Aaron on the back. "How come your ears are so red?"

"Must be the heat. Summer weather makes its way indoors pretty quick on days like this."

Paul nodded and picked up a piece of leather lying on the workbench near him. "Just never saw your ears turn so red before."

Aaron just kept on working.

While Harvey guided his horse and buggy down Highway C, Allison sat in amazement, studying her surroundings. Everything looked so different from what she was used to seeing in Pennsylvania. There were no rolling hills—just a multitude of trees with Amish and English houses built on the land that had been cleared. Most of the homes looked old, and many were a bit rundown. Few had flowers in abundance, the way most Amish places did back home. The two-story gray and white home that loomed before them as they turned onto a graveled driveway was an exception. A bounty of irises danced in the breeze near the vegetable garden growing to the left of the house, and two pots of pink flowers graced the front porch.

Harvey had no more than guided the horse to the hitching rail when the front door opened. A middle-aged woman followed by a young boy and a girl hurried over to the buggy.

Allison climbed down and was surprised when the woman

gave her a hug. "I'm your aunt Mary, and these are my youngest children: Sarah, who is twelve, and Dan, who's ten."

Allison noticed immediately that Aunt Mary had the same dark hair and brown eyes with little green flecks that she had. Since Allison barely remembered her mother, she couldn't be sure her mother's sister looked like Mama, but Papa had said they were identical twins. Mama probably would have looked much like Aunt Marry if she were still alive.

"It's nice to meet you, Aunt Mary," Allison said. She turned to face the children. "You, too, Cousin Sarah and Dan."

"Actually, we have met before," Aunt Mary said. "I came to Pennsylvania for your mamm's funeral."

Allison stared at the ground, struggling to remember the past. "Sorry, but I. . .I don't remember."

"You were quite young then, so I don't expect you would remember." Aunt Mary put her arm around Allison's shoulder. "Shall we go inside and have a glass of freshly squeezed lemonade? It's turned into a real scorcher today, and nothing cools a parched throat quite like cold lemonade."

Allison licked her lips, realizing that they were parched and she was rather thirsty. "That would be real nice."

"I'll put the horse away and bring in her luggage," Harvey said as Allison, Aunt Mary, and the two younger children headed for the house.

"Sounds good. When you're done, come join us in the kitchen," his mother called over her shoulder.

Allison began to relax. *Aunt Mary seems so pleasant—much different than Aunt Catherine. Of course, I'd best wait until I get to know her better to make any decisions.*

As Allison sat around the supper table that evening, she was amazed at the camaraderie between family members. Aunt Mary made no sharp remarks—only smiles and encouraging words. Uncle Ben was kind and friendly, but then Papa and her brothers had always been that way, too. It was Aunt Catherine who had made Allison feel as though she could do nothing right. No jokes were tolerated at Aunt Catherine's table, and she often hurried them through their meals, saying more chores needed to be done.

Allison had never been able to talk about her feelings with Aunt Catherine, either, and Papa sure didn't have much time to listen. Here, everyone seemed interested in what others in the family had to say.

She glanced at Cousin Harvey, who sat beside his fifteen-year-old brother, Walter. The younger teenaged boy had been in the fields with their father when Allison had arrived. This was the first chance she'd had to meet him. Both Harvey and Walter seemed polite and easygoing, and so did Dan and Sarah. Could the whole family be as pleasant as they seemed?

"Allison brought us some peanut brittle," Aunt Mary said to Uncle Ben. "Since it's your favorite candy, I hope you'll let the rest of us have some."

He chuckled, and his crimson beard jiggled up and down. "I'll share, but only a *bissel*."

"Ah, Dad," Walter said with a frown, "don't you think we deserve more than a little?"

Uncle Ben jiggled his eyebrows playfully. "Well, maybe." He

smiled at Allison. "It was sure nice of your daed's sister to send the peanut brittle. She must be a very *gedankevoll* woman."

Allison almost choked on the piece of chicken she'd put in her mouth. If Uncle Ben knew Aunt Catherine the way she did, he might not think she was so thoughtful.

"Are you all right?" Aunt Mary asked, patting Allison on the back.

"I'm fine. I almost choked on a piece of meat, but I'm okay." Allison reached for her glass and took a gulp of water.

"I met your aunt Catherine at your mamm's funeral," Aunt Mary said. "You said earlier that you don't remember me being there, right?"

Allison nodded. "I was only seven when Mama died, so I don't remember much of anything about that time."

"Are you saying you don't remember your mamm at all?" Uncle Ben asked with raised eyebrows.

"I have a few vague memories of her from before the accident, but that's all."

"Martha and I were so close when we were growing up," Aunt Mary said in a wistful tone. "It was hard on both of us when I moved to Missouri. We kept in touch through letters until her passing. I sure miss my twin sister."

"What made you move to Missouri?" Allison asked, not wishing to talk about her mother's death.

"That was my fault," Uncle Ben interjected. "I wanted to get away from all the tourists in Lancaster County. Since I had a brother who'd moved to Missouri, shortly after Mary and I got married, we packed up our things, hired a driver, and moved here to Webster County."

Allison wondered if her life would be any different if Aunt Mary and Uncle Ben still lived in Pennsylvania. Aunt Catherine wouldn't have needed to move in with them after Mama died if Aunt Mary had lived closer. She took another sip of water. *Oh, well. As Papa always says, "Since you can't change the past, you may as well make the best of the present." So I will try to enjoy my summer here,* she resolved.

Chapter 3

Before church the following morning, Allison stepped into the Kings' barn and was surprised to see how few people filled the backless wooden benches. At home, twice as many people would have attended, but then this Amish community was much smaller than hers in Lancaster County.

As she lowered herself to a bench on the women's side, someone touched her arm. She glanced to the left. A young, blond-haired woman smiled and said, "Hi. My name's Katie Esh." Her vivid blue eyes sparkled like ripples of water on a hot summer day, and a small dimple was set in the middle of her chin. Allison thought Katie was the prettiest young woman she'd ever seen. Not plain and ordinary like her. That's what Aunt Catherine had always said about Allison, anyway.

"What's your name?" Katie asked, nudging Allison's arm.

"Oh, I'm Allison Troyer, visiting from Pennsylvania."

"How long will you be here?"

"Until the end of August. I'm staying with my aunt and uncle, Mary and Ben King."

Katie leaned closer and whispered in Allison's ear, "Looks like the service is getting ready to start. We can talk later, jah?"

Allison nodded and sat up straight, thinking about the way Aunt Catherine expected her to behave in church. She remembered one time when she'd been sitting next to Sally and had been caught whispering. Aunt Catherine had marched up to them and plucked Allison right off the bench. Allison had spent the next three hours sitting beside Aunt Catherine, worried that she might receive a spanking if she moved wrong or did anything Aunt Catherine disapproved of.

Allison glanced over her shoulder at Aunt Mary, sitting a few rows behind. *I wonder what kind of mother she is to her children. Is she really kind and gentle, the way she appeared to be last night, or does she have a mean streak like Aunt Catherine?*

Aaron's mind drifted from the sermon Bishop John was preaching as he glanced at the women's side of the room and spotted Allison Troyer staring out the open barn door. Would she rather be outdoors, or was she bored with the service? As much as Aaron hated to admit it, Allison had his full attention. Maybe it was the fact that she'd mentioned yesterday how she liked the smell of leather. Aaron smiled to himself. *Or maybe it's because–*

Aaron felt a jab to his ribs, and he looked over at his brother Joseph and frowned. "What'd you poke me for?" he whispered.

"Church is over," Joseph said with a smirk. "You looked like you were off in some other world, so I figured I'd better bring you back to this one."

Aaron grunted. "Very funny."

A short time later, Aaron followed the men up to the house, where the common meal would be served. He'd no more than taken a seat when he felt another sharp jab to the ribs. He glanced to the left and saw Gabe sitting beside him. "What'd you prod me for?"

Gabe snickered. "I was wondering why you're making cow eyes at that new girl, Allison."

"I'm not!" Aaron bit off the end of a fingernail and was about to flick it over his shoulder onto the floor, when Gabe grabbed his hand.

"That's a nasty habit, and we're not outside, so you'd better not do that."

"You're right." Aaron slipped the sliver of fingernail into his pants pocket.

"Are you ever planning to quit that awful habit?" Gabe questioned.

"Maybe someday—if I feel like it."

"Falling in love might make you give up your crude ways."

Aaron elbowed his friend. "A lot you know; I'm not crude."

"Jah, well, I know a man with a crush when I see one."

"I don't have a crush on anyone. I barely know her."

"Who?"

"Allison Troyer. That's who we were talking about, right?"

Gabe put his finger in the small of Aaron's back. "Since you barely know her, why don't you remedy that by going over and talking to her? Or are you too much of a chicken?"

"I'm not scared of anything."

"Then prove it."

Joseph, sitting on the other side of Aaron, nodded his blond head in agreement. "I think it's about time you took an interest in some nice young woman."

"Just so you two will get off my back, I will go speak to Allison," Aaron said, his jaw tight. "But it's not because I have an interest in her." He hopped off the bench and strolled across the room, heading for the kitchen. He stopped a few feet from the table where Allison and Katie were serving a group of men. His heart hammered so hard he feared it might break through his chest, and he took in a couple of deep breaths in order to steady his nerves. He couldn't march right up to Allison and start yammering away. What would he say? What if she thought he was trying to make a play for her? Then again, he didn't want Gabe and Joseph to think he was a coward.

Aaron took a step back and bumped a table leg, jostling Bishop Frey's glass of water.

"Whoa there! What do you think you're doing, boy?" the man asked as he blotted the table with his napkin.

"S–s–sorry, Bishop. I didn't realize you were behind me." Aaron glanced around. Everyone in the room seemed to be staring at him, including Allison.

Oh, great. She probably thinks I'm a real klutz. Aaron slunk away, knowing he would probably be in for more ribbing from Gabe.

He figured a little teasing from his friend would be better than facing Allison and feeling more foolish than he already did. No, he wasn't about to start up a conversation with her now.

Allison watched from the sidelines as a group of young men got a baseball game going in the field behind the Kings' place. She longed to join them but figured, since she was new here, it would seem forward if she asked to be part of the game. Besides, none of the other young women had joined the fellows.

"What are you doing over here?" Katie asked, stepping up to Allison. "I figured you'd be up on the porch with some of the women, visiting and sipping iced tea."

Allison shook her head. "To tell you the truth, I'd like to play baseball, but since the next best thing to playing the game is watching, I decided to stand here by the fence and watch."

"If you'd rather play ball, why aren't you?"

Allison shrugged. "I wasn't invited."

"Me neither, but I'd play if I wanted to, invited or not." Katie grinned. "Who do you think is the cutest fellow here today?"

"I. . .I haven't given it much thought."

Katie leaned closer to Allison. "Can you keep a secret?"

"Jah, sure."

"I think the cutest fellow here is Joseph Zook." Katie pointed across the field. "He's the one with curly blond hair. That's his brother Aaron with dark hair. They don't look much alike, because Joseph looks like his real daed, and Aaron takes after his mamm."

Katie rushed on. "There's going to be a young people's gathering tonight at the Kauffmans' place. Do you think you might attend?"

"I guess that all depends on whether Harvey's planning to go."

"I'm sure he will; he usually does."

"Tell me about your family," Allison said, changing the subject.

Katie smiled. "Let's see now. There's me; my younger sister, Mary Alice; and my older brother, Elam, still living at home, and I've got three other brothers who are married and out on their own. What about you, Allison?" she asked. "How many *kinner* are in your family?"

Allison opened her mouth to reply when the ball *whooshed* toward her. Instinctively, she reached up and caught it.

"Wow, that was *wunderbaar!*" her cousin Harvey exclaimed. "Never knew a girl could catch a ball so well. And with only one hand."

An eager smile sprang to Allison's lips. She wondered if she should tell Harvey she was an expert ballplayer or let him think she had caught it by accident. If she had remembered to pack her new baseball glove when she'd left home, she'd probably be even more anxious to join their game.

"Allison wants to be part of your game," Katie spoke up. "She told me that she'd rather play ball than visit."

Harvey tipped his head and grinned at Allison. "Is that so?"

She nodded and handed him the ball. "I've been playing baseball with my brothers since I was a little girl."

"Maybe you'd like to be on Aaron Zook's team. He's one player short, and if you don't mind playing with a bunch of rowdy fellows, we'd be happy to have you."

Allison looked over at Katie. "Would you like to play, too?"

Katie shook her head. "You go ahead. I'll stand here and cheer you on."

Allison followed Harvey across the field to where Aaron stood. Harvey explained the situation.

Aaron's dark eyebrows drew together, making Allison wonder if he disapproved.

"You can play left field," he finally said.

For the next hour, Allison caught several fly balls, hit three home runs, and chocked up more points for Aaron's team than any other player.

When the game ended, she headed toward Katie, but Aaron stepped in front of her. He swiped a grimy hand across his sweaty forehead. "A lot of women I know like to play ball, and they do okay, but I've never met anyone who could catch the way you did today."

She grinned at him. "I've always liked playing ball."

He shuffled his feet in the dirt. "I. . .uh. . .guess I'll go get myself something cold to drink."

Allison nodded. "I worked up quite a thirst out there, so maybe I'll do the same."

Aaron hesitated and stared at the ground. "Maybe I'll see you tonight at the young people's gathering."

"Jah, maybe so."

Chapter 4

I am glad you were willing to go with me tonight," Harvey said as he helped Allison into his open buggy. "It'll be a good chance for you to get to know some of the other young people in our district."

Allison nodded. "I did get acquainted with Katie Esh after church today, as well as some of the fellows who were involved in the ball game."

Harvey chuckled. "I still can't get over how well you played. I'll bet Aaron Zook was glad I suggested you be on his team."

"I don't know about that, but I did enjoy playing."

They rode in silence. The only sounds were the steady *clippety-clop* of the horse's hooves and the *whoosh* of the wind whipping against their faces.

"Seemed like you and Katie Esh hit it off pretty well today,"

Harvey said, breaking the quiet.

Allison nodded. "Katie seems real nice."

"Several of the guys would agree with you on that. Some I know of have been interested in Katie ever since they were in school."

"I can understand that. Katie's very pretty." Allison stared down at her hands. Her friend back home was being courted by Peter, and her new friend here had a boyfriend, too. If only some young man would take an interest in her, she might not feel like such a misfit.

"Think you might get up the nerve to ask someone to ride home in your buggy tonight?" Joseph asked Aaron as the two of them entered the Kauffmans' barn.

Aaron shook his head.

"If you were to ask someone, who would it be?"

"I just said I wouldn't be asking anyone."

"You never said that; only shook your head."

"Same difference."

"But if you were to ask someone, who would it be?"

"That's my business, don't you think?"

Joseph pulled off his straw hat. "Aren't you the testy one tonight? I was only making sure you aren't interested in the same girl I am."

"I'm not interested in Katie Esh, so don't worry. You've got the green light to ask her yourself."

A wave of heat washed over Joseph's cheeks. Could his older

brother read his mind? Aaron had always been able to stay one up on him when they were boys. Maybe things weren't so different now. "How'd you know I was interested in Katie?"

"It doesn't take a genius to see that you're smitten with her. You act like a lovesick *hund* every time she's around."

"I'm no puppy dog."

"But you are lovesick, right?"

Joseph wrinkled his nose. "If you're not willing to tell me who you'd like to take home tonight, I'm not willing to say how I feel about Katie."

"Suit yourself, because I'm not telling you a thing. Besides, I already know how you feel about Katie." Aaron sauntered off toward the refreshment table, leaving Joseph alone.

When Joseph glanced across the barn and saw Katie sitting on a bale of straw, he began rehearsing what he should say to her. *Should I come right out and ask if I can give her a ride home tonight, or would it be better if I dropped a couple of hints to see what she might be thinking?*

Drawing in a deep breath for added courage, he made his way to Katie's side. She looked up at him and smiled. "I'm glad to see you made it, Joseph. I saw Aaron over at the refreshment table, but I wasn't sure if you were here."

He took a seat beside her and decided to plunge ahead before he lost his nerve. "I. . .uh, came in my own buggy tonight, and I was hoping—" A trickle of sweat rolled down Joseph's nose, and he reached up to wipe it away.

"You were hoping what?"

He licked his lips and swallowed hard.

"Do you need something to drink?"

"No, no. I'm just feeling a little nervous, is all."

"How come?"

You. You're the reason I've got a passel of butterflies tromping around in my stomach. Joseph drew in a quick breath and plastered a smile on his face. His mother had always said a friendly smile was the best remedy for a case of nerves. "I. . .uh. . .was wondering. . ."

Katie leaned a little closer to Joseph. "What were you wondering?"

"Would you be willing to ride home with me in my buggy tonight?"

Her eyes widened. "You want me to go to your house after the gathering?"

"No, no," he stammered. "I'd like to give you a ride home to your house. That is, if you're willing."

Katie's smile stretched from ear to ear. "Jah, Joseph. I'm more than willing."

Allison stepped into the Kauffmans' barn, and the first person she spotted was Aaron Zook. He stood next to the refreshment table, holding a paper cup in one hand and a cookie in the other. She was tempted to go over and talk to him but thought that would seem too forward. Besides, Aaron could very well have a girlfriend, and Allison didn't want to do anything that might cause trouble between them if he did.

Glancing around the barn, she discovered Katie sitting on a bale of straw talking to Joseph Zook. Since they both had blond hair and blue eyes, they made quite a striking pair. Allison remembered Katie had mentioned earlier that she had her eye on Joseph. From the looks of the smile she saw on Joseph's face, she had a hunch he might be asking if he could give Katie a ride home.

Katie looked over at Allison just then and motioned her to come over. Allison hesitated until Joseph headed over to the refreshment table. Then she scurried over and took a seat on the bale of straw next to Katie.

"I'm glad you could make it tonight," Katie said.

Allison smiled. "Aunt Mary thought it would be good for me to come so I can get better acquainted with everyone."

Katie nodded and glanced over at Joseph. "Do you have a steady boyfriend back home?"

"Oh, no," Allison was quick to reply.

"Someday you will, I'm sure." Katie released a contented sigh. "Joseph Zook just asked if I'd like a ride home in his buggy tonight."

"What'd you say?"

"I said I'd be willing, of course." Katie nudged Allison's arm. "From the way some of the fellows are watching you, I'd say you might have your pick of whose buggy you get to ride home in."

Allison's eyebrows shot up. "What do you mean? I haven't noticed anyone staring at me."

"If you keep your eyes open, you will."

With a quick glance around the room, Allison scanned the faces of the young men present. Katie was right—one man was watching her. She hadn't seen him in church. The young man had shiny black hair worn a bit longer than any of the other fellows. When he caught her looking at him, he winked and lifted his hand.

Allison looked away. "Who is that guy leaning against the wall over there?" she asked Katie.

"Where?"

Allison nodded with her head and said quietly, "Over there by the back wall. The one with the hair black as coal."

"Oh, that's James Esh, my cousin. He's kind of wild, but I think he's harmless enough." Katie leaned closer to Allison. "Was he staring at you?"

"Jah. He winked at me."

Before Katie could respond, Joseph showed up with a plate of cookies and some pretzels, which he handed to Katie.

"Danki, Joseph." Katie scooted over, and he plunked down beside her.

Joseph glanced over at Allison and smiled. "I was impressed with how well you played ball today."

Allison smiled. "Danki."

"My brother Aaron wasn't too happy about being one player short at the beginning of the game, but after you joined, his team sure racked up the points."

"I was glad I could play. It was fun. We don't usually play ball after church in my district back home."

Just then, James showed up, carrying a plate of cookies. "Since we haven't been properly introduced, I thought I'd come over and say hello," he said, offering Allison a crooked grin.

"I'm Allison Troyer."

"And I'm—"

"My pushy cousin James," Katie cut in.

James's dark brows drew together as he scowled at her. "I can speak on my own behalf, you know." He squeezed onto the bale of straw beside Allison and handed her the cookies. "I thought you might be hungry."

Allison took one with chocolate frosting. "Danki."

Allison, James, Katie, and Joseph visited until the song leader called out the first song—"Mocking Bird Hill." James kept time to the music by tapping his finger on Allison's arm. His attention made her feel nervous, but she felt flattered, too.

When the singing ended, Allison decided to leave the stuffy barn and breathe some fresh air. Maybe she would join the group that had begun a game of volleyball.

"Hey, where are you going?" James called.

"Outside."

"Mind if I come with you?"

"No."

James joined Allison under a maple tree, where she stood staring up at the moonlit sky. "Sure is pretty tonight," he whispered against her ear. "Some of those stars are so bright they look like headlights in the sky."

Allison nodded. Being this close to James made her feel jittery as a june bug.

"Say, I was wondering if you'd be willing to let me take you home tonight."

Allison shivered even though the evening air was quite warm and muggy. Should she allow James to escort her back to Aunt Mary's? She'd only met him and didn't know anything about him other than the little bit Katie had shared. Still, if she accepted the ride, it would leave Cousin Harvey free to escort someone home without her tagging along.

"What's your answer?" James prompted.

"I. . .I guess it would be okay, but I need to speak with my cousin first."

"What for?"

"I can't take off without telling him. He'd probably be worried."

James pointed to a buggy parked near the end of the barn. "That's my rig—the one with the fancy silver trim. If Harvey's okay with me taking you home, then meet me over there."

Allison hurried off to look for her cousin. She found him talking to a young woman he introduced as Clara Weaver. From the affectionate looks the young couple gave each other, Allison figured Clara must be Harvey's girlfriend.

"Someone has asked to give me a ride home," Allison said to Harvey. "If you don't mind me going, then you won't have to bother taking me back home."

Harvey quirked an eyebrow. "Whose buggy are you riding in?"

"James Esh. He's Katie's cousin."

"I know who he is, and I'd rather you didn't ride in his buggy."

"Why not?"

Harvey leaned closer to Allison. "James is kind of wild; I'm not sure he can be trusted. I can't stop you from riding home in his buggy, but I don't think it's a good idea."

"He seems nice enough to me," Allison said. "Besides, I think I'm old enough to take care of myself."

Harvey shrugged. "Suit yourself. I'll see you at home then."

Aaron stood in the shadows watching James help Allison into his buggy. A feeling of frustration welled up in him. He'd spent most of the evening watching Allison and James as they sat together on a bale of straw, and now the fellow was obviously taking her home. He scuffed the toe of his boot in the dirt. *James isn't right for Allison. He's a big flirt, and he's way too wild.*

Aaron knew that James, who had recently turned twenty-one, was still going through his *rumschpringe*. The unruly fellow had a mind of his own and liked to show off with his fancy buggy and unmanageable horse.

He shouldn't be using that spirited gelding for a buggy horse, Aaron fumed. *And he shouldn't be escorting a woman home in a buggy pulled by that crazy critter.*

When James backed his buggy away from the barn, Aaron slunk back into the shadows and ambled toward his buggy. *Don't know why I care what Allison does. It's none of my business if she's interested in James or any other fellow.*

"I hope things are going well at the young people's gathering this evening," Mary said to Ben as the two of them sat at the kitchen table drinking lemonade.

"I'm sure everyone's having a good time." Ben reached across the table and patted her hand. "Remember how much fun we used to have when we attended young people's functions?"

Mary smiled at the memory of the evening when Ben had asked for the first time if he could give her a ride home in his buggy. She'd known from that moment that they would one day get married. "I wonder how Harvey will work things out if he wants to give some young woman a ride home tonight," she said.

"What do you mean?"

"Since he escorted Allison to the gathering, he'll have to bring her home."

Ben shrugged his broad shoulders. "Maybe Allison will catch some young fellow's eye, and he'll ask to give her a ride home."

Mary took a sip of lemonade. "I hope it's someone nice and not one of those fellows like James Esh or Brian Stutzman who likes to show off."

"I'm sure if someone like that were to offer Allison a ride home, her answer would be no."

On the ride home, Harvey's words of warning echoed in Allison's head. She'd chosen to ignore her cousin's advice, not wishing to judge James without getting to know him. After all, it wasn't as if he was asking to court her. It was a ride home in his buggy—nothing more.

"You don't talk much, do you?" James asked, breaking into Allison's thoughts.

She shrugged. "I do when there's something to say."

He chuckled and reached for her hand. "A pretty girl like you doesn't need to say anything as far as I'm concerned."

She eased her hand away and tucked a wayward strand of hair back under her kapp. She wasn't used to receiving such compliments and wasn't sure how to respond. "Your horse is nice looking, and he trots very well," she said, for lack of anything better to say.

"As far as I'm concerned, he's one of the finest. He can get pretty feisty when he wants to, though."

"I've ridden bareback a time a two, though never on a spirited horse."

James glanced over at her, and his dark eyebrows drew together. "You like to ride horses?"

She nodded. *Does he think I'm a tomboy? Should I have kept that information to myself?*

"Besides owning a high-spirited horse, I also own a car," James said.

"You do?"

He nodded. "I was thinking maybe sometime you'd like to ride to Springfield with me, and we can do something fun. There's not much to do around here."

"Oh, I don't know."

"You haven't joined the church yet, have you?"

"No, I. . .I don't feel quite ready."

"That means you're still going through rumschpringe, so you ought to be able to go most anywhere with me." He reached across the seat and touched her arm. "Think about it, okay?"

Allison gave a quick nod. Being with James made her feel nervous, yet she felt an attraction to him.

They rode in silence. The only sounds were the steady *clop-clop* of the horse's hooves and the creaking of the crickets coming from the woods along the road. When they turned up the driveway leading to Aunt Mary and Uncle Ben's place, James pulled back on the reins. The horse and buggy came to a halt, and he slipped one arm around Allison's shoulders. "I'd really like to see you again. If you're not interested in going to Springfield, maybe we could go on a picnic sometime." He smiled.

Allison swallowed hard. "That sounds nice, but my aunt mentioned last night that she'll need help with her garden this summer. I'll probably be kept pretty busy."

"You can't work every minute."

"That's true. I guess I'll just have to see how it goes."

James leaned toward her suddenly and bent his head. Before Allison knew what had happened, his lips touched hers with a kiss that took her breath away. Except for her father's occasional pecks on the cheek, she'd never been kissed and hadn't known quite what to expect.

He tickled her under the chin. "I hope to see you again, Allison."

No words would come, so Allison merely nodded and hopped down from the buggy. Then she sprinted up the driveway toward the house without looking back. Her heart pounded so hard, she feared it might explode. As she reached the porch, she heard James call to his horse, "Giddyup there, boy!"

A slight breezed swept under the eaves of the porch and pushed the mugginess away. "That was my first kiss," she murmured.

Chapter 5

Allison pulled the log-cabin-patterned quilt up over her bed and straightened the pillows. She picked up her faceless doll, placed it at the foot of the bed, and took a seat. Tears gathered in her eyes as she stroked the small kapp perched on the doll's head. Looking at it reminded her of home.

After the pleasant welcome Allison had received last Saturday, she thought she might do okay here. Yet now she found herself missing Papa, Peter, and Sally—everyone but Aunt Catherine. It was actually a relief to be out from under her aunt's scrutinizing eyes and sharp tongue.

Allison's thoughts shifted to the evening before and how James Esh had brought her home from the singing and then stolen a kiss. She was flattered by his attention and wondered if he'd offer to give her a ride home from the next young people's gathering. If he did, what should her response be? Despite the fact that she found James attractive and exciting, his boldness frightened her.

A vision of Aaron Zook flashed across Allison's mind—brunette hair, dark eyes, square jaw, and a shy-looking smile. It seemed odd that Aaron hadn't said more than a quick hello to her last night, since after church he'd asked if she'd be attending. Maybe he had only asked out of politeness.

Allison hadn't seen Aaron with any young woman last night, so if he had a girlfriend, she must not have been at the gathering.

A knock on the bedroom door startled Allison, and she jumped up. "Come in."

The door opened and Aunt Mary stepped into the room. "I was wondering if you were up yet."

"Jah, I'm up. I was just getting ready to do up my hair." Allison moved over to the small mirror hanging above her dresser. She picked up her comb, made a part down the middle of her hair, rolled it back on the sides, and secured it into a bun.

"Did you have fun at the young people's gathering last night?" Aunt Mary asked. "Since I was in bed when you got home, I didn't get the chance to ask."

"It was okay."

"When Harvey came downstairs this morning, he mentioned that James Esh gave you a ride home last night."

Allison nodded. She hoped the warmth she felt on her cheeks wouldn't let Aunt Mary know how embarrassed she felt over the kiss James had given her.

"In case you didn't know, James hasn't joined the church yet."

Aunt Mary's brows furrowed. "You might watch yourself around James, because from what I've heard, he's kind of wild."

"I don't think James is really interested in me, but I'll be careful, Aunt Mary."

"I hope so, dear one." Aunt Mary moved over to the bed and picked up the faceless doll. "It looks like this poor thing is in need of repair."

Allison set her kapp on the back of her head. "According to my daed, my mamm made it for me when I was little. I don't remember that, but I've kept it because it reminds me that I had a mamm once."

Aunt Mary patted Allison's arm. "I'm sorry about that." She took a seat on the edge of the bed and placed the doll in her lap. "Is there a reason this poor thing is in such bad shape?"

"I. . .I don't know how to fix it." Allison sighed. "I asked Aunt Catherine several times to repair the doll, but she said she wasn't much of a seamstress and was too busy to mess with something as unimportant as a faceless doll."

"Are you saying no one has ever taught you to sew?"

Allison nodded. "Whenever I tried on my own, I either managed to stick myself with the needle, or the thread never seemed to hold."

"Would you like to learn to use my treadle machine?"

Allison nibbled on the inside of her cheek. Truth be told, she'd never had a desire to sew.

"We could begin by repairing your faceless doll. Then later, when we have more time, I'd be happy to show you how to make a doll from scratch."

"Well, I—"

"I haven't made a faceless doll for some time, since most Amish children don't play with that kind of doll much anymore." Aunt Mary smiled. "I think it would be fun for you to make one, though. You might even want to sell some dolls at the farmers' market or in one of the gift shops in Seymour."

The thought of making some money appealed to Allison, but she wasn't sure she wanted to learn how to sew in order to accomplish that. *Of course,* she reminded herself, *the reason Papa sent me here is so I can learn to do more womanly things. If I'm ever to find a husband, I'll need to know how to sew, whether I like it or not.*

"Jah, okay," she finally said. "I'd be happy if you could show me how to use the sewing machine."

"Has the mail come yet?" Herman asked as he entered the kitchen after finishing his morning chores.

Catherine, who was sitting at the table, nodded and motioned to a stack of letters on the counter.

"Any word from Allison?"

"Not a thing."

Herman compressed his lips. "That's strange. I thought for sure there would be a letter from her by now."

"Your sister-in-law is probably keeping the girl too busy to write. She's supposed to be learning how to run a home, after all."

Herman noticed the bitter tone in his sister's voice. Was she jealous because Mary possessed homemaking skills she didn't?

Or could she be angry because having Allison gone meant she was stuck doing all the housework on her own?

"Is there any iced tea?" he asked.

Catherine shook her head. "I didn't make any cold tea today. Just some hot peppermint tea to soothe my stomach."

"What's wrong with your stomach? Are you feeling *grank?*"

"I don't think I'm sick; just a bit of indigestion is all." She shrugged. "It's probably those greasy sausage links I ate for breakfast. Never did care much for sausage."

"Then why'd you fix them?"

"That's what you and Peter said you wanted this morning."

In all the years Herman's sister had been living with them, he had never known her to cater to anyone's whims. Maybe she thought, with Allison gone and him missing her so much, she needed to be more agreeable.

"I'd better change out of these grubby clothes," he said. "I hope your stomach settles down soon."

Catherine grunted.

Herman stomped up the stairs, wondering why he'd bothered to say anything positive to Catherine. She seemed determined to spend the rest of her days finding fault and complaining about something or other. *Which is one of the reasons I sent Allison away for the summer. If I had the time, I'd take a vacation from that negative sister of mine myself!*

Aaron had just finished his chores in the barn and was about to head to the harness shop, when he spotted his collie crouched in the weeds near the garden. He moved closer to see if the dog had a mouse or some other critter cornered and discovered Rufus had a kitten between his paws. "Come here and leave that poor animal alone!"

The collie released a pathetic whimper and backed away slowly. Aaron figured the cat would take off like a flash, but it just lay there, still as could be.

"Rufus, if you killed Bessie's kitten, she'll have your hide. Mine, too, for letting you run free." Aaron squatted in front of the tiny gray kitten and was relieved to see that it was still breathing. After a quick examination, he realized there were no teeth marks.

Aaron returned to the barn, placed the cat with its mother, and then tied Rufus up for the rest of the day.

When Aaron entered the harness shop a short time later, he found Paul at his workbench, assembling an enormous leather harness for a Belgian draft horse.

"How come you're late?" Paul asked.

"I caught Rufus with one of Bessie's kittens. I knew if I didn't get the critter away from him quickly it would soon be dead."

"You'd better keep that dog tied. At least until the kittens are big enough to fend for themselves."

"He's tied up now."

"That's good, because Bessie would have a conniption if something happened to one of her cats." Paul motioned to a tub sitting off to one side. "Better get started cleaning and oiling James Esh's saddle. He dropped it by on Friday afternoon while you were up at the house getting our lunches."

The mention of James's name set Aaron's teeth on edge. He'd never liked that fellow much. Ever since they were children,

James had been a showoff and a bit of a rebel. Aaron hadn't liked the way James had looked at Allison last night at the young people's gathering, either. He especially didn't like seeing the two of them drive away in James's buggy after the gathering was over. *I hope he didn't try anything funny with Allison. If only I'd had the nerve to ask about giving her a ride myself.*

Aaron balled his fingers into tight fists. *What am I thinking? I'm not interested in a relationship with Allison. Courting leads to marriage, and I'm not getting married!*

"Aaron, did you hear what I said?"

Aaron whirled around. "Huh?"

Paul pointed to the tub. "The saddle needs to be cleaned."

"Jah, okay. I'll see that it gets done." Aaron set to work, but it was hard to concentrate when he kept thinking about Allison.

He shook his head in an attempt to get himself thinking straight. Why was he thinking about a woman who would be leaving in a few months—especially when he was dead set against love and marriage? *It's probably because she took an interest in the harness shop.*

Aaron and Paul worked in silence for the rest of the morning, interrupted only by an English customer who dropped off two broken bridles and a worn-out harness that needed to be replaced. By noon, Aaron had James's saddle finished, and he'd also done some work at the riveting machine on a new harness for Noah Hertzler.

"I think I'll go up to the house and see if your mamm's got lunch ready," Paul said as he headed for the door.

"Did you plan to bring the food back, or should we close the shop and eat in Mom's kitchen today?" Aaron asked.

"I'll bring it back." Paul nodded toward the finished saddle. "James Esh said he'd be here around noon, and I don't want to miss him." The door closed behind him, but a few minutes later it opened again.

"Came to get my saddle," James announced as he stepped into the building. The straw hat he wore was shaped a little different than most Amish men's in their area, and it had a bright red band around the middle.

Anything to let everyone know he's going through his running-around years, Aaron thought. *I wonder if James will decide to jump the fence and go English.*

"Your saddle's ready and waiting," Aaron said, motioning to the workbench across the room.

James sauntered over to the saddle and leaned close, like he was scrutinizing the work Aaron had done. "Hmm. . . Guess it'll be good enough."

Aaron bit back an unkind retort and moved to Paul's desk. He reached into the metal basket and handed James his bill.

James squinted at the piece of paper. "This is pretty high for just a cleaning and oiling, wouldn't you say?"

Aaron shrugged. "I don't set the prices. If you've got a problem with the price, you'd best take it up with Paul."

"Paul, is it? Since when did you start callin' your daed Paul?"

Aaron shrugged. He didn't think he had to explain himself to James.

James glanced around the room. "Where is Paul, anyway?"

"He went up to the house to get our lunch. You can wait if you want to talk to him about the bill."

"Naw, I don't have any time to waste today." James reached

into his pocket and pulled out a couple of large bills. He slapped the money down, then sauntered back to his saddle, which he easily hoisted onto his broad shoulders. He was almost to the door when he pivoted toward Aaron. "Did you know that I escorted that new girl from Pennsylvania home from the gathering last night? Allison Troyer, that's her name."

Aaron gritted his teeth. Did James have to brag about everything he did?

"Allison sure is cute," James said with a crooked grin. "Don't you think so?"

"I hadn't noticed." Aaron's fingers made a fist as he fought for control. He knew it would be wrong to provoke a fight, but at the moment, he felt like punching James in the nose.

Just then, the front door swung open and Paul stepped into the room, carrying a wicker basket. "How are you, James?"

"Doin' real good," James replied with a nod.

"I see you've got what you came for." Paul motioned to the saddle perched on James's shoulders.

"Jah. I'm headed home."

James made no mention of how much the cleaning and oiling had cost, and Aaron figured James had only made an issue of it just to see if he could get a rise out of him. The ornery fellow had a knack for irritating folks—especially Aaron.

"Well, I'd best be on my way. I might stop by the Kings' place sometime soon and see if their niece wants to go out with me." James had his back to Aaron, so Aaron couldn't see the fellow's face, but he had a feeling there was a wily-looking smile plastered there. "See you later, Paul. You, too, Aaron."

When the door shut behind James, Paul placed the basket

on the desk in front of Aaron. "You ready to eat, son? There are a couple of roast beef sandwiches in here, as well as a carton of your mamm's tangy potato salad."

Aaron shook his head. "I'm not hungry."

"You need to eat something. Besides, your mamm worked hard making our lunches. She'd be real disappointed if you didn't eat yours."

"Oh, all right." It would be a shame to let a tasty roast beef sandwich go to waste on account of his dislike for James Esh.

"I just got around to checking for mail, and I discovered a letter in the box for you," Aunt Mary said as she entered the kitchen, where Allison was cutting slices of ham for their lunch.

"Is it from my daed?" Allison asked.

"No, it's from someone named Sally Mast." Aunt Mary placed the mail on one end of the counter. "If you'd like to read it now, I'll take over making the sandwiches."

"Are you sure you wouldn't mind? Sally's my best friend, and I sure do miss her. I'd like to see what she has to say."

"I don't mind at all. Enjoy your letter, and feel free to answer it now, too." Aunt Mary moved over to the counter, took the knife from Allison, and started slicing the ham.

"Danki." Allison could hardly believe how agreeable Aunt Mary seemed to be. If Aunt Catherine had been getting the mail, she wouldn't have told Allison she had a letter until lunch had been served and the dishes had been washed and put away.

Allison thumbed through the mail until she located Sally's

letter. Taking a seat at the table, she opened the envelope and silently read her friend's letter:

Dear Allison,

How are things in Missouri? Do you like it there? Have you made any new friends?

I miss you. We all do—your daed, Peter, and the rest of your family.

Allison grimaced. *Sally didn't mention anything about Aunt Catherine missing me. She's probably hoping I'll decide to stay here in Missouri and never come home.*

"Is everyone all right at home?" Aunt Mary asked. "That frown you're wearing makes me think something might be wrong."

"Nothing's wrong," Allison said with a shake of her head. "Sally's letter says I'm missed."

"And I'm sure you're missing your family back home, too."

"Everyone but Aunt Catherine," Allison mumbled.

"What was that?"

"Oh, nothing. It wasn't important." Allison returned to the letter:

I probably shouldn't say anything just yet, but I think Peter's on the verge of asking me to marry him. If he does, I'll want you to be one of my attendants.

Write back soon and tell me all about Webster County. I want to know about everything you're doing.

Your best friend for always,
Sally

Allison was pleased to hear that Sally and Peter might be getting married soon, but she couldn't help feeling a pang of envy, wondering if she would ever become a bride. She moved over to the desk across the room and took out a writing tablet and a pen. Returning to the table, she wrote a letter to her friend:

Dear Sally,

It was good hearing from you. I'm glad things are going well for you and Peter. Be sure and let me know when he asks you to marry him. I miss you a lot, but I'm making some new friends here, too, which helps me not to feel so homesick.

Things are so different from what I'm used to in Lancaster County. They drive only open buggies, which is fine during the warmer months, but I have to wonder how they manage during the cold winter months.

Aunt Mary is going to teach me to sew, but we'll have to see how that goes; I'll probably make a mess of things. I still prefer doing outdoor things better than household chores, but maybe I'll learn to like some domestic things, too.

A young man named James gave me a ride home from a young people's gathering awhile back. Don't tell anyone, but he gave me my first kiss. It wasn't quite what I expected, but it felt good to know he found me attractive enough to kiss. I've always felt so plain, and since I'm a tomboy, I didn't think anyone would ever want to kiss me.

"Lunch is about ready now," Aunt Mary said, touching Allison's shoulder.

Allison quickly folded the letter, slipped it into an envelope, and jumped up from the table. She would finish writing later.

Chapter 6

Keep your legs pumping while you hold the material just so," Aunt Mary said as she showed Allison how to use her treadle sewing machine.

It looked easy enough when Aunt Mary did it, but when Allison tried, things didn't go nearly so well. On her first attempt, she either pumped the treadle too fast or too slow. Then when she thought she had the hang of things, she pushed the hand wheel backwards and stitched right off the piece of cloth.

On Allison's next attempt, she stitched the end of her apron to the material. "I don't know how that happened," she muttered, pulling the thread from the scrap of fabric. "Makes me wonder if I'll ever get the hang of things."

"Try it again," Aunt Mary encouraged. "I'm sure you'll get it soon enough."

Allison pumped up and down with her feet as she guided the wheel with one hand and directed the cotton material with the other. When the thread snapped, so did her patience. "I'm no good at this!" She pushed her chair away from the machine and stood. "I'd rather do something else, if you don't mind."

Aunt Mary put her arm around Allison. "You'll catch on if you give it a chance. The more you practice, the better you'll get."

Allison shrugged. "Can it wait until later? It's such a nice day. I wouldn't mind going fishing if there's someplace nearby— and if I can borrow someone's pole."

"There's a pond up the road that has some good bass in it. I'm sure Harvey wouldn't mind if you used his pole. But I don't think it's a good idea for you to go fishing alone."

"I'll be fine. I go fishing by myself a lot back home."

"Maybe so, but I'd feel better if you took one of your cousins with you," Aunt Mary insisted. "Dan's out in the garden pulling weeds with Sarah, but I'm sure he'd be happy to join you at the pond for a while."

Allison figured it wouldn't be so bad to have her ten-year-old cousin tag along. At least she'd have someone to talk to if the fish weren't biting. "That's fine with me," she said with a smile.

When Allison left the room, Mary took a seat in front of the sewing machine. *I can't believe a woman Allison's age doesn't know how to sew,* she thought as she picked up the piece of material Allison had been working on. *What kind of a woman is Herman's sister that she's never taught Allison to cook or sew?*

Mary remembered getting a letter from Allison's mother once, where she'd mentioned how unfriendly Catherine had been when they'd gone to visit Herman's family in Ohio. She'd said that Catherine had seemed distant and unhappy. Mary wondered what could have happened in Catherine's past that had left her with such a sour attitude. Whatever it was, it shouldn't have kept Catherine from teaching Allison the necessary skills for becoming a homemaker.

The back door opened with a bang, interrupting Mary's thoughts. She went to the kitchen, thinking maybe Allison had come back inside. Instead, she found her daughter Sarah.

"Hi, Mama." Sarah swiped at the perspiration on her forehead and sighed. "It's hot out in the garden, so I decided to come inside for somethin' cold to drink."

"Would you like iced tea or lemonade?" Mary asked.

"Water's fine and dandy." Sarah grimaced. "Dan left me alone to pull all the weeds while he took off for the pond with Allison. He sure doesn't care about helpin' me one iota."

"When Allison said she wanted to go fishing, I suggested that Dan go along," Mary explained. "I didn't think it would be a good idea for her to go traipsing off by herself when she doesn't know the area very well."

"Guess that makes sense."

"I suppose I should have asked if you wanted to go fishing, too."

Sarah wrinkled her nose. "No way! I don't like fishin'!"

"Why not?"

Sarah held up one finger. "Too many bugs bite you." A second finger came up. "On a day like this, the sun's too hot to sit for hours waitin' and hopin' a fish might snag your line." She extended a third finger. "If you do catch any fish, you've gotta touch their slimy bodies!"

Mary chuckled. One young woman living in this house was certainly no tomboy!

Aaron rubbed at a kink in his lower back and glanced at the clock on the far wall. It was almost three thirty, and there hadn't been a single customer since noon. Paul had taken Mom, Grandpa, Grandma, and the girls into Springfield for the day, since both Grandpa and Grandma had doctor's appointments. Joseph, Zachary, and Davey were helping one of their neighbors in the fields. That left Aaron alone in the shop, which was just fine with him. But he was tired of working, and for the last several days he'd been itching to go fishing. Since things were slow, there would be no harm in heading to the pond. The folks had said they might go out for supper after their shopping and appointments were done, so Aaron was sure they wouldn't be back until late evening. That left him plenty of time.

He removed his work apron, hung it on a wall peg, turned off the gas lamps, and put the CLOSED sign in the front window. *Think I'll untie Rufus and take him along. The poor critter deserves some fun in the sun.*

Allison and Dan had been sitting on the grassy banks by the

pond for nearly an hour without getting a single bite, and Allison's patience was beginning to wane. "Are you sure there's any fish in here?" she asked her young cousin.

Dan's head bobbed up and down. "Oh, jah. Me and my daed have taken plenty of bass and catfish out of this here pond."

Allison sighed. "Maybe they're just not hungry today."

"We could move to a different spot."

"You mean cast our lines in over there?" Allison pointed to the other side of the pond.

Dan shook his blond head. "There's another pond about a mile down the road. Might be better fishin' over there."

Allison reeled in her line and stood. "I guess it's worth a try. Let's hop in the buggy, and you can show me the way."

When they arrived at the other pond, Allison noticed a lot more trees grew near the water than at the first pond. The trees offered plenty of shade, and it had turned into a hot, muggy day.

"Let's sit over there on a log," Dan suggested.

Allison followed as he led her to a place with several downed trees. She took a seat on one of the logs and lifted her face to the cloudless sky. She drew in a deep breath and closed her eyes, letting her imagination believe it was fall and a cool breeze was moving the stale air away. She could almost hear the rustling wind clicking the branches of the trees together. She could almost feel the crackle of leaves as she rubbed them between her fingers.

A sharp jab to the ribs halted Allison's musings, and her eyes snapped open.

"Hey, are ya gonna sit there with your eyes closed all day?" Dan pointed to her fishing pole. "Or did ya come here to fish?"

"I came here to fish, same as you." She baited her hook and had no more than thrown her line into the water when she heard loud barking.

"Great! Now all the fish will be scared away," Dan grumbled.

Allison glanced to her left and saw a young Amish man with a fishing pole step into the clearing. A collie romped beside him, barking and wagging its tail.

"Wouldn't ya know Aaron Zook would have to show up with that yappy dog of his?" Dan scowled. "Now we'll never catch any fish."

Allison shielded her eyes from the glare of the sun. Sure enough, Aaron seemed to be heading their way.

Aaron halted when he realized Allison and her cousin Dan were sitting on a log near the pond. He hadn't expected to run into anyone here—especially not her. With the exception of Aaron's mother, most of the women he knew didn't care much for fishing. Maybe Allison had only come along to keep Dan company.

Rufus's tail swished back and forth, and he let out a couple of excited barks. The next thing Aaron knew, the dog took off on a run, heading straight for Allison.

"Come back here, Rufus!" Aaron shouted. The collie kept running, and by the time Aaron caught up to him, the crazy mutt had his head lying in Allison's lap.

She stroked the critter behind its ears and smiled up at Aaron.

"Sorry about that," he panted. "Don't know what got into

that mutt of mine. I told him to stop, but he seems to take pleasure in ignoring me."

"It's all right. I like dogs—at least the friendly ones."

Dan frowned and moved farther down the log. "Not me. Most dogs are loud and like to get underfoot." He pointed to his fishing pole. "And they scare away the fish with their stupid barking."

"Sorry," Aaron mumbled. "I'll try to make sure Rufus stays quiet."

"Let Allison keep pettin' him, and you won't have to worry about him barkin' or runnin' around," Dan said.

Aaron hunkered down beside the log. "You could be right about that. I've never seen my dog take to anyone so quickly."

"I've always wanted a dog," Allison said in a wistful tone. "But Aunt Catherine would never allow it."

"You've got no dogs at your place?" Dan's raised brows showed his obvious surprise.

"Nope. Just a few cats to keep the mice down." Allison stroked Rufus's other ear, and the dog burrowed his head deeper into her lap.

"Who's Aunt Catherine?" Aaron wanted to know.

"She's my daed's older sister. She came to live with us soon after my mamm was killed."

Aaron's forehead wrinkled. "Mind if I ask how your mamm died?"

"A car ran into her buggy." Allison frowned. "At least that's what I was told. I was only seven at the time and don't remember anything about the accident, even though I supposedly witnessed the whole thing."

"Sorry to hear that." Aaron started to bite off a fingernail but stopped himself in time. "When my real daed died, it was sure hard on my mamm."

"I can imagine. It was hard on my daed to lose my mamm, too. How'd your daed die?" Allison asked.

"He'd gone into town to pick up a stove he planned to give to my mamm," Aaron grimaced. He hated to think about this, much less talk about it, but he figured he ought to answer Allison's questions. "On the way home, the buggy my daed was driving got hit by a truck. The stove flew forward, killing him instantly. At least that's what my mamm was told when the sheriff came to tell her about the accident."

"That's *baremlich*," Allison said as her eyes widened.

"You're right; it was a terrible thing," Dan put in. "I can't imagine losin' either of my parents. "I'd miss 'em something awful."

"Do you mind if we talk about something else?" Allison asked. She looked like she was on the verge of tears.

"Jah, sure," Aaron was quick to say. "What shall we talk about?"

Tears stung the back of Allison's eyes, and she tried to think of something to talk about besides death. The idea of dying scared her because she wasn't sure where her soul would go when it was time to leave this earth. Allison knew some folks felt confident that they would go to heaven, but she'd never understood how anyone could have that assurance. Did going to church every other Sunday guarantee that one would spend eternity with the

Lord, or could there be more to it? Did following the church rules give one that confidence?

"I. . .uh. . .guess if I'm going to fish, I'd better see about getting my hook baited," she said, pushing Rufus away gently.

The dog whined and flopped on the ground beside Allison as she leaned over and picked up the jar of worms sitting by Dan's feet. "They sure are fat little things, aren't they?" She held up the glass container and wrinkled her nose.

"Would you like me to put one on your hook?" Aaron asked, taking a seat on the log next to her.

"Thanks anyway, but I've been baiting my own hooks since I was a young girl." Allison's cheeks warmed. She could have kicked herself for blurting that out. Aaron must think she was a real tomboy.

Dan grunted and shot her a look of impatience. "If you two are gonna keep on yammerin', then I'm movin' to the other side of the pond where it's quiet."

"No need to move; I'll quit talking." Allison baited her hook and cast the line into the water. Aaron did the same.

They sat in silence, with only the sound of the breeze rustling the trees and Rufus's occasional snorts.

"Did you enjoy the young people's gathering last Sunday night?" Aaron asked suddenly.

"It was okay." Allison shifted on the log, almost bumping his arm. "Many of the songs were new to me, though."

"Not the same as you sing back home?"

"Just the hymns. The others were different."

Dan grunted again. "I thought you two weren't gonna talk anymore."

Aaron scowled at the boy. "We sat here for quite a spell without saying a word, and nobody had a nibble. Maybe a bit of chitchat will liven up the fish."

"*Puh!*" Dan stood and plunked down on a large boulder several feet away.

"He thinks he knows a lot for someone so young," Aaron muttered. "Reminds me of the way James Esh used to be when he was a boy." He looked at Allison pointedly. "Speaking of James, I understand that you rode home with him the other night."

She gave a quick nod and glanced at her cousin, who had lifted his face to the sun. *I hope Dan's not listening to this conversation. He might repeat it to someone outside the family.*

"Somebody should have warned you about James," Aaron continued.

"What do you mean?"

"He hasn't joined the church and is still in his rumschpringe. I really have to wonder if he'll ever settle down."

Allison's forehead wrinkled. "Do you think he'll leave the faith and never come back?"

"Maybe so." Aaron released his grip on the pole and rubbed the bridge of his nose. "It's a shame the way some fellows like James get into all sorts of trouble during their running-around years."

"I take it you're not one of the rowdy ones?"

He shook his head. "I've never had the desire to do anything more than get involved in an occasional buggy race. For me, having fun means fishing, hunting, or playing ball."

"Same here," she blurted out. "I. . .I mean—"

"Hey, I've got a bite!" Dan hollered. He jumped off the rock and moved closer to the pond.

Allison cupped one hand around her mouth. "Be careful, Dan! You're getting awful close to the water."

The boy looked at her over his shoulder, but his line jerked hard. He lurched forward, and—*splash*—into the water he went!

Chapter 7

On the drive home from the pond, Allison's thoughts began to wander. Until Dan had fallen into the water, she'd been having fun—even without catching any fish. It had felt nice to sit in the warm sun and get to know Aaron a little better. He didn't brag the way James did. If she had the opportunity to be with Aaron more, they might become friends. Of course, they could never be more than friends. Over the summer, there wouldn't be much chance of them developing a lasting relationship, even if she were to become a woman someone might want to marry.

"Are you mad at me, Allison?"

Dan's sudden question drove Allison's thoughts aside, and she turned to look at him. "Of course not. I know you didn't fall into the pond on purpose."

"That's for certain sure." Dan shivered beneath the quilt

Allison had wrapped around his small frame. "That old catfish didn't wanna be caught, so he tried to take me into the water with him."

Allison laughed. "I think your foot slipped when the fish tugged on your line, and then you lost your balance."

Wrinkles formed in Dan's forehead. "Sure hope Mama won't be angry at me for gettin' my clothes all wet."

The boy's comment made Allison worry about her aunt's response. Would Aunt Mary be upset when she saw her water-logged son? Would she blame Allison for the accident? Aunt Catherine certainly would have. She thought everything was Allison's fault. Even something as silly as Aunt Catherine stubbing her toe on the porch step a few years ago had been blamed on Allison. She'd been walking ahead of her aunt that day as they carried groceries into the house. Aunt Catherine had said she wouldn't have stubbed her toe if Allison hadn't been dawdling.

Then there was the time Allison got her dress caught on the buggy wheel while climbing out. She'd landed in a mud puddle, and Aunt Catherine had been madder than a hornet. She would have spanked Allison for messing up her clothes if Papa hadn't stopped her, saying it was an accident and that Allison didn't deserve to be punished for something that wasn't her fault.

Pushing her thoughts aside and feeling the need to reassure her cousin, Allison reached across the buggy seat and patted Dan's knee. "I'll explain to your mamm about you falling in the pond."

"Danki."

Dan remained quiet for the rest of the ride, and Allison kept her focus on driving the buggy and making sure the horse cooperated with her commands. The shoulder of the road wasn't wide in this area, like it was in most places back home. Of course, there wasn't nearly as much traffic to deal with in Webster County.

When Allison guided the horse and buggy onto the Kings' property, she noticed a buggy parked out front and figured they must have company. *Good. If there's someone here visiting, Aunt Mary probably won't let on that she's mad when she finds out what happened to Dan.*

Dan clambered out of the buggy as soon as it came to a stop and hurried toward the house. Allison knew she should get the horse unhitched and into the barn right away, so she decided to let Dan tell his version of the pond mishap first. When she got to the house, she would explain things in more detail if necessary.

As Aaron traveled home from the pond, he thought about how much he'd enjoyed being with Allison. Even if they couldn't develop a lasting relationship, it would be nice to get to know her better while she was here for the summer. They'd begun a good visit this afternoon until Dan's little mishap had cut things short.

I wonder if Allison would enjoy working in the harness shop. Aaron slapped the side of his head, nearly knocking his straw hat off. *Don't get any dumb ideas. It would never work, even if she could stay here. I wouldn't be able to forget how things were for Mom when Dad died. I could never trust that it wouldn't happen to me.*

As Aaron turned onto his property, he noticed light shining

through the harness shop windows. He'd thought he had shut off all the lanterns before he'd left.

He brought the horse to a stop in front of the building, hopped out of the buggy, and dashed inside. He discovered only one gas lamp lit—the one directly above Paul's desk.

Paul was seated in his oak chair, going over a stack of invoices. He squinted at Aaron. "Where have you been?"

Aaron shifted from one foot to the other, feeling like a young boy caught doing something bad. "I went fishing this afternoon."

Paul's heavy eyebrows drew together as he fingered the edge of his full beard. "You went fishing when you should have been working?"

Aaron nodded. "There hadn't been any customers since noon, so I didn't think there'd be any harm in closing the shop a few hours early."

Paul pushed his chair aside and stood. "I left you in charge today because I thought I could trust you to take care of things in my absence." He motioned to the front door. "Then I come home and find the shop door is locked, the CLOSED sign's in the window, and you're nowhere to be found."

Aaron opened his mouth to defend himself, but Paul cut him off. "I know you're expecting to take over this shop someday, but your irresponsible actions don't give me any indication that you're close to being ready for something like that."

"I work plenty hard." Aaron pursed his lips. "I think I always do a good job, too."

"That's true, but you're often late to work, and sometimes you look for excuses to slack off. You can't coast along in life if you expect to support a wife and family someday."

"I don't think I'm coasting. Besides, I'm not planning to get married, so I won't have to worry about supporting a wife or a family."

"I've heard you say that before, Aaron. Would you care to explain?"

Aaron shook his head and started to walk away, but he halted and turned back around. "Say, how come you're home early from Springfield? I thought you were planning to eat supper out."

"Emma came down with a *bauchweh*."

"What's wrong with Emma? Has she got the flu?"

"I suppose she might, but more than likely her bellyache's from eating too much candy earlier in the day. Our driver, Larry Porter, always has a bag of chocolates he likes to hand out to the kinner." Paul grunted. "Emma ate way too much candy before either your mamm or I realized it."

"I remember once when Davey was a little guy and got into Mom's candy dish," Aaron said. "The little *schtinker* polished off every last piece. Mom said she didn't have the heart to give him a *bletsching* because suffering with an upset stomach was punishment enough."

"Sometimes the direct consequences of one's transgressions are worse than a spanking."

"I guess that's true." Aaron moved toward the door.

"Before you go up to the house, I'd like to say one more thing," Paul said.

Out of respect, Aaron halted. "What'd you want to say?"

"Just wanted you to know that I love you. That's the only reason I want to be sure you get your priorities straight."

Aaron nodded.

"Tell your mamm to ring the supper bell when it's time to eat."

"Jah, okay." Aaron opened the door and stepped outside. "I'm not a baby," he muttered under his breath, "and I wish he'd quit treating me like one."

Allison entered the house and was pleased to discover Katie Esh sitting at the kitchen table, talking with Aunt Mary. "I'm sorry about bringing Dan home soaking wet," Allison apologized.

"It's not the first time he's fallen into the pond, and it probably won't be the last." Aunt Mary smiled. "He's in the bathroom, taking a warm bath."

Allison looked down at the muddy footprints leading from the kitchen door to the hallway. "Since I'm the one who took Dan fishing, I'd better mop up the mess he left behind."

"Nonsense," her aunt said, pushing away from the table. "You sit with Katie and visit. I'll see to the floor."

Allison was amazed at her aunt's generosity. If this had happened in Aunt Catherine's kitchen, the woman would have been grumpier than an old goat.

Katie smiled and motioned to the chair beside her. "How about a glass of cold milk to go with the carrot cake I brought over?"

Allison glanced at Aunt Mary, who was at the sink, dampening the mop. "When are you planning to serve supper?"

"Not for an hour or so. Ben, Harvey, and Walter will probably work in the fields until it's nearly dark, so feel free to eat some of Katie's cake."

A hunk of moist carrot cake did sound appealing, so Allison poured a glass of milk and helped herself to a slice of cake.

"I came by to visit with you, but your aunt said you and Dan had gone fishing. How'd it go?" Katie asked.

"Not so good. We didn't catch a single fish."

Katie snickered. "From the looks of Dan when he came through the door, I'd say the fish caught him."

Allison laughed, too. "Aaron and I rescued my waterlogged cousin before the fish could reel him in too far."

Katie's pale eyebrows lifted in obvious surprise. "Aaron Zook?"

"Jah."

"I didn't realize you were meeting him at the pond," Aunt Mary said.

"Oh, I wasn't," Allison was quick to say. "He and his collie showed up. It was shortly after they arrived that Dan fell in the water." She leaned closer to Katie. "Do you know if Aaron has a girlfriend?"

"Nope, he sure doesn't." Katie blinked a couple of times. "Why, are you interested in Aaron?"

"No, of course not. I barely know him." Allison quickly forked a piece of cake into her mouth. "*Umm. . .* This is sure good."

"I'm glad you like it."

"Next to chocolate, carrot's my favorite kind of cake."

"What kind of pie do you like?" Katie asked.

"Most any except for mincemeat."

Katie wrinkled her nose. "Me, neither. I never have understood why my *mamm* likes mincemeat pie so well."

Aunt Mary swished the mop past the table and stopped long enough to grab a sliver of cake. "My favorite pie is strawberry."

Allison's mouth watered at the mention of sweet, juicy strawberries, so ripe the juice ran down your chin.

As if she could read Allison's mind, Katie leaned over and said, "We've got a big strawberry patch. Why don't you plan to come over some Saturday toward the end of the month and help me pick some? They should be ripe by then."

"That sounds like fun."

Katie smiled. "In the meantime, let's set this Thursday evening aside, and the two of us can go on a picnic in the woods near my house. I'll furnish the meal," she quickly added.

Allison glanced at Aunt Mary, who had finished mopping and was now peeling potatoes. "Would that be all right with you?"

"I have no problem with it."

Allison smiled. She could hardly believe how agreeable her mother's twin sister seemed to be. She hated to keep comparing Aunt Mary to Aunt Catherine, but they were as different as winter and summer. What made the difference? What was the reason for Aunt Mary's sweet disposition?

Chapter 8

Allison sat at the kitchen table, reading the letter she'd just received from her father:

> Dear Allison,
>
> Except for that one letter you wrote soon after you arrived in Missouri, I haven't heard anything from you, and I'm wondering why. I'm anxious to hear how things are going and what it's like for you there.
>
> We're getting along okay here. We went to Gerald and Norma's for supper the other night, and all your brothers were there except for Clarence and his family. They couldn't make it because Esther's been quite tired during this pregnancy.

A wave of homesickness washed over Allison. She'd always

enjoyed spending time with her brothers, especially family dinners at one of their homes. All of her siblings except Peter were married, and from what Sally had said in her last letter, Allison figured it wouldn't be long before they were, too. Then she'd be the only one of her siblings not married.

Directing her focus back to the letter, Allison read on:

> *The weather has been hot and muggy. We could sure use a good rain. Peter and I are keeping busy as usual with the dairy, and Aunt Catherine stays busy with the household chores. We all miss you and hope you're having a good time. Write back soon.*
>
> *Love,*
> *Papa*

Allison shook her head. "You might miss me, Papa, but I'm sure Aunt Catherine doesn't."

"What was that you were saying?" Aunt Mary asked as she stepped into the room.

Allison's cheeks warmed. "I was reading a letter from my daed that came in today's mail."

"How's my brother-in-law doing? I'll bet he's missing you already."

Allison nodded. "He says everyone misses me, but I don't think Aunt Catherine does."

Aunt Mary took a seat at the table. "What makes you think that?"

"Aunt Catherine has never shown much interest in me except to find fault. That's why I can't cook or sew very well."

"Still, that's no reason to believe she doesn't care about you."

Allison shrugged.

"Speaking of sewing, would you like to try to make a faceless doll after we've had lunch?" Aunt Mary asked.

"Do you think I'm ready for that?"

"You've been practicing at the machine nearly every day this week, and you've been able to make several potholders." A wide smile spread across Aunt Mary's face. "I think you're ready to try making a doll."

"Okay."

Aunt Mary squeezed Allison's shoulder. "I'll leave you alone to answer your daed's letter, but I'll be back when it's time to start lunch."

"I probably should answer his letter right away," Allison agreed. "He seemed a little worried because I haven't written but one letter since I've been here."

Aunt Mary's forehead creased. "I guess that's my fault for keeping you so busy."

"It's not your fault. I've enjoyed staying busy." Allison smiled.

Aunt Mary motioned to the desk in the corner of the room. "There's a book of stamps, envelopes, and plenty of paper in there, so use whatever you need."

"Danki."

When Aunt Mary left the room, Allison hurried over to the desk. Maybe she would write Sally a letter after she finished writing Papa. She was anxious to let them both know how things had been going.

"I thought you were out in the fields," Aaron said when Joseph stepped into the harness shop.

"I was, but I'm here now."

"What happened? Did one of the mules' straps break?"

"Nope. I came to see Papa. Mom wanted me to tell him that she'll be taking Emma into Seymour to see the doctor."

Aaron frowned. "Is our little sister still feeling poorly?"

"Afraid so. That bellyache she's had for the last couple of days doesn't seem to be going away."

"I thought it was just the flu."

"If it is, it's lasting longer than most flu bugs do." Joseph glanced around the room. "Where is Papa, anyway?"

Aaron motioned toward the back of the shop. "Paul's in the supply room."

"I'll give him Mom's message. Then I need to get back to the house and grab something cold to drink for me, Zachary, and Davey." Joseph started to walk away but turned back around. "Say, I've been wondering about something."

"What's that?"

"Why have you started calling our daed by his first name?"

"Paul's not our real daed, Joseph. Have you forgotten that?"

"Of course not, but we've been calling him Papa ever since he married Mom."

Aaron shrugged.

Joseph's eyebrows drew together, and he took a step closer to Aaron. "What's Papa think of you calling him Paul?"

"He hasn't said anything, so he probably doesn't care." Aaron squinted at Joseph. "You were so little when our real daed died, you probably don't remember him."

"You're right, I don't, but what's that got to do with—"

"Paul's been our stepfather so long, you probably think of him as your real daed."

"That's right. He's always treated us like he's our real daed, too." Joseph nudged Aaron's arm. "Don't you think Paul acts like a real daed to us?"

"What I think is that he favors you and the younger kinner."

Joseph's mouth dropped open. "You're kidding, right?"

"No, I'm not."

"Well, if you think that, then your thinking is just plain *lecherich*." Joseph headed for the back room.

Aaron resumed work on the bridle he was making for Gabe. "A lot you know, Joseph," he mumbled under his breath. "My thinking is not ridiculous!"

When Joseph entered the supply room, he spotted his stepfather down on his knees, rummaging through a box of old harnesses.

"Joseph, what are you doing here?" Papa asked when Joseph cleared his throat.

"I came up to the house to get something and saw Mom hitching one of the horses to a buggy. She asked me to let you know she's taking Emma into Seymour to see the doctor. I guess whatever's been ailing her has gotten worse."

Papa's forehead wrinkled as he rose to his feet. "Emma's been feeling poorly ever since she ate too much candy the day we went to Springfield. If it's the flu, it's lasted a lot longer than normal."

"That's what Mom thinks, too, which is why she decided it was time to take Emma to see the doctor."

Papa rubbed his back. "Does she want me to go with her?"

Joseph shook his head. "I don't think so. She just asked if I'd let you know where she was going so you wouldn't worry."

"Danki for delivering the message." Papa moved toward the door leading to the main part of the shop. "I guess I should see how Aaron's doing, and you'd better get back out to the fields to check on your brothers."

"Jah. No telling what those two are up to." Joseph hesitated, wondering if he should say something about the conversation he'd just had with Aaron.

"Is there something else?" Papa asked.

"Uh, well. . .I've been wondering about something."

"What's that?"

"I was wondering how you feel about Aaron calling you Paul here of late."

Papa pulled his fingers through the ends of his beard. "To be perfectly honest, it kind of hurts."

"Then how come you let him get away with it?"

"Aaron's a grown man now, and there's not much I can do if he's made up his mind to call me Paul. After all, I'm not his real daed."

"Maybe not by blood, but you've been like a real daed to us ever since you married Mom," Joseph was quick to say. "I think

Aaron's being disrespectful by calling you Paul."

Papa shrugged as he gave his left earlobe a quick tug. "That may be, but I won't try to force Aaron to call me Papa. So unless he changes his mind, I've decided to just accept it and try to be Aaron's friend."

Joseph wanted to say more, but he figured his daed had made up his mind. And since it really wasn't his business, the best thing to do was to drop the subject and get on back to work.

"Is this the way the doll's hair is supposed to attach to its head?" Allison asked as she lifted a brown piece of material for her aunt's inspection.

Aunt Mary nodded. "You've got it pinned in exactly the right place. Now stitch that section of hair to the top of the head, and you'll be ready to put the rest of the body together."

Pumping her legs up and down and guiding the wheel of the treadle machine with one hand, Allison carefully sewed the hair in place.

"I thought I might go to the farmers' market this Saturday to sell some of my quilted pillows and our garden produce," Aunt Mary said. "If you finish with the doll by then, maybe you'd like to go along and try to sell it. That would give you an idea of whether there's a market for more."

Allison finished the seam and cut the thread before she looked up. "I. . .I don't think I'm quite ready for anything like that yet."

Aunt Mary gave Allison's shoulder a gentle squeeze. "Maybe

some other time—when you have more than one doll made."

"Maybe so. I'll have to wait and see how well my sewing goes."

"Are you ready to take a break? I thought a glass of your uncle Ben's homemade root beer might taste good about now."

"That does sound refreshing." Allison stood and arched her back. "I think after all that pumping on the treadle machine I worked up a thirst."

Aunt Mary chuckled. "Let's round up the kinner and have our snack out on the front porch. I'm sure they need a break from their garden chores, too."

A short time later, Allison, Aunt Mary, Sarah, and Dan sat in chairs on the front porch, enjoying tall glasses of root beer and some peanut butter cookies.

"This is real good." Dan made a slurping sound and swiped his tongue across his upper lip where some foamy root beer had gathered. "It would be even better if we had a batch of vanilla ice cream so we could make frosty floats."

"We'll see about making some homemade ice cream soon," his mother said.

"How about this Saturday night?" Sarah suggested. "We can invite Grandpa and Grandma King over. What do you think about that, Mama?"

"That sounds like a fine idea, but you and I will be at the farmers' market all day Saturday. We could do it on Friday evening, though." Aunt Mary glanced over at Allison and smiled. "Maybe we can have an outdoor barbecue and invite some of our friends and family. It would be a nice way of giving everyone a chance to get to know you better."

"A barbecue sounds real nice," Allison said.

"Can we invite the Hiltys?" Sarah asked. "I'd like my friend Bessie to be here."

"Jah, maybe so. And we can ask Gabe and Melinda Swartz." Aunt Mary looked over at Allison. "Melinda's about your age, but she wasn't at our last preaching service because she was feeling sick." She eased out of her chair. "I'll pick up the ingredients we need for the ice cream sometime before Friday, but for now, I think I'd better see about making some corn bread and beans for supper."

Allison started to get up, but her aunt motioned her to sit back down. "Take your time and finish your root beer. When you're done, you can make the coleslaw while Sarah sets the table."

Chapter 9

Allison had never made coleslaw before, but she'd seen Aunt Catherine do it and figured it couldn't be that hard. Just chop up some cabbage, add a little mayonnaise, some vinegar, salt, and pepper. She watched with anticipation as Uncle Ben forked some of her coleslaw into his mouth. After the first bite, he puckered his lips and quickly reached for his glass of water. "Whew! How come there's so much vinegar in this?"

"I don't think there's that much." Aunt Mary spooned some onto her plate and took a bite. Her eyes widened, but she swallowed it down.

Dan grimaced when he ate some. "Papa's right. This stuff is awful!" He jumped up from the table, ran over to the garbage can, and spit out the coleslaw.

"Dan, you're being rude," Uncle Ben said sternly. "And I

never said the coleslaw was awful."

Allison's face burned with embarrassment. She couldn't even make a simple thing like coleslaw without ruining it. "I–I'm so sorry," she stammered. "I should have asked how much vinegar to use."

"You mean *you* made the coleslaw?" Walter pointed at Allison as his eyebrows lifted high on his forehead.

She nodded and tears sprang to her eyes. "I thought it would be easy, but I. . .I guess I was wrong."

"What were you tryin' to do, make us all sick?" Walter wrapped his fingers around his throat and coughed several times.

"There's too much pepper in it, too," Sarah sputtered. She grabbed her glass of water and gulped half of it down.

"That will be enough about the coleslaw," Uncle Ben admonished. "I'm sure Allison didn't ruin it on purpose. Too much vinegar probably spilled from the bottle before she realized what had happened."

"I tried pouring some of that stuff onto a piece of cotton when I got a nosebleed a couple weeks ago," Harvey put in. "It ran out all over the counter."

Allison was sure everyone was just trying to make her feel better, but their comments hadn't helped. "No wonder Aunt Catherine never let me do much in the kitchen," she mumbled. "She was probably afraid I'd make everyone sick."

"I'm sure that's not true," Aunt Mary said kindly. "All you need is a little more practice. By the end of the summer, you'll probably be able to cook so well that your aunt Catherine will be happy to let you take over her kitchen when you return home."

"I doubt she'd let anyone take her place in the kitchen." Allison sniffed. "Besides, it's not just cooking I can't do well."

"With my *fraa* as your teacher," Uncle Ben said, looking over at Aunt Mary and giving her a wink, "I can almost guarantee that you'll be ready to get married and run a house of your own by the end of summer."

Sarah's head bobbed up and down. "Now we just need to find Allison a husband."

The telephone on Paul's desk rang sharply, and Aaron reached for it since Paul was outside talking to a customer. "Zook's Harness Shop," he said. At least Paul hadn't insisted on changing the name of their business to Hilty after he'd married Aaron's mother. He'd been the one to suggest they put a phone in the shop, too, since it wasn't allowed inside their home.

"Aaron, is that you?"

Aaron knew by the tone of his mother's voice that she was upset about something. "Jah, Mom, it's me. What's wrong?"

"Would you please put Paul on the phone?"

"He's outside talking to Noah Hertzler right now. Can I give him a message?"

"The doctor thinks Emma's problem is her appendix. He wants us to take her to the hospital right away."

Aaron gripped the receiver tightly. "If it bursts open, she could be in big trouble. Isn't that right?"

"I'm afraid so."

"Do you want Paul to hire a driver and pick you and Emma

up in Seymour, or are you coming home first?"

"There's no time to waste. I've hired a driver in town, so please ask your daed to get a driver and meet us at the hospital in Springfield."

"Okay, Mom. I'll be praying for Emma."

"Danki."

Aaron hung up the phone and dashed outside to give Paul the news. "Mom just called. She wants you to hire a driver and meet her and Emma at the hospital in Springfield."

Deep lines formed in Paul's forehead. "Why are they going to the hospital?"

"The doctor thinks Emma's appendix is about to burst, so Mom hired a driver to take them to the hospital."

Paul's face blanched, and he turned to Noah. "Sorry, but I've got to go."

"Of course you do. We can talk some other time." Noah headed for his buggy, calling over his shoulder, "We'll be praying for Emma. Be sure to let us know how she's doing."

"We will." Paul nodded at Aaron. "Run back inside and phone one of our English neighbors to see if they can give me a ride to Springfield. I'll go up to the house and let your mamm's folks know what's happening. Bessie can help Grandma get supper going while your brothers finish helping the neighbor in his fields."

"What do you need me to do after I'm done making the phone call?" Aaron asked.

"Complete whatever you're working on in the harness shop." Paul gave his beard a couple of pulls. "Then maybe you should hang out there the rest of the evening so you can answer the phone. We'll call again to let you know how things are going at the hospital."

"Jah, okay. By the time you get back from the house, I should have a driver lined up for you." Aaron sent up a quick prayer and rushed back to the harness shop.

"Where's your aunt Catherine?" Herman asked when he found Peter in the kitchen, frying some eggs.

"She came out of her room long enough to say she wasn't feeling well; then she went back to bed."

Herman frowned. "She's been feeling poorly for several weeks, but she won't go to the doctor." He lifted his bedraggled straw hat from his head and hung it on a wall peg near the back door. "That woman is the most *glotzkeppich* person I know."

Peter nodded. "She can be pretty stubborn."

"If she doesn't get better soon, I might have to ask Allison to return home earlier than planned."

"How come?"

Herman motioned to the stove. "You have to ask?"

"I'm doing okay with breakfast." Peter handed Herman a plate of eggs.

"Jah, but who's going to clean up this mess?" Herman pointed to the broken egg shells and spilled juice on the counter.

Peter grimaced. "I see your point. It's one thing to fry up some eggs and bacon, but I don't really have the time to cook and clean. Not with all the other chores I have to do."

"Maybe I should make an appointment for Catherine to see

the doctor," Herman said as he took a seat at the table.

Carrying a platter full of bacon, Peter took the seat opposite him. "You think she'd go if you did?"

"Probably not." Herman grunted. "Guess I'll wait a few more days. If she's not feeling better by the end of the week, I may take her to the doctor whether she likes it or not."

Aaron paced in front of Paul's desk, waiting for some word on his sister's condition. Paul had phoned shortly after he'd arrived at the hospital, saying the doctors had determined it was Emma's appendix and that she'd be going in for surgery soon. That had been several hours ago, and Aaron was getting worried.

At six o'clock Joseph had brought out a meatloaf sandwich, but that still sat on the desk, untouched. Aaron had no appetite. Not when his little sister's life could be in jeopardy. He'd tried to get some work done, but all he could do was pray and pace.

At nine o'clock the phone rang, and he grabbed the receiver. "Zook's Harness Shop." He didn't know why he was answering it that way. Nobody would be calling the shop at this time of night for anything related to business.

"Hi, Aaron, it's me. I wanted to let you know that Emma's out of surgery. She's in the recovery room."

"How'd it go, Mom?"

"The doctor said things went well, and Emma should recover fine."

"Had her appendix burst?"

"No, but it was getting close."

Aaron sighed. "I'm glad you got her there in time."

"So are we." There was a brief pause, and Aaron could hear his mother say something to Paul, but he couldn't make out the words. A few seconds later she said, "We've decided to stay here tonight. Could you make sure Grandma and Grandpa are okay and settled in at the *daadihaus?*"

"Sure, Mom. I'll head up to their house right now and check on them."

"Oh, and your daed said to open the shop without him in the morning because we're not sure how long we'll be here."

Aaron gritted his teeth. He was tempted to remind Mom that Paul wasn't his daed. . .not his real one, anyway. "No problem," he said instead. "I can manage fine on my own."

"Danki, Aaron. I knew we could count on you."

"I'll be here bright and early tomorrow, so let me know if you need anything," he said. "I could hire a driver and send one of the brothers or close up the shop and come to the hospital myself."

"We'll let you know, son."

"Okay. Bye, Mom."

Aaron hung up the phone and sank onto the wooden stool behind the desk. *Thank You, Lord, for bringing Emma through her surgery. Now please heal her quickly.*

"I'm going out to the shop to see what's taking Aaron so long," Joseph said to his younger brother, Zachary, who sat on the front porch reading a book. "Since Bessie and Davey are both in bed, and we've checked on Grandma and Grandpa, I thought maybe you, me, and Aaron could play a game of Dutch Blitz while we wait for Mom and Papa to get home."

"Can we make a batch of popcorn and have some cold apple cider?" Zachary asked.

"Jah, sure. I don't see why not."

"I'll get the popcorn and popper out while you get Aaron."

"Okay. Be back soon." Joseph sprinted across the yard, singing a few lines from "Scattered Seed," one of his favorite songs from schooldays. " *'In the furrows of life, scatter seed; small may be thy spirit field, but a goodly crop 'twill yield; sow the kindly word and deed, scatter seed!'* "

By the time Joseph reached the harness shop, he'd sung himself into a good frame of mind. Earlier, he'd been down in the dumps, worried that Emma's appendix might rupture and she might die. He'd been praying for his little sister all day and felt confident that his prayers would be answered and Emma would be okay.

A shaft of light illuminated the harness shop as Joseph opened the door. Aaron sat at their dad's desk, with his head in his hands.

"What's wrong, Aaron?" Joseph asked as he stepped into the building. "Have you got a *koppweh*?"

Aaron lifted his head. "No, I don't have a headache. I just got off the phone with Mom, and I was praying."

"How come you were praying? What did Mom have to say? How's Emma? Is she going to be all right? Did they have to do surgery?"

"Slow down with the questions." Aaron frowned. "I can only answer one at a time."

"You don't have to be so testy." Joseph pulled a wooden stool over to the desk and took a seat. "Why don't you start by telling me how Emma is doing?"

"She had surgery to remove her appendix."

"Had it ruptured?"

"No, but I guess it was getting real close." Aaron rubbed the bridge of his nose. "I hate to think of what would have happened if Mom hadn't gotten Emma to the hospital in time."

Joseph nodded. "Are Mom and Papa coming home soon?"

"Mom said they planned to spend the night with Emma, and they probably won't be home until sometime tomorrow. Paul wants me to open the shop in the morning." Aaron nodded toward the window. "Mom also said I should check on Grandma and Grandpa."

"It's already been done." Joseph smiled. "Davey and Bessie have gone to bed, so I thought it would be fun if you, me, and Zachary played a game of Dutch Blitz."

"You and Zachary go ahead if you want to," Aaron said with a shake of his head, "but I'm going to hang out here awhile and try to get some more work done."

Joseph's eyebrows shot up. "Are you kidding me? You've been out here all day."

"So what? There's a lot to be done—especially with Paul being gone most of the day."

Joseph winced at his brother's caustic tone.

"Guess I'll head back to the house," Joseph said, stepping down from his stool. No point in making an issue of Aaron's attitude. "If you change your mind about playing a game with me and Zachary, we'll be in the kitchen."

"I won't change my mind." Aaron grabbed a stack of invoices and thumbed quickly through them. "You and Zachary will probably be fast asleep by the time I come up to the house."

Joseph shrugged. He wondered if Aaron had decided to stay in the harness shop late because there was so much work to be done, or was he just being unsocial? Joseph turned and took one last look around the harness shop. When he was a boy, he used to feel a bit jealous whenever Aaron got to help out here. Now, he couldn't care less about working in the harness shop.

Chapter 10

I hope Bessie and her family can come to our barbecue Friday evening," Sarah said to Allison as they sat beside each other in one of Uncle Ben's open buggies. They were heading toward the Hiltys' place, and Allison was driving.

"Sure will be fun to have some homemade ice cream." Sarah smacked her lips. "I love ice cream!"

"Does your family make it often?" Allison asked.

"Oh, jah. During the summer we make it a lot. Doesn't your family make ice cream?"

"We do on occasion, but since most of my brothers are married, we don't make it as much as we did when they all lived at home."

Sarah wrinkled her nose. "The only part of ice cream makin' I don't like is the crankin'."

Allison grinned. "That can be hard, especially toward the

end when the ice cream starts to freeze up."

They rode in companionable silence the rest of the way. As soon as Allison brought the buggy to a stop, Sarah jumped out and ran over to greet her friend Bessie, who sat under a tree in the front yard, playing with her dolls.

Allison tied the horse to the hitching rail near the barn and joined the girls on the lawn. She'd been tempted to drop by the harness shop to see Aaron but couldn't think of a good excuse.

"I invited Bessie and her family to our barbecue on Friday evening, but Bessie's not sure if they can come," Sarah said.

"I'm sorry to hear that."

"It's not that we don't wanna come. My little sister Emma's in the hospital," Bessie explained. "Her appendix got sick, and she had to have it taken out."

"Will Emma be okay?" Allison remembered the day Peter's appendix had ruptured. He'd been thirteen years old at the time, and Papa had been afraid he might not make it. But after several days in the hospital, Peter had recovered nicely.

"I think Emma will be all right, but she's gonna be laid up at home for a while." Bessie turned to Sarah. "That means they probably won't be able to go over to your place on Friday."

"Say, I've got an idea," Sarah said to her friend. "Maybe one of your brothers can take you to the barbecue."

Bessie grabbed Sarah's hand. "Aaron's in the harness shop. Let's go see if he thinks he can go."

Struggling with an oversized piece of leather, Aaron looked up when the front door swooshed open. He was surprised to see Bessie step inside the harness shop with Sarah and Allison.

"Hey, Aaron. Look who's here," Bessie said.

"What brings you by the harness shop on this hot morning?" Aaron asked, looking at Allison.

"They came to invite us to a barbecue at their place on Friday evening," Bessie said before Allison could reply.

Aaron dropped the leather to his workbench and stepped forward. "Didn't you tell them about Emma?"

" 'Course I did."

"Even if our little sister comes home from the hospital by Friday, she won't be up to going to any barbecue."

"I realize that," Bessie said in an exasperated tone. "But that don't mean we can't go."

Aaron glanced at Allison, and she offered him a pleasant smile. "Would it be possible for you or one of your brothers to bring Bessie over?" she asked. "I think she's really looking forward to it."

"That's a nice idea," Aaron replied, "but somebody's got to stay here with Grandma and Grandpa Raber if Mom and Paul are still at the hospital with Emma."

Bessie's lower lip protruded. "I'm sure Grandpa and Grandma can manage on their own for a couple of hours."

Aaron contemplated the idea. Grandpa's arthritis had gotten so bad over the years that he could barely walk, and Grandma's bad back made it difficult for her to do much. While it was true that they could manage a few hours alone, he would feel better if someone were at home in case a need arose.

"I'll talk to Mom about it when she calls later today. If they don't mind you going, someone can probably drive you over to the Kings' place on Friday evening."

Bessie smiled and reached for Sarah's hand. "While you're here, would you like to go out to the barn and see the baby goat that was born a few days ago?"

"Sure!" Sarah turned to Allison. "Would ya like to come along?"

Allison shook her head. "You two go along. I'll visit with Aaron awhile."

Sarah and Bessie scampered out the door, and Allison moved toward the workbench where Aaron stood.

"Are you minding the shop on your own today?" she asked.

"Jah. Probably will be until Emma gets out of the hospital."

She leaned close to the piece of leather he'd been working on. "Is harness making hard work?"

"Sometimes, but I enjoy what I do." Aaron motioned to the leather. "It's a good feeling to make a bridle or harness."

"The harness shop back home repairs shoes, too," Allison said. "Do you do that?"

Aaron shook his head. "Paul thought about doing some shoe repair, but we get enough business with saddles, harnesses, and bridles. I doubt he'll ever do shoes."

Allison drew in a deep breath as she scanned the room. "I can't get over how nice it smells in here."

"You really think so?"

"I do. I think it would be fun to work in a place like this."

"You might not say that if you knew what all was involved."

"Why don't you show me?"

"All right." As Aaron gave Allison a tour of the shop, he

demonstrated how he connected a breast strap to a huge, three-way snap that required some fancy looping, pointed out numerous tools they used, and showed her two oversized sewing machines run by an air compressor. He was surprised to see how much interest she took in everything.

"These are much bigger than the treadle sewing machine Aunt Mary uses." Allison smiled, and her cheeks turned a light shade of pink. "She's been teaching me how to sew, and I've learned to make a faceless doll."

"I'll bet that required some hand stitching, too."

She nodded. "Tiny snaps had to be sewn on the clothes."

"Nothing like the big ones we use here." He motioned to the riveting machine. "That's where we punch shiny rivets into our leather straps."

Allison followed as Aaron moved to the front of the store. "What were you working on when the girls and I first came in?"

"I was getting ready to cut some leather, but the thing's so long and heavy, I may need to wait until Paul's here and can help me with it."

Allison's eyes lit up like copper pennies. "I'd be happy to help."

"You wouldn't mind holding one end while I do the cutting?"

"Not at all."

Aaron handed one end of the leather to Allison, and she held it while he made the necessary cuts. They'd just finished when the shop door flew open, and Sarah rushed into the room. "The *gees* have all escaped! Bessie and I need your help gettin' them back in their pens!"

Aaron grimaced. How was he supposed to get any work done if he had to waste time chasing after a bunch of goats?

Allison smiled and said, "I'm sure Aaron has a lot of work to do here in the harness shop, but I'd be happy to help you round up the goats."

"That's okay. I can take the time to get those gees back where they belong." Aaron didn't want Allison to think he was willing to let the girls round up the goats on their own.

Allison placed her end of the leather onto the nearest workbench, and they headed out the door.

Out in the yard, they were greeted by a scene of total chaos. Six goats frolicked on the grass, four goats raced up and down the driveway, and two more kicked up their heels on the porch. Aaron could only imagine how much damage those goats would do if they didn't get back in their pen quickly. The two on the porch needed to be corralled first, as one of the goats had jumped onto a chair and was nibbling away at the petunias dangling from a pot that hung from the porch ceiling.

"Bessie, why don't you and Sarah try to catch the goats in the yard, while I capture the ones on the porch?" Aaron called to his sister.

"Jah, okay!" Bessie hollered in response.

He glanced over at Allison. "If you'd like to join in, you can take your pick of whatever goat you want to chase."

With no hesitation, Allison headed for the porch. Aaron was right on her heels. By the time they reached their destination, both goats were standing on chairs, and Mom's pot of flowers was half eaten.

"Stupid gees! You're nothing but trouble," Aaron fumed.

He lunged for one goat at the same time Allison did. The goat slipped between them and darted off the porch. *Smack!*—their heads came together.

"Ouch!" Allison pulled back like she'd been stung by a hornet.

"Yow!" Aaron did the same.

"Are you okay?" Allison asked, rubbing her forehead.

He fingered the pulsating spot on his head and nodded. "I think I'll live. How about you?"

"I've got a little bump, but the skin's not broken."

Aaron fought the urge to touch the swollen red spot on Allison's forehead. "Sorry about that," he mumbled. "Guess I should have told you which goat I was going for."

"It's okay; no permanent damage has been done."

Pulling his gaze away from Allison, Aaron turned to see Sarah, Bessie, and eight frolicking goats leaping around the yard like a bunch of frogs. The goats that had been on the porch now joined the six in the yard, and the four that had been in the driveway were still slipping and sliding in the gravel.

"I guess I'd better see if my brothers can help out," he said.

Allison nodded. "We're going to need all the help we can get."

Chapter 11

"I am glad you were free to go on a picnic with me this evening," Katie said to Allison as they rode in Katie's buggy toward one of the ponds off Highway C. "This will give us a chance to get to know each other better."

"Sorry we couldn't have left earlier, but Aunt Mary needed my help getting some things ready for tomorrow evening's barbecue."

"That's okay. I had plenty of chores to do at my place today, too." Katie flicked the reins, and the horse broke into a trot. "I'm glad I got an invitation to your aunt and uncle's barbecue." She smiled. "You mentioned that the Hiltys were invited, so I'm hoping Joseph will be there."

"You've heard about little Emma's surgery, haven't you?"

Katie nodded. "It's a shame about her appendix."

"Sarah and I stopped by the harness shop yesterday to invite the family to the barbecue. That's when I heard about it. Aaron said maybe he or one of his brothers might bring Bessie over."

"If only one brother can come, I hope it will be Joseph," Katie said wistfully.

Allison chuckled. "I think you've got a one-track mind, and it leads to only one place."

"Where's that?"

"Joseph Zook."

Katie's face heated up. She cared for Joseph a lot, but she didn't feel she knew Allison well enough to discuss her deepest feelings. "Sure is a pretty evening," she said as they pulled onto the dirt road that led to the pond.

"Jah, it's real nice." Allison grinned. "Would you like to hear about my embarrassing experience while Sarah and I were at the Zooks' place?"

"Jah, sure. What happened?"

"The goats got out, and Aaron and I bumped heads trying to capture the same goat."

"Were either of you hurt?"

"We each got a bump, but it was nothing serious."

"Did you manage to get the goats okay?"

"Finally. . .after Aaron called his brothers to help."

"Joseph, too?"

"Jah. Joseph, Zachary, and Davey."

"It can be a real chore to get goats back in their pen," Katie said. "I can see why you'd need extra help."

"The breeze blowing against my face sure feels good," Allison said, changing the subject. "It's been so hot and muggy all week, and it makes it hard not to become cranky."

"Don't you have hot, humid weather in Lancaster County?"

"We do, but I've never gotten used to it." Allison drew in a deep breath and released it with a sigh. "On the really hot days of summer, I find myself envying the English with their air-conditioning."

"You'd never leave the Amish faith so you could have electricity, would you?"

"No, of course not," Allison said with a shake of her head.

"We're here!" Katie halted the horse. "Would you mind getting the picnic basket from the backseat while I tether Sandy to a tree?"

"Sure." Allison climbed down from the buggy and reached under the seat. She grasped the wicker basket with one hand and the quilt lying beside it with the other hand. As soon as Katie had the horse secured, they headed for the pond.

When they took seats on the quilt, they bowed for silent prayer. Then Katie opened the picnic basket and removed fried chicken, deviled eggs, dill pickles, and potato salad. She had also brought a thermos of iced tea, and for dessert, a pan of brownies with thick chocolate frosting.

"Everything looks so good," Allison said. "But there's so much food!"

Katie smiled. "Just eat what you can."

Allison reached for a piece of chicken and practically devoured it. "Umm. . .this is so good. I wish I could cook as well as you do."

Katie tipped her head and stared at Allison. "All the women I know can cook really well."

"Not me. Aunt Catherine has never allowed me to do much in the kitchen except dishes and mopping the floors. Whenever I would try to cook anything, she would scrutinize everything so much, I would get nervous and end up ruining it."

"How come she was so critical?"

Allison shrugged. "My aunt likes to be in charge. She's often said she can't be bothered with the messes I make in her kitchen."

"How does she expect you to learn the necessary things in order to run a house of your own someday?"

"I don't know, but Aunt Mary apparently doesn't think that way. She's been more than willing to teach me how to cook and sew." Allison wrinkled her nose. "I don't know if I'll ever learn, though. You should have tasted the awful coleslaw I made the other night. I put in too much vinegar, and I'm sure from the things Walter said that he thought I was trying to make them all sick."

"I doubt anyone in your aunt's family would think such a thing." Katie reached for a deviled egg and was about to take a bite, when she heard voices nearby. She turned and spotted two young Amish men with fishing poles heading toward the pond. Her heart skipped a beat. It was Aaron and his brother, Joseph.

She jumped up and ran over to them. "Allison and I are having a picnic supper. There's still plenty of food left if you'd like to join us."

Aaron glanced over at Allison, then back to Katie. "Thanks anyway, but we've already had our supper," he said before Joseph could respond. "Fact is, my bruder and I just came here to do a little fishing, so don't let us bother you."

"It won't be a bother," Katie insisted.

"See, Aaron, they don't mind us joining them. Besides, I think I could eat a little something," Joseph put in.

Aaron thumped his younger brother on the back. "You must have a hollow leg."

Joseph shrugged, leaned his fishing pole against a tree, and joined Katie on the quilt.

Allison waited anxiously to see what Aaron would do and was pleased when he followed Katie and Joseph.

"Did you bring your fishing pole along?" Aaron asked Allison as he took a seat on the edge of the quilt near her.

She shook her head. "Katie and I just came to eat and visit."

"Then we showed up and ruined your picnic." Joseph winked at Katie, and she swatted him playfully on the arm.

A stab of jealousy pierced Allison's heart. Katie and Joseph obviously cared for each other, and Allison longed to have someone look at her the way Joseph looked at Katie, with love and respect.

"How's your little sister doing?" Katie asked Aaron. "Is she still in the hospital?"

He nodded. "She's doing well and will probably be home soon."

"I'm glad she's going to be okay," Allison spoke up.

"Me, too."

"Will either one of you be at the barbecue Allison's aunt and uncle are having tomorrow evening?" Katie asked.

"I thought I might go," they said at the same time.

Joseph grinned at Katie. "You'll be there, too, I hope."

She nodded. "Definitely."

"Glad to hear it," Joseph said as he helped himself to some potato salad and chicken.

Katie extended the container of chicken to Aaron. "How about you? Wouldn't you like to try a piece?"

He shook his head. "I'm still full from supper."

"Who's watching things at home while you and Joseph are here?" Allison asked.

"Paul came home from Springfield and left Mom to stay with Emma," Aaron replied. "Since I've been taking care of things in Paul's absence, he said Joseph and I could go fishing for a few hours this evening."

"That was nice of him," Katie said.

They continued to visit while Joseph ate. When the food was put away, the men invited the women to join them at the pond.

Aaron squatted beside Allison and extended his pole. "Would you like to fish awhile?"

She smiled and eagerly reached for it but pulled her hand back in time. "I'd better just watch."

"How come? You fished the other day and even baited your own hook."

"That's true, but if my aunt Catherine had seen me do that, she wouldn't have approved."

"Why not?"

"She thinks fishing isn't very ladylike."

"That's lecherich. My mamm likes to fish, and she's a lady.

Of course, she doesn't go fishing as often as she used to now that my grandma and grandpa need her help so much more."

"Don't you have other family to help with their care?" Allison asked.

"My brothers and I try to help out as much as we can, just like we've been doing while Emma's in the hospital." Aaron wedged his pole between his knees, leaned back on his elbows, and lifted his face toward the sky. "Ever wonder what heaven is like?"

"Sometimes." Allison thought about heaven a lot, wondering whether she would ever get there. Even though she'd attended church since she was a baby, she'd never felt as if she knew God in a personal way. For that matter, Allison didn't think God knew her, either. She envied people like Aunt Mary, who read her Bible every day and seemed to walk closely with the Lord. She often wondered how her mother had felt about spiritual things when she was alive.

"I know there's supposed to be streets of gold in heaven," Aaron said, "but I'm hoping there will be fishing holes, too."

Allison smiled and was about to reply, when Aaron leaned forward and hollered, "Hey! I've got a bite!"

She watched with envy as he gripped his pole and started playing the fish. "I think it's a big one!" he hollered.

"Don't fall in the water like my cousin Dan did."

"I won't; don't worry." Aaron moved closer to the edge of the pond, reeling in his catch a little at a time. Soon a nice-sized bass lay at his feet, and he knelt beside it with a satisfied smile.

Allison knew it would sound silly, but she almost offered to remove the hook. She caught herself before the words popped out. She glanced over at Katie, who sat beside Joseph with a contented smile. Katie didn't seem the least bit interested in fishing, but she could cook, and if that's what a man wanted in a wife, then Allison would need to learn to do the same.

Aaron extended the pole toward Allison. "Now it's your turn."

"What?"

"I know you like to fish, so quit trying to fool me and fish."

Allison drew in a deep breath, savoring the musty aroma of the pond and the fishy smell of the bass he'd landed. Oh, how she longed to grip that fishing pole and throw the line into the water. It would feel so satisfying to snag a big old bass or tasty catfish. "I'll just watch," she mumbled.

"Okay, suit yourself." Aaron cast out his line once more, and they sat in silence.

Allison could hardly contain herself when Aaron reeled in another bass, followed by a couple of plump catfish. Her fingers itched to grab hold of the fishing pole and cast her line into the water.

"Hey, Joseph," Aaron called to his brother, "I'll bet you can't top the size of my last fish!"

"I'm not tryin' to," Joseph shot back. "I've got three nice catfish, and I'm not a bit worried about their size."

Aaron chuckled. "All my brother worries about is trying to make an impression on Katie Esh." His face sobered. "Speaking of the Esh family. . .Katie's cousin James isn't coming to your barbecue tomorrow night, is he?"

"I don't know who all my aunt and uncle have invited."

"It would be just my luck if James was there." Aaron bit off the end of a fingernail and spit it onto the ground.

Allison wrinkled her nose. "Do you have to do that? I think it's *ekelhaft.*"

Aaron examined his hands and frowned. "You're right. It is a disgusting habit, but I do it whenever I'm nervous or upset."

"Would you be upset if James came to the barbecue?"

"Guess I would, but it's not my decision who comes."

Allison wasn't sure what Aaron had against James, but she didn't think it was her place to ask.

Chapter 12

Allison didn't know why, but thinking about the barbecue that would begin in less than an hour made her feel jittery as a june bug. Could it be because she was excited about seeing Aaron again? Or maybe she was worried over who else might be in attendance.

If James shows up, how should I act around him? Allison asked herself as she sliced tomatoes. *I don't want to hurt his feelings, but I'm really not interested in having him court me.* She grunted. "Guess I'll have to cross that bridge when I come to it."

"What was that?"

Allison whirled around. She'd thought she was alone in the kitchen. Aunt Mary had gone outside to see if Uncle Ben had the barbecue lit. Sarah and Dan were supposed to be setting the picnic tables. Walter was outside somewhere, too. She'd certainly never expected Harvey to come into the kitchen. But here he was, looking at her like she'd taken leave of her senses.

"I. . .uh. . .was talking to myself," she mumbled, quickly turning back to cutting the tomatoes.

He chuckled. "No need to look so flustered. We all talk to ourselves sometimes."

Allison smiled. She still couldn't get over how easygoing this family seemed to be. If Aunt Catherine had caught Allison talking to herself, she would have made an issue of it.

"I came in to get the hamburger buns," Harvey said, moving toward the ample-sized bread box.

"Have any of the guests arrived yet?" Allison asked.

"Not that I know of, but I'm sure they'll be here soon."

"And you don't know who all is coming?"

"Nope. Just heard that Mom and Dad had invited the Hiltys, Eshes, Swartzes, and Hertzlers."

"Which Eshes?"

Harvey shrugged. "I'm not sure."

"So you don't know whether James was invited?"

"Nope."

Allison went to the refrigerator and removed a jar of pickles. "I guess we'll know soon enough."

Harvey stared at her in a strange way. "You're not interested in James, I hope."

"Why do you ask?"

"Well, I know he brought you home the night of the last young people's gathering, and Clara said she saw James in Seymour one day and that he'd mentioned that he might ask you out."

Allison shook her head. "He hasn't."

"That's good to hear." Harvey started across the room. "Oh, Mom said to tell you to bring out the stuff you're cutting up as soon as you're done."

"I will." Allison turned back to her chore as Harvey went out the back door. *Now if I can just relax and have a good time. It's plain silly for me to get all worked up over who's coming and who's not.*

Aaron clucked to his horse to get him moving faster, then glanced over at Joseph, who sat on the seat beside him. Bessie was in the back of the buggy and had been practicing her yodeling ever since they'd left home. Earlier today, she'd mentioned that Gabe's wife, Melinda, had been teaching her some special yodeling techniques. Aaron figured Bessie had a long way to go before she could yodel half as well as Melinda.

His thoughts shifted gears. He was glad Emma had come home from the hospital today and that Mom and Paul hadn't minded him and Joseph escorting Bessie to the barbecue. It meant he would see Allison again, and that thought pleased him more than he cared to admit. He'd never met anyone like her before. If he weren't so set against marriage, he might even want to court her. Since Allison would be returning to Pennsylvania at the end of summer, what harm could there be in them doing a few things together? Surely she wouldn't have any expectations of love or romance.

Aaron gripped the reins tighter. *I wonder if James will be at the barbecue tonight.*

"You're awfully quiet," Joseph said, breaking into Aaron's thoughts.

"It's kind of hard to talk with Bessie in the backseat, cackling away."

"You're right." Joseph glanced over his shoulder. "Our little sister seems determined to master the art of yodeling."

Aaron nodded. "She'll need a lot more practice."

"Melinda started yodeling when she was a girl, and she sure does it well. In time, Bessie will get the hang of it."

"Maybe so."

"I don't know about you, but I'm sure looking forward to the barbecue and all that good food." Joseph gave his stomach a couple of pats.

"More than likely what you're really looking forward to is spending time with Katie."

"Jah, that, too."

"You're not thinking of marrying the girl, are you?"

Joseph's ears turned pink. "Uh. . .I'd sure like to, but—"

"Maybe someday, when you're both a little older?"

Joseph nodded. "I'll probably need to find myself a better job before then."

"You're not happy working part-time at the Christmas tree farm and working the fields for our neighbors when you can?"

"Not really. I don't think I'd want to spend the rest of my life flagging trees, pulling weeds, or traipsing through the dusty fields behind a pair of stubborn mules."

"Noah Hertzler has worked at Osborn's Christmas Tree Farm for several years, and he seems happy enough. Maybe Hank Osborn will hire you full-time."

"Jah, well, one man's pleasure is another man's pain. I'm not really looking to work there full-time."

"You hate it that much?"

"I don't hate it. Just don't like it well enough to keep doing it forever." Joseph looked over at Aaron. "I need something that provides more of a challenge—the way your work in the harness shop does."

Aaron frowned. "You've never shown any interest in working in the harness shop before."

Joseph bumped Aaron's arm. "I'd just like to find something that's more of a challenge for me."

"The harness shop can be challenge, all right." Aaron drew in a breath and released it quickly. He hoped Joseph didn't want to work at the harness shop. If he did, Paul might decide to turn the shop over to him when he was ready to retire, and not give it to Aaron, the way his real dad had wanted. Of course, there was always Zachary and Davey to consider. One of them might want in on their real dad's shop. If that proved to be the case, where would it leave Aaron? "Maybe you should consider carpentry or painting. There's always a need for that," he said.

"Naw. Those jobs don't interest me, either."

"Maybe you could go to work on a dairy farm. That's what Allison's daed does for a living. He runs the farm with one of his sons."

Joseph shook his head. "I don't think so. Cows are too smelly for my taste."

"Oddle-lei-de-tee! Oddle-lei-de-tee!" Bessie's shrill voice grew louder and louder, until Aaron thought he would scream.

"Would you quiet down back there? I can hardly think, and

all that howling is giving me a headache!"

Bessie finally quieted, but Aaron figured it was only because she was afraid he might head back home if she didn't.

A short time later, they pulled onto the Kings' property, and Aaron parked the buggy near the barn. "I'll get the horse put in the corral and join you and Bessie up at the house," he said.

"Jah, okay." Joseph grabbed Bessie's hand, and they sprinted across the yard.

Allison stepped onto the back porch in time to see Bessie and Joseph enter the yard. She felt a keen sense of disappointment when she realized Aaron wasn't with them. She'd hoped he would come to the barbecue but figured he must have responsibilities that had kept him at home.

At least Katie will be happy this evening, since Joseph is here, Allison thought. *Guess I shouldn't be so envious, but it's hard to see Katie and Joseph all smiles when they're together.*

Determined to be pleasant, Allison stepped forward and greeted her guests. "Sarah's in the house helping Aunt Mary make some lemonade. I'm sure she'll be glad to see you," she said, smiling at Bessie.

"I'll go inside and help 'em." Bessie bounded away, and Allison turned to Joseph. "You and Bessie are the first to arrive, but I'm sure Katie and her family will be here shortly."

Joseph grinned. "I hope so."

Allison motioned to the barbecue grill across the lawn. "Uncle Ben's got the chicken cooking, and he'll be doing up some burgers, too. We should be able to eat soon, I expect."

"It sure smells good." Joseph sniffed the air. "Guess I'll wander over there and say hello."

When he sauntered off, Allison moved over to the picnic tables and spotted Aaron coming out of the barn. Her heart did a little flip-flop, and she drew in a quick breath to steady her nerves.

"When Bessie and Joseph showed up without you, I didn't think you'd come," she said when Aaron walked into the yard.

"I put my horse in the corral, then stopped off at the barn to talk to Harvey and Walter. They were checking on the new horse their daed recently bought."

Allison smiled. "Jah, I know."

Aaron shifted from one foot to the other as he glanced around, kind of nervous-like. "Where is everyone? Are we the only ones here?"

"You, Joseph, and Bessie are the first to arrive, but I'm sure the others will be along soon."

Aaron took a seat on one of the picnic benches, and Allison sat across from him. Feeling a bit nervous and shy all of a sudden, she fiddled with the napkin in front of her.

Aaron cleared his throat. "Uh, I was wondering. . . ."

"Jah?"

"Do you think you might be free to—"

A buggy rumbled into the yard and a deep male voice hollered, "Whoa there! Hold up, you crazy critter!"

Allison's mouth dropped open when she saw James Esh in his fancy buggy, with his unruly horse trotting at full speed straight for the barn.

Chapter 13

As James's horse and buggy thundered into the barn, everyone in the yard took off on a run.

"That crazy fellow is going to hurt himself if he keeps pulling stunts like that," Aaron mumbled as he sprinted along beside Joseph.

"Jah," Joseph agreed. "He had no call to be running his horse like that. I'm sure he could have gotten the animal stopped in time if he'd had a mind to."

"The way James raced into the barn, his horse could have been injured," Uncle Ben added.

"I hope James isn't hurt," Allison said breathlessly.

It would serve him right if he did get hurt. Aaron bit back the words on his tongue and drew in a sharp breath. His attitude wasn't right; he really didn't want to see anyone hurt, no matter how irritating they could be.

By the time they reached the barn, James, who appeared to be unharmed, was backing his horse and buggy out the door. "Get back, everyone!" he shouted. "I'm comin' through!"

When James had maneuvered the buggy out of the barn, Allison stepped up to him and asked, "Are you all right? Is your horse okay?"

"I'm fine, and my horse wasn't hurt. I was just trying to give everyone a little thrill for the day."

"You could have picked a better way to do it," Aaron said, stepping up to James. "Someone could have been trampled by that crazy horse of yours."

James leveled Aaron with a piercing look. "You think so?"

Aaron nodded.

James glanced over at Allison and smiled. "I told you my horse was a spirited one."

Allison stood silently, a peculiar expression on her face. Was she impressed with James's brazen behavior? Did she find him exciting?

Just then, two more buggies rolled into the yard—the Eshes and Hiltys had arrived.

"Why are we all standing here?" James asked. "Let's head over to the picnic tables and eat ourselves full!"

As Allison moved over to one of the picnic tables, she thought about how foolish James had been to run his horse into the barn like that. He'd said he'd been trying to give them a thrill, but she figured he was probably showing off, the way her brother Peter did when he was trying to impress Sally. *Could James have been trying to impress me?* she wondered. She thought about how he'd kissed her the night he'd given her a ride home from the young people's gathering. Maybe James didn't mind her tomboy ways. Maybe he accepted her as she was.

Allison grimaced. *But James hasn't joined the church, so it's not likely that he's ready to settle down. Besides, I'll be going home in a few months, so there wouldn't be much point in starting a relationship with James or anyone else, even if they are interested in me.*

She glanced over at Aaron, who had taken a seat at the picnic table across from her. Truth be told, it was Aaron she wished would take an interest in her, not James. But that was about as unlikely as Aunt Catherine saying she missed Allison and begging her to come home. Aaron had given no indication that he was interested in her in a romantic way.

"Sure is a nice night, isn't it?" James asked, plopping onto the bench beside Allison.

"Jah." Allison glanced at Gabe and Melinda Swartz, who sat across from Aaron. They looked happy and content. Katie and Joseph were all smiles, too. Allison couldn't help but envy the two couples who were obviously in love.

"Maybe you young people would like to play a game of croquet after we're done eating," Aunt Mary suggested, smiling at Allison. "Later, after everyone feels hungry again, we'll start cranking the homemade ice cream."

"Croquet sounds like fun," Katie spoke up. She turned to Joseph. "Don't you think so?"

He nodded with an eager expression. "I've always enjoyed

battin' the ball around."

Katie jabbed Joseph in the ribs. "It's not baseball we'll be playing, silly. We're supposed to hit the ball through the metal wickets, using a mallet."

Joseph jiggled his eyebrows. "I knew that."

Allison felt James's warm breath on her neck as he leaned over and whispered, "Why don't you and me take a walk down the road while the others play croquet? We can get to know each other better if we're alone."

The back of Allison's neck heated up. What would everyone think if she went off with James? What if he tried to kiss her again? "I'd really like to join the game," she replied. "If you don't want to play, maybe you can find something else to do until the ice cream is made."

"I can't think of anything I'd rather do than spend time with you," James said, offering her a crooked grin. "So if it means hitting a ball through some silly wicket, then that's what I'll do."

Aaron pushed macaroni salad around on his plate as irritation welled in his soul. He didn't like seeing James sitting beside Allison, whispering in her ear like she was his girlfriend. Couldn't she see what that pushy fellow was up to? Didn't she realize all James wanted was a summer romance with no strings attached?

Aaron clenched his fists. *If I'd come in my own buggy, and Joseph and Bessie had a way home, I'd head out now so I wouldn't have to watch James carry on like a lovesick cow.*

"You're not eating much." Gabe leaned across the table and

pointed at Aaron's plate. "If you're gonna beat me at croquet, then you'd better do something to build up your strength, don't you think?"

Aaron shrugged. He was in no mood for Gabe's ribbing. Truth was he wasn't sure he wanted to get in on the game.

"You look like you're sucking on a bunch of tart cherries," Gabe said. "Is something bothering you?"

"I'm just not hungry."

"I'll bet he's saving room for that homemade ice cream." Melinda reached for the dish of deviled eggs and took two.

Gabe looked over at his wife and smiled. "Now that Melinda's eating for two, she takes second helpings of everything."

Melinda needled him in the ribs with her elbow. "That's not so, and you know it."

Aaron's mouth fell open. "I—I didn't know you two were expecting a *boppli*."

Melinda nodded, and Gabe's smile widened. "The baby should be born in October. I'm hoping for a boy to help me in the woodworking shop."

"Congratulations."

"Danki," Melinda said. "I'm really looking forward to being a *mudder*."

Aaron grabbed his glass of iced tea and took a big drink. He would never know what it was like to have a loving wife and a baby of his own.

The young women teamed up to play the first round of croquet against the men. Aunt Mary sat on the sidelines with Katie's mother, Doris, while the children played a game of tag. Uncle Ben and Katie's father, Amos, had taken a walk to the barn.

Allison went first, since she was the guest of honor. Then it was Katie's turn, followed by Melinda, Sarah, and Katie's fifteen-year-old sister, Mary Alice. Next, the young men took turns.

"It sure is obvious that the fellows are trying to win this game," Melinda said to Allison when Gabe hit his ball through the middle wicket, leaving everyone else two wickets behind.

"I guess it doesn't matter who wins as long as everyone has fun." Allison wouldn't have admitted it, but she'd intentionally not played as well as she would have at home. She was trying to act like a woman and not a tomboy.

"I didn't get much chance to visit with you at the last preaching service," Melinda said to Allison. "But I understand you're from Pennsylvania."

Allison nodded and took aim with her mallet. She gave the ball a light tap, but it missed the wicket by several inches.

"How long will you be in Webster County?" Melinda asked as Katie took her turn.

"Just until the end of summer."

"Do you like animals?" came the next question from Gabe's pretty, blond-haired wife.

"Some. I like dogs, although I've never had one as a pet."

"Really?"

"My aunt Catherine doesn't care much for pets," Allison explained.

"You'll have to go over to Melinda and Gabe's sometime," Katie said after she'd taken her turn. "Melinda's got more pets than you'll see at the zoo."

Allison's interest was piqued. She couldn't imagine having that many pets.

"I have an animal shelter where I care for orphaned animals or those that have been hurt and need a place to stay while they're recuperating," Melinda explained. "Gabe's a woodworker, and he's built lots of cages for me to keep my animals in."

"Is that so?"

Melinda nodded as Katie explained, "Melinda used to work at the veterinary clinic in Seymour, so Dr. Franklin sends all his orphaned patients to her once he's done all he can for them."

"There must never be a dull moment at your place," Allison said.

"That's for sure. I think my folks were glad when I married Gabe and they no longer had to put up with all my animals and the crazy stunts they pulled." Melinda giggled. "Now it's Gabe's job to help me round up any runaway critters."

Allison thought the idea of having a safe haven for animals was wonderful. She figured Gabe must be a caring husband to have built cages for Melinda, not to mention him being willing to run after a bunch of stray animals.

"All right," Sarah shouted, interrupting the conversation, "let's see if anyone can catch up with me now!"

Allison scanned the yard and was surprised to see her cousin's red ball lying a few feet from the final set of wickets. Apparently Sarah had made it through the previous four without Allison realizing it.

The women stood on the edge of the grass while the men took their turns, each with a determined look on his face. Aaron swung his mallet, and his ball ended up right next to Sarah's.

"This is gonna be a close game," Harvey shouted. "It's your turn, Allison, so do your best!"

Allison lined up her mallet, pulled both arms back, and let loose with a swing that sent the ball sailing through the air. Aaron was on his way to the sidelines when—*whack!*—her ball hit him square in the knee.

Aaron crumpled to the ground with a muffled groan.

Allison gasped and rushed forward, but James caught her hand. "Don't worry about him; he's probably faking it."

"These balls are awfully hard, and I'm sure it hurts real bad," she said. By this time everyone had gathered around Aaron, and Allison couldn't see how he was doing.

"Aw, he'll be okay," James insisted. "A little ice on his knee and he'll be just fine."

Allison wasn't convinced. She had smacked her ball with a lot of force—enough to knock Aaron down. She pulled her hand free and started to move away, but James grabbed her elbow and said, "Say, Allison, did you know there's to be another young people's gathering next Sunday night?"

She shook her head, wondering why he'd brought the gathering up now. Didn't James care that Aaron had been hurt?

"How would you like to take another ride home in my buggy after the get-together on Sunday night?" James asked.

Allison opened her mouth to respond, but before she could get a word out, Aaron limped through the crowd and announced, "That won't be possible because Allison's riding home with me!" Before Allison could respond, he turned and hobbled off toward the house.

"Can I have a word with you?" Allison asked as she stepped onto the porch.

Dropping into a chair near the door, Aaron merely nodded.

"Is your leg okay?"

"It'll be fine. I think it's just badly bruised."

"I'm really sorry. I didn't realize I had hit the ball so hard or that you were standing in line with where the ball would head."

"No problem. It's not like you did it on purpose or anything." Aaron looked up at her. "If it had been James's ball that clobbered me, I'd have figured he did it intentionally."

"Speaking of James, I was wondering why you told him you'd be taking me home from the young people's gathering next week." Allison moistened her lips with the tip of her tongue. "I'm curious about whether you meant it or not."

"Of course I meant it. Wouldn't have said it if I didn't."

"Do you mind if I ask why?"

He shrugged. "Just didn't want to see you with James. He's trouble with a capital *T*."

"You don't have to protect me from James," Allison said. "I'm perfectly capable of making my own decisions and speaking on my own behalf."

Aaron stared at her. "Are you saying you'd prefer to ride home with James on Sunday night?"

"I–I'm not saying that at all," she stammered, her face turning a light shade of red.

Aaron rubbed the sore spot on his knee. "So, do you want a ride home after the gathering or not?"

Allison looked a bit hesitant, but finally nodded. "Jah, okay." She moved toward the door. "I'll go inside and get you some ice."

"Danki."

Allison stepped into the house, and Aaron grimaced, wondering why he felt so befuddled whenever he was in Allison's presence.

Chapter 14

Even though the barbecue at her aunt and uncle's had been over a week ago, Allison's mind was still in a jumble over what had transpired during the game of croquet. Aaron's announcement that he'd be taking her home after the young people's gathering had taken her completely by surprise. As she sat in the Kauffmans' barn during the gathering, she wondered if Aaron had extended the invitation only to irritate James, or if he'd been trying to protect her from James's flirtatious ways. Aaron obviously didn't care much for James, but she wasn't sure why. Was there some kind of a rift going on between them, or maybe a clash of personalities?

"Allison, did you hear what I said?"

Allison jumped at the sound of a woman's voice. Katie stood beside her holding two glasses of root beer.

"I was deep in thought and didn't hear you," Allison said.

"I thought maybe you would have fallen asleep." Katie handed one of the glasses to Allison. "Here's some cold root beer for you."

"Danki." Allison reached for the glass and took a sip. The frothy soda pop tasted sweet, and the coolness felt good on her parched lips. It was another warm evening, and summer was only beginning. She hated to think what the weather would be like by August.

"I'm surprised you're not sitting with Joseph," Allison commented as Katie took a seat beside her.

"Joseph isn't here yet, but Aaron showed up awhile ago. I figured you might be with him." Katie gave her a knowing look. "Since he's taking you home tonight, I thought you would probably spend at least part of the evening together."

Allison shook her head. "Truth be told, I'm not sure Aaron really wants to take me home."

"Are you kidding? Last week during our game of croquet he made it clear that was his intention."

"That's true, but I'm not convinced he made the announcement because he enjoys being with me."

"What makes you say that?"

"He acts so moody and sometimes kind of distant whenever I'm around."

"Aaron does tend to be a bit temperamental, but he has many good qualities, too."

"Such as?"

"Let's see. . . He's kind, dependable, and he works at the harness shop. Aaron's nothing like my lazy cousin James." Katie smiled. "I think Aaron will make a good husband and father someday. He just needs to find the right woman."

Ever since Aaron had arrived at the young people's gathering, he'd hung around the refreshment table, trying to work up the nerve to take a plate of food over to Allison. A few minutes ago, he'd seen Katie head over to the bale of straw where Allison sat, but he didn't feel right about interrupting their conversation. Besides, he didn't want to give anyone the impression that he and Allison were a courting couple. It was bad enough that he'd foolishly announced that he'd be taking her home tonight. He'd already taken too much ribbing about that from Gabe, who seemed to take pleasure in telling Aaron how great life was now that he was married to Melinda and they were expecting a baby.

Aaron glanced across the room and saw James swagger into the barn. His straw hat was tipped way back on his head, he had a red bandanna tied around his neck, and he wore a pair of blue jeans with holes in the knees. *Anything to draw attention to himself.*

After a quick survey of the room, James headed toward Allison and Katie. Aaron clenched his fists and waited to see what would happen. Sure enough, James marched right up to Allison, bent over, and whispered something in her ear.

Aaron grabbed a handful of pretzels and inched his way closer to the bale of straw Allison and Katie shared.

Suddenly Katie stood, said something to Allison, and headed for the barn door. That's when Aaron noticed Joseph had arrived. Apparently Katie cared more about being with his brother than she did about protecting Allison from her over-confident cousin.

Katie had been gone only a few seconds when James plunked down next to Allison.

Aaron halted and leaned against the wall. He was close enough now that he could hear what James said to Allison.

"I was wondering if I could give you a ride home again tonight," James said.

Allison shook her head. "I'm riding home with Aaron."

"I think you'd enjoy riding home with me more."

"I really can't."

"Come on, Allison; I won't take no for an answer."

That did it! With no thought of the consequences, Aaron marched over, seized James by the collar, and pulled him to his feet. "I believe you're sitting in my seat!"

Aaron didn't know who was more surprised—James, whose face had turned red as a ripe tomato; Allison, whose eyes were huge as saucers; or himself, because he'd never done anything quite so bold.

"Don't get yourself in a snit," James snarled. "I wasn't sayin' anything to Allison that she didn't want to hear."

Aaron held his arms tightly against his sides. It was all he could do to keep from punching James in the nose. "You're nothing but trouble, and if I ever catch you bothering Allison again, I'll—"

"You'll what? Put my lights out?" James glared at Aaron like he was daring him to land the first punch.

"You know I won't fight you," Aaron mumbled. "But I can

make trouble in other ways if you don't back off."

James stepped forward so that he was nose to nose with Aaron. "What are you gonna do—run to the bishop or one of the other ministers and tell 'em what a bad fellow I am?"

Aaron glanced around the room, feeling as if all eyes were on him. Sure enough, everyone within earshot was watching them.

"Why don't you leave now, James?" Aaron said through clenched teeth. "Knowing the kind of things you usually do for entertainment, I'm sure an evening of singing and games would only bore you."

James looked over at Allison. "Do you want me to go?"

She stared at her hands, folded in her lap, and nodded slowly. "Jah, it might be best."

"Okay, but only for you, Allison." He threw Aaron an icy stare. "This ain't the end of it, ya know."

As James walked away, Allison sat, too numb to say a word. What was wrong with James for talking to Aaron like that? And why had Aaron gotten so defensive? Surely he couldn't be jealous of James.

"That was some scene you had going on with James there, brother," Joseph said, stepping up to Aaron. "If I hadn't known better, I'd have thought you were going to start a fight with him."

"That fellow can be so cocky sometimes. I wish he would have stayed home tonight." Aaron's face had turned cherry red, and his voice quavered.

"James has always been a bit overbearing, but he's gotten worse in the last few years," Katie said as she joined the group.

"Why do you think that is?" Joseph questioned.

Katie shrugged. "I'm not sure, but I suppose it might have something to do with the fact that James's daed turned his wheel shop over to James's older brother Dennis a few years ago."

"Why would that make James act so brazen?" Allison asked.

"Because James thought the blacksmith shop should belong to him." Katie slowly shook her head. "Some folks do strange things out of jealousy."

Aaron cleared his throat real loud. "Are we just going to stand around here all night talking about James, or should we get something to eat?"

Joseph thumped Aaron on the back. "You're right; all this speculating about James is getting us nowhere. Let's head over to the refreshment table."

Katie smiled at Joseph. "I brought a plate of brownies tonight."

He licked his lips. "Umm. . .can't wait."

The couple hurried off, and Allison and Aaron followed.

"I don't know about you, but I can't wait for summer to be over," Peter said to Herman as the two of them strolled toward the barn to begin their nightly milking process.

"What's the matter? Can't stand the hot, muggy weather?"

Peter shook his head. "It's not that. I'm just anxious for Allison to return."

"I didn't think you would miss your sister so much—especially since you've been spending so much time with Sally lately." Herman needled Peter in the ribs with his elbow.

"Jah, well, I'm hoping Aunt Catherine will be a little nicer once Allison returns home. I think she misses her, Dad."

"I've noticed that she's been crankier than normal lately, but I'm not sure it's because she misses Allison."

Peter stopped walking and turned to face Herman. "What do you think's the reason for her sour mood?"

"Even though she tries to hide it, I think that pain in her stomach that she complains about may have gotten worse."

"Has she seen the doctor yet?"

Herman shook his head. "Stubborn woman still refuses to go."

"Would it help if I asked Sally's mamm, Dorothy, to speak to Aunt Catherine? She's got an easygoing way about her, and maybe she could convince Aunt Catherine to see the doctor."

Herman smiled and thumped Peter on the back. "That's the best idea you've had in weeks."

Peter turned on the diesel engine for their milking machine. "I'll talk to Dorothy about it when I go over to see Sally later this week."

Chapter 15

Allison climbed into Aaron's buggy and settled herself on the passenger's side. Even though she'd been with Aaron a few times, she'd never felt as nervous as she did right now. She glanced at him as he stepped in and took the seat beside her. Their gazes met, and the moment seemed awkward. Was Aaron nervous, too? Would this be the only time he would offer her a ride home, or might he repeat the invitation?

Aaron gave Allison a brief smile and picked up the reins. "Mind if I trot the horse once we get on the main road?"

She shook her head. "I don't mind at all. The breezy air might help cool us off."

"It has been a hot day," Aaron agreed. "We could use a good rain to lower the temperature some."

They pulled onto Highway C, and the buggy picked up speed

when Aaron gave his horse the signal to trot.

"Ah, that feels better," Allison said as the air lifted the strings of her kapp.

Aaron pointed to his trotting horse. "I think he's enjoying it, too."

Allison smiled. "How's your sister Emma doing since she came home from the hospital?"

"She's doing real well. We're all thankful they got her to the hospital before her appendix burst."

"That was a good thing. My youngest brother's appendix burst when he was a teenager. He was pretty sick for a spell."

"I guess the infection spreads quickly when someone's appendix bursts."

"That's what I understand."

"Do you miss Pennsylvania much?" Aaron asked, changing the subject.

"I miss Papa and my brothers." Allison figured it would be best not to mention that she didn't miss Aunt Catherine. Aaron might think she didn't appreciate her aunt stepping in to help after her mother had died.

"It won't be long before summer will be over, and then you'll be on your way home," Aaron said.

"I hope I'm ready to go by August."

Aaron tipped his head and quirked an eyebrow.

"If I can't sew or cook well enough, it'll be hard to go home and face my daed. The only reason he sent me here was so Aunt Mary could teach me how to be a woman."

Aaron's cheeks turned red and he looked away. "I'd say you're already a woman."

Allison felt the heat of a blush stain her cheeks as well. She might look like a woman on the outside, but she had a long way to go before she would be ready to take on the responsibility of becoming a wife. Even if she did manage to accomplish that task, she would need to find a man who'd be willing to marry her.

"Why would you have to come all this way so you could learn to cook and sew?" he asked. "Isn't there someone in your family who could have taught you the necessary skills?"

"My aunt Catherine, but she hasn't taught me much."

"How come?"

"I'm not really sure, but she acts like she doesn't want me in her kitchen."

"I guess some women are territorial when it comes to their kitchen."

Allison nodded. "Only thing is, it's not really *her* kitchen. She wouldn't even be living with us if my mamm hadn't died."

Aaron's forehead wrinkled. "I've been wondering something."

"What's that?"

"It's about James Esh."

"What about him?"

"As I'm sure you know, James hasn't been baptized or joined the church. Even though he's in his twenties, he's still running wild like some kid who's *ab im kopp*."

Allison felt a surge of guilt. She hadn't been baptized or joined the church yet, either. Did that mean she, too, was crazy? Her reluctance to join the church, however, wasn't because she was going through rumschpringe and wanted to experience things the modern world had to offer. It had more to do with her lack of faith in God. The truth was Allison didn't think it would be right for anyone to join the church when they felt so empty and faceless inside. Maybe James felt as faceless as she did and had acted wild and arrogant in order to hide behind his feelings.

They rode in silence the rest of the way home, and Allison was glad Aaron had dropped the subject of James. It made her uncomfortable to think about the way James had carried on at the gathering tonight. It had also convinced her that James wouldn't be a good choice for a boyfriend, even if there was a certain charm about him.

When they pulled into Uncle Ben's driveway, Aaron stopped the buggy and came around to help Allison down. She had planned to step out on her own, but before she could make a move, he put his hands around her waist and lifted her out of the buggy as if she weighed no more than a feather. He held her like that for several seconds, and Allison's heart pounded so hard it echoed in her ears.

"I heard that your uncle's going to rebuild his barn soon," Aaron said as he set Allison on the ground and took a step back.

Allison nodded. "I believe Uncle Ben plans to start sometime in the next few weeks."

"I imagine there'll be a work frolic then."

"Probably so."

"Most of the men in our community will be there to help." Aaron removed his straw hat and fanned his face with the brim. "Whew! Sure can't believe how hot it still is, even with the sun almost down."

"It will be hard to sleep tonight," she said, turning toward the house. "Maybe I'll sleep outside on the porch where it's not so stifling."

"You like sleeping outdoors?" Aaron asked as he strode up the path beside her.

"I do. My friend Sally and I used to sleep on her front porch when we were younger. It was great fun to listen to the music of the crickets while we lay awake visiting and watching for shooting stars."

Aaron leaned on the porch railing as Allison moved toward the door.

Should I invite him in for a glass of cold milk and some cookies? No, he might think I'm being too forward. Allison reached for the doorknob. "I appreciate the ride home, Aaron. Danki."

"You're welcome. Maybe we can do it again sometime."

"I'd like that."

Aaron shuffled his feet across the wooden planks. "Well, *gut nacht* then."

"Good night, Aaron." Allison shut the door and hurried up the stairs to her room, anxious to write Sally a letter.

As Aaron drove away, a vision of the moon shining down on Allison's pretty face stuck in his mind. He was attracted to her; there was no denying it. Would it be a mistake if he tried to pursue a relationship with her?

Aaron halted his thoughts when another horse and buggy passed him and the driver shouted, "Can't that old nag of yours go any faster than that? That poor critter must be half dead."

James. Aaron gritted his teeth and gripped the reins as he fought to keep from hollering something mean in return. It would only give James the satisfaction of knowing he'd been able to get Aaron riled.

Aaron kept his horse going at a steady pace as he watched James's buggy disappear over the next hill. He was probably in a hurry to get someplace, but it sure couldn't have been home, since James lived in the opposite direction.

He's probably heading for Seymour, Aaron thought. *Probably plans to hang out there until the wee hours of the morning.* He clicked his tongue to get his horse moving up the hill. *It's not my problem what James does or how he spends his time. I've got my own life to worry about.*

When Aaron descended the hill, he was surprised to see James's buggy pulled off to the shoulder of the road. "Guess you must have struck out with Allison, since you're headed for home so soon, huh?" James called.

Aaron ground his teeth together and kept going. *I won't give that ornery fellow the satisfaction of goading me into an argument.*

"That Allison, she's really something, isn't she?" James hollered as Aaron's rig went past.

Keep going. Don't look back. Don't give him what he wants. He's not worth it.

"Giddyup there, boy!" James whipped his horse and buggy past Aaron again. This time James just laughed and kept on going.

Aaron held his horse steady and felt relieved when he came to his driveway. At least he didn't have to put up with James's antagonizing anymore.

"Weren't you surprised when Aaron spoke up to my cousin like that tonight?" Katie asked Joseph as they headed down the road in his open buggy.

"I sure was," he said with a nod. "I didn't know my bruder could be so feisty."

"I think it's because he likes Allison."

Joseph looked over at Katie and raised his eyebrows. "What makes you think that?"

Katie gently nudged him in the ribs. "Think about it. Aaron did ask to give Allison a ride home tonight."

"True, but I believe he may have only asked her in order to get a rise out of James."

"Why would he do that?"

"Aaron and James have never gotten along well. From the time we were kinner, James has always thought he was stronger, smarter, and better looking than Aaron." Joseph grunted. "Of course, that arrogant fellow thinks he's better than anyone."

Katie sighed. "I hate to say it, but I have to agree. Ever since James and I were kinner he's been a show-off."

"Enough about James now." Joseph reached for her hand. "Let's talk about us, shall we?"

"What about us?"

"I love you, Katie," Joseph whispered against her ear. "Have ever since we were kinner."

Katie shivered as Joseph's warm breath tickled her neck. "I. . .I love you, too."

"Really?"

"I wouldn't have said so if I didn't."

"Enough to marry me?"

Katie's jaw dropped. She'd thought Joseph might have strong feelings for her, but she'd never expected a proposal of marriage—not so soon, anyway.

"You look surprised. Didn't you figure if I was declaring my love for you that a proposal would be next?"

She moistened her lips with the tip of her tongue. "Well, I—"

"What's wrong? Don't you want to marry me?"

"It's not that." She paused and drew in a quick breath.

"What's the problem?"

"The thing is. . ." How could she say this without hurting Joseph's feelings?

"The thing is what?"

"Well, we're so young, and—"

"We both know what we want, and we love each other. I don't see why our age should matter."

"Do you think our folks will agree with that?"

A light danced in Joseph's eyes as he looked at Katie. "When we tell 'em how much we love each other, I'm sure they'll understand and give us their blessing. After all, they were young and in love once, too."

She nodded. "I guess that's true."

"If our folks have no objections, will you agree to be my wife?"

She leaned her head against his shoulder. "Jah, Joseph. I'd be honored to marry you."

Chapter 16

Throughout the next several weeks, Allison kept busy helping her aunt and cousins in the garden, practicing her cooking skills, and making potholders and faceless dolls. Yet despite her busy days, thoughts of Aaron occupied her mind. She kept comparing him to James, wondering if Aaron might be right for her. She knew from the things James had said that he was interested in her. She wasn't sure about Aaron, though. Did he enjoy her company as much as she did his? It had seemed so when he'd brought her home from the last young people's gathering, but she didn't want to get her hopes up.

"Your sewing abilities have improved," Aunt Mary commented as she stepped up to the treadle machine where Allison worked on a dark green dress for a faceless doll.

Allison looked up and smiled. "I'd never be able to sew a

straight seam if you hadn't been willing to work with me."

Aunt Mary placed a gentle hand on Allison's shoulder. "You've been a good student."

"Do you think I'm ready to sell some of these at the farmers' market?" Allison motioned to the two dolls lying on the end of the sewing table.

"I believe so. Sarah and I plan to take some fresh produce to the market this Saturday. Would you like to share our table?"

"I think I would." Allison picked up one of the dolls and studied its faceless form. Every time she looked at one of these dolls, it reminded her that she felt faceless and would continue to feel that way until she figured out some way to get closer to God.

As though sensing Allison's troubled spirit, Aunt Mary pulled a chair over and sat down. "Is something bothering you? You look kind of sad today."

Tears welled in Allison's eyes, and she blinked, trying to dispel them. "Being with you and your family has made me realize there's something absent in my life."

"Are you missing your mamm? Is that the problem?"

"I don't remember her well enough to miss her, but I do miss *having* a mother."

"That's understandable. You've had your aunt Catherine through most of your growing-up years, and now you have me." Aunt Mary patted Allison's hand affectionately. "I'm here for you whenever you need anything or just want to talk. I hope you won't be too shy to ask."

Allison's throat clogged, making it difficult for her to speak. There were so many things she wanted to say—questions she wished to ask, things she would never feel comfortable discussing with Aunt Catherine. "I–I've never said this to anyone before," she began shakily, "but I feel faceless, just like these dolls."

"I'm afraid I don't understand. Why would you feel faceless?"

"I–I don't know God personally, the way you seem to." Allison swallowed hard. "Sometimes I feel so empty inside, like I'm all alone. It's as if my life has no real purpose."

"We're never alone, Allison. God is always there if we just look for Him. Jeremiah 29:13 says: 'And ye shall seek me, and find me, when ye shall search for me with all your heart.' "

Allison pursed her lips. "How can I seek God when I don't feel as if He knows me?"

"Jeremiah 1:5 says: 'Before I formed thee in the belly I knew thee; and before thou camest forth out of the womb I sanctified thee.' " Aunt Mary smiled. "Isn't it wonderful to know that God knew us even before we were born?"

Allison could only nod in reply, wondering why no one had ever told her this before. Had she not been listening during the times she'd been in church?

"God not only knew us before we were born," Aunt Mary went on to say, "but He loved us so much that He sent Jesus to die for our sins. By Christ's blood, God made a way for us to get to heaven. All we need to do is ask Him to forgive our sins and yield our lives to Him."

Allison had heard some of those things in church. She knew that Jesus was God's Son and had come to earth as a baby. When He grew up and became a man, He traveled around the country, teaching, preaching, and healing people of their diseases. Some men were jealous and plotted to have Jesus killed. She also knew the Bible made it clear that Jesus had died on a cross and was raised to life after three days. What she hadn't realized was that He had done it for the sins of the world—hers included.

She swallowed and drew in a shaky breath. "I. . .I sin every time I think or say something bad about Aunt Catherine. Even my anger toward God for taking my mamm away is a sin. He must be disappointed in me."

Aunt Mary shook her head. "God loves you, Allison. You're His child, and He wants you to come to Him." She took Allison's hand and gently squeezed her fingers. "Would you like to pray and ask God to forgive your sins? Would you like to invite Jesus into your heart right now?"

A shuddering sob escaped Allison's lips. "Jah, I surely would."

When Aaron's mother stepped into the harness shop, he looked up from the riveting machine. A strand of brown hair had come loose from her bun, and dark circles shadowed her eyes. She looked tired. Probably had spent another night helping Grandma Raber take care of Grandpa, whose arthritis seemed to be getting worse all the time.

"What brings you to the harness shop?" he asked. "Paul's not here. He went to town for some supplies."

"I know he did." Aaron's mother moved closer. "I was supposed to go over to Leah Swartz's this morning to work on a quilt with her and a couple other women. But since neither Grandma nor Grandpa are feeling well, I didn't want to leave Bessie alone to care for them and Emma, too."

"But Emma's doing better, isn't she?" Aaron knew his

mother didn't get away much anymore, and he figured it would do her good to spend the day with Gabe's mother and whoever else would attend the quilting bee.

"Jah, but Emma still tires easily, and I don't want her overdoing."

"Can't you take her with you?"

"I don't think she's up to a whole day out yet." Mom glanced around the room. "Since you have no customers at the moment, I was hoping you'd be free to run over to Leah's and let her know I won't be coming after all."

Aaron chewed on the inside of his cheek as he contemplated his mother's request. "Paul won't like it if he gets back from Seymour and finds the shop closed."

Mom pursed her lips. "I wish you'd quit calling him *Paul*. Ever since he and I got married, you've been calling him *Papa*. Why the change now?"

"Just doesn't feel right to be calling him *Papa* anymore. Especially since he's not my real *daed*."

"But he's been like a real *daed* to you, Aaron. I think it's rude and unkind of you to call him by his first name."

Aaron shrugged. "He doesn't seem to mind."

"Maybe he does and he's just not saying so."

"Can't we talk about something else?"

She nodded. "Let's get back to our discussion about you delivering my message to Leah."

"Can't you send Davey or Zachary?"

"I could, but they aren't home. Zachary's helping Joseph at the tree farm today, and Davey went fishing with Samuel Esh."

The mention of the name *Esh* set Aaron's teeth on edge.

Samuel was James's younger brother, and Aaron was concerned that the boy might follow in his unruly brother's footsteps. "Might not be a good idea for Davey to hang around Samuel," he said.

Mom's dark eyebrows drew together. "Why would you say something like that?"

"Samuel's brother James is nothing but trouble. If Samuel goes down the same path, he could lead Davey astray."

"For a boy of only fourteen, your youngest brother has a good head on his shoulders. I don't think he would be easily swayed, even if Samuel were to suggest they do something wrong."

"I hope you're right, but no one, not even my levelheaded little bruder, is exempt from trouble if it comes knocking at the right moment." Aaron felt so upset over the thought of Davey hanging around Samuel that he was tempted to chomp off the end of a fingernail. Instead, he reached for another hunk of leather and positioned it under the riveter.

Mom frowned. "You seem distressed, and I have a feeling it goes deeper than your concern for Davey."

"Maybe so."

"Would you like to talk about it?"

He shrugged.

"Does it involve Allison Troyer?"

"What?" Aaron nearly dropped the piece of leather, but he rescued it before it hit the floor. "Why would you think that?"

Mom pulled a wooden stool over to the machine and took a seat. "I heard that you escorted Allison home from the last young people's gathering."

"Joseph's a *blappermaul*," Aaron grumbled. "He ought to keep quiet about things that are none of his business."

"Your brother did mention what happened at the gathering, but that's no reason for you to call him a blabbermouth." She touched Aaron's shoulder. "You've been acting strange ever since Allison arrived in Webster County."

Aaron grunted.

"Are you planning to court Allison?"

"No way!" Aaron wasn't about to admit that the thought of courting Allison had crossed his mind.

"She seems like a nice girl, and since you've never had a steady girlfriend—"

"There wouldn't be much point in me courting Allison."

"Why not?"

"She'll be leaving at the end of summer."

"Maybe she will decide to stay."

He shrugged. "Even if she were to stay, I can't court her."

"Why not?"

"She might expect me to marry her someday." He shook his head. "I'm never getting married. Plain and simple."

Mom clucked her tongue. "You've been saying that ever since you were little, but I figured once you found the right girl you'd decide to settle down and start a family of your own."

"Nope."

"Mind if I ask why?"

Aaron did mind. He didn't want to talk about the one thing that had troubled him ever since his real dad had been killed. But he knew if he didn't offer some sort of explanation, Mom would keep plying him with questions.

"I. . .uh. . .haven't found anyone who'd be willing to work in the harness shop with me," he mumbled.

"There's a lot more to marriage than working side by side on harnesses." Mom's lips compressed. "Paul and I still have a good marriage, and I'm not helping in the shop anymore."

Aaron tried to focus on the piece of leather he'd been punching holes in, but it was hard to concentrate when Mom sat beside him, saying things he'd rather not hear.

"Does the idea of marriage scare you, Aaron? Is that why you're shying from it?"

He looked up and met his mother's penetrating gaze. Did she know what he was thinking? Could she sense his fear?

"Aaron, please share your thoughts with me."

His mouth went dry, and he swallowed a couple of times. "I. . .I'm scared of falling in love, getting married, and having my wife snatched away from me the way Dad was from you!"

Mom's mouth dropped open. "Oh, Aaron, I'm sorry we've never talked about this before. I can see by your pained expression that you're deeply disturbed."

Aaron was about to respond, but she rushed on. "Life is full of disappointments, but we have to take some risks. None of us can predict the future, for only God knows what's to come."

"If you had known Dad's buggy would be hit by a car and that you'd be left to raise four boys on your own, would you have married him?"

She nodded as tears filled her dark eyes. "I wouldn't give up a single moment of the time I had with your daed."

"You really mean that?"

"I do. And look how God has blessed me, despite my loss. I found a wonderful husband in Paul, and now besides my four terrific sons, I have two sweet daughters. As much as it hurt when I lost your daed, I've had the joy and privilege of finding love again."

"I. . .I see what you mean." Aaron gulped in a quick breath. "But how can I pursue a relationship with Allison when she's going home at the end of summer?"

"If you're meant to be together, then the distance between here and Pennsylvania won't keep you apart." Mom squeezed Aaron's shoulder. "As I said before, Allison might decide to remain here, or you may decide to relocate there. It's something you need to pray about, don't you think?"

Aaron nodded. Was it possible that he could set his fears aside and find the same kind of happiness Mom had found? Was Allison the woman he might find it with?

The minute Herman entered the house he knew his sister was in a foul mood. She stood in the middle of the room, holding a mop in one hand and wearing a frown on her face that could have stopped the clock on the kitchen wall from ticking.

"I hope you wiped your feet before you entered the house," Catherine growled. "Because if you didn't, then you can turn right around and head back outside." She pointed to the muddy boot prints marring the floor. "When Peter came in awhile ago, that's what he left behind."

Herman's face heated up. He was tempted to tell Catherine that she could get more bees with honey than vinegar but decided it was best to keep his tongue. "I'll be right back," he mumbled as he went out the door.

A few seconds later he returned, having left his boots on the back porch. "I came in to see if there's any coffee brewing," he said.

She gave a curt nod toward the stove. "Help yourself."

Herman tiptoed around the spot she was mopping and removed a mug from the cupboard. Then he poured himself some coffee, added a teaspoon of sugar, and took a drink. "Ugh! This coffee is way too strong! How many scoops did you put in?"

"If you don't like the way I brew coffee, then you ought to start making it yourself!"

He poured the rest of the coffee down the sink. "Guess maybe I'll do that from now on."

Catherine kept mopping. He could tell from the determined set of her jaw that she had no more to say on the subject.

"I thought after Allison left that there'd be less work for me to do, but I find instead that there's more," Catherine grumbled.

"Why would there be more?"

"Because you and Peter never wipe your feet or pick up after yourselves."

"I forget sometimes, but I'll try to do better."

"I shouldn't be expected to do all this work by myself, you know."

"Do you want me to ask Allison to come home?"

She shook her head. "She wasn't a lot of help anyway."

"Maybe that's because you didn't let her do much of anything."

Catherine opened her mouth to reply, but only a groan came out, and she doubled over.

Herman dashed across the room. "What's wrong? Have you got a crick in your back?"

She gritted her teeth and placed both hands against her stomach. "It's not my back; the pain's in my stomach."

He pulled out a chair and helped her over to the table. "I think it's time you see the doctor, don't you?"

She nodded slowly, as a deep frown marred her forehead. "I was planning to anyway. Sally's mamm came over the other day, and she talked me into making an appointment."

"Have you done that?"

"Not yet."

"How come?"

"Just haven't gotten around to it."

"Do you want me to make the appointment for you?"

"No, I'll do it today."

Herman breathed a sigh of relief. If Catherine got in to see the doctor, they would soon know the cause of her pain. He just prayed it was nothing serious.

Chapter 17

Allison had just placed her faceless dolls on the table she and Aunt Mary had set up at the farmers' market when she caught sight of Aaron heading her way. Her heart lurched. Would he be as happy to see her as she was to see him?

"I didn't know you were going to be here today," he said, stopping in front of the table and leaning on the edge of it.

"I didn't expect to see you, either. I figured you'd be working at the harness shop."

"I usually do work on Saturdays, but Paul said I could have the day off." Aaron grinned. "I can't figure out why, but lately he's been nicer to me."

"Maybe he appreciates all the hard work you did at the shop while he and your mamm were in Springfield during your sister's hospital stay."

"That could be." He glanced around. "Are you here alone?"

She shook her head. "Aunt Mary and Sarah are getting some produce and baked goods from the buggy. I'll be sharing this table with them."

Aaron picked up one of Allison's dolls. "Looks like you've been hard at work. This is real nice."

"It took me awhile, but I think I'm finally getting a feel for the treadle machine."

He nodded and placed the doll back on the table. "I would say so."

"Are you planning to sell anything today, or did you just come to look around?"

"Actually, I came to see Gabe. He's supposed to be selling some of his wooden items here today. Melinda will probably sell her drawings and maybe some of her grandpa's homemade jam."

"I didn't know Melinda was an artist," Allison said with interest. "With all her animals to care for, plus keeping house and cooking for a husband, I wonder how she finds the time to draw."

"Melinda makes time to do whatever she feels is important."

"Maybe she won't be able to do so much once the boppli is born."

Aaron chuckled. "Knowing Melinda, she'll try to do everything she's doing now, and then some."

"Aunt Mary's like that," Allison said. "She keeps busy all the time and is good at everything she does."

Aaron motioned to the faceless dolls. "Looks to me like you're able to do lots of things, too."

Allison shook her head. "I'm good at baseball, fishing, and

most outdoor chores; but my sewing skills are just average, and I still can't cook very well." She grimaced. "You should have tasted the buttermilk biscuits I made the other night. They were chewy like leather."

He snickered. "I doubt they were that bad."

"Let's just say nobody had seconds."

"Speaking of food, how would you like to go across the street with me at noon and have a juicy burger at the fast-food restaurant?"

"I'd like that." Allison couldn't get over how relaxed Aaron seemed to be. All the times she'd been with him before, he'd seemed kind of nervous and hesitant, like he might be holding back from something. The way he looked at her now made her feel like he really wanted to be with her.

"Guess I'll head over to Gabe's table now," he said. "I'll be back to pick you up for lunch a little before noon."

"I'll be right here."

As Aaron headed across the parking lot, he thought about his conversation with Allison. He couldn't get over how contented she looked this morning. He wondered if something had happened since he'd last seen her. Maybe she was just excited about being at the farmers' market and trying to sell some of her dolls.

Aaron spotted Gabe and Melinda's table on the other side of the open field. He jogged over to it and tapped his friend on the shoulder. "How's it going?"

Gabe nodded at his wife. "Why don't you ask her? She's the

one who's selling everything this morning."

Melinda smiled. "Most people have been buying Grandpa's rhubarb-strawberry jam, but I have sold a couple of my drawings."

"At least you've got people coming over to your table," Aaron said.

"How come you're not working today?" Gabe asked.

"Paul gave me the day off, and since I knew you were planning to be at the market, I figured I'd come by and see you."

"Anything in particular you wanted to see me about?"

Aaron placed his hands on the table and leaned closer to Gabe. "I was wondering if I could hire you to do a job for me."

Gabe's eyebrows lifted. "What kind of job?"

"I need a dog run built for Rufus. He's not happy being tied up all the time, and if I let him run free, he chases Bessie's kittens."

"A dog on the loose can be a problem," Gabe agreed.

"You're right," Melinda put in. "Remember when Gabe built a dog run for my brother's dog? Jericho was chasing my animals all over the place, and he kept breaking free from his chain."

Aaron nodded. "Gabe did a good job, which is why I want him to build a run for Rufus. I'll pay whatever it costs."

"Sorry, but you can't hire me," Gabe said.

"How come? Are you too busy at your shop?"

"You're my good friend, Aaron. I'll gladly build the dog run as a favor, with no money involved."

"That's real nice of you. I'll pay for all the supplies, of course."

"Sounds fine. When do you want me to start?"

"Whenever you have the time. There's no rush, but the

sooner I get Rufus in his own run, the sooner Bessie will quit bugging me."

Gabe chuckled. "I'll come over and talk about where the run should be built some evening after work. How's that sound?"

"Sounds fine to me." Aaron rubbed his clean-shaven chin. "Say, I've got an idea. Why don't you and Melinda join Allison and me for some fishing at Rabers' pond one night next week? If you drop by my place before we go, I can show you where I was thinking the dog run could be built."

"I think that would be fun," Melinda said. "I love going to the pond, where there's so much wildlife. It will give me a chance to get to know Allison better, too."

Aaron smiled. "I still need to ask Allison, but I'm hoping she'll say yes."

Allison sat in a booth at the restaurant, with Aaron in the seat across from her. They both had double cheeseburgers and an order of fries. This felt like a real date, and she couldn't seem to calm her racing heart. Was it her imagination, or did the look of admiration on Aaron's face mean he was beginning to care for her? Maybe he didn't mind that she was a tomboy. She hoped that was the case. And she hoped. . . . What was she hoping for—that she could stay in Webster County and be courted by Aaron? After that first young people's gathering when James had brought her home and then stolen a kiss, she'd thought he might ask to court her. She was glad he hadn't. She'd been so flattered by his attention, she might have said yes. After hearing all the negative things others had said about James, she knew he wasn't the sort of fellow she would want to court her.

It's strange, she thought. *James hasn't been around lately.* The last time Allison had seen him was at their preaching service a few weeks ago, but she hadn't had a chance to speak with him, and he'd hightailed it out of there as soon as the service was over.

Allison bit into another fry and tried to imagine what it would be like if she and Aaron were married. *Would he be willing to teach me how to work in the harness shop? I'll never find out if Aaron and I can have a future together if I go back to Pennsylvania at the end of summer. If Aaron asked me to stay, I'd write Papa a letter and see what he thought of the idea.*

"There's something about you that looks different today," Aaron said, breaking into Allison's thoughts.

She smiled. "Actually, I am different, and for the first time in my life, I feel carefree and happy."

"In what way?"

"I accepted Jesus as my Savior last week."

His forehead wrinkled. "You've never done that before?"

She shook her head. "I'd heard some of our ministers talk about how Jesus had been crucified on the cross, but until Aunt Mary explained things to me, I didn't realize He had died for my sins."

"I suppose there might be some in our community who don't understand about having a personal relationship with Christ," Aaron said. "But my mamm started reading the Bible to me, my brothers, and sisters as soon as we were old enough to comprehend things. I confessed my sins when I was fifteen and joined the church by the time I was eighteen." He reached for his glass of root beer. "Of course, that doesn't mean I'm the perfect Christian. I've had my share of problems along the way."

"I doubt there's anyone in this world who hasn't had problems," Allison said. "But with God's help, I feel like I'll be able to deal with anything that comes my way."

He smiled. "That's where Bible reading and prayer come in. I'm trying to remember to do both every day."

"Me, too. As Aunt Mary says, 'It's the only way to stay close to God.' " She blotted her lips with the paper napkin. "I used to feel like the dolls I make—faceless and without a purpose. Now that I know God in a personal way, I think my purpose in life is to share His love through my actions as well as my words."

It seemed as though Aaron wanted to say something more, but they were interrupted when Gabe and Melinda walked up to their table.

"It looks like you two are about done eating," Gabe said, thumping Aaron on the shoulder.

"Just about."

"Mind if we join you?"

Aaron looked over at Allison as if he was waiting for her approval. When she nodded and slid over, he said, "Sure, have a seat."

Melinda slipped in beside Allison, and Gabe plunked down next to Aaron. "What'd Allison say about going fishing?" he asked, reaching over and grabbing one of Aaron's fries.

Aaron's ears turned red. "I. . .uh. . .haven't asked her yet."

"The fellows want to take us fishing some evening this week," Melinda said before either Aaron or Gabe could explain. "I hope you can go, because I'd like the chance to get better acquainted with you."

"I plan to take my canoe along," Aaron said quickly. "Haven't had the chance to use it yet this summer."

Allison smiled. "That sounds like fun. Jah, I'd like to go."

"Mama, there's something I need to talk to you about," Katie said as she and her mother stood at their kitchen counter, rolling out pie dough.

"What's that, daughter?"

Katie moistened her lips with the tip of her tongue, wondering how best she could say what was on her mind. "Well, uh—"

"*Raus mitt*," her mother said. "If there's something on your mind, then just out with it."

Katie drew in a quick breath to steady her nerves and plunged ahead. "The other night, when Joseph brought me home from the young people's gathering. . ."

"Joseph Zook?"

"Jah."

"I didn't realize he'd brought you home."

Katie nodded. "It's not the first time, either."

Mama's eyebrows lifted. "It's not?"

"No. We've. . .uh. . .been kind of courting here of late, and—"

"I see."

"And the thing is. . ." Katie paused for another quick breath.

"The other night Joseph asked if I would marry him, and I said—"

"I hope you said no!"

Katie swallowed a couple of times. "I love him, Mama, and he loves me."

Mama dropped the rolling pin and placed both hands on her hips. "Joseph Zook is a nice enough boy, and I have no problem with him courting you, but you're both too young to be thinking about marriage right now."

"But, Mama, I know several others who've gotten married when they were eighteen, and—"

Mama shook her head forcibly. "Besides the fact that you're both too young, Joseph only has a part-time job working at the Osborns' tree farm. How does he expect to support a wife and kinner when he's not working full-time?"

The tears Katie had been trying to hold back stung like wildfire. She knew her mother was right about Joseph needing a full-time job, but she didn't know what could be done about it. "Maybe I could speak to Joseph about finding a better job," she murmured. "If he did find one, then would you give us your blessing?"

"We'll have to see about that." Mama grabbed the rolling pin and pushed the pie dough back and forth really hard. She was obviously upset. Katie wondered if she should have brought up the subject of marrying Joseph at all.

She gripped her rolling pin tightly. *The next time Joseph and I are alone together, I'll see if he's willing to look for a better job.*

Chapter 18

Excitement welled in Allison's soul as Aaron and Gabe lifted the canoe from the back of the larger market wagon he'd driven to the pond. It would be fun to sit in the boat and fish in the deepest part of the pond rather than trying to do it from shore.

"Sure is a beautiful evening," Melinda commented.

Allison nodded.

Melinda spread a quilt on the ground and motioned Allison to come over. "Let's have a seat so we can visit while the men put the canoe in the water and get our fishing gear ready to use."

Allison dropped to the quilt, and Melinda did the same.

"Oh, look, there's a little squirrel over by that tree," Melinda said excitedly.

"You really like animals, don't you?"

"Jah, almost as much as I think Aaron likes you." Melinda winked at Allison.

"What?"

"I've seen the way he looks at you. Gabe told me that Aaron's decided to give up the nasty habit of biting his nails." Melinda grinned. "A change like that could only come about for one reason. He wants to impress someone. I'm guessing it's you."

The back of Allison's neck radiated with heat, and she knew it wasn't from the warmth of the evening sun. "Has Aaron told Gabe he has an interest in me?"

Melinda shrugged. "I don't know about that, but I do know Aaron has never shown much interest in any woman until you came along."

Allison shifted on the quilt, tucking her legs under her long blue dress. "Even if Aaron does care for me, I'll be leaving at the end of summer."

"You can always write to each other."

"I suppose, but it would be hard to develop a lasting relationship with me living in Pennsylvania and him living here."

"I guess that depends on how you feel about Aaron," Melinda said.

Allison felt the warmth on her neck spread quickly to her face. "I'd like to come by your place sometime and see all those animals you care for," she said, quickly changing the subject.

"I'd like that." Melinda grinned. "How about next Monday morning? Would you be free to come over then?"

Allison nodded. "Sounds good to me."

"Who's ready for the first canoe ride?" Gabe called, interrupting their conversation.

Allison shielded her eyes from the sun filtering through the trees and realized that the canoe was already in the water.

"Why don't you go ahead?" Melinda suggested. "I'd like to draw awhile, and Gabe can fish from shore while he keeps me company."

Since Allison had come to realize that Aaron didn't think it was unladylike for her to fish, she didn't need any coaxing. She scrambled to her feet and started for the pond.

"Wait a minute!" Melinda called. She rushed over to Allison and handed her a couple of large safety pins.

"What are these for?"

"To pin your skirt between your legs."

Allison tipped her head in question. "Why would I want to do that?"

"In case the canoe tips over and you end up going for a swim you hadn't planned on." Melinda smiled. "My aunt Susie, who recently got married and moved to an Amish community in Montana, showed me how to do that when we were young girls."

"I don't plan on moving around much in the canoe, so I doubt it will tip over."

"Even so, it never hurts to be prepared."

Allison shrugged and took the pins. She bent over and attached them to the inside of her dress, laughing as she did so.

Melinda snickered. "It's real fashionable, don't you think?"

"Jah, sure." Allison wondered what Aaron would think of her getup, but she decided not to worry about it and just try to have fun. She trotted off toward the pond, and when she reached the canoe, she took hold of Aaron's hand and stepped carefully in.

Aaron's gaze went to her safety-pinned skirt, but he never said a word. He just grabbed a paddle, hollered for Gabe to let go of the canoe, and propelled them toward the middle of the pond.

It had been hard for Aaron not to laugh when Allison got into the canoe with her dress pinned between her knees, but he wasn't about to say anything. She might take it wrong, and he didn't want to ruin their evening together.

When they reached the middle of the pond, they baited their hooks, cast their lines into the water, and sat in companionable silence. It was peaceful with the ripple of water lapping the sides of the canoe and the warble of birds serenading them from the nearby trees.

I could get used to being with Allison, Aaron thought as she leaned her head back and closed her eyes. *Can I really set my fears about marriage aside and try to build a relationship with her? I want to. I've never wanted anything so much or felt this happy being with anyone before. But she'll be leaving for Pennsylvania in a few months, and then what?*

Aaron cleared his throat, and Allison's eyes popped open. "What's wrong? Have you got a nibble?" she asked, glancing at the end of his pole.

"No. I wanted to ask you something."

"What is it?"

"I was wondering. . . ." Aaron fought the temptation to bite off a fingernail. Why did he feel so tongue-tied when all he wanted to do was ask her a simple question?

"What were you wondering?"

He drew in a deep breath for added courage. "I enjoy your company and would like to court you, Allison. I was hoping you might consider staying here longer instead of leaving in August like you'd planned."

Allison's eyes glowed with a look of happiness. "To tell you the truth, I had been thinking about writing my daed and asking if he would mind if I stayed here longer."

"You'd really consider doing that?"

"Jah. And I'm pleased that you want to court me, because I enjoy being with you." She smiled sweetly, and Aaron knew he wanted to kiss her.

He leaned toward her, and when the canoe rocked gently, he grabbed both sides, hoping to hold it steady. It finally settled, and he inched forward until his lips were inches from hers. He felt relief when Allison made no move to resist. Maybe she wanted the kiss as much as he did.

Aaron extended his arms and reached for Allison, but before he could get his hands around her waist, the boat rocked harder. He tried to steady it, but there wasn't time. In one quick movement, the canoe flipped over. *Splash!*—they plunged into the chilly water.

Aaron kicked his way to the top and panicked when saw no sign of Allison. He dove under, taking in a nose full of water, frantically searching for Allison. Where was she? Why hadn't she surfaced when he did? Could she have hit her head on a rock and been knocked unconscious? No, the water level was too deep in the middle of the pond. It wasn't likely that she could have gone under that far.

The water in the pond was murky, and Aaron couldn't see much at all. He surfaced again and gulped in a breath of air. Treading water, he scanned the area around the canoe, which was turned upside down and bobbing like a cork. "Allison! Where are you?"

He heard Melinda's terrified shouts from shore, and then water splashing. Aaron was relieved to see Gabe swimming toward him. "I can't find Allison! You've got to help me find her!"

Gabe had just reached the canoe when one side of it lifted, and Allison popped her head out. "What's all the yelling about?"

"Thank the Lord you're okay," Aaron hollered as relief flooded his soul. "I was afraid you had drowned."

She shook her head. "I had all the air I needed under the canoe."

"Do you know how to swim?" Gabe asked.

"Of course I do. I'm able to tread water, too."

Aaron held the edge of the canoe while Allison swam out. "Let's get this thing turned over," he called to Gabe.

Gabe grabbed hold, and they lifted it together. A few seconds later, the canoe was in an upright position.

"We'll hold it steady while you climb in," Aaron instructed, nodding at Allison.

"I might be safer out here," she said in a teasing voice. "Besides, the cool water feels kind of good."

"You'd better do as Aaron says," Gabe put in, "or we'll be here all day arguing with him."

"Okay, but please don't let go of the canoe. I've already had one drink of pond water, and it's all I need for the day."

Gabe steadied the canoe with both hands, while Aaron held on with one hand. The other hand he used to give Allison a boost. When she was safely inside, he handed her the paddle, which he'd found floating nearby. "Do you think you can row this slowly back to shore?" he asked.

"I'm sure I can, but what about you? And what about our fishing gear?"

Aaron glanced at the shadowy water. "I'm afraid it's at the bottom of the pond, but that's not important. I'm just relieved that you're all right."

"I'm glad you're okay, too."

"Gabe and I will swim alongside of you. I don't want to chance tipping the canoe again by me trying to climb in."

Allison looked like she might argue the point, but Gabe intervened once more. "Aaron's right. You'll do better on your own. We're both good swimmers; we can help steady the boat if you run into a problem."

"Okay." Allison grabbed the paddle and soon had the canoe gliding along.

Aaron was exhausted when they finally got to dry land, but he was thankful the accident had happened while they were in a small pond and not a larger body of water. He and Gabe steadied the canoe as Allison climbed out.

Melinda came running, eyes wide and mouth open. "That was so scary! I'm glad everyone's okay."

"Just sopping wet." Allison grabbed the edge of her dress and wrung out the excess water. "I must look a mess."

Aaron gazed at her as affection welled in his chest. Any other woman would have probably cried or complained about her plight, but not Allison. Her dress was completely soaked, and her hair had come loose from its bun, spilling from her white kapp, which hung down her back by the narrow strips of material tied under her chin. Yet she had been able to laugh about it. At that moment, Aaron knew he had fallen hopelessly in love with Allison Troyer.

Allison shivered as a chill ran through her body, but she didn't utter a word of complaint. Aaron had almost kissed her, and if the canoe hadn't capsized, she was sure he would have.

Melinda draped a quilt around Allison's shoulders. "I think we should go, Gabe," she said, glancing at her husband. "The three of you need to get out of those wet clothes."

"I'll be okay if I sit in the sun awhile," Allison argued.

"What sun?" Aaron pointed to the clouds overhead. "Looks like our sun is gone, and rain might be on the way."

"We can't get any wetter than we are," Gabe said with a chuckle.

"Except for me," Melinda reminded.

Gabe shook his head, sending a spray of water all over her navy blue dress. "Now everyone's wet."

Melinda planted both hands on her ever-widening hips and scowled at him, but Allison could see by the twinkle in Melinda's eyes that she wasn't really upset by her husband's antics. "Just for that, I'm going to yodel all the way home," Melinda announced.

"Go ahead. I'm not Grandpa Stutzman; I like it whenever you yodel."

"Well, see if you like this." Melinda cupped her hands around her mouth and let loose with a terrible shriek. "Oh-lee-oh-lee-oh-lee-de-tee!" She held the last note and made it go so high that Gabe covered his ears. Allison and Aaron did the same.

"Enough already! I'm sorry I got water on your dress," Gabe apologized.

Allison laughed, and Aaron reached for her hand. "Now that's true love, wouldn't you say?"

She gazed at his handsome face, still dripping with pond water. *What I'm feeling for you—that's true love.*

Chapter 19

On Saturday morning, Allison awoke to hammers pounding against wood and the deep murmur of men's voices. She climbed out of bed, rushed over to the window, and pulled the dark curtain aside. There were at least a dozen men in the yard, moving back and forth from the barn to the plywood-covered sawhorses where all their supplies were laid out. She'd almost forgotten this was the day they'd be tearing down Uncle Ben's rickety old barn. If everything went well, construction on the new barn would begin next week.

Allison thought about the previous night's discussion with Aunt Mary and Uncle Ben about the possibility of her staying with them longer than originally planned. She was pleased when they'd said they would be happy to have her stay as long as she wanted. After that, Allison had hurried to her room and written a letter to her father, asking if he would mind if she stayed awhile longer. She hoped he would have no objections.

Pulling her thoughts back to the present, Allison hurried to get washed and dressed. She knew Aunt Mary would need her more than ever today, as it would be the women's job to feed the men and see that they had plenty of water and snacks to sustain them throughout the day.

Allison entered the kitchen and found Aunt Mary and Sarah bustling around. "Sorry I'm late," she apologized. "Until I woke up to all that pounding, I'd forgotten the men would begin tearing down the old barn today."

Aunt Mary smiled. "That's all right. You're here now, and we can certainly use another pair of hands."

"What would you like me to do?"

"The menfolk have had their breakfast already, so after you eat, you can make a batch of gingerbread."

Allison wished she could do something that had nothing to do with food, but she nodded agreeably and headed for the refrigerator to get some milk.

"Want me to see if the mail's here yet?" Sarah asked her mother.

"That would be fine." Aunt Mary nodded at some envelopes lying on the table. "If the mailman hasn't come yet, please put those bills in the box for him to pick up."

Sarah grabbed the mail off the table and was almost to the door when Allison remembered the letter she'd written to her father.

"I've got a letter that needs to go out," she said. "Would you wait a minute while I run upstairs and get it?"

"Sure."

"Did you write your daed a letter?" Aunt Mary asked.

"Jah. I asked him if he'd mind if I stay on here longer, and I told him you said it would be okay."

Her aunt smiled. "I hope he agrees."

Allison nodded. "Me, too."

As Aaron pulled his buggy into the Kings' yard, he noticed Gabe's rig in front of him. They both pulled up to the hitching rail near the corral and unhooked their horses from the buggies.

"I was going to start work on Rufus's dog run today," Gabe said. "But I figured I was needed here more, tearing down the barn."

"That's okay. Rufus has waited this long, so a little longer won't matter." Aaron led his horse to the corral, and Gabe followed.

"From the looks of all the men milling around, I'd say every Amish shop in Webster County must be closed for the day," Gabe commented.

Aaron nodded. "Paul didn't think twice about closing the harness shop so we could both come here to work. He should be along shortly and so should my brothers."

Gabe pointed across the yard. "I think my daed's here already."

"Guess we'd better go see what jobs we're needed to do."

Sometime later, while Aaron was hauling a stack of wood

from the old barn to the pile across the yard, he spotted Allison heading that way. She smiled and waved, but since his hands were full, he could only nod and smile in response.

"I was wondering if you'd be here today," she said when she caught up to him.

"Wouldn't have missed it." He grinned at her. "I've been looking forward to seeing how you look in dry clothes."

Allison's cheeks turned crimson. "I did look pretty awful in those sopping clothes after our dunking in the pond, didn't I?"

He dropped the wood to the growing pile and chuckled. "Guess I didn't look so good myself."

"I wrote a letter to my daed last night," Allison said, changing the subject. "I asked if he would mind if I stayed here longer."

"How much longer are you thinking?"

"As long as Aunt Mary and Uncle Ben are willing to put up with me."

Aaron moved closer to her. "I'm glad to hear that. I hope your daed says you can stay indefinitely."

"We'll have to see about that." Allison motioned to what remained of the barn. "I wish I could help the menfolk tear the wood off the walls instead of serving them cold drinks and meals."

He chuckled and shook his head. "Why would someone as pretty as you want to get her hands all dirty?"

She thumped his arm playfully. "Are you teasing me?"

"Jah, I sure am." The truth was, Aaron was impressed with Allison's willingness to help the men, and if he had his way, she'd be working alongside of him today. He was fairly certain

Allison's uncle would never go for that. Except for Paul, most men he knew thought a woman's place was in the kitchen.

Allison released a sigh. "I suppose I should get back inside. I've got two loaves of gingerbread baking, and if I'm not careful, they'll be overdone."

"I'll look forward to sampling a piece," Aaron said as he moved toward the work site. Suddenly he turned back around. "Say, how would you like to go over to Katie Esh's place and pick strawberries with me one evening next week? Katie's mamm told my mamm that the berries are coming to an end. If we don't get them soon, they'll be gone."

"I'd like that. Katie had mentioned that idea to me several weeks ago, but I haven't been over there yet." Allison smiled. "I made plans to visit Melinda and see the animals she's taking care of on Monday morning, but I think the rest of my week is fairly free."

"I have a hunch you'll like seeing all her critters." Aaron reached under his straw hat and scratched the side of his head. "Guess I'd better ask Joseph to join us for the strawberry picking. He and Katie have begun courting, and this could be like a double date."

"That sounds good to me." Allison flashed him another smile and headed for the house.

Aaron started toward the old barn as he hummed a song the young people sometimes sang at their singings. He thought about the words and how they related to the way he felt about Allison. *"Every minute of the day I'm thinkin' 'bout you; and without you, life is just a crazy dream. Every breath I take I'm hopin' that you're hopin' that I'm hopin' you'll stay here with me."*

As Joseph headed to the work site, he spotted Katie coming around the corner of the house, and his heart skipped a beat. He loved her so much and wished they could be married this fall. But if he didn't find a better job soon, he saw no way he could adequately support a wife, much less any children they might be blessed with.

"I was hoping you'd be here today," she said breathlessly.

"I wouldn't have missed it for anything." He smiled. "It's not just the work that brought me here, either."

Katie's cheeks turned pink, and tears gathered in the corners of her eyes.

Joseph felt immediate concern. "What's wrong?"

"I—I talked to mamm the other night—about us wanting to get married."

Joseph's spine went rigid. The tears he saw in Katie's eyes probably meant things hadn't gone so well. "What'd your mamm say?"

"Besides the fact that she thinks we're too young, she doesn't feel that you're making enough money working at your part-time job to support a wife and family."

"What about your daed? What'd he have to say about this?"

Katie's chin quivered. "I talked to him this morning, and he agreed with Mama."

Joseph groaned. "As much as I hate to say this, I think your folks are right."

"Have you changed your mind about marrying me?"

"Of course not, but until I'm able to find a full-time job that pays a decent wage, I know I won't be ready for marriage."

Katie's gaze dropped to the ground. "I see."

"I hope it won't be long until I can find the right job, and as soon as I do, I'll speak to my folks about us getting married, and you can talk to yours again." He reached for her hand. "Doesn't that make sense to you?"

She lifted her gaze to meet his, and a few tears spilled over onto her cheeks. "Jah, it does."

Joseph motioned to the place where the old barn was being torn down. "In the meantime, I'd better get busy. If I don't, my daed will probably come looking for me."

She smiled shakily. "I'd best get into the kitchen and find out what I need to do as well."

"See you later, Katie." As Joseph walked away, he determined in his heart that he would find a full-time job as soon as possible.

When Herman entered the living room and found Catherine sprawled on the sofa, he felt immediate concern. "Are you hurting again, or just tired?" he asked, moving to stand beside her.

She stared up at him with a pinched expression. "I've just been lying here, thinking."

"About what?"

"About the appointment I had with the doctor earlier this week." Her eyelids fluttered. "What if this pain I've been having is something serious? What if—"

"Didn't you tell me the doctor said he didn't think it was serious?"

She nodded. "He thinks I've got irritable bowel syndrome, and that a change in my diet and some medication might help. Of course, he'll know more after I have some tests run and he gets the results."

Herman took a seat in the chair across from her. "We'll just have to pray it's nothing serious."

"Humph! A lot of good prayer has ever done me."

Herman was about to respond, when Peter stepped into the room. "Papa, are you coming back to the barn? I think Bossy's about to deliver her calf."

"I'd better go, Catherine," Herman said, rising to his feet. "We can talk more about this later."

Chapter 20

When Allison pulled her horse and buggy into the Swartzes' driveway on Monday morning, she was surprised to see so many empty animal cages stacked along the side of the barn. From what she'd heard about Melinda's animal shelter, she figured all the cages would be full.

She spotted Melinda and waved to her.

Melinda hurried out to meet Allison, just as Allison hitched the horse to the hitching rail.

"*Wie geht's?*" Allison asked.

"I'm doing well. How about you?"

"Real good." Allison smiled. "Guess what?"

"What?"

"I think I may be staying in Webster County longer than originally planned."

"That's wunderbaar." Melinda led the way as Allison took her horse to the corral. "How much longer will you be staying?"

"I'm not sure. Maybe indefinitely if my daed agrees to it."

"It would be nice if you could stay, but won't you miss your family back home?"

"I will miss my papa and my brothers, and of course my friend Sally Mast. But I've got family here, too, and I've made several new friends. I was really homesick when I first came here, but now I want to stay." Allison smiled. "Besides, I can go home for visits, and maybe Papa and my brothers can come visit here, too."

Melinda gave Allison a knowing look. "Does this decision to stay have anything to do with Aaron Zook?"

Allison's face heated up as she stared at the toes of her sneakers. "Jah."

"I thought so." Melinda squeezed Allison's shoulder. "You're in love with him, aren't you?"

"I do care for Aaron," Allison admitted, "but—but I'm not sure—"

Before Allison could finish her sentence, a ball of white fur darted in front of her and raced for the barn.

"There goes my cat, Snow," Melinda said with a laugh. "She's either after a mouse or is trying to get away from some other critter."

"Have you had the cat long, or is she one of your newer pets?"

"Oh, I've had Snow since my nineteenth birthday. She's kept things livened up for me ever since." Melinda motioned to the barn. "She's got a litter of kittens that are little characters, too."

Allison's interest was piqued. "Can I see them?"

"Jah, sure." Melinda led the way to the barn.

When Allison stepped inside, she spotted several kittens sleeping in a pile of straw. "They're so cute," she said, kneeling next to them.

Melinda dropped down beside her. "Would you like one?"

"You mean it?"

"Of course. I need to find good homes for them, and I'm guessing by the look on your face that you might like to have one."

"I've never had a pet before, and if Aunt Mary and Uncle Ben don't object, I'd love to have a kitten." Allison picked a gray and white one out of the litter and held it against her chest.

"I can't believe you've never had a pet of your own!"

"We've had a few barn cats to keep the mice down, but Aunt Catherine wouldn't allow me or my brothers to make pets out of them."

Melinda frowned. "That's a shame. I make pets out of almost any animal that comes into my care." She rose to her feet. "Speaking of which, would you like me to show you the rest of my menagerie?"

Allison nodded. That was, after all, why she'd come to see Melinda.

Herman fiddled with the edge of his straw hat as he waited for Catherine's doctor to give them the results of her tests. The solemn expression on the doctor's face indicated the news wasn't good.

"I'm sorry to have to tell you this, Catherine," Dr. Rawlings said, placing both hands on his desk, "but the results of your tests reveal that you have colon cancer, and it appears to be spreading."

Herman drew in a sharp breath, but Catherine just sat with a stoic expression.

"There are a couple of treatment options," the doctor said. "I'd like to go over them with you now."

"How long have I got to live?" Catherine's blunt question jolted Herman to the core.

"That all depends on how well your body responds to the treatment plan," Dr. Rawlings replied. "We'll want to start with surgery, and then add chemo, and maybe—"

"Can you guarantee that surgery, chemo, or anything else you have on that list of yours will make me well again?"

He shook his head. "There are no guarantees, but—"

"Then forget about the treatment plan."

The doctor blinked a couple of times. "What?"

"If there are no guarantees, then I'm not putting myself through any kind of treatment that will probably make me feel worse than I do now."

Herman placed his hand on Catherine's arm. "Think about what you're saying. Without treatment, you'll die."

"Humph! Seems to me like I'm going to die anyway."

"But if the treatment will extend your life, then—"

"*If* is a little word, and it sounds like my chances are little or none." Catherine compressed her lips, the way she always did when she was trying to make a point. "It's my life, and I'll live and die the way I choose."

"You should listen to your brother," the doctor put in. "I'm sure he's got your best interest at heart."

"Puh!" She waved a hand. "The only thing he's thinking about is who's going to look after his house and cook his meals once I'm dead and gone."

Herman's mouth dropped open. "That's not true, Catherine."

Dr. Rawlings looked at her steadily. "I'd like you to give serious consideration to what I've said."

She stalked out of the room.

"I'll talk to her," Herman said to the doctor. "See if I can't make her listen to reason."

The doctor nodded. "If your sister changes her mind, have her call my office for another appointment."

By the time Herman left the doctor's office, Catherine was already heading down the hall. "Wait up!" he called. "We need to talk about this."

She whirled around, her eyes flashing and her lips set in a determined line. "You're not going to talk me into going under the knife or taking any kind of treatment."

"But, Catherine. . ."

She shook her head vigorously. "And whatever you do, I don't want you telling Allison about this or bringing her home early on account of me. Is that clear?"

"I won't say anything now," he promised, "but if the time comes that I feel she's needed, I'll bring her home."

"She won't be needed." Catherine turned and rushed out the door.

"I'm glad we're finally getting to do this," Katie said as Allison climbed down from her uncle's buggy.

"Me, too. I love ripe, juicy strawberries, and Aunt Mary said if I bring enough home she'll teach me to make a strawberry pie."

"I'm sure there'll be plenty for that." Katie pointed to the garden, where clusters of fat strawberries grew in abundance. "I was surprised to see you drive in alone. I figured Aaron and Joseph would stop by your aunt and uncle's place on the way over and give you a ride."

Allison shook her head. "When I saw Aaron on Sunday, I told him I would drive myself, since I knew he'd be working at the harness shop until suppertime and Joseph would be doing the same at the Christmas tree farm." She glanced at the road in front of the Eshes' place. "I hope they get here soon."

Katie nodded and her cheeks turned pink. "I always look forward to spending time with Joseph, and I hope—" Her voice trailed off.

"What do you hope?"

"Oh, nothing." Katie shielded her eyes from the evening sun filtering through the trees. "We don't have to wait until the fellows arrive to start picking. I can run into the house and get some containers right now."

"That's fine with me," Allison replied. "The sooner I get started, the more berries I'll have to take home to Aunt Mary."

Katie nodded and hurried off.

Allison strolled around the edge of the garden, breathing in the pungent aroma of dill weed and feasting her eyes on the colorful vegetables growing among a few scattered weeds. All kinds of produce would soon be ready for harvest—long skinny pole beans, leafy green carrot tops, an abundance of plump tomatoes, and several kinds of squash.

She bent down and plucked a fat, red berry off the vine, then popped it into her mouth. "Umm. . .this is wunderbaar." She swished the juice around on her tongue, savoring the succulent sweetness and allowing it to trickle down her throat.

When Allison heard the screen door slam shut, she glanced up at the house. Katie stepped onto the back porch, holding two plastic containers. When she reached the berry patch, she handed one to Allison. "I see someone's been sampling the goods already; there's berry juice on your chin."

Allison rubbed the spot Katie had pointed to and laughed. "I'm guilty."

"Shall we start picking?"

"Sure." Allison knelt at the end of the first row, and Katie took the next row over.

"Maybe we can get our containers filled before Aaron and Joseph show up," Katie said.

Allison plucked off several berries and placed them in her container, being careful not to crush any. "Guess what?" she asked.

"What?"

"I went to visit Melinda Swartz Monday morning, and she gave me one of her cat's kittens."

"That was nice. I take it your aunt and uncle were okay with you bringing it home?"

Allison nodded. "They didn't have a problem with it at all."

"What'd you name the kitten?" Katie asked.

"Since it followed me around the whole time I was visiting Melinda, I decided to call it Shadow."

Katie smiled. "That sounds like an appropriate name."

They worked in silence for a time; then Allison said, "I haven't seen your cousin James lately. He wasn't at church last week, and he didn't come to help tear down Uncle Ben's barn on Saturday." James had been on Allison's mind ever since she'd made things right with God. He seemed angry and brash, thinking only of himself. Since God could change anyone's heart, and she knew it wasn't His will that any should perish, she hoped James might find the same peace in his heart as she'd found by accepting Jesus as her Savior.

"James doesn't care much for church these days, and he doesn't worry about helping anyone." Katie wrinkled her nose. "He probably drove that fancy car of his to Springfield for the day so he could have some fun."

"Maybe James is away on a trip or something. That might be why he hasn't been around."

"Could be. You never know what that fellow might be up to. It makes me sick to say this, but I wouldn't be surprised if he doesn't decide to jump the fence."

"You mean, 'go English'?"

Katie nodded.

Allison looked up when she heard horse's hooves clomping against the pavement. She hoped it was Aaron and Joseph. Sure enough, Aaron's buggy slowed. They were just turning up the driveway.

"They're here!" Katie scrambled to her feet and rushed over to the hitching rail near her father's barn. Allison followed, her heart hammering with excitement. She hoped what she felt for Aaron wasn't just a silly crush. She hoped she hadn't misinterpreted his feelings for her.

"Sorry we're late," Aaron apologized as he and Joseph jumped down from the buggy. "Paul and I had a harness that needed to be fixed while the customer waited, and that made us late for supper."

"It's okay. You're here now." Katie gave Joseph a deep-dimpled smile.

"Would you rather I hitch my horse to the rail or put him in the corral?" Aaron asked her.

"Whatever you want is fine. My daed's still out in the fields with my brother Elam, so none of the workhorses are in the corral yet."

"We'll meet you in the garden when we get the horse unhitched," Joseph said.

Aaron waved his brother aside. "You go on ahead. I don't need any help."

"Let's go then." Joseph reached for Katie's hand, and Allison followed as the happy couple hurried toward the berry patch.

Soon Katie and Joseph were on their knees together, and Allison returned to the spot where she'd been working. Rhythmically, she picked one berry after another, but her thoughts were on Aaron. She glanced up every once in a while, wondering what was taking him so long.

Several minutes later, Aaron finally showed up. His straw hat was tipped way back on his head, and his face was red and sweaty.

"What happened?" she asked as he knelt beside her. "You look like you've been running."

"Something spooked my horse, and he pulled away from me. I

had to chase him down before I could get him into the corral."

Since the barn was out of sight of the garden, Allison hadn't heard or seen the incident, but she imagined it must have looked pretty funny. She held back the laughter bubbling in her throat and pointed to her half-full bucket of berries. "You can help fill mine if you want. When it's full, we can get another container for you to take home."

"Sounds good." Aaron wiped his forehead with his shirtsleeve and started picking.

During the next hour, they cleaned out most of the ripe berries. When they were done, they sat in wicker chairs on the back porch, drinking cold milk and eating the brownies Katie's mother had made.

As the sun began to set, Allison stood and smoothed the wrinkles in her dress. "Guess I'd better be going. Uncle Ben and Aunt Mary will worry if I'm out after dark."

Aaron jumped up. "I've got an idea. Why don't I drive you home in your buggy, and Joseph can take our rig?"

"How will you get home once you've dropped me off?" she questioned.

Aaron rubbed the bridge of his nose as he contemplated the problem.

"I know how we can make it work," Joseph spoke up. "I'll stay and visit with Katie awhile, and that'll give you a chance to take Allison home. When I'm ready to head out, I'll swing by the Kings' place and pick you up."

"That's fine by me." Aaron glanced at Allison. "Are you okay with it?"

She nodded. "Of course."

The breeze hitting Allison's face as they traveled in the buggy helped her cool off, but when Aaron guided the horse to a wide spot alongside the road and slipped his arm across her shoulders, her face heated up.

He grinned at her. "I hope you don't mind that I stopped, but it's hard to talk with the wind in our faces and the horse snorting the way he does. It's not very romantic, either."

Allison smiled. "I don't mind stopping."

"I really enjoy being with you," Aaron said, leaning closer. He smelled good, like ripe strawberries and fresh wind.

She opened her mouth to reply, but his lips touched hers before she could get a word out. The kiss was gentle yet firm, and Allison slipped her hands around Aaron's neck as she leaned into him, enjoying the pleasant moment they shared.

The *clomp-clomp* of horse's hooves, followed by a horn honking, broke the spell, and she reluctantly pulled away. "I think a buggy and a car must be coming."

Aaron nodded and reached for her hand. "Just sit tight and let 'em pass."

As the two vehicles drew closer, Allison's mouth dropped open. The horse was trotting fast in one lane, and the car, going the same way, sped along in the other lane.

"That car is attempting to pass, but the *mupsich* fellow in the buggy is trying to race him," Aaron said with a shake of his head.

Allison sat, too stunned to say a word. She could hardly

believe the buggy driver would try to keep up with a car. It really did make him look stupid.

"I should have known. That's James Esh in his fancy rig," Aaron mumbled. "He hasn't got a lick of sense."

The buggy raced past them so quickly, Allison felt a chilly breeze. Suddenly, the horse whinnied, reared up, and swerved into the side of the car.

Chapter 21

Allison gasped as she watched James's buggy careen into the car, bounce away, swerve back and forth, and finally flip over on its side. The panicked horse broke free and tore off down the road, and James flew out of the buggy, landing in the ditch.

The car screeched to a stop, the Englisher jumped out, and Allison and Aaron hopped down from the buggy. "I didn't hit that fellow on purpose," the middle-aged man said in a trembling voice. "He was trying to keep me from passing and kept swerving all over the road." He raked shaky fingers through his thinning brown hair and winced as his gaze came to rest on James, who lay motionless in a twisted position.

From where Allison stood, she couldn't see the extent of James's injuries. As the man and Aaron rushed over to him, she could only stand, too dazed to move. She saw the English man bend down and touch the side of James's neck; then he reached into his shirt pocket and pulled out a cell phone. Aaron's lips moved, but she wasn't able to make out his words.

Taking short, quick breaths, Allison leaned against her buggy. Her heart pounded wildly as a vision from the past threatened to suffocate her. . . .

"Mama!" Allison gasped as she watched a car slam into her mother's buggy, thrusting it to the middle of the road before it toppled on its side with a sickening clatter.

"Mama! Mama!" Allison rushed into the road, but someone—maybe the English man who'd driven the car—pushed her aside. She swallowed against the bitter taste of fear in her mouth. "Oh, Mama, please don't die. You've got to be all right!"

Allison struggled to bring her thoughts back to the present and had to lean over and place both hands on her knees in order to slow the rate of her heartbeat. "I remember," she murmured. "I remember seeing Mama's accident on that hot summer day when she pulled out of our driveway."

She glanced over at James and saw that the lower part of his body had been covered with a quilt. Aaron must have taken it from the back of the buggy without her realizing it.

When Aaron and the English man joined Allison, she noticed that Aaron stood in such a way that her view of James was blocked. She wondered if Aaron was trying to shield her from seeing the extent of James's injuries.

"Is. . .is he dead?" Allison's voice was little more than a

gravelly croak, and the moisture on her cheeks dribbled all the way to her chin.

"There's a faint pulse, but it doesn't look good," the English man answered before Aaron could reply. "I've called 911 on my cell phone, and an ambulance is on its way."

"I. . .I need to see James. There's something I must tell him." Allison stepped around Aaron, but he grabbed her arm.

"He doesn't seem to be conscious, and there's really nothing we can do but wait for help to arrive."

"Shouldn't we get him up off the ground?"

"That's not a good idea," the English man said with a shake of his head. "He's likely got internal injuries, and from the looks of his left leg, I'd say he has at least one broken bone."

Allison swallowed around the lump in her throat. "I have to talk to James."

Aaron shook his head. "You don't want to go over there, believe me. He's been seriously injured, and—"

"And it's not a pretty sight," the Englisher interrupted. "You'd better listen and wait in the buggy."

"No, I won't! I can't!" Allison pulled away from Aaron's grasp.

"Then let me go with you," he offered.

"I'd rather do this alone." Without waiting for Aaron's reply, she rushed over to James and knelt beside his mangled body. Her heart lurched at the sight of his head, twisted awkwardly to one side and covered in blood. His left leg was bent at an odd, distorted angle, and his arms were scraped and bleeding.

"James. Can you hear me?"

There was no response—no indication that he was even alive.

Heavenly Father, Allison prayed, *help me get through to him. Please don't let it be too late for James.* With her eyes closed, Allison quoted Jeremiah 29:13, the same verse that Aunt Mary had shared with her. " 'And ye shall seek me, and find me, when ye shall search for me with all your heart.' "

Allison heard a muffled moan, and her eyes popped open. James's eyes were barely slits, but at least they were open. She hoped he could see her.

"James, have you ever asked God to forgive your sins? Have you accepted Jesus as your personal Savior?" she whispered, leaning close to his ear.

His only response was another weak moan.

She laid a gentle hand on James's chest. It was the only place on his body where there was no blood showing. "If you can hear me, James, blink your eyes once."

His eyelids closed then opened slowly again.

"I'm going to pray with you now. If you believe the words I say, then repeat them in your mind."

James closed his eyes, but the slight rise and fall of his chest let Allison know he was still breathing.

"Dear Lord," she prayed, "I know I'm a sinner, and I ask Your forgiveness for the wrongs I have done. I believe Jesus died for my sins, and that His blood saves me now."

When Allison finished the prayer, James opened his eyes and blinked once. Had she gotten through to him? Had he sought forgiveness for his sins and yielded his life to the Lord?

Sirens blared in the distance, but Allison felt a strange sense of peace. She had done all she could for the man who lay before her. James's life was in God's hands.

As Herman sat on a bale of straw inside his barn, confusing thoughts swirled in his brain like a raging tornado. Catherine had cancer but refused any kind of treatment. Short of a miracle, she was going to die. She didn't want Allison to come home.

He let his head fall forward into his open palms. *Why, God? Why? I know Catherine hasn't been the best sister or even such a good aunt to my kinner. But she's always seen that we had meals on the table and kept the house clean, organized, and running smoothly so I could be about my dairy business. Even though my sister and I don't always see eye to eye on things, I don't want her to die.*

"Papa, what's wrong?"

Herman jumped at the sound of Peter's voice. He looked up and slowly shook his head. "I took your aunt Catherine to see the doctor again today. He gave us some bad news."

"What kind of bad news?"

"Your aunt's got colon cancer."

Peter's face blanched. "Ach, no!"

"The doctor says it's spreading to other parts of her body." Herman's voice shook with emotion. "The worst of it is she refuses to take any kind of treatment."

"But that's lecherich! Even if treatment won't cure her cancer, I'm sure it can give her more time."

Herman nodded. "That's what I believe, too. Even though we both think your aunt's decision is ridiculous, unless we can get her to change her mind, I'm afraid we'll have to abide by her wishes."

Peter sank to the bale of straw beside Herman. "Does anyone

else in the family know about this yet?"

"So far, just you and me." Herman released a shuddering sigh. "I'll tell your brothers and their wives about it sometime this week, but I'm not sure what to do about Allison."

"What do you mean?"

"My stubborn sister doesn't want Allison to know."

"Why not?"

Herman shrugged. "I don't know. She wouldn't say; just insisted I not tell Allison or ask that she come home."

"Isn't Aunt Catherine going to need some help? I mean, with her not feeling well, and—"

"There'll come a time when she won't be able to do much at all. I'm hoping that won't happen until after Allison returns home."

"So you're not going to tell her about Aunt Catherine's diagnosis?"

Herman shook his head. "Not yet, but I will when it becomes necessary."

"I guess all we can do right now is pray," Peter said. "Pray that Aunt Catherine comes to her senses and agrees to take whatever treatment the doctor thinks she should have."

Herman nodded. "Prayer is all we have right now."

As Aaron watched Allison kneeling beside James's wounded body, a pang of jealousy crept into his soul. Only moments ago, she and Aaron had been kissing. Now she was at James's side, whispering in his ear.

I feel bad for the poor fellow and hate being a witness to such a terrible accident. Even though I've never cared much for James, I find no pleasure in him getting hurt or possibly dying. Aaron hoped James's injuries weren't life threatening and had even been praying on his behalf. Yet he couldn't set his feelings of rejection aside as he witnessed Allison bent over James. She obviously had strong feelings for the man.

Aaron gritted his teeth. *If it were me lying there hurt, would she care so much?* He was tempted to move closer so he could hear what she was saying, but that might make things worse. If Allison did love James, she would probably see Aaron's coming over as interference. She needed this time to express her feelings and possibly say her last good-byes. No, Aaron would not disturb their time together, no matter how much he wanted to know what was being said.

Blaring sirens drove his thoughts aside, and he felt relief when the ambulance and a police car approached the scene of the accident. Two paramedics rushed over to James, while a policeman headed for the English man, waiting beside his car.

Aaron stepped forward, knowing he'd been a witness to the crash and needed to tell the police everything he'd seen.

Just before Aaron approached the uniformed officer, he glanced over his shoulder. The paramedics had lifted James onto a stretcher, and Allison followed as they headed for the ambulance. Was she planning to go with them to the hospital?

Aaron squeezed his eyes shut. *Lord, please be with James, and if Allison's in love with James, then give me the strength to let her go.*

Chapter 22

Allison drew in a deep breath and tried to steady her nerves. Today was the day the men in the community had originally planned to build Uncle Ben's new barn. Instead, they stood at the cemetery, saying good-bye to James Esh. The barn raising would have to wait another week or so.

Allison was confident that James had heard the prayer she'd offered on his behalf, but she grieved for his family. It didn't seem right that a young man in the prime of his life had been killed in such a senseless, tragic accident.

She pitied Clarence and Vera Esh. James was the only one of their children who had never been baptized and joined the Amish church. Allison hoped for the chance to speak with James's parents later on and explain how she'd been able to pray with their son. It might offer some measure of comfort if they knew James had been given the opportunity to make things right with God before he died.

Allison glanced at her friend Katie, who stood with her folks next to James's family. Katie's eyes were downcast, as were the rest of the family's. Vera Esh leaned her head on her husband's shoulder and trembled with obvious grief.

Allison felt moisture on her cheek and realized that she, too, was crying. She knew it was partly in sympathy for James's family, but she also grieved for her mother's passing. It had been hard to witness James's tragic accident, and remembering the crash that had taken her mother's life was nearly Allison's undoing. Even now, as she tried to focus on the verses of scripture Bishop Frey quoted, she could picture Mama lying in the road after being tossed from her buggy when the car had smashed into it. There'd been no chance for good-byes, no opportunity to touch her dear mama one last time. Allison's brothers Ezra and Gerald had insisted that she and Peter go up to the house while Papa waited with Mama until the ambulance arrived. Peter went willingly, but Allison remembered sobbing and begging to stay. Ezra had threatened to carry her if she didn't cooperate, so Allison had remained in the house all afternoon, waiting for some word on her mother's condition. Papa and her other brothers, Darin and Milton, hadn't returned from the hospital until that evening, bringing the grim news that Mama had passed away. That's when Allison's world had fallen apart, and then her memory of the accident had completely shut down.

With a determination to leave the past behind, Allison's gaze went to Aaron, standing between Joseph and Zachary, looking very somber. Allison hoped Aaron would look her way so she could offer a nod of encouragement, but the one time he glanced in her direction, he frowned and looked quickly away.

Ever since the evening of James's accident, Aaron had seemed distant toward Allison, and she didn't know why. She hadn't been allowed to accompany James to the hospital, since she wasn't a family member. Also, the police had wanted to ask her about the things she had witnessed. So Allison, Aaron, and the English man who'd driven the vehicle that collided with James's buggy had taken seats in the police car to answer questions, while James had been rushed to Springfield. It wasn't until the following morning that Allison learned James had died en route to the hospital.

Allison hadn't realized at first that Aaron was acting differently toward her. He'd only said a few words and seemed almost as if he were in daze when she'd joined him in the police car for questioning. She'd thought he was upset over witnessing the horrible crash. But then Joseph showed up, and Aaron suggested his brother take Allison home while he drove over to James's house to tell his parents what had happened. Later, when Aaron came back to Uncle Ben and Aunt Mary's to pick up Joseph, Allison had hoped they could talk. However, Aaron had said he and his brother needed to get home, and they'd left in a hurry. Aaron didn't come around the rest of the week.

Allison squeezed her eyes shut as a silent prayer floated through her mind. *What's gone wrong between Aaron and me? Lord, please give me the opportunity to speak with Aaron today. If it's Your will for us to be a couple, then make things right between us again.*

Another thought popped into Allison's mind. Maybe Aaron wasn't upset with her at all. He might be grieving over James's death and feeling guilty for the unkind words he'd said about

James when he was alive. Not that those things weren't true. Allison had seen for herself how wild James was, and she'd never doubted anything Aaron had said. Still, she knew it wasn't right to talk about someone behind his back. If Aaron felt guilty, that might be the reason for his distant attitude. She prayed that was all there was to it and hoped she would have a chance to speak with Aaron after the funeral dinner. If there was any possibility of them having a permanent relationship, they needed to clear the air.

Aaron tried to concentrate on the words of Bishop Frey, who stood at the head of James's casket. But it was hard not to think about Allison and how their relationship had crumbled on the night of James's death. Aaron had thought they were drawing closer and that she might be falling in love with him. But when he'd seen her reaction to the accident, heard the panic in her voice when she insisted on seeing James, and watched her bend over James's body as though she was his girlfriend, he'd been hit with the realization that Allison had deep feelings for James.

Aaron clenched his fingers as he held his hands rigidly at his sides. *That's what I get for allowing myself to fall in love with her. It was stupid to think Allison might become my wife someday. I wish I'd never gone anywhere with her now.* He swallowed around the lump in his throat as a sense of despair crept into his soul, pushing cracks of doubt that threatened his confidence and caused the notion that he'd finally found the perfect woman for him to crumble. *From now on, I'm going to concentrate on my work and forget about Allison loving me, for it's obviously not meant to be. Even if Allison chose to be with me now, I'd be her second choice.*

Aaron turned his thoughts to the harness shop. He'd had a disagreement with his stepfather yesterday morning. Paul had said Aaron was careless and sometimes seemed lazy. Aaron had become angry and reminded Paul that he wasn't his real father and didn't have the right to tell him what to do.

I shouldn't have lost my temper like that, Aaron berated himself. *Paul's a good man, and I know he loves my mamm. I'm sure he cares about everyone in the family—including me. I should have apologized right away, and I'll need to do that when we get home. Life's too short to allow hard feelings to come between family members.*

Aaron pulled his thoughts aside and concentrated on the bishop's final words. It wasn't right that he'd let his mind wander during the graveside service. No matter how much of a scoundrel James Esh had been, he'd passed from this world into the next and deserved everyone's respect during the last phase of his funeral.

Allison kept busy during the funeral dinner, which was held at Clarence and Vera Esh's house. She helped the women serve the meal and clean up afterward, and was pleased to see that all the strawberry pies she and Aunt Mary had made had been eaten. By the time the last dish was put away, some people had already headed for home. Allison hoped Aaron and his family were not among those that had gone already.

Allison stepped onto the front porch and scanned the yard.

Some of the older men sat in chairs under a leafy maple tree, a group of children played nearby, and several women had gathered in another area to visit. There was no sign of Aaron or anyone from his family, though. Maybe he was in the barn.

Allison headed that way, kicking up dust with each step she took. It had been a humid, hot summer, and they needed rain. Inside the barn, she spotted Joseph and Katie sitting on a bale of straw next to Gabe and Melinda. She hurried over and tapped Joseph on the shoulder. "Is Aaron still here? I need to speak with him."

Joseph shook his head. "Sorry, but he left when our folks did. Grandpa and Grandma Raber were tired and needed to get home. I guess Aaron didn't feel like hanging around because he followed them in his buggy. Emma, Bessie, and Zachary rode with him. Davey and I are the only ones from our family still here."

Allison felt a keen sense of disappointment. "I plan to take some of my faceless dolls to the gift shop at the bed-and-breakfast in Seymour on Monday morning," she said. "Maybe I'll drop by the harness shop and speak to him on my way into town."

"I'm sure Aaron will be glad to see you," Joseph replied.

Allison nodded, but she wasn't so sure he would be pleased to see her. She was prepared to exit the barn when Katie said, "How's Shadow doing?"

"Fine. He seems right at home in Uncle Ben's barn."

"That's probably because there are plenty of mice for him to chase," Gabe said with a snicker.

"Won't you sit and visit awhile?" Melinda asked, patting the bale of straw.

"I'd better not," Allison replied. "Aunt Mary and the rest of the family will be ready to leave soon, and I don't want to keep them waiting."

"Gabe and I would like to get together with you and Aaron and go fishing again." Melinda rubbed her protruding stomach and glanced over at Katie. "Maybe you and Joseph can join us."

Katie and Joseph nodded, but Allison shrugged and said, "I'll have to wait and see. Right now I need to speak with Clarence and Vera Esh."

Joseph watched Katie out of the corner of his eye. He sensed that she wanted to speak with him alone, but Melinda seemed to be monopolizing the conversation.

"You should have seen how excited Allison was when I gave her that kitten," Melinda said with an enthusiastic nod. "She said she'd never had a pet before."

"She could have taken her pick of any critter at our place." Gabe nudged Melinda with his elbow. "Why didn't you pawn a few other animals off on Allison that day?"

She nudged him right back. "Very funny."

Katie cleared her throat. "I don't mean to be rude, but I need some fresh air, so I think I'll head outside and take a walk."

"That's fine," Melinda said. "We'll just sit here and visit with Joseph awhile."

Joseph jumped to his feet. "Actually, I think I could use a bit of fresh air, too."

Gabe gave him a knowing smile. "You go right ahead."

Joseph followed Katie to the barn door, and when they

stepped outside, he turned to her and said, "Should we take a walk down by the creek?"

"That'd be nice," she said with a nod. "Hopefully no one else is there right now."

They walked in silence until the water came into view, and Joseph was relieved to see that there wasn't a soul in sight. He motioned to a nearby log. "Should we take a seat?"

Katie sat down and released a sigh. "This has been such a trying day. I still can't get over the pitiful look on my aunt Vera's face during the graveside services."

Joseph nodded. "Losing a loved one is never easy, but I think it's especially hard for parents to lose a child."

She shuddered, and when she looked at Joseph, tears glistened in her eyes. "I can't imagine how it would be if I ever lost you."

"I wouldn't want to lose you, either." He reached for her hand. "I've been doing a lot of thinking in the past few days, and I've made a decision."

"What's that?"

"If the main reason your folks don't want you to marry me is because I don't have a good job, then I'm going to ask my daed if he'll hire me at the harness shop."

Katie's brows lifted high on her forehead. "But Aaron's worked there for several years. I thought the shop was supposed to be his someday. Isn't that what you told me once?"

"That's true," he agreed, "but Papa's got lots of work right now, so I'm sure he could use another pair of hands. And as far as who gets the shop—"

Joseph halted his words when his younger brother, Davey,

and Melinda's brother Isaiah showed up on the scene.

"What are you two doin' down here at the creek?" Davey asked.

"We're talking. What's it look like?"

Davey snickered. Isaiah did the same.

"Knock it off." Joseph hoped his little brother wasn't going to say or do something to embarrass him in front of Katie.

Isaiah picked up a flat rock and pitched it into the creek. "Sure is hot today. Makes me wish I could go swimmin' in this old creek."

"I don't suppose it would hurt if we went wading." Davey dropped to the ground and removed his shoes and socks. Then he rolled his pant legs up to the knees and plodded into the water.

Isaiah followed suit.

Joseph looked over at Katie and rolled his eyes.

"I guess I'd better get back to the house," she said, rising to her feet. "I should see how Aunt Vera and Uncle Clarence are doing."

"Jah, okay."

As Joseph and Katie walked away, he leaned close to her ear and whispered, "I'll be talking to my daed sometime this week, and I'll let you know what he has to say about me working for him."

Allison spotted James's folks standing under a maple tree, talking to one of their church ministers. She waited patiently until the minister moved away, then she hurried over to Vera and Clarence.

"Hello, Allison," Vera said. "I heard you were with our son when he died, and I was hoping for the chance to talk to you."

Allison nodded. "I'm not sure if James understood everything I said, but I did get the chance to speak with him before the ambulance came."

"Vera and I had hoped our son would settle down and marry a nice Amish woman from our community," Clarence spoke up. "We'd have even been happy if he'd found an Amish woman from outside this community." He slowly shook his head. "It's so hard for us to accept his death."

Vera's hands trembled as she dabbed at the corners of her eyes with a handkerchief. "My biggest fear is that James didn't make it to heaven."

Allison gave Vera's arm a gentle squeeze. "I can't say for sure what was in James's heart when he died, but I had the chance to pray with him. When I asked if he wanted to seek forgiveness for his sins, he blinked twice."

"What are you saying?" Clarence asked.

"I'm saying that when I prayed the prayer of forgiveness out loud, I think James repeated it in his mind."

Tears welled in Vera's eyes and ran down her cheeks. "Danki, Allison. I'm glad you were there for James in his last moments, and I'm thankful you cared enough to offer that prayer on his behalf."

Allison swallowed around the lump in her throat. She wished she could have prayed with her mother before she'd died. Deep in her heart, she felt confident that Mama had known Jesus personally and made it to heaven. She had such a sweet spirit; she had to know Jesus.

Chapter 23

Aunt Mary, could I speak with you a minute?" Allison asked before she headed out after breakfast the following morning.

"Of course." Aunt Mary dried her hands on a towel and turned to face Allison. "What did you wish to say?"

"I wanted you to know I remembered my mamm's accident."

"You did?"

"Jah. The day I witnessed James's accident, it all came rushing back to me."

Aunt Mary stepped forward and gave Allison a hug. "I know it must have been painful, but I hope it helped you find some sort of closure."

Allison nodded as tears welled in her eyes. "It brought back all the fear and sorrow I felt that day, but it also helped me remember Mama."

"I'm glad."

Allison smiled, despite her tears. "I want you to know how much I appreciate all you've been teaching me. Getting to know you and your family has given me a taste of what life would have been like for me if my mamm had lived."

"Having you here has been good for us as well." Aunt Mary patted Allison's back. "We're all pleased that you've decided to stay longer."

"I just hope Papa's okay with it. I still haven't had a letter from him in response to my request. It makes me worry that he might say no."

"I'm sure a letter will come soon, and then your fears will be put to rest." Aunt Mary handed Allison a tissue. "Now dry your eyes and be on your way to town."

"I hope the bed-and-breakfast will be willing to buy some of my dolls," Allison said as she set her black outer bonnet in place over her white kapp.

"They've bought other things made by the Amish in this area, so I'm sure they'll be interested in your dolls, as well."

Allison smiled and scurried out the door. Thanks to Uncle Ben, she found her horse and buggy all ready to go. With a quick wave to Aunt Mary, Allison clucked to the horse and guided her buggy down the driveway. She was excited about taking some of her dolls to the bed-and-breakfast, but nervous about stopping at the harness shop to speak with Aaron. Would he be glad to see her? Would he be too busy to talk? Could they get their relationship back to where it had been before James's accident?

Allison thought of Proverbs 18:24, which she'd read that morning: *"A man that hath friends must shew himself friendly: and there is a friend that sticketh closer than a brother.*" She wanted to be Aaron's friend, even if she couldn't be his girlfriend. She knew if he was grieving over James's death, he really needed a friend.

As Allison's horse and buggy proceeded down Highway C, she tried to focus on other things. It was a warm morning, already muggy and buzzing with insects. She'd been swatting at flies ever since she left her aunt and uncle's place.

Allison wondered what it would be like to spend a winter in Webster County. Since the Amish who lived here only drove open buggies, they would have to bundle up in order to be protected when the weather turned cold and snowy. Even so, she longed to stay in this small Amish community, where she could be close to the family and friends she had come to care about. What if, for some reason, Papa didn't want her to stay? What if he insisted she return to Pennsylvania at the end of summer?

Halting her negatives thoughts, Allison guided the horse to turn at the entrance of the Hiltys' place. She stopped in front of the hitching post by the harness shop and stepped down from the buggy. It was time to see Aaron.

"I'm going up to the house to speak with your mamm, but I'll be back soon," Paul called to Aaron. "Is there anything I can bring you to eat or drink?"

Aaron looked up from a tub of dye and smiled. He hadn't had a chance to apologize to his stepfather for the harsh words he'd spoken the other morning, but he would do that as soon as Paul returned to the shop. "How about a couple of Mom's oatmeal cookies?"

"Sure, I can do that." Paul opened the door and had just stepped outside when Allison walked in.

"Guder mariye, Paul," she said. "I'm on my way to Seymour and thought I'd drop by and see Aaron a few minutes. If he's not too busy, that is."

Paul nodded. "Aaron's dying some leather straps, but you're welcome to talk to him."

As Allison moved toward Aaron, his breath caught in his throat. He waited for Paul to shut the door, then held up his hands, encased in rubber gloves that were dark with stain. "Better not get too close. This stuff is hard to scrub off. Just ask my mamm; she's had to deal with trying to get dye off my clothes, as well as my skin, ever since I was a boy and first came to work in this shop."

"I'll be careful."

"What did you want to see me about?" he asked.

Allison leaned against one of their workbenches. "We haven't had a chance to talk since the night of James's accident. I had wanted to speak with you after the funeral dinner, but Joseph said you'd gone home with your folks."

Aaron nodded.

She cleared her throat. "You've been acting kind of distant, and I'm wondering if something's wrong."

Aaron draped the piece of leather he'd just stained over a rung on the wooden drying rack and stood. Should he tell her what he thought about her reaction to James? Would it do any good to share his feelings?

"Are you upset about James?" Allison questioned.

He nodded. Maybe she had figured things out already.

"If you're feeling guilty because you said unkind things about James before he died, all you need to do is confess it to God."

Aaron's mouth dropped open. "What?"

"You seemed so glum during the funeral service. I wondered if it was because you felt remorse and wished you could have made things right between you and James before he died."

"I do feel bad for speaking against him," Aaron admitted.

"It's easy to let things slip off our tongue when we're upset. I should know; I've done plenty of it in the past—especially things I said to Aunt Catherine." Allison took a step toward Aaron, but he held up his hands.

"Stain, remember?"

"Right." Her smile seemed to light up the room. "So the reason you didn't say much when you took me home after the accident was because you felt bad about the way things had been between you and James?"

"Actually, I wasn't talking much because I was upset over *you* and James."

"Me and James?"

"Jah. The way you acted when he was thrown from his buggy made me think you had strong feelings for him."

Allison's mouth dropped open. "You thought that?"

He nodded. "You were determined to speak with James, and then you wanted to ride to the hospital in the ambulance with him. It made me believe—"

"I did care about James, but not in the way you think," she interrupted.

"How was it then?"

"I cared about his soul—where he would spend eternity if he died."

Aaron shifted from one foot to the other. Was Allison saying she had rushed to James's side in order to speak to him about God?

"I told James he could be forgiven of his sins, and then I prayed, asking him to repeat the prayer in his mind. I believe in my heart that James understood and accepted Christ as his Savior."

"I. . .I see." Aaron felt as if someone had squeezed all the air out of his lungs. If Allison wasn't in love with James, was it possible that she cared for him?

She stepped forward and touched his arm. "Are you okay? Have I said something to upset you?"

He pulled the rubber gloves off his hands and let them fall to the floor, then quickly reached for her hand. "I've been so dumb thinking you loved James." He lowered his gaze. "It's taken me a long time to deal with my feelings about my daed's death and how it affected my mamm. I was scared of falling in love, because I was worried if I got married, I might lose my wife, the way Mom lost Dad." He drew in a deep breath and lifted his gaze. "After talking to my mamm several weeks ago, I realized that God gave her a second chance at love with Paul and that it wouldn't be good for me to live my life in fear of the unknown."

"That's true."

"I've always told everyone that I'd never get married because I couldn't find the kind of woman I needed. But the truth is I've been too scared." He paused and moistened his lips. "Then you came along, and that all changed."

Allison's forehead wrinkled. "I. . .I'm glad you feel that way, but how can you think I'm the kind of woman you need? I can barely cook, and the things I enjoy doing most are considered men's jobs."

Aaron lifted her chin with his thumb. "That's what I like about you—you're not afraid to try some things other women might shy away from." He drew her into his arms, not even caring about what would happen if Paul stepped through the door. "I'm glad you came by today," he murmured against her ear.

"Jah, me, too."

"Catherine, you've got to listen to reason," Herman said as he pulled out a chair at the kitchen table and sat beside her.

She shook her head. "There is no need to bring Allison home early."

He held out the letter he'd recently received. "She wants to stay longer than originally planned."

Catherine shrugged. "She can do whatever she likes."

"But you're going to need her help," he argued.

"I'll do what I can for as long as I can." She took a sip from her cup of tea. "If I need any help, I'll ask some of the women in our community."

Herman was sure Sally's mother, Dorothy, and several other women would be willing to help out, but they couldn't be there all the time. Besides, Allison deserved to know about her aunt's cancer, and he was sure once she heard, she would want to return home.

"Can I talk to you a minute?" Joseph asked when he stepped out of the barn and spotted his stepfather heading for the harness shop.

"Jah, sure. What's up, son?"

Joseph hurried to his side. "I was wondering. . . ."

"You seem nervous. Is there something wrong?"

"Not wrong exactly." Joseph cleared his throat a couple of times. "It's just that. . .well, I know you and Aaron have been pretty busy in the harness shop lately, and I was wondering if you might need an extra pair of hands."

"You mean *your* hands?"

Joseph nodded. "My job at Osborn's tree farm is only part-time, and so's the farm work I do for the neighbors."

Papa studied Joseph intently. "Are you looking for full-time work? Is that what you're saying?"

"Jah. I need something steady and reliable. Something I can count on all year long."

Papa squinted as he gave his earlobe a tug. "You've never shown much interest in the harness shop before. You'd have a lot to learn."

"I know."

"Do you mind telling me why the sudden desire to work there?"

"I just told you—I need to find a full-time job."

"And why is that, Joseph?"

"Well, I—"

"Is there a woman involved in this decision?"

"Jah. I've asked Katie Esh to marry me, but her folks won't give their blessing unless I have a full-time job."

Papa's brows furrowed. "Is that the only reason?"

"What do you mean?"

"Don't they have any concerns about the fact that you and Katie are only eighteen?"

"I suppose they do, but—"

"Don't you think it would be better if you and Katie waited a few years to be married?"

"Katie and I are in love, and we want to be married as soon as possible."

"Even if you did have a full-time job, I don't think you're mature enough to be a husband right now."

Joseph's spine went rigid. In all the years Paul had been married to Mom, he'd never made Joseph feel as small as he did right now. "I'm not immature. I'm a hard worker, and I make good decisions."

"Do you now?" Papa gave his earlobe another quick pull. "Was it a good decision when you bought that very spirited gelding a few months ago and then it kicked one of the other horses because it has such a mean streak?"

"I had no way of knowing the horse was mean when I bought him."

"A knowledgeable horseman would have known. Would have asked more questions before buying such a horse."

Joseph grunted. "So you're saying I shouldn't marry Katie because I made one mistake when I bought a spirited horse?"

"I'm not saying that at all. I just think you need to wait a few

years before you settle down to marriage and raising a family."
Papa sighed. "If you really want to work at the harness shop, I'll
have Aaron train you in his spare time, but that doesn't mean
you have my blessing to marry Katie right now."

"Just forget it." Joseph kicked at the stones beneath his feet.
"I'll find a job somewhere else."

Papa put his hand on Joseph's shoulder. "I didn't say you
couldn't come to work for me. If you really want to work in
the harness shop, then I'd like to have you here." He smiled.
"Maybe someday, after I retire, you and Aaron can run the shop
together."

Joseph compressed his lips as he mulled things over. *If I
learn the harness business and prove that I'm hard-working and reliable,
maybe Papa will change his mind about me marrying Katie.* "I'll think
things over and let you know." He hurried away before Papa
could say anything more.

As Aaron walked past the front window of the harness shop, he
spotted Paul talking with Joseph. His brother appeared to be quite
upset. So did Paul, for that matter. Surely they couldn't have had
a disagreement. Joseph and Paul had always gotten along so well.
For many years, Aaron had struggled with jealousy toward his
brother because of his and Paul's special relationship. Easygoing,
happy-go-lucky Joseph had stuck to Paul like sticky tape when he'd
first come to work for Mom in the harness shop. Aaron could
still remember the irritation he'd felt every time he'd seen Joseph
sitting beside Paul, looking up at him with adoration. And Paul

had seemed equally mesmerized with Joseph. Zachary and Davey, too, for that matter. It was as if Paul had taken their father's place right from the start. Back then, Aaron had thought Paul was buttering Joseph and Zachary up just so he could get close to Mom. He figured Paul was trying to worm his way into her heart so he could get his hands on the harness shop. But later, when Paul had taken more of an interest in Aaron and shown that he really loved Mom, Aaron had decided that Paul wasn't after the harness shop at all.

"I brought our lunches," Paul said when he stepped into the shop a few minutes later.

"Danki." Aaron took his lunch pail from Paul and placed it on the nearest workbench. "I saw you talking to Joseph outside. Is everything okay?"

Paul shrugged. "Jah, sure. Why do you ask?"

"Both of you looked kind of upset, and I wondered what was going on."

"Joseph asked if I might consider hiring him to work here in the harness shop."

Aaron's mouth dropped open, and his heart raced. Did Joseph want his job? Was he hoping to get his hands on the harness shop after Paul retired?

"You look surprised."

"I am. I mean, Joseph's never shown much interest in the shop before. He's usually avoided coming in here because he doesn't care for all the strong odors."

"I know, but some things change. People change." Paul thumped Aaron on the back. "We've got a lot of work right now. I think we should give your brother a chance, and I told him you'd be the one to train him."

Aaron's face heated up. "Me? Why me?"

"Because he's your brother, and I know you'll do a good job teaching him what he needs to know."

Aaron was getting prepared to argue the point, but the telephone rang.

"I'd better see who that is." Paul hurried over to his desk and picked up the phone.

Aaron slumped against the workbench. He had no appetite for lunch now. And he definitely did not want to train his brother to work in the harness shop!

Chapter 24

Allison awoke with a feeling of anticipation. Uncle Ben's barn raising was today, and Aaron would be here, along with most of the Amish men in their community. It would be a long day, and the men would be arriving soon, so she needed to hurry and get downstairs to help Aunt Mary and Sarah in the kitchen. Several women would be coming with their husbands, so they would have plenty of help throughout the day.

Allison headed down the stairs and met her aunt in the hallway. "Guder mariye," Aunt Mary said. "Did you sleep well?"

"Jah. And you?"

"I slept fine, except I'm wishing I had gone to bed earlier last night. I'll need a lot of energy to get through this day."

"I'll help wherever I'm needed."

"I know you will." Aunt Mary squeezed Allison's arm. "You've been a big help since you came here, and I'll be real pleased if your daed says you can stay longer."

Allison smiled. "Me, too."

"Oh, I almost forgot—when I was in Seymour at the chiropractor's yesterday, I was telling the doctor's receptionist about your faceless dolls. She has a friend who works at a gift shop in Branson, and she's interested in selling some of your dolls in her shop."

"That would be wunderbaar." A sense of excitement welled in Allison's soul. She had never been excited about much of anything when she was at home. Maybe that was because every time she showed the least bit of enthusiasm, Aunt Catherine threw cold water on it. "I've got several dolls made up, so maybe I could run them by the chiropractor's office on Monday morning."

"I might go with you," Aunt Mary said as they entered the kitchen. "Then I can see if the doctor has time to work on my back. After today, I'll probably need another adjustment."

"If you're hurting, why don't you rest awhile and let me take over? I'm sure there will be plenty of other women here to help, too."

Aunt Mary shook her head. "I wouldn't dream of putting all the responsibility on your shoulders. I'll be fine as long as I don't lift anything heavy."

"We'll just have to see that you don't." Allison gave Aunt Mary a hug, grabbed her choring apron from the wall peg by the back door, and hurried to the refrigerator. There was so much to be thankful for, and she was eager to begin the day.

"How come you two are wearin' such scowls on your faces? Is it because you're not anxious to spend the day workin' up a sweat?" Zachary asked, glancing first at Aaron and then Joseph as they headed for the Kings' place in Aaron's buggy.

"I'm not wearing a scowl," Joseph mumbled.

Zachary nudged Joseph with his bony elbow. "I would think you'd be wearin' a smug expression today."

"Why's that?" Joseph asked.

" 'Cause your *aldi* will be there, and I'll bet you can't wait to see her." He snickered. "The same goes for you, Aaron. I'll bet you're in *lieb* with Allison, huh?"

"Knock it off, or we'll put you in the backseat," Aaron warned. He was in no mood for his little brother's teasing.

Zachary's forehead wrinkled. "Maybe I should have ridden with Papa and Davey."

"That might have been for the best." Joseph bumped Zachary's shoulder. "At least they'd be the ones putting up with you now, and Aaron and I would be riding in peace and quiet."

Zachary's right; I am in love, Aaron thought as he snapped the reins to get the horse moving faster. *But I'm not about to admit that to my little brother. I haven't even told Gabe yet how deeply I've come to care for Allison.*

Aaron thought about his best friend, who would soon become a father. At one time, the idea of having children had scared Aaron to death. Not anymore. Now that he and Allison had worked things out, he was hopeful they might have a future together. If they ever decided to get married, he hoped Allison would be willing to live in Missouri. He had no desire to move, especially not to an area where there were so many tourists. Of course, with Joseph working at the harness shop, Aaron needed to accept the fact that Paul might give the place over to Joseph instead of him. If that happened, Aaron might need to move away so he wouldn't have to watch the shop that was supposed to be his be run by someone else.

"I'm glad we're finally here," Joseph said as they pulled onto the Kings' property. "You want me and Zachary to help you with the horse, or should the two of us start working on the barn?"

"I can manage on my own," Aaron replied. "I'll join you as soon as I get the horse situated in the corral."

"Okay." Joseph jumped down, and Zachary did the same. As soon as they had moved away, Aaron drove his rig to the area where several other buggies were parked. He'd just gotten the horse unhitched when Gabe showed up.

"Are you all set for a good day's work?" Gabe asked with a smile.

"Sure. How about you?"

"Jah. I'm happy whenever I'm building anything."

"I'm sure that's true. You've enjoyed working with wood ever since we were boys."

"I can probably get started on Rufus's dog run some evening next week," Gabe said. "Would that work okay for you?"

"Whenever you have the time."

"You look kind of down in the dumps today," Gabe commented. "Is there anything going on I should know about?"

Aaron grunted. "Is there anything you don't already know?"

Gabe slapped him playfully on the back. "Are you sayin' I'm nosy?"

"I'm not saying that at all. You just seem to have a way of knowing what's going on around our community."

Gabe chuckled. "Guess that's because so many of my customers like to share the local news."

"Jah, well, you need to be careful you don't blab everything you hear. Some folks don't like others knowing their business."

"Like you? Is that what you're saying?"

Aaron shrugged and led his horse into the corral.

"Are you going to tell me what's put such a sour look on your face this morning or not?"

Aaron closed the corral gate and turned to face his friend. "If you must know, my brother is coming to work in the harness shop."

Gabe's eyebrows lifted. "Which brother?"

"Joseph."

"But I thought he already had a job working at Hank Osborn's Christmas tree farm."

"He does, but it's only part-time, and he asked Paul about working in the harness shop so he'd have steady work." Aaron grimaced. "Paul said yes, and the worst part is, he wants me to train Joseph."

"So that's what's got you looking so down-in-the-mouth?"

"Right. If Joseph learns the harness trade, then he might be looking to own it some day."

Gabe's forehead wrinkled. "But it's been promised to you. Am I right about that?"

"That's true, but things can change." Aaron grunted. "Joseph and Paul have always been very close. I wouldn't be surprised if Paul doesn't decide to give the shop to Joseph instead of me."

Gabe shook his head. "I don't think that's going to happen."

"If it does, I'll probably move away."

"Where would you go?"

Aaron shrugged. "Maybe to Pennsylvania. There are plenty of harness shops there, so I'm sure I'd be able to find a job."

A slow smile spread over Gabe's face. "Does Allison Troyer have anything to do with the reason you would choose Pennsylvania?"

Aaron shrugged. "Maybe."

"I knew it! You're in love with her, aren't you?" Gabe thumped Aaron on the back. "By this time next year, you could be an old married man."

"We'll have to see how it goes." Aaron glanced around, hoping to catch a glimpse of Allison, but she was nowhere in sight. He figured she was probably inside with the women fixing snacks or getting the noon meal going. Maybe they could spend a few minutes together after lunch. If not, he would make a point to speak to her before he went home.

Gabe motioned to the group of men wielding hammers and saws. "I suppose we've gabbed long enough, so let's get to work!"

"Why don't you and I serve that table over there?" Allison suggested to Katie as she motioned to the wooden plank set on two sawhorses where Aaron and Joseph sat with several other young men.

"That's fine with me," Katie said.

When Allison set the plate in front of Aaron, he leaned over and whispered, "It's good to see you. Have you been working hard all morning?"

"Not nearly as hard as you. It's awful hot today. Have you been getting enough to drink?"

He nodded. "Sarah and Bessie have brought water to the crew several times this morning."

"Are you gonna pass those sandwiches over, or did ya plan to spend your lunch hour gabbin'?" Zachary, who sat across from Aaron, held out his hand. "I'm starvin' to death here."

Aaron grabbed a ham sandwich, plunked it on his paper plate, and handed the platter to the next man in line. "Maybe there won't be any sandwiches left by the time they get around to you, little bruder."

"Don't pay him any mind, Zachary," Allison put in. "There's plenty more sandwiches in the kitchen." She enjoyed this bantering between Aaron and his younger brother. It reminded her of all the times she and Peter had teased each other. Of course, whenever Aunt Catherine had caught them fooling around, they'd always been reprimanded.

Allison moved back to the serving table to get a bag of potato chips. When she returned, she was surprised to see that Aaron wasn't in his seat. Surely he couldn't have finished eating already. He hadn't even had dessert.

"*Psst. . .*Allison—over here."

When Allison turned, she saw Aaron crouched in the flower bed near the back porch. "What are you doing down there?"

"I spotted this and wondered if it was yours." He held a tiny white kapp between his thumb and index finger.

Allison squinted. It looked like one of the head coverings she had made for her faceless dolls. But how would it have gotten in the flower bed? "Let me have a look at that." She took the tiny hat from Aaron and studied the stitching. It had obviously been done by hand, not on the treadle machine. She knew immediately whose it was. "This isn't one I made. It belongs on the little doll my mamm sewed for me before she died." She slowly shook her head. "I don't understand how it got out of my room and ended up in the flower bed, though. I always keep the doll at the foot of my bed."

Aaron stood. "Maybe one of the kinner who came with their folks today wandered into your room and discovered the doll."

"I guess I should go inside and take a look." Allison started to turn around, but Aaron touched her arm.

"Uh. . .before you go, I was wondering if we could plan another day of fishing soon. Maybe we could invite an old married couple along as chaperones."

"You mean Gabe and Melinda?"

"Jah. We had fun with them the last time, don't you think?"

"Except for our little dunking in the pond," she said with a grin.

He chuckled. "We'll try not to let that happen again."

"When did you want to go?"

"Well, I was thinking—"

"Hey, Allison, the mail just came and there's a letter for you," her cousin Dan interrupted. He held the envelope out to her.

Allison took the letter. "Danki, Dan."

He stood there, as though waiting for something. "Well, aren't ya gonna open it? It could be important, ya know."

Allison glanced at the envelope. The return address was Papa's. Maybe this was the letter she had been hoping for.

She took a seat on the porch steps and was about to rip it open when Aaron said, "Guess I'll let you read your letter in private." He glanced at the picnic tables. "And I'd better get back to the table before all the food's gone."

"Oh, okay. I'll talk to you later then."

Aaron smiled and walked away.

Allison glanced at her young cousin. "Shouldn't you be eating your lunch, too?"

"I'm done."

"Then haven't you got something else to do?"

Dan shrugged his shoulders. "If I go back to the table, Papa will see me. Then he'll expect me to haul more nails and stuff to the men." He wrinkled his nose. "Why can't they see that I'm capable of doin' some real work for a change?"

"I'm sure they appreciate any help you can give them." Anxious to read Papa's letter, Allison decided the only way she was going to have any privacy was to go upstairs. "I've got to run up to my room a minute, Dan. Why don't you ask Aaron or Joseph if there's something you can do to help them this afternoon?"

Dan's lips curved into a smile. "That's a good idea. I think Aaron likes me, so he might let me help him pound nails." He turned and darted away.

Allison hurried into the house and rushed upstairs to her room. As she took a seat on her bed, she realized that her faceless doll was missing. Aaron was probably right—one of the children here today had most likely come into her room, spotted the doll, and taken it somewhere to play.

She placed the little kapp on the table beside her bed and ripped open the letter from Papa:

> *Dear Allison,*
>
> *I haven't mentioned this before, but your aunt Catherine has been having pains in her stomach for some time. Thanks to Sally's mom, she finally agreed to see the doctor. At first, the doctor thought the pain she was having was from an irritable bowel. But then he ran some tests, and a few weeks ago we got the results. There's no easy way to say this, but my sister has colon cancer, and the doctor says it's spreading quickly.*

Allison clapped her hands over her mouth. Muffled words came out from between her splayed fingers. "Aunt Catherine is sick with cancer? No, it can't be."

She sat for several seconds, trying to digest what she had read. Aunt Catherine had always been a healthy woman. Even when Allison and the rest of the family had come down with a cold or the flu, Aunt Catherine had remained unaffected by the bug. Allison used to think her aunt was too mean to get sick.

Needing to know more, she turned her attention back to the letter:

> *I received your letter asking if you could stay in Webster County longer than planned. I'd fully intended to tell you to stay as long as you like, but now things have changed. You*

*see, Aunt Catherine has refused to have surgery or undergo
any kind of treatment. She asked me not to tell you about her
illness and insisted that I not ask you to come home. At first
I agreed to her request, but she's getting weaker every day and
suffers with more pain. This morning she couldn't get out of
bed because of the pain. Peter and I are fending for ourselves,
but I'm hoping you will set your plans aside and come home
as soon as possible.*

Love,
Papa

Allison let the letter slip from her fingers as a cold chill
rippled across her shoulders. "Oh, dear God, please don't let
Aunt Catherine die before I get home. I need the chance to
speak with her."

Chapter 25

As if in a daze, Allison made her way back downstairs. She found Aunt Mary in the kitchen with Katie's mother and a few other ladies from their community.

"I need to speak with you," Allison said, stepping up to her aunt.

"Certainly. What did you need?" Aunt Mary asked with a pleasant smile.

"Can we find somewhere private to talk?"

"Jah, sure." Aunt Mary led the way to her room and took a seat on her bed, motioning for Allison to join her. "What's this all about?" she asked.

Allison swallowed around the lump in her throat. "I got a letter from my daed today, with some very bad news."

Aunt Mary's eyes widened. "What kind of bad news?"

"Aunt Catherine has colon cancer, and it–it's spreading."

"I'm so sorry to hear of this."

"I've got to go home," Allison said with a catch in her voice. "Papa and Peter need my help. So does Aunt Catherine."

"We'll be sad to see you go, but I certainly understand." Aunt Mary clasped Allison's hand. "Maybe you can return to Webster County when things are better."

Allison shook her head. "I don't think things are going to get better. Papa says Aunt Catherine has refused all forms of treatment, so I'm sure it's just a matter of time before she dies." She drew in a shuddering breath. "I need to speak to her about Jesus. I need to be sure she's accepted Him as her Savior."

Aunt Mary nodded. "Jah, that's the most important thing."

"Could I talk to you for a minute?" Joseph asked Katie when she brought a jug of water out to him. "Someplace in private?"

"Of course." She motioned to the side of the house, where there was a shady maple tree. "How about over there?"

"That'll be fine."

Katie led the way, and Joseph followed. When they were under the tree, she turned to him and smiled. "Is everything okay?"

Joseph wiped the sweat from his forehead and grimaced. "I asked my daed the other day if I could go to work in his harness shop, and he said I could. But when I told him that I needed the job so I could marry you, he wasn't so pleased."

"How come? Doesn't he like me? Does he think I won't

make you a good wife?"

"It's not that. Papa likes you just fine. He just thinks we're too young, that's all."

Katie swallowed against the burning in her throat. "I guess no one thinks we're ready for marriage."

"After thinking and praying about things, I think they may be right." Joseph reached for her hand. "To tell you the truth, I really don't want to work in the harness shop, but I would if it meant we could be married soon."

She shook her head. "I wouldn't want you working at a job you didn't enjoy. As much as I dislike saying this, I think it's best that we wait until we're both a bit older and you've found a job you really like."

He nodded and smiled. "Is it any wonder I love you so much, Katie Esh? You're exactly what I need."

She stared lovingly into his eyes. "You're what I need, Joseph Zook."

Aaron had just returned to the work site with a can of nails when he spotted Joseph heading his way. He figured this might be a good time to confront Joseph about working at the harness shop, since he hadn't been able to say what was on his mind as they'd traveled here this morning. Not with Zachary's big ears listening to everything they said.

"We need to talk," Aaron said when Joseph approached him. "Meet me over by the buggy shed."

Joseph's eyes narrowed. "What's up?"

"I want to discuss something with you."

"Jah, okay."

Joseph headed for the buggy shed, and Aaron did the same. He was relieved to see no one else was about.

"What did you want to talk to me about?" Joseph asked, leaning against the side of the shed.

"It's about working in the harness shop."

"Oh, that."

"If you really want to work in the shop, there's nothing I can do, but if you've got it in your head that you'd like to own the place someday, then I take exception."

Joseph's mouth dropped open like a broken window hinge. "Own the place? Ach, Aaron, no such thought has ever entered my mind."

"Then how come you asked Paul if you could work there?"

"Because I need a full-time job." Joseph grunted. " 'Course that's not so much the case now."

Aaron wrinkled his forehead. "I'm confused. What are you talking about?"

"As you've probably guessed, I'm in love with Katie, and we were hoping to get married soon."

"From the way you get all starry-eyed whenever Katie's around, I kind of figured you were in love," Aaron said. "But I had no idea you were thinking of getting married."

"Thinking and wanting is about as far as it's gone." Joseph slowly shook his head. "Her folks said I'd need to have a full-time job and that they thought we were too young to be thinking about marriage. When I mentioned it to Papa, he said pretty much the same thing." He shrugged and released a groan. "I figured after three negative votes, there wasn't much point in talkin' to Mama about it."

"Let me get this straight. You thought if you had a full-time job you'd be able to marry Katie?"

Joseph nodded.

"I have to agree with the others. There's a lot more to marriage than just being in love, Joseph."

"Humph! What makes you such an expert on the subject of love and marriage? Until recently, I've never seen you take much interest in any woman."

"Things are different now, and I need to be sure my job at the harness shop is secure—in case I should decide to marry."

"Well, you needn't worry about that, because I've changed my mind about working there. I've never really cared much for the smells in that shop, and spending eight or nine hours a day cutting and dying leather really isn't what would make me happy."

"What would make you happy?"

Joseph shrugged. "I haven't figured that out yet. But when I do, you'll be one of the first to know."

Aaron chuckled. "After Katie, you mean?"

"Jah. After her."

"I'm glad we had this little talk," Aaron said. "I feel much better about things, and now I'm free to ask—" Aaron stopped talking when he noticed Allison heading his way. He needed to get rid of Joseph so he could speak to her in private.

As if he could read Aaron's mind, Joseph said, "Well, I'd better get back to the work site." He offered Aaron a wide smile. "See you later, big brother."

As Allison passed Joseph on her way to speak with Aaron, she hoped he wouldn't detain her with small talk. To her relief, he merely smiled and moved swiftly over to the work site. She hurried over to where Aaron stood by the buggy shed, hoping for the right words and praying she wouldn't break down in front of him.

"Allison, I was hoping I'd get the chance to talk to you again," Aaron said. "I just got some good news."

"I could use some good news about now," she said. "What's your good news?"

"Joseph was planning to work at the harness shop, but he informed me that he's changed his mind."

Allison had no idea why that was good news to Aaron, but she knew if she didn't say what was on her mind quickly, she might lose her nerve. "I came over here to tell you what was in that letter I got from my daed this morning."

"Did he give you an answer about staying on here longer?"

She nodded, as tears stung the backs of her eyes. "He said he would have been fine with the idea, but things have changed at home, so he couldn't give his approval."

Aaron frowned. "What's changed?"

"My aunt Catherine has colon cancer, and it's spreading to other parts of her body." She swallowed hard. "I'm needed at home to care for my family."

Aaron stood for several seconds, rocking back and forth on his heels. "I'm sorry to hear about your aunt, but couldn't your daed find someone to—"

Allison shook her head. "I'm not just needed to cook and clean for them. I need to go home so I can tell Aunt Catherine about Jesus."

Aaron looked at Allison like she'd taken leave of her senses. "She doesn't know about Jesus?"

"She knows *about* Him, but I don't believe she knows Him in a personal way."

"I see. Then I guess it's important for someone to tell her."

Allison nodded. "Aunt Catherine and I have never been close, and I'm not even sure she'll listen to anything I have to say. But I have to try, Aaron." Tears clouded her vision and dribbled onto her cheeks.

"You will write to me, won't you?"

"Of course. I'll write as often as I can."

"I'll write you, too." Aaron pulled her into his arms and gently patted her back. "Will you come back to Missouri?"

"I. . .I'm not sure. I want to, but I'll have to wait and see how things go." She sniffed. While she wouldn't tell Aaron, she believed that once she returned home, she would never see him again.

Chapter 26

As Allison stood with Aunt Mary in front of Lazy Lee's Gas Station on Monday morning, tears welled in her eyes and mixed with the raindrops that had begun to fall. The much-needed rain they'd been praying for was finally here, and it seemed fitting that the clouds overhead would add their tears to her own. Instead of taking her homemade Amish dolls to the chiropractor's office so the receptionist could offer them to a gift shop in Branson, Allison now waited for a bus that would take her home.

It pained her to leave Aunt Mary and her family, and it especially hurt to be going away from Aaron. It had been hard to tell him she was returning to Pennsylvania, and even more difficult to admit she didn't know when or if she might return to Missouri. Even though she and Aaron had promised to write to each other, it wouldn't be easy to carry on a long-distance relationship. She wished she could have offered Aaron a guarantee that she would come back, but there were no guarantees. She didn't know how long she would be needed at home, and if Aunt Catherine died, Papa would need someone to cook and keep house for him.

Allison could still see the forlorn look on Aaron's face when they'd said good-bye yesterday in front of the buggy shed. She had longed to say she loved him and ask if he would wait for her, in case she was able to return to Missouri. But that wouldn't have been fair. As much as it hurt, she would have to let Aaron go. He deserved the freedom to move on with his life and find someone else to marry.

"We'll surely miss you," Aunt Mary said, breaking into Allison's thoughts. "We'll be praying that God might offer a miracle for your daed's sister."

Allison nodded. "It would be wunderbaar if she was healed of her cancer, but as I've mentioned before, I'm more worried about healing for her soul."

"We'll be praying about that, too." Aunt Mary smiled and slipped her arm around Allison's waist. "I'll ask God to give you the chance to witness to your aunt Catherine, just as you did with James."

"Danki, I'm praying for that, too." Allison glanced over her shoulder. A part of her had secretly hoped Aaron would come to see her off this morning. But maybe it was for the best that he hadn't shown up. A tearful good-bye in front of Aunt Mary or anyone else waiting for the bus would have been too difficult.

"I appreciate your willingness to see if you can sell the dolls I'm leaving with you, and I'm also glad you gave Bessie permission to take my kitten," Allison said, hoping the change of subject might lessen her pain. "There wouldn't be much point in me taking the dolls with me, and since Aunt Catherine doesn't like pets, I couldn't take Shadow."

"I don't mind keeping the dolls or your cat," Aunt Mary replied. "But I do hope you will continue making faceless dolls when you get home."

Allison shook her head. "I doubt there'll be enough time for that, since I'll have so many chores to do. Not to mention that I'll be needed to help care for Aunt Catherine as she nears the end."

"I understand, but if you do find any free time, sewing might be good therapy for you."

"I'll have to see how it goes." Allison looked at the piece of luggage sitting at her feet. All the clothes she had brought to Missouri were inside the suitcase, but one important item was missing—the little faceless doll her mother had made for her before she died. It didn't feel right leaving without that precious doll; yet all that remained of it was the small white kapp Aaron had found in the flower bed.

After Allison had made a thorough search of the room, she'd resigned herself to the fact that someone had indeed taken it. She had questioned everyone in Aunt Mary's family and searched the house and barn, but the doll hadn't turned up anywhere.

"If you ever find the faceless doll my mamm made, would you mail it to me?" Allison asked Aunt Mary.

"Of course, and I'll ask everyone in the family to keep an eye out for it."

The rumble of the bus pulling into the parking lot brought a fresh set of tears to Allison's eyes. She was about to leave Webster County behind, along with so many people she had come to love. At least she was returning home a little better equipped to run a house, and for that she felt thankful.

While Allison's suitcase was being loaded into the baggage compartment, she turned and gave Aunt Mary a hug. "Danki for everything—especially for showing me how to find the Lord." Her voice broke and she swallowed hard. "Come visit us sometime if you can."

Aunt Mary nodded as tears trickled down her cheeks. "I'll be praying that you'll be able to come back here again, too."

"There's something I need to tell you," Herman said as he took a seat on the sofa beside his sister.

"What is it?" Catherine asked, barely giving him a glance.

"I wrote Allison a letter the other day and told her about your condition."

"Figured you would," she mumbled. "Never could trust you to keep your word."

Herman fought the urge to argue with her. Catherine always had to be right. He cleared his throat a couple of times. "The thing is I asked if Allison would come home."

"You did what?" Catherine's voice trembled, and her usually pale face turned crimson.

"Allison is needed here, and—"

"I told you I didn't want her help."

"I know what you said, but I also know that you can no longer keep up with things around here."

"Write her back and tell her not to come."

"It's too late for that; she called me the same day she got my letter and said she's coming home. Fact is, she should be on the bus by now and will be here in a couple of days."

Catherine folded her arms and stared straight ahead. "Then I guess there's nothing more to be said."

As Aaron guided his horse and buggy into Lazy Lee's, he scanned the parking lot, filled with numerous mud puddles. There was no sign of Allison or her aunt out front. Had he arrived too late to say one final good-bye?

A vision of Allison's face popped into his head. He could still see her sad expression when she'd told him she was leaving. He could still smell the aroma of peaches from her freshly shampooed hair and hear the pain in her voice as she'd murmured, "I'll write you as often as I can."

Aaron pulled on the reins and halted his horse near the back of the station, where a hitching rail had been erected for Amish buggies. Maybe the bus hadn't come yet. Allison might be waiting inside, out of the rain. He jumped down from the buggy, tied the horse to the rail, and dashed into the building.

Aaron glanced around the place, noting the numerous racks of fast-food items and shelves full of oil cans, wiper blades, and other things the Englishers used on their cars. A man and a woman sat at one of the tables near the front of the store, eating sub sandwiches. But there was no sign of Allison or Mary. Could they have gone to the ladies' room?

"Has the bus come in yet?" Aaron asked the middle-aged man behind the counter.

"Yep. Came and left again."

"How long ago?" It was a crazy notion, but if the bus wasn't too far ahead, Aaron thought maybe he could catch up to it along the highway.

"It's been a good ten or fifteen minutes now," the station attendant replied.

Aaron's heart took a nosedive. He was too late. There was no hope of him catching the bus; it was well on its way to Springfield. He'd thought saying good-bye to Allison yesterday would be good enough, but this morning as he was getting ready for work, he'd changed his mind. With Paul's permission, he had hitched his horse to a buggy and headed for Seymour, with the need to see Allison burning in his soul. He needed to hold her one last time and let her know how much he loved her.

"You wantin' to buy anything?"

The question from the store clerk halted Aaron's thoughts. "Uh. . .no. Just came in to see if the bus had come yet."

"As I said before, you've missed it."

With shoulders slumped and head down, Aaron shuffled to the front door, feeling like a heavy chunk of leather was weighing him down. Would he ever see Allison again?

Chapter 27

I want you to be prepared for the way things are at home," Allison's father said as their English neighbor drove them from the bus station to their home in his minivan.

Allison turned in her seat and faced her father. "What do you mean, Papa?" His grave expression let her know things weren't good.

"Your aunt Catherine won't accept any of the treatments her doctor's suggested, and she won't even talk about her illness."

"Why not? Doesn't she realize the treatments might prolong her life?"

"I think she's afraid of the negative side effects the treatments could cause." He pulled his fingers through the side of his hair. "To tell you the truth, I don't think she cares about prolonging her life."

"Oh, but—"

"This is her decision, and I've agreed to abide by it." He reached for Allison's hand. "She's irritable and tries to do more than she can. Then she exhausts herself and ends up unable to do anything except rest for the next several days. Peter and I can fend for ourselves when it's necessary, but we don't have time to cook decent meals or keep the place clean. And someone needs to be at the house to take care of my sister when she's having a bad day."

"Maybe she will rest more with me there to do the cleaning and cooking."

Papa nodded soberly. "That's what I'm hoping for, and I thank you for coming."

"You're welcome." Allison leaned her head against the seat and tried to relax. The days ahead would be full of trials. She could only hope she was up to the task.

"Wie geht's?" Gabe asked as he stepped into the harness shop.

Aaron pulled his fingers through the back of his hair. "I'm doin' okay. How about you?"

"Can't complain." Gabe moved toward the workbench where Aaron stood. "I came over to start working on Rufus's dog run. It's about time I got around to it, wouldn't you say?"

"I suppose."

"You don't sound too enthused. I figured you'd be desperate to get your mutt in a dog run."

Aaron gave a noncommittal shrug.

"You seem really *nunner* today."

"You'd be down, too, if the woman you loved had moved to Pennsylvania," Aaron mumbled.

Gabe shook his head. "Allison didn't *move* to Pennsylvania, Aaron. She lives there and had to return because her aunt is sick."

"I know that, but she was planning to stay here—at least longer than she'd originally intended."

"She's only been gone a few days. I wouldn't think you'd miss her so much already."

"Jah, well, how would you know what I'm feeling? You're married to the woman you love, and you know she'll be waiting for you when you come home every night." Aaron removed his work apron and hung it on a wall peg. It was past quitting time, and Paul had already gone up to the house. Aaron had figured he would stay and work awhile longer, hoping to keep his hands busy and his mind off the emptiness he'd felt since Allison left. Now that Gabe was here, he figured he might as well quit for the day. Truth be told, he was tired and didn't feel like working longer, anyway.

Gabe rested his hand on Aaron's slumped shoulder. "Don't you remember how things were with Melinda and me during our courtship? There was a time when I didn't know if she was going to remain true to the Amish faith, or if she would choose to go English and become a vet." He shook his head. "Don't think that wasn't stressful. Believe me, I know more of how you're feeling than you can imagine."

Aaron knew his friend was probably right, but it didn't relieve his anxiety any. It had taken a lot for him to get past his feelings about marriage and start courting Allison. Knowing they might never be together hurt worse than a kick in the head by an unruly mule.

"Have you had supper yet?" he asked, feeling the need to change the subject.

"Melinda and I had an early supper," Gabe replied. "But feel free to go have your meal. I'll get started on the dog run, and when you're done, you can join me. If you don't have anything else to do, that is."

"I'm not all that hungry, so I'll go inside and tell my mamm I won't be joining them at the table this evening. Then I'll come back out to help you with the dog run."

Gabe clucked his tongue. "You've got to eat, Aaron. Pining for Allison and starving yourself won't solve a thing."

Aaron knew his friend was only showing concern, but it irked him. He didn't want anyone's sympathy, and he didn't need to be told what to do.

As he opened the shop door and stepped out, a blast of hot, muggy air hit him full in the face. He grimaced. "Sure wish it would cool off and rain again. I'm sick of this sweltering weather!"

He kicked at the stones beneath his feet. *I hope I get a letter from Allison soon. I really do miss her.*

Allison thought she had prepared herself for this moment, but the sight that greeted her when she and Papa stepped into the house made her stomach clench. Aunt Catherine lay on the sofa with a wet washrag on her forehead and a hot water bottle on her stomach. Her skin had a grayish-yellow tinge, her eyes were rimmed with dark circles, and she looked skinny and frail. This wasn't the robust, healthy woman Allison had seen three months ago. It made her wonder how long Aunt Catherine had been sick and hadn't said anything. She might have been in pain for some time. That could be the reason she'd been so crabby much of the time.

Allison approached the sofa, and her aunt struggled to sit. "That's okay. Don't get up on my account." Allison leaned over and took hold of Aunt Catherine's hand. Aunt Catherine squeezed it in return, but there wasn't much strength in her fingers. A tear trickled down Allison's cheek, and she sniffed.

"We'll have no tears around here. You shouldn't have come home." Aunt Catherine's words were clipped, and if it hadn't been for the knowledge that her aunt was hurting, Allison would have felt offended. "I told your daed not to write that letter, but he insisted on bringing you back to take care of me."

Allison wasn't sure if Aunt Catherine didn't want her here because she didn't like her, or if her harsh words were because she felt bad about Allison having to leave Missouri. It didn't matter. Allison was home now, and she had a job to do. Many times in the past she'd let Aunt Catherine's sharp tongue bother her, but with God's help, she would care for her aunt's physical and spiritual needs without complaint.

"Have you heard anything from Allison?" Melinda asked Mary

as she and Katie stepped into Mary's living room for a quilting bee.

Mary nodded. "I got a letter this morning."

"How's she doing? I've only had one letter, and that was right after she first got home," Katie said.

"She's doing all right, but she's very busy keeping house, cooking, and taking care of her aunt."

"Is her aunt's health any better?" Melinda wanted to know.

Mary shook her head. "I'm afraid not. Allison said Catherine is still refusing any kind of treatment other than some pills for her pain."

"That's a shame," Melinda's mother, Faith, put in from across the room. "It seems that so many people have cancer these days."

"If only there wasn't so much pain and suffering in this world," Melinda said, taking a seat in front of the quilting frame. "It breaks my heart to see even the animals I care for when they suffer with some incurable disease."

"Sickness and death were brought into this world when Adam and Eve sinned," Vera Esh spoke up. Her eyes misted. "But someday, God will wipe away all our tears."

"And there will be no more pain and suffering," Mary said, reaching for her well-used thimble. "In the meantime, we can do our part to alleviate some of the misery our friends and family must endure by being there for them and lifting them up in prayer."

All heads nodded in agreement, and Mary lifted a silent prayer on behalf of her brother-in-law, Herman, and the whole Troyer family.

"If you keep jabbing that pitchfork the way you're doing, you'll put a hole in the floor instead of spreading straw in the places it needs to be spread," Peter said when he stepped into the stall Herman had been cleaning.

Herman set the pitchfork aside and straightened. "I guess I *was* going at it pretty good." He reached around to rub a sore spot in his lower back and grimaced.

"If you're back's actin' up, why don't you let me take over?" Peter offered.

"Actually, I think I'm hurting in here more than here." Herman touched his chest, and then his back.

"Because of Aunt Catherine, you mean?"

"Jah, that and the fact that Allison had to cut her time short in Missouri in order to come back and care for things here."

"I think the two of us could have managed okay on our own," Peter said. "It's Aunt Catherine who needs the most looking after right now."

Herman nodded. "I'm afraid it's only going to get worse. Have you noticed the determined set of my sister's jaw when she tries to do something? She attempts to cover up her pain, but I'm no *narr*."

"Of course you're not a fool, Papa."

Herman grimaced. "That sister of mine is hurting more than she'll admit, but I sure wish I hadn't had to ask Allison to come home. She's been so sad since she arrived. I don't think it's just because she feels bad about Aunt Catherine's condition, either."

"You think she's missing Aunt Mary and her family?"

"Jah, and maybe a few others besides."

Peter tipped his head to one side. "You don't think Allison found a boyfriend while she was there, do you?"

Herman shrugged. "I can't be sure, but from the way she's been acting, it's my guess that she's missing more than just her family in Webster County."

Peter stabbed a chunk of straw with the pitchfork and dropped it to the floor. "Allison hasn't had very good luck getting boyfriends in the past, so if she did find one while she was visiting Aunt Mary's family, she's probably none too happy about giving up that relationship." He stuck the pitchfork into the pile of straw again. "Want me to ask her about it?"

Herman shrugged. "She might not appreciate it, but if you feel so inclined, go right ahead."

"I think I will," Peter said with a nod. "As soon as I figure out the best way to ask."

Over the next several weeks, Allison established a routine. Up early every morning to fix breakfast so Papa and Peter could get out to the milking barn. Clean up the kitchen. Take a tray of hot cereal up to Aunt Catherine, who now ate most of her meals in bed. Do the laundry whenever it was needed. Dust, sweep, and shake rugs in every part of the house. Bake bread and desserts, while making sure that each meal was fixed on time.

Allison had to squeeze in a few minutes before bed at night to read her Bible. And she had been negligent about letter writing. She'd only written to Aaron twice, once to let him know she'd arrived home safely, and another letter earlier this week to tell him how her aunt was doing and that she missed him. She'd also written to Aunt Mary and Uncle Ben, as well as to Katie and Melinda. Aunt Mary had sent several letters in return, and she'd had two letters from Katie, but only one from Melinda. Allison figured that was because Melinda had recently given birth to a baby boy, which she'd learned about when she'd received a letter from Aaron last week. He had also said he missed her and had been praying for her aunt.

"I wish I could see that boppli of Melinda's," Allison said with a yawn. For that matter, she wished she could see all her friends and family back in Missouri—especially Aaron, whom she missed more than she was willing to admit.

A knock sounded on Allison's bedroom door.

"Come in," she called.

The door opened, and Peter stuck his head inside. "I was hoping you were still awake."

"I was just getting ready to read a few verses from the Bible before I go to bed," Allison replied.

"Mind if I come in so we can talk awhile?"

"Be my guest," Allison said, motioning him into the room.

Peter stepped inside and took a seat on the end of Allison's bed. "I'm worried about you, Allison."

"Why would you be worried about me? Aunt Catherine's the sick one here."

His forehead wrinkled. "I know that, but you've been

working hard night and day. I'm afraid if you don't slow down some you're going to collapse."

She shook her head. "You sound more like Papa now, and not my little bruder."

"I'm not your little brother, Allison. In case you've forgotten, I'm two years older than you."

"I know, but you're my youngest brother, just the same."

Peter smiled, but then his face sobered. "I wish you hadn't felt it necessary to come home so you could take care of us."

"I love you and Papa, so I wouldn't have it any other way." She shrugged. "Besides, I wanted to be here for Aunt Catherine during her time of need."

Deep wrinkles formed in his forehead. "I don't think she's got long for this world, do you?"

Allison shook her head. "Short of a miracle, Aunt Catherine's going to die soon, and I want to be sure she knows Jesus in a personal way before she goes."

"How can you care so much after all the mean things she's said to you over the years?"

"The way I felt about Aunt Catherine changed after I accepted Jesus as my Savior."

Peter nodded slowly. "You have changed a lot since you came home from Missouri."

Allison stared at her Bible, lying on the table beside her bed. "I used to feel faceless, like my life had no purpose. But after Aunt Mary explained to me that God sent Jesus to die for my sins and that He does have a purpose for my life, everything changed." She smiled. "I'm planning to be baptized and join the church this fall."

"That's good to hear."

"Have you ever confessed your sins and asked Jesus to come into your heart, Peter?" Allison asked pointedly.

He nodded. "I made that confession before the People when I was baptized and joined the church."

"I guess the truth of God's plan of salvation never hit home with me until Aunt Mary explained things," Allison said.

Peter reached across the bed and touched Allison's arm. "Mind if I ask you a personal question?"

"What do you want to know?"

"I was wondering why you wrote and asked Papa if you could stay in Missouri longer."

Allison's face heated up, and she blinked a couple of times to keep her tears from spilling over. "I liked it there. I—"

"Did you fall in love with someone? Is that why you wanted to stay?"

She nodded slowly. If she spoke the words, she knew she would dissolve into a puddle of tears.

"I don't suppose you want to tell me who you're in love with?"

She shook her head. "It's over between us, so there's no point in even talking about it."

"That's okay; you don't have to." Peter stood. "Maybe things will work out so you can go back to Missouri after Aunt Catherine—"

Allison held up her hand. "Don't even say it, Peter. My place is here now, and it will always be so for as long as Papa needs me."

Peter opened his mouth as if to say something more, but he closed it again and hurried out of the room.

Allison reached for her Bible, feeling a strong need to read a passage or two before she fell asleep. *I don't want Aaron to get his hopes up about me going back there, because unless God provides a miracle, it doesn't look like Aunt Catherine will make it. If she dies, Papa will need me here more than ever.*

As Allison read John 3:16 and reflected on how God had sent His only Son to die for the sins of the world, she felt a sense of urgency. She had tried on several occasions to witness to Aunt Catherine, but every time she brought up the subject of heaven, Aunt Catherine either said she was tired and wanted to sleep, or became irritable and shouted at Allison to leave the room.

"Dear Lord," Allison prayed, "please give me the opportunity to speak with Aunt Catherine about You soon."

Chapter 28

By the first of November, Aunt Catherine had become so weak she spent most of her time in bed. The pain in her body had intensified, and the medication brought little relief. Allison knew if she was going to get through to Aunt Catherine with the message of forgiveness, it would have to be soon. In desperation, Allison formulated a plan. She would make Aunt Catherine a faceless doll and attach a verse of scripture to it, the way Melinda's stepfather did with the desserts he baked to give to folks he felt had a need. Maybe the verse would touch Aunt Catherine's heart in a way Allison couldn't do with words.

Allison headed for the treadle sewing machine, which she discovered was covered with dust. It had obviously been some time since it had been put to use. Carefully, she cut out a girl doll, using the pattern Aunt Mary had given her. She also cut enough material to make a dark blue dress with a black cape and apron, a pair of black stockings, and a small white kapp. It made her think of the doll Mama had made—the one that went missing while she was in Missouri. She'd clung to the doll during her growing-up years, and even though she missed it, she realized what she missed most was not an inanimate object, but people—her aunt, uncle, cousins. . .and especially Aaron.

Allison closed her eyes and drew in a weary breath. She felt so tired and discouraged. Nothing she'd said or done had seemed to please Aunt Catherine. To make things worse, she missed Aaron so much she felt as if her heart could break in two. The only good thing that had happened in her life lately was that she'd been baptized and joined the church a few weeks ago. But even that positive happening hadn't filled the void Allison had felt since she'd left her family and friends in Missouri.

Should I continue to write Aaron letters? she wondered. *Or would it be better if I made a clean break?* Allison continued to ponder the situation as she sewed the doll. Maybe she should wait until after Christmas to make a decision. Or would it be better to do it now, while it was fresh on her mind?

"The letter can wait," she murmured as she slipped a piece of muslin under the pressure foot of the treadle machine. "Right now I need to concentrate on making this doll and deciding which verse of scripture to attach to it."

"Let's get these stalls mucked out now, and then we'll go outside and get that hay unloaded that we've got on the wagon," Herman said to Peter as they entered the barn.

"Good idea," Peter agreed. "The cows aren't as agreeable when they come in for the night and find dirty stalls."

Herman chuckled. "I think it would take more than a clean stall to put some of our cows in an agreeable mood."

"Jah—like Aunt Catherine. She's rarely in a good mood."

"She's got a good excuse for being grumpy these days," Herman said as he handed Peter a shovel.

Peter nodded as he began to muck out the first stall. "Remember when you and I talked about whether Allison has a boyfriend back in Missouri?"

"Jah." Herman lifted a clean bale of straw onto his shoulders and carried it to the stall.

"Well, I had a talk with her about that a few days ago, and I keep forgetting to tell you what she said."

"What did she say?"

"She admitted that she's in love with someone, but she wouldn't say who, and she said it was over between them." Peter grunted as he scooped a shovelful of cow manure into the wheelbarrow. "I think Allison believes her place is here now, caring for us. She's certainly doing a good job, too," he added.

"You're right about that. She may have left Lancaster County a tomboy, but she came home a woman, capable of running a household by herself." Herman set the bale of straw on the floor and grabbed a pitchfork. "I'm just sorry to hear she began a relationship that was over before it really had a chance to begin."

"When I mentioned her returning to Missouri, she said she felt obligated to us. She thinks once Aunt Catherine is gone, she'll be needed here even more."

Herman nodded. "We'll have to see about that when the time comes."

"What are you doing over there?" Aaron asked his youngest sister, Emma, as he stepped into the barn and discovered her huddled in one corner near some bales of straw. Since he'd heard their mother call Emma a few minutes ago, he figured the child must have sneaked off to the barn to play with the kittens when she should have been inside helping set the table for supper.

Emma jumped, like she'd been caught doing something bad, and she looked up at Aaron with both hands behind her back.

"What have you got that you don't want me to see?" he asked, taking a step closer.

She backed away, until her legs bumped the bale of straw. "Nothin'. Just girl stuff."

"What kind of girl stuff would you need to hide?"

She hung her head but gave no reply.

"Emma, hold out your hands so I can see."

Her shoulders trembled, and Aaron guessed she was close to tears.

"If you've got something you're not supposed to have, you'd better give it to me."

"I. . .I didn't mean to keep it. I was only gonna borrow it, but then—"

"Borrow what, Emma?"

The child sniffed, and when she looked up at Aaron, he saw

tears in her eyes. "I borrowed this—from Allison Troyer."

Aaron's mouth dropped open as Emma extended her hands, revealing a faceless doll with no kapp on its head. He knew immediately it was the one Allison's mother had given her when she was a young girl. The one Allison's aunt had told him was missing.

"Why, Emma? Why would you take something that wasn't yours?"

Her voice quavered when she spoke. "I–I've asked Mama to make me a doll, but she always says she's too busy takin' care of Grandma and Grandpa Raber. I think she loves them more'n she does me."

Aaron's heart went out to Emma, even though he knew what she had done was wrong. He knelt in front of the little girl and gathered her into his arms. "If I had known you wanted a doll so badly, I would have asked Allison to make you one. She sews faceless dolls and sells them."

Emma opened her mouth as if to say something, but he cut her off. "As far as our mamm loving her folks more than she does you, that's just plain silly. Grandpa and Grandma have some health problems, and she wants to care for them during their old age. But you're her little girl, and she loves you very much." He patted her gently on the back. "Remember when you were in the hospital because of your appendix?"

"Jah."

"Mom and Paul. . .uh. . .your daed, came to see you every day. Fact is, during the first twenty-four hours after your surgery they never left the hospital. Did you know that?"

She hiccupped on a sob. "Huh-uh."

"Do you think they would have done that if they didn't love you?"

"I guess not."

Aaron took the doll from his sister. "This isn't yours, and taking it was wrong. You'll need to tell Mom what you've done."

Tears streamed down Emma's cheeks. "Do I have to, Aaron? What if she gives me a bletsching?"

Aaron gently squeezed her shoulders. "I haven't known our mamm to give out too many spankings over the years, but I'm sure you'll receive whatever punishment she feels you deserve. And if Mom knows how important having a faceless doll is to you, she'll either find the time to sew a doll or she'll buy one for you. Why don't you ask after you've told her what you've done?"

"I. . .I will."

Aaron stood. "I'll see that this doll is sent to Allison, and I'll be sure and tell her how sorry you are for taking it."

She nodded. "Jah, please tell her that, for I surely wish I hadn't done it."

He pointed to the barn door. "Run into the house now and set things straight with Mom. I'll be in shortly."

Emma hesitated, gave Aaron a quick hug around his legs, and darted out the door.

Aaron stared at the bedraggled-looking doll. "Allison will sure be surprised when I mail her this." He smiled. "Maybe I'll wait and send it to her for Christmas."

Allison crept quietly into her aunt's room, unsure if she would find her asleep or not.

The floor squeaked, and Aunt Catherine's eyes fluttered open. Allison smiled, but Aunt Catherine only stared at her with a vacant look. *Doesn't she know who I am? How close might she be to dying?*

"Aunt Catherine, I brought you something," Allison said as she approached the bed.

No response.

"It's a faceless doll, and I made it myself." She held the doll in front of her aunt's face.

Aunt Catherine moaned, as though she were in terrible pain.

"Are you hurting real bad? Is there something I can get for you?"

"I–I've always wanted one."

"What do you want?"

"A faceless doll." Aunt Catherine lifted a shaky hand as tears gathered in the corner of her eyes.

Allison handed the doll to her aunt, and the woman clutched it to her chest with a trembling sob. "My mamm wouldn't allow dolls in the house when I was a girl—not even the faceless kind."

"I–I'm so sorry." Allison's throat clogged with tears. Through all the years Aunt Catherine had lived with them, she'd never thought about how things must have been for her aunt when she was a child. Allison knew Aunt Catherine had grown up with seven brothers and no sisters, but she didn't have any idea the poor woman had been denied the pleasure of owning a doll. All this time, Allison had focused only on how mean Aunt

Catherine was and how she'd never felt that the woman cared for her. Maybe if she'd shown love first, it would have been given in return.

"Wh-what's this?" Aunt Catherine asked, touching the slip of paper pinned to the back of the doll's skirt.

"A verse of scripture," Allison replied. "It's one Aunt Mary quoted to me one day, and then I asked Jesus to forgive my sins. Would you like me to read it to you?"

Aunt Catherine's expression turned stony, and Allison feared she might throw the doll aside or yell at Allison to get out of the room. Instead, her aunt began to cry. First it came out in a soft whine, but then it turned to convulsing sobs. "I've sinned many times over the years." She drew in a raspy breath. "When I learned I had cancer, I wanted to die quickly, but now that my time's getting close, I'm afraid because I. . .I don't know where my soul will go. Oh, Allison, I'm so scared. I don't think I'll make it to heaven."

Aunt Catherine's confession was almost Allison's undoing. She took a seat on the edge of the bed and reached for her aunt's hand. "You can go to heaven, Aunt Catherine. The Bible says we have all sinned and come short of the glory of God. But He provided a way for us to get to heaven, through the blood of His Son, Jesus." She paused to gauge her aunt's reaction. Aunt Catherine lay staring vacantly like she had when Allison first came into the room.

"I used to feel faceless before God," Allison went on to say. "I know now that I'm not faceless. The Bible tells us in Jeremiah 29:13: 'And ye shall seek me, and find me, when ye shall search for me with all your heart.' " She smiled. "I had been searching for Jesus for some time, but it wasn't until I accepted Him as my personal Savior that I felt a sense of peace and purpose for my life. I have every confidence that if I were to die today, my soul would enter into the place where my heavenly Father lives."

"Heaven," Aunt Catherine murmured, as if she were being drawn back into the conversation.

Allison nodded. "Romans 10:9 says, 'That if thou shalt confess with thy mouth the Lord Jesus, and shalt believe in thine heart that God hath raised him from the dead, thou shalt be saved.' Aunt Catherine, would you like me to pray with you, so you can confess your sins and tell the Lord you believe in Him as your Savior?"

"Jah, I would."

Aunt Catherine closed her eyes, and Allison did the same. Allison prayed the same prayer Aunt Mary had prayed with her and that Allison had prayed with James. Aunt Catherine repeated each word. When the prayer ended, a look of peace flooded the woman's face. Allison knew that no matter when the Lord chose to take Aunt Catherine home, she would go to heaven and spend eternity with Him.

Chapter 29

As Allison headed down the driveway toward their mailbox in early December, she let her tears flow unchecked. Yesterday had been Aunt Catherine's funeral. Despite any negative feelings Allison had harbored toward her aunt in the past, she would miss her. Aunt Catherine had been given the chance to make peace with God, and for that Allison felt grateful.

Allison thought about Aunt Catherine's final days on earth and the request she'd made one week before her death. *"Peanut brittle. Let me taste some peanut brittle,"* she'd said.

Even though her aunt had been too weak to chew the hard candy, Allison had honored the appeal. Using the recipe she'd found tucked inside Aunt Catherine's cookbook, Allison had made a batch of peanut brittle.

She could still see the contented expression on her aunt's face when she'd placed a small piece of it between her lips. "*Umm. . .good.*"

Allison knew from that day on, whenever she ate peanut brittle, she would think of Aunt Catherine and the precious moments they had spent together over the last few months.

Allison glanced at the letter in her hand. She had planned to wait until after Christmas to write Aaron and tell him she would be staying in Pennsylvania. But why prolong things? Wouldn't it be better if she made a clean break so Aaron could move on with his life? Now that Aunt Catherine was gone, Papa needed Allison more than ever. As much as it hurt to tell Aaron good-bye, she knew it would be best if he found someone else.

Allison opened the mailbox flap, placed the letter inside, and lifted the red flag. With tears blurring her vision, she turned toward the house. *This is for the best—jah, it truly is.*

Aaron's hands trembled as he read the letter he had just received from Allison. She wasn't coming back to Webster County. Her aunt had died, and her father needed someone to cook and clean for him.

"Doesn't Allison know I need her, too?" he mumbled. "I don't want to court anyone else. It's her I love."

Aaron thought about the doll Allison's mother had made and how he'd discovered his sister had taken it. He had planned to send the doll to Allison for Christmas, but he wondered if it would be best to put it in the mail now and be done with it.

As the reality of never seeing Allison set in, he sank to the stool behind his workbench and groaned. "It isn't fair."

"What's wrong, son? You look like you've lost your best friend," Paul said, moving across the room to stand beside Aaron.

"I have lost a friend." Aaron handed the letter to his stepfather. "Allison's not coming back to Missouri. Her aunt passed away, and she says her daed needs her there."

"I'm sorry about her aunt—and sorry Allison won't be returning to Webster County." Paul placed his hand on Aaron's shoulder. "You care for her a lot, don't you, son?"

Aaron nodded. There was no use denying it, but there wasn't much point in talking about it, either.

"From what I could tell when Allison was visiting for the summer, she seems a lot like your mamm," Paul said.

"She's the kind of woman I've always wanted but never thought I would find." Aaron grunted. "I wish now that I'd never met her."

Paul pulled another stool over beside Aaron and took a seat. "This isn't an impossible situation, you know."

"As far as I can tell, it is."

Paul shook his head. "Have you forgotten that I used to live in Lancaster County?"

"No, I haven't forgotten. I remember when you first came here for your brother's funeral and decided to stay so you could help Mom in the harness shop."

"That's right. I thought I would only be here a few months— just until your mamm got her strength back after Davey was born. Then I figured I'd be on my way back to Pennsylvania, where I worked at my cousin's harness shop."

"But you ended up staying and marrying Mom."

Paul nodded. "That's right. I loved your mamm so much—and would have done just about anything to marry her." He squeezed Aaron's shoulder. "There is a way for you and Allison to be together."

"What way's that?"

"I could see if my cousin would be willing to hire you at his harness shop, and then you could move to Pennsylvania to be near Allison."

Aaron's mouth dropped open. He'd thought about moving to Pennsylvania once—when he believed Joseph might want to take over the harness shop. "I couldn't leave you in the lurch," he mumbled. "Mom's not able to help out here anymore, and there's too much work for one man. Besides, this shop is supposed to be mine someday. That's the way my real daed wanted it, you know."

"I realize that, Aaron, but what about what you want?"

"What do you mean?"

"Is owning this harness shop more important to you than being with Allison?"

Aaron didn't have to think about that very long. He loved Allison so much it hurt. "Well, no, but I still wouldn't feel right about leaving you to run the place all alone."

Paul pursed his lips, as though deep in thought. "Guess I could see if Zachary might want to work here—although he's never really shown much interest in the harness shop, and I'd have to train him."

Aaron thought about Joseph and how he had asked about working in the harness shop but suddenly changed his mind. Just last week Joseph had found a new job working at the local buggy shop. He liked it there and really seemed to have found his niche. Aaron figured it was just a matter of time before Katie received her parents' blessing to marry Joseph.

"What about asking Davey to work here?" Aaron suggested. "Do you think he might want to be your apprentice?"

Paul pulled his fingers through the ends of his beard and pressed his lips together. "Between Zachary and Davey, I'm sure one of them would be willing to take your place so you can be with the woman you love."

Aaron blew out his breath. "You really think it could work?"

"Don't see why not." Paul patted Aaron on the back. "When love's involved, there's got to be a way."

Aaron rubbed his chin thoughtfully. "Guess I'll have to give this matter some serious consideration."

"It wouldn't hurt to pray about it, too."

Aaron nodded. "I'll definitely be praying."

Paul started to walk away, but Aaron called out to him, "Can I ask you a question?"

Paul turned around. "Sure, Aaron."

Aaron rubbed the bridge of his nose as he contemplated the best way to say what was on his mind. "I've. . .uh. . .been thinking about the way I've been calling you *Paul* for a while, and I'd like to go back to calling you *Papa* again, if you don't mind."

Paul's face broke into a wide smile. "I don't mind at all."

"I'm glad to hear it, because I've come to realize that even though you're not my real daed, you love me and my *brieder* just like our real daed would."

Paul clasped Aaron's shoulder and gave him a hug. "You and your brothers are like real sons to me."

Chapter 30

For the next several weeks, Allison forced herself to act cheerful in front of Papa and Peter. Last week Sally had come for a visit and told her that she and Peter planned to be married soon. Allison was happy about that. Even so, whenever she was alone in the house, she allowed her grief to surface. With Peter soon to be married, Papa would be lonely and would need Allison more than ever. There was no way she would be able to return to Missouri; she needed to accept that fact.

But oh, how she missed Aaron and her family in Webster County. She missed making faceless dolls and spending time with Melinda and Katie. She even missed her cooking lessons and housekeeping chores. Of course, she had cooking and cleaning to do here, but it wasn't nearly as much fun as it had been under Aunt Mary's tutelage.

Allison stirred the pot of stew sitting on the back burner of the stove and sighed. If only she could forget about Aaron. Truth was she wished they'd never met, because it was too painful to find love and then lose it.

The back door slammed shut and she jumped.

"Sorry. Didn't mean to frighten you," Papa said, brushing the snow off his woolen jacket.

"I didn't think you'd be in so soon. Supper won't be ready for another half hour or so."

"That's okay. I'm not all that hungry yet." He ambled over to the sink and turned on the faucet.

"Where's Peter?" Allison asked.

"He went over to Sally's house for supper."

"So it's just the two of us?"

"Jah."

When Papa finished washing up, he pulled out a chair at the kitchen table. "Why don't you turn down the burner and come have a seat? I have a couple of things I've been meaning to give you." He motioned to the chair across from him.

Allison seated herself, curious as to what he had for her.

Papa reached into his shirt pocket and pulled out two envelopes. "This one is from your aunt Catherine."

Allison squinted at the envelope. "But how—"

"She gave it to me before she died—while she was still able to stay focused enough to talk, she told our bishop's wife what she wanted her to write." He handed Allison the envelope. "She said she wanted you to know a few things, but not until after she was gone."

"What things?"

"Why don't you open the letter and find out?"

Allison opened the envelope and read the letter out loud:

"Dear Allison,

It's never been easy for me to admit when I'm wrong,
but there's something I need to confess. Remember when John
Miller used to come around, wanting to spend time with you?
Then just when you showed an interest in him, he quit coming
around. That was my fault, Allison. I sent John away."

Allison looked over at Papa. "Why would Aunt Catherine
have sent John away?"

"Because she was jealous."

"Jealous? Of me having a boyfriend?"

He nodded. "I think you'd better read on."

Allison focused her gaze on her aunt's letter again:

"I was jealous because someone was interested in you,
which meant you had the possibility of marriage. I, on the
other hand, was destined to be an old maid the minute my
parents were killed in a horrible fire that destroyed our home
and left me and my four younger brothers as orphans. I was
the oldest and felt it was my duty to care for them.

"Jeremiah King had been courting me for several months,
and he'd even hinted that he had marriage on his mind. Soon
after my folks were killed, however, Jeremiah informed me
that he'd found someone else he loved more than me. Turned
out that someone else was my best friend, Annie. From that
moment on, I vowed never to love again.

"I became bitter because I'd been jilted by the only man

I'd ever loved, and I felt obligated to take care of my brothers. Then, when your daed lost his wife and asked me to move to Pennsylvania to care for his brood, my bitterness increased. That's why I've been so critical of everything you've done. I suppose I felt that if I couldn't be happy, I didn't want anyone else to be, either. So when John Miller started coming around, I told him you didn't care for him and sent him packing.

"I know what I did was wrong, and I hope you'll find it in your heart to forgive me someday. I really do love you, Allison, and I thank you for showing me the way to salvation.

"With deepest appreciation,
"Aunt Catherine"

A lump clogged Allison's throat, and she blinked against stinging tears. "Oh, Papa, I had no idea any of that had happened to Aunt Catherine, or that John was seriously interested in me."

"How did you feel about him, Allison? Were you in love with John?"

"At the time I thought he was pretty cute, but I never really got to know him well enough to decide if I could love him or not." She shrugged. "It doesn't matter now, because John married Sharon Yoder, and they've moved to Illinois."

Papa reached for Allison's hand and gave her fingers a gentle squeeze. "One of the reasons I sent you to visit your aunt and uncle in Missouri was to get you away from my sister's bitter attitude. I could see how it was affecting you."

"That's true. Aunt Catherine and I never got along very well—not until her last days." She looked at the letter she'd placed on the table and sighed. "I wish Aunt Catherine would have told me all this to my face. We could have talked about it, and I would have said, 'I forgive you,' and I would have asked her to forgive me for the way I'd behaved during my growing-up years."

"I guess she didn't feel comfortable saying those things to your face, so that's why she asked our bishop's wife to write her thoughts down in a letter." Papa pulled a second envelope from his pocket. "This is for you, too—an early Christmas present."

Allison tipped her head. "What is it? A letter?"

He leaned across the table and handed it to her. "Take a look."

When Allison tore open the envelope, her mouth fell open. Surely this couldn't be!

Aaron held a piece of leather out to Zachary. "You didn't get it stained right. Now you'll have to do it over again."

Zachary's eyebrows drew together. "You're too picky, ya know that? I'll bet Papa will be easier to work with than you."

"That's what you think." Aaron ruffled his brother's brown hair. "Papa knows the harness business well, and he expects only the best. So you'd better learn to listen if you're going to work here."

Zachary leaned across the workbench and lowered his voice. "I would never admit this to Papa, but harness work ain't my first choice for an occupation."

"What would you rather be doing?"

"Well, since Joseph quit working at Osborn's Christmas Tree Farm, I've thought I might like to go to work there."

Aaron's eyebrows drew together. "If you'd rather work there, then why'd you agree to work here?"

Zachary shrugged. "Papa said you're in love with Allison Troyer, and I didn't wanna be the one blamed for keepin' you two apart."

Aaron grimaced. He still hadn't decided what he should do about going to Pennsylvania. He did love Allison, but he hadn't had a letter from her in several weeks, and in the one he'd received, she'd suggested he find someone else. She hadn't even said she missed him. Had she found someone else, or had he misjudged her feelings for him in the first place? Maybe it would be best if he forgot about her and made a fresh start with someone else.

Who am I kidding? he silently moaned. *There's no one I'd rather be with than Allison. Still, if she's not interested in me, then I guess I'll have to deal with it. Maybe I should tell Zachary he's free to take a job at the tree farm and just be satisfied working here for the rest of my life without a helpmate.*

The bell above the front door jingled, but Aaron didn't bother to go up front to see who'd come in. Paul was working at his desk, so he could wait on the customer.

A few seconds later, Paul called, "Zachary, can I see you a minute?"

Zachary looked at Aaron and shrugged. "Guess I'd best go see what the boss wants, or I'll be in trouble."

Aaron went back to work on the bridle he was making for Ben King and tried not to think about Zachary's admission that he didn't really want to do harness work.

"Hello, Aaron."

Aaron looked up, and his breath caught in his throat. "Allison? Wh-what are you doing here?"

She took a few steps toward him. "I came to see you."

"But. . .I thought. . .I mean. . .I was going to. . ." Aaron knew he was stammering, but he seemed powerless to say anything intelligent. Allison looked so sweet, standing there smiling at him. He wanted to reach out and hug her.

"My daed gave me an early Christmas present—a bus ticket to Webster County, Missouri." She smiled. "I have to return for my brother's wedding in a few weeks, but then I'll come back here for good."

Aaron's heartbeat picked up speed. "You. . .you really mean that?"

She nodded.

"I thought you had to stay in Pennsylvania to care for your daed."

"I believed that, too, but after Peter and Sally are married, they've agreed to move in with Papa. Peter thinks it will be easier for him to keep working at the dairy farm if he lives nearby. Sally will quit her job at the Plain and Fancy Farm after she and Peter are married, and she told my daed that she'll be more than happy to take care of him and his house."

Aaron could hardly contain himself. "Do you know what this means, Allison?"

"I hope it means we can begin courting again—if you haven't found someone else, that is."

He shook his head and reached for her hand. "Never!"

"I'm so glad to hear it."

"It also means I can stay right here and keep working for

Paul in the harness shop. Fact is, I'd be happy to work here even if I never get to call the shop my own."

Allison tipped her head and squinted. "What do you mean?"

"I was thinking about moving to Pennsylvania so I could be near you, but I wasn't sure you'd want me."

"Of course I want you, Aaron."

He pulled her into his arms and drew in a deep breath, relishing the pleasant aroma of her clean-smelling hair. "I'd even thought about showing up at your door and surprising you after the first of the year, but you've surprised me instead." Aaron pulled slowly away from Allison and moved over to the other side of the room. He took a small cardboard box from one of the shelves and handed it to Allison. "This is a special present for you."

"What kind of present?"

"Open it, and see for yourself."

She lifted the lid on the box and gasped. "My faceless doll! Oh, Aaron, where did you find it?"

"I found it in my little sister's hands, but I'll explain that later. Right now, I'd like to ask you a question."

"What question is that?"

"Will you marry me after we've had a suitable time of courting?"

Tears welled in Allison's eyes and threatened to spill over. "You. . .really want me to be your wife?"

"Jah, if you're willing."

She nodded and gave in to her tears, allowing them to trickle down her cheeks. "I'd be happy to marry you, Aaron, but there's one condition."

"What might that be?"

"That I'm allowed to work here in the harness shop with you."

Aaron chuckled as relief flooded his soul. "Now that's a deal I can't refuse." He drew Allison into his arms, thanking God for the way He had worked everything out and looking forward to spending the rest of his days on a journey of love with this special woman.

Epilogue

two years later

Allison sat in front of her treadle sewing machine, hum-ming softly as she sewed another faceless doll. She glanced across the room, where her dark-haired, one-year-old daughter, Catherine, sat on the floor, playing with the doll Allison's mother had made many years ago.

She reached for the verse she planned to attach to the doll she was making. On each doll she sewed, she included a passage of scripture: *"Ye shall seek me, and find me, when ye shall search for me with all your heart. . .saith the* Lord*" Jeremiah 29:13–14.*

Aaron stepped into the kitchen and bent to kiss her. "How are my two favorite women?"

"We're doing just fine," Allison replied with a smile. "I was sitting here at my sewing machine, thinking how my coming to Webster County changed my life."

He swooped their daughter into his arms and took a seat in the rocking chair beside the stove. "Want to tell me and Catherine how your life has changed?"

"If I hadn't come here to stay with my mamm's twin sister, I might never have found the Lord as my Savior." She lifted the pressure foot and pulled the doll free, holding it up for her husband's inspection. "And I would never have learned to make these faceless friends."

He nodded. "Anything else?"

Allison left the sewing machine and reached for Aaron's hand. Then she placed both of their hands on their daughter's head. "If I hadn't moved to Webster County, I wouldn't be married to the new owner of Zook's Harness Shop, and I wouldn't now be the mamm of this sweet little girl I love so much." She chuckled and stroked the child's soft cheek; then she moved her hand to touch Aaron's bearded face. "Of course, I love Catherine's daed quite a lot, too."

"I love you both, too." Aaron grinned. "It sure was a nice surprise when my daed decided it was time to retire and turn the shop over to us, wasn't it?"

Allison nodded. "The Lord is good, and nothing He does surprises me." She pointed to the doll nestled in little Catherine's arms. "I'm glad I no longer feel faceless before God." She smiled and blinked back tears of joy. "No matter how long I'm allowed to journey this earth, I pray that I can share the joy of the Lord with everyone who receives one of my little faceless friends."

Recipe for Aunt Catherine's Peanut Brittle

Ingredients:

- 2 cups sugar
- ½ cup water
- 1 cup white Karo syrup
- 1 tsp. butter
- 3 cups raw peanuts
- 1 tsp. vanilla
- 2 tsp. baking soda

In a kettle over medium heat, cook the sugar, water, and Karo syrup to the hardball stage. Add the butter and peanuts. Stir and cook just until mixture turns brown. Remove from stove. Add vanilla and soda. Spread over a large, buttered cookie sheet and cool. Cut or break into pieces and serve.

About the Author

New York Times bestselling and award-winning author **Wanda E. Brunstetter** is one of the founders of the Amish fiction genre. She has written more than 100 books translated in four languages. With over 11 million copies sold, Wanda's stories consistently earn spots on the nation's most prestigious bestseller lists and have received numerous awards.

Wanda's ancestors were part of the Anabaptist faith, and her novels are based on personal research intended to accurately portray the Amish way of life. Her books are well-read and trusted by many Amish, who credit her for giving readers a deeper understanding of the people and their customs.

When Wanda visits her Amish friends, she finds herself drawn to their peaceful lifestyle, sincerity, and close family ties. Wanda enjoys photography, ventriloquism, gardening, bird-watching, beach-combing, and spending time with her family. She and her husband, Richard, have been blessed with two grown children, six grandchildren, and two great-grandchildren. To learn more about Wanda, visit her website at www.wandabrunstetter.com.

Other Books by Wanda E. Brunstetter:

Prairie State Friends Series
The Decision
The Gift
The Restoration

Sisters of Holmes County Series
A Sister's Secret
A Sister's Test
A Sister's Hope

Kentucky Brothers Series
The Journey
The Healing
The Struggle

Indiana Cousins Series
A Cousin's Promise
A Cousin's Prayer
A Cousin's Challenge

Brides of Lehigh Canal Series
Kelly's Chance
Betsy's Return
Sarah's Choice

The Discovery–A Lancaster County Saga
Goodbye to Yesterday
The Silence of Winter
The Hope of Spring
The Pieces of Summer
A Revelation in Autumn
A Vow for Always

Daughters of Lancaster County Series
The Storekeeper's Daughter
The Quilter's Daughter
The Bishop's Daughter

Brides of Lancaster County Series
A Merry Heart
Looking for a Miracle
Plain and Fancy
The Hope Chest

Amish Cooking Class Series
The Seekers
The Blessing
The Celebration
Amish Cooking Class Cookbook

The Half-Stitched Amish Quilting Club Series
The Half-Stitched Amish Quilting Club
The Tattered Quilt
The Healing Quilt

The Prayer Jars Series
The Hope Jar
The Forgiving Jar
The Healing Jar

Amish Greenhouse Mystery Series
The Crow's Call
The Mockingbird's Song
The Robin's Greeting (coming March 2021)

Nonfiction
The Simple Life
A Celebration of the Simple Life
Wanda E. Brunstetter's Amish Friends Cookbook
Wanda E. Brunstetter's Amish Friends Cookbook, Vol. 2
Amish Friends Harvest Cookbook
Amish Friends Christmas Cookbook
Amish Friends Gatherings Cookbook
Amish Friends From Scratch Cookbook

Children's Books
Rachel Yoder—Always Trouble Somewhere Series (8 books)
The Wisdom of Solomon
Mattie and Mark Miller. . .Double Trouble Series (5 books)

Other Books
Amish Front Porch Stories
The Brides of the Big Valley
The Beloved Christmas Quilt
Lydia's Charm
Amish White Christmas Pie
Woman of Courage
The Amish Millionaire
The Christmas Secret
The Lopsided Christmas Cake
The Farmers' Market Mishap
Twice as Nice Amish Romance Collection